IN SEARCH OF
LOST TIME

IN SEARCH OF
LOST TIME

VOLUME I

SWANN'S WAY

MARCEL PROUST

TRANSLATED BY
C. K. SCOTT MONCRIEFF AND TERENCE KILMARTIN
REVISED BY D. J. ENRIGHT

THE MODERN LIBRARY

NEW YORK

MARCEL PROUST

Marcel Proust was born in the Parisian suburb of Auteuil on July 10, 1871. His father, Adrien Proust, was a doctor celebrated for his work in epidemiology; his mother, Jeanne Weil, was a stockbroker's daughter of Jewish descent. He lived as a child in the family home on Boulevard Malesherbes in Paris, but spent vacations with his aunt and uncle in the town of Illiers near Chartres, where the Prousts had lived for generations and which became the model for the Combray of his great novel. (In recent years it was officially renamed Illiers-Combray.) Sickly from birth, Marcel was subject from the age of nine to violent attacks of asthma, and although he did a year of military service as a young man and studied law and political science, his invalidism disqualified him from an active professional life.

During the 1890s Proust contributed sketches to *Le Figaro* and to a short-lived magazine, *Le Banquet*, founded by some of his school friends in 1892. *Pleasures and Days*, a collection of his stories, essays, and poems, was published in 1896. In his youth Proust led an active social life, penetrating the highest circles of wealth and aristocracy. Artistically and intellectually, his influences included the aesthetic criticism of John Ruskin, the philosophy of Henri Bergson, the music of Wagner, and the fiction of Anatole France (on whom he modeled his character Bergotte). An affair begun in 1894 with the composer and pianist Reynaldo Hahn marked the beginning of Proust's often anguished acknowledgment of his homosexuality. Following the publication of Emile Zola's letter in defense of Colonel Dreyfus in 1898, Proust became "the first Dreyfusard," as he later phrased it. By the time Dreyfus was finally vindicated of charges of treason, Proust's social circles had been torn apart by the anti-Semitism and political hatreds stirred up by the affair.

Proust was very attached to his mother, and after her death in 1905 he spent some time in a sanitorium. His health worsened progressively, and he withdrew almost completely from society and devoted himself to writing. Proust's early work had done nothing to establish his reputation as a major writer. In an unfinished novel, *Jean Santeuil* (not published until 1952), he laid some of the groundwork for *In Search of Lost Time*, and in *Against Sainte-Beuve*, written in 1908–09, he stated as his aesthetic credo: "A book is the product of a different self from the one we manifest in our habits, in society, in our vices. If we mean to try to understand this self it is only in our inmost depths, by endeavoring to reconstruct it there, that the quest can be achieved." He appears to have begun work on his long masterpiece sometime around 1908, and the first volume, *Swann's Way*, was published in 1913. In 1919 the second volume, *Within a Budding Grove*, won the Goncourt Prize, bringing Proust great and instantaneous fame. Two subsequent sections—*The Guermantes Way* (1920–21) and *Sodom and Gomorrah* (1921)—appeared in his lifetime. (Of the depiction of homosexuality in the latter, his friend André Gide complained: "Will you never portray this form of Eros for us in the aspect of youth and beauty?") The remaining volumes were published following Proust's death on November 18, 1922: *The Captive* in 1923, *The Fugitive* in 1925, and *Time Regained* in 1927.

SWANN'S WAY

CONTENTS

*Numerals in the text refer the reader to explanatory notes,
which follow the text.*

Note on the Translation (1981)

C. K. Scott Moncrieff's version of *À la recherche du temps perdu* has in the past fifty years earned a reputation as one of the great English translations, almost as a masterpiece in its own right. Why then should it need revision? Why tamper with a work that has been enjoyed and admired, not to say revered, by several generations of readers throughout the English-speaking world?

The answer is that the original French edition from which Scott Moncrieff worked (the "abominable" edition of the *Nouvelle Revue Française*, as Samuel Beckett described it in a marvellous short study of Proust which he published in 1931) was notoriously imperfect. This was not so much the fault of the publishers and printers as of Proust's methods of composition. Only the first volume (*Du côté de chez Swann*) of the novel as originally conceived—and indeed written—was published before the 1914–1918 war. The second volume was set up in type, but publication was delayed, and moreover by that time Proust had already begun to reconsider the scale of the novel; the remaining eight years of his life (1914–1922) were spent in expanding it from its original 500,000 words to more than a million and a quarter. The margins of proofs and typescripts were covered with scribbled corrections and insertions, often overflowing on to additional sheets which were glued to the galleys or to one another to form interminable strips—what Françoise in the novel calls the narrator's *"paperoles."* The unravelling and deciphering of these copious additions cannot have been an enviable task for editors and printers.

Furthermore, the last three sections of the novel (*La prisonnière, La fugitive*—originally called *Albertine disparue*—and *Le temps retrouvé*) had not yet been published at the time of Proust's death in November 1922 (he was still correcting a typed copy of *La prisonnière* on his deathbed). Here the original editors had to take it upon themselves to prepare a coherent text from a manuscript littered with sometimes hasty corrections, revisions and afterthoughts and leaving a number of unresolved contradictions, obscurities and chronological inconsistencies. As a result of all this the original editions—even of the volumes published in Proust's lifetime—pullulate with errors, misreadings and omissions.

In 1954 a revised three-volume edition of *À la recherche* was published in Gallimard's Bibliothèque de la Pléiade. The editors, M. Pierre Clarac and M. André Ferré, had been charged by Proust's heirs with the task of "establishing a text of his novel as faithful as possible to his intentions." With infinite care and patience they examined all the relevant material—manuscripts, notebooks, typescripts, proofs, as well as the original edition—and produced what is generally agreed to be a virtually impeccable transcription of Proust's text. They scrupulously avoided the arbitrary emendations, the touchings-up, the wholesale reshufflings of paragraphs in which the original editors indulged, confining themselves to clarifying the text wherever necessary, correcting errors due to haste or inadvertence, eliminating careless repetitions and rationalising the punctuation (an area where Proust was notoriously casual). They justify and explain their editorial decisions in detailed critical notes, occupying some 200 pages over the three volumes, and print all the significant variants as well as a number of passages that Proust did not have time to work into his book.

The Pléiade text differs from that of the original edition, mostly in minor though none the less significant ways, throughout the novel. In the last three sections (the third Pléiade volume) the differences are sometimes considerable. In particular, MM. Clarac and Ferré have included a number of passages, sometimes of a paragraph or two, sometimes of several pages, which the original editors omitted for no good reason.

The present translation is a reworking, on the basis of the Pléiade edition, of Scott Moncrieff's version of the first six sections of À la recherche—or the first eleven volumes of the twelve-volume English edition. A post-Pléiade version of the final volume, Le temps retrouvé (originally translated by Stephen Hudson after Scott Moncrieff's death in 1930), was produced by the late Andreas Mayor and published in 1970; with some minor emendations, it is incorporated in this edition. There being no indication in Proust's manuscript as to where La fugitive should end and Le temps retrouvé begin, I have followed the Pléiade editors in introducing the break some pages earlier than in the previous editions, both French and English—at the beginning of the account of the Tansonville episode.

The need to revise the existing translation in the light of the Pléiade edition has also provided an opportunity of correcting mistakes and misinterpretations in Scott Moncrieff's version. Translation, almost by definition, is imperfect; there is always "room for improvement," and it is only too easy for the latecomer to assume the beau rôle. I have refrained from officious tinkering for its own sake, but a translator's loyalty is to the original author, and in trying to be faithful to Proust's meaning and tone of voice I have been obliged, here and there, to make extensive alterations.

A general criticism that might be levelled against Scott Moncrieff is that his prose tends to the purple and the precious—or that this is how he interpreted the tone of the original: whereas the truth is that, complicated, dense, overloaded though it often is, Proust's style is essentially natural and unaffected, quite free of preciosity, archaism or self-conscious elegance. Another pervasive weakness of Scott Moncrieff's is perhaps the defect of a virtue. Contrary to a widely held view, he stuck very closely to the original (he is seldom guilty of short-cuts, omissions or loose paraphrases), and in his efforts to reproduce the structure of those elaborate sentences with their spiralling subordinate clauses, not only does he sometimes lose the thread but he wrenches his syntax into oddly unEnglish shapes: a whiff of Gallicism clings to some of the longer periods, obscuring the sense and falsifying the tone. A corollary to this is a tendency to translate French idioms and turns of phrase literally, thus making them sound weirder, more outlandish, than they would to a French reader. In endeavouring to rectify these weaknesses, I hope I have preserved the undoubted felicity of much of Scott Moncrieff while doing the fullest possible justice to Proust.

I should like to thank Professor J. G. Weightman for his generous help and advice and Mr D. J. Enright for his patient and percipient editing.

TERENCE KILMARTIN

Terence Kilmartin intended to make further changes to the translation as published in 1981 under the title *Remembrance of Things Past*. But, as Proust's narrator observed while reflecting on the work he had yet to do, when the fortress of the body is besieged on all sides the mind must at length succumb. "It was precisely when the thought of death had become a matter of indifference to me that I was beginning once more to fear death . . . as a threat not to myself but to my book."

C. K. Scott Moncrieff excelled in description, notably of landscape and architecture, but he was less adroit in translating dialogue of an informal, idiomatic nature. At ease with intellectual and artistic discourse and the finer feelings, and alert to sallies of humorous fantasy, he was not always comfortable with workaday matters and the less elevated aspects of human behaviour. It was left to Kilmartin to elucidate the significance of Albertine's incomplete but alarming outburst—". . . *me faire casser* . . ." —in *The Captive*, a passage Scott Moncrieff rendered totally incomprehensible, perhaps through squeamishness, perhaps through ignorance of low slang. Other misunderstandings of colloquialisms and failures to spot secondary meanings remained to be rectified. And some further intervention was prompted by Scott Moncrieff's tendency to spell out things for the benefit of the English reader: an admirable intention (shared by Arthur Waley in his *Tale of Genji*), though the effect could be to clog Proust's flow and make his drift harder to follow.

The present revision or re-revision has taken into account the second Pléiade edition of *À la recherche du temps perdu*, published in four volumes between 1987 and 1989 under the direction of Jean-Yves Tadié. This both adds, chiefly in the form of drafts and variants, and relocates material: not always helpfully from the viewpoint of the common (as distinct from specialist) reader, who may be surprised to encounter virtually the same passage in two different locations when there was doubt as to where Proust would finally have placed it. But the new edition clears up some long-standing misreadings: for example, in correcting Cambremer's admiring "niece" in *Time Regained* to his "mother," an identification which accords with a mention some thousand pages earlier in the novel.

Kilmartin notes that it is only too easy for the latecomer, tempted to make his mark by "officious tinkering," to "assume the *beau rôle*." The caveat, so delicately worded, is one to take to heart. I am much indebted to my wife, Madeleine, without whose collaboration I would never have dared to assume a role that is melancholy rather than (in any sense) *beau*.

D. J. ENRIGHT

À M. Gaston Calmette.
Comme un témoignage de profonde
et affectueuse reconnaissance.
M . P .

Part One

COMBRAY

I

For a long time I would go to bed early. Sometimes, the candle barely out, my eyes closed so quickly that I did not have time to tell myself: "I'm falling asleep." And half an hour later the thought that it was time to look for sleep would awaken me; I would make as if to put away the book which I imagined was still in my hands, and to blow out the light; I had gone on thinking, while I was asleep, about what I had just been reading, but these thoughts had taken a rather peculiar turn; it seemed to me that I myself was the immediate subject of my book: a church, a quartet, the rivalry between François I and Charles V. This impression would persist for some moments after I awoke; it did not offend my reason, but lay like scales upon my eyes and prevented them from registering the fact that the candle was no longer burning. Then it would begin to seem unintelligible, as the thoughts of a previous existence must be after reincarnation; the subject of my book would separate itself from me, leaving me free to apply myself to it or not; and at the same time my sight would return and I would be astonished to find myself in a state of darkness, pleasant and restful enough for my eyes, but even more, perhaps, for my mind, to which it appeared incomprehensible, without a cause, something dark indeed.

I would ask myself what time it could be; I could hear the whistling of trains, which, now nearer and now

1

further off, punctuating the distance like the note of a bird in a forest, showed me in perspective the deserted countryside through which a traveller is hurrying towards the nearby station; and the path he is taking will be engraved in his memory by the excitement induced by strange surroundings, by unaccustomed activities, by the conversation he has had and the farewells exchanged beneath an unfamiliar lamp that still echo in his ears amid the silence of the night, and by the happy prospect of being home again.

I would lay my cheeks gently against the comfortable cheeks of my pillow, as plump and fresh as the cheeks of childhood. I would strike a match to look at my watch. Nearly midnight. The hour when an invalid, who has been obliged to set out on a journey and to sleep in a strange hotel, awakened by a sudden spasm, sees with glad relief a streak of daylight showing under his door. Thank God, it is morning! The servants will be about in a minute: he can ring, and someone will come to look after him. The thought of being assuaged gives him strength to endure his pain. He is certain he heard footsteps: they come nearer, and then die away. The ray of light beneath his door is extinguished. It is midnight; someone has just turned down the gas; the last servant has gone to bed, and he must lie all night suffering without remedy.

I would fall asleep again, and thereafter would reawaken for short snatches only, just long enough to hear the regular creaking of the wainscot, or to open my eyes to stare at the shifting kaleidoscope of the darkness, to savour, in a momentary glimmer of consciousness, the sleep which lay heavy upon the furniture, the room, that whole of which I formed no more than a small part and whose insensibility I should very soon return to share. Or else while sleeping I had drifted back to an earlier stage in my life, now for ever outgrown, and had come under the thrall of one of my childish terrors, such as that old terror of my great-uncle's pulling my curls which was effectually dispelled on the day—the dawn of a new era to me— when they were finally cropped from my head. I had forgotten that event during my sleep, but I remembered it again immediately I had succeeded in waking myself up to escape my great-uncle's fingers, and as a measure of precaution I would bury the whole of my head in the pillow before returning to the world of dreams.

Sometimes, too, as Eve was created from a rib of Adam, a woman would be born during my sleep from some misplacing of my thigh. Conceived from the pleasure I was on the point of enjoying, she it was, I imagined, who offered me that pleasure. My body, conscious that its own warmth was permeating hers, would strive to become one with her, and I would awake. The rest of humanity seemed very remote in comparison with this woman whose company I had left but a moment ago; my cheek was still warm from her kiss, my body ached beneath the weight of hers. If, as would sometimes happen, she had the features of some woman whom I had known in waking hours, I would abandon myself altogether to this end: to find her again, like people who set out on a journey to see with their eyes some city of their desire, and imagine that one can taste in reality what has charmed one's fancy. And then, gradually, the memory of her would fade away, I had forgotten the girl of my dream.

When a man is asleep, he has in a circle round him the chain of the hours, the sequence of the years, the order of the heavenly bodies. Instinctively he consults them when he awakes, and in an instant reads off his own position on the earth's surface and the time that has elapsed during his slumbers; but this ordered procession is apt to grow confused, and to break its ranks. Suppose that, towards morning, after a night of insomnia, sleep descends upon him while he is reading, in quite a different position from that in which he normally goes to sleep, he has only to lift his arm to arrest the sun and turn it back in its course, and, at the moment of waking, he will have no idea of the time, but will conclude that he has just gone to bed. Or suppose that he dozes off in some even more abnormal and divergent position, sitting in an armchair, for instance, after dinner: then the world will go hurtling out of orbit, the magic chair will carry him at full speed through time and space, and when he opens his eyes again he will imagine that he went to sleep months earlier in another place. But for me it was enough if, in my own bed, my sleep was so heavy as completely to relax my consciousness; for then I lost all sense of the place in which I had gone to sleep, and when I awoke in the middle of the night, not knowing where I was, I could not even be sure at first who I was; I had only the most rudimentary sense of existence, such as may lurk and flicker in the depths of an animal's consciousness; I was more destitute than the cave-dweller; but then the memory— not yet of the place in which I was, but of various other places where I had lived and might now very possibly be—would come like a rope let down from heaven to draw me up out of the abyss of not-being, from which I could never have escaped by myself: in a flash I would traverse centuries of civilisation, and out of a blurred glimpse of oil-lamps, then of shirts with turned-down collars, would gradually piece together the original components of my ego.

Perhaps the immobility of the things that surround us is forced upon them by our conviction that they are themselves and not anything else, by the immobility of our conception of them. For it always happened that when I awoke like this, and my mind struggled in an unsuccessful attempt to discover where I was, everything revolved around me through the darkness: things, places, years. My body, still too heavy with sleep to move, would endeavour to construe from the pattern of its tiredness the position of its various limbs, in order to deduce therefrom the direction of the wall, the location of the furniture, to piece together and give a name to the house in which it lay. Its memory, the composite memory of its ribs, its knees, its shoulder-blades, offered it a series of rooms in which it had at one time or another slept, while the unseen walls, shifting and adapting themselves to the shape of each successive room that it remembered, whirled round it in the dark. And even before my brain, hesitating at the threshold of times and shapes, had reassembled the circumstances sufficiently to identify the room, it— my body—would recall from each room in succession the style of the bed, the position of the doors, the angle at which the daylight came in at the windows, whether there was a passage outside, what I had had in my mind when I went to sleep and found there when I awoke. The stiffened side on which I lay would, for instance, in trying to fix its position, imagine itself to be lying face to the wall in a big bed with a canopy; and at once I would say to myself, "Why, I must have fallen asleep before Mamma came to say good night," for I was in the country at my grandfather's, who died years ago; and my body, the side upon which I was lying, faithful guardians of a past which my mind should never have forgotten, brought back before my eyes the glimmering flame of the night-light in its urn-shaped bowl of Bohemian glass that hung by chains from the ceiling, and the chimney-piece of Siena marble in my bedroom at Combray, in my grand-parents' house, in those far distant days which at this moment I imagined to be in the present without being able to picture them exactly, and which would become plainer in a little while when I was properly awake.

Then the memory of a new position would spring up, and the wall would slide away in another direction; I was in my room in Mme de Saint-Loup's house in the coun-try; good heavens, it must be ten o'clock, they will have finished dinner! I must have overslept myself in the little nap which I always take when I come in from my walk with Mme de Saint-Loup, before dressing for the evening. For many years have now elapsed since the Combray days when, coming in from the longest and latest walks, I would still be in time to see the reflection of the sunset glowing in the panes of my bedroom window. It is a very different kind of life that one leads at Tansonville, at Mme de Saint-Loup's, and a different kind of pleasure that I derive from taking walks only in the evenings, from visiting by moonlight the roads on which I used to play as a child in the sunshine; as for the bedroom in which I must have fallen asleep instead of dressing for dinner, I can see it from the distance as we return from our walk,

with its lamp shining through the window, a solitary bea-
con in the night.

These shifting and confused gusts of memory never
lasted for more than a few seconds; it often happened
that, in my brief spell of uncertainty as to where I was, I
did not distinguish the various suppositions of which it
was composed any more than, when we watch a horse
running, we isolate the successive positions of its body as
they appear upon a bioscope. But I had seen first one and
then another of the rooms in which I had slept during my
life, and in the end I would revisit them all in the long
course of my waking dream: rooms in winter, where on
going to bed I would at once bury my head in a nest woven out of the most diverse materials—the corner of my
pillow, the top of my blankets, a piece of a shawl, the
edge of my bed, and a copy of a children's paper—which
I had contrived to cement together, bird-fashion, by dint
of continuous pressure; rooms where, in freezing weather,
I would enjoy the satisfaction of being shut in from the
outer world (like the sea-swallow which builds at the end
of a dark tunnel and is kept warm by the surrounding
earth), and where, the fire keeping in all night, I would
sleep wrapped up, as it were, in a great cloak of snug and
smoky air, shot with the glow of the logs intermittently
breaking out again in flame, a sort of alcove without
walls, a cave of warmth dug out of the heart of the room
itself, a zone of heat whose boundaries were constantly
shifting and altering in temperature as gusts of air traversed them to strike freshly upon my face, from the corners of the room or from parts near the window or far
from the fireplace which had therefore remained cold;—
or rooms in summer, where I would delight to feel myself

a part of the warm night, where the moonlight striking
upon the half-opened shutters would throw down to the
foot of my bed its enchanted ladder, where I would fall
asleep, as it might be in the open air, like a titmouse
which the breeze gently rocks at the tip of a sunbeam;—
or sometimes the Louis XVI room, so cheerful that I
never felt too miserable in it, even on my first night, and
in which the slender columns that lightly supported its
ceiling drew so gracefully apart to reveal and frame the
site of the bed;—sometimes, again, the little room with
the high ceiling, hollowed in the form of a pyramid out of
two separate storeys, and partly walled with mahogany, in
which from the first moment, mentally poisoned by the
unfamiliar scent of vetiver, I was convinced of the hostil-
ity of the violet curtains and of the insolent indifference
of a clock that chattered on at the top of its voice as
though I were not there; in which a strange and pitiless
rectangular cheval-glass, standing across one corner of the
room, carved out for itself a site I had not looked to find
tenanted in the soft plenitude of my normal field of vision; in which my mind, striving for hours on end to
break away from its moorings, to stretch upwards so as to
take on the exact shape of the room and to reach to the
topmost height of its gigantic funnel, had endured many a
painful night as I lay stretched out in bed, my eyes staring upwards, my ears straining, my nostrils flaring, my
heart beating; until habit had changed the colour of the
curtains, silenced the clock, brought an expression of pity
to the cruel, slanting face of the glass, disguised or even
completely dispelled the scent of vetiver, and appreciably
reduced the apparent loftiness of the ceiling. Habit! that
skilful but slow-moving arranger who begins by letting

our minds suffer for weeks on end in temporary quarters, but whom our minds are none the less only too happy to discover at last, for without it, reduced to their own devices, they would be powerless to make any room seem habitable.

Certainly I was now well awake; my body had veered round for the last time and the good angel of certainty had made all the surrounding objects stand still, had set me down under my bedclothes, in my bedroom, and had fixed, approximately in their right places in the uncertain light, my chest of drawers, my writing-table, my fireplace, the window overlooking the street, and both the doors. But for all that I now knew that I was not in any of the houses of which the ignorance of the waking moment had, in a flash, if not presented me with a distinct picture, at least persuaded me of the possible presence, my memory had been set in motion; as a rule I did not attempt to go to sleep again at once, but used to spend the greater part of the night recalling our life in the old days at Combray with my great-aunt, at Balbec, Paris, Doncières, Venice, and the rest; remembering again all the places and people I had known, what I had actually seen of them, and what others had told me.

At Combray, as every afternoon ended, long before the time when I should have to go to bed and lie there, unsleeping, far from my mother and grandmother, my bedroom became the fixed point on which my melancholy and anxious thoughts were centred. Someone had indeed had the happy idea of giving me, to distract me on evenings when I seemed abnormally wretched, a magic lantern, which used to be set on top of my lamp while we waited for dinner-time to come; and, after the fashion of

the master-builders and glass-painters of Gothic days, it
substituted for the opaqueness of my walls an impalpable
iridescence, supernatural phenomena of many colours, in
which legends were depicted as on a shifting and transi-
tory window. But my sorrows were only increased
thereby, because this mere change of lighting was enough
to destroy the familiar impression I had of my room,
thanks to which, save for the torture of going to bed, it
had become quite endurable. Now I no longer recognised
it, and felt uneasy in it, as in a room in some hotel or
chalet, in a place where I had just arrived by train for the
first time.

Riding at a jerky trot, Golo, filled with an infamous
design, issued from the little triangular forest which softened with dark green the slope of a hill, and advanced fit-
fully towards the castle of poor Geneviève de Brabant.
This castle was cut off short by a curved line which was
in fact the circumference of one of the transparent ovals
in the slides which were pushed into position through a
slot in the lantern. It was only the wing of a castle, and in
front of it stretched a moor on which Geneviève stood
dreaming, wearing a blue girdle. The castle and the moor
were yellow, but I could tell their colour without waiting
to see them, for before the slides made their appearance
the old-gold sonorous name of Brabant had given me an
unmistakable clue. Golo stopped for a moment and listened sadly to the accompanying patter read aloud by my
great-aunt, which he seemed perfectly to understand, for
he modified his attitude with a docility not devoid of a
degree of majesty, so as to conform to the indications
given in the text; then he rode away at the same jerky
trot. And nothing could arrest his slow progress. If the

lantern were moved I could still distinguish Golo's horse advancing across the window-curtains, swelling out with their curves and diving into their folds. The body of Golo himself, being of the same supernatural substance as his steed's, overcame every material obstacle—everything that seemed to bar his way—by taking it as an ossature and absorbing it into himself: even the doorknob—on which, adapting themselves at once, his red cloak or his pale face, still as noble and as melancholy, floated invincibly—would never betray the least concern at this transvertebration.

And, indeed, I found plenty of charm in these bright projections, which seemed to emanate from a Merovingian past and shed around me the reflections of such ancient history. But I cannot express the discomfort I felt at this intrusion of mystery and beauty into a room which I had succeeded in filling with my own personality until I thought no more of it than of myself. The anaesthetic effect of habit being destroyed, I would begin to think— and to feel—such melancholy things. The doorknob of my room, which was different to me from all the other doorknobs in the world, inasmuch as it seemed to move of its own accord and without my having to turn it, so unconscious had its manipulation become—lo and behold, it was now an astral body for Golo. And as soon as the dinner-bell rang I would hurry down to the dining-room, where the big hanging lamp, ignorant of Golo and Bluebeard but well acquainted with my family and the dish of stewed beef, shed the same light as on every other evening; and I would fall into the arms of my mother, whom the misfortunes of Geneviève de Brabant had made all the dearer to me, just as the crimes of Golo had driven

me to a more than ordinarily scrupulous examination of
my own conscience.

But after dinner, alas, I was soon obliged to leave
Mamma, who stayed talking with the others, in the garden if it was fine, or in the little parlour where everyone
took shelter when it was wet. Everyone except my grandmother, who held that "It's a pity to shut oneself indoors
in the country," and used to have endless arguments with
my father on the very wettest days, because he would
send me up to my room with a book instead of letting me
stay out of doors. "That is not the way to make him
strong and active," she would say sadly, "especially this
little man, who needs all the strength and will-power that
he can get." My father would shrug his shoulders and
study the barometer, for he took an interest in meteorol-
ogy, while my mother, keeping very quiet so as not to
disturb him, looked at him with tender respect, but not
too hard, not wishing to penetrate the mysteries of his superior mind. But my grandmother, in all weathers, even
when the rain was coming down in torrents and Françoise
had rushed the precious wicker armchairs indoors so that
they should not get soaked, was to be seen pacing the deserted rain-lashed garden, pushing back her disordered
grey locks so that her forehead might be freer to absorb
the health-giving draughts of wind and rain. She would
say, "At last one can breathe!" and would trot up and
down the sodden paths—too straight and symmetrical for
her liking, owing to the want of any feeling for nature in
the new gardener, whom my father had been asking all
morning if the weather were going to improve—her keen,
jerky little step regulated by the various effects wrought
upon her soul by the intoxication of the storm, the power

of hygiene, the stupidity of my upbringing and the sym-
metry of gardens, rather than by any anxiety (for that was
quite unknown to her) to save her plum-coloured skirt
from the mudstains beneath which it would gradually disappear to a height that was the constant bane and despair
of her maid.

When these walks of my grandmother's took place
after dinner there was one thing which never failed to
bring her back to the house: this was if (at one of those
points when her circular itinerary brought her back,
moth-like, in sight of the lamp in the little parlour where
the liqueurs were set out on the card-table) my great-aunt
called out to her: "Bathilde! Come in and stop your husband drinking brandy!" For, simply to tease her (she had
brought so different a type of mind into my father's family that everyone made fun of her), my great-aunt used to
make my grandfather, who was forbidden liqueurs, take
just a few drops. My poor grandmother would come
in and beg and implore her husband not to taste the
brandy; and he would get angry and gulp it down all the
same, and she would go out again sad and discouraged,
but still smiling, for she was so humble of heart and so
gentle that her tenderness for others and her disregard for
herself and her own troubles blended in a smile which,
unlike those seen on the majority of human faces, bore no
trace of irony save for herself, while for all of us kisses
seemed to spring from her eyes, which could not look
upon those she loved without seeming to bestow upon
them passionate caresses. This torture inflicted on her by
my great-aunt, the sight of my grandmother's vain entreaties, of her feeble attempts, doomed in advance, to remove the liqueur-glass from my grandfather's hands—all

these were things of the sort to which, in later years, one can grow so accustomed as to smile at them and to take the persecutor's side resolutely and cheerfully enough to persuade oneself that it is not really persecution; but in those days they filled me with such horror that I longed to strike my great-aunt. And yet, as soon as I heard her "Bathilde! Come in and stop your husband drinking brandy," in my cowardice I became at once a man, and did what all we grown men do when face to face with suffering and injustice: I preferred not to see them; I ran up to the top of the house to cry by myself in a little room beside the schoolroom and beneath the roof, which smelt of orris-root and was scented also by a wild cur-rant-bush which had climbed up between the stones of the outer wall and thrust a flowering branch in through the half-opened window. Intended for a more special and a baser use, this room, from which, in the daytime, I could see as far as the keep of Roussainville-le-Pin, was for a long time my place of refuge, doubtless because it was the only room whose door I was allowed to lock, whenever my occupation was such as required an invio-lable solitude: reading or day-dreaming, tears or sensual pleasure. Alas! I did not realise that my own lack of will-power, my delicate health, and the consequent uncertainty as to my future, weighed far more heavily on my grand-mother's mind than any little dietary indiscretion by her husband in the course of those endless perambulations, afternoon and evening, during which we used to see her handsome face passing to and fro, half raised towards the sky, its brown and wrinkled cheeks, which with age had acquired almost the purple hue of tilled fields in autumn, covered, if she were "going out," by a half-lifted veil,

while upon them either the cold or some sad reflection invariably left the drying traces of an involuntary tear.

My sole consolation when I went upstairs for the
night was that Mamma would come in and kiss me after I
was in bed. But this good night lasted for so short a time,
she went down again so soon, that the moment in which I
heard her climb the stairs, and then caught the sound of
her garden dress of blue muslin, from which hung little
tassels of plaited straw, rustling along the double-doored
corridor, was for me a moment of the utmost pain; for it
heralded the moment which was to follow it, when she
would have left me and gone downstairs again. So much
so that I reached the point of hoping that this good night
which I loved so much would come as late as possible, so
as to prolong the time of respite during which Mamma
would not yet have appeared. Sometimes when, after kissing me, she opened the door to go, I longed to call her
back, to say to her "Kiss me just once more," but I knew
that then she would at once look displeased, for the concession which she made to my wretchedness and agitation
in coming up to give me this kiss of peace always annoyed my father, who thought such rituals absurd, and
she would have liked to try to induce me to outgrow the
need, the habit, of having her there at all, let alone get
into the habit of asking her for an additional kiss when
she was already crossing the threshold. And to see her
look displeased destroyed all the calm and serenity she
had brought me a moment before, when she had bent her
loving face down over my bed, and held it out to me like
a host for an act of peace-giving communion in which my
lips might imbibe her real presence and with it the power
to sleep. But those evenings on which Mamma stayed so

short a time in my room were sweet indeed compared to those on which we had people to dinner, and therefore she did not come at all. Our "people" were usually limited to M. Swann, who, apart from a few passing strangers, was almost the only person who ever came to the house at Combray, sometimes to a neighbourly dinner (but less frequently since his unfortunate marriage, as my family did not care to receive his wife) and sometimes after dinner, uninvited. On those evenings when, as we sat in front of the house round the iron table beneath the big chestnut-tree, we heard, from the far end of the garden, not the shrill and assertive alarm bell which assailed and deafened with its ferruginous, interminable, frozen sound any member of the household who set it off on entering "without ringing," but the double tinkle, timid, oval, golden, of the visitors' bell, everyone would at once exclaim "A visitor! Who in the world can it be?" but they knew quite well that it could only be M. Swann. My great-aunt, speaking in a loud voice to set an example, in a tone which she endeavoured to make sound natural, would tell the others not to whisper so; that nothing could be more offensive to a stranger coming in, who would be led to think that people were saying things about him which he was not meant to hear; and then my grandmother, always happy to find an excuse for an additional turn in the garden, would be sent out to reconnoitre, and would take the opportunity to remove surreptitiously, as she passed, the stakes of a rose-tree or two, so as to make the roses look a little more natural, as a mother might run her hand through her boy's hair after the barber has smoothed it down, to make it look naturally wavy.

We would all wait there in suspense for the report which my grandmother would bring back from the enemy lines, as though there might be a choice between a large number of possible assailants, and then, soon after, my grandfather would say: "I recognise Swann's voice." And indeed one could tell him only by his voice, for it was difficult to make out his face with its arched nose and green eyes, under a high forehead fringed with fair, almost red hair, done in the Bressant style,[1] because in the garden we used as little light as possible, so as not to attract mosquitoes; and I would slip away unobtrusively to order the liqueurs to be brought out, for my grandmother made a great point, thinking it "nicer," of their not being allowed to seem anything out of the ordinary, which we kept for visitors only. Although a far younger man, M. Swann was very attached to my grandfather, who had been an intimate friend of Swann's father, an excellent but eccentric man the ardour of whose feelings and the current of whose thoughts would often be checked or diverted by the most trifling thing. Several times in the course of a year I would hear my grandfather tell at table the story, which never varied, of the behaviour of M. Swann the elder upon the death of his wife, by whose bedside he had watched day and night. My grandfather, who had not seen him for a long time, hastened to join him at the Swanns' family property on the outskirts of Combray, and managed to entice him for a moment, weeping profusely, out of the death-chamber, so that he should not be present when the body was laid in its coffin. They took a turn or two in the park, where there was a little sunshine. Suddenly M. Swann seized my grandfather by the arm and cried, "Ah, my dear old friend, how fortunate we are to be walking here together on such a charming day! Don't you see how pretty they are, all these trees, my hawthorns, and my new pond, on which you have never congratulated me? You look as solemn as the grave. Don't you feel this little breeze? Ah! whatever you may say, it's good to be alive all the same, my dear Amédée!" And then, abruptly, the memory of his dead wife returned to him, and probably thinking it too complicated to inquire into how, at such a time, he could have allowed himself to be carried away by an impulse of happiness, he confined himself to a gesture which he habitually employed whenever any perplexing question came into his mind: that is, he passed his hand across his forehead, rubbed his eyes, and wiped his glasses. And yet he never got over the loss of his wife, but used to say to my grandfather, during the two years by which he survived her, "It's a funny thing, now; I very often think of my poor wife, but I cannot think of her for long at a time." "Often, but a little at a time, like poor old Swann," became one of my grandfather's favourite sayings, which he would apply to all manner of things. I should have assumed that this father of Swann's had been a monster if my grandfather, whom I regarded as a better judge than myself, and whose word was my law and often led me in the long run to pardon offences which I should have been inclined to condemn, had not gone on to exclaim, "But, after all, he had a heart of gold."

For many years, during the course of which—especially before his marriage—M. Swann the younger came often to see them at Combray, my great-aunt and my grandparents never suspected that he had entirely ceased to live in the society which his family had frequented, and

that, under the sort of incognito which the name of
Swann gave him among us, they were harbouring—with
the complete innocence of a family of respectable
innkeepers who have in their midst some celebrated high-
wayman without knowing it—one of the most distinguished members of the Jockey Club, a particular friend
of the Comte de Paris and of the Prince of Wales, and
one of the men most sought after in the aristocratic world
of the Faubourg Saint-Germain.

Our utter ignorance of the brilliant social life which
Swann led was, of course, due in part to his own reserve
and discretion, but also to the fact that middle-class people in those days took what was almost a Hindu view of
society, which they held to consist of sharply defined
castes, so that everyone at his birth found himself called
to that station in life which his parents already occupied,
and from which nothing, save the accident of an exceptional career or of a "good" marriage, could extract you
and translate you to a superior caste. M. Swann the elder
had been a stockbroker; and so "young Swann" found
himself immured for life in a caste whose members' for-
tunes, as in a category of tax-payers, varied between such
and such limits of income. One knew the people with
whom his father had associated, and so one knew his own
associates, the people with whom he was "in a position"
to mix. If he knew other people besides, those were
youthful acquaintances on whom the old friends of his
family, like my relatives, shut their eyes all the more
good-naturedly because Swann himself, after he was left
an orphan, still came most faithfully to see us; but we
would have been ready to wager that the people outside
our acquaintance whom Swann knew were of the sort to

whom he would not have dared to raise his hat if he had
met them while he was walking with us. Had it been absolutely essential to apply to Swann a social coefficient
peculiar to himself, as distinct from all the other sons of
other stockbrokers in his father's position, his coefficient
would have been rather lower than theirs, because, being
very simple in his habits, and having always had a
"craze" for antiques and pictures, he now lived and
amassed his collections in an old house which my grandmother longed to visit but which was situated on the
Quai d'Orléans, a neighbourhood in which my great-aunt
thought it most degrading to be quartered. "Are you really a connoisseur at least?" she would say to him; "I ask
for your own sake, as you are likely to have fakes palmed
off on you by the dealers," for she did not, in fact, endow
him with any critical faculty, and had no great opinion of
the intelligence of a man who, in conversation, would
avoid serious topics and showed a very dull preciseness,
not only when he gave us kitchen recipes, going into the
most minute details, but even when my grandmother's
sisters were talking to him about art. When challenged by
them to give an opinion, or to express his admiration for
some picture, he would remain almost disobligingly silent,
and would then make amends by furnishing (if he could)
some fact or other about the gallery in which the picture
was hung, or the date at which it had been painted. But
as a rule he would content himself with trying to amuse
us by telling us about his latest adventure with someone
whom we ourselves knew, such as the Combray chemist,
or our cook, or our coachman. These stories certainly
used to make my great-aunt laugh, but she could never
decide whether this was on account of the absurd role

which Swann invariably gave himself therein, or of the wit that he showed in telling them: "I must say you really are a regular character, M. Swann!"

As she was the only member of our family who could be described as a trifle "common," she would always take care to remark to strangers, when Swann was mentioned, that he could easily, had he so wished, have lived in the Boulevard Haussmann or the Avenue de l'Opéra, and that he was the son of old M. Swann who must have left four or five million francs, but that it was a fad of his. A fad which, moreover, she thought was bound to amuse other people so much that in Paris, when M. Swann called on New Year's Day bringing her a little packet of marrons glacés, she never failed, if there were strangers in the room, to say to him: "Well, M. Swann, and do you still live next door to the bonded warehouse, so as to be sure of not missing your train when you go to Lyons?" and she would peep out of the corner of her eye, over her glasses, at the other visitors.

But if anyone had suggested to my great-aunt that this Swann, who, in his capacity as the son of old M. Swann, was "fully qualified" to be received by any of the "best people," by the most respected barristers and solicitors of Paris (though he was perhaps a trifle inclined to let this hereditary privilege go by default), had another almost secret existence of a wholly different kind; that when he left our house in Paris, saying that he must go home to bed, he would no sooner have turned the corner than he would stop, retrace his steps, and be off to some salon on whose like no stockbroker or associate of stock-brokers had ever set eyes—that would have seemed to my aunt as extraordinary as, to a woman of wider reading, the thought of being herself on terms of intimacy with Aristaeus and of learning that after having a chat with her he would plunge deep into the realms of Thetis, into an empire veiled from mortal eyes, in which Virgil depicts him as being received with open arms; or—to be content with an image more likely to have occurred to her, for she had seen it painted on the plates we used for biscuits at Combray—as the thought of having had to dinner Ali Baba, who, as soon as he finds himself alone and unobserved, will make his way into the cave, resplendent with its unsuspected treasures.

One day when he had come to see us after dinner in Paris, apologising for being in evening clothes, Françoise told us after he had left that she had got it from his coachman that he had been dining "with a princess." "A nice sort of princess," retorted my aunt, shrugging her shoulders without raising her eyes from her knitting, serenely sarcastic.

Altogether, my great-aunt treated him with scant ceremony. Since she was of the opinion that he ought to feel flattered by our invitations, she thought it only right and proper that he should never come to see us in summer without a basket of peaches or raspberries from his garden, and that from each of his visits to Italy he should bring back some photographs of old masters for me.

It seemed quite natural, therefore, to send for him whenever a recipe for some special sauce or for a pineapple salad was needed for one of our big dinner-parties, to which he himself would not be invited, being regarded as insufficiently important to be served up to new friends who might be in our house for the first time. If the conversation turned upon the princes of the House of France, "gentlemen you and I will never know, will we, and don't want to, do we?" my great-aunt would say tartly to Swann, who had, perhaps, a letter from Twickenham in his pocket; she would make him push the piano into place and turn over the music on evenings when my grandmother's sister sang, manipulating this person who was elsewhere so sought after with the rough simplicity of a child who will play with a collectors' piece with no more circumspection than if it were a cheap gewgaw. Doubtless the Swann who was a familiar figure in all the clubs of those days differed hugely from the Swann created by my great-aunt when, of an evening, in our little garden at Combray, after the two shy peals had sounded from the gate, she would inject and vitalise with everything she knew about the Swann family the obscure and shadowy figure who emerged, with my grandmother in his wake, from the dark background and who was identified by his voice. But then, even in the most insignificant details of our daily life, none of us can be said to constitute a material whole, which is identical for everyone, and need only be turned up like a page in an account-book or the record of a will; our social personality is a creation of the thoughts of other people. Even the simple act which we describe as "seeing someone we know" is to some extent an intellectual process. We pack the physical outline of the person we see with all the notions we have already formed about him, and in the total picture of him which we compose in our minds those notions have certainly the principal place. In the end they come to fill out so completely the curve of his cheeks, to follow so exactly the line of his nose, they blend so harmoniously in the sound of his voice as if it were no more than a transparent envelope, that each time we see the face or hear the voice it is these notions which we recognise and to which we listen. And so, no doubt, from the Swann they had constructed for themselves my family had left out, in their ignorance, a whole host of details of his life in the world of fashion, details which caused other people, when they met him, to see all the graces enthroned in his face and stopping at the line of his aquiline nose as at a natural frontier; but they had contrived also to put into this face divested of all glamour, vacant and roomy as an untenanted house, to plant in the depths of these undervalued eyes, a lingering residuum, vague but not unpleasing—half-memory and half-oblivion—of idle hours spent together after our weekly dinners, round the card-table or in the garden, during our companionable country life. Our friend's corporeal envelope had been so well lined with this residuum, as well as various earlier memories of his parents, that their own special Swann had become to my family a complete and living creature; so that even now I have the feeling of leaving someone I know for another quite different person when, going back in memory, I pass from the Swann whom I knew later and more intimately to this early Swann—this early Swann in whom I can distinguish the charming mistakes of my youth, and who in fact is less like his successor than he is like the other people I knew at that time, as though one's life were a picture gallery in which all the portraits of any one period had a marked family likeness, a similar tonality— this early Swann abounding in leisure, fragrant with the scent of the great chestnut-tree, of baskets of raspberries and of a sprig of tarragon.

And yet one day, when my grandmother had gone to

ask some favour of a lady whom she had known at the Sacré Cœur (and with whom, because of our notions of caste, she had not cared to keep up any degree of intimacy in spite of several common interests), the Marquise de Villeparisis, of the famous house of Bouillon, this lady had said to her:

"I believe you know M. Swann very well; he's a great friend of my nephew and niece, the des Laumes."

My grandmother had returned from the call full of praise for the house, which overlooked some gardens, and in which Mme de Villeparisis had advised her to rent a flat, and also for a repairing tailor and his daughter who kept a little shop in the courtyard, into which she had gone to ask them to put a stitch in her skirt, which she had torn on the staircase. My grandmother had found these people perfectly charming: the girl, she said, was a jewel, and the tailor the best and most distinguished man she had ever seen. For in her eyes distinction was a thing wholly independent of social position. She was in ecstasies over some answer the tailor had made to her, saying to Mamma:

"Sévigné would not have put it better!" and, by way of contrast, of a nephew of Mme de Villeparisis whom she had met at the house:

"My dear, he is so common!"

Now, the effect of the remark about Swann had been, not to raise him in my great-aunt's estimation, but to lower Mme de Villeparisis. It appeared that the deference which, on my grandmother's authority, we owed to Mme de Villeparisis imposed on her the reciprocal obligation to do nothing that would render her less worthy of our regard, and that she had failed in this duty by becoming

aware of Swann's existence and in allowing members of
her family to associate with him. "What! She knows
Swann? A person who, you always made out, was related
to Marshal MacMahon!" This view of Swann's social position which prevailed in my family seemed to be confirmed later on by his marriage with a woman of the
worst type, almost a prostitute, whom, to do him justice,
he never attempted to introduce to us—for he continued
to come to our house alone, though more and more seldom—but from whom they felt they could establish, on
the assumption that he had found her there, the circle,
unknown to them, in which he ordinarily moved.

But on one occasion my grandfather read in a newspaper that M. Swann was one of the most regular atten-
dants at the Sunday luncheons given by the Duc de
X——, whose father and uncle had been among our most
prominent statesmen in the reign of Louis-Philippe. Now
my grandfather was curious to learn all the smallest details which might help him to take a mental share in the
private lives of men like Molé, the Duc Pasquier, or the
Duc de Broglie. He was delighted to find that Swann associated with people who had known them. My great-
aunt, on the other hand, interpreted this piece of news in
a sense discreditable to Swann; for anyone who chose his
associates outside the caste in which he had been born
and bred, outside his "proper station," automatically lowered himself in her eyes. It seemed to her that such a one
abdicated all claim to enjoy the fruits of the splendid connections with people of good position which prudent parents cultivate and store up for their children's benefit, and
she had actually ceased to "see" the son of a lawyer of
our acquaintance because he had married a "Highness"

and had thereby stepped down—in her eyes—from the respectable position of a lawyer's son to that of those adventurers, upstart footmen or stable-boys mostly, to whom, we are told, queens have sometimes shown their favours. She objected, therefore, to my grandfather's plan of questioning Swann, when next he came to dine with us, about these people whose friendship with him we had discovered. At the same time my grandmother's two sisters, elderly spinsters who shared her nobility of character but lacked her intelligence, declared that they could not conceive what pleasure their brother-in-law could find in talking about such trifles. They were ladies of lofty aspirations, who for that reason were incapable of taking the least interest in what might be termed gossip, even if it had some historical import, or, generally speaking, in anything that was not directly associated with some aesthetic or virtuous object. So complete was their negation of interest in anything which seemed directly or indirectly connected with worldly matters that their sense of hearing—having finally come to realise its temporary futility when the tone of the conversation at the dinner-table became frivolous or merely mundane without the two old ladies' being able to guide it back to topics dear to themselves—would put its receptive organs into abeyance to the point of actually becoming atrophied. So that if my grandfather wished to attract the attention of the two sisters, he had to resort to some such physical stimuli as alienists adopt in dealing with their distracted patients: to wit, repeated taps on a glass with the blade of a knife, accompanied by a sharp word and a compelling glance, violent methods which these psychiatrists are apt to bring with them into their everyday life among the sane, either from force of professional habit or because they think the whole world a trifle mad.

Their interest grew, however, when, the day before Swann was to dine with us, and when he had made them a special present of a case of Asti, my great-aunt, who had in her hand a copy of the *Figaro* in which to the name of a picture then on view in a Corot exhibition were added the words, "from the collection of M. Charles Swann," asked: "Did you see that Swann is 'mentioned' in the *Figaro*?"

"But I've always told you," said my grandmother, "that he had a great deal of taste."

"You would, of course," retorted my great-aunt, "say anything just to seem different from *us*." For, knowing that my grandmother never agreed with her, and not being quite confident that it was her own opinion which the rest of us invariably endorsed, she wished to extort from us a wholesale condemnation of my grandmother's views, against which she hoped to force us into solidarity with her own. But we sat silent. My grandmother's sisters having expressed a desire to mention to Swann this reference to him in the *Figaro*, my great-aunt dissuaded them. Whenever she saw in others an advantage, however trivial, which she herself lacked, she would persuade herself that it was no advantage at all, but a drawback, and would pity so as not to have to envy them.

"I don't think that would please him at all; I know very well that I should hate to see my name printed like that, as large as life, in the paper, and I shouldn't feel at all flattered if anyone spoke to me about it."

She did not, however, put any very great pressure upon my grandmother's sisters, for they, in their horror

of vulgarity, had brought to such a fine art the conceal-
ment of a personal allusion in a wealth of ingenious cir-
cumlocution, that it would often pass unnoticed even by
the person to whom it was addressed. As for my mother,
her only thought was of trying to induce my father to
speak to Swann, not about his wife but about his daughter, whom he worshipped, and for whose sake it was understood that he had ultimately made his unfortunate
marriage.

"You need only say a word; just ask him how she is.
It must be so very hard for him."

My father, however, was annoyed: "No, no; you have
the most absurd ideas. It would be utterly ridiculous."

But the only one of us in whom the prospect of
Swann's arrival gave rise to an unhappy foreboding was
myself. This was because on the evenings when there
were visitors, or just M. Swann, in the house, Mamma
did not come up to my room. I dined before the others,
and afterwards came and sat at table until eight o'clock,
when it was understood that I must go upstairs; that frail
and precious kiss which Mamma used normally to bestow
on me when I was in bed and just going to sleep had to
be transported from the dining-room to my bedroom
where I must keep it inviolate all the time that it took me
to undress, without letting its sweet charm be broken,
without letting its volatile essence diffuse itself and evaporate; and it was precisely on those very evenings when I
needed to receive it with special care that I was obliged to
take it, to snatch it brusquely and in public, without even
having the time or the equanimity to bring to what I was
doing the single-minded attention of lunatics who compel
themselves to exclude all other thoughts from their minds

while they are shutting a door, so that when the sickness of uncertainty sweeps over them again they can triumphantly oppose it with the recollection of the precise moment when they shut the door.

We were all in the garden when the double tinkle of the visitors' bell sounded shyly. Everyone knew that it must be Swann, and yet they looked at one another inquiringly and sent my grandmother to reconnoitre.

"See that you thank him intelligibly for the wine," my grandfather warned his two sisters-in-law. "You know how good it is, and the case is huge."

"Now, don't start whispering!" said my great-aunt. "How would you like to come into a house and find everyone muttering to themselves?"

"Ah! There's M. Swann," cried my father. "Let's ask him if he thinks it will be fine tomorrow."

My mother fancied that a word from her would wipe out all the distress which my family had contrived to cause Swann since his marriage. She found an opportunity to draw him aside for a moment. But I followed her: I could not bring myself to let her out of my sight while I felt that in a few minutes I should have to leave her in the dining-room and go up to my bed without the consoling thought, as on ordinary evenings, that she would come up later to kiss me.

"Now, M. Swann," she said, "do tell me about your daughter. I'm sure she already has a taste for beautiful things, like her papa."

"Come along and sit down here with us all on the verandah," said my grandfather, coming up to him. My mother had to abandon her quest, but managed to extract from the restriction itself a further delicate thought, like good poets whom the tyranny of rhyme forces into the discovery of their finest lines.

"We can talk about her again when we are by ourselves," she said, or rather whispered to Swann. "Only a mother is capable of understanding these things. I'm sure that hers would agree with me."

And so we all sat down round the iron table. I should have liked not to think of the hours of anguish which I should have to spend that evening alone in my room, without being able to go to sleep: I tried to convince myself that they were of no importance since I should have forgotten them next morning, and to fix my mind on thoughts of the future which would carry me, as on a bridge, across the terrifying abyss that yawned at my feet. But my mind, strained by this foreboding, distended like the look which I shot at my mother, would not allow any extraneous impression to enter. Thoughts did indeed enter it, but only on the condition that they left behind them every element of beauty, or even of humour, by which I might have been distracted or beguiled. As a surgical patient, thanks to a local anaesthetic, can look on fully conscious while an operation is being performed upon him and yet feel nothing, I could repeat to myself some favourite lines, or watch my grandfather's efforts to talk to Swann about the Duc d'Audiffret-Pasquier, without being able to kindle any emotion from the one or amusement from the other. Hardly had my grandfather begun to question Swann about that orator when one of my grandmother's sisters, in whose ears the question echoed like a solemn but untimely silence which her natural politeness bade her interrupt, addressed the other with:

"Just fancy, Flora, I met a young Swedish governess today who told me some most interesting things about the co-operative movement in Scandinavia. We really must have her to dine here one evening."

"To be sure!" said her sister Flora, "but I haven't wasted my time either. I met such a clever old gentleman at M. Vinteuil's who knows Maubant quite well, and Maubant has told him every little thing about how he gets up his parts. It's the most interesting thing I ever heard. He's a neighbour of M. Vinteuil's, and I never knew; and he is so nice besides."

"M. Vinteuil is not the only one who has nice neighbours," cried my aunt Céline in a voice that was loud because of shyness and forced because of premeditation, darting, as she spoke, what she called a "significant glance" at Swann. And my aunt Flora, who realised that this veiled utterance was Céline's way of thanking Swann for the Asti, looked at him also with a blend of congratulation and irony, either because she simply wished to underline her sister's little witticism, or because she envied Swann his having inspired it, or because she imagined that he was embarrassed, and could not help having a little fun at his expense.

"I think it would be worth while," Flora went on, "to have this old gentleman to dinner. When you get him going on Maubant or Mme Materna he will talk for hours on end."

"That must be delightful," sighed my grandfather, in whose mind nature had unfortunately forgotten to include any capacity whatsoever for becoming passionately interested in the Swedish co-operative movement or in the methods employed by Maubant to get up his parts, just as it had forgotten to endow my grandmother's two sisters with a grain of that precious salt which one has oneself to "add to taste" in order to extract any savour from a narrative of the private life of Molé or of the Comte de Paris.

"By the way," said Swann to my grandfather, "what I was going to tell you has more to do than you might think with what you were asking me just now, for in some respects there has been very little change. I came across a passage in Saint-Simon this morning which would have amused you. It's in the volume which covers his mission to Spain; not one of the best, little more in fact than a journal, but at least a wonderfully well written journal, which fairly distinguishes it from the tedious journals we feel bound to read morning and evening."

"I don't agree with you: there are some days when I find reading the papers very pleasant indeed," my aunt Flora broke in, to show Swann that she had read the note about his Corot in the *Figaro*.

"Yes," aunt Céline went one better, "when they write about things or people in whom we are interested."

"I don't deny it," answered Swann in some bewilderment. "The fault I find with our journalism is that it forces us to take an interest in some fresh triviality or other every day, whereas only three or four books in a lifetime give us anything that is of real importance. Suppose that, every morning, when we tore the wrapper off our paper with fevered hands, a transmutation were to take place, and we were to find inside it—oh! I don't know; shall we say Pascal's *Pensées*?" He articulated the title with an ironic emphasis so as not to appear pedantic. "And then, in the gilt and tooled volumes which we open once in ten years," he went on, showing that contempt for

worldly matters which some men of the world like to affect, "we should read that the Queen of the Hellenes had
arrived at Cannes, or that the Princesse de Léon had
given a fancy dress ball. In that way we should arrive at a
happy medium." But at once regretting that he had allowed himself to speak of serious matters even in jest, he
added ironically: "What a fine conversation we're having!
I can't think why we climb to these lofty heights," and
then, turning to my grandfather: "Well, Saint-Simon tells
how Maulévrier had had the audacity to try to shake
hands with his sons. You remember how he says of
Maulévrier, 'Never did I find in that coarse bottle anything but ill-humour, boorishness, and folly.' "

"Coarse or not, I know bottles in which there is
something very different," said Flora briskly, feeling
bound to thank Swann as well as her sister, since the
present of Asti had been addressed to them both. Céline
laughed.

Swann was puzzled, but went on: " 'I cannot say
whether it was ignorance or cozenage,' writes Saint-Simon. 'He tried to give his hand to my children. I noticed
it in time to prevent him.' "

My grandfather was already in ecstasies over "ignorance or cozenage," but Mlle Céline—the name of Saint-
Simon, a "man of letters," having arrested the complete
paralysis of her auditory faculties—was indignant:

"What! You admire that? Well, that's a fine thing, I
must say! But what's it supposed to mean? Isn't one man
as good as the next? What difference can it make whether
he's a duke or a groom so long as he's intelligent and
kind? He had a fine way of bringing up his children, your
Saint-Simon, if he didn't teach them to shake hands with

all decent folk. Really and truly, it's abominable. And you
dare to quote it!"

And my grandfather, utterly depressed, realising how
futile it would be, against this opposition, to attempt to
get Swann to tell him the stories which would have
amused him, murmured to my mother: "Just tell me
again that line of yours which always comforts me so
much on these occasions. Oh, yes: 'What virtues, Lord,
Thou makest us abhor!'[2] How good that is!"

I never took my eyes off my mother. I knew that
when they were at table I should not be permitted to stay
there for the whole of dinner-time, and that Mamma, for
fear of annoying my father, would not allow me to kiss
her several times in public, as I would have done in my
room. And so I promised myself that in the dining-room,
as they began to eat and drink and as I felt the hour approach, I would put beforehand into this kiss, which was
bound to be so brief and furtive, everything that my own
efforts could muster, would carefully choose in advance
the exact spot on her cheek where I would imprint it, and
would so prepare my thoughts as to be able, thanks to
these mental preliminaries, to consecrate the whole of the
minute Mamma would grant me to the sensation of her
cheek against my lips, as a painter who can have his subject for short sittings only prepares his palette, and from
what he remembers and from rough notes does in advance everything which he possibly can do in the sitter's
absence. But tonight, before the dinner-bell had sounded,
my grandfather said with unconscious cruelty: "The little
man looks tired; he'd better go up to bed. Besides, we're
dining late tonight."

And my father, who was less scrupulous than my

grandmother or my mother in observing the letter of a treaty, went on: "Yes; run along; off to bed."

I would have kissed Mamma then and there, but at that moment the dinner-bell rang.

"No, no, leave your mother alone. You've said good night to one another, that's enough. These exhibitions are absurd. Go on upstairs."

And so I must set forth without viaticum; must climb each step of the staircase "against my heart,"[3] as the saying is, climbing in opposition to my heart's desire, which was to return to my mother, since she had not, by kissing me, given my heart leave to accompany me. That hateful staircase, up which I always went so sadly, gave out a smell of varnish which had, as it were, absorbed and crystallised the special quality of sorrow that I felt each evening, and made it perhaps even crueller to my sensibility because, when it assumed this olfactory guise, my intellect was powerless to resist it. When we have gone to sleep with a raging toothache and are conscious of it only as of a little girl whom we attempt, time after time, to pull out of the water, or a line of Molière which we repeat incessantly to ourselves, it is a great relief to wake up, so that our intelligence can disentangle the idea of toothache from any artificial semblance of heroism or rhythmic cadence. It was the converse of this relief which I felt when my anguish at having to go up to my room invaded my consciousness in a manner infinitely more rapid, instantaneous almost, a manner at once insidious and brutal, through the inhalation—far more poisonous than moral penetration—of the smell of varnish peculiar to that staircase.

Once in my room I had to stop every loophole, to

close the shutters, to dig my own grave as I turned down
the bed-clothes, to wrap myself in the shroud of my
nightshirt. But before burying myself in the iron bed
which had been placed there because, on summer nights,
I was too hot among the rep curtains of the four-poster, I
was stirred to revolt, and attempted the desperate
stratagem of a condemned prisoner. I wrote to my mother
begging her to come upstairs for an important reason
which I could not put in writing. My fear was that
Françoise, my aunt's cook who used to be put in charge
of me when I was at Combray, might refuse to take my
note. I had a suspicion that, in her eyes, to carry a message to my mother when there was a guest would appear
as flatly inconceivable as for the door-keeper of a theatre
to hand a letter to an actor upon the stage. On the subject
of things which might or might not be done she possessed
a code at once imperious, abundant, subtle, and uncompromising on points themselves imperceptible or irrelevant, which gave it a resemblance to those ancient laws
which combine such cruel ordinances as the massacre of
infants at the breast with prohibitions of exaggerated refinement against "seething the kid in his mother's milk,"
or "eating of the sinew which is upon the hollow of the
thigh." This code, judging by the sudden obstinacy which
she would put into her refusal to carry out certain of our
instructions, seemed to have provided for social complexi-
ties and refinements of etiquette which nothing in
Françoise's background or in her career as a servant in a
village household could have put into her head; and we
were obliged to assume that there was latent in her some
past existence in the ancient history of France, noble and
little understood, as in those manufacturing towns where

old mansions still testify to their former courtly days, and chemical workers toil among delicately sculptured scenes from *Le Miracle de Théophile* or *Les quatres fils Aymon*.[4]

In this particular instance, the article of her code which made it highly improbable that—barring an outbreak of fire—Françoise would go down and disturb Mamma in the presence of M. Swann for so unimportant a person as myself was one embodying the respect she showed not only for the family (as for the dead, for the clergy, or for royalty), but also for the stranger within our gates; a respect which I should perhaps have found touching in a book, but which never failed to irritate me on her lips, because of the solemn and sentimental tones in which she would express it, and which irritated me more than usual this evening when the sacred character with which she invested the dinner-party might have the effect of making her decline to disturb its ceremonial. But to give myself a chance of success I had no hesitation in lying, telling her that it was not in the least myself who had wanted to write to Mamma, but Mamma who, on saying good night to me, had begged me not to forget to send her an answer about something she had asked me to look for, and that she would certainly be very angry if this note were not taken to her. I think that Françoise disbelieved me, for, like those primitive men whose senses were so much keener than our own, she could immediately detect, from signs imperceptible to the rest of us, the truth or falsehood of anything that we might wish to conceal from her. She studied the envelope for five minutes as though an examination of the paper itself and the look of my handwriting could enlighten her as to the nature of the contents, or tell her to which article of her

code she ought to refer the matter. Then she went out
with an air of resignation which seemed to imply: "It's
hard lines on parents having a child like that."

A moment later she returned to say that they were
still at the ice stage and that it was impossible for the
butler to deliver the note at once, in front of everybody;
but that when the finger-bowls were put round he would
find a way of slipping it into Mamma's hand. At once my
anxiety subsided; it was now no longer (as it had been a
moment ago) until tomorrow that I had lost my mother,
since my little note—though it would annoy her, no
doubt, and doubly so because this stratagem would make
me ridiculous in Swann's eyes—would at least admit me,
invisible and enraptured, into the same room as herself,
would whisper about me into her ear; since that forbidden
and unfriendly dining-room, where but a moment ago the
ice itself—with burned nuts in it—and the finger-bowls
seemed to me to be concealing pleasures that were baleful
and of a mortal sadness because Mamma was tasting of
them while I was far away, had opened its doors to me
and, like a ripe fruit which bursts through its skin, was
going to pour out into my intoxicated heart the sweetness
of Mamma's attention while she was reading what I had
written. Now I was no longer separated from her; the bar-
riers were down; an exquisite thread united us. Besides,
that was not all: for surely Mamma would come.

As for the agony through which I had just passed, I
imagined that Swann would have laughed heartily at it if
he had read my letter and had guessed its purpose;
whereas, on the contrary, as I was to learn in due course,
a similar anguish had been the bane of his life for many
years, and no one perhaps could have understood my feel-

ings at that moment so well as he; to him, the anguish
that comes from knowing that the creature one adores is
in some place of enjoyment where oneself is not and cannot follow—to him that anguish came through love, to
which it is in a sense predestined, by which it will be
seized upon and exploited; but when, as had befallen me,
it possesses one's soul before love has yet entered into
one's life, then it must drift, awaiting love's coming,
vague and free, without precise attachment, at the disposal of one sentiment today, of another tomorrow, of filial piety or affection for a friend. And the joy with which
I first bound myself apprentice, when Françoise returned
to tell me that my letter would be delivered, Swann, too,
had known well—that false joy which a friend or relative
of the woman we love can give us, when, on his arrival at
the house or theatre where she is to be found, for some
ball or party or "first night" at which he is to meet her,
he sees us wandering outside, desperately awaiting some
opportunity of communicating with her. He recognises us,
greets us familiarly, and asks what we are doing there.
And when we invent a story of having some urgent message to give to his relative or friend, he assures us that
nothing could be simpler, takes us in at the door, and
promises to send her down to us in five minutes. How we
love him—as at that moment I loved Françoise—the
good-natured intermediary who by a single word has
made supportable, human, almost propitious the inconceivable, infernal scene of gaiety in the thick of which we
had been imagining swarms of enemies, perverse and seductive, beguiling away from us, even making laugh at
us, the woman we love! If we are to judge of them by
him—this relative who has accosted us and who is him-

self an initiate in those cruel mysteries—then the other
guests cannot be so very demoniacal. Those inaccessible
and excruciating hours during which she was about to
taste of unknown pleasures—suddenly, through an unexpected breach, we have broken into them; suddenly we
can picture to ourselves, we possess, we intervene upon,
we have almost created, one of the moments the succession of which would have composed those hours, a moment as real as all the rest, if not actually more important
to us because our mistress is more intensely a part of it:
namely, the moment in which he goes to tell her that we
are waiting below. And doubtless the other moments of
the party would not have been so very different from this
one, would be no more exquisite, no more calculated to
make us suffer, since this kind friend has assured us that
"Of course, she will be delighted to come down! It will be
far more amusing for her to talk to you than to be bored
up there." Alas! Swann had learned by experience that the
good intentions of a third party are powerless to influence
a woman who is annoyed to find herself pursued even
into a ballroom by a man she does not love. Too often,
the kind friend comes down again alone.

My mother did not appear, but without the slightest
consideration for my self-respect (which depended upon
her keeping up the fiction that she had asked me to let
her know the result of my search for something or other)
told Françoise to tell me, in so many words: "There is no
answer"—words I have so often, since then, heard the
hall-porters in grand hotels and the flunkeys in gambling-
clubs and the like repeat to some poor girl who replies in
bewilderment: "What! he said nothing? It's not possible.
You did give him my letter, didn't you? Very well, I shall

wait a little longer." And, just as she invariably protests that she does not need the extra gas-jet which the porter offers to light for her, and sits on there, hearing nothing further except an occasional remark on the weather which the porter exchanges with a bell-hop whom he will send off suddenly, when he notices the time, to put some customer's wine on the ice, so, having declined Françoise's offer to make me some tea or to stay beside me, I let her go off again to the pantry, and lay down and shut my eyes, trying not to hear the voices of my family who were drinking their coffee in the garden.

But after a few seconds I realised that, by writing that note to Mamma, by approaching—at the risk of making her angry—so near to her that I felt I could reach out and grasp the moment in which I should see her again, I had cut myself off from the possibility of going to sleep until I actually had seen her, and my heart began to beat more and more painfully as I increased my agitation by ordering myself to keep calm and to acquiesce in my ill-fortune. Then, suddenly, my anxiety subsided, a feeling of intense happiness coursed through me, as when a strong medicine begins to take effect and one's pain vanishes: I had formed a resolution to abandon all attempts to go to sleep without seeing Mamma, had made up my mind to kiss her at all costs, even though this meant the certainty of being in disgrace with her for long afterwards—when she herself came up to bed. The calm which succeeded my anguish filled me with extraordinary exhilaration, no less than my sense of expectation, my thirst for and my fear of danger. Noiselessly I opened the window and sat down on the foot of my bed. I hardly dared to move in case they should hear me from below.

Outside, things too seemed frozen, rapt in a mute intent-
ness not to disturb the moonlight which, duplicating each
of them and throwing it back by the extension in front of
it of a shadow denser and more concrete than its substance, had made the whole landscape at once thinner and
larger, like a map which, after being folded up, is spread
out upon the ground. What had to move—a leaf of the
chestnut-tree, for instance—moved. But its minute quivering, total, self-contained, finished down to its minutest
gradation and its last delicate tremor, did not impinge
upon the rest of the scene, did not merge with it, remained circumscribed. Exposed upon this surface of silence which absorbed nothing of them, the most distant
sounds, those which must have come from gardens at the
far end of the town, could be distinguished with such exact "finish" that the impression they gave of coming from
a distance seemed due only to their "pianissimo" execution, like those movements on muted strings so well performed by the orchestra of the Conservatoire that, even
though one does not miss a single note, one thinks none
the less that they are being played somewhere outside, a
long way from the concert hall, so that all the old sub-
scribers—my grandmother's sisters too, when Swann had
given them his seats—used to strain their ears as if they
had caught the distant approach of an army on the march,
which had not yet rounded the corner of the Rue de
Trévise.

I was well aware that I had placed myself in a position than which none could be counted upon to involve
me in graver consequences at my parents' hands; consequences far graver, indeed, than a stranger would have
imagined, and such as (he would have thought) could fol-

low only some really shameful misdemeanour. But in the upbringing which they had given me faults were not classified in the same order as in that of other children, and I had been taught to place at the head of the list (doubtless because there was no other class of faults from which I needed to be more carefully protected) those in which I can now distinguish the common feature that one succumbs to them by yielding to a nervous impulse. But such a phrase had never been uttered in my hearing; no one had yet accounted for my temptations in a way which might have led me to believe that there was some excuse for my giving in to them, or that I was actually incapable of holding out against them. Yet I could easily recognise this class of transgressions by the anguish of mind which preceded as well as by the rigour of the punishment which followed them; and I knew that what I had just done was in the same category as certain other sins for which I had been severely punished, though infinitely more serious than they. When I went out to meet my mother on her way up to bed, and when she saw that I had stayed up in order to say good night to her again in the passage, I should not be allowed to stay in the house a day longer, I should be packed off to school next morning; so much was certain. Very well: had I been obliged, the next moment, to hurl myself out of the window, I should still have preferred such a fate. For what I wanted now was Mamma, to say good night to her. I had gone too far along the road which led to the fulfilment of this desire to be able to retrace my steps.

I could hear my parents' footsteps as they accompanied Swann to the gate, and when the clanging of the bell assured me that he had really gone, I crept to the window. Mamma was asking my father if he had thought the lobster good, and whether M. Swann had had a second helping of the coffee-and-pistachio ice. "I thought it rather so-so," she was saying. "Next time we shall have to try another flavour."

"I can't tell you," said my great-aunt, "what a change I find in Swann. He is quite antiquated!" She had grown so accustomed to seeing Swann always in the same stage of adolescence that it was a shock to her to find him suddenly less young than the age she still attributed to him. And the others too were beginning to remark in Swann that abnormal, excessive, shameful and deserved senescence of bachelors, of all those for whom it seems that the great day which knows no morrow must be longer than for other men, since for them it is void of promise, and from its dawn the moments steadily accumulate without any subsequent partition among offspring.

"I fancy he has a lot of trouble with that wretched wife of his, who lives with a certain Monsieur de Charlus, as all Combray knows. It's the talk of the town."

My mother observed that, in spite of this, he had looked much less unhappy of late. "And he doesn't nearly so often do that trick of his, so like his father, of wiping his eyes and drawing his hand across his forehead. I think myself that in his heart of hearts he no longer loves that woman."

"Why, of course he doesn't," answered my grandfather. "He wrote me a letter about it, ages ago, to which I took care to pay no attention, but it left no doubt as to his feelings, or at any rate his love, for his wife. Hullo! you two; you never thanked him for the Asti," he went on, turning to his sisters-in-law.

"What! we never thanked him? I think, between you and me, that I put it to him quite neatly," replied my aunt Flora.

"Yes, you managed it very well; I admired you for it," said my aunt Céline.

"But you did it very prettily, too."

"Yes; I was rather proud of my remark about 'nice neighbours.' "

"What! Do you call that thanking him?" shouted my grandfather. "I heard that all right, but devil take me if I guessed it was meant for Swann. You may be quite sure he never noticed it."

"Come, come; Swann isn't a fool. I'm sure he understood. You didn't expect me to tell him the number of bottles, or to guess what he paid for them."

My father and mother were left alone and sat down for a moment; then my father said: "Well, shall we go up to bed?"

"As you wish, dear, though I don't feel at all sleepy. I don't know why; it can't be the coffee-ice—it wasn't strong enough to keep me awake like this. But I see a light in the servants' hall: poor Françoise has been sitting up for me, so I'll get her to unhook me while you go and undress."

My mother opened the latticed door which led from the hall to the staircase. Presently I heard her coming upstairs to close her window. I went quietly into the passage; my heart was beating so violently that I could hardly move, but at least it was throbbing no longer with anxiety, but with terror and joy. I saw in the well of the stair a light coming upwards, from Mamma's candle. Then I saw Mamma herself and I threw myself upon her.

For an instant she looked at me in astonishment, not real-ising what could have happened. Then her face assumed an expression of anger. She said not a single word to me; and indeed I used to go for days on end without being spoken to, for far more venial offences than this. A single word from Mamma would have been an admission that further intercourse with me was within the bounds of possibility, and that might perhaps have appeared to me more terrible still, as indicating that, with such a punish-ment as was in store for me, mere silence and black looks would have been puerile. A word from her then would have implied the false calm with which one addresses a servant to whom one has just decided to give notice; the kiss one bestows on a son who is being packed off to en-list, which would have been denied him if it had merely been a matter of being angry with him for a few days. But she heard my father coming from the dressing-room, where he had gone to take off his clothes, and, to avoid the scene which he would make if he saw me, she said to me in a voice half-stifled with anger: "Off you go at once. Do you want your father to see you waiting there like an idiot?" But I implored her again: "Come and say good night to me," terrified as I saw the light from my father's candle already creeping up the wall, but also making use of his approach as a means of blackmail, in the hope that my mother, not wishing him to find me there, as find me he must if she continued to refuse me, would give in and say: "Go back to your room. I will come."

Too late: my father was upon us. Instinctively I mur-mured, though no one heard me, "I'm done for!"

I was not, however. My father used constantly to refuse to let me do things which were quite clearly al-

lowed by the more liberal charters granted me by my
mother and grandmother, because he paid no heed to
"principles," and because for him there was no such thing
as the "rule of law." For some quite irrelevant reason, or
for no reason at all, he would at the last moment prevent
me from taking some particular walk, one so regular, so
hallowed, that to deprive me of it was a clear breach of
faith; or again, as he had done this evening, long before
the appointed hour he would snap out: "Run along up
to bed now; no excuses!" But at the same time, because
he was devoid of principles (in my grandmother's sense),
he could not, strictly speaking, be called intransigent. He
looked at me for a moment with an air of surprise and
annoyance, and then when Mamma had told him, not
without some embarrassment, what had happened, said to
her: "Go along with him, then. You said just now that
you didn't feel very sleepy, so stay in his room for a little.
I don't need anything."

"But, my dear," my mother answered timidly,
"whether or not I feel sleepy is not the point; we mustn't
let the child get into the habit . . ."

"There's no question of getting into a habit," said my
father, with a shrug of the shoulders; "you can see quite
well that the child is unhappy. After all, we aren't gaol-
ers. You'll end by making him ill, and a lot of good that
will do. There are two beds in his room; tell Françoise to
make up the big one for you, and stay with him for the
rest of the night. Anyhow, I'm off to bed; I'm not so
nervy as you. Good night."

It was impossible for me to thank my father; he
would have been exasperated by what he called mawkish-
ness. I stood there, not daring to move; he was still in

front of us, a tall figure in his white nightshirt, crowned with the pink and violet cashmere scarf which he used to wrap around his head since he had begun to suffer from neuralgia, standing like Abraham in the engraving after Benozzo Gozzoli which M. Swann had given me, telling Sarah that she must tear herself away from Isaac. Many years have passed since that night. The wall of the staircase up which I had watched the light of his candle gradually climb was long ago demolished. And in myself, too, many things have perished which I imagined would last for ever, and new ones have arisen, giving birth to new sorrows and new joys which in those days I could not have foreseen, just as now the old are hard to understand. It is a long time, too, since my father has been able to say to Mamma: "Go along with the child." Never again will such moments be possible for me. But of late I have been increasingly able to catch, if I listen attentively, the sound of the sobs which I had the strength to control in my father's presence, and which broke out only when I found myself alone with Mamma. In reality their echo has never ceased; and it is only because life is now growing more and more quiet round about me that I hear them anew, like those convent bells which are so effectively drowned during the day by the noises of the street that one would suppose them to have stopped, until they ring out again through the silent evening air.

Mamma spent that night in my room: when I had just committed an offence for which I expected to be banished from the household, my parents gave me a far greater concession than I could ever have won as the reward of a good deed. Even at the moment when it manifested itself in this crowning mercy, my father's behaviour towards me still retained that arbitrary and unwarranted quality which was so characteristic of him and which arose from the fact that his actions were generally dictated by chance expediencies rather than based on any formal plan. And perhaps even what I called his severity, when he sent me off to bed, deserved that title less than my mother's or my grandmother's attitude, for his nature, which in some respects differed more than theirs from my own, had probably prevented him from realising until then how wretched I was every evening, something which my mother and grandmother knew well; but they loved me enough to be unwilling to spare me that suffering, which they hoped to teach me to overcome, so as to reduce my nervous sensibility and to strengthen my will. Whereas my father, whose affection for me was of another kind, would not, I suspect, have had the same courage, for as soon as he had grasped the fact that I was unhappy he had said to my mother: "Go and comfort him."

Mamma stayed that night in my room, and it seemed that she did not wish to mar by recrimination those hours which were so different from anything that I had had a right to expect, for when Françoise (who guessed that something extraordinary must have happened when she saw Mamma sitting by my side, holding my hand and letting me cry unchided) said to her: "But, Madame, what is young master crying for?" she replied: "Why, Françoise, he doesn't know himself: it's his nerves. Make up the big bed for me quickly and then go off to your own." And thus for the first time my unhappiness was regarded no longer as a punishable offence but as an involuntary ailment which had been officially recognised, a

nervous condition for which I was in no way responsible:
I had the consolation of no longer having to mingle ap-
prehensive scruples with the bitterness of my tears; I
could weep henceforth without sin. I felt no small degree
of pride, either, in Françoise's presence at this return to
humane conditions which, not an hour after Mamma had
refused to come up to my room and had sent the snub-
bing message that I was to go to sleep, raised me to the
dignity of a grown-up person, brought me of a sudden to
a sort of puberty of sorrow, a manumission of tears. I
ought to have been happy; I was not. It struck me that
my mother had just made a first concession which must
have been painful to her, that it was a first abdication on
her part from the ideal she had formed for me, and that
for the first time she who was so brave had to confess
herself beaten. It struck me that if I had just won a victory it was over her, that I had succeeded, as sickness or
sorrow or age might have succeeded, in relaxing her will,
in undermining her judgment; and that this evening
opened a new era, would remain a black date in the calendar. And if I had dared now, I should have said to
Mamma: "No, I don't want you to, you mustn't sleep
here." But I was conscious of the practical wisdom, of
what would nowadays be called the realism, with which
she tempered the ardent idealism of my grandmother's
nature, and I knew that now the mischief was done she
would prefer to let me enjoy the soothing pleasure of her
company, and not to disturb my father again. Certainly
my mother's beautiful face seemed to shine again with
youth that evening, as she sat gently holding my hands
and trying to check my tears; but this was just what I felt
should not have been; her anger would have saddened me

less than this new gentleness, unknown to my childhood experience; I felt that I had with an impious and secret finger traced a first wrinkle upon her soul and brought out a first white hair on her head. This thought redoubled my sobs, and then I saw that Mamma, who had never allowed herself to indulge in any undue emotion with me, was suddenly overcome by my tears and had to struggle to keep back her own. When she realised that I had noticed this, she said to me with a smile: "Why, my little chick, my little canary, he's going to make Mamma as silly as himself if this goes on. Look, since you can't sleep, and Mamma can't either, we mustn't go on in this stupid way; we must do something; I'll get one of your books." But I had none there. "Would you like me to get out the books now that your grandmother is going to give you for your birthday? Just think it over first, and don't be disappointed if there's nothing new for you then."

I was only too delighted, and Mamma went to fetch a parcel of books of which I could not distinguish, through the paper in which they were wrapped, any more than their short, wide format but which, even at this first glimpse, brief and obscure as it was, bade fair to eclipse already the paintbox of New Year's Day and the silkworms of the year before. The books were *La Mare au Diable, François le Champi, La Petite Fadette* and *Les Maîtres Sonneurs*. My grandmother, as I learned afterwards, had at first chosen Musset's poems, a volume of Rousseau, and *Indiana*; for while she considered light reading as unwholesome as sweets and cakes, she did not reflect that the strong breath of genius might have upon the mind even of a child an influence at once more dangerous and less invigorating than that of fresh air and sea

breezes upon his body. But when my father had almost
called her an imbecile on learning the names of the books
she proposed to give me, she had journeyed back by herself to Jouy-le-Vicomte to the bookseller's, so that there
should be no danger of my not having my present in time
(it was a boiling hot day, and she had come home so unwell that the doctor had warned my mother not to allow
her to tire herself so), and had fallen back upon the four
pastoral novels of George Sand. "My dear," she had said
to Mamma, "I could not bring myself to give the child
anything that was not well written."

The truth was that she could never permit herself to
buy anything from which no intellectual profit was to be
derived, above all the profit which fine things afford us
by teaching us to seek our pleasures elsewhere than in the
barren satisfaction of worldly wealth. Even when she had
to make someone a present of the kind called "useful,"
when she had to give an armchair or some table-silver or
a walking-stick, she would choose antiques, as though
their long desuetude had effaced from them any semblance of utility and fitted them rather to instruct us in
the lives of the men of other days than to serve the common requirements of our own. She would have liked me
to have in my room photographs of ancient buildings or
of beautiful places. But at the moment of buying them,
and for all that the subject of the picture had an aesthetic
value, she would find that vulgarity and utility had too
prominent a part in them, through the mechanical nature
of their reproduction by photography. She attempted by a
subterfuge, if not to eliminate altogether this commercial
banality, at least to minimise it, to supplant it to a certain
extent with what was art still, to introduce, as it were,

several "thicknesses" of art: instead of photographs of Chartres Cathedral, of the Fountains of Saint-Cloud, or of Vesuvius, she would inquire of Swann whether some great painter had not depicted them, and preferred to give me photographs of "Chartres Cathedral" after Corot, of the "Fountains of Saint-Cloud" after Hubert Robert, and of "Vesuvius" after Turner, which were a stage higher in the scale of art. But although the photographer had been prevented from reproducing directly these masterpieces or beauties of nature, and had there been replaced by a great artist, he resumed his odious position when it came to reproducing the artist's interpretation. Accordingly, having to reckon again with vulgarity, my grandmother would endeavour to postpone the moment of contact still further. She would ask Swann if the picture had not been engraved, preferring, when possible, old engravings with some interest of association apart from themselves, such, for example, as show us a masterpiece in a state in which we can no longer see it today (like Morghen's print of Leonardo's "Last Supper" before its defacement). It must be admitted that the results of this method of interpreting the art of making presents were not always happy. The idea which I formed of Venice, from a drawing by Titian which is supposed to have the lagoon in the background, was certainly far less accurate than what I should have derived from ordinary photographs. We could no longer keep count in the family (when my great-aunt wanted to draw up an indictment of my grandmother) of all the armchairs she had presented to married couples, young and old, which on a first attempt to sit down upon them had at once collapsed beneath the weight of their recipients. But my grandmother would have thought it sordid

to concern herself too closely with the solidity of any
piece of furniture in which could still be discerned a
flourish, a smile, a brave conceit of the past. And even
what in such pieces answered a material need, since it did
so in a manner to which we are no longer accustomed,
charmed her like those old forms of speech in which we
can still see traces of a metaphor whose fine point has
been worn away by the rough usage of our modern
tongue. As it happened, the pastoral novels of George
Sand which she was giving me for my birthday were regular lumber-rooms full of expressions that have fallen out
of use and become quaint and picturesque, and are now
only to be found in country dialects. And my grandmother had bought them in preference to other books, as
she would more readily have taken a house with a Gothic
dovecot or some other such piece of antiquity as will exert
a benign influence on the mind by giving it a hankering
for impossible journeys through the realms of time.

Mamma sat down by my bed; she had chosen
François le Champi, whose reddish cover and incomprehensible title gave it, for me, a distinct personality and a
mysterious attraction. I had not then read any real novels.
I had heard it said that George Sand was a typical novelist. This predisposed me to imagine that *François le
Champi* contained something inexpressibly delicious. The
narrative devices designed to arouse curiosity or melt to
pity, certain modes of expression which disturb or sadden
the reader, and which, with a little experience, he may
recognise as common to a great many novels, seemed to
me—for whom a new book was not one of a number of
similar objects but, as it were, a unique person, absolutely
self-contained—simply an intoxicating distillation of the

peculiar essence of *François le Champi*. Beneath the everyday incidents, the ordinary objects and common words, I
sensed a strange and individual tone of voice. The plot
began to unfold: to me it seemed all the more obscure because in those days, when I read, I used often to day-
dream about something quite different for page after
page. And the gaps which this habit left in my knowledge
of the story were widened by the fact that when it was
Mamma who was reading to me aloud she left all the
love-scenes out. And so all the odd changes which take
place in the relations between the miller's wife and the
boy, changes which only the gradual dawning of love can
explain, seemed to me steeped in a mystery the key to
which (I readily believed) lay in that strange and melliflu-
ous name of *Champi*, which invested the boy who bore it,
I had no idea why, with its own vivid, ruddy, charming
colour. If my mother was not a faithful reader, she was
none the less an admirable one, when reading a work in
which she found the note of true feeling, in the respectful
simplicity of her interpretation and the beauty and sweetness of her voice. Even in ordinary life, when it was not
works of art but men and women whom she was moved
to pity or admire, it was touching to observe with what
deference she would banish from her voice, her gestures,
from her whole conversation, now the note of gaiety
which might have distressed some mother who had once
lost a child, now the recollection of an event or anniversary which might have reminded some old gentleman of
the burden of his years, now the household topic which
might have bored some young man of letters. And so,
when she read aloud the prose of George Sand, prose
which is everywhere redolent of that generosity and moral

distinction which Mamma had learned from my grandmother to place above all other qualities in life, and which
I was not to teach her until much later to refrain from
placing above all other qualities in literature too, taking
pains to banish from her voice any pettiness or affectation
which might have choked that powerful stream of language, she supplied all the natural tenderness, all the lavish sweetness which they demanded to sentences which
seemed to have been composed for her voice and which
were all, so to speak, within the compass of her sensibility. She found, to tackle them in the required tone, the
warmth of feeling which pre-existed and dictated them,
but which is not to be found in the words themselves,
and by this means she smoothed away, as she read, any
harshness or discordance in the tenses of verbs, endowing
the imperfect and the preterite with all the sweetness to
be found in generosity, all the melancholy to be found
in love, guiding the sentence that was drawing to a close
towards the one that was about to begin, now hastening,
now slackening the pace of the syllables so as to bring
them, despite their differences of quantity, into a uniform
rhythm, and breathing into this quite ordinary prose a
kind of emotional life and continuity.

My aching heart was soothed; I let myself be borne
upon the current of this gentle night on which I had my
mother by my side. I knew that such a night could not be
repeated; that the strongest desire I had in the world,
namely, to keep my mother in my room through the sad
hours of darkness, ran too much counter to general requirements and to the wishes of others for such a concession as had been granted me this evening to be anything
but a rare and artificial exception. Tomorrow night my

anguish would return and Mamma would not stay by my side. But when my anguish was assuaged, I could no longer understand it; besides, tomorrow was still a long way off; I told myself that I should still have time to take preventive action, although that time could bring me no access of power since these things were in no way dependent upon the exercise of my will, and seemed not quite inevitable only because they were still separated from me by this short interval.

And so it was that, for a long time afterwards, when I lay awake at night and revived old memories of Combray, I saw no more of it than this sort of luminous panel, sharply defined against a vague and shadowy background, like the panels which the glow of a Bengal light or a searchlight beam will cut out and illuminate in a building the other parts of which remain plunged in darkness: broad enough at its base, the little parlour, the dining-room, the opening of the dark path from which M. Swann, the unwitting author of my sufferings, would emerge, the hall through which I would journey to the first step of that staircase, so painful to climb, which constituted, all by itself, the slender cone of this irregular pyramid; and, at the summit, my bedroom, with the little passage through whose glazed door Mamma would enter; in a word, seen always at the same evening hour, isolated from all its possible surroundings, detached and solitary against the dark background, the bare minimum of scenery necessary (like the décor one sees prescribed on the title-page of an old play, for its performance in the provinces) to the drama of my undressing; as though all

Combray had consisted of but two floors joined by a slender staircase, and as though there had been no time there
but seven o'clock at night. I must own that I could have
assured any questioner that Combray did include other
scenes and did exist at other hours than these. But since
the facts which I should then have recalled would have
been prompted only by voluntary memory, the memory
of the intellect, and since the pictures which that kind of
memory shows us preserve nothing of the past itself, I
should never have had any wish to ponder over this
residue of Combray. To me it was in reality all dead.

Permanently dead? Very possibly.

There is a large element of chance in these matters,
and a second chance occurrence, that of our own death,
often prevents us from awaiting for any length of time the
favours of the first.

I feel that there is much to be said for the Celtic belief that the souls of those whom we have lost are held
captive in some inferior being, in an animal, in a plant, in
some inanimate object, and thus effectively lost to us until the day (which to many never comes) when we happen
to pass by the tree or to obtain possession of the object
which forms their prison. Then they start and tremble,
they call us by our name, and as soon as we have recognised them the spell is broken. Delivered by us, they have
overcome death and return to share our life.

And so it is with our own past. It is a labour in vain
to attempt to recapture it: all the efforts of our intellect
must prove futile. The past is hidden somewhere outside
the realm, beyond the reach of intellect, in some material
object (in the sensation which that material object will

give us) of which we have no inkling. And it depends on chance whether or not we come upon this object before we ourselves must die.

Many years had elapsed during which nothing of Combray, except what lay in the theatre and the drama of my going to bed there, had any existence for me, when one day in winter, on my return home, my mother, seeing that I was cold, offered me some tea, a thing I did not ordinarily take. I declined at first, and then, for no particular reason, changed my mind. She sent for one of those squat, plump little cakes called "petites madeleines," which look as though they had been moulded in the fluted valve of a scallop shell. And soon, mechanically, dispirited after a dreary day with the prospect of a depressing morrow, I raised to my lips a spoonful of the tea in which I had soaked a morsel of the cake. No sooner had the warm liquid mixed with the crumbs touched my palate than a shiver ran through me and I stopped, intent upon the extraordinary thing that was happening to me. An exquisite pleasure had invaded my senses, something isolated, detached, with no suggestion of its origin. And at once the vicissitudes of life had become indifferent to me, its disasters innocuous, its brevity illusory—this new sensation having had the effect, which love has, of filling me with a precious essence; or rather this essence was not in me, it *was* me. I had ceased now to feel mediocre, contingent, mortal. Whence could it have come to me, this all-powerful joy? I sensed that it was connected with the taste of the tea and the cake, but that it infinitely transcended those savours, could not, indeed, be of the same nature. Where did it come from? What did it mean? How could I seize and apprehend it?

I drink a second mouthful, in which I find nothing more than in the first, then a third, which gives me rather less than the second. It is time to stop; the potion is losing its virtue. It is plain that the truth I am seeking lies not in the cup but in myself. The drink has called it into being, but does not know it, and can only repeat indefinitely, with a progressive diminution of strength, the same message which I cannot interpret, though I hope at least to be able to call it forth again and to find it there presently, intact and at my disposal, for my final enlightenment. I put down the cup and examine my own mind. It alone can discover the truth. But how? What an abyss of uncertainty, whenever the mind feels overtaken by itself; when it, the seeker, is at the same time the dark region through which it must go seeking and where all its equipment will avail it nothing. Seek? More than that: create. It is face to face with something which does not yet exist, which it alone can make actual, which it alone can bring into the light of day.

And I begin again to ask myself what it could have been, this unremembered state which brought with it no logical proof, but the indisputable evidence, of its felicity, its reality, and in whose presence other states of consciousness melted and vanished. I want to try to make it reappear. I retrace my thoughts to the moment at which I drank the first spoonful of tea. I rediscover the same state, illuminated by no fresh light. I ask my mind to make one further effort, to bring back once more the fleeting sensation. And so that nothing may interrupt it in its course I shut out every obstacle, every extraneous idea, I stop my ears and screen my attention from the sounds from the next room. And then, feeling that my mind is

tiring itself without having any success to report, I compel it for a change to enjoy the distraction which I have
just denied it, to think of other things, to rest and refresh
itself before making a final effort. And then for the second time I clear an empty space in front of it; I place in
position before my mind's eye the still recent taste of that
first mouthful, and I feel something start within me,
something that leaves its resting-place and attempts to
rise, something that has been anchored at a great depth; I
do not know yet what it is, but I can feel it mounting
slowly; I can measure the resistance, I can hear the echo
of great spaces traversed.

Undoubtedly what is thus palpitating in the depths of
my being must be the image, the visual memory which,
being linked to that taste, is trying to follow it into my
conscious mind. But its struggles are too far off, too confused and chaotic; scarcely can I perceive the neutral glow
into which the elusive whirling medley of stirred-up
colours is fused, and I cannot distinguish its form, cannot
invite it, as the one possible interpreter, to translate for
me the evidence of its contemporary, its inseparable
paramour, the taste, cannot ask it to inform me what special circumstance is in question, from what period in my
past life.

Will it ultimately reach the clear surface of my
consciousness, this memory, this old, dead moment which
the magnetism of an identical moment has travelled so
far to importune, to disturb, to raise up out of the
very depths of my being? I cannot tell. Now I feel nothing; it has stopped, has perhaps sunk back into its darkness, from which who can say whether it will ever rise

again? Ten times over I must essay the task, must lean
down over the abyss. And each time the cowardice that
deters us from every difficult task, every important enterprise, has urged me to leave the thing alone, to drink my
tea and to think merely of the worries of today and my
hopes for tomorrow, which can be brooded over
painlessly.

And suddenly the memory revealed itself. The taste
was that of the little piece of madeleine which on Sunday
mornings at Combray (because on those mornings I did
not go out before mass), when I went to say good morning to her in her bedroom, my aunt Léonie used to give
me, dipping it first in her own cup of tea or tisane. The
sight of the little madeleine had recalled nothing to my
mind before I tasted it; perhaps because I had so often
seen such things in the meantime, without tasting them,
on the trays in pastry-cooks' windows, that their image
had dissociated itself from those Combray days to take its
place among others more recent; perhaps because, of
those memories so long abandoned and put out of mind,
nothing now survived, everything was scattered; the
shapes of things, including that of the little scallop-shell
of pastry, so richly sensual under its severe, religious
folds, were either obliterated or had been so long dormant
as to have lost the power of expansion which would have
allowed them to resume their place in my consciousness.
But when from a long-distant past nothing subsists, after
the people are dead, after the things are broken and scattered, taste and smell alone, more fragile but more enduring, more immaterial, more persistent, more faithful,
remain poised a long time, like souls, remembering, wait-

ing, hoping, amid the ruins of all the rest; and bear un-
flinchingly, in the tiny and almost impalpable drop of
their essence, the vast structure of recollection.

And as soon as I had recognised the taste of the piece
of madeleine soaked in her decoction of lime-blossom
which my aunt used to give me (although I did not yet
know and must long postpone the discovery of why this
memory made me so happy) immediately the old grey
house upon the street, where her room was, rose up like a
stage set to attach itself to the little pavilion opening on to
the garden which had been built out behind it for my
parents (the isolated segment which until that moment
had been all that I could see); and with the house the
town, from morning to night and in all weathers, the
Square where I used to be sent before lunch, the streets
along which I used to run errands, the country roads we
took when it was fine. And as in the game wherein the
Japanese amuse themselves by filling a porcelain bowl
with water and steeping in it little pieces of paper which
until then are without character or form, but, the moment
they become wet, stretch and twist and take on colour
and distinctive shape, become flowers or houses or people,
solid and recognisable, so in that moment all the flowers
in our garden and in M. Swann's park, and the water-
lilies on the Vivonne and the good folk of the village and
their little dwellings and the parish church and the whole
of Combray and its surroundings, taking shape and solidity, sprang into being, town and gardens alike, from my
cup of tea.

II

Combray at a distance, from a twenty-mile radius, as we
used to see it from the railway when we arrived there in
the week before Easter, was no more than a church epito-
mising the town, representing it, speaking of it and for it
to the horizon, and as one drew near, gathering close
about its long, dark cloak, sheltering from the wind, on
the open plain, as a shepherdess gathers her sheep, the
woolly grey backs of its huddled houses, which the remains of its mediaeval ramparts enclosed, here and there,
in an outline as scrupulously circular as that of a little
town in a primitive painting. To live in, Combray was a
trifle depressing, like its streets, whose houses, built of the
blackened stone of the country, fronted with outside
steps, capped with gables which projected long shadows
downwards, were so dark that as soon as the sun began to
go down one had to draw back the curtains in the sitting-
room windows; streets with the solemn names of saints,
not a few of whom figured in the history of the early
lords of Combray, such as the Rue Saint-Hilaire, the Rue
Saint-Jacques, in which my aunt's house stood, the Rue
Sainte-Hildegarde, which ran past her railings, and the
Rue du Saint-Esprit, on to which the little garden gate
opened; and these Combray streets exist in so remote a
corner of my memory, painted in colours so different
from those in which the world is decked for me today,
that in fact one and all of them, and the church which
towered above them in the Square, seem to me now more
unreal than the projections of my magic lantern; and at
times I feel that to be able to cross the Rue Saint-Hilaire
again, to engage a room in the Rue de l'Oiseau, in the old

hostelry of the Oiseau Flesché, from whose basement windows used to rise a smell of cooking which rises still in my mind, now and then, in the same warm and intermittent gusts, would be to secure a contact with the Beyond more marvellously supernatural than it would be to make Golo's acquaintance and to chat with Geneviève de Brabant.

My grandfather's cousin—by courtesy my great-aunt—with whom we used to stay, was the mother of that aunt Léonie who, since her husband's (my uncle Octave's) death, had gradually declined to leave, first Combray, then her house in Combray, then her bedroom, and finally her bed, and now never "came down," but lay perpetually in a vague state of grief, physical debility, illness, obsession and piety. Her private apartment looked out over the Rue Saint-Jacques, which ran a long way further to end in the Grand-Pré (as distinct from the Petit-Pré, a green space in the centre of the town where three streets met) and which, monotonous and grey, with the three high sandstone steps before almost every one of its doors, seemed like a deep furrow carved by some sculptor of Gothic images out of the block of stone from which he might have fashioned a calvary or a crib. My aunt's life was now practically confined to two adjoining rooms, in one of which she would spend the afternoon while the other was being aired. They were rooms of that country order which—just as in certain climes whole tracts of air or ocean are illuminated or scented by myriads of protozoa which we cannot see—enchants us with the countless odours emanating from the virtues, wisdom, habits, a whole secret system of life, invisible, superabundant and profoundly moral, which their atmosphere holds in solution; smells natural enough indeed, and weather-tinted like those of the neighbouring countryside, but already humanised, domesticated, snug, an exquisite, limpid jelly skilfully blended from all the fruits of the year which have left the orchard for the store-room, smells changing with the season, but plenishing and homely, offsetting the sharpness of hoarfrost with the sweetness of warm bread, smells lazy and punctual as a village clock, roving and settled, heedless and provident, linen smells, morning smells, pious smells, rejoicing in a peace which brings only additional anxiety, and in a prosaicness which serves as a deep reservoir of poetry to the stranger who passes through their midst without having lived among them. The air of those rooms was saturated with the fine bouquet of a silence so nourishing, so succulent, that I never went into them without a sort of greedy anticipation, particularly on those first mornings, chilly still, of the Easter holidays, when I could taste it more fully because I had only just arrived in Combray: before I went in to say good morning to my aunt I would be kept waiting a moment in the outer room where the sun, wintry still, had crept in to warm itself before the fire, which was already alight between its two bricks and plastering the whole room with a smell of soot, turning it into one of those great rustic open hearths, or one of those canopied mantelpieces in country houses, beneath which one sits hoping that in the world outside it is raining or snowing, hoping almost for a catastrophic deluge to add the romance of being in winter quarters to the comfort of a snug retreat; I would pace to and fro between the prie-dieu and the stamped velvet armchairs, each one always draped in its crocheted antimacassar, while the fire, bak-

ing like dough the appetising smells with which the air of
the room was thickly clotted and which the moist and
sunny freshness of the morning had already "raised" and
started to "set," puffed them and glazed them and fluted
them and swelled them into an invisible though not impalpable country pie, an immense "turnover" to which,
barely waiting to savour the crisper, more delicate, more
reputable but also drier aromas of the cupboard, the chest
of drawers and the patterned wall-paper, I always returned with an unconfessed gluttony to wallow in the
central, glutinous, insipid, indigestible and fruity smell of
the flowered bedspread.

In the next room I could hear my aunt talking quietly
to herself. She never spoke except in low tones, because
she believed that there was something broken inside her
head and floating loose there, which she might displace
by talking too loud; but she never remained for long, even
when alone, without saying something, because she believed that it was good for her throat, and that by keeping
the blood there in circulation it would make less frequent
the chokings and the pains from which she suffered; besides, in the life of complete inertia which she led, she
attached to the least of her sensations an extraordinary
importance, endowed them with a Protean ubiquity which
made it difficult for her to keep them to herself, and, failing a confidant to whom she might communicate them,
she used to promulgate them to herself in an unceasing
monologue which was her sole form of activity. Unfortunately, having formed the habit of thinking aloud, she did
not always take care to see that there was no one in the
adjoining room, and I would often hear her saying to herself: "I must not forget that I never slept a wink"—for

"never sleeping a wink" was her great claim to distinction, and one admitted and respected in our household vocabulary: in the morning Françoise would not "wake" her, but would simply "go in" to her; during the day, when my aunt wished to take a nap, we used to say just that she wished to "ponder" or to "rest"; and when in conversation she so far forgot herself as to say "what woke me up," or "I dreamed that," she would blush and at once correct herself.

After waiting a minute, I would go in and kiss her; Françoise would be making her tea; or, if my aunt felt agitated, she would ask instead for her tisane, and it would be my duty to shake out of the chemist's little package on to a plate the amount of lime-blossom required for infusion in boiling water. The drying of the stems had twisted them into a fantastic trellis, in the interlacings of which the pale flowers opened, as though a painter had arranged them there, grouping them in the most decorative poses. The leaves, having lost or altered their original appearance, resembled the most disparate things, the transparent wing of a fly, the blank side of a label, the petal of a rose, which had all been piled together, pounded or interwoven like the materials for a nest. A thousand trifling little details—a charming prodigality on the part of the chemist—details which would have been eliminated from an artificial preparation, gave me, like a book in which one reads with astonished delight the name of a person one knows, the pleasure of finding that these were sprigs of real lime-trees, like those I had seen, when coming from the train, in the Avenue de la Gare, altered indeed, precisely because they were not imitations but themselves, and because they had aged. And as each new character is

merely a metamorphosis from something earlier, in these
little grey balls I recognised green buds plucked before
their time; but beyond all else the rosy, lunar, tender
gleam that lit up the blossoms among the frail forest of
stems from which they hung like little golden roses—
marking, as the glow upon an old wall still marks the
place of a vanished fresco, the difference between those
parts of the tree which had and those which had not been
"in colour"—showed me that these were indeed petals
which, before filling the chemist's bag with their spring
fragrance, had perfumed the evening air. That rosy can-
dleglow was still their colour, but half-extinguished and
deadened in the diminished life which was now theirs,
and which may be called the twilight of a flower.
Presently my aunt would dip a little madeleine in the
boiling infusion, whose taste of dead leaves or faded blossom she so relished, and hand me a piece when it was
sufficiently soft.

At one side of her bed stood a big yellow chest of
drawers of lemon-wood, and a table which served at once
as dispensary and high altar, on which, beneath a statue
of the Virgin and a bottle of Vichy-Célestins, might be
found her prayer-books and her medical prescriptions, everything that she needed for the performance, in bed, of
her duties to soul and body, to keep the proper times for
pepsin and for vespers. On the other side her bed was
bounded by the window: she had the street in full view,
and would while away the time by reading in it from
morning to night, like the Persian princes of old, the daily
but immemorial chronicles of Combray, which she would
discuss in detail later with Françoise.

Scarcely had I been five minutes with my aunt before

she would send me away for fear that I might tire her. She would hold out for me to kiss her sad, pale, lacklustre forehead, on which at this early hour she would not yet have arranged the false hair and through which the bones shone like the points of a crown of thorns or the beads of a rosary, and she would say to me: "Now, my poor child, off you go and get ready for mass; and if you see Françoise downstairs, tell her not to stay too long amusing herself with you; she must come up soon to see if I need anything."

Françoise, who had been for many years in my aunt's service and did not at that time suspect that she would one day be transferred entirely to ours, was a little inclined to neglect my aunt during the months which we spent there. There had been in my early childhood, before we first went to Combray, and when my aunt Léonie used still to spend the winter in Paris with her mother, a time when I knew Françoise so little that on New Year's Day, before going into my great-aunt's house, my mother would put a five-franc piece into my hand and say: "Now, be careful. Don't make any mistake. Wait until you hear me say 'Good morning, Françoise,' and tap you on the arm, before you give it to her." No sooner had we arrived in my aunt's dark hall than we saw in the gloom, beneath the frills of a snowy bonnet as stiff and fragile as if it had been made of spun sugar, the concentric ripples of a smile of anticipatory gratitude. It was Françoise, motionless and erect, framed in the small doorway of the corridor like the statue of a saint in its niche. When we had grown more accustomed to this religious darkness we could discern in her features the disinterested love of humanity, the tender respect for the gentry, which the hope

of receiving New Year bounty intensified in the nobler regions of her heart. Mamma pinched my arm sharply and
said in a loud voice: "Good morning, Françoise." At this
signal my fingers parted and I let fall the coin, which
found a receptacle in a shy but outstretched hand. But
since we had begun to go to Combray there was no one I
knew better than Françoise. We were her favourites, and
in the first years at least she showed for us not only the
same consideration as for my aunt, but a keener relish,
because we had, in addition to the prestige of belonging
to "the family" (for she had for those invisible bonds
which the community of blood creates between the members of a family as much respect as any Greek tragedian),
the charm of not being her customary employers. And so
with what joy would she welcome us, with what sorrow
complain that the weather was still so bad for us, on the
day of our arrival, just before Easter, when there was often an icy wind; while Mamma inquired after her daughter and her nephews, and if her grandson was a nice boy,
and what they were going to do with him, and whether he
took after his granny.

And later, when no one else was in the room,
Mamma, who knew that Françoise was still mourning for
her parents, who had been dead for years, would speak to
her kindly about them, asking her endless little questions
concerning their lives.

She had guessed that Françoise was not over-fond of
her son-in-law, and that he spoiled the pleasure she found
in visiting her daughter, with whom she could not talk so
freely when he was there. And so, when Françoise was
going to their house, some miles from Combray, Mamma
would say to her with a smile: "Tell me, Françoise, if

Julien has had to go away, and you have Marguerite to yourself all day, you'll be very sorry, but you will make the best of it, won't you?"

And Françoise answered, laughing: "Madame knows everything; Madame is worse than the X-rays" (she pronounced the "x" with an affectation of difficulty and a self-mocking smile that someone so ignorant should employ this learned term) "that they brought here for Mme Octave, and which can see what's in your heart"—and she went off, overwhelmed that anyone should be caring about her, perhaps anxious that we should not see her in tears: Mamma was the first person who had given her the heart-warming feeling that her peasant existence, with its simple joys and sorrows, might be an object of interest, might be a source of grief or pleasure to someone other than herself.

My aunt resigned herself to doing without Françoise to some extent during our visits, knowing how much my mother appreciated the services of so active and intelligent a maid, one who looked as smart at five o'clock in the morning in her kitchen, under a bonnet whose stiff and dazzling frills seemed to be made of porcelain, as when dressed for high mass; who did everything in the right way, toiling like a horse, whether she was well or ill, but without fuss, without the appearance of doing anything; the only one of my aunt's maids who when Mamma asked for hot water or black coffee would bring them actually boiling. She was one of those servants who, in a household, seem least satisfactory at first to a stranger, doubtless because they take no pains to make a conquest of him and show him no special attention, knowing very well that they have no real need of him, that he will cease to be invited to the house sooner than they will be dismissed from it, but who, on the other hand, are most prized by masters and mistresses who have tested and proved their real capacity, and care nothing for that superficial affability, that servile chit-chat which may impress a stranger favourably, but often conceals an incurable incompetence.

When Françoise, having seen that my parents had everything they required, first went upstairs again to give my aunt her pepsin and to find out from her what she would take for lunch, it was rare indeed for her not to be called upon to give an opinion, or to furnish an explanation, in regard to some important event.

"Just fancy, Françoise, Mme Goupil went by more than a quarter of an hour late to fetch her sister: if she loses any more time on the way I shouldn't be at all surprised if she arrived after the Elevation."

"Well, there'd be nothing wonderful in that," would be the answer.

"Françoise, if you had come in five minutes ago, you would have seen Mme Imbert go past with some asparagus twice the size of Mother Callot's: do try to find out from her cook where she got them. You know you've been serving asparagus with everything this spring; you might be able to get some like those for our visitors."

"I shouldn't be surprised if they came from the Curé's," Françoise would say.

"I'm sure you wouldn't, my poor Françoise," my aunt would reply, shrugging her shoulders. "From the Curé's, indeed! You know quite well that he never grows anything but wretched little twigs of asparagus. I tell you these ones were as thick as my arm. Not your arm, of course, but my poor arm, which has grown so much thinner again this year . . . Françoise, didn't you hear that bell just now that nearly split my skull?"

"No, Mme Octave."

"Ah, my poor girl, your skull must be very thick; you may thank God for that. It was Maguelone come to fetch Dr Piperaud. He came out with her at once and they went off along the Rue de l'Oiseau. There must be some child ill."

"Oh, dear God!" Françoise would sigh, for she could not hear of any calamity befalling a person unknown to her, even in some distant part of the world, without beginning to lament.

"Françoise, who were they tolling the knell for just now? Oh dear, of course, it would be for Mme Rousseau. And to think that I had forgotten that she passed away the other night. Ah! it's time the good Lord called me too; I don't know what has become of my head since I lost my poor Octave. But I'm wasting your time, my good girl."

"Not at all, Mme Octave, my time is not so precious; the one who made it doesn't charge us for it. I'm just going to see if my fire's going out."

Thus Françoise and my aunt between them made a critical evaluation, in the course of these morning sessions, of the earliest events of the day. But sometimes these events assumed so mysterious or so alarming a character that my aunt felt she could not wait until it was time for Françoise to come upstairs, and then a formidable and quadruple peal would resound through the house.

"But, Mme Octave, it's not yet time for your pepsin," Françoise would begin. "Are you feeling faint?"

"No, no, Françoise," my aunt would reply, "that is to say, yes; you know quite well that there's very seldom a time when I don't feel faint; one day I shall pass away like Mme Rousseau, before I know where I am; but that's not why I rang. Would you believe that I've just seen, as plain as I can see you, Mme Goupil with a little girl I didn't know from Adam. Run and get a pennyworth of salt from Camus. It's not often that Théodore can't tell you who a person is."

"But that must be M. Pupin's daughter," Françoise would say, preferring to stick to an immediate explanation, since she had been twice already into Camus's shop that morning.

"M. Pupin's daughter! Oh, that's a likely story, my poor Françoise. Do you think I wouldn't have recognised M. Pupin's daughter!"

"But I don't mean the big one, Mme Octave; I mean the little lass, the one who goes to school at Jouy. It be-seems I've seen her once already this morning."

"Ah! that's probably it," my aunt would say. "She must have come over for the holidays. Yes, that's it. No need to ask, she will have come over for the holidays. But then we shall soon see Mme Sazerat come along and ring her sister's door-bell for lunch. That will be it! I saw the boy from Galopin's go by with a tart. You'll see that the tart was for Mme Goupil."

"Once Mme Goupil has company, Mme Octave, you won't have long to wait before you see all her folk going home to their lunch, for it's not so early as it was," Françoise would say, for she was anxious to return downstairs to look after our own meal, and was not sorry to leave my aunt with the prospect of such a diversion.

"Oh! not before midday," my aunt would reply in a tone of resignation, darting an anxious glance at the clock, but furtively, so as not to let it be seen that she, who had renounced all earthly joys, yet found a keen satisfaction in learning that Mme Goupil was expecting company to lunch, though, alas, she must wait a little more than an hour still before enjoying the spectacle. "And it will come in the middle of my lunch!" she would murmur to herself. Her lunch was such a distraction in itself that she did not wish for any other at the same time. "I hope you won't forget to give me my creamed eggs on one of the flat plates?" she would add. These were the only plates which had pictures on them, and my aunt used to amuse herself at every meal by reading the caption on whichever one had been sent up to her that day. She would put on her spectacles and spell out: "Ali Baba and the Forty Thieves," "Aladdin and his Wonderful Lamp," and smile, and say: "Very good, very good."

"I would have gone across to Camus . . ." Françoise would hazard, seeing that my aunt had no longer any intention of sending her there.

"No, no; it's not worth while now; it's certainly the Pupin girl. My poor Françoise, I'm sorry to have brought you upstairs for nothing."

But it was not for nothing, as my aunt well knew, that she had rung for Françoise, since at Combray a person whom one "didn't know from Adam" was as incredible a being as any mythological deity, and indeed no one could remember, on the various occasions when one of these startling apparitions had occurred in the Rue du

Saint-Esprit or in the Square, exhaustive inquiries ever having failed to reduce the fabulous monster to the proportions of a person whom one "did know," either personally or in the abstract, in his or her civil status as being more or less closely related to some family in Combray. It would turn out to be Mme Sauton's son back from military service, or the Abbé Perdreau's niece home from her convent, or the Curé's brother, a tax-collector at Châteaudun, who had just retired on a pension or had come over to Combray for the holidays. They had on first appearance aroused the exciting thought that there might be in Combray people whom one "didn't know from Adam," simply because they had not been recognised or identified at once. And yet long beforehand Mme Sauton and the Curé had given warning that they expected their "strangers." Whenever I went upstairs on returning home of an evening, to tell my aunt about our walk, if I was rash enough to say to her that we had passed, near the Pont-Vieux, a man whom my grandfather didn't know: "A man grandfather didn't know from Adam!" she would exclaim. "That's a likely story." None the less, she would be a little disturbed by the news, would wish to have it cleared up, and so my grandfather would be summoned. "Who can it have been that you passed near the Pont-Vieux, uncle? A man you didn't know from Adam?"

"Why, of course I knew him," my grandfather would answer. "It was Prosper, Mme Bouillebœuf's gardener's brother."

"Ah, good," my aunt would say, reassured but slightly flushed; shrugging her shoulders and smiling ironically, she would add: "You see, he told me that you passed a man you didn't know from Adam!" After which I would be warned to be more circumspect in future, and not to upset my aunt so by thoughtless remarks. Everyone was so well known in Combray, animals as well as people, that if my aunt had happened to see a dog go by which she "didn't know from Adam" she never stopped thinking about it, devoting all her inductive talents and her leisure hours to this incomprehensible phenomenon.

"That will be Mme Sazerat's dog," Françoise would suggest, without any real conviction, but in the hope of appeasement, and so that my aunt should not "split her head."

"As if I didn't know Mme Sazerat's dog!" My aunt's critical mind would not be fobbed off so easily.

"Well then, it must be the new dog M. Galopin brought back from Lisieux."

"Oh, if that's what it is!"

"They say he's a very friendly animal," Françoise would go on, having got the story from Théodore, "as clever as a Christian, always in a good temper, always friendly, always well-behaved. You don't often see an animal so gentlemanly at that age. Mme Octave, I've got to leave you now; I haven't time to dilly-dally; it's nearly ten o'clock and my fire not lighted yet, and I've still got to scrape my asparagus."

"What, Françoise, more asparagus! It's a regular mania for asparagus you've got this year. You'll make our Parisians sick of it."

"No, no, Mme Octave, they like it well enough. They'll be coming back from church soon as hungry as hunters, and they won't turn their noses up at their asparagus, you'll see."

"Church! Why, they must be there now; you'd better not lose any time. Go and look after your lunch."

While my aunt was gossiping on in this way with Françoise I accompanied my parents to mass. How I loved our church, and how clearly I can see it still! The old porch by which we entered, black, and full of holes as a colander, was worn out of shape and deeply furrowed at the sides (as also was the font to which it led us) just as if the gentle friction of the cloaks of peasant-women coming into church, and of their fingers dipping into the holy water, had managed by age-long repetition to acquire a destructive force, to impress itself on the stone, to carve grooves in it like those made by cart-wheels upon stone gate-posts which they bump against every day. Its memorial stones, beneath which the noble dust of the Abbots of Combray who lay buried there furnished the choir with a sort of spiritual pavement, were themselves no longer hard and lifeless matter, for time had softened them and made them flow like honey beyond their proper margins, here oozing out in a golden stream, washing from its place a florid Gothic capital, drowning the white violets of the marble floor, and elsewhere reabsorbed into their limits, contracting still further a crabbed Latin inscription, bringing a fresh touch of fantasy into the arrangement of its curtailed characters, closing together two letters of some word of which the rest were disproportionately distended. Its windows were never so sparkling as on days when the sun scarcely shone, so that if it was dull outside you could be sure it would be fine inside the church. One of them was filled from top to bottom by a solitary figure, like the king on a playing-card, who lived up there beneath his canopy of stone, between earth and

heaven, and in whose slanting blue gleam, on weekdays
sometimes, at noon, when there was no service (at one of
those rare moments when the airy, empty church, more
human somehow and more luxurious, with the sun showing off all its rich furnishings, had an almost habitable
air, like the entrance hall—all sculptured stone and
painted glass—of some hotel in the mediaeval style), you
might see Mme Sazerat kneel for an instant, laying down
on the seat next to hers a neatly corded parcel of little
cakes which she had just bought at the baker's and was
taking home for lunch. In another, a mountain of pink
snow, at whose foot a battle was being fought, seemed to
have frozen against the very glass itself, which it swelled
and distorted with its cloudy sleet, like a window to
which snowflakes have drifted and clung, illumined by
the light of dawn—the same, doubtless, that tinged the
reredos of the altar with hues so fresh that they seemed
rather to be thrown on it momentarily by a light shining
from outside and shortly to be extinguished than painted
and permanently fastened on the stone. And all of them
were so old that you could see, here and there, their sil-
very antiquity sparkling with the dust of centuries and
showing in its threadbare brilliance the texture of their
lovely tapestry of glass. There was one among them
which was a tall panel composed of a hundred little rectangular panes, of blue principally, like an enormous pack
of cards of the kind planned to beguile King Charles VI;
but, either because a ray of sunlight had gleamed through
it or because my own shifting glance had sent shooting
across the window, whose colours died away and were
rekindled by turns, a rare and flickering fire—the next
instant it had taken on the shimmering brilliance of a

peacock's tail, then quivered and rippled in a flaming and
fantastic shower that streamed from the groin of the dark
and stony vault down the moist walls, as though it were
along the bed of some grotto glowing with sinuous stalac-
tites that I was following my parents, who preceded me
with their prayer-books clasped in their hands. A moment
later the little lozenge panes had taken on the deep transparency, the unbreakable hardness of sapphires clustered
on some enormous breastplate behind which, however,
could be distinguished, dearer than all such treasures, a
fleeting smile from the sun, which could be seen and felt
as well here, in the soft, blue stream with which it bathed
the jewelled windows, as on the pavement of the Square
or the straw of the market-place; and even on our first
Sundays, when we had come down before Easter, it would
console me for the blackness and bareness of the earth
outside by quickening into blossom, as in some springtime in old history among the heirs of Saint Louis, this
dazzling, gilded carpet of forget-me-nots in glass.

There were two tapestries of high warp representing
the coronation of Esther (tradition had it that the weaver
had given to Ahasuerus the features of one of the kings of
France and to Esther those of a lady of Guermantes
whose lover he had been), to which the colours, in melt-
ing into one another, had added expression, relief and
light: a touch of pink over the lips of Esther had strayed
beyond their outline; the yellow of her dress was spread
so unctuously, so thickly, as to have acquired a kind of
solidity, and stood out boldly against the receding background; while the green of the trees, still bright in the
lower parts of the panel of silk and wool, but quite
"gone" at the top, brought out in a paler tone, above the

dark trunks, the yellowing upper branches, gilded and half-obliterated by the sharp though sidelong rays of an invisible sun.

All this, and still more the treasures which had come to the church from personages who to me were almost legendary figures (such as the golden cross wrought, it was said, by Saint Eloi and presented by Dagobert, and the tomb of the sons of Louis the Germanic in porphyry and enamelled copper), because of which I used to advance into the church, as we made our way to our seats, as into a fairy-haunted valley, where the rustic sees with amazement in a rock, a tree, a pond, the tangible traces of the little people's supernatural passage—all this made of the church for me something entirely different from the rest of the town: an edifice occupying, so to speak, a four-dimensional space—the name of the fourth being Time—extending through the centuries its ancient nave, which, bay after bay, chapel after chapel, seemed to stretch across and conquer not merely a few yards of soil, but each successive epoch from which it emerged triumphant, hiding the rugged barbarities of the eleventh century in the thickness of its walls, through which nothing could be seen of the heavy arches, long stopped and blinded with coarse blocks of ashlar, except where, near the porch, a deep cleft had been hollowed out by the tower staircase, and veiling it even there by the graceful Gothic arcades which crowded coquettishly around it like a row of grown-up sisters who, to hide him from the eyes of strangers, arrange themselves smilingly in front of a rustic, peevish and ill-dressed younger brother; raising up into the sky above the Square a tower which had looked down upon Saint Louis, and seemed to see him still; and

thrusting down with its crypt into a Merovingian darkness, through which, guiding us with groping finger-tips
beneath the shadowy vault, powerfully ribbed like an immense bat's wing of stone, Théodore and his sister would
light up for us with a candle the tomb of Sigebert's little
daughter, in which a deep cavity, like the bed of a fossil,
had been dug, or so it was said, "by a crystal lamp which,
on the night when the Frankish princess was murdered,
had detached itself, of its own accord, from the golden
chains by which it was suspended on the site of the present apse and, with neither the crystal being broken nor
the light extinguished, had buried itself in the stone,
which had softly given way beneath it."

And then the apse of Combray: what can one say of
that? It was so crude, so devoid of artistic beauty, even of
religious feeling. From the outside, since the street crossing which it commanded was on a lower level, its great
wall was thrust upwards from a basement of unfaced ashlar, jagged with flints, in which there was nothing particularly ecclesiastical, the windows seemed to have been
pierced at an abnormal height, and its whole appearance
was that of a prison wall rather than of a church. And
certainly in later years, when I recalled all the glorious
apses that I had seen, it would never have occurred to me
to compare with any one of them the apse of Combray.
Only, one day, turning out of a little street in some country town, I came upon three alley-ways that converged,
and facing them an old wall, rough-hewn and unusually
high, with windows pierced in it far overhead and the
same asymmetrical appearance as the apse of Combray.
And at that moment I did not say to myself, as I might
have done at Chartres or at Rheims, with what power the

religious feeling had been expressed therein, but instinctively I exclaimed: "The Church!"

The church! Homely and familiar, cheek by jowl in the Rue Saint-Hilaire, upon which its north door opened, with its two neighbours, Mme Loiseau's house and M. Rapin's pharmacy, against which its walls rested without interspace, a simple citizen of Combray, which might have had its number in the street had the streets of Combray borne numbers, and at whose door one felt that the postman ought to stop on his morning rounds, before going into Mme Loiseau's and after leaving M. Rapin's, there existed, none the less, between the church and everything in Combray that was not the church a clear line of demarcation which my mind has never succeeded in crossing. In vain might Mme Loiseau deck her window-sills with fuchsias, which developed the bad habit of letting their branches trail at all times and in all directions, head downwards, and whose flowers had no more important business, when they were big enough to taste the joys of life, than to go and cool their purple, congested cheeks against the dark front of the church, to me such conduct sanctified the fuchsias not at all; between the flowers and the blackened stone against which they leaned, if my eyes could discern no gap, my mind preserved the impression of an abyss.

The steeple of Saint-Hilaire could be distinguished from a long way off, inscribing its unforgettable form upon a horizon against which Combray had not yet appeared; when from the train which brought us down from Paris at Easter-time my father caught sight of it, as it slipped into every fold of the sky in turn, its little iron weathercock veering in all directions, he would say:

"Come on, get your wraps together, we're there." And on one of the longest walks we used to take from Combray there was a spot where the narrow road emerged suddenly on to an immense plain, closed at the horizon by a jagged ridge of forest above which rose the solitary point of Saint-Hilaire's steeple, so slender and so pink that it seemed to be no more than scratched on the sky by the finger-nail of a painter anxious to give to such a landscape, to so pure a piece of nature, this little sign of art, this single indication of human existence. As one drew near it and could see the remains of the square tower, half in ruins, which still stood by its side, though without rivalling it in height, one was struck most of all by the dark-red tone of its stones; and on a misty morning in autumn one might have thought it, rising above the violet thunder-cloud of the vineyards, a ruin of purple, almost the colour of Virginia creeper.

Often in the Square, as we came home, my grandmother would make me stop to look up at it. From the tower windows, placed two by two, one pair above another, with that right and original proportion in their spacing which gives beauty and dignity not only to human faces, it released, it let fall at regular intervals, flocks of jackdaws which would wheel noisily for a while, as though the ancient stones which allowed them to disport themselves without seeming to see them, becoming of a sudden untenantable and discharging some element of extreme perturbation, had struck them and driven them out. Then, having crisscrossed in all directions the violet velvet of the evening air, they would return, suddenly calmed, to absorb themselves in the tower, baleful no longer but benignant, some perching here and there (not seeming to move, but perhaps snapping up some passing insect) on the points of turrets, as a seagull perches with an angler's immobility on the crest of a wave. Without quite knowing why, my grandmother found in the steeple of Saint-Hilaire that absence of vulgarity, pretension, and niggardliness which made her love, and deem rich in beneficent influences, nature itself—when the hand of man had not, as did my great-aunt's gardener, trimmed it—and the works of genius. And certainly every part of the church that one saw distinguished it from any other building by a kind of innate thoughtfulness, but it was in its steeple that it seemed most truly to find itself, to affirm its individual and responsible existence. It was the steeple that spoke for the church. I think, too, that in a confused way my grandmother found in the steeple of Combray what she prized above anything else in the world, namely, a natural air and an air of distinction. Ignorant of architecture, she would say:

"My dears, laugh at me if you like; it is not conventionally beautiful, but there is something in its quaint old face that pleases me. If it could play the piano, I'm sure it wouldn't sound tinny." And when she gazed up at it, when her eyes followed the gentle tension, the fervent inclination of its stony slopes which drew together as they rose, like hands joined in prayer, she would absorb herself so utterly in the effusion of the spire that her gaze seemed to leap upwards with it; her lips at the same time curving in a friendly smile for the worn old stones of which the setting sun now illumined no more than the topmost pinnacles and which, at the point where they entered that sunlit zone and were softened by it, seemed to have mounted suddenly far higher, to have become truly re-

mote, like a song taken up again in a "head voice," an octave above.

It was the steeple of Saint-Hilaire that shaped and
crowned and consecrated every occupation, every hour of
the day, every view in the town. From my bedroom window I could discern no more than its base, which had
been freshly covered with slates; but when, on a Sunday,
I saw these blaze like a black sun in the hot light of a
summer morning, I would say to myself: "Good heavens!
nine o'clock! I must get ready for mass at once if I am to
have time to go in and kiss aunt Léonie first," and I
would know exactly what was the colour of the sunlight
upon the Square, I could feel the heat and dust of the
market, the shade thrown by the awning of the shop into
which Mamma would perhaps go on her way to mass,
penetrating its odour of unbleached calico, to purchase a
handkerchief or something which the draper, bowing from
the waist, would order to be shown to her while, in readiness for shutting up, he went into the back shop to put
on his Sunday coat and to wash his hands, which it was
his habit, every few minutes, even in the most melancholy
circumstances, to rub together with an air of enterprise,
cunning, and success.

And again, after mass, when we looked in to tell
Théodore to bring a larger loaf than usual because our
cousins had taken advantage of the fine weather to come
over from Thiberzy for lunch, we had in front of us the
steeple which, baked golden-brown itself like a still larger,
consecrated loaf, with gummy flakes and droplets of sunlight, thrust its sharp point into the blue sky. And in the
evening, when I came in from my walk and thought of
the approaching moment when I must say good night to

my mother and see her no more, the steeple was by contrast so soft and gentle, there at the close of day, that it looked as if it had been thrust like a brown velvet cushion against the pallid sky which had yielded beneath its pressure, had hollowed slightly to make room for it, and had correspondingly risen on either side; while the cries of the birds that wheeled around it seemed to intensify its silence, to elongate its spire still further, and to invest it with some quality beyond the power of words.

Even when our errands lay in places behind the church, from which it could not be seen, the view seemed always to have been composed with reference to the steeple, which would loom up here and there among the houses, and was perhaps even more affecting when it appeared thus without the church. And, indeed, there are many others which look best when seen in this way, and I can call to mind vignettes of housetops with surmounting steeples in quite another category of art than those formed by the dreary streets of Combray. I shall never forget, in a quaint Norman town not far from Balbec, two charming eighteenth-century houses, dear to me and venerable for many reasons, between which, when one looks up at it from the fine garden which descends in terraces to the river, the Gothic spire of a church (itself hidden by the houses) soars into the sky with the effect of crowning and completing their façades, but in a style so different, so precious, so annulated, so pink, so polished, that one sees at once that it no more belongs to them than would the purple, crinkled spire of some sea-shell spun out into a turret and gay with glossy colour to a pair of handsome, smooth pebbles between which it had been washed up on the beach. Even in Paris, in one of the ugliest parts of the

town, I know a window from which one can see, across a
first, a second, and even a third layer of jumbled roofs,
street beyond street, a violet dome, sometimes ruddy,
sometimes too, in the finest "prints" which the atmosphere makes of it, of an ashy solution of black, which is,
in fact, none other than the dome of Saint-Augustin, and
which imparts to this view of Paris the character of some
of the Piranesi views of Rome. But since into none of
these little etchings, whatever the discernment my memory may have been able to bring to their execution, was it
able to contribute an element I have long lost, the feeling
which makes us not merely regard a thing as a spectacle,
but believe in it as in a unique essence, so none of them
keeps in its thrall a whole section of my inmost life as
does the memory of those aspects of the steeple of Combray from the streets behind the church. Whether one
saw it at five o'clock when going to call for letters at the
post-office, some doors away from one, on the left, raising
abruptly with its isolated peak the ridge of housetops; or
whether, if one were looking in to ask for news of Mme
Sazerat, one's eyes followed that ridge which had now become low again after the descent of its other slope, and
one knew that it would be the second turning after the
steeple; or again if, pressing further afield, one went to
the station and saw it obliquely, showing in profile fresh
angles and surfaces, like a solid body surprised at some
unknown point in its revolution; or if, seen from the
banks of the Vivonne, the apse, crouched muscularly and
heightened by the perspective, seemed to spring upwards
with the effort which the steeple was making to hurl its
spire-point into the heart of heaven—it was always to the
steeple that one must return, always the steeple that dom-

inated everything else, summoning the houses from an unexpected pinnacle, raised before me like the finger of God, whose body might have been concealed below among the crowd of humans without fear of my confusing it with them. And so even today, if, in a large provincial town, or in a quarter of Paris which I do not know very well, a passer-by who is "putting me on the right road" shows me in the distance, as a point to aim at, some hospital belfry or convent steeple lifting the peak of its ecclesiastical cap at the corner of the street which I am to take, my memory need only find in it some dim resemblance to that dear and vanished outline, and the passer-by, should he turn round to make sure that I have not gone astray, may be amazed to see me still standing there, oblivious of the walk that I had planned to take or the place where I was obliged to call, gazing at the steeple for hours on end, motionless, trying to remember, feeling deep within myself a tract of soil reclaimed from the waters of Lethe slowly drying until the buildings rise on it again; and then no doubt, and then more anxiously than when, just now, I asked him to direct me, I seek my way again, I turn a corner . . . but . . . the goal is in my heart . . .

On our way home from mass we would often meet M. Legrandin, who, detained in Paris by his professional duties as an engineer, could only (except in the regular holiday seasons) visit his house at Combray between Saturday evenings and Monday mornings. He was one of that class of men who, apart from a scientific career in which they may well have proved brilliantly successful, have acquired an entirely different kind of culture, literary or artistic, for which their professional specialisation has no use but by which their conversation profits. More let-

tered than many men of letters (we were not aware at this
period that M. Legrandin had a distinct reputation as a
writer, and were greatly astonished to find that a well-
known composer had set some verses of his to music), endowed with greater "facility" than many painters, they
imagine that the life they are obliged to lead is not that
for which they are really fitted, and they bring to their
regular occupations either an indifference tinged with fantasy, or a sustained and haughty application, scornful, bitter, and conscientious. Tall and handsome of bearing,
with a fine, thoughtful face, drooping fair moustaches,
blue eyes, an air of disenchantment, an almost exaggerated refinement of courtesy, a talker such as we had never
heard, he was in the sight of my family, who never ceased
to quote him as an example, the very pattern of a gentleman, who took life in the noblest and most delicate manner. My grandmother alone found fault with him for
speaking a little too well, a little too much like a book, for
not using a vocabulary as natural as his loosely knotted
bow-ties, his short, straight, almost schoolboyish coat. She
was astonished, too, at the furious tirades which he was
always launching at the aristocracy, at fashionable life, at
snobbishness—"undoubtedly," he would say, "the sin of
which St Paul is thinking when he speaks of the unforgiv-
able sin against the Holy Ghost."

Worldly ambition was a thing which my grandmother
was so little capable of feeling, or indeed of understanding, that it seemed to her futile to apply so much heat to
its condemnation. Besides, she did not think it in very
good taste for M. Legrandin, whose sister was married to
a country gentleman of Lower Normandy, near Balbec, to
deliver himself of such violent attacks upon the nobility,

going so far as to blame the Revolution for not having guillotined them all.

"Well met, my friends!" he would say as he came towards us. "You are lucky to spend so much time here; tomorrow I have to go back to Paris, to squeeze back into my niche. Oh, I admit," he went on, with the gentle, ironical, disillusioned, rather absent-minded smile that was peculiar to him, "I have every useless thing in the world in my house there. The only thing wanting is the necessary thing, a great patch of open sky like this. Always try to keep a patch of sky above your life, little boy," he added, turning to me. "You have a soul in you of rare quality, an artist's nature; never let it starve for lack of what it needs."

When, on our return home, my aunt would send to ask us whether Mme Goupil had indeed arrived late for mass, not one of us could inform her. Instead, we increased her anxiety by telling her that there was a painter at work in the church copying the window of Gilbert the Bad. Françoise was at once dispatched to the grocer's, but returned empty-handed owing to the absence of Théodore, whose dual profession of cantor, with a share in the upkeep of the church, and of grocer's assistant gave him not only relations with all sections of society, but an encyclopaedic knowledge of their affairs.

"Ah!" my aunt would sigh, "I wish it were time for Eulalie to come. She is really the only person who will be able to tell me."

Eulalie was a limping, energetic, deaf spinster who had "retired" after the death of Mme de la Bretonnerie, with whom she had been in service since her childhood, and had then taken a room beside the church from which

she would incessantly emerge either to attend some service or, when there was no service, to say a prayer by
herself or to give Théodore a hand; the rest of her time
she spent in visiting sick persons like my aunt Léonie, to
whom she would relate everything that had occurred at
mass or vespers. She was not above adding occasional
pocket-money to the small annuity paid to her by the
family of her former employers by going from time to
time to look after the Curé's linen, or that of some other
person of note in the clerical world of Combray. Above a
mantle of black cloth she wore a little white coif that
seemed almost to attach her to some Order, and an infirmity of the skin had stained part of her cheeks and her
crooked nose the bright red colour of balsam. Her visits
were the one great distraction in the life of my aunt
Léonie, who now saw hardly anyone else, except the
Curé. My aunt had by degrees dropped every other visitor's name from her list, because they were all guilty of
the fatal error, in her eyes, of falling into one or other of
the two categories of people she most detested. One
group, the worse of the two, and the one of which she rid
herself first, consisted of those who advised her not to
"coddle" herself, and preached (even if only negatively
and with no outward signs beyond an occasional disapproving silence or doubting smile) the subversive doctrine
that a sharp walk in the sun and a good red beefsteak
would do her more good (when she had had only two
wretched mouthfuls of Vichy water on her stomach for
fourteen hours!) than her bed and her medicines. The
other category was composed of people who appeared to
believe that she was more seriously ill than she thought,
in fact that she was as seriously ill as she said. And so, of

those whom she had allowed upstairs to her room, after
considerable hesitation and only at Françoise's urgent request, and who in the course of their visit had shown how
unworthy they were of the honour which had been done
them by venturing a timid: "Don't you think that if you
were just to stir out a little on really fine days . . . ?" or
who, on the other hand, when she said to them: "I'm
very low, very low; nearing the end, I'm afraid" had
replied: "Ah, yes, when one has no strength left! Still, you
may last a while yet," all alike might be certain that her
doors would never be opened to them again. And if
Françoise was amused by the look of consternation on my
aunt's face whenever she saw from her bed any of these
people in the Rue du Saint-Esprit looking as if they were
coming to see her, or whenever she heard her door-bell
ring, she would laugh far more heartily, as at a clever
trick, at my aunt's devices (which never failed) for having
them sent away, and at their look of discomfiture when
they had to turn back without having seen her, and would
be filled with secret admiration for her mistress, whom
she felt to be superior to all these people since she did not
wish to receive them. In short, my aunt demanded that
whoever came to see her must at one and the same time
approve of her way of life, commiserate with her in her
sufferings, and assure her of ultimate recovery.

In all this Eulalie excelled. My aunt might say to her
twenty times in a minute: "The end is come at last, my
poor Eulalie!," twenty times Eulalie would retort: "Knowing your illness as you do, Mme Octave, you will live to
be a hundred, as Mme Sazerin said to me only yesterday." For one of Eulalie's most rooted beliefs, and one
that the formidable number of rebuttals which experience

had brought her was powerless to eradicate, was that Mme Sazerat's name was really Mme Sazerin.

"I do not ask to live to a hundred," my aunt would say, for she preferred to have no definite limit fixed to the number of her days.

And since besides this Eulalie knew, as no one else knew, how to distract my aunt without tiring her, her visits, which took place regularly every Sunday, unless something unforeseen occurred to prevent them, were for my aunt a pleasure the prospect of which kept her on those days in a state of expectation, agreeable enough to begin with, but swiftly changing to the agony of a hunger too long unsatisfied if Eulalie happened to be a little late. For, if unduly prolonged, the rapture of waiting for Eulalie became a torture, and my aunt would never stop looking at the time, and yawning, and complaining of each of her symptoms in turn. Eulalie's ring, if it sounded from the front door at the very end of the day, when she was no longer expecting it, would almost make her ill. For the fact was that on Sundays she thought of nothing else but this visit, and the moment our lunch was ended Françoise would be impatient for us to leave the dining-room so that she might go upstairs to "occupy" my aunt. But— especially after the fine weather had definitely set in at Combray—the proud hour of noon, descending from the steeple of Saint-Hilaire which it blazoned for a moment with the twelve points of its sonorous crown, would long have echoed about our table, beside the blessed bread which too had come in, after church, in its familiar way, and we would still be seated in front of our Arabian Nights plates, weighed down by the heat of the day, and even more by our heavy meal. For upon the permanent

foundation of eggs, cutlets, potatoes, preserves, and biscuits, which she no longer even bothered to announce,
Françoise would add—as the labour of fields and or-
chards, the harvest of the tides, the luck of the markets,
the kindness of neighbours, and her own genius might
provide, so that our bill of fare, like the quatrefoils that
were carved on the porches of cathedrals in the thirteenth
century, reflected to some extent the rhythm of the seasons and the incidents of daily life—a brill because the
fish-woman had guaranteed its freshness, a turkey because
she had seen a beauty in the market at Roussainville-le-
Pin, cardoons with marrow because she had never done
them for us in that way before, a roast leg of mutton because the fresh air made one hungry and there would be
plenty of time for it to "settle down" in the seven hours
before dinner, spinach by way of a change, apricots because they were still hard to get, gooseberries because in
another fortnight there would be none left, raspberries
which M. Swann had brought specially, cherries, the first
to come from the cherry-tree which had yielded none for
the last two years, a cream cheese, of which in those days
I was extremely fond, an almond cake because she had
ordered one the evening before, a brioche because it was
our turn to make them for the church. And when all this
was finished, a work composed expressly for ourselves,
but dedicated more particularly to my father who had a
fondness for such things, a chocolate cream, Françoise's
personal inspiration and speciality would be laid before
us, light and fleeting as an "occasional" piece of music
into which she had poured the whole of her talent. Anyone who refused to partake of it, saying: "No, thank you,
I've finished; I'm not hungry any more," would at once

have been relegated to the level of those Philistines who, even when an artist makes them a present of one of his works, examine its weight and material, whereas what is of value is the creator's intention and his signature. To have left even the tiniest morsel in the dish would have shown as much discourtesy as to rise and leave a concert hall before the end of a piece under the composer's very eyes.

At length my mother would say to me: "Now, don't stay here all day; you can go up to your room if you are too hot outside, but get a little fresh air first; don't start reading immediately after your food." And I would go and sit down beside the pump and its trough, ornamented here and there, like a Gothic font, with a salamander, which impressed on the rough stone the mobile relief of its tapering allegorical body, on the bench without a back, in the shade of a lilac-tree, in that little corner of the garden which opened, through a service door, on to the Rue du Saint-Esprit, and from whose neglected soil there rose, in two stages, jutting out from the house itself, and as it were a separate building, my aunt's back-kitchen. One could see its red-tiled floor gleaming like porphyry. It seemed not so much the cave of Françoise as a little temple of Venus. It would be overflowing with the offerings of the dairyman, the fruiterer, the greengrocer, come sometimes from distant villages to dedicate to the goddess the first-fruits of their fields. And its roof was always crowned with a cooing dove.

In earlier days I did not linger in the sacred grove which surrounded this temple, for, before going upstairs to read, I used to steal into the little sitting-room that my uncle Adolphe, a brother of my grandfather and an old

soldier who had retired from the service as a major, occupied on the ground floor, a room which, even when its
opened windows let in the heat, if not actually the rays of
the sun which seldom penetrated so far, would never fail
to emit that oddly cool odour, suggestive at once of
woodlands and the ancient régime, which sets the nostrils
quivering when one goes into an abandoned shooting-
lodge. But for some years now I had not gone into my
uncle Adolphe's sanctum, for he no longer came to Combray on account of a quarrel which had arisen between
him and my family, through my fault, in the following
circumstances:

Once or twice a month, in Paris, I used to be sent to
pay him a visit, as he was finishing his luncheon, wearing
a simple jacket and waited upon by his manservant in a
tunic of striped drill, purple and white. He would complain that I had not been to see him for a long time, that
he was being neglected; he would offer me a biscuit or a
tangerine, and we would go through a drawing-room in
which no one ever sat, whose fire was never lighted,
whose walls were decorated with gilded mouldings, its
ceiling painted blue in imitation of the sky, and its furniture upholstered in satin, as at my grandparents', only
yellow; then we would enter what he called his "study," a
room whose walls were hung with prints which showed,
against a dark background, a pink and fleshy goddess
driving a chariot, or standing upon a globe, or wearing a
star on her brow—pictures which were popular under the
Second Empire because there was thought to be something about them that suggested Pompeii, which were
then generally despised, and which are now becoming
fashionable again for one single and consistent reason

(notwithstanding all the others that are advanced), namely, that they suggest the Second Empire. And there I would stay with my uncle until his man came with a message from the coachman, asking him at what time he would like the carriage. My uncle would then become lost in meditation, while his servant stood there agape, not daring to disturb him by the least movement, curiously awaiting his answer, which never varied. For in the end, after a supreme crisis of hesitation, my uncle would utter, infallibly, the words: "A quarter past two," which the servant would echo with amazement, but without disputing them: "A quarter past two! Very good, sir . . . I'll go and tell him . . ."

At this date I was a lover of the theatre: a Platonic lover, since my parents had not yet allowed me to enter one, and so inaccurate was the picture I had formed in my mind's eye of the pleasures to be enjoyed there that I almost believed that each of the spectators looked, as through a stereoscope, at a scene that existed for himself alone, though similar to the thousand other scenes presented to the rest of the audience individually.

Every morning I would hasten to the Morris column to see what new plays it announced. Nothing could be more disinterested or happier than the day-dreams with which these announcements filled my imagination, day-dreams which were conditioned by the associations of the words forming the titles of the plays, and also by the colour of the bills, still damp and wrinkled with paste, on which those words stood out. Nothing, unless it were such strange titles as the *Testament de César Girodot* or *Oedipus Rex*, inscribed not on the green bills of the Opéra-Comique but on the wine-coloured bills of the

Comédie-Française, nothing seemed to me to differ more profoundly from the sparkling white plume of the *Diamants de la Couronne* than the sleek, mysterious satin of the *Domino Noir*; and since my parents had told me that, for my first visit to the theatre, I should have to choose between these two pieces, I would study exhaustively and in turn the title of one and the title of the other (for these were all that I knew of either), attempting to snatch from each a foretaste of the pleasure it promised, and to compare this with the pleasure latent in the other, until in the end I succeeded in conjuring up such vivid and compelling pictures of, on the one hand, a play of dazzling arrogance, and on the other a gentle, velvety play, that I was as little capable of deciding which of them I should prefer to see as if, at the dinner-table, I had been obliged to choose between rice *à l'Impératrice* and the famous chocolate cream.

All my conversations with my friends bore upon actors, whose art, although as yet I had no experience of it, was the first of all its numberless forms in which Art itself allowed me to anticipate its enjoyment. Between one actor's tricks of intonation and inflection and another's, the most trifling differences would strike me as being of an incalculable importance. And from what I had been told of them I would arrange them in order of talent in lists which I used to recite to myself all day and which ended up by hardening in my brain and hampering it by their immovability.

And later, in my schooldays, whenever I ventured in class, as soon as the master's head was turned, to communicate with some new friend, I would always begin by asking him whether he had already been to the theatre, and whether he agreed that our greatest actor was Got, our second Delaunay, and so on. And if, in his judgment, Febvre came below Thiron, or Delaunay below Coquelin, the sudden volatility which the name of Coquelin, forsaking its stony rigidity, would acquire in my mind, in order to move up to second place, the miraculous agility, the fecund animation with which the name of Delaunay would suddenly be endowed, to enable it to slip down to fourth, would stimulate and fertilise my brain with a sense of budding and blossoming life.

But if the thought of actors preoccupied me so, if the sight of Maubant coming out of the Théâtre-Français one afternoon had plunged me into the throes and sufferings of love, how much more did the name of a star blazing outside the doors of a theatre, how much more, seen through the window of a brougham passing by in the street, its horses' headbands decked with roses, did the face of a woman whom I took to be an actress, leave me in a state of troubled excitement, impotently and painfully trying to form a picture of her private life.

I classified the most distinguished in order of talent: Sarah Bernhardt, Berma, Bartet, Madeleine Brohan, Jeanne Samary; but I was interested in them all. Now my uncle knew many of them personally, and also ladies of another class, not clearly distinguished from actresses in my mind. He used to entertain them at his house. And if we went to see him on certain days only, that was because on the other days ladies might come whom his family could not very well have met—so they at least thought, for my uncle, on the contrary, was only too willing to pay pretty widows (who had perhaps never been married) and countesses (whose high-sounding titles were probably no more than *noms de guerre*) the compliment of presenting them to my grandmother, or even of presenting to them some of the family jewels, a propensity which had already embroiled him more than once with my grandfather. Often, if the name of some actress were mentioned in conversation, I would hear my father say to my mother with a smile: "One of your uncle's friends," and thinking of the weary and fruitless novitiate eminent men would go through, perhaps for years on end, on the doorstep of some such lady who refused to answer their letters and had them sent packing by the hall-porter, it struck me that my uncle could have spared from such torments a youngster like me by introducing him to the actress, unapproachable by all the world, who was for him an intimate friend.

And so—on the pretext that some lesson, the hour of which had been altered, now came at such an awkward time that it had already more than once prevented me, and would continue to prevent me, from seeing my uncle—one day, not one of the days which he set apart for our visits, taking advantage of the fact that my parents had had lunch earlier than usual, I slipped out and, instead of going to read the playbills on their column, for which purpose I was allowed to go out unaccompanied, ran round to his house. I noticed in front of his door a carriage and pair, with red carnations on the horses' blinkers and in the coachman's buttonhole. As I climbed the staircase I could hear laughter and a woman's voice, and, as soon as I had rung, silence and the sound of shutting doors. The manservant seemed embarrassed when he let me in, and said that my uncle was extremely busy and probably could not see me; he went in, however, to announce my arrival, and the same voice I had heard before said: "Oh, yes! Do let him come in, just for a moment; I should so enjoy it. Isn't that his photograph there on your desk? And his mother (your niece, isn't she?) beside it? The image of her, isn't he? I should so like to see the little chap, just for a second."

I could hear my uncle grumbling angrily; finally the manservant ushered me in.

On the table was the same plate of biscuits that was always there; my uncle wore the same jacket as on other days, but opposite him, in a pink silk dress with a great necklace of pearls about her throat, sat a young woman who was just finishing a tangerine. My uncertainty whether I ought to address her as Madame or Mademoiselle made me blush, and not daring to look too much in her direction, in case I should be obliged to speak to her, I hurried across to embrace my uncle. She looked at me and smiled; my uncle said "My nephew!" without telling her my name or giving me hers, doubtless because, since his difficulties with my grandfather, he had endeavoured as far as possible to avoid any association of his family with this other class of acquaintance.

"How like his mother he is," said the lady.

"But you've never seen my niece except in photographs," my uncle answered brusquely.

"I beg your pardon, dear friend, I passed her on the staircase last year when you were so ill. It's true I only saw her for a moment, and your staircase is rather dark; but I could see well enough to admire her. This young gentleman has her beautiful eyes, and also *this*," she went on, tracing a line with one finger across the lower part of her forehead. "Tell me," she asked my uncle, "is your niece's name the same as yours?"

"He takes most after his father," muttered my uncle, who was no more anxious to effect an introduction by proxy by mentioning Mamma's name than to bring the two together in the flesh. "He's his father all over, and also like my poor mother."

"I haven't met his father," said the lady in pink, bowing her head slightly, "and I never knew your poor mother. You will remember it was just after your great sorrow that we got to know one another."

I felt somewhat disillusioned, for this young lady was in no way different from other pretty women whom I had seen from time to time at home, in particular the daughter of one of our cousins to whose house I went every New Year's Day. Apart from being better dressed, my uncle's friend had the same quick and kindly glance, the same frank and friendly manner. I could find no trace in her of the theatrical appearance which I admired in photographs of actresses, nothing of the diabolical expression which would have been in keeping with the life she must lead. I had difficulty in believing that she was a courtesan, and certainly I should never have believed her to be an ultra-fashionable one, had I not seen the carriage and pair, the pink dress, the pearl necklace, had I not been aware, too, that my uncle knew only those of the top flight. But I asked myself how the millionaire who gave her her carriage and her house and her jewels could find any pleasure in flinging his money away upon a woman of so simple and respectable an appearance. And yet, when I thought of what her life must be like, its immoral-

ity disturbed me more, perhaps, than if it had stood before me in some concrete and recognisable form, by being
thus invisible, like the secret of some novel or some scandal which had driven out of the home of her genteel parents and dedicated to the service of all mankind, which
had brought to a bright bloom of beauty and raised to
fame or notoriety, this woman the play of whose features,
the intonations of whose voice, reminiscent of so many
others I already knew, made me regard her, in spite of
myself, as a young lady of good family, when she was no
longer of any family at all.

We had moved by this time into the "study," and
my uncle, who seemed a trifle embarrassed by my presence, offered her a cigarette.

"No, thank you, my dear," she said. "You know I
only smoke the ones the grand duke sends me. I told him
that they made you jealous." And she drew from a case
cigarettes covered with gilt lettering in a foreign language.
"But of course," she began again suddenly, "I must have
met this young man's father with you. Isn't he your
nephew? How on earth could I have forgotten? He was so
nice, so exquisitely charming to me," she added, with an
air of warmth and modesty. But when I thought to myself, knowing my father's coldness and reserve, what must
actually have been the brusque greeting which she
claimed to have found so charming, I was embarrassed, as
though at some indelicacy on his part, by the contrast between the excessive recognition bestowed on it and his
want of geniality. It has since struck me as one of the
most touching aspects of the part played in life by these
idle, painstaking women that they devote their generosity,
their talent, a disposable dream of sentimental beauty

(for, like artists, they never seek to realise the value of their dreams, or to enclose them in the four-square frame of everyday life), and a wealth that counts for little, to the fashioning of a fine and precious setting for the rough, ill-polished lives of men. And just as this one filled the smoking-room, where my uncle was entertaining her in his jacket, with the aura of her charming person, her dress of pink silk, her pearls, the elegance that derives from the friendship of a grand duke, so in the same way she had taken some casual remark of my father's, had delicately fashioned it, given it a "turn," a precious title, and embellishing it with a gem-like glance from her sparkling eyes, tinged with humility and gratitude, had given it back transformed into a jewel, a work of art, into something "exquisitely charming."

"Look here, my boy, it's time you were off," said my uncle.

I rose. I had an irresistible desire to kiss the hand of the lady in pink, but I felt that to do so would require as much audacity as a forcible abduction. My heart beat loud while I repeated to myself "Shall I do it, shall I not?" and then I ceased to ask myself what I ought to do so as at least to do something. With a blind, insensate gesture, divested of all the reasons in its favour that I had thought of a moment before, I seized and raised to my lips the hand she held out to me.

"Isn't he delicious! Quite a ladies' man already; he takes after his uncle. He'll be a perfect 'gentleman,' " she added, clenching her teeth so as to give the word a kind of English accentuation. "Couldn't he come to me some day for 'a cup of tea,' as our friends across the Channel say? He need only send me a 'blue' in the morning?"

I had not the least idea what a "blue" might be.[5] I did not understand half the words which the lady used, but my fear lest there should be concealed in them some question which it would be impolite of me not to answer made me keep on listening to them with close attention, and I was beginning to feel extremely tired.

"No, no, it's impossible," said my uncle, shrugging his shoulders. "He's kept very busy, he works extremely hard. He brings back all the prizes from his school," he added in a lower voice, so that I should not hear this falsehood and interrupt with a contradiction. "Who knows? he may turn out a little Victor Hugo, a kind of Vaulabelle, don't you know."

"Oh, I love artistic people," replied the lady in pink. "There's no one like them for understanding women. Apart from a few superior people like yourself. But please forgive my ignorance. Who or what is Vaulabelle? Is it those gilt books in the little glass case in your drawing-room? You know you promised to lend them to me. I'll take great care of them."

My uncle, who hated lending people books, said nothing, and ushered me out into the hall. Madly in love with the lady in pink, I covered my old uncle's tobacco-stained cheeks with passionate kisses, and while with some embarrassment he gave me to understand without actually saying that he would rather I did not tell my parents about this visit, I assured him with tears in my eyes that his kindness had made so strong an impression upon me that some day I would most certainly find a way of expressing my gratitude. So strong an impression, indeed, had it made upon me that two hours later, after a string of mysterious utterances which did not strike me as giving

my parents a sufficiently clear idea of the new importance
with which I had been invested, I found it simpler to tell
them in the minutest detail of the visit I had paid that afternoon. In doing this I had no thought of causing my
uncle any unpleasantness. How could I have thought such
a thing, since I did not wish it? And I could not suppose
that my parents would see any harm in a visit in which I
myself saw none. Every day of our lives does not some
friend or other ask us to make his apologies, without fail,
to some woman to whom he has been prevented from
writing, and do not we forget to do so, feeling that this
woman cannot attach much importance to a silence that
has none for ourselves? I imagined, like everyone else,
that the brains of other people were lifeless and submissive receptacles with no power of specific reaction to anything that might be introduced into them; and I had not
the least doubt that when I deposited in the minds of my
parents the news of the acquaintance I had made at my
uncle's I should at the same time transmit to them the
kindly judgment I myself had based on the introduction.
Unfortunately my parents had recourse to principles entirely different from those which I intended them to adopt
when they came to form their estimate of my uncle's conduct. My father and grandfather had "words" with him of
a violent order; as I learned indirectly. A few days later,
passing my uncle in the street as he drove by in an open
carriage, I felt at once all the grief, the gratitude, the remorse which I should have liked to convey to him. Beside
the immensity of these emotions I considered that merely
to raise my hat to him would be incongruous and petty,
and might make him think that I regarded myself as
bound to show him no more than the commonest form of

courtesy. I decided to abstain from so inadequate a gesture, and turned my head away. My uncle thought that in
doing so I was obeying my parents' orders; he never for-
gave them; and though he did not die until many years
later, not one of us ever set eyes on him again.

And so I no longer went into the little sitting-room
(now kept shut) of my uncle Adolphe; instead, after hanging about on the outskirts of the back-kitchen until
Françoise appeared on its threshold and announced: "I'm
going to let my kitchen-maid serve the coffee and take up
the hot water; it's time I went off to Mme Octave," I
would then decide to go indoors, and would go straight
upstairs to my room to read. The kitchen-maid was an
abstract personality, a permanent institution to which an
invariable set of functions assured a sort of fixity and continuity and identity throughout the succession of transi-
tory human shapes in which it was embodied; for we
never had the same girl two years running. In the year in
which we ate such quantities of asparagus, the kitchen-
maid whose duty it was to prepare them was a poor sickly
creature, some way "gone" in pregnancy when we arrived
at Combray for Easter, and it was indeed surprising that
Françoise allowed her to run so many errands and to do
so much work, for she was beginning to find difficulty in
bearing before her the mysterious basket, fuller and larger
every day, whose splendid outline could be detected beneath the folds of her ample smock. This last recalled the
cloaks in which Giotto shrouds some of his allegorical figures, of which M. Swann had given me photographs. He
it was who pointed out the resemblance, and when he inquired after the kitchen-maid he would say: "Well, how
goes it with Giotto's Charity?" And indeed the poor girl,

whose pregnancy had swelled and stoutened every part of
her, even including her face and her squarish, elongated
cheeks, did distinctly suggest those virgins, so sturdy and
mannish as to seem matrons rather, in whom the Virtues
are personified in the Arena Chapel. And I can see now
that those Virtues and Vices of Padua resembled her in
another respect as well. For just as the figure of this girl
had been enlarged by the additional symbol which she
carried before her, without appearing to understand its
meaning, with no awareness in her facial expression of its
beauty and spiritual significance, as if it were an ordinary,
rather heavy burden, so it is without any apparent suspicion of what she is about that the powerfully built housewife who is portrayed in the Arena Chapel beneath the
label "Caritas," and a reproduction of whose portrait
hung upon the wall of my schoolroom at Combray, em-
bodies that virtue, for it seems impossible that any
thought of charity can ever have found expression in her
vulgar and energetic face. By a fine stroke of the painter's
invention she is trampling all the treasures of the earth
beneath her feet, but exactly as if she were treading
grapes in a wine-press to extract their juice, or rather as if
she had climbed on to a heap of sacks to raise herself
higher; and she is holding out her flaming heart to God,
or shall we say "handing" it to him, exactly as a cook
might hand up a corkscrew through the skylight of her
basement kitchen to someone who has called down for it
from the ground-floor window. The "Invidia," again,
should have had some look of envy on her face. But in
this fresco, too, the symbol occupies so large a place and
is represented with such realism, the serpent hissing between the lips of Envy is so huge, and so completely fills

her wide-opened mouth, that the muscles of her face are
strained and contorted, like those of a child blowing up
a balloon, and her attention—and ours too for that
matter—is so utterly concentrated on the activity of her
lips as to leave little time to spare for envious thoughts.

Despite all the admiration M. Swann professed for
these figures of Giotto, it was a long time before I could
find any pleasure in contemplating on the walls of our
schoolroom (where the copies he had brought me were
hung) that Charity devoid of charity, that Envy who
looked like nothing so much as a plate in some medical
book, illustrating the compression of the glottis or the
uvula by a tumour of the tongue or by the introduction of
the operator's instrument, a Justice whose greyish and
meanly regular features were identical with those which
characterised the faces of certain pious, desiccated ladies
of Combray whom I used to see at mass and many of
whom had long been enrolled in the reserve forces of Injustice. But in later years I came to understand that the
arresting strangeness, the special beauty of these frescoes
derived from the great part played in them by symbolism,
and the fact that this was represented not as a symbol (for
the thought symbolised was nowhere expressed) but as a
reality, actually felt or materially handled, added something more precise and more literal to the meaning of the
work, something more concrete and more striking to the
lesson it imparted. Similarly, in the case of the poor
kitchen-maid, was not one's attention incessantly drawn
to her belly by the weight which dragged it down; and in
the same way, again, are not the thoughts of the dying often turned towards the practical, painful, obscure, visceral
aspect, towards that "seamy side" of death which is, as it

happens, the side that death actually presents to them and forces them to feel, and which far more closely resembles a crushing burden, a difficulty in breathing, a destroying thirst, than the abstract idea to which we are accustomed to give the name of Death?

There must have been a strong element of reality in those Virtues and Vices of Padua, since they appeared to me to be as alive as the pregnant servant-girl, while she herself seemed scarcely less allegorical than they. And, quite possibly, this lack (or seeming lack) of participation by a person's soul in the virtue of which he or she is the agent has, apart from its aesthetic meaning, a reality which, if not strictly psychological, may at least be called physiognomical. Since then, whenever in the course of my life I have come across, in convents for instance, truly saintly embodiments of practical charity, they have generally had the cheerful, practical, brusque and unemotioned air of a busy surgeon, the sort of face in which one can discern no commiseration, no tenderness at the sight of suffering humanity, no fear of hurting it, the impassive, unsympathetic, sublime face of true goodness.

While the kitchen-maid—who, all unawares, made the superior qualities of Françoise shine with added lustre, just as Error, by force of contrast, enhances the triumph of Truth—served coffee which (according to Mamma) was nothing more than hot water, and then carried up to our rooms hot water which was barely lukewarm, I would be lying stretched out on my bed with a book in my hand. My room quivered with the effort to defend its frail, transparent coolness against the afternoon sun behind its almost closed shutters through which, however, a gleam of daylight had contrived to insinuate

its golden wings, remaining motionless in a corner between glass and woodwork, like a butterfly poised upon a
flower. It was hardly light enough for me to read, and my
sense of the day's brightness and splendour was derived
solely from the blows struck down below, in the Rue de
la Cure, by Camus (whom Françoise had assured that my
aunt was not "resting" and that he might therefore make
a noise) upon some dusty packing-cases which, reverber-
ating in the sonorous atmosphere that accompanies hot
weather, seemed to scatter broadcast a rain of blood-red
stars; and also from the flies who performed for my benefit, in their tiny chorus, as it were the chamber music of
summer, evoking it quite differently from a snatch of human music which, heard by chance in high summer, will
remind you of it later, whereas the music of the flies is
bound to the season by a more compelling tie—born of
the sunny days, and not to be reborn but with them, containing something of their essential nature, it not merely
calls up their image in our memory, but guarantees their
return, their actual, circumjacent, immediately accessible
presence.

This dim coolness of my room was to the broad daylight of the street what the shadow is to the sunbeam,
that is to say equally luminous, and presented to my
imagination the entire panorama of summer, which my
senses, if I had been out walking, could have tasted and
enjoyed only piecemeal; and so it was quite in harmony
with my state of repose which (thanks to the enlivening
adventures related in my books) sustained, like a hand
reposing motionless in a stream of running water, the
shock and animation of a torrent of activity.

But my grandmother, even if the weather, after growing too hot, had broken, and a storm, or just a shower, had burst over us, would come up and beg me to go outside. And as I did not wish to interrupt my reading, I would go on with it in the garden, under the chestnut-tree, in a hooded chair of wicker and canvas in the depths of which I used to sit and feel that I was hidden from the eyes of anyone who might be coming to call upon the family.

And then my thoughts, too, formed a similar sort of recess, in the depths of which I felt that I could bury myself and remain invisible even while I looked at what went on outside. When I saw an external object, my consciousness that I was seeing it would remain between me and it, surrounding it with a thin spiritual border that prevented me from ever touching its substance directly; for it would somehow evaporate before I could make contact with it, just as an incandescent body that is brought into proximity with something wet never actually touches its moisture, since it is always preceded by a zone of evaporation. On the sort of screen dappled with different states and impressions which my consciousness would simultaneously unfold while I was reading, and which ranged from the most deeply hidden aspirations of my being to the wholly external view of the horizon spread out before my eyes at the bottom of the garden, what was my primary, my innermost impulse, the lever whose incessant movements controlled everything else, was my belief in the philosophic richness and beauty of the book I was reading, and my desire to appropriate them for myself, whatever the book might be. For even if I had bought it at Combray, having seen it outside Borange's—whose grocery lay too far from our house for Françoise to be

able to shop there, as she did at Camus's, but was better
stocked as a stationer and bookseller—tied with string to
keep it in its place in the mosaic of monthly serials and
pamphlets which adorned either side of his doorway, a
doorway more mysterious, more teeming with suggestion
than that of a cathedral, it was because I had recognised it
as a book which had been well spoken of by the school-
master or the school-friend who at that particular time
seemed to me to be entrusted with the secret of truth and
beauty, things half-felt by me, half-incomprehensible, the
full understanding of which was the vague but permanent
object of my thoughts.

Next to this central belief which, while I was reading,
would be constantly reaching out from my inner self to
the outer world, towards the discovery of truth, came the
emotions aroused in me by the action in which I was taking part, for these afternoons were crammed with more
dramatic events than occur, often, in a whole lifetime.
These were the events taking place in the book I was
reading. It is true that the people concerned in them were
not what Françoise would have called "real people." But
none of the feelings which the joys or misfortunes of a
real person arouse in us can be awakened except through
a mental picture of those joys or misfortunes; and the ingenuity of the first novelist lay in his understanding that,
as the image was the one essential element in the complicated structure of our emotions, so that simplification of
it which consisted in the suppression, pure and simple, of
real people would be a decided improvement. A real person, profoundly as we may sympathise with him, is in a
great measure perceptible only through our senses, that is
to say, remains opaque, presents a dead weight which our

sensibilities have not the strength to lift. If some misfortune comes to him, it is only in one small section of the complete idea we have of him that we are capable of feeling any emotion; indeed it is only in one small section of the complete idea he has of himself that he is capable of feeling any emotion either. The novelist's happy discovery was to think of substituting for those opaque sections, impenetrable to the human soul, their equivalent in immaterial sections, things, that is, which one's soul can assimilate. After which it matters not that the actions, the feelings of this new order of creatures appear to us in the guise of truth, since we have made them our own, since it is in ourselves that they are happening, that they are holding in thrall, as we feverishly turn over the pages of the book, our quickened breath and staring eyes. And once the novelist has brought us to this state, in which, as in all purely mental states, every emotion is multiplied ten-fold, into which his book comes to disturb us as might a dream, but a dream more lucid and more abiding than those which come to us in sleep, why then, for the space of an hour he sets free within us all the joys and sorrows in the world, a few of which only we should have to spend years of our actual life in getting to know, and the most intense of which would never be revealed to us because the slow course of their development prevents us from perceiving them. It is the same in life; the heart changes, and it is our worst sorrow; but we know it only through reading, through our imagination: in reality its alteration, like that of certain natural phenomena, is so gradual that, even if we are able to distinguish, successively, each of its different states, we are still spared the actual sensation of change.

Next to, but distinctly less intimate a part of myself
than this human element, would come the landscape,
more or less projected before my eyes, in which the plot
of the story was taking place, and which made a far
stronger impression on my mind than the other, the actual landscape which met my eyes when I raised them
from my book. Thus for two consecutive summers I sat
in the heat of our Combray garden, sick with a longing
inspired by the book I was then reading for a land of
mountains and rivers, where I could see innumerable
sawmills, where beneath the limpid currents fragments of
wood lay mouldering in beds of watercress; and near by,
rambling and clustering along low walls, purple and red
flowers. And since there was always lurking in my mind
the dream of a woman who would enrich me with her
love, that dream in those two summers was quickened
with the fresh coolness of running water; and whoever she
might be, the woman whose image I called to mind, flowers, purple and red, would at once spring up on either
side of her like complementary colours.

This was not only because an image of which we
dream remains for ever stamped, is adorned and enriched,
by the association of colours not its own which may
happen to surround it in our mental picture; for the landscapes in the books I read were to me not merely landscapes more vividly portrayed in my imagination than any
which Combray could spread before my eyes but otherwise of the same kind. Because of the choice that the author had made of them, because of the spirit of faith in
which my mind would exceed and anticipate his printed
word, as it might be interpreting a revelation, they
seemed to me—an impression I hardly ever derived from

the place where I happened to be, especially from our garden, that undistinguished product of the strictly conventional fantasy of the gardener whom my grandmother so despised—to be actually part of nature itself, and worthy to be studied and explored.

Had my parents allowed me, when I read a book, to pay a visit to the region it described, I should have felt that I was making an enormous advance towards the ultimate conquest of truth. For even if we have the sensation of being always enveloped in, surrounded by our own soul, still it does not seem a fixed and immovable prison; rather do we seem to be borne away with it, and perpetually struggling to transcend it, to break out into the world, with a perpetual discouragement as we hear endlessly all around us that unvarying sound which is not an echo from without, but the resonance of a vibration from within. We try to discover in things, which become precious to us on that account, the reflection of what our soul has projected on to them; we are disillusioned when we find that they are in reality devoid of the charm which they owed, in our minds, to the association of certain ideas; sometimes we mobilise all our spiritual forces in a glittering array in order to bring our influence to bear on other human beings who, we very well know, are situated outside ourselves where we can never reach them. And so, if I always imagined the woman I loved in the setting I most longed at the time to visit, if I wished that it were she who showed it to me, who opened to me the gates of an unknown world, it was not by the mere hazard of a simple association of thoughts; no, it was because my dreams of travel and of love were only moments—which I isolate artificially today as though I were cutting sec-

tions at different heights in a jet of water, iridescent but
seemingly without flow or motion—in a single, undeviat-
ing, irresistible outpouring of all the forces of my life.

Finally, continuing to trace from the inside outwards
these states simultaneously juxtaposed in my consciousness, and before reaching the horizon of reality which enveloped them, I discover pleasures of another kind, those
of being comfortably seated, of sniffing the fragrance of
the air, of not being disturbed by any visitor, and, when
an hour chimed from the steeple of Saint-Hilaire, of seeing what was already spent of the afternoon fall drop by
drop until I heard the last stroke which enabled me to
add up the total, after which the long silence that followed seemed to herald the beginning, in the blue sky
above me, of all that part of the day that still remained to
me for reading, until the good dinner which Françoise
was even now preparing and which would strengthen and
refresh me after the strenuous pursuit of the hero through
the pages of my book. And as each hour struck, it would
seem to me that a few moments only had passed since the
hour before; the latest would inscribe itself close to its
predecessor on the sky's surface, and I was unable to believe that sixty minutes could have been squeezed into the
tiny arc of blue which was comprised between their two
golden figures. Sometimes it would even happen that this
precocious hour would sound two strokes more than the
last; there must then have been an hour which I had not
heard strike; something that had taken place had not
taken place for me; the fascination of my book, a magic as
potent as the deepest slumber, had deceived my enchanted ears and had obliterated the sound of that golden
bell from the azure surface of the enveloping silence.

Sweet Sunday afternoons beneath the chestnut-tree in the
garden at Combray, carefully purged by me of every
commonplace incident of my personal existence, which I
had replaced with a life of strange adventures and aspirations in a land watered with living streams, you still recall
that life to me when I think of you, and you embody it in
effect by virtue of having gradually encircled and enclosed
it—while I went on with my reading and the heat of the
day declined—in the crystalline succession, slowly changing and dappled with foliage, of your silent, sonorous, fragrant, limpid hours.

Sometimes I would be torn from my book in the
middle of the afternoon by the gardener's daughter, who
came running wildly, overturning an orange-tree in its
tub, cutting a finger, breaking a tooth, and screaming
"They're coming, they're coming!" so that Françoise and
I should run too and not miss anything of the show. That
was on the days when the cavalry from the local garrison
passed through Combray on their way to manoeuvres, going as a rule by the Rue Sainte-Hildegarde. While our
servants, sitting in a row on their chairs outside the garden railings, stared at the people of Combray taking their
Sunday walk and were stared at in return, the gardener's
daughter, through the gap between two distant houses in
the Avenue de la Gare, had spied the glitter of helmets.
The servants had then hurried in with their chairs, for
when the troopers paraded down the Rue Sainte-Hildegarde they filled it from side to side, and their jostling
horses scraped against the walls of the houses, covering
and submerging the pavements like banks which present
too narrow a channel to a river in flood.

"Poor boys," Françoise would exclaim, in tears almost before she had reached the railings, "poor boys, to be mown down like grass in a meadow. It's just shocking to think of," she would add, laying a hand over her heart, where presumably she had felt the shock.

"A fine sight, isn't it, Mme Françoise, all these young fellows not caring two straws for their lives?" the gardener would ask, just to "draw" her. And he would not have spoken in vain.

"Not caring for their lives, is it? Why, what in the world should we care for if it's not our lives, the only gift the Lord never offers us a second time? Alas, dear God! You're right all the same, they don't care! I can remember them in '70; in those wretched wars they've no fear of death left in them; they're nothing more nor less than madmen; and then they aren't worth the price of a rope to hang them with; they're not men any more, they're lions." For by her way of thinking, to compare a man with a lion, which she used to pronounce "lie-on," was not at all complimentary.

The Rue Sainte-Hildegarde turned too sharply for us to be able to see them approaching at any distance, and it was only through the gap between the two houses in the Avenue de la Gare that we could glimpse more helmets flashing past in the sunlight. The gardener wanted to know whether there were still many to come, and he was thirsty besides, with the sun beating down upon his head. So then, suddenly, his daughter would leap out as though from a beleaguered city, would make a sortie, turn the street corner, and after having risked her life a hundred times over, would reappear bringing us, together with a jug of liquorice-water, the news that there were still at least a thousand of them, pouring along without a break from the direction of Thiberzy and Méséglise. Françoise and the gardener, reconciled, would discuss the line to be followed in the event of war.

"Don't you see, Françoise," he would say, "revolution would be better, because then no one would need to join in unless he wanted to."

"Oh, yes, I can see that, certainly; it's more straightforward."

The gardener believed that, as soon as war was declared, all the railways would be shut down.

"Yes, to be sure; to stop people running away," Françoise would say.

And the gardener would assent, with "Ay, they're the cunning ones," for he would not allow that war was anything but a kind of trick which the State attempted to play on the people, or that there was a man in the world who would not run away from it if he had the chance to do so.

But Françoise would hasten back to my aunt, and I would return to my book, and the servants would take their places again outside the gate to watch the dust settle on the pavement and the excitement caused by the passage of the soldiers subside. Long after calm had been restored, an abnormal tide of humanity would continue to darken the streets of Combray. And in front of every house, even those where it was not the custom, the servants, and sometimes even the masters, would sit and watch, festooning the doorsteps with a dark, irregular fringe, like the border of shells and sea-weed which a stronger tide than usual leaves on the beach, as though trimming it with embroidered crape, when the sea itself has retreated.

Except on such days as these, however, I would as a
rule be left to read in peace. But the interruption and the
commentary which a visit from Swann once occasioned in
the course of my reading, which had brought me to the
work of an author quite new to me, Bergotte, resulted in
the consequence that for a long time afterwards it was not
against a wall gay with spikes of purple blossom, but
against a wholly different background, the porch of a
Gothic cathedral, that I saw the figure of one of the
women of whom I dreamed.

I had heard Bergotte spoken of for the first time by a
friend older than myself whom I greatly admired, Bloch.
Hearing me confess my admiration for the *Nuit d'Octobre*,
he had burst out in a loud bray of laughter like a bugle-
call, and said to me: "You really must conquer your vile
taste for A. de Musset, Esquire. He is a bad egg, one of
the very worst, a pretty detestable specimen. I am bound
to admit, natheless, that he, and even the man Racine,
did, each of them, once in his life, compose a line which
is not only fairly rhythmical but has also what is in my
eyes the supreme merit of meaning absolutely nothing.
One is 'La blanche Oloossone et la blanche Camyre,' and
the other 'La fille de Minos et de Pasiphaë' They were
submitted to my judgment, as evidence for the defence of
these two runagates, in an article by my revered master,
old Leconte, beloved of the immortal gods. By which token, here is a book which I haven't the time to read just
now, recommended, it appears, by that colossal fellow. He
regards, or so they tell me, its author, one Bergotte, as a
most subtle scribe; and, albeit he exhibits on occasion a
critical mansuetude that is not easily explicable, still his
word has weight with me as it were the Delphic Oracle.

Read you then this lyrical prose, and, if the titanic rhymester who composed *Bhagavat* and the *Lévrier de Magnus* speaks not falsely, then, by Apollo, you may taste, *cher maître*, the ambrosial joys of Olympus." It was in an ostensible vein of sarcasm that he had asked me to call him, and that he himself called me, *"cher maître."* But, as a matter of fact, we each derived a certain satisfaction from the mannerism, being still at the age in which one believes that one gives a thing real existence by giving it a name.

Unfortunately I was unable to set at rest by further talks with Bloch, in which I might have insisted upon an explanation, the doubts he had engendered in me when he told me that fine lines of poetry (from which I expected nothing less than the revelation of truth itself) were all the finer if they meant absolutely nothing. For, as it happened, Bloch was not invited to the house again. At first he had been well received there. It is true that my grandfather made out that, whenever I formed a strong attachment to any one of my friends and brought him home with me, that friend was invariably a Jew; to which he would not have objected on principle—indeed his own friend Swann was of Jewish extraction—had he not found that the Jews whom I chose as friends were not usually of the best type. And so whenever I brought a new friend home my grandfather seldom failed to start humming the "O, God of our fathers" from *La Juive*, or else "Israel, break thy chains," singing the tune alone, of course, to an "um-ti-tum-ti-tum, tra-la"; but I used to be afraid that my friend would recognise it and be able to reconstruct the words.

Before seeing them, merely on hearing their names,

about which, as often as not, there was nothing particularly Hebraic, he would divine not only the Jewish origin of such of my friends as might indeed be Jewish, but even at times some skeleton in their family cupboard.

"And what's the name of this friend of yours who is coming this evening?"

"Dumont, grandpapa."

"Dumont! Oh, I don't like the sound of that."

And he would sing:

> Archers, be on your guard!
> Watch without rest, without sound.

And then, after a few adroit questions on points of detail, he would call out "On guard! on guard," or, if it were the victim himself who had already arrived, and had been unwittingly obliged, by subtle interrogation, to admit his origins, then my grandfather, to show us that he had no longer any doubts, would merely look at us, humming under his breath the air of

> What! do you hither guide the feet
> Of this timid Israelite?

or of

> Sweet vale of Hebron, dear paternal fields,

or, perhaps, of

> Yes, I am of the chosen race.

These little eccentricities on my grandfather's part implied no ill-will whatsoever towards my friends. But

Bloch had displeased my family for other reasons. He had begun by irritating my father, who, seeing him come in with wet clothes, had asked him with keen interest:

"Why, M. Bloch, is there a change in the weather? Has it been raining? I can't understand it; the barometer was set fair."

Which drew from Bloch nothing more than: "Sir, I am absolutely incapable of telling you whether it has rained. I live so resolutely apart from physical contingencies that my senses no longer trouble to inform me of them."

"My poor boy," said my father after Bloch had gone, "your friend is out of his mind. Why, he couldn't even tell me what the weather was like. As if there could be anything more interesting! He's an imbecile."

Next Bloch had displeased my grandmother because once, after lunch, when she complained of not feeling very well, he had stifled a sob and wiped tears from his eyes.

"How can he possibly be sincere," she observed to me. "Why, he doesn't know me. Unless he's mad, of course."

And finally he had upset the whole household when he arrived an hour and a half late for dinner and covered with mud from head to foot, and made not the least apology, saying merely: "I never allow myself to be influenced in the smallest degree either by atmospheric disturbances or by the arbitrary divisions of what is known as time. I would willingly reintroduce the use of the opium pipe or the Malay kris, but I know nothing about that of those infinitely more pernicious and moreover flatly bourgeois implements, the umbrella and the watch."

In spite of all this he would still have been received at Combray. He was, of course, hardly the friend my parents would have chosen for me; they had, in the end, decided that the tears which he had shed on hearing of my grandmother's indisposition were genuine enough; but they knew, either instinctively or from experience, that our impulsive emotions have but little influence over the course of our actions and the conduct of our lives; and that regard for moral obligations, loyalty to friends, patience in finishing our work, obedience to a rule of life, have a surer foundation in habits solidly formed and blindly followed than in these momentary transports, ardent but sterile. They would have preferred for me, instead of Bloch, companions who would have given me no more than it is proper to give according to the laws of middle-class morality, who would not unexpectedly send me a basket of fruit because they happened, that morning, to have thought of me with affection, but who, being incapable of inclining in my favour, by a simple impulse of their imagination and sensibility, the exact balance of the duties and claims of friendship, would be equally incapable of loading the scales to my detriment. Even our faults will not easily divert from the path of their duty towards us those conventional natures of which the model was my great-aunt who, estranged for years from a niece to whom she never spoke, yet made no change in the will in which she had left that niece the whole of her fortune, because she was her next-of-kin and it was the "proper thing" to do.

But I was fond of Bloch; my parents wished me to be happy; and the insoluble problems which I set myself on such texts as the beauty stripped of meaning of *La fille de*

Minos et de Pasiphaë made me more exhausted and unwell than further talks on the subject would have done, unwholesome as those talks might seem to my mother's mind. And he would still have been received at Combray but for one thing. That same night, after dinner, having informed me (a piece of news which had a great influence on my later life, making it happier at one time and then more unhappy) that no woman ever thought of anything but love, and that there was not one of them whose resistance could not be overcome, he had gone on to assure me that he had heard it said on unimpeachable authority that my great-aunt herself had led a tempestuous life in her younger days and had been known as a kept woman. I could not refrain from passing on so important a piece of information to my parents; the next time Bloch called he was not admitted, and afterwards, when I met him in the street, he greeted me with extreme coldness.

But in the matter of Bergotte he had spoken truly.

For the first few days, like a tune with which one will soon be infatuated but which one has not yet "got hold of," the things I was to love so passionately in Bergotte's style did not immediately strike me. I could not, it is true, lay down the novel of his which I was reading, but I fancied that I was interested in the subject alone, as in the first dawn of love when we go every day to meet a woman at some party or entertainment which we think is in itself the attraction. Then I observed the rare, almost archaic expressions he liked to employ at certain moments, in which a hidden stream of harmony, an inner prelude, would heighten his style; and it was at such points as these, too, that he would begin to speak of the "vain dream of life," of the "inexhaustible torrent of fair

forms," of the "sterile and exquisite torment of understanding and loving," of the "moving effigies which enno-
ble for all time the charming and venerable fronts of our
cathedrals," that he would express a whole system of philosophy, new to me, by the use of marvellous images that
one felt must be the inspiration for the harp-song which
then arose and to which they provided a sublime accompaniment. One of these passages of Bergotte, the third or
fourth which I had detached from the rest, filled me with
a joy to which the meagre joy I had tasted in the first
passage bore no comparison, a joy that I felt I was experi-
encing in a deeper, vaster, more integral part of myself,
from which all obstacles and partitions seemed to have
been swept away. For what had happened was that, while
I recognised in this passage the same taste for uncommon
phrases, the same musical outpouring, the same idealist
philosophy which had been present in the earlier passages
without my having recognised them as being the source of
my pleasure, I now had the impression of being con-
fronted not by a particular passage in one of Bergotte's
works, tracing a purely bi-dimensional figure upon the
surface of my mind, but rather by the "ideal passage" of
Bergotte, common to every one of his books, to which all
the earlier, similar passages, now becoming merged in it,
had added a kind of density and volume by which my
own understanding seemed to be enlarged.

I was not quite Bergotte's sole admirer; he was the
favourite writer also of a friend of my mother's, a very
well-read lady; while Dr du Boulbon had kept all his patients waiting until he finished Bergotte's latest volume;
and it was from his consulting room, and from a house in
a park near Combray, that some of the first seeds were

scattered of that taste for Bergotte, a rare growth in those days but now universally acclimatised, that one finds flowering everywhere throughout Europe and America, even in the smallest villages, rare still in its refinement, but in that alone. What my mother's friend and, it would seem, Dr du Boulbon liked above all in the writings of Bergotte was just what I liked, the same melodic flow, the old-fashioned phrases, and certain others, quite simple and familiar, but so placed by him, so highlighted, as to hint at a particular quality of taste on his part; and also, in the sad parts of his books, a sort of roughness, a tone that was almost harsh. And he himself, no doubt, realised that these were his principal attractions. For in his later books, if he had hit upon some great truth, or upon the name of an historic cathedral, he would break off his narrative, and in an invocation, an apostrophe, a long prayer, would give free rein to those exhalations which, in the earlier volumes, had been immanent in his prose, discernible only in a rippling of its surface, and perhaps even more delightful, more harmonious when they were thus veiled, when the reader could give no precise indication of where their murmuring began or where it died away. These passages in which he delighted were our favourites also. For my own part I knew all of them by heart. I was disappointed when he resumed the thread of his narrative. Whenever he spoke of something whose beauty had until then remained hidden from me, of pine-forests or of hailstorms, of Notre-Dame Cathedral, of *Athalie* or of *Phèdre*, by some piece of imagery he would make their beauty explode into my consciousness. And so, realising that the universe contained innumerable elements which my feeble senses would be powerless to discern did he not bring

them within my reach, I longed to have some opinion,
some metaphor of his, upon everything in the world, and
especially upon such things as I might some day have an
opportunity of seeing for myself; and among these, more
particularly still upon some of the historic buildings of
France, upon certain seascapes, because the emphasis with
which he referred to them in his books showed that he regarded them as rich in significance and beauty. But, alas,
upon almost everything in the world his opinion was unknown to me. I had no doubt that it would differ entirely
from my own, since his came down from an unknown
sphere towards which I was striving to raise myself; convinced that my thoughts would have seemed pure foolishness to that perfected spirit, I had so completely obliterated them all that, if I happened to find in one of his
books something which had already occurred to my own
mind, my heart would swell as though some deity had, in
his infinite bounty, restored it to me, had pronounced it
to be beautiful and right. It happened now and then that
a page of Bergotte would express precisely those ideas
which I often used to write to my grandmother and my
mother at night, when I was unable to sleep, so much so
that this page of his had the appearance of a collection of
epigraphs for me to set at the head of my letters. And so
too, in later years, when I began to write a book of my
own, and the quality of some of my sentences seemed so
inadequate that I could not make up my mind to go on
with the undertaking, I would find the equivalent in
Bergotte. But it was only then, when I read them in his
pages, that I could enjoy them; when it was I myself who
composed them, in my anxiety that they should exactly
reproduce what I had perceived in my mind's eye, and in

my fear of their not turning out "true to life," how could
I find time to ask myself whether what I was writing was
pleasing! But in fact there was no other kind of prose, no
other sort of ideas, that I really liked. My feverish and
unsatisfactory attempts were themselves a token of love, a
love which brought me no pleasure but was none the less
profound. And so, when I came suddenly upon similar
phrases in the writings of another, that is to say stripped
of their familiar accompaniment of scruples and repres-
sions and self-tormentings, I was free to indulge to the
full my own appetite for such things, like a cook who, for
once having no dinner to prepare for other people, at last
has the time to enjoy his food. When, one day, I came
across in a book by Bergotte some joke about an old family servant which the writer's solemn and magnificent
prose made even more comical, but which was in principle the same joke I had often made to my grandmother
about Françoise, and when, another time, I discovered
that he considered not unworthy of reflection in one of
those mirrors of absolute truth which were his writings a
remark similar to one which I had had occasion to make
about our friend M. Legrandin (and moreover my remarks on Françoise and M. Legrandin were among those
which I would most resolutely have sacrificed for Bergotte's sake, in the belief that he would find them quite
without interest), then it was suddenly revealed to me
that my own humble existence and the realms of the true
were less widely separated than I had supposed, that at
certain points they actually coincided, and in my new-
found confidence and joy I had wept upon his printed
page as in the arms of a long-lost father.

From his books I had formed an impression of

Bergotte as a frail and disappointed old man, who had lost some of his children and had never got over the loss. And so I would read, or rather sing his sentences in my mind, with rather more *dolce*, rather more *lento* than he himself had perhaps intended, and his simplest phrase would strike my ears with something peculiarly gentle and loving in its intonation. More than anything else I cherished his philosophy, and had pledged myself to it in life-long devotion. It made me impatient to reach the age when I should be eligible for the class at school called "Philosophy." But I did not wish to do anything else there but exist and be guided exclusively by the mind of Bergotte, and if I had been told then that the metaphysicians to whom I was actually to become attached there would resemble him in nothing, I should have been struck down by the despair of a young lover who has sworn lifelong fidelity, when a friend speaks to him of the other mistresses he will have in time to come.

One Sunday, while I was reading in the garden, I was interrupted by Swann, who had come to call upon my parents.

"What are you reading? May I look? Why, it's Bergotte! Who has been telling you about him?"

I said it was Bloch.

"Oh, yes, that boy I saw here once, who looks so like the Bellini portrait of Mahomet II. It's an astonishing likeness; he has the same arched eyebrows and hooked nose and prominent cheekbones. When he has a little beard he'll be Mahomet himself. Anyhow, he has good taste, for Bergotte is a delightful soul." And seeing how much I seemed to admire Bergotte, Swann, who never spoke at all about the people he knew, made an exception in my favour and said: "I know him well. If you would like him to write a few words on the title-page of your book I could ask him for you."

I dared not accept such an offer, but bombarded Swann with questions about his friend. "Can you tell me, please, who is his favourite actor?"

"Actor? No, I can't say. But I do know this: there's not a man on the stage whom he thinks equal to Berma— he puts her above everyone. Have you seen her?"

"No, sir, my parents don't allow me to go to the theatre."

"That's a pity. You should insist. Berma in *Phèdre*, in the *Cid*; she's only an actress, if you like, but you know I don't believe very much in the '*hierarchy*' of the arts." (As he spoke I noticed, what had often struck me before in his conversations with my grandmother's sisters, that whenever he spoke of serious matters, whenever he used an expression which seemed to imply a definite opinion upon some important subject, he would take care to isolate, to sterilise it by using a special intonation, mechanical and ironic, as though he had put the phrase or word between inverted commas, and was anxious to disclaim any personal responsibility for it; as who should say "the '*hierarchy*,' don't you know, as silly people call it." But then, if it was so absurd, why did he use the word?) A moment later he went on: "Her acting will give you as noble an inspiration as any masterpiece of art, as—oh, I don't know—" and he laughed, "shall we say the Queens of Chartres?" Until then I had supposed that this horror of having to give a serious opinion was something Parisian and refined, in contrast to the provincial dogmatism of my grandmother's sisters; and I imagined also

that it was characteristic of the mental attitude of the circle in which Swann moved, where, by a natural reaction
from the lyrical enthusiasms of earlier generations, an excessive importance was now given to precise and petty
facts, formerly regarded as vulgar, and anything in the
nature of "phrase-making" was proscribed. But now I
found myself slightly shocked by this attitude of Swann's.
He appeared unwilling even to risk having an opinion,
and to be at his ease only when he could furnish, with
meticulous accuracy, some precise detail. But did he not
realise that to postulate that the accuracy of his information was of some importance was tantamount to profess-
ing an opinion? I thought again of the dinner that night
when I had been so unhappy because Mamma would not
be coming up to my room, and when he had dismissed
the balls given by the Princesse de Léon as being of no
importance. And yet it was to just that sort of amusement
that he devoted his life. I found all this contradictory.
What other life did he set apart for saying in all serious-
ness what he thought about things, for formulating judgments which he would not put between inverted commas,
and for no longer indulging with punctilious politeness in
occupations which at the same time he professed to find
absurd? I noticed, too, in the manner in which Swann
spoke to me of Bergotte, something which, to do him justice, was not peculiar to himself, but was shared at the
time by all that writer's admirers, including my mother's
friend and Dr du Boulbon. Like Swann, they would say
of Bergotte: "He has a delightful mind, so individual, he
has a way of his own of saying things, which is a little
far-fetched, but so agreeable. You never need to look for
the signature, you can tell his work at once." But none of

them would go so far as to say "He's a great writer, he has great talent." They did not even credit him with talent at all. They did not do so, because they did not know. We are very slow to recognise in the peculiar physiognomy of a new writer the model which is labelled "great talent" in our museum of general ideas. Simply because that physiognomy is new and strange, we can find in it no resemblance to what we are accustomed to call talent. We say rather originality, charm, delicacy, strength; and then one day we realise that it is precisely all this that adds up to talent.

"Are there any books in which Bergotte has written about Berma?" I asked M. Swann.

"I think he has, in that little essay on Racine, but it must be out of print. Still, perhaps there has been a second impression. I'll find out. In fact I can ask Bergotte himself all you want to know next time he comes to dine with us. He never misses a week, from one year's end to another. He's my daughter's greatest friend. They go and look at old towns and cathedrals and castles together."

As I was still completely ignorant of the social hierarchy, the fact that my father found it impossible for us to see anything of Swann's wife and daughter had for a long time had the effect, in making me imagine them as separated from us by an enormous gulf, of enhancing their prestige in my eyes. I was sorry that my mother did not dye her hair and redden her lips, as I had heard our neighbour Mme Sazerat say that Mme Swann did, to gratify not her husband but M. de Charlus; and I felt that, to her, we must be an object of scorn, which distressed me particularly on account of the daughter, such a pretty little girl, as I had heard, of whom I used often to

dream, ascribing to her each time the same arbitrarily
chosen and enchanting features. But when, that day, I
learned that Mlle Swann was a creature living in such rare
and fortunate circumstances, bathed, as in her natural element, in such a sea of privilege that, if she should ask her
parents whether anyone were coming to dinner, she would
be answered by those two syllables, radiant with light, by
the name of that golden guest who was to her no more
than an old friend of the family, Bergotte, that for her the
intimate conversation at table, corresponding to what my
great-aunt's conversation was for me, would be the words
of Bergotte on all those subjects which he had not been
able to take up in his writings, and on which I should
have liked to hear him pronounce his oracles, and that,
above all, when she went to visit other towns, he would
be walking by her side, unrecognised and glorious, like
the gods who came down of old to dwell among
mortals—then I realised both the rare worth of a creature
such as Mlle Swann and, at the same time, how coarse
and ignorant I should appear to her; and I felt so keenly
how sweet and how impossible it would be for me to become her friend that I was filled at once with longing and
despair. Henceforth, more often than not when I thought
of her, I would see her standing before the porch of a
cathedral, explaining to me what each of the statues
meant, and, with a smile which was my highest commendation, presenting me as her friend to Bergotte. And invariably the charm of all the fancies which the thought of
cathedrals used to inspire in me, the charm of the hills
and valleys of the Ile-de-France and of the plains of Normandy, would be reflected in the picture I had formed in
my mind's eye of Mlle Swann; nothing more remained

but to know and to love her. The belief that a person has
a share in an unknown life to which his or her love may
win us admission is, of all the prerequisites of love, the
one which it values most highly and which makes it set
little store by all the rest. Even those women who claim
to judge a man by his looks alone, see in those looks the
emanation of a special way of life. That is why they fall
in love with soldiers or with firemen; the uniform makes
them less particular about the face; they feel they are em-
bracing beneath the gleaming breastplate a heart different
from the rest, more gallant, more adventurous, more tender; and so it is that a young king or a crown prince may
make the most gratifying conquests in the countries that
he visits, and yet lack entirely that regular and classic
profile which would be indispensable, I dare say, for a
stockbroker.

While I was reading in the garden, a thing my great-
aunt would never have understood my doing save on a
Sunday, that being the day on which it is unlawful to indulge in any serious occupation, and on which she herself
would lay aside her sewing (on a week-day she would
have said, "What! still amusing yourself with a book? It
isn't Sunday, you know!"—putting into the word "amusing" an implication of childishness and waste of time), my
aunt Léonie would be gossiping with Françoise until it
was time for Eulalie to arrive. She would tell her that she
had just seen Mme Goupil go by "without an umbrella,
in the silk dress she had made for her the other day at
Châteaudun. If she has far to go before vespers, she may
get it properly soaked."

"Maybe, maybe" (which meant "maybe not"), was

the answer, for Françoise did not wish definitely to exclude the possibility of a happier alternative.

"Heavens," said my aunt, slapping herself on the
forehead, "that reminds me I never heard if she got to
church this morning before the Elevation. I must remember to ask Eulalie . . . Françoise, just look at that black
cloud behind the steeple, and how poor the light is on the
slates. You may be certain it will rain before the day is
out. It couldn't possibly go on like that, it's been too hot.
And the sooner the better, for until the storm breaks my
Vichy water won't go down," she added, since, in her
mind, the desire to accelerate the digestion of her Vichy
water was of infinitely greater importance than her fear of
seeing Mme Goupil's new dress ruined.

"Maybe, maybe."

"And you know that when it rains in the Square
there's none too much shelter." Suddenly my aunt turned
pale. "What, three o'clock!" she exclaimed. "But vespers
will have begun already, and I've forgotten my pepsin!
Now I know why that Vichy water has been lying on my
stomach." And pouncing on a prayer-book bound in purple velvet with gilt clasps, out of which in her haste she
let fall a shower of those pictures bordered in a lace fringe
of yellowish paper which mark the pages of feast-days,
my aunt, while she swallowed her drops, began at full
speed to mutter the words of the sacred text, its meaning
slightly clouded by the uncertainty whether the pepsin,
when taken so long after the Vichy, would still be able to
catch up with it and send it down. "Three o'clock! It's
unbelievable how time flies."

A little tap on the window-pane, as though something
had struck it, followed by a plentiful light falling sound,

as of grains of sand being sprinkled from a window overhead, gradually spreading, intensifying, acquiring a regular rhythm, becoming fluid, sonorous, musical, immeasurable, universal: it was the rain.

"There, Françoise, what did I tell you? How it's
coming down! But I think I heard the bell at the garden
gate: go along and see who can be outside in this
weather."

Françoise went and returned. "It's Mme Amédée"
(my grandmother). "She said she was going for a walk.
And yet it's raining hard."

"I'm not at all surprised," said my aunt, raising her
eyes to the heavens. "I've always said that she was not in
the least like other people. Well, I'm glad it's she and not
myself who's outside in all this."

"Mme Amédée is always the exact opposite of everyone else," said Françoise, not unkindly, refraining until
she should be alone with the other servants from stating
her belief that my grandmother was "slightly batty."

"There's Benediction over! Eulalie will never come
now," sighed my aunt. "It will be the weather that's
frightened her away."

"But it's not five o'clock yet, Mme Octave, it's only
half-past four."

"Only half-past four! And here am I, obliged to draw
back the curtains just to get a tiny streak of daylight. At
half-past four! Only a week before the Rogation-days.
Ah, my poor Françoise, the good Lord must be sorely
vexed with us. The world is going too far these days. As
my poor Octave used to say, we have forgotten God too
often, and he is taking his revenge."

A bright flush animated my aunt's cheeks; it was Eulalie. As ill luck would have it, scarcely had she been admitted to the presence when Françoise reappeared and, with a smile that was meant to indicate her full participation in the pleasure which, she had no doubt, her tidings would give my aunt, articulating each syllable so as to show that, in spite of her having to translate them into indirect speech, she was repeating, as a good servant should, the very words which the new visitor had condescended to use, said: "His reverence the Curé would be delighted, enchanted, if Mme Octave is not resting just now, and could see him. His reverence don't wish to disturb Mme Octave. His reverence is downstairs; I told him to go into the parlour."

Had the truth been known, the Curé's visits gave my aunt no such ecstatic pleasure as Françoise supposed, and the air of jubilation with which she felt bound to illuminate her face whenever she had to announce his arrival did not altogether correspond to the sentiments of her invalid. The Curé (an excellent man, with whom I now regret not having conversed more often, for, even if he cared nothing for the arts, he knew a great many etymologies), being in the habit of showing distinguished visitors over his church (he had even planned to compile a history of the Parish of Combray), used to weary her with his endless commentaries which, incidentally, never varied in the least degree. But when his visit synchronised exactly with Eulalie's it became frankly distasteful to my aunt. She would have preferred to make the most of Eulalie, and not to have the whole of her circle about her at one time. But she dared not send the Curé away, and had to content herself with making a sign to Eulalie not to leave when he did, so that she might have her to herself for a little after he had gone.

"What is this I have been hearing, Father, about a painter setting up his easel in your church, and copying one of the windows? Old as I am, I can safely say that I have never heard of such a thing in all my life! What is the world coming to! And the ugliest thing in the whole church, too."

"I will not go so far as to say that it's quite the ugliest, for although there are certain things in Saint-Hilaire which are well worth a visit, there are others that are very old now in my poor basilica, the only one in all the diocese that has never even been restored. God knows our porch is dirty and antiquated, but still it has a certain majesty. I'll even grant you the Esther tapestries, which personally I wouldn't give a brass farthing for, but which the experts place immediately after the ones at Sens. I can quite see, too, that apart from certain details which are— well, a trifle realistic—they show features which testify to a genuine power of observation. But don't talk to me about the windows. Is it common sense, I ask you, to leave up windows which shut out all the daylight and even confuse the eyes by throwing patches of colour, to which I should be hard put to it to give a name, on to a floor in which there are not two slabs on the same level and which they refuse to renew for me because, if you please, those are the tombstones of the Abbots of Combray and the Lords of Guermantes, the old Counts, you know, of Brabant, direct ancestors of the present Duc de Guermantes and of the Duchess too since she was a Mademoiselle de Guermantes who married her cousin?"

(My grandmother, whose steadfast refusal to take any interest in "persons" had ended in her confusing all their names and titles, whenever anyone mentioned the Duchesse de Guermantes used to make out that she must be related to Mme de Villeparisis. The whole family would then burst out laughing; and she would attempt to justify herself by harking back to some invitation to a christening or funeral: "I feel sure that there was a Guermantes in it somewhere." And for once I would side with the others against her, refusing to believe that there could be any connexion between her school-friend and the descendant of Geneviève de Brabant.)

"Look at Roussainville," the Curé went on. "It's nothing more nowadays than a parish of tenant farmers, though in olden times the place must have had a considerable importance from its trade in felt hats and clocks. (I'm not certain, by the way, of the etymology of Roussainville. I'm rather inclined to think that the name was originally Rouville, from *Radulfi villa*, analogous, don't you see, to Châteauroux, *Castrum Radulfi*, but we'll talk about that some other time.) Anyway, the church there has superb windows, almost all modern, including that most imposing 'Entry of Louis-Philippe into Combray' which would be more in keeping, surely, at Combray itself and which is every bit as good, I understand, as the famous windows at Chartres. Only yesterday I met Dr Percepied's brother, who goes in for these things, and he told me that he regarded it as a very fine piece of work. But, as I said to this artist, who, by the way, seems to be a most civil fellow, and is a regular virtuoso, it appears, with the brush, what on earth do you find so extraordinary in this window, which is if anything a little dingier than the rest?"

"I am sure that if you were to ask the Bishop," said my aunt in a resigned tone, for she had begun to feel that she was going to be "tired," "he would never refuse you a new window."

"You may depend upon it, Mme Octave," replied the Curé. "Why, it was his Lordship himself who started the outcry about the window, by proving that it represented Gilbert the Bad, a Lord of Guermantes and a direct descendant of Geneviève de Brabant who was a daughter of the House of Guermantes, receiving absolution from Saint Hilaire."

"But I don't see where Saint Hilaire comes in."

"Why yes, have you never noticed, in the corner of the window, a lady in a yellow robe? Well, that's Saint Hilaire, who is also known, you will remember, in certain parts of the country as Saint Illiers, Saint Hélier, and even, in the Jura, Saint Ylie. But these various corruptions of *Sanctus Hilarius* are by no means the most curious that have occurred in the names of the blessed. Take, for example, my good Eulalie, the case of your own patron, *Sancta Eulalia*; do you know what she has become in Burgundy? Saint Eloi, nothing more nor less! The lady has become a gentleman. Do you hear that, Eulalie—after you're dead they'll make a man of you!"

"His Reverence will always have his little joke."

"Gilbert's brother, Charles the Stammerer, was a pious prince, but, having early in life lost his father, Pepin the Mad, who died as a result of his mental infirmity, he wielded the supreme power with all the arrogance of a

man who has not been subjected to discipline in his
youth, so much so that, whenever he saw a man in a
town whose face he didn't like, he would massacre the
entire population. Gilbert, wishing to be avenged on
Charles, caused the church at Combray to be burned
down, the original church, that was, which Théodebert,
when he and his court left the country residence he had
near here, at Thiberzy (which is, of course, *Theodeberciacus*), to go and fight the Burgundians, had promised to
build over the tomb of Saint Hilaire if the saint brought
him victory. Nothing remains of it now but the crypt,
into which Théodore has probably taken you, for Gilbert
burned all the rest. Finally, he defeated the unlucky
Charles with the aid of William the Conqueror," (the
Curé pronounced it "Will'am"), "which is why so many
English still come to visit the place. But he does not appear to have managed to win the affection of the people
of Combray, for they fell upon him as he was coming out
from mass, and cut off his head. Théodore has a little
book he lends people that tells the whole story.

"But what is unquestionably the most remarkable
thing about our church is the view from the belfry, which
is full of grandeur. Certainly in your case, since you are
not very strong, I should never recommend you to climb
our ninety-seven steps, just half the number they have in
the famous cathedral at Milan. It's quite tiring enough for
the most active person, especially as you have to bend
double if you don't wish to crack your skull, and you collect all the cobwebs off the staircase on your clothes. In
any case you should be well wrapped up," he went on,
without noticing my aunt's indignation at the mere suggestion that she could ever be capable of climbing into his

belfry, "for there's a strong breeze there once you get to the top. Some people even assure me that they have felt the chill of death up there. However, on Sundays there are always clubs and societies who come, often from a long way off, to admire our beautiful panorama, and they always go home charmed. For instance, next Sunday, if the weather holds, you'll be sure to find a lot of people there, for Rogation-tide. No doubt about it, the view from up there is entrancing, with what you might call vistas over the plain, which have quite a special charm of their own. On a clear day you can see as far as Verneuil. And then another thing; you can see at the same time places which you normally see one without the other, as, for instance, the course of the Vivonne and the irrigation ditches at Saint-Assise-lès-Combray, which are separated by a screen of tall trees, or again, the various canals at Jouy-le-Vicomte, which is *Gaudiacus vice comitis*, as of course you know. Each time I've been to Jouy I've seen a bit of canal in one place, and then I've turned a corner and seen another, but when I saw the second I could no longer see the first. I tried to put them together in my mind's eye; it was no good. But from the top of Saint-Hilaire it's quite another matter—a regular network in which the place is enclosed. Only you can't see any water; it's as though there were great clefts slicing up the town so neatly that it looks like a loaf of bread which still holds together after it has been cut up. To get it all quite perfect you would have to be in both places at once; up at the top of the steeple of Saint-Hilaire and down there at Jouy-le-Vicomte."

The Curé had so exhausted my aunt that no sooner had he gone than she was obliged to send Eulalie away.

"Here, my poor Eulalie," she said in a feeble voice, drawing a coin from a small purse which lay ready to her hand. "This is just something so that you won't forget me in your prayers."

"Oh, but, Mme Octave, I don't think I ought to; you know very well that I don't come here for that!" So Eulalie would answer, with the same hesitation and the same embarrassment, every Sunday as though it were the first, and with a look of vexation which delighted my aunt and never offended her, for if it happened that Eulalie, when she took the money, looked a little less peevish than usual, my aunt would remark afterwards, "I cannot think what has come over Eulalie; I gave her the same as I always give, and she did not look at all pleased."

"I don't think she has very much to complain of, all the same," Françoise would sigh grimly, for she had a tendency to regard as petty cash all that my aunt might give her for herself or her children, and as treasure riotously squandered on an ungrateful wretch the little coins slipped Sunday after Sunday into Eulalie's hand, but so discreetly that Françoise never managed to see them. It was not that she wanted for herself the money my aunt bestowed on Eulalie. She already enjoyed a sufficiency of all that my aunt possessed, in the knowledge that the wealth of the mistress automatically elevates and enhances the maid in the eyes of the world, and that she herself was renowned and glorified throughout Combray, Jouy-le-Vicomte, and other places, on account of my aunt's many farms, her frequent and prolonged visits from the Curé, and the astonishing number of bottles of Vichy water which she consumed. Françoise was avaricious only for my aunt; had she had control over my

aunt's fortune (which would have more than satisfied her
highest ambition) she would have guarded it from the assaults of strangers with a maternal ferocity. She would,
however, have seen no great harm in what my aunt,
whom she knew to be incurably generous, allowed herself
to give away, had she given only to those who were already rich. Perhaps she felt that such persons, not being
actually in need of my aunt's presents, could not be suspected of simulating affection for her on that account.
Besides, presents offered to persons of great wealth and
position, such as Mme Sazerat, M. Swann, M. Legrandin
and Mme Goupil, to persons of the "same rank" as my
aunt, and who would naturally "mix with her," seemed to
Françoise to be included among the ornamental customs
of that strange and brilliant life led by rich people, who
hunt and shoot and give balls and pay each other visits, a
life which she would contemplate with an admiring smile.
But it was by no means the same thing if the beneficiaries
of my aunt's generosity were of the class whom Françoise
would label "folk like me" or "folk no better than me"
and who were those she most despised, unless they called
her "Madame Françoise" and considered themselves her
inferiors. And when she saw that, despite all her warn-
ings, my aunt continued to do exactly as she pleased, and
to fling money away with both hands (or so at least
Françoise believed) on undeserving creatures, she began
to find that the presents she herself received from my
aunt were very small compared to the imaginary riches
squandered upon Eulalie. There was not, in the neighbourhood of Combray, a farm of such prosperity and importance that Françoise doubted Eulalie's ability to buy
it, without thinking twice, out of the capital which her

visits to my aunt "brought in." (It must be said that Eulalie had formed an exactly similar estimate of the vast and secret hoards of Françoise.) Every Sunday, after Eulalie had left, Françoise would utter malevolent prophecies about her. She hated Eulalie, but was at the same time afraid of her, and so felt bound, when she was there, to show her a friendly face. She would make up for it, however, after the other's departure; never, it is true, alluding to her by name, but hinting at her in Sibylline oracles or in maxims of a comprehensive character, like those of Ecclesiastes, so worded that their special application could not escape my aunt. After peering round the edge of the curtain to see whether Eulalie had shut the front-door behind her, "Flatterers know how to make themselves agreeable and to feather their nests, but patience, one fine day the good Lord will be avenged upon them!" she would declaim, with the sidelong, insinuating glance of Joas thinking exclusively of Athalia when he says:

> The prosperity of the wicked
> Drains away like a torrent.

But when the Curé had come as well, and by his interminable visit had drained my aunt's strength, Françoise would follow Eulalie from the room, saying: "Mme Octave, I will leave you to rest; you look really tired out."

And my aunt would answer her not a word, breathing a sigh so faint that it seemed it must prove her last, and lying there with closed eyes, as though already dead. But hardly had Françoise arrived downstairs when four peals of a bell pulled with the utmost violence reverberated through the house, and my aunt, sitting bolt upright

in her bed, would call out: "Has Eulalie gone yet? Would
you believe it; I forgot to ask her whether Mme Goupil
arrived in church before the Elevation. Run after her,
quick!"

But Françoise would return alone, having failed to
overtake Eulalie.

"It is most provoking," my aunt would say, shaking
her head. "The one important thing that I had to ask
her."

In this way life went by for my aunt Léonie, always
the same, in the gentle uniformity of what she called,
with a pretence of deprecation but with a deep tenderness,
her "little jog-trot." Respected by all and sundry, not
merely in her own house, where every one of us, having
learned the futility of recommending a healthier mode of
life, had become gradually resigned to its observance, but
in the village as well, where, three streets away, a trades-
man who had to hammer nails into a packing-case would
send first to Françoise to make sure that my aunt was not
"resting." This "jog-trot" was none the less brutally disturbed on one occasion that year. Like a fruit hidden
among its leaves, which has grown and ripened unobserved and falls of its own accord, there came upon us
one night the kitchen-maid's confinement. Her pains were
unbearable, and, as there was no midwife in Combray,
Françoise had to set off before dawn to fetch one from
Thiberzy. My aunt was unable to rest owing to the cries
of the girl, and as Françoise, though the distance was not
great, was very late in returning, her services were greatly
missed. And so, in the course of the morning, my mother
said to me: "Run upstairs and see if your aunt wants anything."

I went into the first of her two rooms, and through
the open door of the other saw my aunt lying on her side
asleep; I could hear her snoring gently. I was about to slip
away when the noise of my entry must have broken into
her sleep and made it "change gear," as they say of motor-cars, for the music of her snore stopped for a second
and began again on a lower note; then she awoke and half
turned her face, which I could see for the first time; a
kind of horror was imprinted on it; plainly she had just
escaped from some terrifying dream. She could not see me
from the position in which she was lying, and I stood
there not knowing whether I ought to go forward or withdraw; but all at once she seemed to return to a sense of
reality, and to grasp the falsehood of the visions that had
terrified her; a smile of joy, of pious thanksgiving to God
who is pleased to grant that life shall be less cruel than
our dreams, feebly illumined her face, and, with the habit
she had formed of speaking to herself half-aloud when she
thought herself alone, she murmured: "God be praised!
we have nothing to worry us here but the kitchen-maid's
baby. And I've been dreaming that my poor Octave had
come back to life and was trying to make me take a walk
every day!" She stretched out a hand towards her rosary,
which was lying on the small table, but sleep was once
again overcoming her, and did not leave her the strength
to reach it; she fell asleep, her mind at rest, and I crept
out of the room on tiptoe without either her or anyone
else ever knowing what I had seen and heard.

When I say that, apart from such rare happenings as
this confinement, my aunt's daily routine never under-
went any variation, I do not include those which, repeated
at regular intervals and in identical form, did no more

than print a sort of uniform pattern upon the greater uniformity of her life. Thus, for instance, every Saturday, as Françoise had to go in the afternoon to market at Roussainville-le-Pin, the whole household would have to have lunch an hour earlier. And my aunt had so thoroughly acquired the habit of this weekly exception to her general habits, that she clung to it as much as to the rest. She was so well "routined" to it, as Françoise would say, that if, on a Saturday, she had had to wait for her lunch until the regular hour, it would have "upset" her as much as if on an ordinary day she had had to put her lunch forward to its Saturday hour. Incidentally this acceleration of lunch gave Saturday, for all of us, an individual character, kindly and rather attractive. At the moment when ordinarily there is still an hour to be lived through before the meal-time relaxation, we knew that in a few seconds we should see the arrival of premature endives, a gratuitous omelette, an unmerited beefsteak. The recurrence of this asymmetrical Saturday was one of those minor events, intra-mural, localised, almost civic, which, in uneventful lives and stable orders of society, create a kind of national tie and become the favourite theme for conversation, for pleasantries, for anecdotes which can be embroidered as the narrator pleases; it would have provided the ready-made kernel for a legendary cycle, had any of us had an epic turn of mind. Early in the morning, before we were dressed, without rhyme or reason, save for the pleasure of proving the strength of our solidarity, we would call to one another good-humouredly, cordially, patriotically, "Hurry up, there's no time to waste; don't forget it's Saturday!" while my aunt, conferring with Françoise and reflecting that the day would be even longer than usual,

would say, "You might cook them a nice bit of veal, seeing that it's Saturday." If, at half-past ten, someone ab-
sent-mindedly pulled out a watch and said, "I say, an
hour-and-a-half still before lunch," everyone else would
be delighted to be able to retort at once: "Why, what are
you thinking about? Have you forgotten that it's Saturday?" And a quarter of an hour later we would still be
laughing about it and reminding ourselves to go up and
tell aunt Léonie of this absurd mistake, to amuse her.
The very face of the sky appeared to undergo a change.
After lunch the sun, conscious that it was Saturday,
would blaze an hour longer in the zenith, and when
someone, thinking that we were late in starting for our
walk, said, "What, only two o'clock!" on registering the
passage of the twin strokes from the steeple of Saint-
Hilaire (which as a rule met no one at that hour upon the
highways, deserted for the midday meal or for the nap
which follows it, or on the banks of the bright and ever-
flowing stream, which even the angler had abandoned,
and passed unaccompanied across the vacant sky, where
only a few loitering clouds remained to greet them) the
whole family would respond in chorus: "Why, you're for-
getting we had lunch an hour earlier; you know very well
it's Saturday."

The surprise of a "barbarian" (for so we termed everyone who was not acquainted with Saturday's special
customs) who had called at eleven o'clock to speak to my
father and had found us at table, was an event which
caused Françoise as much merriment as anything that had
ever happened in her life. But if she found it amusing
that the nonplussed visitor should not have known beforehand that we had our lunch an hour earlier on Saturdays,

it was still more irresistibly funny that my father himself
(wholeheartedly as she sympathised with the rigid chau-
vinism which prompted him) should never have dreamed
that the barbarian could fail to be aware of the fact, and
so had replied, with no further enlightenment of the
other's surprise at seeing us already in the dining-room:
"After all, it's Saturday!" On reaching this point in the
story, Françoise would pause to wipe the tears of merriment from her eyes, and then, to add to her own enjoyment, would prolong the dialogue, inventing a further
reply for the visitor to whom the word "Saturday" had
conveyed nothing. And so far from our objecting to these
interpolations, we would feel that the story was not yet
long enough, and would rally her with: "Oh, but surely
he said something else. There was more to it than that,
the first time you told it." My great-aunt herself would
lay aside her needlework, and raise her head and look on
at us over her glasses.

The day had yet another characteristic feature,
namely, that during May we used to go out on Saturday
evenings after dinner to the "Month of Mary" devotions.

As we were liable, there, to meet M. Vinteuil, who
held very strict views on "the deplorable slovenliness of
young people, which seems to be encouraged these days,"
my mother would first see that there was nothing out of
order in my appearance, and then we would set out for
the church. It was in the "Month of Mary" that I remember having first fallen in love with hawthorns. Not only
were they in the church, where, holy ground as it was, we
had all of us a right of entry, but arranged upon the altar
itself, inseparable from the mysteries in whose celebration
they participated, thrusting in among the tapers and the

sacred vessels their serried branches, tied to one another horizontally in a stiff, festal scheme of decoration still further embellished by the festoons of leaves, over which were scattered in profusion, as over a bridal train, little clusters of buds of a dazzling whiteness. Though I dared not look at it except through my fingers, I could sense that this formal scheme was composed of living things, and that it was Nature herself who, by trimming the shape of the foliage, and by adding the crowning ornament of those snowy buds, had made the decorations worthy of what was at once a public rejoicing and a solemn mystery. Higher up on the altar, a flower had opened here and there with a careless grace, holding so unconcernedly, like a final, almost vaporous adornment, its bunch of stamens, slender as gossamer and entirely veiling each corolla, that in following, in trying to mimic to myself the action of their efflorescence, I imagined it as a swift and thoughtless movement of the head, with a provocative glance from her contracted pupils, by a young girl in white, insouciant and vivacious.

M. Vinteuil had come in with his daughter and had sat down beside us. He belonged to a good family, and had once been piano-teacher to my grandmother's sisters; so that when, after losing his wife and inheriting some property, he had retired to the neighbourhood of Combray, we used often to invite him to our house. But with his intense prudishness he had given up coming so as not to be obliged to meet Swann, who had made what he called "a most unsuitable marriage, as seems to be the fashion these days." My mother, on hearing that he composed, told him out of the kindness of her heart that, when she came to see him, he must play her something of his own. M. Vinteuil would have liked nothing better, but he carried politeness and consideration for others to such scrupulous lengths, always putting himself in their place, that he was afraid of boring them, or of appearing egotistical, if he carried out or even allowed them to sus-¹ pect what were his own desires. On the day when my parents had gone to pay him a visit, I had accompanied them, but they had allowed me to remain outside, and as M. Vinteuil's house, Montjouvain, stood at the foot of a bushy hillock where I went to hide, I had found myself on a level with his drawing-room, upstairs, and only a few feet away from its window. When the servant came in to tell him that my parents had arrived, I had seen M. Vinteuil hurriedly place a sheet of music in a promi-nent position on the piano. But as soon as they entered the room he had snatched it away and put it in a corner. He was afraid, no doubt, of letting them suppose that he was glad to see them only because it gave him a chance of playing them some of his compositions. And every time that my mother, in the course of her visit, had returned to the subject he had hurriedly protested: "I can't think who put that on the piano; it's not the proper place for it at all," and had turned the conversation aside to other top-ics, precisely because they were of less interest to himself.

His one and only passion was for his daughter, and she, with her somewhat boyish appearance, looked so ro-bust that it was hard to restrain a smile when one saw the precautions her father used to take for her health, with spare shawls always in readiness to wrap round her shoul-ders. My grandmother had drawn our attention to the gentle, delicate, almost timid expression which might of-ten be caught flitting across the freckled face of this oth-

erwise stolid child. Whenever she spoke, she heard her
own words with the ears of those to whom she had addressed them, and became alarmed at the possibility of a
misunderstanding, and one would see in clear outline, as
though in a transparency, beneath the mannish face of the
"good sort" that she was, the finer features of a tearful
girl.

When, before turning to leave the church, I genu-
flected before the altar, I was suddenly aware of a bitter-
sweet scent of almonds emanating from the hawthorn-
blossom, and I then noticed on the flowers themselves
little patches of a creamier colour, beneath which I imagined that this scent must lie concealed, as the taste of an
almond cake lay beneath the burned parts, or that of Mlle
Vinteuil's cheeks beneath their freckles. Despite the motionless silence of the hawthorns, this intermittent odour
came to me like the murmuring of an intense organic life
with which the whole altar was quivering like a hedgerow
explored by living antennae, of which I was reminded by
seeing some stamens, almost red in colour, which seemed
to have kept the springtime virulence, the irritant power
of stinging insects now transmuted into flowers.

On leaving the church we would stay chatting for a
moment with M. Vinteuil in front of the porch. Boys
would be chasing one another in the Square, and he
would intervene, taking the side of the little ones and lec-
turing the big. If his daughter said in her gruff voice how
glad she had been to see us, immediately it would seem as
though a more sensitive sister within her had blushed at
this thoughtless, schoolboyish utterance which might have
made us think that she was angling for an invitation to
the house. Her father would then arrange a cloak over her

shoulders, they would clamber into a little dog-cart which she herself drove, and home they would both go to Montjouvain. As for ourselves, the next day being Sunday, with no need to be up and stirring before high mass, if it was a moonlight night and warm, my father, in his thirst for glory, instead of taking us home at once would lead us on a long walk round by the Calvary, which my mother's utter incapacity for taking her bearings, or even for knowing which road she might be on, made her regard as a triumph of his strategic genius. Sometimes we would go as far as the viaduct, whose long stone strides began at the railway station and to me typified all the wretchedness of exile beyond the last outposts of civilisation, because every year, as we came down from Paris, we were warned to take special care when we got to Combray not to miss the station, to be ready before the train stopped, since it would start again in two minutes and proceed across the viaduct out of the lands of Christendom, of which Combray, to me, represented the furthest limit. We would return by the Boulevard de la Gare, which contained the most attractive villas in the town. In each of their gardens the moonlight, copying the art of Hubert Robert, scattered its broken staircases of white marble, its fountains, its iron gates temptingly ajar. Its beams had swept away the telegraph office. All that was left of it was a column, half shattered but preserving the beauty of a ruin which endures for all time. I would by now be dragging my weary limbs and ready to drop with sleep; the balmy scent of the lime-trees seemed a reward that could be won only at the price of great fatigue and was not worth the effort. From gates far apart the watchdogs, awakened by our steps in the silence, would set up an antiphonal barking such as I still hear at times of an evening, and among which the Boulevard de la Gare (when the public gardens of Combray were constructed on its site) must have taken refuge, for wherever I may be, as soon as they begin their alternate challenge and response, I can see it again with its lime-trees, and its pavement glistening beneath the moon.

Suddenly my father would bring us to a standstill and ask my mother—"Where are we?" Exhausted by the walk but still proud of her husband, she would lovingly confess that she had not the least idea. He would shrug his shoulders and laugh. And then, as though he had produced it with his latchkey from his waistcoat pocket, he would point out to us, where it stood before our eyes, the back-gate of our own garden, which had come, hand-in-hand with the familiar corner of the Rue du Saint-Esprit, to greet us at the end of our wanderings over paths unknown. My mother would murmur admiringly "You really are wonderful!" And from that instant I did not have to take another step; the ground moved forward under my feet in that garden where for so long my actions had ceased to require any control, or even attention, from my will. Habit had come to take me in her arms and carry me all the way up to my bed like a little child.

Although Saturday, by beginning an hour earlier and by depriving her of the services of Françoise, passed more slowly than other days for my aunt, yet the moment it was past and a new week begun, she would look forward with impatience to its return, as something that embodied all the novelty and distraction which her frail and disordered body was still able to endure. This was not to say, however, that she did not long, at times, for some greater

change, that she did not experience some of those exceptional moments when one thirsts for something other than
what is, and when those who, through lack of energy or
imagination, are unable to generate any motive power in
themselves, cry out, as the clock strikes or the postman
knocks, for something new, even if it is worse, some emotion, some sorrow; when the heartstrings, which contentment has silenced, like a harp laid by, yearn to be
plucked and sounded again by some hand, however
rough, even if it should break them; when the will, which
has with such difficulty won the right to indulge without
let or hindrance in its own desires and woes, would gladly
fling the reins into the hands of imperious circumstance,
however cruel. Of course, since my aunt's strength, which
was completely drained by the slightest exertion, returned
but drop by drop into the depths of her repose, the reservoir was very slow in filling, and months would go by before she reached that slight overflow which other people
siphon off into activity of various kinds and which she
was incapable of knowing or deciding how to use. And I
have no doubt that then—just as a desire to have her
potatoes served with béchamel sauce for a change would
be formed, ultimately, from the pleasure she found in the
daily reappearance of those mashed potatoes of which she
never "tired"—she would extract from the accumulation
of those monotonous days which she treasured so much a
keen expectation of some domestic cataclysm, momentary
in its duration but violent enough to compel her to put
into effect, once for all, one of those changes which she
knew would be beneficial to her health but to which she
could never make up her mind without some such stimulus. She was genuinely fond of us; she would have en-

joyed the long luxury of weeping for our untimely decease; coming at a moment when she felt well and was
not in a perspiration, the news that the house was being
destroyed by a fire in which all the rest of us had already
perished and which soon would leave not a single stone
standing upon another, but from which she herself would
still have plenty of time to escape without undue haste,
provided that she rose at once from her bed, must often
have haunted her dreams, as a prospect which combined
with the two minor advantages of letting her taste the full
savour of her affection for us in long years of mourning,
and of causing universal stupefaction in the village when
she should sally forth to conduct our obsequies, crushed
but courageous, moribund but erect, the paramount and
priceless boon of forcing her at the right moment, with no
time to be lost, no room for weakening hesitations, to go
off and spend the summer at her charming farm of
Mirougrain, where there was a waterfall. Inasmuch as no
such event had ever occurred, though she must often have
pondered its eventuality as she lay alone absorbed in her
interminable games of patience (and though it would have
plunged her in despair from the first moment of its realisation, from the first of those little unforeseen contingencies, the first word of calamitous news, whose accents can
never afterwards be expunged from the memory, everything that bears upon it the imprint of actual, physical
death, so terribly different from the logical abstraction of
its possibility) she would fall back from time to time, to
add an interest to her life, upon imaginary calamities
which she would follow up with passion. She would beguile herself with a sudden pretence that Françoise had
been robbing her, that she had set a trap to make certain,

and had caught her betrayer red-handed; and being in the habit, when she made up a game of cards by herself, of playing her own and her adversary's hands at once, she would first stammer out Françoise's awkward excuses, and then reply to them with such a fiery indignation that any of us who happened to intrude upon her at one of these moments would find her bathed in perspiration, her eyes blazing, her false hair askew and exposing the baldness of her brows. Françoise must often, from the next room, have heard these mordant sarcasms levelled at herself, the mere framing of which in words would not have relieved my aunt's feelings sufficiently, had they been allowed to remain in a purely immaterial form, without the degree of substance and reality which she added to them by muttering them half-aloud. Sometimes, however, even these counterpane dramas would not satisfy my aunt; she must see her work staged. And so, on a Sunday, with all the doors mysteriously closed, she would confide to Eulalie her doubts of Françoise's integrity and her determination to be rid of her, and another time she would confide to Françoise her suspicions of the disloyalty of Eulalie, to whom the front-door would very soon be closed for good. A few days later she would be sick of her latest confidante and once more "as thick as thieves" with the traitor, but before the next performance, the two would yet again have changed roles. But the suspicions which Eulalie might occasionally arouse in her were no more than a flash in the pan that soon subsided for lack of fuel, since Eulalie was not living with her in the house. It was a very different matter in the case of Françoise, of whose presence under the same roof as herself my aunt was perpetually conscious, though for fear of catching

cold were she to leave her bed, she would never dare go
down to the kitchen to establish whether there were any
grounds for her suspicions. Gradually her mind came to
be exclusively occupied with trying to guess what
Françoise might at any given moment be doing behind
her back. She would detect a furtive look on Françoise's
face, something contradictory in what she said, some desire which she appeared to be concealing. And she would
show her that she was unmasked, with a single word,
which made Françoise turn pale and which my aunt
seemed to find a cruel satisfaction in driving deep into her
unhappy servant's heart. And the very next Sunday a dis-
closure by Eulalie—like one of those discoveries that suddenly open up an unsuspected field of exploration for
some new science that has got into something of a rut—
proved to my aunt that her own worst suspicions fell a
long way short of the appalling truth. "But Françoise
ought to know that," said Eulalie, "now that you've given
her a carriage."

"Now that I've given her a carriage!" gasped my
aunt.

"Oh, I know nothing about it, I just thought, well, I
saw her go by yesterday in a barouche, as proud as Lu-
cifer, on her way to Roussainville market. I supposed that
it must be Mme Octave who had given it to her."

And so by degrees Françoise and my aunt, the quarry
and the hunter, had reached the point of constantly trying
to forestall each other's ruses. My mother was afraid lest
Françoise should develop a genuine hatred of my aunt,
who did everything in her power to hurt her. However
that might be, Françoise had come, more and more, to
pay an infinitely scrupulous attention to my aunt's least

word and gesture. When she had to ask her anything she would hesitate for a long time over how best to go about it. And when she had uttered her request, she would watch my aunt covertly, trying to guess from the expression on her face what she thought of it and how she would reply. And so it was that—whereas an artist who, reading the memoirs of the seventeenth century, and, wishing to bring himself nearer to the great Louis, considers that he is making progress in that direction by constructing a pedigree that traces his own descent from some historic family, or by engaging in correspondence with one of the reigning sovereigns of Europe, is actually turning his back on what he mistakenly seeks under identical and therefore moribund forms—an elderly provincial lady, by doing no more than yield wholeheartedly to her own irresistible eccentricities and a cruelty born of idleness, could see, without ever having given a thought to Louis XIV, the most trivial occupations of her daily life, her morning toilet, her lunch, her afternoon nap, assume, by virtue of their despotic singularity, something of the interest that was to be found in what Saint-Simon called the "mechanics" of life at Versailles; and was able, too, to persuade herself that her silences, a suggestion of good humour or of haughtiness on her features, would provide Françoise with matter for a mental commentary as tense with passion and terror as did the silence, the good humour or the haughtiness of the King when a courtier, or even his greatest nobles, had presented a petition to him in an avenue at Versailles.

One Sunday, when my aunt had received simultaneous visits from the Curé and from Eulalie, and had been left alone, afterwards, to rest, the whole family went

upstairs to bid her good evening, and Mamma ventured
to condole with her on the unlucky coincidence that always brought both visitors to her door at the same time.

"I hear that things worked out badly again today,
Léonie," she said kindly, "you had all your friends here at
once."

And my great-aunt interrupted with: "The more the
merrier," for, since her daughter's illness, she felt herself
in duty bound to cheer her up by always drawing her attention to the brighter side of things. But my father had
begun to speak.

"I should like to take advantage," he said, "of the
whole family's being here together to tell you a story, so
as not to have to begin all over again to each of you sepa-
rately. I'm afraid we are in M. Legrandin's bad books: he
would hardly say 'How d'ye do' to me this morning."

I did not wait to hear the end of my father's story,
for I had been with him myself after mass when we had
met M. Legrandin; instead, I went downstairs to the
kitchen to ask about the menu for our dinner, which was
of fresh interest to me daily, like the news in a paper, and
excited me as might the programme of a coming festivity.

As M. Legrandin had passed close by us on our way
from church, walking by the side of a lady, the owner of
a country house in the neighbourhood, whom we knew
only by sight, my father had saluted him in a manner at
once friendly and reserved, without stopping in his walk;
M. Legrandin had barely acknowledged the courtesy, and
then with an air of surprise, as though he had not recognised us, and with that distant look characteristic of people who do not wish to be agreeable and who, from the
suddenly receding depths of their eyes, seem to have

caught sight of you at the far end of an interminably straight road and at so great a distance that they content themselves with directing towards you an almost imperceptible movement of the head, commensurate with your doll-like dimensions.

Now, the lady who was walking with Legrandin was a virtuous and highly respected person; there could be no question of his being out for amorous adventure and embarrassed at being detected, and my father wondered how he could possibly have displeased our friend.

"I should be all the more sorry to feel that he was vexed with us," he said, "because among all those people in their Sunday best there is something about him, with his little cutaway coat and his soft neckties, so little 'dressed-up,' so genuinely simple; an air of innocence, almost, which is really attractive."

But the vote of the family council was unanimous, that my father had imagined the whole thing, or that Legrandin, at the moment in question, had been preoccupied in thinking about something else. In any case my father's fears were dispelled no later than the following evening. Returning from a long walk, we saw Legrandin near the Pont-Vieux (he was spending a few days more in Combray because of the holidays). He came up to us with outstretched hand: "Do you know, master booklover," he asked me, "this line of Paul Desjardins?

Now are the woods all black, but still the sky is blue.

Isn't that a fine rendering of a moment like this? Perhaps you have never read Paul Desjardins. Read him, my boy, read him; in these days he is converted, they tell me, into a preaching friar, but he used to have the most charming water-colour touch—

Now are the woods all black, but still the sky is blue.

May you always see a blue sky overhead, my young friend; and then, even when the time comes, as it has come for me now, when the woods are all black, when night is fast falling, you will be able to console yourself, as I do, by looking up at the sky." He took a cigarette from his pocket and stood for a long time with his eyes fixed on the horizon. "Good-bye, friends!" he suddenly exclaimed, and left us.

At the hour when I usually went downstairs to find out what there was for dinner, its preparation would already have begun, and Françoise, a commanding officer with all the forces of nature for her subalterns, as in the fairy-tales where giants hire themselves out as scullions, would be stirring the coals, putting the potatoes to steam, and, at the right moment, finishing over the fire those culinary masterpieces which had been first got ready in some of the great array of vessels, triumphs of the potter's craft, which ranged from tubs and boilers and cauldrons and fish kettles down to jars for game, moulds for pastry, and tiny pannikins for cream, through an entire collection of pots and pans of every shape and size. I would stop by the table, where the kitchen-maid had shelled them, to inspect the platoons of peas, drawn up in ranks and numbered, like little green marbles, ready for a game; but what most enraptured me were the asparagus, tinged with ultramarine and pink which shaded off from their heads, finely stippled in mauve and azure, through a series of imperceptible gradations to their white feet—still stained a little by the soil of their garden-bed—with an iridescence that was not of this world. I felt that these celestial hues indicated the presence of exquisite creatures who had been pleased to assume vegetable form and who, through the disguise of their firm, comestible flesh, allowed me to discern in this radiance of earliest dawn, these hinted rainbows, these blue evening shades, that precious quality which I should recognise again when, all night long after a dinner at which I had partaken of them, they played (lyrical and coarse in their jesting like one of Shakespeare's fairies) at transforming my chamber pot into a vase of aromatic perfume.

Poor Giotto's Charity, as Swann had named her, charged by Françoise with the task of preparing them for the table, would have them lying beside her in a basket, while she sat there with a mournful air as though all the sorrows of the world were heaped upon her; and the light crowns of azure which capped the asparagus shoots above their pink jackets were delicately outlined, star by star, as, in Giotto's fresco, are the flowers encircling the brow or patterning the basket of his Virtue at Padua. And meanwhile Françoise would be turning on the spit one of those chickens such as she alone knew how to roast, chickens which had wafted far abroad from Combray the savour of her merits, and which, while she was serving them to us at table, would make the quality of sweetness predominate for the moment in my private conception of her character, the aroma of that cooked flesh which she knew how to make so unctuous and so tender seeming to me no more than the proper perfume of one of her many virtues.

But the day on which I went down to the kitchen while my father consulted the family council about our strange meeting with Legrandin was one of those days when Giotto's Charity, still very weak and ill after her recent confinement, had been unable to rise from her bed; Françoise, being without assistance, had fallen behind. When I went in, I saw her in the scullery which opened on to the back yard, in the process of killing a chicken which, by its desperate and quite natural resistance, accompanied by Françoise, beside herself with rage as she attempted to slit its throat beneath the ear, with shrill cries of "Filthy creature! Filthy creature!," made the saintly meekness and unction of our servant rather less prominent than it would do, next day at dinner, when it made its appearance in a skin gold-embroidered like a chasuble, and its precious juice was poured out drop by drop as from a pyx. When it was dead, Françoise collected its streaming blood, which did not, however, drown her rancour, for she gave vent to another burst of rage, and gazing down at the carcass of her enemy, uttered a final "Filthy creature!"

I crept out of the kitchen and upstairs, trembling all over; I could have prayed, then, for the instant dismissal of Françoise. But who would have baked me such hot rolls, made me such fragrant coffee, and even . . . roasted me such chickens? And, as it happened, everyone else had already had to make the same cowardly reckoning. For my aunt Léonie knew (though I was still in ignorance of this) that Françoise, who, for her own daughter or for her nephews, would have given her life without a murmur, showed a singular implacability in her dealings with the rest of the world. In spite of which my aunt had kept her,

for, while conscious of her cruelty, she appreciated her
services. I began gradually to realise that Françoise's
kindness, her compunction, her numerous virtues, concealed many of these kitchen tragedies, just as history reveals to us that the reigns of the kings and queens who
are portrayed as kneeling with their hands joined in
prayer in the windows of churches were stained by op-
pression and bloodshed. I came to recognise that, apart
from her own kinsfolk, the sufferings of humanity inspired in her a pity which increased in direct ratio to the
distance separating the sufferers from herself. The tears
that flowed from her in torrents when she read in a newspaper of the misfortunes of persons unknown to her were
quickly stemmed once she had been able to form a more
precise mental picture of the victims. One night, shortly
after her confinement, the kitchen-maid was seized with
the most appalling pains; Mamma heard her groans, and
rose and awakened Françoise, who, quite unmoved, declared that all the outcry was mere malingering, that the
girl wanted to "play the mistress." The doctor, who had
been afraid of some such attack, had left a marker in a
medical dictionary which we had, at the page on which
the symptoms were described, and had told us to turn up
this passage to discover the first aid to be adopted. My
mother sent Françoise to fetch the book, warning her not
to let the marker drop out. An hour elapsed, and
Françoise had not returned; my mother, supposing that
she had gone back to bed, grew vexed, and told me to go
myself to the library and fetch the volume. I did so, and
there found Françoise who, in her curiosity to know what
the marker indicated, had begun to read the clinical account of these after-pains, and was violently sobbing, now

that it was a question of a prototype patient with whom she was unacquainted. At each painful symptom mentioned by the writer she would exclaim: "Oh, oh, Holy Virgin, is it possible that God wishes a wretched human creature to suffer so? Oh, the poor girl!"

But when I had called her, and she had returned to the bedside of Giotto's Charity, her tears at once ceased to flow; she could find no stimulus for that pleasant sensation of tenderness and pity with which she was familiar, having been moved to it often enough by the perusal of newspapers, nor any other pleasure of the same kind, in her boredom and irritation at being dragged out of bed in the middle of the night for the kitchen-maid; so that at the sight of those very sufferings the printed account of which had moved her to tears, she relapsed into ill-tempered mutterings, mingled with bitter sarcasm, saying, when she thought that we were out of earshot: "Well, she should have been careful not to do what got her into this! She enjoyed it well enough, I dare say, so she'd better not put on any airs now! All the same, he must have been a godforsaken young fellow to go with the likes of *her*. Dear, dear, it's just as they used to say in my poor mother's day:

> Frogs and snails and puppy-dogs' tails,
>   And dirty sluts in plenty,
> Smell sweeter than roses in young men's noses
>   When the heart is one-and-twenty."

Although, when her grandson had a slight cold in his head, she would set off at night, even if she were unwell, instead of going to bed, to see whether he had everything he needed, covering ten miles on foot before daybreak so as to be back in time for work, this same love for her own people, and her desire to establish the future greatness of her house on a solid foundation, found expression, in her policy with regard to the other servants, in one unvarying maxim, which was never to let any of them set foot in my aunt's room; indeed she showed a sort of pride in not allowing anyone else to come near my aunt, preferring, when she herself was ill, to get out of bed and to administer the Vichy water in person, rather than to concede to the kitchen-maid the right of entry into her mistress's presence. There is a species of hymenoptera observed by Fabre, the burrowing wasp, which in order to provide a supply of fresh meat for her offspring after her own decease, calls in the science of anatomy to amplify the resources of her instinctive cruelty, and, having made a collection of weevils and spiders, proceeds with marvellous knowledge and skill to pierce the nerve-centre on which their power of locomotion (but none of their other vital functions) depends, so that the paralysed insect, beside which she lays her eggs, will furnish the larvae, when hatched, with a docile, inoffensive quarry, incapable either of flight or of resistance, but perfectly fresh for the larder: in the same way Françoise had adopted, to minister to her unfaltering resolution to render the house uninhabitable to any other servant, a series of stratagems so cunning and so pitiless that, many years later, we discovered that if we had been fed on asparagus day after day throughout that summer, it was because their smell gave the poor kitchen-maid who had to prepare them such violent attacks of asthma that she was finally obliged to leave my aunt's service.

.   .   .

Alas! we had definitely to alter our opinion of
M. Legrandin. On one of the Sundays following our
meeting with him on the Pont-Vieux, after which my father had been forced to confess himself mistaken, as mass
drew to an end and, with the sunshine and the noise of
the outer world, something else invaded the church, an
atmosphere so far from sacred that Mme Goupil, Mme
Percepied (everyone, in fact, who not so long before,
when I arrived a little late, had been sitting motionless,
engrossed in their prayers, and who I might even have
thought oblivious of my entry had not their feet moved
slightly to push away the little kneeling-bench which was
preventing me from getting to my chair) had begun to
discuss with us out loud all manner of utterly mundane
topics as though we were already outside in the Square,
we saw Legrandin on the sunbaked threshold of the porch
dominating the many-coloured tumult of the market, being introduced by the husband of the lady we had seen
him with on the previous occasion to the wife of another
large landed proprietor of the district. Legrandin's face
wore an expression of extraordinary zeal and animation;
he made a deep bow, with a subsidiary backward movement which brought his shoulders sharply up into a position behind their starting-point, a gesture in which he
must have been trained by the husband of his sister,
Mme de Cambremer. This rapid straightening-up caused
a sort of tense muscular wave to ripple over Legrandin's
rump, which I had not supposed to be so fleshy; I cannot
say why, but this undulation of pure matter, this wholly
carnal fluency devoid of spiritual significance, this wave
lashed into a tempest by an obsequious alacrity of the
basest sort, awoke my mind suddenly to the possibility of

a Legrandin altogether different from the one we knew.
The lady gave him some message for her coachman, and
as he walked over to her carriage the impression of shy
and respectful happiness which the introduction had
stamped upon his face still lingered there. Rapt in a sort
of dream, he smiled, then began to hurry back towards
the lady; as he was walking faster than usual, his shoulders swayed backwards and forwards, right and left, in
the most absurd fashion; and altogether he looked, so utterly had he abandoned himself to it, to the exclusion of
all other considerations, as though he were the passive,
wire-pulled puppet of his own happiness. Meanwhile we
were coming out through the porch and were about to
pass close beside him; he was too well bred to turn his
head away, but he fixed his eyes, which had suddenly
changed to those of a seer lost in the profundity of his vision, on so distant a point of the horizon that he could
not see us and so had no need to acknowledge our presence. His face was as artless as ever above his plain, sin-
gle-breasted jacket, which looked as though conscious of
having been led astray and plunged willy-nilly into surroundings of detested splendour. And a spotted bow-tie,
stirred by the breezes of the Square, continued to float in
front of Legrandin like the standard of his proud isolation
and his noble independence. When we reached the house
my mother discovered that the baker had forgotten to deliver the cream tart and asked my father to go back with
me and tell them to send it up at once. Near the church
we met Legrandin coming towards us with the same lady,
whom he was escorting to her carriage. He brushed past
us, and did not interrupt what he was saying to her, but
gave us, out of the corner of his blue eye, a little sign

which began and ended, so to speak, inside his eyelids
and which, as it did not involve the least movement of his
facial muscles, managed to pass quite unperceived by the
lady; but, striving to compensate by the intensity of his
feelings for the somewhat restricted field in which they
had to find expression, he made that blue chink which
was set apart for us sparkle with all the zest of an affability that went far beyond mere playfulness, almost touched
the border-line of roguery; he subtilised the refinements
of good-fellowship into a wink of connivance, a hint, a
hidden meaning, a secret understanding, all the mysteries
of complicity, and finally elevated his assurances of
friendship to the level of protestations of affection, even
of a declaration of love, lighting up for us alone, with a
secret and languid flame invisible to the chatelaine, an enamoured pupil in a countenance of ice.

Only the day before he had asked my parents to send
me to dine with him on this same Sunday evening.
"Come, and bear your aged friend company," he had said
to me. "Like the nosegay which a traveller sends us from
some land to which we shall never return, come and let
me breathe from the far country of your adolescence the
scent of those spring flowers among which I also used to
wander many years ago. Come with the primrose, the
love-vine, the buttercup; come with the stone-crop,
whereof are posies made, pledges of love, in the Balzacian
flora, come with that flower of the Resurrection morning,
the Easter daisy, come with the snowballs of the guelder-
rose, which begin to perfume the alleys of your great-
aunt's garden ere the last snows of Lent are melted from
its soil. Come with the glorious silken raiment of the lily,
apparel fit for Solomon, and with the polychrome hues of

the pansies, but come, above all, with the spring breeze, still cooled by the last frosts of winter, wafting apart, for the two butterflies that have waited outside all morning, the closed portals of the first Jerusalem rose."

The question was raised at home whether, all things considered, I ought still to be sent to dine with M. Legrandin. But my grandmother refused to believe that he could have been impolite.

"You admit yourself that he appears there at church quite simply dressed and all that; he hardly looks like a man of fashion." She added that in any event, even if, assuming the worst, he had been intentionally rude, it was far better for us to pretend that we had noticed nothing. And indeed my father himself, though more annoyed than any of us by the attitude which Legrandin had adopted, may still have held in reserve a final uncertainty as to its true meaning. It was like every attitude or action which reveals a man's underlying character; they bear no relation to what he has previously said, and we cannot confirm our suspicions by the culprit's own testimony, for he will admit nothing; we are reduced to the evidence of our own senses, and we ask ourselves, in the face of this detached and incoherent fragment of recollection, whether indeed our senses have not been the victims of a hallucination; with the result that such attitudes, which are alone of importance in indicating character, are the most apt to leave us in perplexity.

I dined with Legrandin on the terrace of his house, by moonlight. "There is a charming quality, is there not," he said to me, "in this silence; for hearts that are wounded, as mine is, a novelist whom you will read in time to come asserts that there is no remedy but silence

and shadow. And see you this, my boy, there comes in all
our lives a time, towards which you still have far to go,
when the weary eyes can endure but one kind of light, the
light which a fine evening like this prepares for us in the
stillroom of darkness, when the ears can listen to no music save what the moonlight breathes through the flute of
silence."

I listened to M. Legrandin's words which always
seemed to me so pleasing; but I was preoccupied by the
memory of a lady whom I had seen recently for the first
time and thinking, now that I knew that Legrandin was
on friendly terms with several of the local aristocracy, that
perhaps she also was among his acquaintance, I summoned up all my courage and said to him: "Tell me, sir,
do you by any chance know the lady . . . the ladies of
Guermantes?"—glad, too, in pronouncing this name, to
secure a sort of power over it, by the mere act of drawing
it up out of my day-dreams and giving it an objective existence in the world of spoken things.

But, at the sound of the name Guermantes, I saw in
the middle of each of our friend's blue eyes a little brown
nick appear, as though they had been stabbed by some
invisible pin-point, while the rest of the pupil reacted by
secreting the azure overflow. His fringed eyelids darkened
and drooped. His mouth, set in a bitter grimace, was the
first to recover, and smiled, while his eyes remained full
of pain, like the eyes of a handsome martyr whose body
bristles with arrows.

"No, I don't know them," he said, but instead of
vouchsafing so simple a piece of information, so very un-
remarkable a reply, in the natural conversational tone
which would have been appropriate to it, he enunciated it

with special emphasis on each word, leaning forward, nodding his head, with at once the vehemence which a man imparts, in order to be believed, to a highly improbable statement (as though the fact that he did not know the Guermantes could be due only to some strange accident of fortune) and the grandiloquence of a man who, finding himself unable to keep silence about what is to him a painful situation, chooses to proclaim it openly in order to convince his hearers that the confession he is making is one that causes him no embarrassment, is in fact easy, agreeable, spontaneous, that the situation itself—in this case the absence of relations with the Guermantes family—might very well have been not forced upon, but actually willed by him, might arise from some family tradition, some moral principle or mystical vow which expressly forbade his seeking their society.

"No," he went on, explaining by his words the tone in which they were uttered, "no, I don't know them, I've never wanted to; I've always made a point of preserving complete independence; at heart, you know, I'm a bit of a Jacobin. People are always coming to me about it, telling me I'm mistaken in not going to Guermantes, that I make myself seem ill-bred, uncivilised, an old bear. But that's not the sort of reputation that can frighten me; it's too true! In my heart of hearts I care for nothing in the world now but a few churches, two or three books and pictures, and the light of the moon when the fresh breeze of your youth wafts to my nostrils the scent of gardens whose flowers my old eyes can no longer distinguish."

I did not understand very clearly why, in order to refrain from going to the houses of people whom one did not know, it should be necessary to cling to one's inde-

pendence, or how this could give one the appearance of a
savage or a bear. But what I did understand was that
Legrandin was not altogether truthful when he said that
he cared only for churches, moonlight, and youth; he
cared also, he cared a very great deal, for people who
lived in country houses, and in their presence was so
overcome by fear of incurring their displeasure that he
dared not let them see that he numbered among his
friends middle-class people, the sons of solicitors and
stockbrokers, preferring, if the truth must come to light,
that it should do so in his absence, a long way away, and
"by default." In a word, he was a snob. No doubt he
would never have said any of this in the poetical language
which my family and I so much enjoyed. And if I asked
him, "Do you know the Guermantes family?" Legrandin
the talker would reply, "No, I've never wished to know
them." But unfortunately the talker was now subordinated to another Legrandin, whom he kept carefully hidden in his breast, whom he would never consciously ex-
hibit, because this other could tell compromising stories
about our own Legrandin and his snobbishness; and this
other Legrandin had replied to me already in that
wounded look, that twisted smile, the undue gravity of
the tone of his reply, in the thousand arrows by which
our own Legrandin had instantaneously been stabbed and
prostrated like a St Sebastian of snobbery: "Oh, how you
hurt me! No, I don't know the Guermantes family. Do
not remind me of the great sorrow of my life." And since
this other, irrepressible, blackmailing Legrandin, if he
lacked our Legrandin's charming vocabulary, showed an
infinitely greater promptness in expressing himself, by
means of what are called "reflexes," when Legrandin the

talker attempted to silence him, he had already spoken, and however much our friend deplored the bad impression which the revelations of his *alter ego* must have caused, he could do no more than endeavour to mitigate them.

This is not to say that M. Legrandin was anything but sincere when he inveighed against snobs. He could not (from his own knowledge, at least) be aware that he himself was one, since it is only with the passions of others that we are ever really familiar, and what we come to discover about our own can only be learned from them. Upon ourselves they react only indirectly, through our imagination, which substitutes for our primary motives other, auxiliary motives, less stark and therefore more seemly. Never had Legrandin's snobbishness prompted him to make a habit of visiting a duchess as such. Instead, it would encourage his imagination to make that duchess appear, in his eyes, endowed with all the graces. He would gain acquaintance with the duchess, assuring himself that he was yielding to the attractions of mind and heart which the vile race of snobs could never understand. Only his fellow-snobs knew that he was of their number, for, owing to their inability to appreciate the intervening efforts of his imagination, they saw in close juxtaposition the social activity of Legrandin and its primary cause.

At home, meanwhile, we no longer had any illusions about M. Legrandin, and our relations with him had become much more distant. Mamma was greatly delighted whenever she caught him red-handed in the sin which he never admitted to, which he continued to call the unpardonable sin, snobbery. As for my father, he found it difficult to take Legrandin's airs in so light-hearted and detached a spirit; and when there was talk, one year, of sending me to spend the summer holidays at Balbec with my grandmother, he said: "I simply must tell Legrandin that you're going to Balbec, to see whether he'll offer to introduce you to his sister. He probably doesn't remember telling us that she lived within a mile of the place."

My grandmother, who held that when one went to the seaside one ought to be on the beach from morning to night sniffing the salt breezes, and that one should not know anyone there because visits and excursions are so much time filched from the sea air, begged him on no account to speak to Legrandin of our plans; for already, in her mind's eye, she could see his sister, Mme de Cambremer, alighting from her carriage at the door of our hotel just as we were on the point of going out fishing, and obliging us to remain indoors to entertain her. But Mamma laughed at her fears, thinking to herself that the danger was not so threatening, and that Legrandin would show no undue anxiety to put us in touch with his sister. As it happened, there was no need for any of us to introduce the subject of Balbec, for it was Legrandin himself who, without the least suspicion that we had ever had any intention of visiting those parts, walked into the trap uninvited one evening when we met him strolling on the banks of the Vivonne.

"There are tints in the clouds this evening, violets and blues, which are very beautiful, are they not, my friend?" he said to my father, "a blue, especially, more floral than aerial, a cineraria blue, which it is surprising to see in the sky. And that little pink cloud there, has it not also the tint of some flower, a carnation or hydrangea?

Nowhere, perhaps, except on the shores of the Channel, where Normandy merges into Brittany, have I observed such copious examples of that sort of vegetable kingdom of the atmosphere. Down there, in that unspoiled country near Balbec, there is a charmingly quiet little bay where the sunsets of the Auge Valley, those red-and-gold sunsets (which, by the by, I am very far from despising) seem commonplace and insignificant; but in that moist and gentle atmosphere these celestial bouquets, pink and blue, will blossom all at once of an evening, incomparably lovely, and often lasting for hours before they fade. Others shed their flowers at once, and then it is lovelier still to see the sky strewn with their innumerable petals, sulphur or rose-pink. In that bay, which they call the Bay of Opal, the golden sands appear more charming still from being fastened, like fair Andromeda, to those terrible rocks of the surrounding coast, to that funereal shore, famed for the number of its wrecks, where every winter many a brave vessel falls victim to the perils of the sea. Balbec! the most ancient bone in the geological skeleton that underlies our soil, the true Ar-mor, the sea, the land's end, the accursed region which Anatole France— an enchanter whose works our young friend ought to read—has so well depicted, beneath its eternal fogs, as though it were indeed the land of the Cimmerians in the *Odyssey*. Balbec; yes, they are building hotels there now, superimposing them upon its ancient and charming soil which they are powerless to alter; how delightful it is to be able to make excursions into such primitive and beautiful regions only a step or two away!"

"Indeed! And do you know anyone at Balbec?" inquired my father. "As it happens, this young man is

going to spend a couple of months there with his grandmother, and my wife too, perhaps."

Legrandin, taken unawares by the question at a moment when he was looking directly at my father, was unable to avert his eyes, and so fastened them with steadily
increasing intensity—smiling mournfully the while—
upon the eyes of his questioner, with an air of friendliness and frankness and of not being afraid to look him in
the face, until he seemed to have penetrated my father's
skull as if it had become transparent, and to be seeing at
that moment, far beyond and behind it, a brightly
coloured cloud which provided him with a mental alibi
and would enable him to establish that at the moment
when he was asked whether he knew anyone at Balbec, he
had been thinking of something else and so had not heard
the question. As a rule such tactics make the questioner
proceed to ask, "Why, what are you thinking about?" But
my father, inquisitive, irritated and cruel, repeated: "Have
you friends, then, in the neighbourhood, since you know
Balbec so well?"

In a final and desperate effort, Legrandin's smiling
gaze struggled to the extreme limits of tenderness, vague-
ness, candour and abstraction; but, feeling no doubt that
there was nothing left for it now but to answer, he said to
us: "I have friends wherever there are clusters of trees,
stricken but not defeated, which have come together with
touching perseverance to offer a common supplication to
an inclement sky which has no mercy upon them."

"That is not quite what I meant," interrupted my father, as obstinate as the trees and as merciless as the sky.
"I asked you, in case anything should happen to my
mother-in-law and she wanted to feel that she was not all

alone there in an out-of-the-way place, whether you knew anyone in the neighbourhood."

"There as elsewhere, I know everyone and I know no one," replied Legrandin, who did not give in so easily. "The places I know well, the people very slightly. But the places themselves seem like people, rare and wonderful people, of a delicate quality easily disillusioned by life. Perhaps it is a castle which you encounter upon the cliff's edge standing there by the path where it has halted to contemplate its sorrows beneath an evening sky, still roseate, in which the golden moon is climbing while the homeward-bound fishing-boats, cleaving the dappled waters, hoist its pennant at their mastheads and carry its colours. Or perhaps it is a simple dwelling-house that stands alone, plain and shy-looking but full of romance, hiding from every eye some imperishable secret of happiness and disenchantment. That land which knows not truth," he continued with Machiavellian subtlety, "that land of pure fiction makes bad reading for any boy, and is certainly not what I should choose or recommend for my young friend here, who is already so much inclined to melancholy—for a heart already predisposed to receive its impressions. Climates that breathe amorous secrets and futile regrets may suit a disillusioned old man like myself, but they must always prove fatal to a temperament that is still unformed. Believe me," he went on with emphasis, "the waters of that bay—more Breton than Norman—may exert a sedative influence, though even that is of questionable value, upon a heart which, like mine, is no longer intact, a heart for whose wounds there is no longer anything to compensate. But at your age, my boy, those waters are contra-indicated . . . Good night to you, neighbours," he added, moving away from us with that evasive abruptness to which we were accustomed; and then, turning towards us with a physicianly finger raised in warning, he resumed the consultation: "No Balbec before fifty!" he called out to us, "and even then it must depend on the state of the heart."

My father raised the subject again at our subsequent meetings, torturing him with questions, but it was labour in vain: like that scholarly swindler who devoted to the fabrication of forged palimpsests a wealth of skill and knowledge and industry the hundredth part of which would have sufficed to establish him in a more lucrative but honourable occupation, M. Legrandin, had we insisted further, would in the end have constructed a whole system of landscape ethics and a celestial geography of Lower Normandy sooner than admit to us that his own sister was living within a mile or two of Balbec, sooner than find himself obliged to offer us a letter of introduction, the prospect of which would never have inspired him with such terror had he been absolutely certain—as from his knowledge of my grandmother's character, he really ought to have been—that we would never have dreamed of making use of it.

We used always to return from our walks in good time to pay aunt Léonie a visit before dinner. At the beginning of the season, when the days ended early, we would still be able to see, as we turned into the Rue du Saint-Esprit, a reflection of the setting sun in the windows of the house and a band of crimson beyond the timbers of the Calvary, which was mirrored further on in the pond; a fiery glow that, accompanied often by a sharp tang in the air, would associate itself in my mind with the glow of the fire over which, at that very moment, was roasting the chicken that was to furnish me, in place of the poetic pleasure of the walk, with the sensual pleasures of good feeding, warmth and rest. But in summer, when we came back to the house, the sun would not have set; and while we were upstairs paying our visit to aunt Léonie its rays, sinking until they lay along her window-sill, would be caught and held by the large inner curtains and the loops which tied them back to the wall, and then, split and ramified and filtered, encrusting with tiny flakes of gold the citron-wood of the chest of drawers, would illuminate the room with a delicate, slanting, woodland glow. But on some days, though very rarely, the chest of drawers would long since have shed its momentary incrustations, there would no longer, as we turned into the Rue du Saint-Esprit, be any reflection from the western sky lighting up the window-panes, and the pond beneath the Calvary would have lost its fiery glow, sometimes indeed had changed already to an opalescent pallor, while a long ribbon of moonlight, gradually broadening and splintered by every ripple upon the water's surface, would stretch across it from end to end. Then, as we drew near the house, we would see a figure standing upon the doorstep, and Mamma would say to me: "Good heavens! There's Françoise looking out for us; your aunt must be anxious; that means we're late."

And without wasting time by stopping to take off our things we would dash upstairs to my aunt Léonie's room to reassure her, to prove to her by our bodily presence that all her gloomy imaginings were false, that nothing had happened to us, but that we had gone the

"Guermantes way," and when one took that walk, why, my aunt knew well enough that one could never be sure what time one would be home.

"There, Françoise," my aunt would say, "didn't I tell you that they must have gone the Guermantes way? Good gracious, they must be hungry! And your nice leg of mutton will be quite dried up now after all the hours it's been waiting. What a time to come in! Well, and so you went the Guermantes way?"

"But, Léonie, I supposed you knew," Mamma would answer. "I thought Françoise had seen us go out by the little gate through the kitchen-garden."

For there were, in the environs of Combray, two "ways" which we used to take for our walks, and they were so diametrically opposed that we would actually leave the house by a different door according to the way we had chosen: the way towards Méséglise-la-Vineuse, which we called also "Swann's way" because to get there one had to pass along the boundary of M. Swann's estate, and the "Guermantes way." Of Méséglise-la-Vineuse, to tell the truth, I never knew anything more than the "way," and some strangers who used to come over on Sundays to take the air in Combray, people whom, this time, neither my aunt herself nor any of us "knew from Adam," and whom we therefore assumed to be "people who must have come over from Méséglise." As for Guermantes, I was to know it well enough one day, but that day had still to come; and, during the whole of my boyhood, if Méséglise was to me something as inaccessible as the horizon, which remained hidden from sight, however far one went, by the folds of a landscape which no longer bore the least resemblance to the country round Combray,

Guermantes, on the other hand, meant no more than the
ultimate goal, ideal rather than real, of the "Guermantes
way," a sort of abstract geographical term like the North
Pole or the Equator or the Orient. And so to "take the
Guermantes way" in order to get to Méséglise, or vice
versa, would have seemed to me as nonsensical a proceeding as to turn to the east in order to reach the west. Since
my father used always to speak of the "Méséglise way" as
comprising the finest view of a plain that he knew anywhere, and of the "Guermantes way" as typical of river
scenery, I had invested each of them, by conceiving them
in this way as two distinct entities, with that cohesion,
that unity which belong only to the figments of the mind;
the smallest detail of either of them seemed to me a precious thing exemplifying the special excellence of the
whole, while beside them, before one had reached the sacred soil of one or the other, the purely material paths
amid which they were set down as the ideal view over a
plain and the ideal river landscape, were no more worth
the trouble of looking at than, to a keen playgoer and
lover of dramatic art, are the little streets that run past
the walls of a theatre. But above all I set between them,
far more than the mere distance in miles that separated
one from the other, the distance that there was between
the two parts of my brain in which I used to think of
them, one of those distances of the mind which not only
keep things apart, but cut them off from one another and
put them on different planes. And this distinction was
rendered still more absolute because the habit we had of
never going both ways on the same day, or in the course
of the same walk, but the "Méséglise way" one time and
the "Guermantes way" another, shut them off, so to

speak, far apart from one another and unaware of each other's existence, in the airtight compartments of separate afternoons.

When we had decided to go the Méséglise way we would start (without undue haste, and even if the sky were clouded over, since the walk was not very long and did not take us too far from home), as though we were not going anywhere in particular, from the front-door of my aunt's house, which opened on to the Rue du Saint-Esprit. We would be greeted by the gunsmith, we would drop our letters into the box, we would tell Théodore, from Françoise, as we passed that she had run out of oil or coffee, and we would leave the town by the road which ran along the white fence of M. Swann's park. Before reaching it we would be met on our way by the scent of his lilac-trees, come out to welcome strangers. From amid the fresh little green hearts of their foliage they raised inquisitively over the fence of the park their plumes of white or mauve blossom, which glowed, even in the shade, with the sunlight in which they had bathed. Some of them, half-concealed by the little tiled house known as the Archers' Lodge in which Swann's keeper lived, overtopped its Gothic gable with their pink minaret. The nymphs of spring would have seemed coarse and vulgar in comparison with these young houris, who retained in this French garden the pure and vivid colouring of a Persian miniature. Despite my desire to throw my arms about their pliant forms and to draw down towards me the starry locks that crowned their fragrant heads, we would pass them by without stopping, for my parents had ceased to visit Tansonville since Swann's marriage, and, so as not to appear to be looking into his park, instead of taking the path which skirted his property and then climbed straight up to the open fields, we took another path which led in the same direction, but circuitously, and brought us out beyond it.

One day my grandfather said to my father: "Don't you remember Swann's telling us yesterday that his wife and daughter had gone off to Rheims[6] and that he was taking the opportunity of spending a day or two in Paris? We might go along by the park, since the ladies are not at home; that will make it a little shorter."

We stopped for a moment by the fence. Lilac-time was nearly over; some of the trees still thrust aloft, in tall mauve chandeliers, their delicate sprays of blossom, but in many parts of the foliage which only a week before had been drenched in their fragrant foam, there remained only a dry, hollow, scentless froth, shrivelled and discoloured. My grandfather pointed out to my father in what respects the appearance of the place was still the same, and how far it had altered since the walk that he had taken with old M. Swann on the day of his wife's death; and he seized the opportunity to tell us once again the story of that walk.

In front of us a path bordered with nasturtiums ascended in the full glare of the sun towards the house. But to our right the park stretched across level ground. Overshadowed by the tall trees which stood close around it, an ornamental pond had been dug by Swann's parents; but, even in his most artificial creations, nature is the material upon which man has to work; certain places persist in remaining surrounded by the vassals of their own especial sovereignty, and will flaunt their immemorial insignia in the middle of a park, just as they would have done far from any human interference, in a solitude which must everywhere return to engulf them, springing up out of the necessities of their exposed position and superimposed on the work of man's hands. And so it was that, at the foot of the path which led down to the artificial lake, there might be seen, in its two tiers woven of forget-me-nots and periwinkle flowers, a natural, delicate, blue garland encircling the water's luminous and shadowy brow, while the iris, flourishing its sword-blades in regal profusion, stretched out over agrimony and water-growing crowfoot the tattered fleurs-de-lis, violet and yellow, of its lacustrine sceptre.

The absence of Mlle Swann, which—since it preserved me from the terrible risk of seeing her appear on one of the paths, and of being identified and scorned by this privileged little girl who had Bergotte for a friend and used to go with him to visit cathedrals—made the exploration of Tansonville, now for the first time permissible, a matter of indifference to myself, seemed on the contrary to invest the property, in my grandfather's and my father's eyes, with an added attraction, a transient charm, and (like an entirely cloudless sky when one is going mountaineering) to make the day exceptionally propitious for a walk round it; I should have liked to see their reckoning proved false, to see, by a miracle, Mlle Swann appear with her father, so close to us that we should not have time to avoid her, and should therefore be obliged to make her acquaintance. And so, when I suddenly noticed a straw basket lying forgotten on the grass by the side of a fishing line whose float was bobbing in the water, I made every effort to keep my father and grandfather looking in another direction, away from this sign that she might, after all, be in residence. However, as Swann had told us that it was bad of him to go away just then as he had some people staying in the house, the line might equally belong to one of these guests. Not a footstep was to be heard on any of the paths. Quartering the topmost branches of one of the tall trees, an invisible bird was striving to make the day seem shorter, exploring with a long-drawn note the solitude that pressed it on every side, but it received at once so unanimous an answer, so powerful a repercussion of silence and of immobility, that one felt it had arrested for all eternity the moment which it had been trying to make pass more quickly. The sunlight fell so implacably from a motionless sky that one longed to escape its attentions, and even the slumbering water, whose repose was perpetually disturbed by the insects that swarmed above its surface, dreaming no doubt of some imaginary maelstrom, intensified the uneasiness which the sight of that floating cork had wrought in me by appearing to draw it at full speed across the silent reaches of the reflected sky; now almost vertical, it seemed on the point of plunging down out of sight, and I had begun to wonder whether, setting aside the longing and the terror that I had of making her acquaintance, it was not actually my duty to warn Mlle Swann that the fish was biting—when I was obliged to run after my father and grandfather who were calling me, surprised that I had not followed them along the little path leading up to the open fields into which they had already turned. I found the whole path throbbing with the fragrance of hawthorn-blossom. The hedge resembled a series of chapels, whose walls were no longer visible under the mountains of flowers that were heaped upon their altars;

while beneath them the sun cast a chequered light upon
the ground, as though it had just passed through a
stained-glass window; and their scent swept over me, as
unctuous, as circumscribed in its range, as though I had
been standing before the Lady-altar, and the flowers,
themselves adorned also, held out each its little bunch of
glittering stamens with an absent-minded air, delicate radiating veins in the flamboyant style like those which, in
the church, framed the stairway to the rood-loft or the
mullions of the windows and blossomed out into the
fleshy whiteness of strawberry-flowers. How simple and
rustic by comparison would seem the dog-roses which in
a few weeks' time would be climbing the same path in the
heat of the sun, dressed in the smooth silk of their blushing pink bodices that dissolve in the first breath of wind.

But it was in vain that I lingered beside the
hawthorns—breathing in their invisible and unchanging
odour, trying to fix it in my mind (which did not know
what to do with it), losing it, recapturing it, absorbing
myself in the rhythm which disposed the flowers here and
there with a youthful light-heartedness and at intervals as
unexpected as certain intervals in music—they went on
offering me the same charm in inexhaustible profusion,
but without letting me delve any more deeply, like those
melodies which one can play a hundred times in succession without coming any nearer to their secret. I turned
away from them for a moment so as to be able to return
to them afresh. My eyes travelled up the bank which rose
steeply to the fields beyond the hedge, alighting on a
stray poppy or a few laggard cornflowers which decorated
the slope here and there like the border of a tapestry
whereon may be glimpsed sporadically the rustic theme

which will emerge triumphant in the panel itself; infrequent still, spaced out like the scattered houses which herald the approach of a village, they betokened to me the vast expanse of waving corn beneath the fleecy clouds, and the sight of a single poppy hoisting upon its slender rigging and holding against the breeze its scarlet ensign, over the buoy of rich black earth from which it sprang, made my heart beat like that of a traveller who glimpses on some low-lying ground a stranded boat which is being caulked and made sea-worthy, and cries out, although he has not yet caught sight of it, "The Sea!"

And then I returned to the hawthorns, and stood before them as one stands before those masterpieces which, one imagines, one will be better able to "take in" when one has looked away for a moment at something else; but in vain did I make a screen with my hands, the better to concentrate upon the flowers, the feeling they aroused in me remained obscure and vague, struggling and failing to free itself, to float across and become one with them. They themselves offered me no enlightenment, and I could not call upon any other flowers to satisfy this mysterious longing. And then, inspiring me with that rapture which we feel on seeing a work by our favourite painter quite different from those we already know, or, better still, when we are shown a painting of which we have hitherto seen no more than a pencilled sketch, or when a piece of music which we have heard only on the piano appears to us later clothed in all the colours of the orchestra, my grandfather called me to him, and, pointing to the Tansonville hedge, said to me: "You're fond of hawthorns; just look at this pink one—isn't it lovely?"

And it was indeed a hawthorn, but one whose

blossom was pink, and lovelier even than the white. It, too, was in holiday attire—for one of those days which are the only true holidays, the holy days of religion, because they are not assigned by some arbitrary caprice, as secular holidays are, to days which are not specially ordained for them, which have nothing about them that is essentially festal—but it was attired even more richly than the rest, for the flowers which clung to its branches, one above another, so thickly as to leave no part of the tree undecorated, like the tassels wreathed about the crook of a rococo shepherdess, were every one of them "in colour," and consequently of a superior quality, by the aesthetic standards of Combray, if one was to judge by the scale of prices at the "stores" in the Square, or at Camus's, where the most expensive biscuits were those whose sugar was pink. For my own part, I set a higher value on cream cheese when it was pink, when I had been allowed to tinge it with crushed strawberries. And these flowers had chosen precisely one of those colours of some edible and delicious thing, or of some fond embellishment of a costume for a major feast, which, inasmuch as they make plain the reason for their superiority, are those whose beauty is most evident to the eyes of children, and for that reason must always seem more vivid and more natural than any other tints, even after the child's mind has realised that they offer no gratification to the appetite and have not been selected by the dressmaker. And indeed I had felt at once, as I had felt with the white blossom, but with even greater wonderment, that it was in no artificial manner, by no device of human fabrication, that the festal intention of these flowers was revealed, but that it was Nature herself who had spontaneously expressed it, with

the simplicity of a woman from a village shop labouring
at the decoration of a street altar for some procession, by
overloading the bush with these little rosettes, almost too
ravishing in colour, this rustic pompadour. High up on
the branches, like so many of those tiny rose-trees, their
pots concealed in jackets of paper lace, whose slender
shafts rose in a forest from the altar on major feast-days,
a thousand buds were swelling and opening, paler in
colour, but each disclosing as it burst, as at the bottom of
a bowl of pink marble, its blood-red stain, and suggesting
even more strongly than the full-blown flowers the special, irresistible quality of the thorn-bush which, wherever
it budded, wherever it was about to blossom, could do so
in pink alone. Embedded in the hedge, but as different
from it as a young girl in festal attire among a crowd of
dowdy women in everyday clothes who are staying at
home, all ready for the "Month of Mary" of which it
seemed already to form a part, it glowed there, smiling in
its fresh pink garments, deliciously demure and Catholic.

The hedge afforded a glimpse, inside the park, of an
alley bordered with jasmine, pansies, and verbenas,
among which the stocks held open their fresh plump
purses, of a pink as fragrant and as faded as old Spanish
leather, while a long green hose, coiling across the gravel,
sent up from its sprinkler a vertical and prismatic fan of
multicoloured droplets. Suddenly I stood still, unable to
move, as happens when we are faced with a vision that
appeals not to our eyes only but requires a deeper kind of
perception and takes possession of the whole of our being.
A little girl with fair, reddish hair, who appeared to be returning from a walk, and held a spade in her hand, was
looking at us, raising towards us a face powdered with

pinkish freckles. Her black eyes gleamed, and since I did
not at that time know, and indeed have never since
learned, how to reduce a strong impression to its objective
elements, since I had not, as they say, enough "power of
observation" to isolate the notion of their colour, for a
long time afterwards, whenever I thought of her, the
memory of those bright eyes would at once present itself
to me as a vivid azure, since her complexion was fair; so
much so that, perhaps if her eyes had not been quite so
black—which was what struck one most forcibly on first
seeing her—I should not have been, as I was, so especially enamoured of their imagined blue.

I gazed at her, at first with that gaze which is not
merely the messenger of the eyes, but at whose window
all the senses assemble and lean out, petrified and anxious, a gaze eager to reach, touch, capture, bear off in triumph the body at which it is aimed, and the soul with
the body; then (so frightened was I lest at any moment
my grandfather and my father, catching sight of the girl,
might tear me away from her by telling me to run on in
front of them) with another, an unconsciously imploring
look, whose object was to force her to pay attention to
me, to see, to know me. She cast a glance forwards and
sideways, so as to take stock of my grandfather and my
father, and doubtless the impression she formed was that
we were all ridiculous people, for she turned away with an
indifferent and disdainful air, and stood sideways so as to
spare her face the indignity of remaining within their field
of vision; and while they, continuing to walk on without
noticing her, overtook and passed me, she went on staring
out of the corner of her eye in my direction, without any
particular expression, without appearing to see me, but

with a fixity and a half-hidden smile which I could only interpret, from the notions I had been vouchsafed of good breeding, as a mark of infinite contempt; and her hand, at the same time, sketched in the air an indelicate gesture, for which, when it was addressed in public to a person whom one did not know, the little dictionary of manners which I carried in my mind supplied only one meaning, namely, a deliberate insult.

"Gilberte, come along; what are you doing?" called out in a piercing tone of authority a lady in white whom I had not seen until that moment, while, a little way beyond her, a gentleman in a suit of linen "ducks," whom I did not know either, stared at me with eyes which seemed to be starting from his head. The little girl's smile abruptly faded, and, seizing her spade, she made off without turning to look again in my direction, with an air of docility, inscrutable and sly.

Thus was wafted to my ears the name of Gilberte, bestowed on me like a talisman which might, perhaps, enable me some day to rediscover the girl that its syllables had just endowed with an identity, whereas the moment before she had been merely an uncertain image. So it came to me, uttered across the heads of the stocks and jasmines, pungent and cool as the drops which fell from the green watering-pipe; impregnating and irradiating the zone of pure air through which it had passed—and which it set apart and isolated—with the mystery of the life of her whom its syllables designated to the happy beings who lived and walked and travelled in her company; unfolding beneath the arch of the pink hawthorn, at the height of my shoulder, the quintessence of their familiarity—so exquisitely painful to myself—with her and with the unknown world of her existence into which I should never penetrate.

For a moment (as we moved away and my grandfather murmured: "Poor Swann, what a life they are leading him—sending him away so that she can be alone with her Charlus—for it was he, I recognised him at once! And the child, too; at her age, to be mixed up in all that!") the impression left on me by the despotic tone in which Gilberte's mother had spoken to her without her answering back, by exhibiting her to me as being obliged to obey someone else, as not being superior to the whole world, calmed my anguish somewhat, revived some hope in me, and cooled the ardour of my love. But very soon that love surged up again in me like a reaction by which my humiliated heart sought to rise to Gilberte's level or to bring her down to its own. I loved her; I was sorry not to have had the time and the inspiration to insult her, to hurt her, to force her to keep some memory of me. I thought her so beautiful that I should have liked to be able to retrace my steps so as to shake my fist at her and shout, "I think you're hideous, grotesque; how I loathe you!" But I walked away, carrying with me, then and for ever afterwards, as the first illustration of a type of happiness rendered inaccessible to a little boy of my kind by certain laws of nature which it was impossible to transgress, the picture of a little girl with reddish hair and a freckled skin, who held a spade in her hand and smiled as she directed towards me a long, sly, expressionless stare. And already the charm with which her name, like a whiff of incense, had imbued that archway in the pink hawthorn through which she and I had together heard its sound, was beginning to impregnate, to overlay, to perfume everything with which it had any association: her grandparents, whom my own had had the unutterable good fortune to know, the sublime profession of stockbroker, the melancholy neighbourhood of the Champs-Elysées, where she lived in Paris.

"Léonie," said my grandfather on our return, "I wish we had had you with us this afternoon. You would never have known Tansonville. If I had dared, I would have cut you a branch of that pink hawthorn you used to like so much." And so my grandfather told my aunt about our walk, either to divert her, or because he had not yet given up hope of persuading her to rise from her bed and to go out of doors. For in earlier days she had been very fond of Tansonville, and moreover Swann's visits had been the last that she had continued to receive, at a time when she had already closed her doors to all the world. And just as, when he now called to inquire after her (she was the only person in our household whom he still asked to see), she would send down to say that she was tired at the moment and resting, but that she would be happy to see him another time, so, this evening, she said to my grandfather, "Yes, some day when the weather is fine I shall go for a drive as far as the gate of the park." And in saying this she was quite sincere. She would have liked to see Swann and Tansonville again; but the mere wish to do so sufficed for all that remained of her strength, which its fulfilment would have more than exhausted. Sometimes a spell of fine weather made her a little more energetic, and she would get up and dress; but before she had reached the outer room she would be tired again, and would insist on returning to her bed. The process which had begun in her—and in her a little earlier only than it must come to

all of us — was the great renunciation of old age as it prepared for death, wraps itself up in its chrysalis, which
may be observed at the end of lives that are at all prolonged, even in old lovers who have lived for one another,
in old friends bound by the closest ties of mutual sympathy, who, after a certain year, cease to make the necessary
journey or even to cross the street to see one another,
cease to correspond, and know that they will communicate no more in this world. My aunt must have been perfectly well aware that she would never see Swann again,
that she would never leave the house again, but this ultimate reclusion seemed to be made bearable to her by the
very factor which, to our minds, ought to have made it
more painful; namely, that this reclusion was forced upon
her by the gradual diminution in her strength which she
was able to measure daily and which, by making every
action, every movement exhausting if not actually painful,
gave to inaction, isolation and silence the blessed and
restoring charm of repose.

My aunt did not go to see the pink hawthorn in the
hedge, but at all hours of the day I would ask the rest of
my family whether she was not going to do so, whether
she used not, at one time, to go often to Tansonville, trying to make them speak of Mlle Swann's parents and
grandparents, who appeared to me to be as great and glorious as gods. The name Swann had for me become almost mythological, and when I talked with my family I
would grow sick with longing to hear them utter it; I
dared not pronounce it myself, but I would draw them
into the discussion of matters which led naturally to
Gilberte and her family, in which she was involved, in
speaking of which I would feel myself not too remotely

exiled from her; and I would suddenly force my father (by pretending, for instance, to believe that my grandfather's appointment had been in our family before his day, or that the hedge with the pink hawthorn which my aunt Léonie wished to visit was on common land) to correct my assertions, to say, as though in opposition to me and of his own accord: "No, no, that appointment belonged to *Swann's* father, that hedge is part of *Swann's* park." And then I would be obliged to catch my breath, so suffocating was the pressure, upon that part of me where it was for ever inscribed, of that name which, at the moment when I heard it, seemed to me fuller, more portentous than any other, because it was heavy with the weight of all the occasions on which I had secretly uttered it in my mind. It caused me a pleasure which I was ashamed to have dared to demand from my parents, for so great was this pleasure that to have procured it for me must have caused them a good deal of effort, and with no recompense, since it was no pleasure for them. And so I would turn the conversation, out of tact, and out of scruple too. All the singular seductions with which I had invested the name Swann came back to me as soon as they uttered it. And then it seemed to me suddenly that my parents could not fail to experience the same emotions, that they must find themselves sharing my point of view, that they perceived in their turn, that they condoned, that they even embraced my visionary longings, and I was as wretched as though I had ravished and corrupted the innocence of their hearts.

That year my family fixed the day of our return to Paris rather earlier than usual. On the morning of our departure I had had my hair curled, to be ready to face the

photographer, had had a new hat carefully set upon my
head, and had been buttoned into a velvet jacket; a little
later my mother, after searching everywhere for me,
found me standing in tears on the steep little path near
Tansonville, bidding farewell to my hawthorns, clasping
their sharp branches in my arms and, like a princess in a
tragedy oppressed by the weight of these vain ornaments,
with no gratitude towards the importunate hand which, in
curling all those ringlets, had been at pains to arrange my
hair upon my forehead,[7] trampling underfoot the curl-pa-
pers which I had torn from my head, and my new hat
with them. My mother was not at all moved by my tears,
but she could not suppress a cry at the sight of my bat-
tered headgear and my ruined jacket. I did not, however,
hear her. "Oh, my poor little hawthorns," I was assuring
them through my sobs, "it isn't you who want to make
me unhappy, to force me to leave you. You, you've never
done me any harm. So I shall always love you." And,
drying my eyes, I promised them that, when I grew up, I
would never copy the foolish example of other men, but
that even in Paris, on fine spring days, instead of paying
calls and listening to silly talk, I would set off for the
country to see the first hawthorn-trees in bloom.

Once in the fields, we never left them again during
the rest of our Méséglise walk. They were perpetually traversed, as though by an invisible wanderer, by the wind
which was to me the tutelary genius of Combray. Every
year, on the day of our arrival, in order to feel that I really was at Combray, I would climb the hill to greet it as
it swept through the furrows and swept me along in its
wake. One always had the wind for companion when one
went the Méséglise way, on that gently undulating plain

where for mile after mile it met no rising ground. I knew that Mlle Swann used often to go and spend a few days at Laon; for all that it was many miles away, the distance was counterbalanced by the absence of any intervening obstacle, and when, on hot afternoons, I saw a breath of wind emerge from the furthest horizon, bowing the heads of the corn in distant fields, pouring like a flood over all that vast expanse, and finally come to rest, warm and rustling, among the clover and sainfoin at my feet, that plain which was common to us both seemed then to draw us together, to unite us; I would imagine that the same breath of wind had passed close to her, that it was some message from her that it was whispering to me, without my being able to understand it, and I would kiss it as it passed. On my left was a village called Champieu (*Campus Pagani*, according to the Curé). On my right I could see across the cornfields the two chiselled rustic spires of Saint-André-des-Champs, themselves as tapering, scaly, chequered, honeycombed, yellowing and friable as two ears of wheat.

At regular intervals, amid the inimitable ornamentation of their leaves, which can be mistaken for those of no other fruit-tree, the apple-trees opened their broad petals of white satin, or dangled the shy bunches of their blushing buds. It was on the Méséglise way that I first noticed the circular shadow which apple-trees cast upon the sunlit ground, and also those impalpable threads of golden silk which the setting sun weaves slantingly downwards from beneath their leaves, and which I used to see my father slash through with his stick without ever making them deviate.

Sometimes in the afternoon sky the moon would

creep up, white as a cloud, furtive, lustreless, suggesting an actress who does not have to come on for a while, and watches the rest of the company for a moment from the auditorium in her ordinary clothes, keeping in the background, not wishing to attract attention to herself. I enjoyed finding its image reproduced in books and paintings, though these works of art were very different—at least in my earlier years, before Bloch had attuned my eyes and mind to more subtle harmonies—from those in which the moon would seem fair to me today, but in which I should not have recognised it then. It might, for instance, be some novel by Saintine, some landscape by Gleyre, in which it is silhouetted against the sky in the form of a silver sickle, one of those works as naïvely unformed as were my own impressions, and which it enraged my grandmother's sisters to see me admire. They held that one ought to set before children, and that children showed their own innate good taste in admiring, only such books and pictures as they would continue to admire when their minds were developed and mature. No doubt they regarded aesthetic merits as material objects which an unclouded vision could not fail to discern, without one's needing to nurture equivalents of them and let them slowly ripen in one's own heart.

It was along the Méséglise way, at Montjouvain, a house built on the edge of a large pond against the side of a steep, bushy hill, that M. Vinteuil lived. And so we used often to meet his daughter driving her dogcart at full speed along the road. After a certain year we never saw her alone, but always accompanied by a friend, a girl older than herself with a bad reputation in the neighbourhood, who one day installed herself permanently at Mont-

jouvain. People said: "That poor M. Vinteuil must be
blinded by fatherly love not to see what everyone is talking about—a man who is shocked by the slightest loose
word letting his daughter bring a woman like that to live
under his roof! He says that she is a most superior
woman, with a heart of gold, and that she would have
shown extraordinary musical talent if she had only been
trained. He may be sure it isn't music that she's teaching
his daughter." But M. Vinteuil assured them that it was,
and indeed it is remarkable how people never fail to
arouse admiration for their moral qualities in the relatives
of those with whom they are having carnal relations.
Physical passion, so unjustly decried, compels its victims
to display every vestige that is in them of kindness and
self-abnegation, to such an extent that they shine resplendent in the eyes of their immediate entourage. Dr Percepied, whose hearty voice and bushy eyebrows enabled
him to play to his heart's content the role of mischief-
maker which his looks belied, without in the least degree
compromising his unassailable and quite unmerited reputation of being a kind-hearted old curmudgeon, could
make the Curé and everyone else laugh until they cried
by saying in a gruff voice: "What d'ye say to this, now?
It seems that she plays music with her friend, Mlle Vinteuil. That surprises you, does it? I'm not so sure. It was
Papa Vinteuil who told me all about it yesterday. After
all, she has every right to be fond of music, that girl. I'm
not one to thwart the artistic vocation of a child; nor Vinteuil either, it seems. And then he plays music too, with
his daughter's friend. Why, good lord, it must be a regular musical box, that house! What are you laughing at?
They play too much music, those people, in my opinion.

I met Papa Vinteuil the other day, by the cemetery. It was all he could do to keep on his feet."

Anyone who, like ourselves, had seen M. Vinteuil at that time, avoiding people whom he knew, turning away as soon as he caught sight of them, growing old within a few months, brooding over his sorrows, becoming incapable of any effort not directly aimed at promoting his daughter's happiness, spending whole days beside his wife's grave, could hardly have failed to realise that he was dying of a broken heart, could hardly have supposed that he was unaware of the rumours which were going about. He knew, perhaps he even believed, what his neighbours were saying. There is probably no one, however rigid his virtue, who is not liable to find himself, by the complexity of circumstances, living at close quarters with the very vice which he himself has been most outspoken in condemning—without altogether recognising it beneath the disguise of ambiguous behaviour which it assumes in his presence: the strange remarks, the unaccountable attitude, one evening, of a person whom he has a thousand reasons for loving. But for a man of M. Vinteuil's sensibility it must have been far more painful than for a hardened man of the world to have to resign himself to one of those situations which are wrongly supposed to be the monopoly of Bohemian circles; for they occur whenever a vice which Nature herself has planted in the soul of a child—perhaps by no more than blending the virtues of its father and mother, as she might blend the colour of its eyes—needs to ensure for itself the room and the security necessary for its development. And yet however much M. Vinteuil may have known of his daughter's conduct it did not follow that his adoration of her grew any less. The facts of life do not penetrate to the sphere in which our beliefs are cherished; they did not engender those beliefs, and they are powerless to destroy them; they can inflict on them continual blows of contradiction and disproof without weakening them; and an avalanche of miseries and maladies succeeding one another without interruption in the bosom of a family will not make it lose faith in either the clemency of its God or the capacity of its physician. But when M. Vinteuil thought of his daughter and himself from the point of view of society, from the point of view of their reputation, when he attempted to place himself by her side in the rank which they occupied in the general estimation of their neighbours, then he was bound to give judgment, to utter his own and her social condemnation in precisely the same terms as the most hostile inhabitant of Combray; he saw himself and his daughter in the lowest depths, and his manners had of late been tinged with that humility, that respect for persons who ranked above him and to whom he now looked up (however far beneath him they might hitherto have been), that tendency to search for some means of rising again to their level, which is an almost mechanical result of any human downfall.

One day, when we were walking with Swann in one of the streets of Combray, M. Vinteuil, turning out of another street, found himself so suddenly face to face with us all that he had no time to escape; and Swann, with that condescending charity of a man of the world who, amid the dissolution of all his own moral prejudices, finds in another's shame merely a reason for treating him with a benevolence the expression of which serves to gratify all the more the self-esteem of the bestower because he feels

that it is all the more precious to the recipient, conversed
at great length with M. Vinteuil, with whom for a long
time he had been barely on speaking terms, and invited
him, before leaving us, to send his daughter over one day
to play at Tansonville. It was an invitation which, two
years earlier, would have incensed M. Vinteuil, but which
now filled him with so much gratitude that he felt obliged
to refrain from the indiscretion of accepting. Swann's
friendly regard for his daughter seemed to him to be in itself so honourable, so precious a support that he felt it
would perhaps be advisable not to make use of it, so as to
have the wholly Platonic satisfaction of preserving it.

"What a charming man!" he said to us, after Swann
had gone, with the same enthusiasm and veneration which
make clever and pretty women of the middle classes fall
victims to the charms of a duchess, however ugly and
stupid. "What a charming man! What a pity that he
should have made such a deplorable marriage!"

And then, so strong an element of hypocrisy is there
in even the most sincere people, who lay aside the opinion
they actually hold of a person while they are talking to
him and express it as soon as he is no longer there, my
family joined with M. Vinteuil in deploring Swann's marriage, invoking principles and conventions which (for the
very reason that they were invoking them in common
with him, as though they were all decent people of the
same sort) they appeared to suggest were in no way in-
fringed at Montjouvain. M. Vinteuil did not send his
daughter to visit Swann, an omission which Swann was
the first to regret. For whenever he met M. Vinteuil, he
would remember afterwards that he had been meaning for
a long time to ask him about someone of the same name,

a relation of his, Swann supposed. And on this occasion he had made up his mind not to forget what he had to say to him when M. Vinteuil should appear with his daughter at Tansonville.

Since the Méséglise way was the shorter of the two that we used to take on our walks round Combray, and for that reason was reserved for days of uncertain weather, it followed that the climate of Méséglise was somewhat wet, and we would never lose sight of the fringe of Roussainville wood beneath whose dense thatch of leaves we could take shelter.

Often the sun would disappear behind a cloud, which impinged on its roundness and whose edge it gilded in return. The brightness though not the luminosity would be expunged from a landscape in which all life appeared to be suspended, while the little village of Roussainville carved its white gables in relief upon the sky with an overpowering precision and finish. A gust of wind put up a solitary crow, which flapped away and settled in the distance, while against a greying sky the woods on the horizon assumed a deeper tone of blue, as though painted in one of those monochromes that still decorate the overmantels of old houses.

But on other days the rain with which the barometer in the optician's window had threatened us would begin to fall. Its drops, like migrating birds which fly off in a body at a given moment, would come down out of the sky in serried ranks—never drifting apart, never wandering off on their own during their rapid course, but each one keeping its place and drawing its successor in its wake, so that the sky was more darkened than during the swallows' exodus. We would take refuge among the trees.

And when it seemed that their flight was accomplished, a few last drops, feebler and slower than the rest, would still come down. But we would emerge from our shelter, for raindrops revel amidst foliage, and even when it was almost dry again underfoot, many a stray drop, lingering in the hollow of a leaf, would run down and hang glistening from the point of it until suddenly they splashed on to our upturned faces from the top of the branch.

Often, too, we would hurry to take shelter, huddled together cheek by jowl with its stony saints and patriarchs, under the porch of Saint-André-des-Champs. How French that church was! Over its door the saints, the chevalier kings with lilies in their hands, the wedding scenes and funerals were carved as they might have been in the mind of Françoise. The sculptor had also recorded certain anecdotes of Aristotle and Virgil, precisely as Françoise in her kitchen was wont to hold forth about St Louis as though she herself had known him, generally in order to depreciate, by contrast with him, my grandparents whom she considered less "righteous." One could see that the notions which the mediaeval artist and the mediaeval peasant (who had survived to cook for us in the nineteenth century) had of classical and of early Christian history, notions whose inaccuracy was atoned for by their honest simplicity, were derived not from books, but from a tradition at once ancient and direct, unbroken, oral, distorted, unrecognisable, and alive. Another Combray personality whom I could discern also, potential and presaged, in the Gothic sculptures of Saint-André-des-Champs was young Théodore, the assistant in Camus's shop. And, indeed, Françoise herself was so well aware that she had in him a countryman and contemporary that

when my aunt was too ill for Françoise to be able,
unaided, to lift her in her bed or to carry her to her
chair, rather than let the kitchen-maid come upstairs
and, perhaps, get into my aunt's good books, she would
send for Théodore. And this lad, who was rightly
regarded as a scapegrace, was so abounding in that spirit
which had served to decorate the porch of Saint-André-
des-Champs, and particularly in the feelings of respect
due, in Françoise's eyes, to all "poor invalids," and above
all to her own "poor mistress," that when he bent down
to raise my aunt's head from her pillow, he wore the same
naïve and zealous mien as the little angels in the bas-
reliefs who throng, with tapers in their hands, about the
swooning Virgin, as though those carved stone faces,
naked and grey as trees in winter, were, like them, asleep
only, storing up life and waiting to flower again in countless plebeian faces, reverent and cunning as the face of
Théodore, and glowing with the ruddy brilliance of ripe
apples.

There, too, not affixed to the stone like the little angels, but detached from the porch, of more than human
stature, erect upon her pedestal as upon a footstool that
had been placed there to save her feet from contact with
the wet ground, stood a saint with the full cheeks, the
firm breasts swelling out her draperies like clusters of ripe
grapes inside a sack, the narrow forehead, short and
impudent nose, deep-set eyes, and hardy, stolid, fearless
demeanour of the country-women of those parts. This
similarity, which imparted to the statue a kindliness that I
had not looked to find in it, was corroborated often by
the arrival of some girl from the fields, come, like ourselves, for shelter beneath the porch, whose presence

there—like the leaves of a climbing plant that have grown
up beside some sculpted foliage—seemed deliberately intended to enable us, by confronting it with its type in nature, to form a critical estimate of the truth of the work of
art. Before our eyes, in the distance, a promised or an accursed land, Roussainville, within whose walls I had
never penetrated, Roussainville was now, when the rain
had ceased for us, still being chastised like a village in the
Old Testament by all the slings and arrows of the storm,
which beat down obliquely upon the dwellings of its inhabitants, or else had already received the forgiveness of
the Almighty, who had restored to it the light of his sun,
which fell upon it in frayed, golden shafts, unequal in
length like the rays of a monstrance.

Sometimes, when the weather had completely broken,
we were obliged to go home and to remain shut up indoors. Here and there in the distance, in a landscape
which in the failing light and saturated atmosphere resembled a seascape rather, a few solitary houses clinging
to the lower slopes of a hill plunged in watery darkness
shone out like little boats which have folded their sails
and ride at anchor all night upon the sea. But what mattered rain or storm? In summer, bad weather is no more
than a passing fit of superficial ill-temper on the part of
the permanent, underlying fine weather which, in sharp
contrast to the fluid and unstable fine weather of winter,
having firmly established itself in the soil where it has
materialised in dense masses of foliage on which the rain
may drip without weakening the endurance of their deep-
seated happiness, has hoisted for the entire season, in the
very streets of the village, on the walls of its houses and
its gardens, its silken banners, violet and white. Sitting in

the little parlour, where I would pass the time until dinner with a book, I could hear the water dripping from our
chestnut-trees, but I knew that the shower would merely
burnish their leaves, and that they promised to remain
there, like pledges of summer, all through the rainy night,
ensuring the continuance of the fine weather; I knew that
however much it rained, tomorrow, over the white fence
of Tansonville, the little heart-shaped leaves would ripple,
as numerous as ever; and it was without the least distress
that I watched the poplar in the Rue des Perchamps pray-
ing for mercy, bowing in desperation before the storm;
without the least distress that I heard, at the bottom of
the garden, the last peals of thunder growling among the
lilacs.

If the weather was bad all morning, my parents
would abandon the idea of a walk, and I would remain at
home. But, later on, I formed the habit of going out by
myself on such days, and walking towards Méséglise-la-
Vineuse, during that autumn when we had to come to
Combray to settle my aunt Léonie's estate; for she had
died at last, vindicating at one and the same time those
who had insisted that her debilitating regimen would ultimately kill her and those who had always maintained that
she suffered from a disease that was not imaginary but organic, by the visible proof of which the sceptics would be
obliged to own themselves convinced, once she had succumbed to it; causing by her death no great grief save to
one person alone, but to that one a grief that was savage
in its violence. During the long fortnight of my aunt's last
illness Françoise never left her for an instant, never undressed, allowed no one else to do anything for her, and
did not leave her body until it was actually in its grave.

Then at last we understood that the sort of terror in which Françoise had lived of my aunt's harsh words, her suspicions and her anger, had developed in her a feeling which we had mistaken for hatred and which was really veneration and love. Her true mistress, whose decisions had been impossible to foresee, whose ruses had been so difficult to foil, of whose good nature it had been so easy to take advantage, her sovereign, her mysterious and omnipotent monarch was no more. Compared with such a mistress we were of very little account. The time had long passed since, on first coming to spend our holidays at Combray, we had enjoyed as much prestige as my aunt in Françoise's eyes.

That autumn my parents, so preoccupied with all the legal formalities, the discussions with solicitors and tenants, that they had little time to make excursions, for which in any case the weather was unpropitious, began to let me go for walks without them along the Méséglise way, wrapped up in a huge plaid which protected me from the rain, and which I was all the more ready to throw over my shoulders because I felt that its tartan stripes scandalised Françoise, whom it was impossible to convince that the colour of one's clothes had nothing whatever to do with one's mourning for the dead, and to whom the grief which we had shown on my aunt's death was wholly inadequate, since we had not entertained the neighbours to a great funeral banquet, and did not adopt a special tone when we spoke of her, while I at times might be heard humming a tune. I am sure that in a book—and to that extent my feelings were akin to those of Françoise—such a conception of mourning, in the manner of the *Chanson de Roland* and of the porch of

Saint-André-des-Champs, would have seemed most attractive. But the moment Françoise herself was near me,
some demon would urge me to try to make her angry,
and I would avail myself of the slightest pretext to say to
her that I regretted my aunt's death because she had been
a good woman in spite of her absurdities, but not in the
least because she was my aunt; that she might have been
my aunt and yet have seemed to me so odious that her
death would not have caused me a moment's sorrow—
statements which, in a book, would have struck me as inept.

And if Françoise then, inspired like a poet with a
flood of confused reflections upon bereavement, grief and
family memories, pleaded her inability to rebut my theories, saying: "I don't know how to *espress* myself," I
would gloat over her admission with an ironical and brutal common sense worthy of Dr Percepied; and if she
went on: "All the same she was kith and kindle; there's
always the respect due to kindle," I would shrug my
shoulders and say to myself: "It's really very good of me
to discuss the matter with an illiterate old woman who
makes such howlers," adopting, to deliver judgment on
Françoise, the mean and narrow outlook of the pedant,
whom those who are most contemptuous of him in the
impartiality of their own minds are only too prone to emulate when they are obliged to play a part upon the vulgar
stage of life.

My walks, that autumn, were all the more delightful
because I used to take them after long hours spent over a
book. When I was tired of reading, after a whole morning
in the house, I would throw my plaid across my shoulders
and set out; my body, which in a long spell of enforced

immobility had stored up an accumulation of vital energy, now felt the need, like a spinning-top wound up and let go, to expend it in every direction. The walls of houses, the Tansonville hedge, the trees of Roussainville wood, the bushes adjoining Montjouvain, all must bear the blows of my walking-stick or umbrella, must hear my shouts of happiness, these being no more than expressions of the confused ideas which exhilarated me, and which had not achieved the repose of enlightenment, preferring the pleasures of a lazy drift towards an immediate outlet rather than submit to a slow and difficult course of elucidation. Thus it is that most of our attempts to translate our innermost feelings do no more than relieve us of them by drawing them out in a blurred form which does not help us to identify them. When I try to reckon up all that I owe to the Méséglise way, all the humble discoveries of which it was either the fortuitous setting or the direct inspiration and cause, I am reminded that it was in that same autumn, on one of those walks, near the bushy slope which overlooks Montjouvain, that I was struck for the first time by this discordance between our impressions and their habitual expression. After an hour of rain and wind, against which I had struggled cheerfully, as I came to the edge of the Montjouvain pond, beside a little hut with a tiled roof in which M. Vinteuil's gardener kept his tools, the sun had just reappeared, and its golden rays, washed clean by the shower, glittered anew in the sky, on the trees, on the wall of the hut and the still wet tiles of the roof, on the ridge of which a hen was strutting. The wind tugged at the wild grass growing from cracks in the wall and at the hen's downy feathers, which floated out horizontally to their full extent with the unresisting sub-

missiveness of light and lifeless things. The tiled roof cast
upon the pond, translucent again in the sunlight, a dappled pink reflection which I had never observed before.
And, seeing upon the water, and on the surface of the
wall, a pallid smile responding to the smiling sky, I cried
aloud in my enthusiasm, brandishing my furled umbrella:
"Gosh, gosh, gosh, gosh!" But at the same time I felt that
I was in duty bound not to content myself with these
unilluminating words, but to endeavour to see more
clearly into the sources of my rapture.

And it was at that moment, too—thanks to a peasant
who went past, apparently in a bad enough humour already, but more so when he nearly got a poke in the face
from my umbrella, and who replied somewhat coolly to
my "Fine day, what! Good to be out walking!"—that I
learned that identical emotions do not spring up simultaneously in the hearts of all men in accordance with a pre-
established order. Later on, whenever a long spell of reading had put me in a mood for conversation, the friend to
whom I was longing to talk would at that very moment
have finished indulging himself in the delights of conversation, and wanted to be left to read undisturbed. And if
I had just been thinking of my parents with affection, and
forming resolutions of the kind most calculated to please
them, they would have been using the same interval of
time to discover some misdeed that I had already forgotten, and would begin to scold me severely as I was about
to fling myself into their arms.

Sometimes to the exhilaration which I derived from
being alone would be added an alternative feeling which I
was unable to distinguish clearly from it, a feeling stimu-
lated by the desire to see appear before my eyes a peas-

ant-girl whom I might clasp in my arms. Springing up
suddenly, and without giving me time to trace it accurately to its source among so many thoughts of a very different kind, the pleasure which accompanied this desire
seemed only a degree superior to that which I derived
from them. I found an additional merit in everything that
was in my mind at that moment, in the pink reflection of
the tiled roof, the grass growing out of the wall, the village of Roussainville into which I had long desired to
penetrate, the trees of its wood and the steeple of its
church, as a result of this fresh emotion which made them
appear more desirable only because I thought it was they
that had provoked it, and which seemed only to wish to
bear me more swiftly towards them when it filled my sails
with a potent, mysterious and propitious breeze. But if,
for me, this desire that a woman should appear added
something more exalting to the charms of nature, they in
their turn enlarged what I might have found too restricted
in the charms of the woman. It seemed to me that the
beauty of the trees was hers also, and that her kisses
would reveal to me the spirit of those horizons, of the village of Roussainville, of the books which I was reading
that year; and, my imagination drawing strength from
contact with my sensuality, my sensuality expanding
through all the realms of my imagination, my desire no
longer had any bounds. Moreover—just as in moments of
musing contemplation of nature, the normal actions of the
mind being suspended, and our abstract ideas of things
set aside, we believe with the profoundest faith in the
originality, in the individual existence of the place in
which we may happen to be—the passing figure whom
my desire evoked seemed to be not just any specimen of

the genus "woman," but a necessary and natural product
of this particular soil. For at that time everything that was
not myself, the earth and the creatures upon it, seemed to
me more precious, more important, endowed with a more
real existence than they appear to full-grown men. And
between the earth and its creatures I made no distinction.
I had a desire for a peasant-girl from Méséglise or Roussainville, for a fisher-girl from Balbec, just as I had a desire for Balbec and Méséglise. The pleasure they might
give me would have seemed less genuine, I should no
longer have believed in it, if I had modified the conditions as I pleased. To meet a fisher-girl from Balbec or a
peasant-girl from Méséglise in Paris would have been like
receiving the present of a shell which I had never seen
upon the beach, or of a fern which I had never found
among the woods, would have stripped from the pleasure
she might give me all those other pleasures amidst which
my imagination had enwrapped her. But to wander thus
among the woods of Roussainville without a peasant-girl
to embrace was to see those woods and yet know nothing
of their secret treasure, their deep-hidden beauty. That
girl whom I invariably saw dappled with the shadows of
their leaves was to me herself a plant of local growth,
merely of a higher species than the rest, and one whose
structure would enable me to get closer than through
them to the intimate savour of the country. I could believe this all the more readily (and also that the caresses
by which she would bring that savour to my senses would
themselves be of a special kind, yielding a pleasure which
I could never derive from anyone else) since I was still,
and must for long remain, in that period of life when one
has not yet separated the fact of this sensual pleasure

from the various women in whose company one has
tasted it, when one has not yet reduced it to a general
idea which makes one regard them thenceforward as the
interchangeable instruments of a pleasure that is always
the same. Indeed, that pleasure does not even exist, isolated, distinct, formulated in the consciousness, as the ultimate aim for which one seeks a woman's company, or as
the cause of the preliminary perturbation that one feels.
Scarcely does one think of it as a pleasure in store for one;
rather does one call it *her* charm; for one does not think
of oneself, but only of escaping from oneself. Obscurely
awaited, immanent and concealed, it simply raises to such
a paroxysm, at the moment when at last it makes itself
felt, those other pleasures which we find in the tender
glances, the kisses, of the woman by our side, that it
seems to us, more than anything else, a sort of transport
of gratitude for her kindness of heart and for her touching
predilection for us, which we measure by the blessings
and the happiness that she showers upon us.

Alas, it was in vain that I implored the castle-keep of
Roussainville, that I begged it to send out to meet me
some daughter of its village, appealing to it as to the sole
confidant of my earliest desires when, at the top of our
house in Combray, in the little room that smelt of orris-
root, I could see nothing but its tower framed in the
half-opened window as, with the heroic misgivings of a
traveller setting out on a voyage of exploration or of a
desperate wretch hesitating on the verge of self-destruc-
tion, faint with emotion, I explored, across the bounds of
my own experience, an untrodden path which for all I
knew was deadly—until the moment when a natural trail
like that left by a snail smeared the leaves of the flowering

currant that drooped around me. In vain did I call upon
it now. In vain did I compress the whole landscape into
my field of vision, draining it with an exhaustive gaze
which sought to extract from it a female creature. I might
go as far as the porch of Saint-André-des-Champs: never
did I find there the peasant-girl whom I should not have
failed to meet had I been with my grandfather and thus
unable to engage her in conversation. I would stare interminably at the trunk of a distant tree, from behind which
she would emerge and come to me; I scanned the horizon,
which remained as deserted as before; night was falling; it
was without hope now that I concentrated my attention,
as though to draw up from it the creatures which it must
conceal, upon that sterile soil, that stale, exhausted earth,
and it was no longer with exhilaration but with sullen
rage that I aimed blows at the trees of Roussainville
wood, from among which no more living creatures
emerged than if they had been trees painted on the
stretched canvas background of a panorama, when, unable
to resign myself to returning home without having held in
my arms the woman I so greatly desired, I was yet
obliged to retrace my steps towards Combray, and to admit to myself that the chance of her appearing in my path
grew smaller every moment. And if she had appeared,
would I have dared to speak to her? I felt that she would
have regarded me as mad, and I ceased to think of those
desires which came to me on my walks, but were never
realised, as being shared by others, or as having any existence outside myself. They seemed to me now no more
than the purely subjective, impotent, illusory creations of
my temperament. They no longer had any connection
with nature, with the world of real things, which from

then onwards lost all its charm and significance, and
meant no more to my life than a purely conventional
framework, what the railway carriage on the bench of
which a traveller is reading to pass the time is to the fic-
tional events of his novel.

It is perhaps from another impression which I received at Montjouvain, some years later, an impression
which at the time remained obscure to me, that there
arose, long afterwards, the notion I was to form of
sadism. We shall see, in due course, that for quite other
reasons the memory of this impression was to play an important part in my life. It was during a spell of very hot
weather; my parents, who had been obliged to go away
for the whole day, had told me that I might stay out as
late as I pleased; and having gone as far as the Montjouvain pond, where I enjoyed seeing again the reflection of
the tiled roof of the hut, I had lain down in the shade and
fallen asleep among the bushes on the steep slope overlooking the house, just where I had waited for my parents, years before, one day when they had gone to call on
M. Vinteuil. It was almost dark when I awoke, and I was
about to get up and go away, but I saw Mlle Vinteuil (or
thought, at least, that I recognised her, for I had not seen
her often at Combray, and then only when she was still a
child, whereas she was now growing into a young
woman), who had probably just come in, standing in
front of me, and only a few feet away, in that room in
which her father had entertained mine, and which she had
now made into a little sitting-room for herself. The window was partly open; the lamp was lighted; I could watch
her every movement without her being able to see me;
but if I had moved away I would have made a rustling

sound among the bushes, she would have heard me, and she might have thought that I had been hiding there in order to spy upon her.

She was in deep mourning, for her father had recently died. We had not gone to see her; my mother had not wished it, by reason of a virtue which alone set limits to her benevolence—namely, modesty; but she pitied the girl from the depths of her heart. My mother had not forgotten the sad last years of M. Vinteuil's life, his complete absorption, first in having to play mother and nursery-maid to his daughter, and, later, in the suffering she had caused him; she could see the tortured expression which was never absent from the old man's face in those last years; she knew that he had finally given up hope of finishing the task of copying out the whole of his later work, the modest pieces, we imagined, of an old piano-teacher, a retired village organist, which we assumed were of little value in themselves, though we did not despise them because they meant so much to him and had been the chief motive of his life before he sacrificed them to his daughter; pieces which, being mostly not even written down, but recorded only in his memory, while the rest were scribbled on loose sheets of paper, and quite illegible, must now remain unknown for ever. My mother thought, too, of that other and still more cruel renunciation to which M. Vinteuil had been driven, that of a future of honourable and respected happiness for his daughter; when she called to mind all this utter and crushing misery that had come upon my aunts' old music-teacher, she was moved to very real grief, and shuddered to think of that other grief, so much more bitter, which Mlle Vinteuil must now be feeling, tinged with remorse at having virtually killed her father. "Poor M. Vinteuil," my mother would say, "he lived and died for his daughter, without getting his reward. Will he get it now, I wonder, and in what form? It can only come to him from her."

At the far end of Mlle Vinteuil's sitting-room, on the mantelpiece, stood a small photograph of her father which she went briskly to fetch, just as the sound of carriage wheels was heard from the road outside, then flung herself down on a sofa and drew towards her a little table on which she placed the photograph, as M. Vinteuil had placed beside him the piece of music which he would have liked to play to my parents. Presently her friend came into the room. Mlle Vinteuil greeted her without rising, clasping her hands behind her head and moving to one side of the sofa as though to make room for her. But no sooner had she done this than she evidently felt that she might seem to be imposing on her friend a posture which she might consider importunate. She thought that her friend would perhaps prefer to sit down at some distance from her, upon a chair; she felt that she had been indiscreet; her sensitive heart took fright; stretching herself out again over the whole of the sofa, she closed her eyes and began to yawn, as if to suggest that drowsiness was the sole reason for her recumbent position. Despite the brusque and hectoring familiarity with which she treated her companion, I could recognise in her the obsequious and reticent gestures and sudden scruples that had characterised her father. Presently she rose and came to the window, where she pretended to be trying to close the shutters and not succeeding.

"Leave them open," said her friend. "I'm hot."

"But it's too tiresome! People will see us," Mlle Vinteuil answered.

But then she must have guessed that her friend would think that she had uttered these words simply in order to provoke a reply in certain other words, which she did indeed wish to hear but, from discretion, would have preferred her friend to be the first to speak. And so her face, which I could not see very clearly, must have assumed the expression which my grandmother had once found so delightful, when she hastily went on: "When I say 'see us' I mean, of course, see us reading. It's so tiresome to think that whatever trivial little thing you do someone's eyes are on you."

With an instinctive rectitude and a gentility beyond her control, she refrained from uttering the premeditated words which she had felt to be indispensable for the full realisation of her desire. And perpetually, in the depths of her being, a shy and suppliant maiden entreated and reined back a rough and swaggering trooper.

"Oh, yes, it's so extremely likely that people are looking at us at this time of night in this densely populated district!" said her friend sarcastically. "And what if they are?" she went on, feeling bound to annotate with a fond and mischievous wink these words which she recited out of good-naturedness, as a text which she knew to be pleasing to Mlle Vinteuil, in a tone of studied cynicism. "And what if they are? All the better that they should see us."

Mlle Vinteuil shuddered and rose to her feet. Her sensitive and scrupulous heart was ignorant of the words that ought to flow spontaneously from her lips to match

the scene for which her eager senses clamoured. She
reached out as far as she could across the limitations of
her true nature to find the language appropriate to the vicious young woman she longed to be thought, but the
words which she imagined such a young woman might
have uttered with sincerity sounded false on her own lips.
And what little she allowed herself to say was said in a
strained tone, in which her ingrained timidity paralysed
her impulse towards audacity and was interlarded with:
"You're sure you aren't cold? You aren't too hot? You
don't want to sit and read by yourself? . . .

"Her ladyship's thoughts seem to be rather lubricious
this evening," she concluded, doubtless repeating a phrase
which she had heard used by her friend on some earlier
occasion.

In the V-shaped opening of her crape bodice Mlle
Vinteuil felt the sting of her friend's sudden kiss; she gave
a little scream and broke away; and then they began to
chase one another about the room, scrambling over the
furniture, their wide sleeves fluttering like wings, clucking
and squealing like a pair of amorous fowls. At last Mlle
Vinteuil collapsed on to the sofa, with her friend lying on
top of her. The latter now had her back turned to the little table on which the old music-master's portrait had
been arranged. Mlle Vinteuil realised that her friend
would not see it unless her attention were drawn to it,
and so exclaimed, as if she herself had just noticed it for
the first time: "Oh! there's my father's picture looking at
us; I can't think who can have put it there; I'm sure I've
told them a dozen times that it isn't the proper place for
it."

I remembered the words that M. Vinteuil had used to

my parents in apologising for an obtrusive sheet of music. This photograph was evidently in regular use for ritual profanations, for the friend replied in words which were clearly a liturgical response: "Let him stay there. He can't bother us any longer. D'you think he'd start whining, and wanting to put your overcoat on for you, if he saw you now with the window open, the ugly old monkey?"

To which Mlle Vinteuil replied in words of gentle reproach—"Come, come!"—which testified to the goodness of her nature, not that they were prompted by any resentment at hearing her father spoken of in this fashion (for that was evidently a feeling which she had trained herself, by a long course of sophistries, to keep in close subjection at such moments), but rather because they were a sort of curb which, in order not to appear selfish, she herself applied to the gratification which her friend was attempting to procure for her. It may well have been, too, that the smiling moderation with which she faced and answered these blasphemies, that this tender and hypocritical rebuke appeared to her frank and generous nature as a particularly shameful and seductive form of the wickedness she was striving to emulate. But she could not resist the attraction of being treated with tenderness by a woman who had shown herself so implacable towards the defenceless dead, and, springing on to her friend's lap she held out a chaste brow to be kissed precisely as a daughter would have done, with the exquisite sensation that they would thus, between them, inflict the last turn of the screw of cruelty by robbing M. Vinteuil, as though they were actually rifling his tomb, of the sacred rights of fatherhood. Her friend took Mlle Vinteuil's head between her hands and placed a kiss on her brow with a docility

prompted by the real affection she had for her, as well as
by the desire to bring what distraction she could into the
dull and melancholy life of an orphan.

"Do you know what I should like to do to this old
horror?" she said, taking up the photograph. And she
murmured in Mlle Vinteuil's ear something that I could
not distinguish.

"Oh! You wouldn't dare."

"Not dare to spit on it? On *that*?" said the friend
with studied brutality.

I heard no more, for Mlle Vinteuil, with an air that
was at once languid, awkward, bustling, honest and sad,
came to the window and drew the shutters close; but I
knew now what was the reward that M. Vinteuil, in return for all the suffering that he had endured in his lifetime on account of his daughter, had received from her
after his death.

And yet I have since reflected that if M. Vinteuil had
been able to be present at this scene, he might still, in
spite of everything, have continued to believe in his
daughter's goodness of heart, and perhaps in so doing he
would not have been altogether wrong. It was true that in
Mlle Vinteuil's habits the appearance of evil was so absolute that it would have been hard to find it exhibited to
such a degree of perfection outside a convinced sadist; it
is behind the footlights of a Paris theatre and not under
the homely lamp of an actual country house that one ex-
pects to see a girl encouraging a friend to spit upon the
portrait of a father who has lived and died for her alone;
and when we find in real life a desire for melodramatic effect, it is generally sadism that is responsible for it. It is
possible that, without being in the least inclined towards

sadism, a daughter might be guilty of equally cruel offences as those of Mlle Vinteuil against the memory and
the wishes of her dead father, but she would not give
them deliberate expression in an act so crude in its symbolism, so lacking in subtlety; the criminal element in her
behaviour would be less evident to other people, and even
to herself, since she would not admit to herself that she
was doing wrong. But, appearances apart, in Mlle Vinteuil's soul, at least in the earlier stages, the evil element
was probably not unmixed. A sadist of her kind is an
artist in evil, which a wholly wicked person could not be,
for in that case the evil would not have been external, it
would have seemed quite natural to her, and would not
even have been distinguishable from herself; and as for
virtue, respect for the dead, filial affection, since she
would never have practised the cult of these things, she
would take no impious delight in profaning them. Sadists
of Mlle Vinteuil's sort are creatures so purely sentimental,
so naturally virtuous, that even sensual pleasure appears
to them as something bad, the prerogative of the wicked.
And when they allow themselves for a moment to enjoy it
they endeavour to impersonate, to identify with, the
wicked, and to make their partners do likewise, in order
to gain the momentary illusion of having escaped beyond
the control of their own gentle and scrupulous natures
into the inhuman world of pleasure. And I could understand how she must have longed for such an escape when
I saw how impossible it was for her to effect it. At the
moment when she wished to be thought the very antithe-
sis of her father, what she at once suggested to me were
the mannerisms, in thought and speech, of the poor old
piano-teacher. Far more than his photograph, what she

really desecrated, what she subordinated to her pleasures though it remained between them and her and prevented her from any direct enjoyment of them, was the likeness between her face and his, his mother's blue eyes which he had handed down to her like a family jewel, those gestures of courtesy and kindness which interposed between her vice and herself a phraseology, a mentality which were not designed for vice and which prevented her from recognising it as something very different from the numberless little social duties and courtesies to which she must devote herself every day. It was not evil that gave her the idea of pleasure, that seemed to her attractive; it was pleasure, rather, that seemed evil. And as, each time she indulged in it, it was accompanied by evil thoughts such as ordinarily had no place in her virtuous mind, she came at length to see in pleasure itself something diabolical, to identify it with Evil. Perhaps Mlle Vinteuil felt that at heart her friend was not altogether bad, nor really sincere when she gave vent to those blasphemous utterances. At any rate, she had the pleasure of receiving and returning those kisses, those smiles, those glances, all feigned, perhaps, but akin in their base and vicious mode of expression to those which would have been evinced not by an ordinarily kind, suffering person but by a cruel and wanton one. She could delude herself for a moment into believing that she was indeed enjoying the pleasures which, with so perverted an accomplice, a girl might enjoy who really did harbour such barbarous feelings towards her father's memory. Perhaps she would not have thought of evil as a state so rare, so abnormal, so exotic, one in which it was so refreshing to sojourn, had she been able to discern in herself, as in everyone else, that indif-

ference to the sufferings one causes which, whatever other
names one gives it, is the most terrible and lasting form
of cruelty.

If the Méséglise way was fairly easy, it was a very
different matter when we took the Guermantes way, for
that meant a long walk, and we must first make sure of
the weather. When we seemed to have entered upon a
spell of fine days; when Françoise, in desperation that not
a drop was falling on the "poor crops," gazing up at the
sky and seeing there only an occasional white cloud floating upon its calm blue surface, groaned aloud and exclaimed: "They look just like a lot of dogfish swimming
about and sticking up their snouts! Ah, they never think
of making it rain a little for the poor labourers! And then
when the corn is all ripe, down it will come, pitter-patter
all over the place, and think no more of where it's falling
than if it was the sea!"; when my father had received the
same favourable reply from the gardener and the barometer several times in succession, then someone would say at
dinner: "Tomorrow, if the weather holds, we might go
the Guermantes way." And off we would set, immediately after lunch, through the little garden gate into the
Rue des Perchamps, narrow and bent at a sharp angle,
dotted with clumps of grass among which two or three
wasps would spend the day botanising, a street as quaint
as its name, from which, I felt, its odd characteristics and
cantankerous personality derived, a street for which one
might search in vain through the Combray of today, for
the village school now occupies its site. But in my dreams
of Combray (like those architects, pupils of Viollet-le-
Duc, who, fancying that they can detect, beneath a Re-

naissance rood-screen and an eighteenth-century altar, traces of a Romanesque choir, restore the whole church to the state in which it must have been in the twelfth century) I leave not a stone of the modern edifice standing, but pierce through it and "restore" the Rue des Perchamps. And for such reconstruction memory furnishes me with more detailed guidance than is generally at the disposal of restorers: the pictures which it has preserved—perhaps the last surviving in the world today, and soon to follow the rest into oblivion—of what Combray looked like in my childhood days; pictures which, because it was the old Combray that traced their outlines upon my mind before it vanished, are as moving—if I may compare a humble landscape with those glorious works, reproductions of which my grandmother was so fond of bestowing on me—as those old engravings of the Last Supper or that painting by Gentile Bellini, in which one sees, in a state in which they no longer exist, the masterpiece of Leonardo and the portico of Saint Mark's.

We would pass, in the Rue de l'Oiseau, in front of the old hostelry of the Oiseau Flesché, into whose great courtyard, once upon a time, would rumble the coaches of the Duchesses de Montpensier, de Guermantes and de Montmorency, when they had to come down to Combray for some litigation with their tenants, or to receive homage from them. We would come at length to the Mall, among whose tree-tops I could distinguish the steeple of Saint-Hilaire. And I should have liked to be able to sit down and spend the whole day there reading and listening to the bells, for it was so blissful and so quiet that, when an hour struck, you would have said not that it broke in upon the calm of the day, but that it relieved the day of its superfluity, and that the steeple, with the indolent, painstaking exactitude of a person who has nothing else to do, had simply—in order to squeeze out and let fall the few golden drops which had slowly and naturally accumulated in the hot sunlight—pressed, at a given moment, the distended surface of the silence.

The great charm of the Guermantes way was that we had beside us, almost all the time, the course of the Vivonne. We crossed it first, ten minutes after leaving the house, by a foot-bridge called the Pont-Vieux. And every year, when we arrived at Combray, on Easter Sunday, after the sermon, if the weather was fine, I would run there to see (amid all the disorder that prevails on the morning of a great festival, the sumptuous preparations for which make the everyday household utensils that they have not contrived to banish seem more sordid than usual) the river flowing past, sky-blue already between banks still black and bare, its only companions a clump of premature daffodils and early primroses, while here and there burned the blue flame of a violet, its stem drooping beneath the weight of the drop of perfume stored in its tiny horn. The Pont-Vieux led to a tow-path which at this point would be overhung in summer by the bluish foliage of a hazel tree, beneath which a fisherman in a straw hat seemed to have taken root. At Combray, where I could always detect the blacksmith or grocer's boy through the disguise of a verger's uniform or chorister's surplice, this fisherman was the only person whom I was never able to identify. He must have known my family, for he used to raise his hat when we passed; and then I would be just on the point of asking his name when someone would signal to me to be quiet or I would frighten the fish. We would

follow the tow-path, which ran along the top of a steep
bank several feet above the stream. The bank on the other
side was lower, stretching in a series of broad meadows as
far as the village and the distant railway-station. Over
these were strewn the remains, half-buried in the long
grass, of the castle of the old Counts of Combray, who,
during the Middle Ages, had had on this side the course
of the Vivonne as a barrier against attack from the Lords
of Guermantes and Abbots of Martinville. Nothing was
left now but a few barely visible stumps of towers, hum-
mocks upon the broad surface of the fields, and a few
broken battlements from which, in their day, the cross-
bowmen had hurled their missiles and the watchmen had
gazed out over Novepont, Clairefontaine, Martinville-le-
Sec, Bailleau-l'Exempt, fiefs all of them of Guermantes by
which Combray was hemmed in, but now razed to the
level of the grass and overrun by the boys from the lay
brothers' school who came there for study or recreation—
a past that had almost sunk into the ground, lying by the
water's edge like an idler taking the air, yet giving me
much food for thought, making the name of Combray
connote to me not only the little town of today but an
historic city vastly different, gripping my imagination by
the remote, incomprehensible features which it half-concealed beneath a spangled veil of buttercups. For the buttercups grew past numbering in this spot which they had
chosen for their games among the grass, standing singly,
in couples, in whole companies, yellow as the yolk of
eggs, and glowing with an added lustre, I felt, because,
being powerless to consummate with my palate the pleasure which the sight of them never failed to give me, I
would let it accumulate as my eyes ranged over their

golden expanse, until it became potent enough to produce
an effect of absolute, purposeless beauty; and so it had
been from my earliest childhood, when from the tow-path
I had stretched out my arms towards them before I could
even properly spell their charming name—a name fit for
the Prince in some fairy-tale—immigrants, perhaps, from
Asia centuries ago, but naturalised now for ever in the
village, satisfied with their modest horizon, rejoicing in
the sunshine and the water's edge, faithful to their little
glimpse of the railway-station, yet keeping none the less
like some of our old paintings, in their plebeian simplicity, a poetic scintillation from the golden East.

I enjoyed watching the glass jars which the village
boys used to lower into the Vivonne to catch minnows,
and which, filled by the stream, in which they in their
turn were enclosed, at once "containers" whose transparent sides were like solidified water and "contents"
plunged into a still larger container of liquid, flowing
crystal, conjured up an image of coolness more delicious
and more provoking than they would have done standing
upon a table laid for dinner, by showing it as perpetually
in flight between the impalpable water in which my hands
could not grasp it and the insoluble glass in which my
palate could not enjoy it. I made up my mind to come
there again with a fishing-line; meanwhile I procured
some bread from our picnic basket, and threw pellets of it
into the Vivonne which seemed to bring about a process
of super-saturation, for the water at once solidified round
them in oval clusters of emaciated tadpoles, which until
then it had no doubt been holding in solution, invisible
and on the verge of entering the stage of crystallisation.

Presently the course of the Vivonne became choked

with water-plants. At first they appeared singly—a lily,
for instance, which the current, across whose path it was
unhappily placed, would never leave at rest for a moment,
so that, like a ferry-boat mechanically propelled, it would
drift over to one bank only to return to the other, eter-
nally repeating its double journey. Thrust towards the
bank, its stalk would uncoil, lengthen, reach out, strain
almost to breaking-point until the current again caught it,
its green moorings swung back over their anchorage and
brought the unhappy plant to what might fitly be called
its starting-point, since it was fated not to rest there a
moment before moving off once again. I would still find
it there, on one walk after another, always in the same
helpless state, suggesting certain victims of neurasthenia,
among whom my grandfather would have included my
aunt Léonie, who present year after year the unchanging
spectacle of their odd and unaccountable habits, which
they constantly imagine themselves to be on the point of
shaking off but which they always retain to the end;
caught in the treadmill of their own maladies and eccentricities, their futile endeavours to escape serve only to ac-
tuate its mechanism, to keep in motion the clockwork of
their strange, ineluctable and baneful dietetics. Such as
these was the water-lily, and reminiscent also of those
wretches whose peculiar torments, repeated indefinitely
throughout eternity, aroused the curiosity of Dante, who
would have inquired about them at greater length and in
fuller detail from the victims themselves had not Virgil,
striding on ahead, obliged him to hasten after him at full
speed, as I must hasten after my parents.

But further on the current slackened, at a point where
the stream ran through a property thrown open to the

public by its owner, who had made a hobby of aquatic gardening, so that the little ponds into which the Vivonne was here diverted were aflower with water-lilies. As the banks hereabouts were thickly wooded, the heavy shade of the trees gave the water a background which was ordinarily dark green, although sometimes, when we were coming home on a calm evening after a stormy afternoon, I have seen in its depths a clear, crude blue verging on violet, suggesting a floor of Japanese cloisonné. Here and there on the surface, blushing like a strawberry, floated a water-lily flower with a scarlet centre and white edges. Further on, the flowers were more numerous, paler, less glossy, more thickly seeded, more tightly folded, and disposed, by accident, in festoons so graceful that I would fancy I saw floating upon the stream, as after the sad dismantling of some *fête galante*, moss-roses in loosened garlands. Elsewhere a corner seemed to be reserved for the commoner kinds of lily, of a neat pink or white like rocket-flowers, washed clean like porcelain with housewifely care while, a little further again, others, pressed close together in a veritable floating flower-bed, suggested garden pansies that had settled here like butterflies and were fluttering their blue and burnished wings over the transparent depths of this watery garden—this celestial garden, too, for it gave the flowers a soil of a colour more precious, more moving than their own, and, whether sparkling beneath the water-lilies in the afternoon in a kaleidoscope of silent, watchful and mobile contentment, or glowing, towards evening, like some distant haven, with the roseate dreaminess of the setting sun, ceaselessly changing yet remaining always in harmony, around the less mutable colours of the flowers themselves, with all

that is most profound, most evanescent, most mysterious—all that is infinite—in the passing hour, it seemed
to have made them blossom in the sky itself.

After leaving this park the Vivonne began to flow
again more swiftly. How often have I watched, and
longed to imitate when I should be free to live as I chose,
a rower who had shipped his oars and lay flat on his back
in the bottom of his boat, letting it drift with the current,
seeing nothing but the sky gliding slowly by above him,
his face aglow with a foretaste of happiness and peace!

We would sit down among the irises at the water's
edge. In the holiday sky an idle cloud languorously daw-
dled. From time to time, oppressed by boredom, a carp
would heave itself out of the water with an anxious gasp.
It was time for our picnic. Before starting homewards we
would sit there for a long time, eating fruit and bread and
chocolate, on the grass over which came to us, faint, horizontal, but dense and metallic still, echoes of the bells of
Saint-Hilaire, which had not melted into the air they had
traversed for so long, and, ribbed by the successive palpi-
tation of all their sound-waves, throbbed as they grazed
the flowers at our feet.

Sometimes, at the water's edge and surrounded by
trees, we would come upon what is called a "country
house," lonely and secluded, seeing nothing of the world
but the river which bathed its feet. A young woman
whose pensive face and elegant veils did not suggest a local origin, and who had doubtless come, in the popular
phrase, "to bury herself" there, to taste the bitter sweetness of knowing that her name, and still more the name
of him whose heart she had once held but had been unable to keep, were unknown there, stood framed in a win-

dow from which she had no outlook beyond the boat that
was moored beside her door. She raised her eyes listlessly
on hearing, through the trees that lined the bank, the
voices of passers-by of whom, before they came in sight,
she might be certain that never had they known, nor ever
would know, the faithless lover, that nothing in their past
lives bore his imprint, and nothing in their future would
have occasion to receive it. One felt that in her renunciation of life she had deliberately abandoned those places in
which she might at least have been able to see the man
she loved, for others where he had never trod. And I
watched her, returning from some walk along a path
where she knew that he would not appear, drawing from
her resigned hands long and uselessly elegant gloves.

Never, in the course of our walks along the Guermantes way, were we able to penetrate as far as the source
of the Vivonne, of which I had often thought and which
had in my mind so abstract, so ideal an existence that I
had been as surprised when someone told me that it was
actually to be found in the same department, at a given
number of miles from Combray, as I had been when I
learned that there was another fixed point somewhere on
the earth's surface, where, according to the ancients,
opened the jaws of Hell. Nor could we ever get as far as
that other goal which I so longed to reach, Guermantes
itself. I knew that it was the residence of the Duc and
Duchesse de Guermantes, I knew that they were real personages who did actually exist, but whenever I thought
about them I pictured them either in tapestry, like the
Comtesse de Guermantes in the "Coronation of Esther"
which hung in our church, or else in iridescent colours,
like Gilbert the Bad in the stained-glass window where he

changed from cabbage green, when I was dipping my fingers in the holy water stoup, to plum blue when I had
reached our row of chairs, or again altogether impalpable,
like the image of Geneviève de Brabant, ancestress of the
Guermantes family, which the magic lantern sent wandering over the curtains of my room or flung aloft upon the
ceiling—in short, invariably wrapped in the mystery of
the Merovingian age and bathed, as in a sunset, in the
amber light which glowed from the resounding syllable
"antes." And if in spite of that they were for me, in their
capacity as a duke and duchess, real people, though of an
unfamiliar kind, this ducal personality of theirs was on
the other hand enormously distended, immaterialised, so
as to encircle and contain that Guermantes of which they
were duke and duchess, all that sunlit "Guermantes way"
of our walks, the course of the Vivonne, its water-lilies
and its overshadowing trees, and an endless series of summer afternoons. And I knew that they bore not only the
title of Duc and Duchesse de Guermantes, but that since
the fourteenth century, when, after vain attempts to conquer its earlier lords in battle, they had allied themselves
to them by marriage and so become Counts of Combray,
the first citizens, consequently, of the place, and yet the
only ones who did not reside in it—Comtes de Combray,
possessing Combray, threading it on their string of names
and titles, absorbing it in their personalities, and imbued,
no doubt, with that strange and pious melancholy which
was peculiar to Combray; proprietors of the town, though
not of any particular house there; dwelling, presumably,
outside, in the street, between heaven and earth, like that
Gilbert de Guermantes of whom I could see, in the
stained glass of the apse of Saint-Hilaire, only the reverse

side in dull black lacquer, if I raised my eyes to look for
him on my way to Camus's for a packet of salt.

And then it happened that, along the Guermantes
way, I sometimes passed beside well-watered little enclo-
sures, over whose hedges rose clusters of dark blossom. I
would stop, hoping to gain some precious addition to my
experience, for I seemed to have before my eyes a fragment of that fluvial country which I had longed so much
to see and know since coming upon a description of it by
one of my favourite authors. And it was with that story-
book land, with its imagined soil intersected by a hundred
bubbling watercourses, that Guermantes, changing its aspect in my mind, became identified, after I heard Dr Percepied speak of the flowers and the charming rivulets and
fountains that were to be seen there in the ducal park. I
used to dream that Mme de Guermantes, taking a sudden
capricious fancy to me, invited me there, that all day long
she stood fishing for trout by my side. And when evening
came, holding my hand in hers, as we passed by the little
gardens of her vassals she would point out to me the
flowers that leaned their red and purple spikes along the
tops of the low walls, and would teach me all their names.
She would make me tell her, too, all about the poems that
I intended to compose. And these dreams reminded me
that, since I wished some day to become a writer, it was
high time to decide what sort of books I was going to
write. But as soon as I asked myself the question, and
tried to discover some subject to which I could impart a
philosophical significance of infinite value, my mind
would stop like a clock, my consciousness would be faced
with a blank, I would feel either that I was wholly devoid
of talent or that perhaps some malady of the brain was

hindering its development. Sometimes I would rely on my father to settle it all for me. He was so powerful, in such high favour with people in office, that he made it possible for us to transgress laws which Françoise had taught me to regard as more ineluctable than the laws of life and death, as when we were allowed to postpone for a year the compulsory repointing of the walls of our house, alone among all the houses in that part of Paris, or when he obtained permission from the Minister for Mme Sazerat's son, who had been ordered to some watering-place, to take his baccalaureate two months in advance, among the candidates whose surnames began with "A," instead of having to wait his turn as an "S." If I had fallen seriously ill, if I had been captured by brigands, convinced that my father's understanding with the supreme powers was too complete, that his letters of introduction to the Almighty were too irresistible for my illness or captivity to turn out to be anything but vain illusions, in which no danger actually threatened me, I should have awaited with perfect composure the inevitable hour of my return to comfortable realities, of my deliverance from bondage or restoration to health; and perhaps this lack of genius, this black cavity which gaped in my mind when I ransacked it for the theme of my future writings, was itself no more than an insubstantial illusion, and would vanish with the intervention of my father, who must have agreed with the Government and with Providence that I should be the foremost writer of the day. But at other times, while my parents were growing impatient at seeing me loiter behind instead of following them, my present life, instead of seeming an artificial creation of my father's which he could modify as he chose, appeared, on the contrary, to

be comprised in a larger reality which had not been created for my benefit, from whose judgments there was no
appeal, within which I had no friend or ally, and beyond
which no further possibilities lay concealed. It seemed to
me then that I existed in the same manner as all other
men, that I must grow old, that I must die like them, and
that among them I was to be distinguished merely as one
of those who have no aptitude for writing. And so, utterly
despondent, I renounced literature for ever, despite the
encouragement Bloch had given me. This intimate, spontaneous feeling, this sense of the nullity of my intellect,
prevailed against all the flattering words that might be
lavished upon me, as a wicked man whose good deeds are
praised by all is gnawed by secret remorse.

One day my mother said to me: "You're always talking about Mme de Guermantes. Well, Dr Percepied took
great care of her when she was ill four years ago, and so
she's coming to Combray for his daughter's wedding.
You'll be able to see her in church." It was from Dr Percepied, as it happened, that I had heard most about Mme
de Guermantes, and he had even shown us the number of
an illustrated paper in which she was depicted in the costume she had worn at a fancy dress ball given by the
Princesse de Léon.

Suddenly, during the nuptial mass, the verger, by
moving to one side, enabled me to see in one of the
chapels a fair-haired lady with a large nose, piercing blue
eyes, a billowy scarf of mauve silk, glossy and new and
bright, and a little pimple at the corner of her nose. And
because on the surface of her face, which was red, as
though she had been very hot, I could discern, diluted
and barely perceptible, fragments of resemblance with the

portrait that had been shown to me; because, more especially, the particular features which I remarked in this
lady, if I attempted to catalogue them, formulated themselves in precisely the same terms—*a large nose, blue
eyes*—as Dr Percepied had used when describing in my
presence the Duchesse de Guermantes, I said to myself:
"This lady is like the Duchesse de Guermantes." Now
the chapel from which she was following the service was
that of Gilbert the Bad, beneath the flat tombstones of
which, yellowed and bulging like cells of honey in a
comb, rested the bones of the old Counts of Brabant; and
I remembered having heard it said that this chapel was
reserved for the Guermantes family, whenever any of its
members came to attend a ceremony at Combray; hence
there was only one woman resembling the portrait of
Mme de Guermantes who on that day, the very day on
which she was expected to come there, could conceivably
be sitting in that chapel: it was she! My disappointment
was immense. It arose from my not having borne in
mind, when I thought of Mme de Guermantes, that I was
picturing her to myself in the colours of a tapestry or a
stained-glass window, as living in another century, as being of another substance than the rest of the human race.
Never had it occurred to me that she might have a red
face, a mauve scarf like Mme Sazerat; and the oval curve
of her cheeks reminded me so strongly of people whom I
had seen at home that the suspicion crossed my mind
(though it was immediately banished) that in her causal
principle, in the molecules of her physical composition,
this lady was perhaps not substantially the Duchesse de
Guermantes, but that her body, in ignorance of the name
that people had given it, belonged to a certain female type

which included also the wives of doctors and tradesmen. "So that's Mme de Guermantes—that's all she is!" were the words underlying the attentive and astonished expression with which I gazed upon this image which, naturally enough, bore no resemblance to those that had so often, under the same title of "Mme de Guermantes," appeared in my dreams, since it had not, like the others, been formed arbitrarily by myself but had leapt to my eyes for the first time only a moment ago, here in church; an image which was not of the same nature, was not colourable at will like those others that allowed themselves to be impregnated with the amber hue of a sonorous syllable, but was so real that everything, down to the fiery little spot at the corner of her nose, attested to her subjection to the laws of life, as, in a transformation scene on the stage, a crease in the fairy's dress, a quivering of her tiny finger, betray the physical presence of a living actress, whereas we were uncertain, till then, whether we were not looking merely at a projection from a lantern.

But at the same time, I was endeavouring to apply to this image, which the prominent nose, the piercing eyes pinned down and fixed in my field of vision (perhaps because it was they that had first struck it, that had made the first impression on its surface, before I had had time to wonder whether the woman who thus appeared before me might possibly be Mme de Guermantes), to this fresh and unchanging image, the idea: "It's Mme de Guermantes"; but I succeeded only in making the idea pass between me and the image, as though they were two discs moving in separate planes with a space between. But this Mme de Guermantes of whom I had so often dreamed, now that I could see that she had a real existence inde-

pendent of myself, acquired an even greater power over
my imagination, which, paralysed for a moment by contact with a reality so different from what it had expected,
began to react and to say to me: "Great and glorious before the days of Charlemagne, the Guermantes had the
right of life and death over their vassals; the Duchesse de
Guermantes descends from Geneviève de Brabant. She
does not know, nor would she consent to know, any of
the people who are here today."

And then—oh, marvellous independence of the human gaze, tied to the human face by a cord so loose, so
long, so elastic that it can stray alone as far as it may
choose—while Mme de Guermantes sat in the chapel
above the tombs of her dead ancestors, her gaze wandered
here and there, rose to the capitals of the pillars, and even
rested momentarily upon myself, like a ray of sunlight
straying down the nave, but a ray of sunlight which, at
the moment when I received its caress, appeared conscious of where it fell. As for Mme de Guermantes herself, since she remained motionless, sitting like a mother
who affects not to notice the mischievous impudence and
the indiscreet advances of her children when, in the
course of their play, they accost people whom she does
not know, it was impossible for me to determine whether,
in the careless detachment of her soul, she approved or
condemned the vagrancy of her eyes.

I felt it to be important that she should not leave the
church before I had been able to look at her for long
enough, reminding myself that for years past I had regarded the sight of her as a thing eminently to be desired,
and I kept my eyes fixed on her, as though by gazing at
her I should be able to carry away and store up inside

myself the memory of that prominent nose, those red
cheeks, of all those details which struck me as so many
precious, authentic and singular items of information with
regard to her face. And now that all the thoughts I
brought to bear upon it (especially, perhaps—a form of
the instinct of self-preservation with which we guard everything that is best in ourselves—the familiar desire not
to have been disappointed) made me think it beautiful,
and I set her once again (since they were one and the
same person, this lady who sat before me and that
Duchesse de Guermantes whom I had hitherto conjured
up in my imagination) apart from that common run of
humanity with which the actual sight of her in the flesh
had made me for a moment confound her, I grew indignant when I heard people saying in the congregation
round me: "She's better looking than Mme Sazerat" or
"than Mlle Vinteuil," as though she was in any way comparable with them. And my eyes resting upon her fair
hair, her blue eyes, the lines of her neck, and overlooking
the features which might have reminded me of the faces
of other women, I cried out within myself as I admired
this deliberately unfinished sketch: "How lovely she is!
What true nobility! It is indeed a proud Guermantes, the
descendant of Geneviève de Brabant, that I have before
me!" And the attention which I focused on her face succeeded in isolating it so completely that today, when I call
that marriage ceremony to mind, I find it impossible to
visualise any single person who was present except her,
and the verger who answered me in the affirmative when
I inquired whether the lady was indeed Mme de Guermantes. But I can see her still quite clearly, especially at
the moment when the procession filed into the sacristy,

which was lit up by the intermittent warm sunshine of a
windy and rainy day and in which Mme de Guermantes
found herself in the midst of all those Combray people
whose names she did not even know, but whose inferior-
ity proclaimed her own supremacy too loudly for her not
to feel sincerely benevolent towards them, and whom she
might count on impressing even more forcibly by virtue
of her simplicity and graciousness. And so, since she
could not bring into play the deliberate glances, charged
with a definite meaning, which one directs towards people
one knows, but must allow her absent-minded thoughts
to flow continuously from her eyes in a stream of blue
light which she was powerless to contain, she was anxious
not to embarrass or to appear to be disdainful of those
humbler mortals whom it encountered on its way, on
whom it was constantly falling. I can still see, above her
mauve scarf, puffed and silky, the gentle astonishment in
her eyes, to which she had added, without daring to address it to anyone in particular, but so that everyone
might enjoy his share of it, a rather shy smile as of a
sovereign lady who seems to be making an apology for
her presence among the vassals whom she loves. This
smile fell upon me, who had never taken my eyes off her.
And remembering the glance which she had let fall upon
me during mass, blue as a ray of sunlight that had penetrated the window of Gilbert the Bad, I said to myself:
"She must have taken notice of me." I fancied that I had
found favour in her eyes, that she would continue to
think of me after she had left the church, and would perhaps feel sad that evening, at Guermantes, because of me.
And at once I fell in love with her, for if it is sometimes
enough to make us love a woman that she should look on

us with contempt, as I supposed Mlle Swann to have done, and that we should think that she can never be ours, sometimes, too, it is enough that she should look on us kindly, as Mme de Guermantes was doing, and that we should think of her as almost ours already. Her eyes waxed blue as a periwinkle flower, impossible to pluck, yet dedicated by her to me; and the sun, bursting out again from behind a threatening cloud and darting the full force of its rays on to the Square and into the sacristy, shed a geranium glow over the red carpet laid down for the wedding, across which Mme de Guermantes was smilingly advancing, and covered its woollen texture with a nap of rosy velvet, a bloom of luminosity, that sort of tenderness, of solemn sweetness in the pomp of a joyful celebration, which characterise certain pages of *Lohengrin*, certain paintings by Carpaccio, and make us understand how Baudelaire was able to apply to the sound of the trumpet the epithet "delicious."

How often, after that day, in the course of my walks along the Guermantes way, and with what an intensified melancholy, did I reflect on my lack of qualification for a literary career, and abandon all hope of ever becoming a famous author. The regrets that I felt for this, as I lingered behind to muse awhile on my own, made me suffer so acutely that, in order to banish them, my mind of its own accord, by a sort of inhibition in the face of pain, ceased entirely to think of verse-making, of fiction, of the poetic future on which my lack of talent precluded me from counting. Then, quite independently of all these literary preoccupations and in no way connected with them, suddenly a roof, a gleam of sunlight on a stone, the smell of a path would make me stop still, to enjoy the special

pleasure that each of them gave me, and also because they
appeared to be concealing, beyond what my eyes could
see, something which they invited me to come and take
but which despite all my efforts I never managed to discover. Since I felt that this something was to be found in
them, I would stand there motionless, looking, breathing,
endeavouring to penetrate with my mind beyond the
thing seen or smelt. And if I then had to hasten after my
grandfather, to continue my walk, I would try to recapture them by closing my eyes; I would concentrate on recalling exactly the line of the roof, the colour of the stone,
which, without my being able to understand why, had
seemed to me to be bursting, ready to open, to yield up
to me the secret treasure of which they were themselves
no more than the lids. It was certainly not impressions of
this kind that could restore the hope I had lost of succeeding one day in becoming an author and poet, for each
of them was associated with some material object devoid
of intellectual value and suggesting no abstract truth. But
at least they gave me an unreasoning pleasure, the illusion
of a sort of fecundity, and thereby distracted me from the
tedium, from the sense of my own impotence which I had
felt whenever I had sought a philosophic theme for some
great literary work. But so arduous was the task imposed
on my conscience by these impressions of form or scent
or colour—to try to perceive what lay hidden beneath
them—that I was not long in seeking an excuse which
would allow me to relax so strenuous an effort and to
spare myself the fatigue that it involved. As good luck
would have it, my parents would call me; I felt that I did
not, for the moment, enjoy the tranquillity necessary for
the successful pursuit of my researches, and that it would

be better to think no more of the matter until I reached home, and not to exhaust myself in the meantime to no purpose. And so I would concern myself no longer with the mystery that lay hidden in a shape or a perfume, quite at ease in my mind since I was taking it home with me, protected by its visible covering which I had imprinted on my mind and beneath which I should find it still alive, like the fish which, on days when I had been allowed to go out fishing, I used to carry back in my basket, covered by a layer of grass which kept them cool and fresh. Having reached home I would begin to think of something else, and so my mind would become littered (as my room was with the flowers that I had gathered on my walks, or the odds and ends that people had given me) with a mass of disparate images—the play of sunlight on a stone, a roof, the sound of a bell, the smell of fallen leaves—beneath which the reality I once sensed, but never had the will-power to discover and bring to light, has long since perished. Once, however, when we had prolonged our walk far beyond its ordinary limits, and so had been very glad to be overtaken half-way home, as afternoon darkened into evening, by Dr Percepied who, driving by at full speed in his carriage, had seen and recognised us, stopped, and made us jump in beside him, I received an impression of this sort which I did not abandon without getting to the bottom of it to some extent. I had been set on the box beside the coachman, and we were going like the wind because the doctor had still, before returning to Combray, to call at Martinville-le-Sec to see a patient at whose door it was agreed that we should wait for him. At a bend in the road I experienced, suddenly, that special pleasure which was un-

like any other, on catching sight of the twin steeples of
Martinville, bathed in the setting sun and constantly
changing their position with the movement of the carriage
and the windings of the road, and then of a third steeple,
that of Vieuxvicq, which, although separated from them
by a hill and a valley, and rising from rather higher
ground in the distance, appeared none the less to be
standing by their side.

In noticing and registering the shape of their spires,
their shifting lines, the sunny warmth of their surfaces, I
felt that I was not penetrating to the core of my impression, that something more lay behind that mobility, that
luminosity, something which they seemed at once to contain and to conceal.

The steeples appeared so distant, and we seemed to
be getting so little nearer them, that I was astonished
when, a few minutes later, we drew up outside the church
of Martinville. I did not know the reason for the pleasure
I had felt on seeing them upon the horizon, and the business of trying to discover that reason seemed to me irk-
some; I wanted to store away in my mind those shifting,
sunlit planes and, for the time being, to think of them no
more. And it is probable that, had I done so, those two
steeples would have gone to join the medley of trees and
roofs and scents and sounds I had noticed and set apart
because of the obscure pleasure they had given me which
I had never fully explored. I got down from the box to
talk to my parents while we waited for the doctor to reappear. Then it was time to set off again, and I resumed my
seat, turning my head to look back once more at the
steeples, of which, a little later, I caught a farewell
glimpse at a turn in the road. The coachman, who seemed

little inclined for conversation, having barely acknowledged my remarks, I was obliged, in default of other company, to fall back on my own, and to attempt to recapture
the vision of my steeples. And presently their outlines
and their sunlit surfaces, as though they had been a sort
of rind, peeled away; something of what they had concealed from me became apparent; a thought came into my
mind which had not existed for me a moment earlier,
framing itself in words in my head; and the pleasure
which the first sight of them had given me was so greatly
enhanced that, overpowered by a sort of intoxication, I
could no longer think of anything else. At that moment,
as we were already some way from Martinville, turning
my head I caught sight of them again, quite black this
time, for the sun had meanwhile set. From time to time a
turn in the road would sweep them out of sight; then they
came into view for the last time, and finally I could see
them no more.

Without admitting to myself that what lay hidden
behind the steeples of Martinville must be something
analogous to a pretty phrase, since it was in the form of
words which gave me pleasure that it had appeared to me,
I borrowed a pencil and some paper from the doctor, and
in spite of the jolting of the carriage, to appease my conscience and to satisfy my enthusiasm, composed the following little fragment, which I have since discovered and
now reproduce with only a slight revision here and there.

Alone, rising from the level of the plain, and seemingly lost in
that expanse of open country, the twin steeples of Martinville
rose towards the sky. Presently we saw three: springing into position in front of them with a bold leap, a third, dilatory steeple,
that of Vieuxvicq, had come to join them. The minutes passed,

we were travelling fast, and yet the three steeples were always a long way ahead of us, like three birds perched upon the plain, motionless and conspicuous in the sunlight. Then the steeple of Vieuxvicq drew aside, took its proper distance, and the steeples of Martinville remained alone, gilded by the light of the setting sun which, even at that distance, I could see playing and smiling upon their sloping sides. We had been so long in approaching them that I was thinking of the time that must still elapse before we could reach them when, of a sudden, the carriage turned a corner and set us down at their feet; and they had flung themselves so abruptly in our path that we had barely time to stop before being dashed against the porch.

We resumed our journey. We had left Martinville some little time, and the village, after accompanying us for a few seconds, had already disappeared, when, lingering alone on the horizon to watch our flight, its steeples and that of Vieuxvicq waved once again their sun-bathed pinnacles in token of farewell. Sometimes one would withdraw, so that the other two might watch us for a moment still; then the road changed direction, they veered in the evening light like three golden pivots, and vanished from my sight. But a little later, when we were already close to Combray, the sun having set meanwhile, I caught sight of them for the last time, far away, and seeming no more now than three flowers painted upon the sky above the low line of the fields. They made me think, too, of three maidens in a legend, abandoned in a solitary place over which night had begun to fall; and as we drew away from them at a gallop, I could see them timidly seeking their way, and after some awkward, stumbling movements of their noble silhouettes, drawing close to one another, gliding one behind another, forming now against the still rosy sky no more than a single dusky shape, charming and resigned, and so vanishing in the night.

I never thought again of this page, but at the moment when, in the corner of the box-seat where the doctor's coachman was in the habit of stowing in a hamper the poultry he had bought at Martinville market, I had fin-

ished writing it, I was so filled with happiness, I felt that
it had so entirely relieved my mind of its obsession with
the steeples and the mystery which lay behind them, that,
as though I myself were a hen and had just laid an egg, I
began to sing at the top of my voice.

All day long, during these walks, I had been able to
muse upon the pleasure of being the friend of the
Duchesse de Guermantes, of fishing for trout, of drifting
in a boat on the Vivonne; and, greedy for happiness, I
asked nothing more from life in such moments than that
it should consist always of a series of joyous afternoons.
But when, on our way home, I had caught sight of a farm
on the left of the road, at some distance from two other
farms which were themselves close together, from which,
to return to Combray, we need only turn down an avenue
of oaks bordered on one side by a series of orchard-closes
planted at regular intervals with apple-trees which cast
upon the ground, when they were lit by the setting sun,
the Japanese stencil of their shadows, suddenly my heart
would begin to pound, for I knew that in half an hour we
should be at home, and that, as was the rule on days
when we had taken the Guermantes way and dinner was
in consequence served later than usual, I should be sent
to bed as soon as I had swallowed my soup, and my
mother, kept at table just as though there had been company to dinner, would not come upstairs to say good
night to me in bed. The zone of melancholy which I then
entered was as distinct from the zone in which I had been
bounding with joy a moment before as, in certain skies, a
band of pink is separated, as though by a line invisibly
ruled, from a band of green or black. You may see a bird

flying across the pink; it draws near the border-line, touches it, enters and is lost upon the black. I was now so remote from the longings by which I had just been absorbed—to go to Guermantes, to travel, to live a life of happiness—that their fulfilment would have afforded me no pleasure. How readily would I have sacrificed them all, just to be able to cry all night long in Mamma's arms! Quivering with emotion, I could not take my anguished eyes from my mother's face, which would not appear that evening in the bedroom where I could see myself already lying, and I wished only that I were lying dead. And this state would persist until the morrow, when, the rays of morning leaning their bars of light, like the rungs of the gardener's ladder, against the wall overgrown with nasturtiums, which clambered up it as far as my window-sill, I would leap out of bed to run down at once into the garden, with no thought of the fact that evening must return, and with it the hour when I must leave my mother. And so it was from the Guermantes way that I learned to distinguish between these states which reign alternately within me, during certain periods, going so far as to divide each day between them, the one returning to dispossess the other with the regularity of a fever: contiguous, and yet so foreign to one another, so devoid of means of communication, that I can no longer understand, or even picture to myself, in one state what I have desired or dreaded or accomplished in the other.

So the Méséglise way and the Guermantes way remain for me linked with many of the little incidents of the life which, of all the various lives we lead concurrently, is the most episodic, the most full of vicissitudes; I mean the life of the mind. Doubtless it progresses within

us imperceptibly, and we had for a long time been
preparing for the discovery of the truths which have
changed its meaning and its aspect, have opened new
paths for us; but that preparation was unconscious; and
for us those truths date only from the day, from the
minute when they became apparent. The flowers which
played then among the grass, the water which rippled
past in the sunshine, the whole landscape which surrounded their apparition still lingers around the memory
of them with its unconscious or unheeding countenance;
and, certainly, when they were contemplated at length by
that humble passer-by, by that dreaming child—as the
face of a king is contemplated by a memorialist buried in
the crowd—that piece of nature, that corner of a garden
could never suppose that it would be thanks to him that
they would be elected to survive in all their most
ephemeral details; and yet the scent of hawthorn which
flits along the hedge from which, in a little while, the
dog-roses will have banished it, a sound of echoless footsteps on a gravel path, a bubble formed against the side
of a water-plant by the current of the stream and instantaneously bursting—all these my exaltation of mind has
borne along with it and kept alive through the succession
of the years, while all around them the paths have vanished and those who trod them, and even the memory of
those who trod them, are dead. Sometimes the fragment
of landscape thus transported into the present will detach
itself in such isolation from all associations that it floats
uncertainly in my mind like a flowering Delos, and I am
unable to say from what place, from what time—perhaps,
quite simply, from what dream—it comes. But it is pre-
eminently as the deepest layer of my mental soil, as the

firm ground on which I still stand, that I regard the
Méséglise and Guermantes ways. It is because I believed
in things and in people while I walked along those paths
that the things and the people they made known to me
are the only ones that I still take seriously and that still
bring me joy. Whether it is because the faith which creates has ceased to exist in me, or because reality takes
shape in the memory alone, the flowers that people show
me nowadays for the first time never seem to me to be
true flowers. The Méséglise way with its lilacs, its
hawthorns, its cornflowers, its poppies, its apple-trees, the
Guermantes way with its river full of tadpoles, its water-
lilies and its buttercups, constituted for me for all time
the image of the landscape in which I should like to live,
in which my principal requirements are that I may go
fishing, drift idly in a boat, see the ruins of Gothic fortifi-
cations, and find among the cornfields—like Saint-André-
des-Champs—an old church, monumental, rustic, and
golden as a haystack; and the cornflowers, the hawthorns,
the apple-trees which I may still happen, when I travel, to
encounter in the fields, because they are situated at the
same depth, on the level of my past life, at once establish
contact with my heart. And yet, because there is an element of individuality in places, if I were seized with a desire to revisit the Guermantes way, it would not be satisfied were I to be led to the banks of a river in which there
were water-lilies as beautiful as, or even more beautiful
than, those in the Vivonne, any more than on my return
home in the evening—at the hour when there awakened
in me that anguish which later transfers itself to the passion of love, and may even become its inseparable com-

panion—I should have wished for a mother more beautiful and more intelligent than my own to come and say
good night to me. No: just as the one thing necessary to
send me to sleep contented—in that untroubled peace
which no mistress, in later years, has ever been able to
give me, since one has doubts of them even at the moment when one believes in them, and never can possess
their hearts as I used to receive, in a kiss, my mother's
heart, whole and entire, without qualm or reservation,
without the smallest residue of an intention that was not
for me alone—was that it should be she who came to me,
that it should be her face that leaned over me, her face on
which there was something below the eye that was apparently a blemish, and that I loved as much as all the
rest—so what I want to see again is the Guermantes way
as I knew it, with the farm that stood a little apart from
the two neighbouring farms, huddled side by side, at the
entrance to the oak avenue; those meadows in which,
when they are burnished by the sun to the luminescence
of a pond, the leaves of the apple-trees are reflected; that
whole landscape whose individuality grips me sometimes
at night, in my dreams, with a power that is almost un-
canny, but of which I can discover no trace when I
awake.

No doubt, by virtue of having permanently and indissolubly united so many different impressions in my
mind, simply because they made me experience them at
the same time, the Méséglise and Guermantes ways left
me exposed, in later life, to much disillusionment and
even to many mistakes. For often I have wished to see a
person again without realising that it was simply because

that person recalled to me a hedge of hawthorns in blossom, and I have been led to believe, and to make someone else believe, in a renewal of affection, by what was no more than an inclination to travel. But by the same token, and by their persistence in those of my present-day impressions to which they can still be linked, they give those impressions a foundation, a depth, a dimension lacking from the rest. They invest them, too, with a charm, a significance which is for me alone. When, on a summer evening, the melodious sky growls like a tawny lion, and everyone is complaining of the storm, it is the memory of the Méséglise way that makes me stand alone in ecstasy, inhaling, through the noise of the falling rain, the lingering scent of invisible lilacs.

Thus would I often lie until morning, dreaming of the old days at Combray, of my melancholy and wakeful evenings there, of other days besides, the memory of which had been more recently restored to me by the taste—by what would have been called at Combray the "perfume"—of a cup of tea, and, by an association of memories, of a story which, many years after I had left the little place, had been told me of a love affair in which Swann had been involved before I was born, with a precision of detail which it is often easier to obtain for the lives of people who have been dead for centuries than for those of our own most intimate friends, an accuracy which it seems as impossible to attain as it seemed impossible to speak from one town to another, before we knew of the contrivance by which that impossibility has been overcome. All these memories, superimposed upon one another, now formed a single mass, but had not so far coalesced that I could not discern between them—between

my oldest, my instinctive memories, and those others, inspired more recently by a taste or "perfume," and finally
those which were actually the memories of another person
from whom I had acquired them at second hand—if not
real fissures, real geological faults, at least that veining,
that variegation of colouring, which in certain rocks, in
certain blocks of marble, points to differences of origin,
age, and formation.

It is true that, when morning drew near, I would long
have settled the brief uncertainty of my waking dream; I
would know in what room I was actually lying, would
have reconstructed it around me in the darkness, and—
fixing my bearings by memory alone, or with the assistance of a feeble glimmer of light at the foot of which I
placed the curtains and the window—would have reconstructed it complete and furnished, as an architect and an
upholsterer might do, keeping the original plan of the
doors and windows; would have replaced the mirrors and
set the chest of drawers on its accustomed site. But
scarcely had daylight itself—and no longer the gleam
from a last, dying ember on a brass curtain-rod which I
had mistaken for daylight—traced across the darkness, as
with a stroke of chalk across a blackboard, its first white,
correcting ray, than the window, with its curtains, would
leave the frame of the doorway in which I had erro-
neously placed it, while, to make room for it, the writing-
table, which my memory had clumsily installed where the
window ought to be, would hurry off at full speed,
thrusting before it the fireplace and sweeping aside the
wall of the passage; a little courtyard would occupy the
place where, a moment earlier, my dressing-room had
lain, and the dwelling-place which I had built up for my-

self in the darkness would have gone to join all those other dwellings glimpsed in the whirlpool of awakening, put to flight by that pale sign traced above my window-curtains by the uplifted forefinger of dawn.

Part Two

SWANN IN LOVE

To admit you to the "little nucleus," the "little group,"
the "little clan" at the Verdurins', one condition sufficed,
but that one was indispensable: you must give tacit ad-
herence to a Creed one of whose articles was that the
young pianist whom Mme Verdurin had taken under her
patronage that year and of whom she said "Really, it
oughtn't to be allowed, to play Wagner as well as that!"
licked both Planté and Rubinstein hollow, and that Dr
Cottard was a more brilliant diagnostician than Potain.
Each "new recruit" whom the Verdurins failed to persuade that the evenings spent by other people, in other
houses than theirs, were as dull as ditch-water, saw himself banished forthwith. Women being in this respect
more rebellious than men, more reluctant to lay aside all
worldly curiosity and the desire to find out for themselves
whether other salons might not sometimes be as entertaining, and the Verdurins feeling, moreover, that this
critical spirit and this demon of frivolity might, by their
contagion, prove fatal to the orthodoxy of the little
church, they had been obliged to expel, one after another,
all those of the "faithful" who were of the female sex.

Apart from the doctor's young wife, they were reduced almost exclusively that season (for all that Mme
Verdurin herself was a thoroughly virtuous woman who
came of a respectable middle-class family, excessively rich
and wholly undistinguished, with which she had gradually
and of her own accord severed all connection) to a young

woman almost of the *demi-monde*, a Mme de Crécy, whom Mme Verdurin called by her Christian name, Odette, and pronounced a "love," and to the pianist's aunt, who looked as though she had, at one period, "answered the door": ladies quite ignorant of society, who in their naïvety had so easily been led to believe that the Princesse de Sagan and the Duchesse de Guermantes were obliged to pay large sums of money to other poor wretches in order to have anyone at their dinner-parties, that if somebody had offered to procure them an invitation to the house of either of those noblewomen, the concierge and the cocotte would have contemptuously declined.

The Verdurins never invited you to dinner; you had your "place laid" there. There was never any programme for the evening's entertainment. The young pianist would play, but only if "the spirit moved him," for no one was forced to do anything, and, as M. Verdurin used to say: "We're all friends here. Liberty Hall, you know!" If the pianist suggested playing the Ride of the Valkyries or the Prelude to *Tristan*, Mme Verdurin would protest, not because the music was displeasing to her, but, on the contrary, because it made too violent an impression on her. "Then you want me to have one of my headaches? You know quite well it's the same every time he plays that. I know what I'm in for. Tomorrow, when I want to get up—nothing doing!" If he was not going to play they talked, and one of the friends—usually the painter who was in favour there that year—would "spin," as M. Verdurin put it, "a damned funny yarn that made 'em all split with laughter," and especially Mme Verdurin, who had such an inveterate habit of taking literally the figurative descriptions of her emotions that Dr Cottard (then a promising young practitioner) had once had to reset her jaw, which she had dislocated from laughing too much.

Evening dress was barred, because you were all "good pals" and didn't want to look like the "boring people" who were to be avoided like the plague and only asked to the big evenings, which were given as seldom as possible and then only if it would amuse the painter or make the musician better known. The rest of the time you were quite happy playing charades and having supper in fancy dress, and there was no need to mingle any alien ingredient with the little "clan."

But as the "good pals" came to take a more and more prominent place in Mme Verdurin's life, the bores, the outcasts, grew to include everybody and everything that kept her friends away from her, that made them sometimes plead previous engagements, the mother of one, the professional duties of another, the "little place in the country" or the ill-health of a third. If Dr Cottard felt bound to leave as soon as they rose from table, so as to go back to some patient who was seriously ill, "Who knows," Mme Verdurin would say, "it might do him far more good if you didn't go disturbing him again this evening; he'll have a good night without you; tomorrow morning you can go round early and you'll find him cured." From the beginning of December she was sick with anxiety at the thought that the "faithful" might "defect" on Christmas and New Year's Days. The pianist's aunt insisted that he must accompany her, on the latter, to a family dinner at her mother's.

"You don't suppose she'll die, your mother," exclaimed Mme Verdurin bitterly, "if you don't have dinner with her on New Year's Day, like people in the *provinces!*"

Her uneasiness was kindled again in Holy Week: "Now you, Doctor, you're a sensible, broad-minded man; you'll come of course on Good Friday, just like any other day?" she said to Cottard in the first year of the little "nucleus," in a loud and confident voice, as though there could be no doubt of his answer. But she trembled as she waited for it, for if he did not come she might find herself condemned to dine alone.

"I shall come on Good Friday—to say good-bye to you, for we're off to spend the holidays in Auvergne."

"In Auvergne? To be eaten alive by fleas and vermin! A fine lot of good that will do you!" And after a solemn pause: "If you'd only told us, we would have tried to get up a party, and all gone there together in comfort."

And so, too, if one of the "faithful" had a friend, or one of the ladies a young man, who was liable, now and then, to make them miss an evening, the Verdurins, who were not in the least afraid of a woman's having a lover, provided that she had him in their company, loved him in their company and did not prefer him to their company, would say: "Very well, then, bring your friend along." And he would be engaged on probation, to see whether he was willing to have no secrets from Mme Verdurin, whether he was susceptible of being enrolled in the "little clan." If he failed to pass, the faithful one who had introduced him would be taken on one side, and would be tactfully assisted to break with the friend or lover or mistress. But if the test proved satisfactory, the newcomer would in turn be numbered among the "faithful." And so when, that year, the *demi-mondaine* told M. Verdurin that she had made the acquaintance of such a charming man, M. Swann, and hinted that he would very much like to be allowed to come, M. Verdurin carried the request at once to his wife. (He never formed an opinion on any subject until she had formed hers, it being his special function to carry out her wishes and those of the "faithful" generally, which he did with boundless ingenuity.)

"My dear, Mme de Crécy has something to say to you. She would like to bring one of her friends here, a M. Swann. What do you say?"

"Why, as if anybody could refuse anything to a little angel like that. Be quiet; no one asked your opinion. I tell you you're an angel."

"Just as you like," replied Odette, in an affected tone, and then added: "You know I'm not *fishing for compliments*."[8]

"Very well; bring your friend, if he's nice."

Now there was nothing whatsoever in common between the "little nucleus" and the society which Swann frequented, and true socialites would have thought it hardly worth while to occupy so exceptional a position in the fashionable world in order to end up with an introduction to the Verdurins. But Swann was so fond of women that, once he had got to know more or less all the women of the aristocracy and they had nothing more to teach him, he had ceased to regard those naturalisation papers, almost a patent of nobility, which the Faubourg Saint-Germain had bestowed upon him, except as a sort of negotiable bond, a letter of credit with no intrinsic value but which enabled him to improvise a status for himself in some out-of-the-way place in the country, or in some obscure quarter of Paris, where the good-looking

daughter of a local squire or town clerk had taken his
fancy. For at such times desire, or love, would revive in
him a feeling of vanity from which he was now quite free
in his everyday life (although it was doubtless this feeling
which had originally prompted him towards the career as
a man of fashion in which he had squandered his intellectual gifts on frivolous amusements and made use of his
erudition in matters of art only to advise society ladies
what pictures to buy and how to decorate their houses),
which made him eager to shine, in the eyes of any unknown beauty he had fallen for, with an elegance which
the name Swann did not in itself imply. And he was most
eager when the unknown beauty was in humble circumstances. Just as it is not by other men of intelligence that
an intelligent man is afraid of being thought a fool, so it
is not by a nobleman but by an oaf that a man of fashion
is afraid of finding his social value underrated. Three-
quarters of the mental ingenuity and the mendacious
boasting squandered ever since the world began by people
who are only cheapened thereby, have been aimed at inferiors. And Swann, who behaved simply and casually with
a duchess, would tremble for fear of being despised, and
would instantly begin to pose, when in the presence of a
housemaid.

Unlike so many people who, either from lack of energy or else from a resigned sense of the obligation laid
upon them by their social grandeur to remain moored like
house-boats to a particular point on the shore of life, abstain from the pleasures which are offered to them outside
the worldly situation in which they remain confined until
the day of their death, and are content, in the end, to describe as pleasures, for want of any better, those mediocre

distractions, that just bearable tedium which it encom-
passes, Swann did not make an effort to find attractive the
women with whom he spent his time, but sought to
spend his time with women whom he had already found
attractive. And as often as not they were women whose
beauty was of a distinctly vulgar type, for the physical
qualities which he instinctively sought were the direct opposite of those he admired in the women painted or
sculpted by his favourite masters. Depth of character, or a
melancholy expression, would freeze his senses, which
were, however, instantly aroused at the sight of healthy,
abundant, rosy flesh.

   If on his travels he met a family whom it would have
been more correct for him to make no attempt to cultivate, but among whom he glimpsed a woman possessed
of a special charm that was new to him, to remain on his
"high horse" and to stave off the desire she had kindled
in him, to substitute a different pleasure for the pleasure
which he might have tasted in her company by writing to
invite one of his former mistresses to come and join him,
would have seemed to him as cowardly an abdication in
the face of life, as stupid a renunciation of a new happiness as if, instead of visiting the country where he was, he
had shut himself up in his own rooms and looked at
views of Paris. He did not immure himself in the edifice
of his social relations, but had made of them, so as to be
able to set it up afresh upon new foundations wherever a
woman might take his fancy, one of those collapsible tents
which explorers carry about with them. Any part of it
that was not portable or could not be adapted to some
fresh pleasure he would have given away for nothing,
however enviable it might appear to others. How often

had his credit with a duchess, built up over the years by her desire to ingratiate herself with him without having found an opportunity to do so, been squandered in a moment by his calling upon her, in an indiscreetly worded message, for a recommendation by telegraph which would put him in touch at once with one of her stewards whose daughter he had noticed in the country, just as a starving man might barter a diamond for a crust of bread. Indeed he would laugh about it afterwards, for there was in his nature, redeemed by many rare refinements, an element of caddishness. Then he belonged to that class of intelligent men who have led a life of idleness, and who seek a consolation and perhaps an excuse in the notion that their idleness offers to their intelligence objects as worthy of interest as any that might be offered by art or learning, the notion that "Life" contains situations more interesting and more romantic than all the romances ever written. So, at least, he affirmed, and had no difficulty in persuading even the most sharp-witted of his society friends, notably the Baron de Charlus, whom he liked to entertain with accounts of the intriguing adventures that had befallen him, such as when he had met a woman in a train and taken her home with him, before discovering that she was the sister of a reigning monarch in whose hands were gathered at that moment all the threads of European politics, of which Swann was thus kept informed in the most delightful fashion, or when, by the complex play of circumstances, it depended upon the choice which this conclave was about to make whether he might or might not become the lover of somebody's cook.

It was not only the brilliant phalanx of virtuous dowagers, generals and academicians with whom he was most intimately associated that Swann so cynically compelled to serve him as panders. All his friends were accustomed to receive, from time to time, letters calling on them for a word of recommendation or introduction, with a diplomatic adroitness which, persisting throughout all his successive love affairs and varying pretexts, revealed, more glaringly than the clumsiest indiscretion, a permanent disposition and an identical quest. I used often to be told, many years later, when I began to take an interest in his character because of the similarities which, in wholly different respects, it offered to my own, how, when he used to write to my grandfather (who had not yet become my grandfather, for it was about the time of my birth that Swann's great love affair began, and it made a long interruption in his amatory practices), the latter, recognising his friend's handwriting on the envelope, would exclaim: "Here's Swann asking for something. On guard!" And, either from distrust or from the unconscious spirit of devilry which urges us to offer a thing only to those who do not want it, my grandparents would offer a blunt refusal to the most easily satisfied of his requests, as when he begged them to introduce him to a girl who dined with them every Sunday, and whom they were obliged, whenever Swann mentioned her, to pretend that they no longer saw, although they would be wondering all through the week whom they could invite with her, and often ended up with no one, sooner than get in touch with the man who would so gladly have accepted.

Occasionally a couple of my grandparents' acquaintance, who had been complaining for some time that they no longer saw Swann, would announce with satisfaction, and perhaps with a slight inclination to make my grand-

parents envious of them, that he had suddenly become as
charming as he could possibly be, and was never out of
their house. My grandfather would not want to shatter
their pleasant illusion, but would look at my grandmother
as he hummed the air of:

> What is this mystery?
> I can understand nothing of it,

or of:

> Fugitive vision . . .

or of:

> In matters such as this
> It's better to close one's eyes.

A few months later, if my grandfather asked Swann's
new friend: "What about Swann? Do you still see as
much of him as ever?" the other's face would fall: "Never
mention his name to me again!"

"But I thought you were such friends . . ."

He had been intimate in this way for several months
with some cousins of my grandmother, dining almost every evening at their house. Suddenly, and without any
warning, he ceased to appear. They supposed him to be
ill, and the lady of the house was about to send to inquire
for him when she found in the pantry a letter in his hand,
which her cook had left by accident in the housekeeping
book. In this he announced that he was leaving Paris and
would not be able to come to the house again. The cook
had been his mistress, and on breaking off relations she
was the only member of the household whom he had
thought it necessary to inform.

But when his mistress of the moment was a woman of rank, or at least one whose birth was not so lowly nor her position so irregular that he was unable to arrange for her reception in "society," then for her sake he would return to it, but only to the particular orbit in which she moved or into which he had drawn her. "No good depending on Swann for this evening," people would say. "Don't you remember, it's his American's night at the Opera?" He would secure invitations for her to the most exclusive salons, to those houses where he himself went regularly for weekly dinners or for poker; every evening, after a slight wave imparted to his stiff red hair had tempered with a certain softness the ardour of his bold green eyes, he would select a flower for his buttonhole and set out to meet his mistress at the house of one or other of the women of his circle; and then, thinking of the affection and admiration which the fashionable people, by whom he was so highly sought-after and whom he would meet again there, would lavish on him in the presence of the woman he loved, he would find a fresh charm in that worldly existence which had begun to pall, but whose substance, pervaded and warmly coloured by the bright flame that now flickered in its midst, seemed to him beautiful and rare since he had incorporated in it a new love.

But, whereas each of these liaisons, or each of these flirtations, had been the realisation, more or less complete, of a dream born of the sight of a face or a body which Swann had spontaneously, without effort on his part, found attractive, on the contrary when, one evening at the theatre, he was introduced to Odette de Crécy by an old friend of his, who had spoken of her as a ravishing crea-

ture with whom he might possibly come to an understanding, but had made her out to be harder of conquest
than she actually was in order to appear to have done him
a bigger favour by the introduction, she had struck Swann
not, certainly, as being devoid of beauty, but as endowed
with a kind of beauty which left him indifferent, which
aroused in him no desire, which gave him, indeed, a sort
of physical repulsion, as one of those women of whom all
of us can cite examples, different for each of us, who are
the converse of the type which our senses demand. Her
profile was too sharp, her skin too delicate, her cheekbones were too prominent, her features too tightly drawn,
to be attractive to him. Her eyes were beautiful, but so
large they seemed to droop beneath their own weight,
strained the rest of her face and always made her appear
unwell or in a bad mood. Some time after this introduction at the theatre she had written to ask Swann whether
she might see his collections, which would very much interest her, "an ignorant woman with a taste for beautiful
things," adding that she felt she would know him better
when once she had seen him in his *"home,"*[9] where she
imagined him to be "so comfortable with his tea and his
books," though she had to admit that she was surprised
that he should live in a neighbourhood which must be so
depressing, and was "not nearly *smart* enough for such a
very *smart* man." And when he allowed her to come she
had said to him as she left how sorry she was to have
stayed so short a time in a house into which she was so
glad to have found her way at last, speaking of him as
though he had meant something more to her than the rest
of the people she knew, and appearing to establish between their two selves a kind of romantic bond which had

made him smile. But at the time of life, tinged already with disenchantment, which Swann was approaching, when a man can content himself with being in love for the pleasure of loving without expecting too much in return, this mutual sympathy, if it is no longer as in early youth the goal towards which love inevitably tends, is nevertheless bound to it by so strong an association of ideas that it may well become the cause of love if it manifests itself first. In his younger days a man dreams of possessing the heart of the woman whom he loves; later, the feeling that he possesses a woman's heart may be enough to make him fall in love with her. And so, at an age when it would appear—since one seeks in love before everything else a subjective pleasure—that the taste for a woman's beauty must play the largest part in it, love may come into being, love of the most physical kind, without any foundation in desire. At this time of life one has already been wounded more than once by the darts of love; it no longer evolves by itself, obeying its own incomprehensible and fatal laws, before our passive and astonished hearts. We come to its aid, we falsify it by memory and by suggestion. Recognising one of its symptoms, we remember and re-create the rest. Since we know its song, which is engraved on our hearts in its entirety, there is no need for a woman to repeat the opening strains—filled with the admiration which beauty inspires—for us to remember what follows. And if she begins in the middle— where hearts are joined and where it sings of our existing, henceforward, for one another only—we are well enough attuned to that music to be able to take it up and follow our partner without hesitation at the appropriate passage.

Odette de Crécy came again to see Swann; her visits

grew more frequent, and doubtless each visit revived the sense of disappointment which he felt at the sight of a face whose details he had somewhat forgotten in the interval, not remembering it as either so expressive or, in spite of her youth, so faded; he used to regret, while she was talking to him, that her really considerable beauty was not of the kind which he spontaneously admired. It must be remarked that Odette's face appeared thinner and sharper than it actually was, because the forehead and the upper part of the cheeks, that smooth and almost plane surface, were covered by the masses of hair which women wore at that period drawn forward in a fringe, raised in crimped waves and falling in stray locks over the ears; while as for her figure—and she was admirably built—it was impossible to make out its continuity (on account of the fashion then prevailing, and in spite of her being one of the best-dressed women in Paris) so much did the corsage, jutting out as though over an imaginary stomach and ending in a sharp point, beneath which bulged out the balloon of her double skirts, give a woman the appearance of being composed of different sections badly fitted together; to such an extent did the frills, the flounces, the inner bodice follow quite independently, according to the whim of their designer or the consistency of their material, the line which led them to the bows, the festoons of lace, the fringes of dangling jet beads, or carried them along the busk, but nowhere attached themselves to the living creature, who, according as the architecture of these fripperies drew them towards or away from her own, found herself either strait-laced to suffocation or else completely buried.

But, after Odette had left him, Swann would think

with a smile of her telling how the time would drag until he allowed her to come again; he remembered the anxious, timid way in which she had once begged him that it might not be too long, and the way she had gazed at him then, with a look of shy entreaty which gave her a touching air beneath the bunches of artificial pansies fastened in the front of her round bonnet of white straw, tied with a ribbon of black velvet. "And won't you," she had ventured, "come just once and have tea with me?" He had pleaded pressure of work, an essay—which, in reality, he had abandoned years ago—on Vermeer of Delft. "I know that I'm quite useless," she had replied, "a pitiful creature like me beside a learned great man like you. I should be like the frog in the fable! And yet I should so much like to learn, to know things, to be initiated. What fun it would be to become a regular bookworm, to bury my nose in a lot of old papers!" she had added, with the self-satisfied air which an elegant woman adopts when she insists that her one desire is to undertake, without fear of soiling her fingers, some grubby task, such as cooking the dinner, "really getting down to it" herself. "You'll only laugh at me, but this painter who stops you from seeing me" (she meant Vermeer), "I've never even heard of him; is he alive still? Can I see any of his things in Paris, so as to have some idea of what's going on behind that great brow which works so hard, that head which I feel sure is always puzzling away about things; to be able to say 'There, that's what he's thinking about!' What a joy it would be to be able to help you with your work."

He had excused himself on the grounds of his fear of forming new friendships, which he gallantly described as his fear of being made unhappy. "You're afraid of affec-

tion? How odd that is, when I go about seeking nothing
else, and would give my soul to find it!" she had said, so
naturally and with such an air of conviction that he had
been genuinely touched. "Some woman must have made
you suffer. And you think that the rest are all like her.
She can't have understood you: you're such an exceptional
person. That's what I liked about you from the start; I
felt that you weren't like everybody else."

"And then, besides, you too," he had said to her, "I
know what women are; you must have a whole heap of
things to do, and never any time to spare."

"I? Why, I never have anything to do. I'm always
free, and I always will be free if you want me. At whatever hour of the day or night it may suit you to see me,
just send for me, and I shall be only too delighted to
come. Will you do that? Do you know what would be
nice—if I were to introduce you to Mme Verdurin, where
I go every evening. Just fancy our meeting there, and my
thinking that it was a little for my sake that you had
come."

And doubtless, in thus remembering their conversations, in thinking about her thus when he was alone, he
was simply turning over her image among those of countless other women in his romantic day-dreams; but if,
thanks to some accidental circumstance (or even perhaps
without that assistance, for the circumstance which presents itself at the moment when a mental state, hitherto
latent, makes itself felt, may well have had no influence
whatsoever upon that state), the image of Odette de
Crécy came to absorb the whole of these day-dreams, if
the memory of her could no longer be eliminated from
them, then her bodily imperfections would no longer be

of the least importance, nor would the conformity of her body, more or less than any other, to the requirements of Swann's taste, since, having become the body of the woman he loved, it must henceforth be the only one capable of causing him joy or anguish.

It so happened that my grandfather had known— which was more than could be said of any of their actual acquaintance—the family of these Verdurins. But he had entirely severed his connexion with the "young Verdurin," as he called him, considering him more or less to have fallen—though without losing hold of his millions— among the riff-raff of Bohemia. One day he received a letter from Swann asking whether he could put him in touch with the Verdurins: "On guard! on guard!" my grandfather exclaimed as he read it, "I'm not at all surprised; Swann was bound to finish up like this. A nice lot of people! I cannot do what he asks, because in the first place I no longer know the gentleman in question. Be sides, there must be a woman in it somewhere, and I never get mixed up in such matters. Ah, well, we shall see some fun if Swann begins running after the young Verdurins."

And on my grandfather's refusal to act as sponsor, it was Odette herself who had taken Swann to the house.

The Verdurins had had dining with them, on the day when Swann made his first appearance, Dr and Mme Cottard, the young pianist and his aunt, and the painter then in favour, and these were joined, in the course of the evening, by a few more of the "faithful."

Dr Cottard was never quite certain of the tone in which he ought to reply to any observation, or whether the speaker was jesting or in earnest. And so by way of

precaution he would embellish all his facial expressions
with the offer of a conditional, a provisional smile whose
expectant subtlety would exonerate him from the charge
of being a simpleton, if the remark addressed to him
should turn out to have been facetious. But as he must
also be prepared to face the alternative, he dared not allow this smile to assert itself positively on his features,
and you would see there a perpetually flickering uncertainty, in which could be deciphered the question that he
never dared to ask: "Do you really mean that?" He was
no more confident of the manner in which he ought to
conduct himself in the street, or indeed in life generally,
than he was in a drawing-room; and he might be seen
greeting passers-by, carriages, and anything that occurred
with a knowing smile which absolved his subsequent behaviour of all impropriety, since it proved, if it should
turn out unsuited to the occasion, that he was well aware
of that, and that if he had assumed a smile, the jest was a
secret of his own.

On all those points, however, where a plain question
appeared to him to be permissible, the doctor was unsparing in his endeavours to cultivate the wilderness of his ignorance and uncertainty and to perfect his education.

So it was that, following the advice given him by a
wise mother on his first coming up to the capital from his
provincial home, he would never let pass either a figure of
speech or a proper name that was new to him without an
effort to secure the fullest information upon it.

As regards figures of speech, he was insatiable in his
thirst for knowledge, for, often imagining them to have a
more definite meaning than was actually the case, he
would want to know what exactly was meant by those

which he most frequently heard used: "devilish pretty,"
"blue blood," "living it up," "the day of reckoning," "the
glass of fashion," "to give a free hand," "to be absolutely
floored," and so forth; and in what particular circumstances he himself might make use of them in conversation. Failing these, he would adorn it with puns and other
plays on words which he had learned by rote. As for unfamiliar names which were uttered in his hearing, he used
merely to repeat them in a questioning tone, which he
thought would suffice to procure him explanations for
which he would not ostensibly be seeking.

Since he was completely lacking in the critical faculty
on which he prided himself in everything, the refinement
of good breeding which consists in assuring someone
whom you are obliging, without expecting to be believed,
that it is really you who are obliged to him, was wasted
on Cottard, who took everything he heard in its literal
sense. Blind though she was to his faults, Mme Verdurin
was genuinely irritated, though she continued to regard
him as brilliantly clever, when, after she had invited him
to see and hear Sarah Bernhardt from a stage box, and
had said politely: "It's so good of you to have come, Doctor, especially as I'm sure you must often have heard
Sarah Bernhardt; and besides, I'm afraid we're rather too
near the stage," the doctor, who had come into the box
with a smile which waited before affirming itself or vanishing from his face until some authoritative person
should enlighten him as to the merits of the spectacle,
replied: "To be sure, we're far too near the stage, and one
is beginning to get sick of Sarah Bernhardt. But you expressed a wish that I should come. And your wish is my
command. I'm only too glad to be able to do you this lit-

tle service. What would one not do to please you, you are so kind." And he went on, "Sarah Bernhardt—she's what they call the Golden Voice, isn't she? They say she sets the house on fire. That's an odd expression, isn't it?" in the hope of an enlightening commentary which, however, was not forthcoming.

"D'you know," Mme Verdurin had said to her husband, "I believe we're on the wrong tack when we belittle what we give to the Doctor. He's a scholar who lives in a world of his own; he has no idea what things are worth, and he accepts everything that we say as gospel."

"I never dared to mention it," M. Verdurin had answered, "but I've noticed the same thing myself." And on the following New Year's Day, instead of sending Dr Cottard a ruby that cost three thousand francs and pretending it was a mere trifle, M. Verdurin bought an artificial stone for three hundred, and let it be understood that it was something almost impossible to match.

When Mme Verdurin had announced that they were to see M. Swann that evening, "Swann!" the doctor had exclaimed in a tone rendered brutal by his astonishment, for the smallest piece of news would always take him utterly unawares though he imagined himself to be prepared for any eventuality. And seeing that no one answered him, "Swann! Who on earth is Swann?" he shouted, in a frenzy of anxiety which subsided as soon as Mme Verdurin had explained, "Why, the friend Odette told us about."

"Ah, good, good; that's all right, then," answered the doctor, at once mollified. As for the painter, he was overjoyed at the prospect of Swann's appearing at the Verdurins', because he supposed him to be in love with

Odette, and was always ready to encourage amorous liaisons. "Nothing amuses me more than match-making,"
he confided to Cottard. "I've brought off quite a few,
even between women!"

In telling the Verdurins that Swann was extremely
"smart," Odette had alarmed them with the prospect of
another "bore." When he arrived, however, he made an
excellent impression, an indirect cause of which, though
they did not know it, was his familiarity with the best society. He had, indeed, one of the advantages which men
who have lived and moved in society enjoy over those,
however intelligent, who have not, namely that they no
longer see it transfigured by the longing or repulsion
which it inspires, but regard it as of no importance. Their
good nature, freed from all taint of snobbishness and
from the fear of seeming too friendly, grown independent,
in fact, has the ease, the grace of movement of a trained
gymnast each of whose supple limbs will carry out precisely what is required without any clumsy participation
by the rest of his body. The simple and elementary gestures of a man of the world as he courteously holds out
his hand to the unknown youth who is introduced to him,
or bows discreetly to the ambassador to whom he is introduced, had gradually pervaded the whole of Swann's social deportment without his being conscious of it, so that
in the company of people from a lower social sphere, such
as the Verdurins and their friends, he displayed an instinctive alacrity, made amiable overtures, from which in
their view a "bore" would have refrained. He showed a
momentary coldness only on meeting Dr Cottard; for,
seeing him wink at him with an ambiguous smile, before
they had yet spoken to one another (a grimace which Cot-

tard styled "wait and see"), Swann supposed that the doctor recognised him from having met him already, probably in some haunt of pleasure, though these he himself
very rarely visited, never having lived a life of debauch-
ery. Regarding such an allusion as in bad taste, especially
in front of Odette, whose opinion of himself it might easily alter for the worse, Swann assumed his most icy manner. But when he learned that a lady standing near him
was Mme Cottard, he decided that so young a husband
would not deliberately have hinted at amusements of that
order in his wife's presence, and so ceased to interpret the
doctor's expression in the sense which he had at first suspected. The painter at once invited Swann to visit his studio with Odette; Swann thought him very civil. "Perhaps
you will be more highly favoured than I have been," said
Mme Verdurin in a tone of mock resentment, "perhaps
you'll be allowed to see Cottard's portrait" (which she
had commissioned from the painter). "Take care, Master
Biche," she reminded the painter, whom it was a time-
honoured pleasantry to address as "Master," "to catch
that nice look in his eyes, that witty little twinkle. You
know what I want to have most of all is his smile; that's
what I've asked you to paint—the portrait of his smile."
And since the phrase struck her as noteworthy, she repeated it very loud, so as to make sure that as many as
possible of her guests should hear it, and even made use
of some vague pretext to draw the circle closer before she
uttered it again. Swann begged to be introduced to everyone, even to an old friend of the Verdurins called Saniette, whose shyness, simplicity and good-nature had lost
him most of the consideration he had earned for his skill
in palaeography, his large fortune, and the distinguished

family to which he belonged. When he spoke, his words
came out in a burble which was delightful to hear because
one felt that it indicated not so much a defect of speech
as a quality of the soul, as it were a survival from the age
of innocence which he had never wholly outgrown. All
the consonants which he was unable to pronounce seemed
like harsh utterances of which his gentle lips were incapable. In asking to be introduced to M. Saniette, Swann
gave Mme Verdurin the impression of reversing roles (so
much so that she replied, with emphasis on the distinction: "M. Swann, pray allow me to introduce our friend
Saniette to you") but aroused in Saniette himself a
warmth of devotion, which, however, the Verdurins never
disclosed to Swann, since Saniette rather irritated them,
and they did not feel inclined to provide him with
friends. On the other hand the Verdurins were extremely
touched by Swann's next request, for he felt that he must
ask to meet the pianist's aunt. She wore a black dress, as
was her invariable custom, for she believed that a woman
always looked well in black and that nothing could be
more distinguished; but her face was exceedingly red, as it
always was for some time after a meal. She bowed to
Swann with deference, but drew herself up again with
great dignity. As she was entirely uneducated, and was
afraid of making mistakes in grammar and pronunciation,
she used purposely to speak in an indistinct and garbling
manner, thinking that if she should make a slip it would
be so buried in the surrounding confusion that no one
could be certain whether she had actually made it or not;
with the result that her talk was a sort of continuous,
blurred expectoration, out of which would emerge, at rare
intervals, the few sounds and syllables of which she felt

sure. Swann supposed himself entitled to poke a little mild fun at her in conversation with M. Verdurin, who, however, was rather put out.

"She's such an excellent woman!" he rejoined. "I grant you that she's not exactly brilliant; but I assure you that she can be most agreeable when you chat with her alone."

"I'm sure she can," Swann hastened to concede. "All I meant was that she hardly struck me as 'distinguished,' " he went on, isolating the epithet in the inverted commas of his tone, "and that, on the whole, is something of a compliment."

"For instance," said M. Verdurin, "now this will surprise you: she writes quite delightfully. You've never heard her nephew play? It's admirable, eh, Doctor? Would you like me to ask him to play something, M. Swann?"

"Why, it would be a joy . . ." Swann was beginning to reply, when the doctor broke in derisively. Having once heard it said, and never having forgotten, that in general conversation over-emphasis and the use of formal expressions were out of date, whenever he heard a solemn word used seriously, as the word "joy" had just been used by Swann, he felt that the speaker had been guilty of pomposity. And if, moreover, the word in question happened to occur also in what he called an old "tag," however common it might still be in current usage, the doctor jumped to the conclusion that the remark which was about to be made was ridiculous, and completed it ironically with the cliché he assumed the speaker was about to perpetrate, although in reality it had never entered his mind.

"A joy for ever!" he exclaimed mischievously, throwing up his arms in a grandiloquent gesture.

M. Verdurin could not help laughing.

"What are all those good people laughing at over there? There's no sign of brooding melancholy down in your corner," shouted Mme Verdurin. "You don't suppose I find it very amusing to be stuck up here by myself on the stool of repentance," she went on with mock peevishness, in a babyish tone of voice.

Mme Verdurin was seated on a high Swedish chair of waxed pinewood, which a violinist from that country had given her, and which she kept in her drawing-room although in appearance it suggested a work-stand and clashed with the really good antique furniture which she had besides; but she made a point of keeping on view the presents which her "faithful" were in the habit of making her from time to time, so that the donors might have the pleasure of seeing them there when they came to the house. She tried to persuade them to confine their tributes to flowers and sweets, which had at least the merit of mortality; but she never succeeded, and the house was gradually filled with a collection of foot-warmers, cushions, clocks, screens, barometers and vases, a constant repetition and a boundless incongruity of useless but indestructible objects.

From this lofty perch she would take a spirited part in the conversation of the "faithful," and would revel in all their "drollery"; but, since the accident to her jaw, she had abandoned the effort involved in wholehearted laughter, and had substituted a kind of symbolical dumb-show which signified, without endangering or fatiguing her in any way, that she was "splitting her sides." At the least

witticism aimed by a member of the circle against a bore
or against a former member who was now relegated to the
limbo of bores—and to the utter despair of M. Verdurin,
who had always made out that he was just as affable as
his wife, but who, since his laughter was the "real thing,"
was out of breath in a moment and so was overtaken and
vanquished by her device of a feigned but continuous hilarity—she would utter a shrill cry, shut tight her little
bird-like eyes, which were beginning to be clouded over
by a cataract, and quickly, as though she had only just
time to avoid some indecent sight or to parry a mortal
blow, burying her face in her hands, which completely
engulfed it and hid it from view, would appear to be
struggling to suppress, to annihilate, a laugh which, had
she succumbed to it, must inevitably have left her inanimate. So, stupefied with the gaiety of the "faithful,"
drunk with good-fellowship, scandal and asseveration,
Mme Verdurin, perched on her high seat like a cage-bird
whose biscuit has been steeped in mulled wine, would sit
aloft and sob with affability.

Meanwhile M. Verdurin, after first asking Swann's
permission to light his pipe ("No ceremony here, you understand; we're all pals!"), went and asked the young musician to sit down at the piano.

"Leave him alone; don't bother him; he hasn't come
here to be tormented," cried Mme Verdurin. "I won't
have him tormented."

"But why on earth should it bother him?" rejoined
M. Verdurin. "I'm sure M. Swann has never heard the
sonata in F sharp which we discovered. He's going to
play us the pianoforte arrangement."

"No, no, no, not my sonata!" she screamed, "I don't

want to be made to cry until I get a cold in the head, and
neuralgia all down my face, like last time. Thanks very
much, I don't intend to repeat that performance. You're
all so very kind and considerate, it's easy to see that none
of you will have to stay in bed for a week."

This little scene, which was re-enacted as often as the
young pianist sat down to play, never failed to delight her
friends as much as if they were witnessing it for the first
time, as a proof of the seductive originality of the "Mistress" and of the acute sensitiveness of her musical ear.
Those nearest to her would attract the attention of the
rest, who were smoking or playing cards at the other end
of the room, by their cries of "Hear, hear!" which, as in
Parliamentary debates, showed that something worth listening to was being said. And next day they would commiserate with those who had been prevented from coming
that evening, assuring them that the scene had been even
more amusing than usual.

"Well, all right, then," said M. Verdurin, "he can
play just the andante."

"Just the andante! That really is a bit rich!" cried his
wife. "As if it weren't precisely the andante that breaks
every bone in my body. The Master is really too priceless! Just as though, in the Ninth, he said 'we'll just hear
the finale,' or 'just the overture' of the *Mastersingers*."

The doctor, however, urged Mme Verdurin to let the
pianist play, not because he supposed her to be feigning
when she spoke of the distressing effects that music always had upon her—for he recognised certain neuras-
thenic symptoms therein—but from the habit, common
to many doctors, of at once relaxing the strict letter of a
prescription as soon as it jeopardises something they re-

gard as more important, such as the success of a social
gathering at which they are present, and of which the patient whom they urge for once to forget his dyspepsia or
his flu is one of the essential ingredients.

"You won't be ill this time, you'll find," he told her,
seeking at the same time to influence her with a hypnotic
stare. "And if you are ill, we'll look after you."

"Will you really?" Mme Verdurin spoke as though,
with so great a favour in store for her, there was nothing
for it but to capitulate. Perhaps, too, by dint of saying
that she was going to be ill, she had worked herself into a
state in which she occasionally forgot that it was all a fabrication and adopted the attitude of a genuine invalid.
And it may often be remarked that invalids, weary of
having to make the infrequency of their attacks depend on
their own prudence, like to persuade themselves that they
can do everything that they enjoy, and that does them
harm, with impunity, provided that they place themselves
in the hands of a higher authority who, without putting
them to the least inconvenience, can and will, by uttering
a word or by administering a pill, set them once again on
their feet.

Odette had gone to sit on a tapestry-covered settee
near the piano, saying to Mme Verdurin, "I have my own
little corner, haven't I?"

And Mme Verdurin, seeing Swann by himself on a
chair, made him get up: "You're not at all comfortable
there. Go along and sit by Odette. You can make room
for M. Swann there, can't you, Odette?"

"What charming Beauvais!" said Swann politely,
stopping to admire the settee before he sat down on it.

"Ah! I'm glad you appreciate my settee," replied

Mme Verdurin, "and I warn you that if you expect ever to see another like it you may as well abandon the idea at once. They've never made anything else like it. And these little chairs, too, are perfect marvels. You can look at them in a moment. The emblems in each of the bronze mouldings correspond to the subject of the tapestry on the chair; you know, you'll have a great deal to enjoy if you want to look at them—I can promise you a delightful time, I assure you. Just look at the little friezes round the edges; here, look, the little vine on a red background in this one, the Bear and the Grapes. Isn't it well drawn? What do you say? I think they knew a thing or two about drawing! Doesn't it make your mouth water, that vine? My husband makes out that I'm not fond of fruit, because I eat less of them than he does. But not a bit of it, I'm greedier than any of you, but I have no need to fill my mouth with them when I can feed on them with my eyes. What are you all laughing at now, pray? Ask the doctor; he'll tell you that those grapes act on me like a regular purge. Some people go to Fontainebleau for cures; I take my own little Beauvais cure here. But, M. Swann, you mustn't run away without feeling the little bronze mouldings on the backs. Isn't it an exquisite patina? No, no, you must feel them properly, with your whole hand!"

"If Mme Verdurin is going to start fingering her bronzes," said the painter, "we shan't get any music tonight."

"Be quiet, you wretch! And yet we poor women," she went on, turning towards Swann, "are forbidden pleasures far less voluptuous than this. There is no flesh in the world to compare with it. None. When M. Verdurin did me the honour of being madly jealous . . . Come, you might at least be polite—don't say that you've never been jealous!"

"But, my dear, I've said absolutely nothing. Look here, Doctor, I call you as a witness. Did I utter a word?"

Swann had begun, out of politeness, to finger the bronzes, and did not like to stop.

"Come along; you can caress them later. Now it's you who are going to be caressed, caressed aurally. You'll like that, I think. Here's the young gentleman who will take charge of that."

After the pianist had played, Swann was even more affable towards him than towards any of the other guests, for the following reason:

The year before, at an evening party, he had heard a piece of music played on the piano and violin. At first he had appreciated only the material quality of the sounds which those instruments secreted. And it had been a source of keen pleasure when, below the delicate line of the violin-part, slender but robust, compact and commanding, he had suddenly become aware of the mass of the piano-part beginning to emerge in a sort of liquid rippling of sound, multiform but indivisible, smooth yet restless, like the deep blue tumult of the sea, silvered and charmed into a minor key by the moonlight. But then at a certain moment, without being able to distinguish any clear outline, or to give a name to what was pleasing him, suddenly enraptured, he had tried to grasp the phrase or harmony—he did not know which—that had just been played and that had opened and expanded his soul, as the fragrance of certain roses, wafted upon the moist air of evening, has the power of dilating one's nostrils. Perhaps it was owing to his ignorance of music that he had re-

ceived so confused an impression, one of those that are
none the less the only purely musical impressions, limited
in their extent, entirely original, and irreducible to any
other kind. An impression of this order, vanishing in an
instant, is, so to speak, *sine materia*. Doubtless the notes
which we hear at such moments tend, according to their
pitch and volume, to spread out before our eyes over surfaces of varying dimensions, to trace arabesques, to give
us the sensation of breadth or tenuity, stability or caprice.
But the notes themselves have vanished before these sensations have developed sufficiently to escape submersion
under those which the succeeding or even simultaneous
notes have already begun to awaken in us. And this impression would continue to envelop in its liquidity, its
ceaseless overlapping, the motifs which from time to time
emerge, barely discernible, to plunge again and disappear
and drown, recognised only by the particular kind of
pleasure which they instil, impossible to describe, to rec-
ollect, to name, ineffable—did not our memory, like a
labourer who toils at the laying down of firm foundations
beneath the tumult of the waves, by fashioning for us fac-
similes of those fugitive phrases, enable us to compare
and to contrast them with those that follow. And so,
scarcely had the exquisite sensation which Swann had experienced died away, before his memory had furnished
him with an immediate transcript, sketchy, it is true, and
provisional, which he had been able to glance at while the
piece continued, so that, when the same impression suddenly returned, it was no longer impossible to grasp. He
could picture to himself its extent, its symmetrical arrangement, its notation, its expressive value; he had before him something that was no longer pure music, but

rather design, architecture, thought, and which allowed
the actual music to be recalled. This time he had distinguished quite clearly a phrase which emerged for a few
moments above the waves of sound. It had at once suggested to him a world of inexpressible delights, of whose
existence, before hearing it, he had never dreamed, into
which he felt that nothing else could initiate him; and he
had been filled with love for it, as with a new and strange
desire.

With a slow and rhythmical movement it led him
first this way, then that, towards a state of happiness that
was noble, unintelligible, and yet precise. And then suddenly, having reached a certain point from which he was
preparing to follow it, after a momentary pause, abruptly
it changed direction, and in a fresh movement, more
rapid, fragile, melancholy, incessant, sweet, it bore him
off with it towards new vistas. Then it vanished. He
hoped, with a passionate longing, that he might find it
again, a third time. And reappear it did, though without
speaking to him more clearly, bringing him, indeed, a
pleasure less profound. But when he returned home he
felt the need of it: he was like a man into whose life a
woman he has seen for a moment passing by has brought
the image of a new beauty which deepens his own sensibility, although he does not even know her name or
whether he will ever see her again.

Indeed this passion for a phrase of music seemed, for
a time, to open up before Swann the possibility of a sort
of rejuvenation. He had so long ceased to direct his life
towards any ideal goal, confining himself to the pursuit of
ephemeral satisfactions, that he had come to believe,
without ever admitting it to himself in so many words,

that he would remain in that condition for the rest of his
days. More than this, since his mind no longer entertained any lofty ideas, he had ceased to believe in (although he could not have expressly denied) their reality.
Thus he had grown into the habit of taking refuge in trivial considerations, which enabled him to disregard matters
of fundamental importance. Just as he never stopped to
ask himself whether he would not have done better by not
going into society, but on the other hand knew for certain
that if he had accepted an invitation he must put in an
appearance, and that afterwards, if he did not actually
call, he must at least leave cards upon his hostess, so in
his conversation he took care never to express with any
warmth a personal opinion about anything, but instead
would supply facts and details which were valid enough
in themselves and excused him from showing his real ca-
pacities. He would be extremely precise about the recipe
for a dish, the dates of a painter's birth and death, and
the titles of his works. Sometimes, in spite of himself, he
would let himself go so far as to express an opinion on a
work of art, or on someone's interpretation of life, but
then he would cloak his words in a tone of irony, as
though he did not altogether associate himself with what
he was saying. But now, like a confirmed invalid in
whom, all of a sudden, a change of air and surroundings,
or a new course of treatment, or sometimes an organic
change in himself, spontaneous and unaccountable, seems
to have brought about such an improvement in his health
that he begins to envisage the possibility, hitherto beyond
all hope, of starting to lead belatedly a wholly different
life, Swann found in himself, in the memory of the phrase
that he had heard, in certain other sonatas which he had

made people play to him to see whether he might not
perhaps discover his phrase therein, the presence of one of
those invisible realities in which he had ceased to believe
and to which, as though the music had had upon the
moral barrenness from which he was suffering a sort of
re-creative influence, he was conscious once again of the
desire and almost the strength to consecrate his life. But,
never having managed to find out whose work it was that
he had heard played that evening, he had been unable to
procure a copy and had finally forgotten the quest. He
had indeed, in the course of that week, encountered several of the people who had been at the party with him,
and had questioned them; but most of them had either
arrived after or left before the piece was played; some had
indeed been there at the time but had gone into another
room to talk, and those who had stayed to listen had no
clearer impression than the rest. As for his hosts, they
knew that it was a recent work which the musicians
whom they had engaged for the evening had asked to be
allowed to play; but, as these last had gone away on tour,
Swann could learn nothing further. He had, of course, a
number of musical friends, but, vividly as he could recall
the exquisite and inexpressible pleasure which the little
phrase had given him, and could see in his mind's eye the
forms that it had traced, he was quite incapable of humming it to them. And so, at last, he ceased to think of it.

But that night, at Mme Verdurin's, scarcely had the
young pianist begun to play than suddenly, after a high
note sustained through two whole bars, Swann sensed its
approach, stealing forth from beneath that long-drawn
sonority, stretched like a curtain of sound to veil the mystery of its incubation, and recognised, secret, murmuring,

detached, the airy and perfumed phrase that he had
loved. And it was so peculiarly itself, it had so individual,
so irreplaceable a charm, that Swann felt as though he
had met, in a friend's drawing-room, a woman whom he
had seen and admired in the street and had despaired of
ever seeing again. Finally the phrase receded, diligently
guiding its successors through the ramifications of its fragrance, leaving on Swann's features the reflection of its
smile. But now, at last, he could ask the name of his fair
unknown (and was told that it was the andante of Vinteuil's sonata for piano and violin); he held it safe, could
have it again to himself, at home, as often as he wished,
could study its language and acquire its secret.

And so, when the pianist had finished, Swann crossed
the room and thanked him with a vivacity which delighted Mme Verdurin.

"Isn't he a charmer?" she asked Swann, "doesn't he
just understand his sonata, the little wretch? You never
dreamed, did you, that a piano could be made to express
all that? Upon my word, you'd think it was everything
but the piano! I'm caught out every time I hear it; I think
I'm listening to an orchestra. Though it's better, really,
than an orchestra, more complete."

The young pianist bowed as he answered, smiling
and underlining each of his words as though he were
making an epigram: "You are most generous to me."

And while Mme Verdurin was saying to her husband,
"Run and fetch him a glass of orangeade; he's earned it,"
Swann began to tell Odette how he had fallen in love
with that little phrase. When their hostess, who was some
way off, called out, "Well! It looks to me as though
someone was saying nice things to you, Odette!" she

replied, "Yes, very nice," and he found her simplicity delightful. Then he asked for information about this Vinteuil: what else he had done, at what period in his life he had composed the sonata, and what meaning the little phrase could have had for him—that was what Swann wanted most to know.

But none of these people who professed to admire this musician (when Swann had said that the sonata was really beautiful Mme Verdurin had exclaimed, "Of course it's beautiful! But you don't dare to confess that you don't know Vinteuil's sonata; you have no right not to know it!"—and the painter had added, "Ah, yes, it's a very fine bit of work, isn't it? Not, of course, if you want something 'obvious,' something 'popular,' but, I mean to say, it makes a very great impression on us artists"), none of them seemed ever to have asked himself these questions, for none of them was able to answer them.

Even to one or two particular remarks made by Swann about his favourite phrase: "D'you know, that's a funny thing; I had never noticed it. I may as well tell you that I don't much care about peering at things through a microscope, and pricking myself on pin-points of difference. No, we don't waste time splitting hairs in this house," Mme Verdurin replied, while Dr Cottard gazed at her with open-mouthed admiration and studious zeal as she skipped lightly from one stepping-stone to another of her stock of ready-made phrases. Both he, however, and Mme Cottard, with a kind of common sense which is shared by many people of humble origin, were careful not to express an opinion, or to pretend to admire a piece of music which they confessed to each other, once they were back at home, that they no more understood than they could understand the art of "Master" Biche. Inasmuch as the public cannot recognise the charm, the beauty, even the outlines of nature save in the stereotyped impressions of an art which they have gradually assimilated, while an original artist starts by rejecting those stereotypes, so M. and Mme Cottard, typical, in this respect, of the public, were incapable of finding, either in Vinteuil's sonata or in Biche's portraits, what constituted for them harmony in music or beauty in painting. It appeared to them, when the pianist played his sonata, as though he were striking at random from the piano a medley of notes which bore no relation to the musical forms to which they themselves were accustomed, and that the painter simply flung the colours at random on his canvases. When, in one of these, they were able to distinguish a human form, they always found it coarsened and vulgarised (that is to say lacking in the elegance of the school of painting through whose spectacles they were in the habit of seeing even the real, living people who passed them in the street) and devoid of truth, as though M. Biche had not known how the human shoulder was constructed, or that a woman's hair was not ordinarily purple.

However, when the "faithful" were scattered out of earshot, the doctor felt that the opportunity was too good to be missed, and so (while Mme Verdurin was adding a final word of commendation of Vinteuil's sonata), like a would-be swimmer who jumps into the water so as to learn, but chooses a moment when there are not too many people looking on: "Yes, indeed; he's what they call a musician *di primo cartello!*" he exclaimed with sudden determination.

Swann discovered no more than that the recent appearance of Vinteuil's sonata had caused a great stir among the most advanced school of musicians, but that it was still unknown to the general public.

"I know someone called Vinteuil," said Swann, thinking of the old piano-teacher at Combray who had taught my grandmother's sisters.

"Perhaps he's the man," cried Mme Verdurin.

"Oh, no, if you'd ever set eyes on him you wouldn't entertain the idea."

"Then to entertain the idea is to settle it?" the doctor suggested.

"But it may well be some relation," Swann went on. "That would be bad enough; but, after all, there's no reason why a genius shouldn't have a cousin who's a silly old fool. And if that should be so, I swear there's no known or unknown form of torture I wouldn't undergo to get the old fool to introduce me to the man who composed the sonata; starting with the torture of the old fool's company, which would be ghastly."

The painter understood that Vinteuil was seriously ill at the moment, and that Dr Potain despaired of his life.

"What!" cried Mme Verdurin, "Do people still call in Potain?"

"Ah! Mme Verdurin," Cottard simpered, "you forget that you are speaking of one of my colleagues—I should say one of my masters."

The painter had heard it said that Vinteuil was threatened with the loss of his reason. And he insisted that signs of this could be detected in certain passages in the sonata. This remark did not strike Swann as ridiculous; but it disturbed him, for, since a work of pure music contains none of the logical sequences whose deformation, in spoken or written language, is a proof of insanity, so insanity diagnosed in a sonata seemed to him as mysterious a thing as the insanity of a dog or a horse, although instances may be observed of these.

"Don't speak to me about your masters; you know ten times as much as he does!" Mme Verdurin answered Dr Cottard, in the tone of a woman who has the courage of her convictions and is quite ready to stand up to anyone who disagrees with her. "At least you don't kill your patients!"

"But, Madame, he is in the Academy," replied the doctor with heavy irony. "If a patient prefers to die at the hands of one of the princes of science . . . It's much smarter to be able to say, 'Yes, I have Potain.' "

"Oh, indeed! Smarter, is it?" said Mme Verdurin. "So there are fashions, nowadays, in illness, are there? I didn't know that . . . Oh, you do make me laugh!" she screamed suddenly, burying her face in her hands. "And here was I, poor thing, talking quite seriously and never realising that you were pulling my leg."

As for M. Verdurin, finding it rather a strain to raise a laugh for so little, he was content with puffing out a cloud of smoke from his pipe, reflecting sadly that he could no longer catch up with his wife in the field of amiability.

"D'you know, we like your friend very much," said Mme Verdurin when Odette was bidding her good night. "He's so unaffected, quite charming. If they're all like that, the friends you want to introduce to us, by all means bring them."

M. Verdurin remarked that Swann had failed, all the same, to appreciate the pianist's aunt.

"I dare say he felt a little out of his depth, poor
man," suggested Mme Verdurin. "You can't expect him
to have caught the tone of the house already, like Cottard,
who has been one of our little clan now for years. The
first time doesn't count; it's just for breaking the ice.
Odette, it's agreed that he's to join us tomorrow at the
Châtelet. Perhaps you might call for him?"

"No, he doesn't want that."

"Oh, very well; just as you like. Provided he doesn't
fail us at the last moment."

Greatly to Mme Verdurin's surprise, he never failed
them. He would go to meet them no matter where, sometimes at restaurants on the outskirts of Paris which were
little frequented as yet, since the season had not yet begun, more often at the theatre, of which Mme Verdurin
was particularly fond. One evening at her house he heard
her remark how useful it would be to have a special pass
for first nights and gala performances, and what a nui-
sance it had been not having one on the day of Gam-
betta's funeral. Swann, who never spoke of his brilliant
connexions, but only of those not highly thought of in the
Faubourg Saint-Germain whom he would have considered
it snobbish to conceal, and among whom he had come to
include his connexions in the official world, broke in: "I'll
see to that. You shall have it in time for the *Danicheff* re-
vival. I happen to be lunching with the Prefect of Police
tomorrow at the Elysée."

"What's that? The Elysée?" Dr Cottard roared in a
voice of thunder.

"Yes, at M. Grévy's," replied Swann, a little embarrassed at the effect which his announcement had produced.

"Are you often taken like that?" the painter asked Cottard with mock-seriousness.

As a rule, once an explanation had been given, Cottard would say: "Ah, good, good; that's all right, then," after which he would show not the least trace of emotion. But this time Swann's last words, instead of the usual calming effect, had that of raising to fever-pitch his astonishment at the discovery that a man with whom he himself was actually sitting at table, a man who had no official position, no honours or distinction of any sort, was on visiting terms with the Head of State.

"What's that you say? M. Grévy? You know M. Grévy?" he demanded of Swann, in the stupid and increduluous tone of a constable on duty at the palace who, when a stranger asks to see the President of the Republic, realising at once "the sort of man he is dealing with," as the newspapers say, assures the poor lunatic that he will be admitted at once, and directs him to the reception ward of the police infirmary.

"I know him slightly; we have some friends in common" (Swann dared not add that one of these friends was the Prince of Wales). "Besides, he is very free with his invitations, and I assure you his luncheon-parties are not the least bit amusing. They're very simple affairs, too, you know—never more than eight at table," he went on, trying desperately to cut out everything that seemed to show off his relations with the President in a light too dazzling for the doctor's eyes.

Whereupon Cottard, at once conforming in his mind to the literal interpretation of what Swann was saying, decided that invitations from M. Grévy were very little sought after, were sent out, in fact, into the highways and byways. And from that moment he was no longer surprised to hear that Swann, or anyone else, was "always at the Elysée"; he even felt a little sorry for a man who had to go to luncheon-parties which he himself admitted were a bore.

"Ah, good, good; that's quite all right, then," he said, in the tone of a suspicious customs official who, after hearing your explanations, stamps your passport and lets you proceed on your journey without troubling to examine your luggage.

"I can well believe you don't find them amusing, those luncheons. Indeed, it's very good of you to go to them," said Mme Verdurin, who regarded the President of the Republic as a bore to be especially dreaded, since he had at his disposal means of seduction, and even of compulsion, which, if employed to captivate her "faithful," might easily make them default. "It seems he's as deaf as a post and eats with his fingers."

"Upon my word! Then it can't be much fun for you, going there." A note of pity sounded in the doctor's voice; and then struck by the number—only eight at table—"Are these luncheons what you would describe as 'intimate'?" he inquired briskly, not so much out of idle curiosity as from linguistic zeal.

But so great was the prestige of the President of the Republic in the eyes of Dr Cottard that neither the modesty of Swann nor the malevolence of Mme Verdurin could wholly efface it, and he never sat down to dinner with the Verdurins without asking anxiously, "D'you think we shall see M. Swann here this evening? He's a personal friend of M. Grévy's. I suppose that means he's what you'd call a 'gentleman'?" He even went to the length of offering Swann a card of invitation to the Dental Exhibition.

"This will let you in, and anyone you take with you," he explained, "but dogs are not admitted. I'm just warning you, you understand, because some friends of mine went there once without knowing, and bitterly regretted it."

As for M. Verdurin, he did not fail to observe the distressing effect upon his wife of the discovery that Swann had influential friends of whom he had never spoken.

If no arrangement had been made to go out, it was at the Verdurins' that Swann would find the "little nucleus" assembled, but he never appeared there except in the evenings, and rarely accepted their invitations to dinner, in spite of Odette's entreaties.

"I could dine with you alone somewhere, if you'd rather," she suggested.

"But what about Mme Verdurin?"

"Oh, that's quite simple. I need only say that my dress wasn't ready, or that my cab came late. There's always some excuse."

"How sweet of you."

But Swann told himself that if he could make Odette feel (by consenting to meet her only after dinner) that there were other pleasures which he preferred to that of her company, then the desire that she felt for his would be all the longer in reaching the point of satiety. Besides, as he infinitely preferred to Odette's style of beauty that of a young seamstress, as fresh and plump as a rose, with whom he was smitten, he preferred to spend the first part of the evening with her, knowing that he was sure to see

Odette later on. It was for the same reason that he never allowed Odette to call for him at his house, to take him on to the Verdurins'. The little seamstress would wait for him at a street corner which Rémi, his coachman, knew; she would jump in beside him, and remain in his arms until the carriage drew up at the Verdurins'. He would enter the drawing-room; and there, while Mme Verdurin, pointing to the roses which he had sent her that morning, said: "I'm furious with you," and sent him to the place kept for him beside Odette, the pianist would play to them—for their two selves—the little phrase by Vinteuil which was, so to speak, the national anthem of their love. He would begin with the sustained tremolos of the violin part which for several bars were heard alone, filling the whole foreground; until suddenly they seemed to draw aside, and—as in those interiors by Pieter de Hooch which are deepened by the narrow frame of a half-opened door, in the far distance, of a different colour, velvety with the radiance of some intervening light—the little phrase appeared, dancing, pastoral, interpolated, episodic, belonging to another world. It rippled past, simple and immortal, scattering on every side the bounties of its grace, with the same ineffable smile; but Swann thought that he could now discern in it some disenchantment. It seemed to be aware how vain, how hollow was the happiness to which it showed the way. In its airy grace there was the sense of something over and done with, like the mood of philosophic detachment which follows an outburst of vain regret. But all this mattered little to him; he contemplated the little phrase less in its own light—in what it might express to a musician who knew nothing of the existence of him and Odette when he had composed it, and to all those who would hear it in centuries to come—than as a pledge, a token of his love, which made even the Verdurins and their young pianist think of Odette at the same time as himself—which bound her to him by a lasting tie; so much so that (whimsically entreated by Odette) he had abandoned the idea of getting some professional to play over to him the whole sonata, of which he still knew no more than this one passage. "Why do you want the rest?" she had asked him. "Our little bit; that's all we need." Indeed, agonised by the reflection, as it floated by, so near and yet so infinitely remote, that while it was addressed to them it did not know them, he almost regretted that it had a meaning of its own, an intrinsic and unalterable beauty, extraneous to themselves, just as in the jewels given to us, or even in the letters written to us by a woman we love, we find fault with the water of the stone, or with the words of the message, because they are not fashioned exclusively from the essence of a transient liaison and a particular person.

Often it would happen that he had stayed so long with the young seamstress before going to the Verdurins' that, as soon as the little phrase had been rendered by the pianist, Swann realised that it was almost time for Odette to go home. He used to take her back as far as the door of her little house in the Rue La Pérouse, behind the Arc de Triomphe. And it was perhaps on this account, and so as not to demand the monopoly of her favours, that he sacrificed the pleasure (not so essential to his well-being) of seeing her earlier in the evening, of arriving with her at the Verdurins', to the exercise of this other privilege which she accorded him of their leaving together; a privilege he valued all the more because it gave him the feel-

ing that no one else would see her, no one would thrust
himself between them, no one could prevent him from remaining with her in spirit, after he had left her for the
night.

And so, night after night, she would return home in
Swann's carriage. Once, after she had got down, and
while he stood at the gate murmuring "Till tomorrow,
then," she turned impulsively from him, plucked a last
lingering chrysanthemum from the little garden in front
of the house, and gave it to him before he left. He held it
pressed to his lips during the drive home, and when in
due course the flower withered, he put it away carefully
in a drawer of his desk.

But he never went into her house. Twice only, in the
daytime, had he done so, to take part in the ceremony—
of such vital importance in her life—of "afternoon tea."
The loneliness and emptiness of those short streets (con-
sisting almost entirely of low-roofed houses, self-contained but not detached, their monotony interrupted here
and there by the dark intrusion of some sinister work-
shop, at once an historical witness to and a sordid survival from the days when the district was still one of ill
repute), the snow which still clung to the garden-beds and
the branches of the trees, the unkemptness of the season,
the proximity of nature, had all combined to add an element of mystery to the warmth, the flowers, the luxury
which he had found inside.

From the ground floor, somewhat raised above street
level, leaving on the left Odette's bedroom, which looked
out to the back over another little street running parallel
with her own, he had climbed a staircase that went
straight up between dark painted walls hung with Orien-

tal draperies, strings of Turkish beads, and a huge
Japanese lantern suspended by a silken cord (which last,
however, so that her visitors should not be deprived of
the latest comforts of Western civilisation, was lighted by
a gas-jet inside), to the two drawing-rooms, large and
small. These were entered through a narrow vestibule, the
wall of which, chequered with the lozenges of a wooden
trellis such as you see on garden walls, only gilded, was
lined from end to end by a long rectangular box in which
bloomed, as in a hothouse, a row of large chrysanthemums, at that time still uncommon though by no means
so large as the mammoth specimens which horticulturists
have since succeeded in producing. Swann was irritated,
as a rule, by the sight of these flowers, which had then
been fashionable in Paris for about a year, but it had
pleased him, on this occasion, to see the gloom of the
vestibule shot with rays of pink and gold and white by
the fragrant petals of these ephemeral stars, which kindle
their cold fires in the murky atmosphere of winter afternoons. Odette had received him in a pink silk dressing-
gown, which left her neck and arms bare. She had made
him sit down beside her in one of the many mysterious
little alcoves which had been contrived in the various recesses of the room, sheltered by enormous palms growing
out of pots of Chinese porcelain, or by screens upon
which were fastened photographs and fans and bows of
ribbon. She had said at once, "You're not comfortable
there; wait a minute, I'll arrange things for you," and
with a little simpering laugh which implied that some
special invention of her own was being brought into play,
she had installed behind his head and beneath his feet
great cushions of Japanese silk which she pummelled and

buffeted as though to prove that she was prodigal of these riches, regardless of their value. But when her footman came into the room bringing, one after another, the innumerable lamps which (contained, mostly, in porcelain vases) burned singly or in pairs upon the different pieces of furniture as upon so many altars, rekindling in the twilight, already almost nocturnal, of this winter afternoon the glow of a sunset more lasting, more roseate, more human—filling, perhaps, with romantic wonder the thoughts of some solitary lover wandering in the street below and brought to a standstill before the mystery of the human presence which those lighted windows at once revealed and screened from sight—she had kept a sharp eye on the servant, to see that he set them down in their appointed places. She felt that if he were to put even one of them where it ought not to be the general effect of her drawing-room would be destroyed, and her portrait, which rested upon a sloping easel draped with plush, inadequately lit. And so she followed the man's clumsy movements with feverish impatience, scolding him severely when he passed too close to a pair of jardinières, which she made a point of always cleaning herself for fear that they might be damaged, and went across to examine now to make sure he had not chipped them. She found something "quaint" in the shape of each of her Chinese ornaments, and also in her orchids, the cattleyas especially—these being, with chrysanthemums, her favourite flowers, because they had the supreme merit of not looking like flowers, but of being made, apparently, of silk or satin. "This one looks just as though it had been cut out of the lining of my cloak," she said to Swann, pointing to an orchid, with a shade of respect in her voice for so "chic" a flower, for this elegant, unexpected sister whom nature had bestowed upon her, so far removed from her in the scale of existence, and yet so delicate, so refined, so much more worthy than many real women of admission to her drawing-room. As she drew his attention, now to the fiery-tongued dragons painted on a bowl or stitched on a screen, now to a fleshy cluster of orchids, now to a dromedary of inlaid silverwork with ruby eyes which kept company, upon her mantelpiece, with a toad carved in jade, she would pretend now to be shrinking from the ferocity of the monsters or laughing at their absurdity, now blushing at the indecency of the flowers, now carried away by an irresistible desire to run across and kiss the toad and dromedary, calling them "darlings." And these affectations were in sharp contrast to the sincerity of some of her attitudes, notably her devotion to Our Lady of Laghet, who had once, when Odette was living at Nice, cured her of a mortal illness, and whose medal, in gold, she always carried on her person, attributing to it unlimited powers. She poured out Swann's tea, inquired "Lemon or cream?" and, on his answering "Cream, please," said to him with a laugh: "A cloud!" And as he pronounced it excellent, "You see, I know just how you like it." This tea had indeed seemed to Swann, just as it seemed to her, something precious, and love has such a need to find some justification for itself, some guarantee of duration, in pleasures which without it would have no existence and must cease with its passing, that when he left her at seven o'clock to go and dress for the evening, all the way home in his brougham, unable to repress the happiness with which the afternoon's adventure had filled him, he kept repeating to himself: "How nice it would be to have a little woman like that in whose house one could always be certain of finding, what one never can be certain of finding, a really good cup of tea." An hour or so later he received a note from Odette, and at once recognised that large handwriting in which an affectation of British stiffness imposed an apparent discipline upon ill-formed characters, suggestive, perhaps, to less biased eyes than his, of an untidiness of mind, a fragmentary education, a want of sincerity and will-power. Swann had left his cigarette-case at her house. "If only," she wrote, "you had also forgotten your heart! I should never have let you have that back."

More important, perhaps, was a second visit which he paid her a little later. On his way to the house, as always when he knew that they were to meet, he formed a picture of her in his mind; and the necessity, if he was to find any beauty in her face, of concentrating on the fresh and rosy cheekbones to the exclusion of the rest of her cheeks which were so often drawn and sallow, and sometimes mottled with little red spots, distressed him as proving that the ideal is unattainable and happiness mediocre. He was bringing her an engraving which she had asked to see. She was not very well, and received him in a dressing-gown of mauve crêpe de Chine, drawing its richly embroidered material over her bosom like a cloak. Standing there beside him, her loosened hair flowing down her cheeks, bending one knee in a slightly balletic pose in order to be able to lean without effort over the picture at which she was gazing, her head on one side, with those great eyes of hers which seemed so tired and sullen when there was nothing to animate her, she struck Swann by her resemblance to the figure of Zipporah,

Jethro's daughter, which is to be seen in one of the Sistine frescoes. He had always found a peculiar fascination in tracing in the paintings of the old masters not merely the general characteristics of the people whom he encountered in his daily life, but rather what seems least susceptible of generalisation, the individual features of men and women whom he knew: as, for instance, in a bust of the Doge Loredan by Antonio Rizzo, the prominent cheekbones, the slanting eyebrows, in short, a speaking likeness to his own coachman Rémi; in the colouring of a Ghirlandaio, the nose of M. de Palancy; in a portrait by Tintoretto, the invasion of the cheek by an outcrop of whisker, the broken nose, the penetrating stare, the swollen eyelids of Dr du Boulbon. Perhaps, having always regretted, in his heart, that he had confined his attention to the social side of life, had talked, always, rather than acted, he imagined a sort of indulgence bestowed upon him by those great artists in the fact that they also had regarded with pleasure and had introduced into their works such types of physiognomy as give those works the strongest possible certificate of reality and truth to life, a modern, almost a topical savour; perhaps, also, he had so far succumbed to the prevailing frivolity of the world of fashion that he felt the need to find in an old masterpiece some such anticipatory and rejuvenating allusion to personalities of today. Perhaps, on the other hand, he had retained enough of the artistic temperament to be able to find a genuine satisfaction in watching these individual characteristics take on a more general significance when he saw them, uprooted and disembodied, in the resemblance between an historic portrait and a modern original whom it was not intended to represent. However that might be—and per-

haps because the abundance of impressions which he had
been receiving for some time past, even though they had
come to him rather through the channel of his apprecia-
tion of music, had enriched his appetite for painting as
well—it was with an unusual intensity of pleasure, a
pleasure destined to have a lasting effect upon him, that
Swann remarked Odette's resemblance to the Zipporah of
that Alessandro de Mariano to whom people more willingly give his popular surname, Botticelli, now that it
suggests not so much the actual work of the Master as
that false and banal conception of it which has of late obtained common currency. He no longer based his estimate
of the merit of Odette's face on the doubtful quality of
her cheeks and the purely fleshy softness which he supposed would greet his lips there should he ever hazard a
kiss, but regarded it rather as a skein of beautiful, delicate
lines which his eyes unravelled, following their curves and
convolutions, relating the rhythm of the neck to the effusion of the hair and the droop of the eyelids, as though in
a portrait of her in which her type was made clearly intelligible.

He stood gazing at her; traces of the old fresco were
apparent in her face and her body, and these he tried incessantly to recapture thereafter, both when he was with
Odette and when he was only thinking of her in her absence; and, although his admiration for the Florentine
masterpiece was doubtless based upon his discovery that
it had been reproduced in her, the similarity enhanced her
beauty also, and made her more precious. Swann re-
proached himself with his failure, hitherto, to estimate at
her true worth a creature whom the great Sandro would
have adored, and was gratified that his pleasure in seeing

Odette should have found a justification in his own aesthetic culture. He told himself that in associating the thought of Odette with his dreams of ideal happiness he had not resigned himself to a stopgap as inadequate as he had hitherto supposed, since she satisfied his most refined predilections in matters of art. He failed to observe that this quality would not naturally avail to bring Odette into the category of women whom he found desirable, since, as it happened, his desires had always run counter to his aesthetic taste. The words "Florentine painting" were invaluable to Swann. They enabled him, like a title, to introduce the image of Odette into a world of dreams and fancies which, until then, she had been debarred from entering, and where she assumed a new and nobler form. And whereas the mere sight of her in the flesh, by perpetually reviving his misgivings as to the quality of her face, her body, the whole of her beauty, cooled the ardour of his love, those misgivings were swept away and that love confirmed now that he could re-erect his estimate of her on the sure foundations of aesthetic principle; while the kiss, the physical possession which would have seemed natural and but moderately attractive had they been granted him by a creature of somewhat blemished flesh and sluggish blood, coming, as they now came, to crown his adoration of a masterpiece in a gallery, must, it seemed, prove supernaturally delicious.

And when he was tempted to regret that, for months past, he had done nothing but see Odette, he would assure himself that he was not unreasonable in giving up much of his time to an inestimably precious work of art, cast for once in a new, a different, an especially delectable metal, in an unmatched exemplar which he would contemplate at one moment with the humble, spiritual, disinterested mind of an artist, at another with the pride, the selfishness, the sensual thrill of a collector.

He placed on his study table, as if it were a photograph of Odette, a reproduction of Jethro's daughter. He would gaze in admiration at the large eyes, the delicate features in which the imperfection of the skin might be surmised, the marvellous locks of hair that fell along the tired cheeks; and, adapting to the idea of a living woman what he had until then felt to be beautiful on aesthetic grounds, he converted it into a series of physical merits which he was gratified to find assembled in the person of one whom he might ultimately possess. The vague feeling of sympathy which attracts one to a work of art, now that he knew the original in flesh and blood of Jethro's daughter, became a desire which more than compensated, thenceforward, for the desire which Odette's physical charms had at first failed to inspire in him. When he had sat for a long time gazing at the Botticelli, he would think of his own living Botticelli, who seemed even lovelier still, and as he drew towards him the photograph of Zipporah he would imagine that he was holding Odette against his heart.

It was not only Odette's lassitude, however, that he must take pains to circumvent; it was also, not infrequently, his own. Feeling that, since Odette had had every facility for seeing him, she seemed no longer to have very much to say to him, he was afraid lest the manner—at once trivial, monotonous, and seemingly unalterable—which she now adopted when they were together should ultimately destroy in him that romantic hope, which alone had aroused and sustained his love, that a day might come when she would declare her passion. And so, in an attempt to revitalise Odette's too fixed and unvarying attitude towards him, of which he was afraid of growing weary, he would write to her, suddenly, a letter full of feigned disappointment and simulated anger, which he sent off so that it should reach her before dinner. He knew that she would be alarmed, and that she would reply, and he hoped that, when the fear of losing him clutched at her heart, it would force from her words such as he had never yet heard her utter; and indeed, it was by this device that he had won from her the most affectionate letters she had so far written him. One of them, which she had sent round to him at midday from the Maison Dorée (it was the day of the Paris-Murcie Fête given for the victims of the recent floods in Murcia) began: "My dear, my hand trembles so that I can scarcely write," and had been put in the same drawer as the withered chrysanthemum. Or else, if she had not had time to write to him, when he arrived at the Verdurins' she would come running up to him with an "I've something to say to you!" and he would gaze curiously at the revelation in her face and speech of what she had hitherto kept concealed from him of her heart.

Even before he reached the Verdurins' door, when he caught sight of the great lamp-lit spaces of the drawing-room windows, whose shutters were never closed, he would begin to melt at the thought of the charming creature he would see as he entered the room, basking in that golden light. Here and there the figures of the guests stood out in silhouette, slender and black, between lamp and window, like those little pictures which one sees at regular intervals round a translucent lampshade, the other panels of which are simply naked light. He would try to distinguish Odette's silhouette. And then, when he was once inside, without his being aware of it, his eyes would sparkle suddenly with such radiant happiness that M. Verdurin said to the painter: "Hm. Seems to be warming up." And indeed her presence gave the house what none of the other houses that he visited seemed to possess: a sort of nervous system, a sensory network which ramified into each of its rooms and sent a constant stimulus to his heart.

Thus the simple and regular manifestations of this social organism, the "little clan," automatically provided Swann with a daily rendezvous with Odette, and enabled him to feign indifference to the prospect of seeing her, or even a desire not to see her; in doing which he incurred no very great risk since, even though he had written to her during the day, he would of necessity see her in the evening and accompany her home.

But one evening, when, depressed by the thought of that inevitable dark drive together, he had taken his young seamstress all the way to the Bois, so as to delay as long as possible the moment of his appearance at the Verdurins', he arrived at the house so late that Odette, supposing that he did not intend to come, had already left. Seeing the room bare of her, Swann felt a sudden stab at the heart; he trembled at the thought of being deprived of a pleasure whose intensity he was able for the first time to gauge, having always, hitherto, had that certainty of finding it whenever he wished which (as in the case of all our pleasures) reduced if it did not altogether blind him to its dimensions.

"Did you notice the face he pulled when he saw that

she wasn't here?" M. Verdurin asked his wife. "I think we may say that he's hooked."

"The face he pulled?" exploded Dr Cottard who, having left the house for a moment to visit a patient, had just returned to fetch his wife and did not know whom they were discussing.

"D'you mean to say you didn't meet him on the doorstep—the loveliest of Swanns?"

"No. M. Swann has been here?"

"Just for a moment. We had a glimpse of a Swann tremendously agitated. In a state of nerves. You see, Odette had left."

"You mean to say that she is 'on a friendly footing' with him, that she has 'given the go-ahead'?" inquired the doctor, cautiously trying out the meaning of these phrases.

"Why, of course not, there's absolutely nothing in it; in fact, between you and me, I think she's making a great mistake, and behaving like a silly little fool, which is what she is, in fact."

"Come, come, come!" said M. Verdurin, "How on earth do you know that there's nothing in it? We haven't been there to see, have we now?"

"She would have told me," answered Mme Verdurin with dignity. "I may say that she tells me everything. As she has no one else at present, I told her that she ought to sleep with him. She makes out that she can't, that she did in fact have a crush on him at first, but he's always shy with her, and that makes her shy with him. Besides, she doesn't care for him in that way, she says; it's an ideal love, she's afraid of rubbing the bloom off—but how should I know? And yet it's just what she needs."

"I beg to differ from you," M. Verdurin courteously interrupted. "I don't entirely care for the gentleman. I feel he puts on airs."

Mme Verdurin's whole body stiffened, and her eyes stared blankly as though she had suddenly been turned into a statue; a device which enabled her to appear not to have caught the sound of that unutterable phrase which seemed to imply that it was possible for people to "put on airs" in their house, in other words consider themselves "superior" to them.

"Anyhow, if there's nothing in it, I don't suppose it's because our friend believes she's *virtuous*," M. Verdurin went on sarcastically. "And yet, you never know; he seems to think she's intelligent. I don't know whether you heard the way he lectured her the other evening about Vinteuil's sonata. I'm devoted to Odette, but really—to expound theories of aesthetics to her—the man must be a prize idiot."

"Look here, I won't have you saying nasty things about Odette," broke in Mme Verdurin in her "little girl" manner. "She's sweet."

"But that doesn't prevent her from being sweet. We're not saying anything nasty about her, only that she isn't exactly the embodiment of virtue or intellect. After all," he turned to the painter, "does it matter so very much whether she's virtuous or not? She might be a great deal less charming if she were."

On the landing Swann had run into the Verdurins' butler, who had been somewhere else a moment earlier when he arrived, and who had been asked by Odette to tell Swann in case he still turned up (but that was at least an hour ago) that she would probably stop for a cup of

chocolate at Prévost's on her way home. Swann set off at
once for Prévost's, but every few yards his carriage was
held up by others, or by people crossing the street, loathsome obstacles that he would gladly have crushed beneath
his wheels, were it not that a policeman fumbling with a
note-book would delay him even longer than the actual
passage of the pedestrian. He counted the minutes feverishly, adding a few seconds to each so as to be quite certain that he had not given himself short measure and so,
possibly, exaggerated whatever chance there might actually be of his arriving at Prévost's in time, and of finding
her still there. And then, in a moment of illumination,
like a man in a fever who awakes from sleep and is conscious of the absurdity of the dream-shapes among which
his mind has been wandering without any clear distinction between himself and them, Swann suddenly perceived how foreign to his nature were the thoughts which
had been revolving in his mind ever since he had heard at
the Verdurins' that Odette had left, how novel the
heartache from which he was suffering, but of which he
was only now conscious, as though he had just woken up.
What! all this agitation simply because he would not see
Odette till tomorrow, exactly what he had been hoping,
not an hour before, as he drove towards Mme Verdurin's.
He was obliged to acknowledge that now, as he sat in that
same carriage and drove to Prévost's, he was no longer
the same man, was no longer alone even—that a new
person was there beside him, adhering to him, amalga-
mated with him, a person whom he might, perhaps, be
unable to shake off, whom he might have to treat with
circumspection, like a master or an illness. And yet, from
the moment he had begun to feel that another, a fresh

personality was thus conjoined with his own, life had
seemed somehow more interesting.

He gave scarcely a thought to the likelihood that this
possible meeting at Prévost's (the tension of waiting for
which so ravished and stripped bare the intervening moments that he could find nothing, not one idea, not one
memory in his mind behind which his troubled spirit
might take shelter and repose) would after all, should it
take place, be much the same as all their meetings, of no
great significance. As on every other evening, once he was
in Odette's company, casting furtive glances at her
changeable face and instantly withdrawing his eyes lest
she should read in them the first signs of desire and no
longer believe in his indifference, he would cease to be
able even to think of her, so busy would he be in the
search for pretexts which would enable him not to leave
her immediately and to ensure, without betraying his concern, that he would find her again next evening at the
Verdurins'; pretexts, that is to say, which would enable
him to prolong for the time being, and to renew for one
day more, the disappointment and the torture engendered
by the vain presence of this woman whom he pursued yet
never dared embrace.

She was not at Prévost's; he must search for her,
then, in every restaurant along the boulevards. To save
time, while he went in one direction, he sent in the other
his coachman Rémi (Rizzo's Doge Loredan) for whom he
presently—after a fruitless search—found himself waiting
at the spot where the carriage was to meet him. It did not
appear, and Swann tantalised himself with alternate pictures of the approaching moment, as one in which Rémi

would say to him: "That lady is there," or as one in which Rémi would say to him: "That lady was not in any of the cafés." And so he saw the remainder of the evening stretching out in front of him, single and yet alternative, preceded either by the meeting with Odette which would put an end to his agony, or by the abandonment of all hope of finding her that evening, the acceptance of the necessity of returning home without having seen her.

The coachman returned; but, as he drew up opposite him, Swann asked, not "Did you find the lady?" but "Remind me, tomorrow, to order in some more firewood. I'm sure we must be running short." Perhaps he had persuaded himself that, if Rémi had at last found Odette in some café where she was waiting for him, then the baleful alternative was already obliterated by the realisation, begun already in his mind, of the happy one, and that there was no need for him to hasten towards the attainment of a joy already captured and held in a safe place, which would not escape his grasp again. But it was also from the force of inertia; there was in his soul that want of adaptability that afflicts the bodies of certain people who, when the moment comes to avoid a collision, to snatch their clothes out of reach of a flame, or to perform any other such necessary movement, take their time, begin by remaining for a moment in their original position, as though seeking to find in it a fulcrum, a springboard, a source of momentum. And no doubt, if the coachman had interrupted him with "That lady is there," he would have answered, "Oh, yes, of course, the errand I sent you on, well, I wouldn't have thought it," and would have continued to discuss his supply of firewood, so as to hide from his servant the emotion he had felt, and to give himself time to break away from the thraldom of his anxieties and devote himself to happiness.

The coachman came back, however, with the report that he could not find her anywhere, and added the advice, as an old and privileged servant: "I think, sir, that all we can do now is to go home."

But the air of indifference which Swann could so lightly assume when Rémi uttered his final, unalterable response, fell from him like a cast-off cloak when he saw Rémi attempt to make him abandon hope and retire from the quest.

"Certainly not!" he exclaimed. "We must find the lady. It's most important. She would be extremely put out—it's a business matter—and vexed with me if she didn't see me."

"But I don't see how the lady can be vexed," answered Rémi, "since it was she who left without waiting for you, sir, and said she was going to Prévost's, and then wasn't there."

Meanwhile the restaurants were closing and their lights began to go out. Under the trees of the boulevards there were still a few people strolling to and fro, barely distinguishable in the gathering darkness. From time to time the shadowy figure of a woman gliding up to Swann, murmuring a few words in his ear, asking him to take her home, would make him start. Anxiously he clutched at all these dim forms, as though, among the phantoms of the dead, in the realms of darkness, he had been searching for a lost Eurydice.

Among all the modes by which love is brought into being, among all the agents which disseminate that blessed bane, there are few so efficacious as this gust of feverish agitation that sweeps over us from time to time. For then the die is cast, the person whose company we enjoy at that moment is the person we shall henceforward love. It is not even necessary for that person to have attracted us, up till then, more than or even as much as others. All that was needed was that our predilection should become exclusive. And that condition is fulfilled when—in this moment of deprivation—the quest for the pleasures we enjoyed in his or her company is suddenly replaced by an anxious, torturing need, whose object is the person alone, an absurd, irrational need which the laws of this world make it impossible to satisfy and difficult to assuage—the insensate, agonising need to possess exclusively.

Swann made Rémi drive him to such restaurants as were still open; it was only the hypothesis of a happy outcome that he had envisaged with calm; now he no longer concealed his agitation, the price he set upon their meeting, and promised in case of success to reward his coachman, as though, by inspiring in him a will to succeed which would reinforce his own, he could bring it to pass, by a miracle, that Odette—assuming that she had long since gone home to bed—might yet be found seated in some restaurant on the boulevards. He pursued the search as far as the Maison Dorée, burst twice into Tortoni's and, still without seeing her, had just emerged from the Café Anglais and was striding, wild-eyed, towards his carriage, which was waiting for him at the corner of the Boulevard des Italiens, when he collided with a person coming in the opposite direction: it was Odette. She explained, later, that there had been no room at Prévost's,

that she had gone, instead, to sup at the Maison Dorée, in
an alcove where he must have failed to see her, and that
she was going back to her carriage.

She had so little expected to see him that she started
back in alarm. As for him, he had ransacked the streets of
Paris not because he supposed it possible that he should
find her, but because it was too painful for him to abandon the attempt. But this happiness which his reason had
never ceased to regard as unattainable, that evening at
least, now seemed doubly real; for, since he himself had
contributed nothing to it by anticipating probabilities, it
remained external to himself; there was no need for him
to think it into existence—it was from itself that there
emanated, it was itself that projected towards him, that
truth whose radiance dispelled like a bad dream the loneliness he had so dreaded, that truth on which his happy
musings now dwelt unthinkingly. So will a traveller, arriving in glorious weather at the Mediterranean shore, no
longer certain of the existence of the lands he has left behind, let his eyes be dazzled by the radiance streaming towards him from the luminous and unfading azure of the
sea.

He climbed after her into the carriage which she had
kept waiting, and ordered his own to follow.

She was holding in her hand a bunch of cattleyas, and
Swann could see, beneath the film of lace that covered her
head, more of the same flowers fastened to a swansdown
plume. She was dressed, beneath her cloak, in a flowing
gown of black velvet, caught up on one side to reveal a
large triangle of white silk skirt, and with a yoke, also of
white silk, in the cleft of the low-necked bodice, in which

were fastened a few more cattleyas. She had scarcely recovered from the shock which the sight of Swann had given her, when some obstacle made the horse start to one side. They were thrown forward in their seats; she uttered a cry, and fell back quivering and breathless.

"It's all right," he assured her, "don't be frightened." And he slipped his arm round her shoulder, supporting her body against his own. Then he went on: "Whatever you do, don't utter a word; just make a sign, yes or no, or you'll be out of breath again. You won't mind if I straighten the flowers on your bodice? The jolt has disarranged them. I'm afraid of their dropping out, so I'd just like to fasten them a little more securely."

She was not used to being made so much fuss of by men, and she smiled as she answered: "No, not at all; I don't mind in the least."

But he, daunted a little by her answer, and also, perhaps, to bear out the pretence that he had been sincere in adopting the stratagem, or even because he was already beginning to believe that he had been, exclaimed, "No, no, you mustn't speak. You'll get out of breath again. You can easily answer in signs; I shall understand. Really and truly now, you don't mind my doing this? Look, there's a little—I think it must be pollen, spilt over your dress. Do you mind if I brush it off with my hand? That's not too hard? I'm not hurting you, am I? Perhaps I'm tickling you a bit? I don't want to touch the velvet in case I crease it. But you see, I really had to fasten the flowers; they would have fallen out if I hadn't. Like that, now; if I just tuck them a little further down . . . Seriously, I'm not annoying you, am I? And if I just sniff

them to see whether they've really got no scent? I don't
believe I ever smelt any before. May I? Tell the truth,
now."

Still smiling, she shrugged her shoulders ever so
slightly, as who should say, "You're quite mad; you know
very well that I like it."

He ran his other hand upwards along Odette's cheek;
she gazed at him fixedly, with that languishing and
solemn air which marks the women of the Florentine
master in whose faces he had found a resemblance with
hers; swimming at the brink of the eyelids, her brilliant
eyes, wide and slender like theirs, seemed on the verge of
welling out like two great tears. She bent her neck, as all
their necks may be seen to bend, in the pagan scenes as
well as in the religious pictures. And in an attitude that
was doubtless habitual to her, one which she knew to be
appropriate to such moments and was careful not to forget to assume, she seemed to need all her strength to hold
her face back, as though some invisible force were drawing it towards Swann's. And it was Swann who, before
she allowed it, as though in spite of herself, to fall upon
his lips, held it back for a moment longer, at a little distance, between his hands. He had wanted to leave time
for his mind to catch up with him, to recognise the dream
which it had so long cherished and to assist at its realisation, like a relative invited as a spectator when a prize is
given to a child of whom she has been especially fond.
Perhaps, too, he was fixing upon the face of an Odette
not yet possessed, nor even kissed by him, which he was
seeing for the last time, the comprehensive gaze with
which, on the day of his departure, a traveller hopes to

bear away with him in memory a landscape he is leaving
for ever.

But he was so shy in approaching her that, after this
evening which had begun by his arranging her cattleyas
and had ended in her complete surrender, whether from
fear of offending her, or from reluctance to appear retrospectively to have lied, or perhaps because he lacked the
audacity to formulate a more urgent requirement than this
(which could always be repeated, since it had not annoyed
her on the first occasion), he resorted to the same pretext
on the following days. If she had cattleyas pinned to her
bodice, he would say: "It's most unfortunate; the cattleyas
don't need tucking in this evening; they've not been disturbed as they were the other night. I think, though, that
this one isn't quite straight. May I see if they have more
scent than the others?" Or else, if she had none: "Oh! no
cattleyas this evening; then there's no chance of my indulging in my little rearrangements." So that for some
time there was no change in the procedure which he had
followed on that first evening, starting with fumblings
with fingers and lips at Odette's bosom, and it was thus
that his caresses still began. And long afterwards, when
the rearrangement (or, rather, the ritual pretence of a rearrangement) of her cattleyas had quite fallen into desuetude, the metaphor "Do a cattleya," transmuted into a
simple verb which they would employ without thinking
when they wished to refer to the act of physical possession (in which, paradoxically, the possessor possesses
nothing), survived to commemorate in their vocabulary
the long-forgotten custom from which it sprang. And perhaps this particular manner of saying "to make love" did

not mean exactly the same thing as its synonyms. However jaded we may be about women, however much we
may regard the possession of the most divergent types as
a repetitive and predictable experience, it none the less
becomes a fresh and stimulating pleasure if the women
concerned are—or are thought by us to be—so difficult
as to oblige us to make it spring from some unrehearsed
incident in our relations with them, as had originally been
for Swann the arrangement of the cattleyas. He trem-
blingly hoped, that evening (but Odette, he told himself,
if she was deceived by his stratagem, could not guess his
intention), that it was the possession of this woman that
would emerge for him from their large mauve petals; and
the pleasure which he had already felt and which Odette
tolerated, he thought, perhaps only because she had not
recognised it, seemed to him for that reason—as it might
have seemed to the first man when he enjoyed it amid the
flowers of the earthly paradise—a pleasure which had
never before existed, which he was striving now to create,
a pleasure—as the special name he gave it was to
certify—entirely individual and new.

Now, every evening, when he had taken her home, he
had to go in with her; and often she would come out
again in her dressing-gown and escort him to his carriage,
and would kiss him in front of his coachman, saying:
"What do I care what other people think?" And on
evenings when he did not go to the Verdurins' (which
happened occasionally now that he had opportunities of
seeing Odette elsewhere), when—more and more rarely—
he went into society, she would ask him to come to her
on his way home, however late he might be. It was
spring, and the nights were clear and frosty. Coming

away from a party, he would climb into his victoria,
spread a rug over his knees, tell the friends who were
leaving at the same time and who wanted him to join
them, that he couldn't, that he wasn't going in their direction; and the coachman would set off at a fast trot
without further orders, knowing where he had to go. His
friends would be left wondering, and indeed Swann was
no longer the same man. No one ever received a letter
from him now demanding an introduction to a woman.
He had ceased to pay any attention to women, and kept
away from the places in which they were ordinarily to be
met. In a restaurant, or in the country, his attitude was
the opposite of the one by which, only yesterday, his
friends would have recognised him, and which had
seemed inevitably and permanently his. To such an extent
does passion manifest itself in us as a temporary and distinct character which not only takes the place of our normal character but obliterates the invariable signs by which
it has hitherto been discernible! What was invariable now
was that wherever Swann might be, he never failed to go
on afterwards to Odette. The interval of space separating
her from him was one which he must traverse as inevitably as though it were the irresistible and rapid slope
of life itself. Truth to tell, as often as not, when he had
stayed late at a party, he would have preferred to return
home at once, without going so far out of his way, and to
postpone their meeting until the morrow; but the very
fact of his putting himself to such inconvenience at an abnormal hour in order to visit her, while he guessed that
his friends, as he left them, were saying to one another:
"He's tied hand and foot; there must certainly be a
woman somewhere who insists on his going to her at all

hours," made him feel that he was leading the life of the
class of men whose existence is coloured by a love-affair,
and in whom the perpetual sacrifice they make of their
comfort and of their practical interests engenders a sort of
inner charm. Then, though he may not consciously have
taken this into consideration, the certainty that she was
waiting for him, that she was not elsewhere with others,
that he would see her before he went home, drew the
sting from that anguish, forgotten but latent and ever
ready to be reawakened, which he had felt on the evening
when Odette had left the Verdurins' before his arrival, an
anguish the present assuagement of which was so agreeable that it might almost be called happiness. Perhaps it
was to that hour of anguish that he owed the importance
which Odette had since assumed in his life. Other people
as a rule mean so little to us that, when we have invested
one of them with the power to cause us so much suffering
or happiness, that person seems at once to belong to a
different universe, is surrounded with poetry, makes of
one's life a sort of stirring arena in which he or she will
be more or less close to one. Swann could not ask himself
with equanimity what Odette would mean to him in the
years that were to come. Sometimes, as he looked up from
his victoria on those fine and frosty nights and saw the
bright moonbeams fall between his eyes and the deserted
street, he would think of that other face, gleaming and
faintly roseate like the moon's, which had, one day, risen
on the horizon of his mind, and since then had shed upon
the world the mysterious light in which he saw it bathed.
If he arrived after the hour at which Odette sent her servants to bed, before ringing the bell at the gate of her little garden he would go round first into the other street,

over which, on the ground-floor, among the windows (all exactly alike, but darkened) of the adjoining houses, shone the solitary lighted window of her room. He would rap on the pane, and she would hear the signal, and answer, before going to meet him at the front door. He would find, lying open on the piano, some of her favourite music, the *Valse des Roses*, the *Pauvre Fou* of Tagliafico (which, according to the instructions embodied in her will, was to be played at her funeral); but he would ask her, instead, to give him the little phrase from Vinteuil's sonata. It was true that Odette played vilely, but often the most memorable impression of a piece of music is one that has arisen out of a jumble of wrong notes struck by unskilful fingers upon a tuneless piano. The little phrase continued to be associated in Swann's mind with his love for Odette. He was well aware that his love was something that did not correspond to anything outside itself, verifiable by others besides him; he realised that Odette's qualities were not such as to justify his setting so high a value on the hours he spent in her company. And often, when the cold government of reason stood unchallenged in his mind, he would readily have ceased to sacrifice so many of his intellectual and social interests to this imaginary pleasure. But the little phrase, as soon as it struck his ear, had the power to liberate in him the space that was needed to contain it; the proportions of Swann's soul were altered; a margin was left for an enjoyment that corresponded no more than his love for Odette to any external object and yet was not, like his enjoyment of that love, purely individual, but assumed for him a sort of reality superior to that of concrete things. This thirst for an unknown delight was awakened in him by the little phrase, but without bringing him any precise gratification to assuage it. With the result that those parts of Swann's soul in which the little phrase had obliterated all concern for material interests, those human considerations which affect all men alike, were left vacant by it, blank pages on which he was at liberty to inscribe the name of Odette. Moreover, in so far as Odette's affection might seem a little abrupt and disappointing, the little phrase would come to supplement it, to blend with it its own mysterious essence. Watching Swann's face while he listened to the phrase, one would have said that he was inhaling an anaesthetic which allowed him to breathe more freely. And the pleasure which the music gave him, which was shortly to create in him a real need, was in fact akin at such moments to the pleasure which he would have derived from experimenting with perfumes, from entering into contact with a world for which we men were not made, which appears to us formless because our eyes cannot perceive it, meaningless because it eludes our understanding, to which we may attain by way of one sense only. There was a deep repose, a mysterious refreshment for Swann—whose eyes, although delicate interpreters of painting, whose mind, although an acute observer of manners, must bear for ever the indelible imprint of the barrenness of his life—in feeling himself transformed into a creature estranged from humanity, blinded, deprived of his logical faculty, almost a fantastic unicorn, a chimaera-like creature conscious of the world through his hearing alone. And since he sought in the little phrase for a meaning to which his intelligence could not descend, with what a strange frenzy of intoxication did he strip bare his innermost soul of the whole armour of reason and make it pass unattended through the dark filter of sound! He began to realise how much that was painful, perhaps even how much secret and unappeased sorrow underlay the sweetness of the phrase; and yet to him it brought no suffering. What matter though the phrase repeated that love is frail and fleeting, when his love was so strong! He played with the melancholy which the music diffused, he felt it stealing over him, but like a caress which only deepened and sweetened his sense of his own happiness. He would make Odette play it over to him again and again, ten, twenty times on end, insisting that, as she did so, she must never stop kissing him. Every kiss provokes another. Ah, in those earliest days of love how naturally the kisses spring into life! So closely, in their profusion, do they crowd together that lovers would find it as hard to count the kisses exchanged in an hour as to count the flowers in a meadow in May. Then she would pretend to stop, saying: "How do you expect me to play when you keep on holding me? I can't do everything at once. Make up your mind what you want: am I to play the phrase or play with you?", and he would get angry, and she would burst out laughing, a laugh that was soon transformed and descended upon him in a shower of kisses. Or else she would look at him sulkily, and he would see once again a face worthy to figure in Botticelli's "Life of Moses"; he would place it there, giving to Odette's neck the necessary inclination; and when he had finished her portrait in tempera, in the fifteenth century, on the wall of the Sistine, the idea that she was none the less in the room with him still, by the piano, at that very moment, ready to be kissed and enjoyed, the idea of her material existence, would sweep over him with so violent an intoxication that, with eyes starting from his head and jaws tensed as though to devour her, he would fling himself upon this Botticelli maiden and kiss and bite her cheeks. And then, once he had left her, not without returning to kiss her again because he had forgotten to take away with him the memory of some detail of her fragrance or of her features, as he drove home in his victoria he blessed Odette for allowing him these daily visits which could not, he felt, bring any great joy to her, but which, by keeping him immune from the fever of jealousy—by removing from him any possibility of a fresh outbreak of the heart-sickness which had afflicted him on the evening when he had failed to find her at the Verdurins'—would help him to arrive, without any recurrence of those crises of which the first had been so painful that it must also be the last, at the end of this strange period of his life, of these hours, enchanted almost, like those in which he drove through Paris by moonlight. And, noticing as he drove home that the moon had now changed its position relatively to his own and was almost touching the horizon, feeling that his love, too, was obedient to these immutable natural laws, he asked himself whether this period upon which he had entered would last much longer, whether presently his mind's eye would cease to behold that beloved face save as occupying a distant and diminished position, and on the verge of ceasing to shed on him the radiance of its charm. For Swann was once more finding in things, since he had fallen in love, the charm that he had found when, in his adolescence, he had fancied himself an artist; with this difference, that the charm that lay in them now was conferred by Odette alone. He felt the inspirations of his youth, which had been dissipated by a frivolous life, stirring again in him, but they all bore now the reflection, the stamp of a particular being; and during the long hours which he now found a subtle pleasure in spending at home, alone with his convalescent soul, he became gradually himself again, but himself in thraldom to another.

He went to her only in the evenings, and knew nothing of how she spent her time during the day, any more than of her past; so little, indeed, that he had not even the tiny, initial clue which, by allowing us to imagine what we do not know, stimulates a desire for knowledge. And so he never asked himself what she might be doing, or what her life had been. Only he smiled sometimes at the thought of how, some years earlier, when he did not yet know her, people had spoken to him of a woman who, if he remembered rightly, must certainly have been Odette, as of a tart, a kept woman, one of those women to whom he still attributed (having lived but little in their company) the wilful, fundamentally perverse character with which they had so long been endowed by the imagination of certain novelists. He told himself that as often as not one has only to take the opposite view to the reputation created by the world in order to judge a person accurately, when with such a character he contrasted that of Odette, so kind, so simple, so enthusiastic in the pursuit of ideals, so incapable, almost, of not telling the truth that, when he had once begged her, so that they might dine together alone, to write to Mme Verdurin saying that she was unwell, the next day he had seen her, face to face with Mme Verdurin who asked whether she had recovered, blushing, stammering and in spite of herself revealing in every feature how painful, what a torture it was to her to act a lie and, as in her answer she multiplied the fictitious details of her alleged indisposition, seeming to ask forgiveness, by her suppliant look and her stricken accents, for the obvious falsehood of her words.

On certain days, however, though these were rare, she would call upon him in the afternoon, interrupting his musings or the essay on Vermeer to which he had latterly returned. His servant would come in to say that Mme de Crécy was in the small drawing-room. He would go and join her, and when he opened the door, on Odette's rosy face, as soon as she caught sight of Swann, would appear—changing the curve of her lips, the look in her eyes, the moulding of her cheeks—an all-absorbing smile. Once he was alone he would see that smile again, and also her smile of the day before, and another with which she had greeted him sometime else, and the smile which had been her answer, in the carriage that night, when he had asked her whether she objected to his rearranging her cattleyas; and the life of Odette at all other times, since he knew nothing of it, appeared to him, with its neutral and colourless background, like those sheets of sketches by Watteau upon which one sees here, there, at every corner and at various angles, traced in three colours upon the buff paper, innumerable smiles. But once in a while, illuminating a chink of that existence which Swann still saw as a complete blank, even if his mind assured him that it was not, because he was unable to visualise it, some friend who knew them both and, suspecting that they were in love, would not have dared to tell him anything about her that was of the least importance, would describe how he had glimpsed Odette that very morning walking up the Rue Abbattucci, in a cape trimmed with skunk, a Rembrandt hat, and a bunch of violets in her bosom. Swann would be bowled over by this simple sketch because it suddenly made him realise that Odette had an existence that was not wholly subordinated to his own; he longed to know whom she had been seeking to impress by this costume in which he had never seen her, and he made up his mind to ask her where she had been going at that intercepted moment, as though, in all the colourless life of his mistress—a life almost non-existent, since it was invisible to him—there had been but a single incident apart from all those smiles directed towards himself: namely, her walking abroad beneath a Rembrandt hat, with a bunch of violets in her bosom.

Except when he asked her for Vinteuil's little phrase instead of the *Valse des Roses*, Swann made no effort to induce her to play the things that he himself preferred, or, in literature any more than in music, to correct the manifold errors of her taste. He fully realised that she was not intelligent. When she said how much she would like him to tell her about the great poets, she had imagined that she would immediately get to know whole pages of romantic and heroic verse, in the style of the Vicomte de Borelli, only even more moving. As for Vermeer of Delft, she asked whether he had been made to suffer by a woman, if it was a woman who had inspired him, and once Swann had told her that no one knew, she had lost all interest in that painter. She would often say: "Poetry, you know—well, of course, there'd be nothing like it if it was all true, if the poets believed everything they say. But as often as not you'll find there's no one so calculating as those fellows. I know something about it: I had a friend, once, who was in love with a poet of sorts. In his verses he never spoke of anything but love and the sky and the

stars. Oh! she was properly taken in! He did her out of
more than three hundred thousand francs."

If, then, Swann tried to show her what artistic beauty
consisted in, how one ought to appreciate poetry or painting, after a minute or two she would cease to listen, saying: "Yes . . . I never thought it would be like that."
And he felt that her disappointment was so great that he
preferred to lie to her, assuring her that what he had said
was nothing, that he had only touched the surface, that he
had no time to go into it all properly, that there was more
in it than that. Then she would interrupt sharply: "More
in it? What? . . . Do tell me!", but he did not tell her,
knowing how feeble it would appear to her, how different
from what she had expected, less sensational and less
touching, and fearing lest, disillusioned with art, she
might at the same time be disillusioned with love.

With the result that she found Swann inferior, intellectually, to what she had supposed. "You're always so
reserved; I can't make you out." She was more impressed
by his indifference to money, by his kindness to everyone,
by his courtesy and tact. And indeed it happens, often
enough, to greater men than Swann, to a scientist or an
artist, when he is not misunderstood by the people among
whom he lives, that the feeling on their part which proves
that they have been convinced of the superiority of his intellect is not their admiration for his ideas—for these are
beyond them—but their respect for his kindness. Swann's
position in society also inspired Odette with respect, but
she had no desire that he should attempt to secure invitations for herself. Perhaps she felt that such attempts
would be bound to fail; perhaps she even feared that,
merely by speaking of her to his friends, he might pro-

voke disclosures of an unwelcome kind. At all events she had made him promise never to mention her name. Her reason for not wishing to go into society was, she had told him, a quarrel she had once had with a friend who had avenged herself subsequently by speaking ill of her. "But surely," Swann objected, "not everyone knew your friend." "Yes, but don't you see, it spreads like wildfire; people are so horrid." Swann found this story frankly incomprehensible; on the other hand, he knew that such generalisations as "People are so horrid," and "A word of scandal spreads like wildfire," were generally accepted as true; there must be cases to which they were applicable. Could Odette's be one of these? He teased himself with the question, though not for long, for he too was subject to that mental torpor that had so weighed upon his father, whenever he was faced by a difficult problem. In any event, that world of society which so frightened Odette did not, perhaps, inspire her with any great longings, since it was too far removed from the world she knew for her to be able to form any clear conception of it. At the same time, while in certain aspects she had retained a genuine simplicity (she had, for instance, kept up a friendship with a little dressmaker, now retired from business, up whose steep and dark and fetid staircase she clambered almost every day), she still thirsted to be in the fashion, though her idea of it was not altogether the same as that of society people. For the latter, it emanates from a comparatively small number of individuals, who project it to a considerable distance—more and more faintly the further one is from their intimate centre—within the circle of their friends and the friends of their friends, whose names form a sort of tabulated index. Society people

know this index by heart; they are gifted in such matters
with an erudition from which they have extracted a sort
of taste, of tact, so automatic in its operation that Swann,
for example, without needing to draw upon his knowledge
of the world, if he read in a newspaper the names of the
people who had been at a dinner-party, could tell at once
its exact degree of smartness, just as a man of letters,
simply by reading a sentence, can estimate exactly the literary merit of its author. But Odette was one of those
persons (an extremely numerous category, whatever the
fashionable world may think, and to be found in every
class of society) who do not share these notions, but
imagine smartness to be something quite other, which assumes different aspects according to the circle to which
they themselves belong, but has the special characteristic—common alike to the fashion of which Odette
dreamed and to that before which Mme Cottard bowed—
of being directly accessible to all. The other kind, the
smartness of society people, is, it must be admitted,
accessible also; but there is a time-lag. Odette would say
of someone: "He only goes to smart places."

    And if Swann asked her what she meant by that, she
would answer with a touch of contempt: "Smart places!
Why, good heavens, just fancy, at your age, having to be
told what the smart places are! Well, on Sunday mornings
there's the Avenue de l'Impératrice, and round the lake at
five o'clock, and on Thursdays, the Eden Théâtre, and
the Races on Fridays; then there are the balls . . ."

    "What balls?"

    "Why, silly, the balls people give in Paris; the smart
ones, I mean. For instance, Herbinger, you know who I
mean, the fellow who's in one of the jobbers' offices. Yes,

of course you must know him, he's one of the best-known
men in Paris, that great big fair-haired boy who's such a
toff—always has a flower in his buttonhole, a parting at
the back, light-coloured overcoats. He goes about with
that old frump, takes her to all the first-nights. Well, he
gave a ball the other night, and all the smart people in
Paris were there. I should have loved to go! But you had
to show your invitation at the door, and I couldn't get
one anywhere. Still, I'm just as glad, now, that I didn't
go; I should have been killed in the crush, and seen nothing. It's really just to be able to say you've been to
Herbinger's ball. You know what a braggart I am! However, you may be quite certain that half the people who
tell you they were there are lying . . . But I'm surprised
you weren't there, a regular 'swell' like you."

Swann made no attempt, however, to modify this
conception of fashionable life; feeling that his own came
no nearer to the truth, was just as fatuous and trivial, he
saw no point in imparting it to his mistress, with the result that, after a few months, she ceased to take any interest in the people to whose houses he went, except as a
means of obtaining tickets for the paddock at race-meet-
ings or first-nights at the theatre. She hoped that he
would continue to cultivate such profitable acquaintances,
but in other respects she was inclined to regard them as
anything but smart, ever since she had passed the Marquise de Villeparisis in the street, wearing a black woollen
dress and a bonnet with strings.

"But she looks like an usherette, like an old concierge,
darling! A marquise, her! Goodness knows I'm not a marquise, but you'd have to pay me a lot of money before
you'd get me to go round Paris rigged out like that!"

Nor could she understand Swann's continuing to live
in his house on the Quai d'Orleans, which, though she
dared not tell him so, she considered unworthy of him.

It was true that she claimed to be fond of "antiques,"
and used to assume a rapturous and knowing air when
she confessed how she loved to spend the whole day
"rummaging" in curio shops, hunting for "bric-à-brac"
and "period" things. Although it was a point of honour to
which she obstinately clung, as though obeying some old
family precept, that she should never answer questions or
"account for" how she spent her days, she spoke to
Swann once about a friend to whose house she had been
invited, and had found that everything in it was "of the
period." Swann could not get her to tell him what the period was. But after thinking the matter over she replied
that it was "mediaeval"; by which she meant that the
walls were panelled. Some time later she spoke to him
again of her friend, and added, in the hesitant tone and
with the knowing air one adopts in referring to a person
one has met at dinner the night before and of whom one
had never heard until then, but whom one's hosts seemed
to regard as someone so celebrated and important that
one hopes that one's listener will know who is meant and
be duly impressed: "Her dining-room . . . is . . . eigh-
teenth century!" She herself had thought it hideous, all
bare, as though the house were still unfinished; women
looked frightful in it, and it would never become the fashion. She mentioned it again, a third time, when she
showed Swann a card with the name and address of the
man who had designed the dining-room, and whom she
wanted to send for when she had enough money, to see
whether he couldn't do one for her too; not one like that,

of course, but one of the sort she used to dream of and which unfortunately her little house wasn't large enough to contain, with tall sideboards, Renaissance furniture and fireplaces like the château at Blois. It was on this occasion that she blurted out to Swann what she really thought of his abode on the Quai d'Orléans; he having ventured the criticism that her friend had indulged, not in the Louis XVI style, for although that was not, of course, done, still it might be made charming, but in the "sham-antique."

"You wouldn't have her live like you among a lot of broken-down chairs and threadbare carpets!" she exclaimed, the innate respectability of the bourgeois housewife getting the better of the acquired dilettantism of the cocotte.

People who enjoyed picking up antiques, who liked poetry, despised sordid calculations of profit and loss, and nourished ideals of honour and love, she placed in a class by themselves, superior to the rest of humanity. There was no need actually to have those tastes, as long as one proclaimed them; when a man had told her at dinner that he loved to wander about and get his hands covered with dust in old furniture shops, that he would never be really appreciated in this commercial age since he was not interested in its concerns, and that he belonged to another generation altogether, she would come home saying: "Why, he's an adorable creature, so sensitive, I had no idea," and she would conceive for him an immediate bond of friendship. But on the other hand, men who, like Swann, had these tastes but did not speak of them, left her cold. She was obliged, of course, to admit that Swann was not interested in money, but she would add sulkily:

"It's not the same thing, you see, with him," and, as a matter of fact, what appealed to her imagination was not the practice of disinterestedness, but its vocabulary.

Feeling that, often, he could not give her in reality the pleasures of which she dreamed, he tried at least to ensure that she should be happy in his company, tried not to counteract those vulgar ideas, that bad taste which she displayed on every possible occasion, and which in fact he loved, as he could not help loving everything that came from her, which enchanted him even, for were they not so many characteristic features by virtue of which the essence of this woman revealed itself to him? And so, when she was in a happy mood because she was going to see the *Reine Topaze*,[10] or when her expression grew serious, worried, petulant because she was afraid of missing the flower-show, or merely of not being in time for tea, with muffins and toast, at the Rue Royale tea-rooms, where she believed that regular attendance was indispensable in order to set the seal upon a woman's certificate of elegance, Swann, enraptured as we all are at times by the naturalness of a child or the verisimilitude of a portrait which appears to be on the point of speaking, would feel so distinctly the soul of his mistress rising to the surface of her face that he could not refrain from touching it with his lips. "Ah, so little Odette wants us to take her to the flower-show, does she? She wants to be admired, does she? Very well, we'll take her there, we can but obey." As Swann was a little short-sighted, he had to resign himself to wearing spectacles at home when working, while to face the world he adopted a monocle as being less disfiguring. The first time that she saw it in his eye, she could not contain her joy: "I really do think—for a man, that is to say—it's tremendously smart! How nice you look with it! Every inch a gentleman. All you want now is a title!" she concluded with a tinge of regret. He liked Odette to say these things, just as if he had been in love with a Breton girl, he would have enjoyed seeing her in her coif and hearing her say that she believed in ghosts. Always until then, as is common among men whose taste for the arts develops independently of their sensuality, a weird disparity had existed between the satisfactions which he would accord to both simultaneously; yielding to the seductions of more and more rarefied works of art in the company of more and more vulgar women, taking a little servant-girl to a screened box at the theatre for the performance of a decadent piece he particularly wanted to see, or to an exhibition of Impressionist painting, convinced, moreover, that a cultivated society woman would have understood them no better, but would not have managed to remain so prettily silent. But, now that he was in love with Odette, all this was changed; to share her sympathies, to strive to be one with her in spirit, was a task so attractive that he tried to find enjoyment in the things that she liked, and did find a pleasure, not only in imitating her habits but in adopting her opinions, which was all the deeper because, as those habits and opinions had no roots in his own intelligence, they reminded him only of his love, for the sake of which he had preferred them to his own. If he went again to *Serge Panine*, if he looked out for opportunities of going to see Olivier Métra conduct,[11] it was for the pleasure of being initiated into every one of Odette's ideas and fancies, of feeling that he had an equal share in all her tastes. This charm, which her favourite plays and pictures and places possessed, of drawing him

closer to her, struck him as being more mysterious than
the intrinsic charm of more beautiful things and places
with which she had no connection. Besides, having allowed the intellectual beliefs of his youth to languish, and
his man-of-the-world scepticism having permeated them
without his being aware of it, he felt (or at least he had
felt for so long that he had fallen into the habit of saying)
that the objects we admire have no absolute value in
themselves, that the whole thing is a matter of period and
class, is no more than a series of fashions, the most vulgar
of which are worth just as much as those which are regarded as the most refined. And as he considered that the
importance Odette attached to receiving an invitation to a
private view was not in itself any more ridiculous than the
pleasure he himself had at one time felt in lunching with
the Prince of Wales, so he did not think that the admiration she professed for Monte-Carlo or for the Righi was
any more unreasonable than his own liking for Holland
(which she imagined to be ugly) and for Versailles (which
bored her to tears). And so he denied himself the pleasure
of visiting those places, delighted to tell himself that it
was for her sake, that he wished only to feel, to enjoy
things with her.

Like everything else that formed part of Odette's environment, and was no more, in a sense, than the means
whereby he might see and talk to her more often, he enjoyed the society of the Verdurins. There, since at the
heart of all their entertainments, dinners, musical
evenings, games, suppers in fancy dress, excursions to the
country, theatre outings, even the infrequent "gala
evenings" when they entertained the "bores," there was
the presence of Odette, the sight of Odette, conversation

with Odette, an inestimable boon which the Verdurins bestowed on Swann by inviting him to their house, he was happier in the little "nucleus" than anywhere else, and tried to find some genuine merit in each of its members, imagining that this would lead him to frequent their society from choice for the rest of his life. Not daring to tell himself, lest he should doubt the truth of the suggestion, that he would always love Odette, at least in supposing that he would go on visiting the Verdurins (a proposition which, *a priori*, raised fewer fundamental objections on the part of his intelligence) he saw himself in the future continuing to meet Odette every evening; that did not, perhaps, come quite to the same thing as loving her for ever, but for the moment, while he loved her, to feel that he would not eventually cease to see her was all that he asked. "What a charming atmosphere!" he said to himself. "How entirely genuine is the life these people lead! How much more intelligent, more artistic, they are than the people one knows! And Mme Verdurin, in spite of a few trifling exaggerations which are rather absurd, what a sincere love of painting and music she has, what a passion for works of art, what anxiety to give pleasure to artists! Her ideas about some of the people one knows are not quite right, but then their ideas about artistic circles are still more wrong! Possibly I make no great intellectual demands in conversation, but I'm perfectly happy talking to Cottard, although he does trot out those idiotic puns. And as for the painter, if he is rather disagreeably pretentious when he tries to shock, still he has one of the finest brains that I've ever come across. Besides, what is most important, one feels quite free there, one does what one likes without constraint or fuss. What a flow of good humour there is every day in that drawing-room! No question about it, with a few rare exceptions I never want to go anywhere else again. It will become more and more of a habit, and I shall spend the rest of my life there."

And as the qualities which he supposed to be intrinsic to the Verdurins were no more than the superficial reflection of pleasures which he had enjoyed in their society through his love for Odette, those qualities became more serious, more profound, more vital, when those pleasures were too. Since Mme Verdurin often gave Swann what alone could constitute his happiness—since, on an evening when he felt anxious because Odette had talked rather more to one of the party than to another, and, irritated by this, would not take the initiative of asking her whether she was coming home with him, Mme Verdurin brought peace and joy to his troubled spirit by saying spontaneously: "Odette, you'll see M. Swann home, won't you?"; and since, when the summer holidays were impending and he had asked himself uneasily whether Odette might not leave Paris without him, whether he would still be able to see her every day, Mme Verdurin had invited them both to spend the summer with her in the country—Swann, unconsciously allowing gratitude and self-interest to infiltrate his intelligence and to influence his ideas, went so far as to proclaim that Mme Verdurin was "a great soul." Should one of his old fellow-students from the École du Louvre speak to him of some delightful or eminent people he had come across, "I'd a hundred times rather have the Verdurins" he would reply. And, with a solemnity of diction that was new in him: "They are magnanimous creatures, and magnanimity is, after all, the one thing that matters, the one thing that gives us distinction here on earth. You see, there are only two classes of people, the magnanimous, and the rest; and I have reached an age when one has to take sides, to decide once and for all whom one is going to like and dislike, to stick to the people one likes, and, to make up for the time one has wasted with the others, never to leave them again as long as one lives. And so," he went on, with the slight thrill of emotion which a man feels when, even without being fully aware of it, he says something not because it is true but because he enjoys saying it, and listens to his own voice uttering the words as though they came from someone else, "the die is now cast. I have elected to love none but magnanimous souls, and to live only in an atmosphere of magnanimity. You ask me whether Mme Verdurin is really intelligent. I can assure you that she has given me proofs of a nobility of heart, of a loftiness of soul, to which no one could possibly attain without a corresponding loftiness of mind. Without question, she has a profound understanding of art. But it is not, perhaps, in that that she is most admirable; every little action, ingeniously, exquisitely kind, which she has performed for my sake, every thoughtful attention, every little gesture, quite domestic and yet quite sublime, reveals a more profound comprehension of existence than all your text-books of philosophy."

He might have reminded himself that there were various old friends of his family who were just as simple as the Verdurins, companions of his youth who were just as fond of art, that he knew other "great-hearted" people, and that nevertheless, since he had opted in favour of simplicity, the arts, and magnanimity, he had entirely ceased to see them. But these people did not know

Odette, and, if they had known her, would never have thought of introducing her to him.

And so, in the whole of the Verdurin circle, there was probably not a single one of the "faithful" who loved them, or believed that he loved them, as dearly as did Swann. And yet, when M. Verdurin had said that he did not take to Swann, he had not only expressed his own sentiments, he had divined those of his wife. Doubtless Swann had too exclusive an affection for Odette, of which he had neglected to make Mme Verdurin his regular confidante; doubtless the very discretion with which he availed himself of the Verdurins' hospitality, often refraining from coming to dine with them for a reason which they never suspected and in place of which they saw only an anxiety on his part not to have to decline an invitation to the house of some "bore" or other, and doubtless, too, despite all the precautions which he had taken to keep it from them, the gradual discovery which they were making of his brilliant position in society— doubtless all this contributed to their growing irritation with Swann. But the real, the fundamental reason was quite different. The fact was that they had very quickly sensed in him a locked door, a reserved, impenetrable chamber in which he still professed silently to himself that the Princesse de Sagan was not grotesque and that Cottard's jokes were not amusing, in a word, for all that he never deviated from his affability or revolted against their dogmas, an impermeability to those dogmas, a resistance to complete conversion, the like of which they had never come across in anyone before. They would have forgiven him for associating with "bores" (to whom, as it

happened, in his heart of hearts he infinitely preferred the
Verdurins and all the little "nucleus") had he consented
to set a good example by openly renouncing those "bores"
in the presence of the "faithful." But that was an abjura-
tion which they realised they were powerless to extort
from him.

How different he was from a "newcomer" whom
Odette had asked them to invite, although she herself had
met him only a few times, and on whom they were building great hopes—the Comte de Forcheville! (It turned
out that he was Saniette's brother-in-law, a discovery
which filled all the faithful with amazement: the manners
of the old palaeographer were so humble that they had
always supposed him to be socially inferior to themselves, and had never expected to learn that he came from
a rich and relatively aristocratic background.) Of course,
Forcheville was a colossal snob, which Swann was not; of
course he would never dream of placing, as Swann now
did, the Verdurin circle above all others. But he lacked
that natural refinement which prevented Swann from associating himself with the more obviously false accusa-
tions that Mme Verdurin levelled at people he knew. As
for the vulgar and pretentious tirades in which the painter
sometimes indulged, the commercial traveller's pleasantries which Cottard used to hazard, and for which
Swann, who liked both men sincerely, could easily find
excuses without having either the heart or the hypocrisy
to applaud them, Forcheville by contrast was of an intellectual calibre to be dumbfounded, awestruck by the first
(without in the least understanding them) and to revel in
the second. And as it happened, the very first dinner at

the Verdurins' at which Forcheville was present threw a glaring light upon all these differences, brought out his qualities and precipitated Swann's fall from grace.

There was at this dinner, besides the usual party, a professor from the Sorbonne, one Brichot, who had met M. and Mme Verdurin at a watering-place somewhere and who, if his university duties and scholarly labours had not left him with very little time to spare, would gladly have come to them more often. For he had the sort of curiosity and superstitious worship of life which, combined with a certain scepticism with regard to the object of their studies, earns for some intelligent men of whatever profession, doctors who do not believe in medicine, schoolmasters who do not believe in Latin exercises, the reputation of having broad, brilliant and indeed superior minds. He affected, when at Mme Verdurin's, to choose his illustrations from among the most topical subjects of the day when he spoke of philosophy or history, principally because he regarded those sciences as no more than a preparation for life, and imagined that he was seeing put into practice by the "little clan" what hitherto he had known only from books, and perhaps also because, having had instilled into him as a boy, and having unconsciously preserved, a reverence for certain subjects, he thought that he was casting aside the scholar's gown when he ventured to treat those subjects with a conversational licence which in fact seemed daring to him only because the folds of the gown still clung.

Early in the course of the dinner, when M. de Forcheville, seated on the right of Mme Verdurin who in the "newcomer's" honour had taken great pains with her toilet, observed to her: 'Quite original, that white dress,"

the doctor, who had never taken his eyes off him so curious was he to learn the nature and attributes of what he
called a "de," and who was on the look-out for an opportunity of attracting his attention and coming into closer
contact with him, caught in its flight the adjective
"*blanche*" and, his eyes still glued to his plate, snapped
out, "*Blanche?* Blanche of Castile?" then, without moving
his head, shot a furtive glance to right and left of him,
smiling uncertainly. While Swann, by the painful and futile effort which he made to smile, showed that he
thought the pun absurd, Forcheville had shown at one
and the same time that he could appreciate its subtlety
and that he was a man of the world, by keeping within its
proper limits a mirth the spontaneity of which had
charmed Mme Verdurin.

"What do you make of a scientist like that?" she
asked Forcheville. "You can't talk seriously to him for
two minutes on end. Is that the sort of thing you tell
them at your hospital?" she went on, turning to the doctor. "They must have some pretty lively times there, if
that's the case. I can see that I shall have to get taken in
as a patient!"

"I think I heard the Doctor speak of that old terma-
gant, Blanche of Castile, if I may so express myself. Am I
not right, Madame?" Brichot appealed to Mme Verdurin,
who, swooning with merriment, her eyes tightly closed,
had buried her face in her hands, from behind which
muffled screams could be heard.

"Good gracious, Madame, I would not dream of
shocking the reverent-minded, if there are any such
around this table, *sub rosa* . . . I recognise, moreover,
that our ineffable and Athenian—oh, how infinitely

Athenian—republic is capable of honouring, in the person of that obscurantist old she-Capet, the first of our
strong-arm chiefs of police. Yes, indeed, my dear host,
yes indeed, yes indeed!" he repeated in his ringing voice,
which sounded a separate note for each syllable, in reply
to a protest from M.Verdurin. "The *Chronique de Saint-
Denis*, and the authenticity of its information is beyond
question, leaves us no room for doubt on that point. No
one could be more fitly chosen as patron by a secularised
proletariat than that mother of a saint, to whom, incidentally, she gave a pretty rough time, according to Suger
and other St Bernards of the sort; for with her everyone
got hauled over the coals."

"Who is that gentleman?" Forcheville asked Mme
Verdurin. "He seems first-rate."

"What! Do you mean to say you don't know the famous Brichot? Why, he's celebrated all over Europe."

"Oh, that's Bréchot, is it?" exclaimed Forcheville,
who had not quite caught the name. "You must tell me
all about him," he went on, fastening a pair of goggle
eyes on the celebrity. "It's always interesting to dine with
prominent people. But, I say, you ask one to very select
parties here. No dull evenings in this house, I'm sure."

"Well, you know what it is really," said Mme Verdurin modestly, "they feel at ease here. They can talk
about whatever they like, and the conversation goes off
like fireworks. Now Brichot, this evening, is nothing. I've
seen him, don't you know, when he's been in my house,
simply dazzling; you'd want to go on your knees to him.
Well, anywhere else he's not the same man, he's not in
the least witty, you have to drag the words out of him,
he's even boring."

"That's strange," remarked Forcheville with fitting astonishment.

A sort of wit like Brichot's would have been regarded as out-and-out stupidity by the people among whom Swann had spent his early life, for all that it is quite compatible with real intelligence. And the intelligence of the Professor's vigorous and well-nourished brain might easily have been envied by many of the people in society who seemed witty enough to Swann. But these last had so thoroughly inculcated into him their likes and dislikes, at least in everything that pertained to social life, including that adjunct to social life which belongs, strictly speaking, to the domain of intelligence, namely, conversation, that Swann could not but find Brichot's pleasantries pedantic, vulgar and nauseating. He was shocked, too, being accustomed to good manners, by the rude, almost barrack-room tone the pugnacious academic adopted no matter to whom he was speaking. Finally, perhaps, he had lost some of his tolerance that evening when he saw the cordiality displayed by Mme Verdurin towards this Forcheville fellow whom it had been Odette's unaccountable idea to bring to the house. Somewhat embarrassed vis-à-vis Swann, she asked him on her arrival: "What do you think of my guest?"

And he, suddenly realising for the first time that Forcheville, whom he had known for years, could actually attract a woman and was quite a good-looking man, replied: "Unspeakable!" It did not occur to him to be jealous of Odette, but he did not feel quite so happy as usual, and when Brichot, having begun to tell them the story of Blanche of Castile's mother who, according to him, "had been with Henry Plantagenet for years before

they were married," tried to prompt Swann to beg him to
continue the story by interjecting "Isn't that so,
M. Swann?" in the martial accents people use in order to
put themselves on a level with a country bumpkin or to
put the fear of God into a trooper, Swann cut his story
short, to the intense fury of their hostess, by begging to
be excused for taking so little interest in Blanche of
Castile, as he had something that he wished to ask the
painter. The latter, it appeared, had been that afternoon
to an exhibition of the work of another artist, also a friend
of Mme Verdurin, who had recently died, and Swann
wished to find out from him (for he valued his discrimination) whether there had really been anything more in
these last works than the virtuosity which had struck people so forcibly in his earlier exhibitions.

"From that point of view it was remarkable, but it
did not seem to me to be a form of art which you could
call 'elevated,' " said Swann with a smile.

"Elevated . . . to the purple," interrupted Cottard,
raising his arms with mock solemnity. The whole table
burst out laughing.

"What did I tell you?" said Mme Verdurin to
Forcheville. "It's simply impossible to be serious with
him. When you least expect it, out he comes with some
piece of foolery."

But she observed that Swann alone had not unbent.
For one thing he was none too pleased with Cottard for
having secured a laugh at his expense in front of
Forcheville. But the painter, instead of replying in a way
that might have interested Swann, as he would probably
have done had they been alone together, preferred to win

the easy admiration of the rest with a witty dissertation
on the talent of the deceased master.

"I went up to one of them," he began, "just to see
how it was done. I stuck my nose into it. Well, it's just
not true! Impossible to say whether it was done with glue,
with rubies, with soap, with sunshine, with leaven, with
cack!"

"And one makes twelve!" shouted the doctor, but just
too late, for no one saw the point of his interruption.

"It looks as though it was done with nothing at all,"
resumed the painter. "No more chance of discovering the
trick than there is in the 'Night Watch' or the 'Female
Regents,' and technically it's even better than Rembrandt
or Hals. It's all there—but really, I swear it."

Then, just as singers who have reached the highest
note in their compass continue in a head voice, piano, he
proceeded to murmur, laughing the while, as if, after all,
there had been something irresistibly absurd in the sheer
beauty of the painting: "It smells good, it makes your
head whirl; it takes your breath away; you feel ticklish all
over—and not the faintest clue to how it's done. The
man's a sorcerer; the thing's a conjuring-trick, a miracle,"
bursting into outright laughter, "it's almost dishonest!"
And stopping, solemnly raising his head, pitching his
voice on a basso profundo note which he struggled to
bring into harmony, he concluded, "And it's so sincere!"

Except at the moment when he had called it "better
than the 'Night Watch,' " a blasphemy which had called
forth an instant protest from Mme Verdurin, who regarded the "Night Watch" as the supreme masterpiece
of the universe (conjointly with the "Ninth" and the

"Winged Victory"), and at the word "cack" which had made Forcheville throw a sweeping glance round the table to see whether it was "all right," before he allowed his lips to curve in a prudish and conciliatory smile, all the guests (save Swann) had kept their fascinated and adoring eyes fixed upon the painter.

"I do so love him when he gets carried away like that!" cried Mme Verdurin the moment he had finished, enraptured that the table-talk should have proved so entertaining on the very night that Forcheville was dining with them for the first time. "Hallo, you!" she turned to her husband, "What's the matter with you, sitting there gaping like a great animal? You know he talks well. Anybody would think it was the first time he had ever listened to you," she added to the painter. "If you had only seen him while you were speaking; he was just drinking it all in. And tomorrow he'll tell us everything you said, without missing out a word."

"No, really, I'm not joking!" protested the painter, enchanted by the success of his speech. "You all look as if you thought I was pulling your legs, that it's all eyewash. I'll take you to see the show, and then you can say whether I've been exaggerating; I'll bet you anything you like, you'll come away even more enthusiastic than I am!"

"But we don't suppose for a moment that you're exaggerating. We only want you to go on with your dinner, and my husband too. Give M. Biche some more sole, can't you see his has got cold? We're not in any hurry; you're dashing round as if the house was on fire. Wait a little; don't serve the salad just yet."

Mme Cottard, who was a modest woman and spoke but seldom, was not however lacking in self-assurance when a happy inspiration put the right word in her mouth. She felt that it would be well received, and this gave her confidence, but what she did with it was with the object not so much of shining herself as of helping her husband on in his career. And so she did not allow the word "salad," which Mme Verdurin had just uttered, to pass unchallenged.

"It's not a Japanese salad, is it?" she said in a loud undertone, turning towards Odette.

And then, in her joy and confusion at the aptness and daring of making so discreet and yet so unmistakable an allusion to the new and brilliantly successful play by Dumas, she broke into a charming, girlish laugh, not very loud, but so irresistible that it was some time before she could control it.

"Who is that lady? She seems devilish clever," said Forcheville.

"No, it is not. But we'll make one for you if you'll all come to dinner on Friday."

"You will think me dreadfully provincial," said Mme Cottard to Swann, "but I haven't yet seen this famous *Francillon* that everybody's talking about. The Doctor has been (I remember now, he told me he had the great pleasure of spending the evening with you) and I must confess I didn't think it very sensible for him to spend money on seats in order to see it again with me. Of course an evening at the Théâtre-Français is never really wasted; the acting's so good there always; but we have some very nice friends" (Mme Cottard rarely uttered a proper name, but restricted herself to "some friends of ours" or "one of my friends," as being more "distinguished," speaking in an affected tone and with the self-importance of a person who need give names only when she chooses) "who often have a box, and are kind enough to take us to all the new pieces that are worth going to, and so I'm certain to see *Francillon* sooner or later, and then I shall know what to think. But I do feel such a fool about it, I must confess, for wherever I go I naturally find everybody talking about that wretched Japanese salad. In fact one's beginning to get just a little tired of hearing about it," she went on, seeing that Swann seemed less interested than she had hoped in so burning a topic. "I must admit, though, that it provides an excuse for some quite amusing notions. I've got a friend, now, who is most original, though she's a very pretty woman, very popular in society, very sought-after, and she tells me that she got her cook to make one of these Japanese salads, putting in everything that young M. Dumas says you're to in the play. Then she asked a few friends to come and taste it. I was not among the favoured few, I'm sorry to say. But she told us all about it at her next 'at home'; it seems it was quite horrible, she made us all laugh till we cried. But of course it's all in the telling," Mme Cottard added, seeing that Swann still looked grave.

And imagining that it was perhaps because he had not liked *Francillon*: "Well, I daresay I shall be disappointed with it, after all. I don't suppose it's as good as the piece Mme de Crécy worships, *Serge Panine*. There's a play, if you like; really deep, makes you think! But just fancy giving a recipe for a salad on the stage of the Théâtre-Français! Now, *Serge Panine*! But then, it's like everything that comes from the pen of Georges Ohnet, it's always so well written. I wonder if you know the

Maître des Forges, which I like even better than *Serge Panine*."

"Forgive me," said Swann with polite irony, "but I must confess that my want of admiration is almost equally divided between those masterpieces."

"Really, and what don't you like about them? Are you sure you aren't prejudiced? Perhaps you think he's a little too sad. Well, well, what I always say is, one should never argue about plays or novels. Everyone has his own way of looking at things, and what you find detestable may be just what I like best."

She was interrupted by Forcheville addressing Swann. While Mme Cottard was discussing *Francillon*, Forcheville had been expressing to Mme Verdurin his admiration for what he called the painter's "little speech": "Your friend has such a flow of language, such a memory!" he said to her when the painter had come to a standstill. "I've seldom come across anything like it. He'd make a first-rate preacher. By Jove, I wish I was like that. What with him and M. Bréchot you've got a couple of real characters, though as regards the gift of the gab, I'm not so sure that this one doesn't knock a few spots off the Professor. It comes more naturally with him, it's less studied. Although now and then he does use some words that are a bit realistic, but that's quite the thing nowadays. Anyhow, it's not often I've seen a man hold the floor as cleverly as that—'hold the spittoon' as we used to say in the regiment, where, by the way, we had a man he rather reminds me of. You could take anything you liked—I don't know what—this glass, say, and he'd rattle on about it for hours; no, not this glass, that's a silly thing to say, but something like the battle of Waterloo, or anything of that sort, he'd spin you such a yarn you simply wouldn't believe it. Why, Swann was in the same regiment; he must have known him."

"Do you see much of M. Swann?" asked Mme Verdurin.

"Oh dear, no!" he answered, and then, thinking that if he made himself pleasant to Swann he might find favour with Odette, he decided to take this opportunity of flattering him by speaking of his fashionable friends, but to do so as a man of the world himself, in a tone of good-natured criticism, and not as though he were congratulating Swann upon some unexpected success. "Isn't that so, Swann? I never see anything of you, do I?—But then, where on earth is one to see him? The fellow spends all his time ensconced with the La Trémoïlles, the Laumes and all that lot!" The imputation would have been false at any time, and was all the more so now that for at least a year Swann scarcely went anywhere except to the Verdurins'. But the mere name of a person whom the Verdurins did not know was greeted by them with a disapproving silence. M. Verdurin, dreading the painful impression which the names of these "bores," especially when flung at her in this tactless fashion in front of all the "faithful," were bound to make on his wife, cast a covert glance at her, instinct with anxious solicitude. He saw then that in her determination not to take cognisance of, not to have been affected by the news which had just been imparted to her, not merely to remain dumb, but to have been deaf as well, as we pretend to be when a friend who has offended us attempts to slip into his conversation some excuse which we might appear to be accepting if we heard it without protesting, or when someone utters the name of an enemy the very mention of whom in our presence is forbidden, Mme Verdurin, so that her silence should have the appearance not of consent but of the unconscious silence of inanimate objects, had suddenly emptied her face of all life, of all mobility; her domed forehead was no more than an exquisite piece of sculpture in the round, which the name of those La Trémoïlles with whom Swann was always "ensconced" had failed to penetrate; her nose, just perceptibly wrinkled in a frown, exposed to view two dark cavities that seemed modelled from life. You would have said that her half-opened lips were just about to speak. She was no more than a wax cast, a plaster mask, a maquette for a monument, a bust for the Palace of Industry, in front of which the public would most certainly gather and marvel to see how the sculptor, in expressing the unchallengeable dignity of the Verdurins as opposed to that of the La Trémoïlles or Laumes, whose equals (if not indeed their betters) they were, and the equals and betters of all other "bores" upon the face of the earth, had contrived to impart an almost papal majesty to the whiteness and rigidity of the stone. But the marble at last came to life and let it be understood that it didn't do to be at all squeamish if one went to that house, since the wife was always drunk and the husband so uneducated that he called a corridor a "collidor"!

"You'd need to pay me a lot of money before I'd let any of that lot set foot inside my house," Mme Verdurin concluded, gazing imperiously down on Swann.

She could scarcely have expected him to capitulate so completely as to echo the holy simplicity of the pianist's aunt, who at once exclaimed: "To think of that, now! What surprises me is that they can get anybody to go near them. I'm sure I should be afraid; one can't be too careful. How can people be so common as to go running after them?" But he might at least have replied, like Forcheville: "Gad, she's a duchess; there are still plenty of people who are impressed by that sort of thing," which would at least have permitted Mme Verdurin the retort, "And a lot of good may it do them!" Instead of which, Swann merely smiled, in a manner which intimated that he could not, of course, take such an outrageous statement seriously. M. Verdurin, who was still casting furtive glances at his wife, saw with regret and understood only too well that she was now inflamed with the passion of a Grand Inquisitor who has failed to stamp out heresy; and so, in the hope of bringing Swann round to a recantation (for the courage of one's opinions is always a form of calculating cowardice in the eyes of the other side), challenged him: "Tell us frankly, now, what you think of them yourself. We shan't repeat it to them, you may be sure."

To which Swann answered: "Why, I'm not in the least afraid of the Duchess (if it's the La Trémoïlles you're speaking of). I can assure you that everyone likes going to her house. I wouldn't go so far as to say that she's at all 'profound' " (he pronounced "profound" as if it was a ridiculous word, for his speech kept the traces of certain mental habits which the recent change in his life, a rejuvenation illustrated by his passion for music, had inclined him temporarily to discard, so that at times he

would actually state his views with considerable warmth)
"but I'm quite sincere when I say that she's intelligent,
while her husband is positively a man of letters. They're
charming people."

Whereupon Mme Verdurin, realising that this one in-
fidel would prevent her "little nucleus" from achieving
complete unanimity, was unable to restrain herself, in her
fury at the obstinacy of this wretch who could not see
what anguish his words were causing her, from screaming
at him from the depths of her tortured heart: "You may
think so if you wish, but at least you needn't say so to
us."

"It all depends on what you call intelligence."
Forcheville felt that it was his turn to be brilliant. "Come
now, Swann, tell us what you mean by intelligence."

"There," cried Odette, "that's the sort of big subject
I'm always asking him to talk to me about, and he never
will."

"Oh, but . . ." protested Swann.

"Oh, but nonsense!" said Odette.

"A water-butt?" asked the doctor.

"In your opinion," pursued Forcheville, "does intelligence mean the gift of the gab—you know, glib society
talk?"

"Finish your sweet, so that they can take your plate
away," said Mme Verdurin sourly to Saniette, who was
lost in thought and had stopped eating. And then, perhaps a little ashamed of her rudeness, "It doesn't matter,
you can take your time about it. I only reminded you because of the others, you know; it keeps the servants
back."

"There is," began Brichot, hammering out each sylla-

ble, "a rather curious definition of intelligence by that
gentle old anarchist Fénelon . . ."

"Just listen to this!" Mme Verdurin rallied
Forcheville and the doctor. "He's going to give us
Fénelon's definition of intelligence. Most interesting. It's
not often you get a chance of hearing that!"

But Brichot was keeping Fénelon's definition until
Swann had given his. Swann remained silent, and, by this
fresh act of recreancy, spoiled the brilliant dialectical con-
test which Mme Verdurin was rejoicing at being able to
offer to Forcheville.

"You see, it's just the same as with me!" said Odette
peevishly. "I'm not at all sorry to see that I'm not the
only one he doesn't find quite up to his level."

"Are these de La Trémouailles whom Mme Verdurin
has shown us to be so undesirable," inquired Brichot, articulating vigorously, "descended from the couple whom
that worthy old snob Mme de Sévigné said she was delighted to know because it was so good for her peasants?
True, the Marquise had another reason, which in her case
probably came first, for she was a thorough journalist at
heart, and always on the look-out for 'copy.' And in the
journal which she used to send regularly to her daughter,
it was Mme de La Trémouaille, kept well-informed
through all her grand connections, who supplied the foreign politics."

"No, no, I don't think they're the same family," haz-
arded Mme Verdurin.

Saniette, who ever since he had surrendered his un-
touched plate to the butler had been plunged once more
in silent meditation, emerged finally to tell them, with a
nervous laugh, the story of a dinner he had once had with

the Duc de La Trémoïlle, from which it transpired that the Duke did not know that George Sand was the pseudonym of a woman. Swann, who was fond of Saniette, felt bound to supply him with a few facts illustrative of the Duke's culture proving that such ignorance on his part was literally impossible; but suddenly he stopped short, realising that Saniette needed no proof, but knew already that the story was untrue for the simple reason that he had just invented it. The worthy man suffered acutely from the Verdurins' always finding him so boring; and as he was conscious of having been more than ordinarily dull this evening, he had made up his mind that he would succeed in being amusing at least once before the end of dinner. He capitulated so quickly, looked so wretched at the sight of his castle in ruins, and replied in so craven a tone to Swann, appealing to him not to persist in a refutation which was now superfluous— "All right; all right; anyhow, even if I'm mistaken it's not a crime, I hope"—that Swann longed to be able to console him by insisting that the story was indubitably true and exquisitely funny. The doctor, who had been listening, had an idea that it was the right moment to interject "Se non é vero," but he was not quite certain of the words, and was afraid of getting them wrong.

After dinner, Forcheville went up to the doctor.

"She can't have been at all bad looking, Mme Verdurin; and besides, she's a woman you can really talk to, which is the main thing. Of course she's getting a bit broad in the beam. But Mme de Crécy! There's a little woman who knows what's what, all right. Upon my word and soul, you can see at a glance she's got her wits about her, that girl. We're speaking of Mme de Crécy," he explained, as M. Verdurin joined them, his pipe in his mouth. "I should say that, as a specimen of the female form . . ."

"I'd rather have it in my bed than a slap with a wet fish," the words came tumbling from Cottard, who had for some time been waiting in vain for Forcheville to pause for breath so that he might get in this hoary old joke for which there might not be another cue if the conversation should take a different turn and which he now produced with that excessive spontaneity and confidence that seeks to cover up the coldness and the anxiety inseparable from a prepared recitation. Forcheville knew and saw the joke, and was thoroughly amused. As for M. Verdurin, he was unsparing of his merriment, having recently discovered a way of expressing it by a convention that was different from his wife's but equally simple and obvious. Scarcely had he begun the movement of head and shoulders of a man shaking with laughter than he would begin at once to cough, as though, in laughing too violently, he had swallowed a mouthful of pipe-smoke. And by keeping the pipe firmly in his mouth he could prolong indefinitely the dumb-show of suffocation and hilarity. Thus he and Mme Verdurin (who, at the other side of the room, where the painter was telling her a story, was shutting her eyes preparatory to flinging her face into her hands) resembled two masks in a theatre each representing Comedy in a different way.

M. Verdurin had been wiser than he knew in not taking his pipe out of his mouth, for Cottard, having occasion to leave the room for a moment, murmured a witty euphemism which he had recently acquired and repeated now whenever he had to go to the place in question: "I must just go and see the Duc d'Aumale for a minute," so drolly that M. Verdurin's cough began all over again.

"Do take your pipe out of your mouth. Can't you see that you'll choke if you try to bottle up your laughter like that," counselled Mme Verdurin as she came round with a tray of liqueurs.

"What a delightful man your husband is; he's devilish witty," declared Forcheville to Mme Cottard. "Thank you, thank you, an old soldier like me can never say no to a drink."

"M. de Forcheville thinks Odette charming," M. Verdurin told his wife.

"Ah, as a matter of fact she'd like to have lunch with you one day. We must arrange it, but don't on any account let Swann hear about it. He spoils everything, don't you know. I don't mean to say that you're not to come to dinner too, of course; we hope to see you very often. Now that the warm weather's coming, we're going to dine out of doors whenever we can. It won't bore you, will it, a quiet little dinner now and then in the Bois? Splendid, splendid, it will be so nice . . .

"I say, aren't you going to do any work this evening?" she screamed suddenly to the young pianist, seeing an opportunity for displaying, before a newcomer of Forcheville's importance, at once her unfailing wit and her despotic power over the "faithful."

"M. de Forcheville has been saying dreadful things about you," Mme Cottard told her husband as he reappeared in the room. And he, still following up the idea of Forcheville's noble birth, which had obsessed him all through dinner, said to him: "I'm treating a Baroness just now, Baroness Putbus. Weren't there some Putbuses in the Crusades? Anyhow they've got a lake in Pomerania that's ten times the size of the Place de la Concorde. I'm treating her for rheumatoid arthritis; she's a charming woman. Mme Verdurin knows her too, I believe."

Which enabled Forcheville, a moment later, finding himself alone again with Mme Cottard, to complete his favourable verdict on her husband with: "He's an interesting man, too; you can see that he knows a few people. Gad! they do get to know a lot of things, those doctors."

"I'm going to play the phrase from the sonata for M. Swann," said the pianist.

"What the devil's that? Not the sonata-snake, I hope!" shouted M. de Forcheville, hoping to create an effect.

But Dr Cottard, who had never heard this pun, missed the point of it, and imagined that M. de Forcheville had made a mistake. He dashed in boldly to correct him: "No, no. The word isn't *serpent-à-sonates*, it's *serpent-à-sonnettes*!" he explained in a tone at once zealous, impatient, and triumphant.[12]

Forcheville explained the joke to him. The doctor blushed.

"You'll admit it's not bad, eh, Doctor?"

"Oh! I've known it for ages."

Then they were silent; beneath the restless tremolos of the violin part which protected it with their throbbing sostenuto two octaves above it—and as in a mountainous country, behind the seeming immobility of a vertiginous waterfall, one descries, two hundred feet below, the tiny form of a woman walking in the valley—the little phrase had just appeared, distant, graceful, protected by the long, gradual unfurling of its transparent, incessant and sonorous curtain. And Swann, in his heart of hearts, turned to it as to a confidant of his love, as to a friend of Odette who would surely tell her to pay no attention to this Forcheville.

"Ah! you've come too late!" Mme Verdurin greeted one of the faithful whose invitation had been only "to look in after dinner." "We've been having a simply incomparable Brichot! You never heard such eloquence! But he's gone. Isn't that so, M. Swann? I believe it's the first time you've met him," she went on, to emphasise the fact that it was to her that Swann owed the introduction. "Wasn't he delicious, our Brichot?"

Swann bowed politely.

"No? You weren't interested?" she asked dryly.

"Oh, but I assure you, I was quite enthralled. He's perhaps a little too peremptory, a little too jovial for my taste. I should like to see him a little less confident at times, a little more tolerant, but one feels that he knows a great deal, and on the whole he seems a very sound fellow."

The party broke up very late. Cottard's first words to his wife were: "I've rarely seen Mme Verdurin in such form as she was tonight."

"What exactly is your Mme Verdurin? A bit of a demirep, eh?" said Forcheville to the painter, to whom he had offered a lift.

Odette watched his departure with regret; she dared not refuse to let Swann take her home, but she was moody and irritable in the carriage, and when he asked whether he might come in, replied, "I suppose so," with an impatient shrug of her shoulders.

When all the guests had gone, Mme Verdurin said to her husband: "Did you notice the way Swann laughed, such an idiotic laugh, when we spoke about Mme La Trémoïlle?"

She had remarked, more than once, how Swann and Forcheville suppressed the particle "de" before that lady's name. Never doubting that it was done on purpose, to show that they were not afraid of a title, she had made up her mind to imitate their arrogance, but had not quite grasped what grammatical form it ought to take. And so, the natural corruptness of her speech overcoming her implacable republicanism, she still said instinctively "the de La Trémoïlles," or rather (by an abbreviation sanctified by usage in music hall lyrics and cartoon captions, where the "de" is elided), "the d'La Trémoïlles," but redeemed herself by saying "Madame La Trémoïlle. — The *Duchess*, as Swann calls her," she added ironically, with a smile which proved that she was merely quoting and would not, herself, accept the least responsibility for a classification so puerile and absurd.

"I don't mind saying that I thought him extremely stupid."

M. Verdurin took it up: "He's not sincere. He's a crafty customer, always sitting on the fence, always trying to run with the hare and hunt with the hounds. What a difference between him and Forcheville. There at least you have a man who tells you straight out what he thinks. Either you agree with him or you don't. Not like the other fellow, who's never definitely fish or fowl. Did you notice, by the way, that Odette seemed all for Forcheville, and I don't blame her, either. And besides, if Swann wants to come the man of fashion over us, the champion of distressed duchesses, at any rate the other man has got a title—he's always Comte de Forcheville," he concluded with an air of discrimination, as though, familiar with every page of the history of that dignity, he were making a scrupulously exact estimate of its value in relation to others of the sort.

"I may tell you," Mme Verdurin went on, "that he saw fit to utter some venomous and quite absurd insinuations against Brichot. Naturally, once he saw that Brichot was popular in this house, it was a way of hitting back at us, of spoiling our party. I know his sort, the dear, good friend of the family who runs you down behind your back."

"Didn't I say so?" retorted her husband. "He's simply a failure, one of those small-minded individuals who are envious of anything that's at all big."

In reality there was not one of the "faithful" who was not infinitely more malicious than Swann; but they all took the precaution of tempering their calumnies with obvious pleasantries, with little sparks of emotion and cordiality; while the slightest reservation on Swann's part, undraped in any such conventional formula as "Of course, I don't mean to be unkind," to which he would not have deigned to stoop, appeared to them a deliberate act of treachery. There are certain original and distinguished authors in whom the least outspokenness is thought shocking because they have not begun by flattering the tastes of the public and serving up to it the commonplaces to which it is accustomed; it was by the same process that Swann infuriated M. Verdurin. In his case as in theirs it was the novelty of his language which led his audience to suspect the blackness of his designs.

Swann was still unconscious of the disgrace that threatened him at the Verdurins', and continued to regard all their absurdities in the most rosy light, through the admiring eyes of love.

As a rule he met Odette only in the evenings; he was afraid of her growing tired of him if he visited her during the day as well, but, being reluctant to forfeit the place that he held in her thoughts, he was constantly looking out for opportunities of claiming her attention in ways that would not be displeasing to her. If, in a florist's or a jeweller's window, a plant or an ornament caught his eye, he would at once think of sending them to Odette, imagining that the pleasure which the casual sight of them had given him would instinctively be felt also by her, and would increase her affection for him; and he would order them to be taken at once to the Rue La Pérouse, so as to accelerate the moment when, as she received an offering from him, he might feel himself somehow transported into her presence. He was particularly anxious, always, that she should receive these presents before she went out for the evening, so that her gratitude towards him might give additional tenderness to her welcome when he arrived at the Verdurins', might even—for all he knew—if the shopkeeper made haste, bring him a letter from her before dinner, or herself in person upon his doorstep, come on a little supplementary visit of thanks. As in an earlier phase, when he had tested the reactions of chagrin on Odette's nature, he now sought by those of gratitude to elicit from her intimate scraps of feeling which she had not yet revealed to him.

Often she was plagued with money troubles, and under pressure from a creditor would appeal to him for assistance. He was pleased by this, as he was pleased by anything that might impress Odette with his love for her, or merely with his influence, with the extent to which he could be of use to her. If anyone had said to him at the beginning, "It's your position that attracts her," or at this stage, "It's your money that she's really in love with," he would probably not have believed the suggestion; nor, on the other hand, would he have been greatly distressed by the thought that people supposed her to be attached to him—that people felt them to be united—by ties so binding as those of snobbishness or wealth. But even if he had believed it to be true, it might not have caused him any suffering to discover that Odette's love for him was based on a foundation more lasting than the charms or the qualities which she might see in him: namely, self-interest, a self-interest which would postpone for ever the fatal day when she might be tempted to bring their relations to an end. For the moment, by heaping presents on her, by doing her all manner of favours, he could fall back on advantages extraneous to his person, or to his intellect, as a relief from the endless, killing effort to make himself attractive to her. And the pleasure of being a lover, of living by love alone, the reality of which he was sometimes inclined to doubt, was enhanced in his eyes, as a dilettante of intangible sensations, by the price he was paying for it—as one sees people who are doubtful whether the sight of the sea and the sound of its waves are really enjoyable become convinced that they are—and convinced also of the rare quality and absolute detachment of their own taste—when they have agreed to pay several pounds a day for a room in an hotel from which that sight and that sound may be enjoyed.

One day, when reflections of this sort had brought
him back to the memory of the time when someone had
spoken to him of Odette as of a kept woman, and he was
amusing himself once again with contrasting that strange
personification, the kept woman—an iridescent mixture
of unknown and demoniacal qualities embroidered, as in
some fantasy of Gustave Moreau, with poison-dripping
flowers interwoven with precious jewels—with the Odette
on whose face he had seen the same expressions of pity
for a sufferer, revolt against an act of injustice, gratitude
for an act of kindness, which he had seen in earlier days
on his own mother's face and on the faces of his friends,
the Odette whose conversation so frequently turned on
the things that he himself knew better than anyone, his
collections, his room, his old servant, the banker who kept
all his securities, it happened that the thought of the
banker reminded him that he must call on him shortly to
draw some money. The fact was that if, during the current month, he were to come less liberally to the aid of
Odette in her financial difficulties than in the month before, when he had given her five thousand francs, if he refrained from offering her a diamond necklace for which
she longed, he would be allowing her admiration for his
generosity, her heart-warming gratitude, to decline, and
would even run the risk of giving her to believe that his
love for her (as she saw its visible manifestations grow
smaller) had itself diminished. And then, suddenly, he
wondered whether that was not precisely what was implied by "keeping" a woman (as if, in fact, that notion of
keeping could be derived from elements not at all mysterious or perverse but belonging to the intimate routine of
his daily life, such as that thousand-franc note, a familiar

and domestic object, torn in places and stuck together
again, which his valet, after paying the household accounts and the rent, had locked up in a drawer in the old
writing-desk whence he had extracted it to send it, with
four others, to Odette) and whether it might not be possible to apply to Odette, since he had known her (for he
never suspected for a moment that she could ever have
taken money from anyone before him), that title, which
he had believed so wholly inapplicable to her, of "kept
woman." He could not explore the idea further, for a sudden access of that mental lethargy which was, with him,
congenital, intermittent and providential, happened at that
moment to extinguish every particle of light in his brain,
as instantaneously as, at a later period, when electric
lighting had been everywhere installed, it became possible
to cut off the supply of light from a house. His mind
fumbled for a moment in the darkness, he took off his
spectacles, wiped the glasses, drew his hand across his
eyes, and only saw light again when he found himself face
to face with a wholly different idea, to wit, that he must
endeavour, in the coming month, to send Odette six or
seven thousand francs instead of five because of the surprise and pleasure it would cause her.

In the evening, when he did not stay at home until it
was time to meet Odette at the Verdurins', or rather at
one of the open-air restaurants which they patronised in
the Bois and especially at Saint-Cloud, he would go to
dine in one of those fashionable houses in which at one
time he had been a constant guest. He did not wish to
lose touch with people who, for all that he knew, might
some day be of use to Odette, and thanks to whom he
was often, in the meantime, able to procure for her some

privilege or pleasure. Besides, his long inurement to luxury and high society had given him a need as well as a
contempt for them, with the result that by the time he
had come to regard the humblest lodgings as precisely on
a par with the most princely mansions, his senses were so
thoroughly accustomed to the latter that he could not enter the former without a feeling of acute discomfort. He
had the same regard—to a degree of identity which they
would never have suspected—for the little families with
small incomes who asked him to dances in their flats
("straight upstairs to the fifth floor, and the door on the
left") as for the Princesse de Parme who gave the most
splendid parties in Paris; but he did not have the feeling
of being actually at a party when he found himself herded
with the fathers of families in the bedroom of the lady of
the house, while the spectacle of washstands covered over
with towels, and of beds converted into cloakrooms, with
a mass of hats and greatcoats sprawling over their coun-
terpanes, gave him the same stifling sensation that, nowadays, people who have been used for half a lifetime to
electric light derive from a smoking lamp or a candle that
needs to be snuffed.

If he was dining out, he would order his carriage for
half-past seven. While he changed his clothes, he would
be thinking all the time about Odette, and in this way
was never alone, for the constant thought of Odette gave
the moments during which he was separated from her the
same peculiar charm as those in which she was at his
side. He would get into his carriage and drive off, but he
knew that this thought had jumped in after him and had
settled down on his lap, like a pet animal which he might
take everywhere, and would keep with him at the dinner-

table unbeknown to his fellow-guests. He would stroke
and fondle it, warm himself with it, and, overcome with a
sort of languor, would give way to a slight shuddering
which contracted his throat and nostrils—a new experience, this—as he fastened the bunch of columbines in his
buttonhole. He had for some time been feeling depressed
and unwell, especially since Odette had introduced
Forcheville to the Verdurins, and he would have liked to
go away for a while to rest in the country. But he could
never summon up the courage to leave Paris, even for a
day, while Odette was there. The air was warm; it was
beautiful spring weather. And for all that he was driving
through a city of stone to immure himself in a house
without grass or garden, what was incessantly before his
eyes was a park which he owned near Combray, where, at
four in the afternoon, before coming to the asparagus-bed,
thanks to the breeze that was wafted across the fields
from Méséglise, one could enjoy the fragrant coolness of
the air beneath an arbour in the garden as much as by the
edge of the pond fringed with forget-me-nots and iris,
and where, when he sat down to dinner, the table ran riot
with the roses and the flowering currant trained and
twined by his gardener's skilful hand.

After dinner, if he had an early appointment in the
Bois or at Saint-Cloud, he would rise from table and leave
the house so abruptly—especially if it threatened to rain,
and thus to scatter the "faithful" before their normal
time—that on one occasion the Princesse des Laumes (at
whose house dinner had been so late that Swann had left
before the coffee was served to join the Verdurins on the
Island in the Bois) observed: "Really, if Swann were
thirty years older and had bladder trouble, there might be

some excuse for his running away like that. I must say it's pretty cool of him."

He persuaded himself that the charm of spring which he could not go down to Combray to enjoy might at least be found on the Ile des Cygnes or at Saint-Cloud. But as he could think only of Odette, he did not even know whether he had smelt the fragrance of the young leaves, or if the moon had been shining. He would be greeted by the little phrase from the sonata, played in the garden on the restaurant piano. If there was no piano in the garden, the Verdurins would have taken immense pains to have one brought down either from one of the rooms or from the dining-room. Not that Swann was now restored to favour; far from it. But the idea of arranging an ingenious form of entertainment for someone, even for someone they disliked, would stimulate them, during the time spent in its preparation, to a momentary sense of cordiality and affection. From time to time he would remind himself that another fine spring evening was drawing to a close, and would force himself to notice the trees and the sky. But the state of agitation into which Odette's presence never failed to throw him, added to a feverish ailment which had persisted for some time now, robbed him of that calm and well-being which are the indispensable background to the impressions we derive from nature.

One evening, when Swann had consented to dine with the Verdurins, and had mentioned during dinner that he had to attend next day the annual banquet of an old comrades' association, Odette had exclaimed across the table, in front of Forcheville, who was now one of the "faithful," in front of the painter, in front of Cottard:

"Yes, I know you have your banquet tomorrow; I shan't see you, then, till I get home; don't be too late."

And although Swann had never yet taken serious offence at Odette's friendship for one or other of the "faithful," he felt an exquisite pleasure on hearing her thus avow in front of them all, with that calm immodesty, the fact that they saw each other regularly every evening, his privileged position in her house and the preference for him which it implied. It was true that Swann had often reflected that Odette was in no way a remarkable woman, and there was nothing especially flattering in seeing the supremacy he wielded over someone so inferior to himself proclaimed to all the "faithful"; but since he had observed that to many other men besides himself Odette seemed a fascinating and desirable woman, the attraction which her body held for them had aroused in him a painful longing to secure the absolute mastery of even the tiniest particles of her heart. And he had begun to attach an incalculable value to those moments spent in her house in the evenings, when he held her upon his knee, made her tell him what she thought about this or that, and counted over the only possessions on earth to which he still clung. And so, drawing her aside after this dinner, he took care to thank her effusively, seeking to indicate to her by the extent of his gratitude the corresponding intensity of the pleasures which it was in her power to bestow on him, the supreme pleasure being to guarantee him immunity, for so long as his love should last and he remain vulnerable, from the assaults of jealousy.

When he came away from his banquet, the next evening, it was pouring with rain, and he had nothing but his victoria. A friend offered to take him home in a closed carriage, and as Odette, by the fact of her having invited him to come, had given him an assurance that she was expecting no one else, he could have gone home to bed with a quiet mind and an untroubled heart, rather than set off thus in the rain. But perhaps, if she saw that he seemed not to adhere to his resolution to spend the late evening always, without exception, in her company, she might not bother to keep it free for him on the one occasion when he particularly desired it.

It was after eleven when he reached her door, and as he made his apology for having been unable to come away earlier, she complained that it was indeed very late, that the storm had made her feel unwell and her head ached, and warned him that she would not let him stay more than half an hour, that at midnight she would send him away; a little while later she felt tired and wished to sleep.

"No cattleya, then, tonight?" he asked, "and I've been so looking forward to a nice little cattleya."

She seemed peevish and on edge, and replied: "No, dear, no cattleya tonight. Can't you see I'm not well?"

"It might have done you good, but I won't bother you."

She asked him to put out the light before he went; he drew the curtains round her bed and left. But, when he was back in his own house, the idea suddenly struck him that perhaps Odette was expecting someone else that evening, that she had merely pretended to be tired, so that she had asked him to put the light out only so that he should suppose that she was going to sleep, that the moment he had left the house she had put it on again and

had opened her door to the man who was to spend the
night with her. He looked at his watch. It was about an
hour and a half since he had left her. He went out, took a
cab, and stopped it close to her house, in a little street
running at right angles to that other street which lay at
the back of her house and along which he used sometimes
to go, to tap upon her bedroom window, for her to let
him in. He left his cab; the streets were deserted and
dark; he walked a few yards and came out almost opposite
her house. Amid the glimmering blackness of the row of
windows in which the lights had long since been put out,
he saw one, and only one, from which percolated—between the slats of its shutters, closed like a wine-press
over its mysterious golden juice—the light that filled the
room within, a light which on so many other evenings, as
soon as he saw it from afar as he turned into the street,
had rejoiced his heart with its message: "She is there—
expecting you," and which now tortured him, saying:
"She is there with the man she was expecting." He must
know who; he tiptoed along the wall until he reached the
window, but between the slanting bars of the shutters he
could see nothing, could only hear, in the silence of the
night, the murmur of conversation.

Certainly he suffered as he watched that light, in
whose golden atmosphere, behind the closed sash, stirred
the unseen and detested pair, as he listened to that murmur which revealed the presence of the man who had
crept in after his own departure, the perfidy of Odette,
and the pleasures which she was at that moment enjoying
with the stranger. And yet he was not sorry he had come;
the torment which had forced him to leave his own house
had become less acute now that it had become less vague,

now that Odette's other life, of which he had had, at that
first moment, a sudden helpless suspicion, was definitely
there, in the full glare of the lamp-light, almost within his
grasp, an unwitting prisoner in that room into which,
when he chose, he would force his way to seize it unawares; or rather he would knock on the shutters, as he
often did when he came very late, and by that signal
Odette would at least learn that he knew, that he had
seen the light and had heard the voices, and he himself,
who a moment ago had been picturing her as laughing
with the other at his illusions, now it was he who saw
them, confident in their error, tricked by none other than
himself, whom they believed to be far away but who was
there, in person, there with a plan, there with the knowledge that he was going, in another minute, to knock on
the shutter. And perhaps the almost pleasurable sensation
he felt at that moment was something more than the assuagement of a doubt, and of a pain: was an intellectual
pleasure. If, since he had fallen in love, things had recovered a little of the delightful interest that they had had for
him long ago—though only in so far as they were illuminated by the thought or the memory of Odette—now it
was another of the faculties of his studious youth that his
jealousy revived, the passion for truth, but for a truth
which, too, was interposed between himself and his mistress, receiving its light from her alone, a private and personal truth the sole object of which (an infinitely precious
object, and one almost disinterested in its beauty) was
Odette's life, her actions, her environment, her plans, her
past. At every other period in his life, the little everyday
activities of another person had always seemed meaningless to Swann; if gossip about such things was repeated to

him, he would dismiss it as insignificant, and while he listened it was only the lowest, the most commonplace part of his mind that was engaged; these were the moments when he felt at his most inglorious. But in this strange phase of love the personality of another person becomes so enlarged, so deepened, that the curiosity which he now felt stirring inside him with regard to the smallest details of a woman's daily life, was the same thirst for knowledge with which he had once studied history. And all manner of actions from which hitherto he would have recoiled in shame, such as spying, tonight, outside a window, tomorrow perhaps, for all he knew, putting adroitly provocative questions to casual witnesses, bribing servants, listening at doors, seemed to him now to be precisely on a level with the deciphering of manuscripts, the weighing of evidence, the interpretation of old monuments—so many different methods of scientific investigation with a genuine intellectual value and legitimately employable in the search for truth.

On the point of knocking on the shutters, he felt a pang of shame at the thought that Odette would now know that he had suspected her, that he had returned, that he had posted himself outside her window. She had often told him what a horror she had of jealous men, of lovers who spied. What he was about to do was singularly inept, and she would detest him for ever after, whereas now, for the moment, for so long as he refrained from knocking, even in the act of infidelity, perhaps she loved him still. How often the prospect of future happiness is thus sacrificed to one's impatient insistence upon an immediate gratification! But his desire to know the truth was stronger, and seemed to him nobler. He knew that the re-

ality of certain circumstances which he would have given
his life to be able to reconstruct accurately and in full,
was to be read behind that window, streaked with bars of
light, as within the illuminated, golden boards of one of
those precious manuscripts by whose artistic wealth itself
the scholar who consults them cannot remain unmoved.
He felt a voluptuous pleasure in learning the truth which
he passionately sought in that unique, ephemeral and precious transcript, on that translucent page, so warm, so
beautiful. And moreover, the advantage which he felt—
which he so desperately wanted to feel—that he had over
them lay perhaps not so much in knowing as in being
able to show them that he knew. He raised himself on
tiptoe. He knocked. They had not heard; he knocked
again, louder, and the conversation ceased. A man's
voice—he strained his ears to distinguish whose, among
such of Odette's friends as he knew, it might be—asked:

"Who's there?"

He could not be certain of the voice. He knocked
once again. The window first, then the shutters were
thrown open. It was too late, now, to draw back, and
since she was about to know all, in order not to seem too
miserable, too jealous and inquisitive, he called out in a
cheerful, casual tone of voice:

"Please don't bother; I just happened to be passing,
and saw the light. I wanted to know if you were feeling
better."

He looked up. Two old gentlemen stood facing him
at the window, one of them with a lamp in his hand; and
beyond them he could see into the room, a room that he
had never seen before. Having fallen into the habit, when
he came late to Odette, of identifying her window by the

fact that it was the only one still lit up in a row of windows otherwise all alike, he had been misled this time by
the light, and had knocked at the window beyond hers,
which belonged to the adjoining house. He made what
apology he could and hurried home, glad that the satisfaction of his curiosity had preserved their love intact, and
that, having feigned for so long a sort of indifference towards Odette, he had not now, by his jealousy, given her
the proof that he loved her too much, which, between a
pair of lovers, for ever dispenses the recipient from the
obligation to love enough.

He never spoke to her of this misadventure, and
ceased even to think of it himself. But now and then his
thoughts in their wandering course would come upon this
memory where it lay unobserved, would startle it into life,
thrust it forward into his consciousness, and leave him
aching with a sharp, deep-rooted pain. As though it were
a bodily pain, Swann's mind was powerless to alleviate it;
but at least, in the case of bodily pain, since it is independent of the mind, the mind can dwell upon it, can note
that it has diminished, that it has momentarily ceased.
But in this case the mind, merely by recalling the pain,
created it afresh. To determine not to think of it was to
think of it still, to suffer from it still. And when, in conversation with his friends, he forgot about it, suddenly a
word casually uttered would make him change countenance like a wounded man when a clumsy hand has
touched his aching limb. When he came away from
Odette he was happy, he felt calm, he recalled her smiles,
of gentle mockery when speaking of this or that other
person, of tenderness for himself; he recalled the gravity
of her head which she seemed to have lifted from its axis

to let it droop and fall, as though in spite of herself, upon
his lips, as she had done on the first evening in the carriage, the languishing looks she had given him as she lay
in his arms, nestling her head against her shoulder as
though shrinking from the cold.

But then at once his jealousy, as though it were the
shadow of his love, presented him with the complement,
with the converse of that new smile with which she had
greeted him that very evening—and which now, per-
versely, mocked Swann and shone with love for another—
of that droop of the head, now sinking on to other lips, of
all the marks of affection (now given to another) that she
had shown to him. And all the voluptuous memories
which he bore away from her house were, so to speak, but
so many sketches, rough plans like those which a decora-
tor submits to one, enabling Swann to form an idea of the
various attitudes, aflame or faint with passion, which she
might adopt for others. With the result that he came to
regret every pleasure that he tasted in her company, every
new caress of which he had been so imprudent as to point
out to her the delights, every fresh charm that he found
in her, for he knew that, a moment later, they would go
to enrich the collection of instruments in his torture-
chamber.

A fresh turn was given to the screw when Swann recalled a sudden expression which he had intercepted, a
few days earlier, and for the first time, in Odette's eyes.
It was after dinner at the Verdurins'. Whether it was because Forcheville, aware that Saniette, his brother-in-law,
was not in favour with them, had decided to make a butt
of him and to shine at his expense, or because he had
been annoyed by some awkward remark which Saniette

had made to him, although it had passed unnoticed by
the rest of the party who knew nothing of whatever offensive allusion it might quite unintentionally have concealed, or possibly because he had been for some time
looking for an opportunity of securing the expulsion from
the house of a fellow-guest who knew rather too much
about him, and whom he knew to be so sensitive that he
himself could not help feeling embarrassed at times
merely by his presence in the room, Forcheville replied to
Saniette's tactless utterance with such a volley of abuse,
going out of his way to insult him, emboldened, the
louder he shouted, by the fear, the pain, the entreaties of
his victim, that the poor creature, after asking Mme Verdurin whether he should stay and receiving no answer,
had left the house in stammering confusion, and with
tears in his eyes. Odette had watched this scene impas-
sively, but when the door had closed behind Saniette, she
had forced the normal expression of her face down, so to
speak, by several pegs, in order to bring herself on to the
same level of baseness as Forcheville, her eyes had
sparkled with a malicious smile of congratulation upon his
audacity, of ironical pity for the poor wretch who had
been its victim, she had darted at him a look of complicity in the crime which so clearly implied: "That's finished
him off, or I'm very much mistaken. Did you see how
pathetic he looked? He was actually crying," that
Forcheville, when his eyes met hers, sobering instantaneously from the anger, or simulated anger, with which
he was still flushed, smiled as he explained: "He need
only have made himself pleasant and he'd have been here
still; a good dressing-down does a man no harm, at any
age."

One day when Swann had gone out early in the afternoon to pay a call, and had failed to find the person he wished to see, it occurred to him to go to see Odette instead, at an hour when, although he never called on her then as a rule, he knew that she was always at home resting or writing letters until tea-time, and would enjoy seeing her for a moment without disturbing her. The porter told him that he believed Odette to be in; Swann rang the bell, thought he heard the sound of footsteps, but no one came to the door. Anxious and irritated, he went round to the other little street at the back of her house and stood beneath her bedroom window: the curtains were drawn and he could see nothing; he knocked loudly upon the pane, and called out; no one opened. He could see that the neighbours were staring at him. He turned away, thinking that after all he had perhaps been mistaken in believing that he heard footsteps; but he remained so preoccupied with the suspicion that he could not think of anything else. After waiting for an hour, he returned. He found her at home; she told him that she had been in the house when he rang, but had been asleep; the bell had awakened her, she had guessed that it must be Swann, and had run to meet him, but he had already gone. She had, of course, heard him knocking at the window. Swann could at once detect in this story one of those fragments of literal truth which liars, when caught off guard, console themselves by introducing into the composition of the falsehood which they have to invent, thinking that it can be safely incorporated and will lend the whole story an air of verisimilitude. It was true that when Odette had just done something she did not wish to disclose, she would take pains to bury it deep down inside herself. But as

soon as she found herself face to face with the man to
whom she was obliged to lie, she became uneasy, all her
ideas melted like wax before a flame, her inventive and
her reasoning faculties were paralysed, she might ransack
her brain but could find only a void; yet she must say
something, and there lay within her reach precisely the
fact which she had wished to conceal and which, being
the truth, was the one thing that had remained. She broke
off from it a tiny fragment, of no importance in itself, assuring herself that, after all, it was the best thing to do,
since it was a verifiable detail and less dangerous, therefore, than a fictitious one. "At any rate, that's true," she
said to herself, "which is something to the good. He may
make inquiries, and he'll see that it's true, so at least it
won't be that that gives me away." But she was wrong; it
was what gave her away; she had failed to realise that this
fragmentary detail of the truth had sharp edges which
could not be made to fit in, except with those contiguous
fragments of the truth from which she had arbitrarily detached it, edges which, whatever the fictitious details in
which she might embed it, would continue to show, by
their overlapping angles and by the gaps she had forgotten to fill in, that its proper place was elsewhere.

"She admits that she heard me ring and then knock,
that she knew it was me, and that she wanted to see me,"
Swann thought to himself. "But that doesn't fit in with
the fact that she didn't let me in."

He did not, however, draw her attention to this in-
consistency, for he thought that if left to herself Odette
might perhaps produce some falsehood which would give
him a faint indication of the truth. She went on speaking,
and he did not interrupt her, but gathered up, with an ea-

ger and sorrowful piety, the words that fell from her lips,
feeling (and rightly feeling, since she was hiding the truth
behind them as she spoke) that, like the sacred veil, they
retained a vague imprint, traced a faint outline, of that infinitely precious and, alas, undiscoverable reality—what
she had been doing that afternoon at three o'clock when
he had called—of which he would never possess any
more than these falsifications, illegible and divine traces,
and which would exist henceforward only in the secretive
memory of this woman who could contemplate it in utter
ignorance of its value but would never yield it up to him.
Of course it occurred to him from time to time that
Odette's daily activities were not in themselves passionately interesting, and that such relations as she might
have with other men did not exhale naturally, universally
and for every rational being a spirit of morbid gloom capable of infecting with fever or of inciting to suicide. He
realised at such moments that that interest, that gloom,
existed in him alone, like a disease, and that once he was
cured of this disease, the actions of Odette, the kisses that
she might have bestowed, would become once again as innocuous as those of countless other women. But the consciousness that the painful curiosity which he now
brought to them had its origin only in himself was not
enough to make Swann decide that it was unreasonable to
regard that curiosity as important and to take every possible step to satisfy it. The fact was that Swann had
reached an age whose philosophy—encouraged, in his
case, by the current philosophy of the day, as well as by
that of the circle in which he had spent much of his life,
the group that surrounded the Princesse des Laumes,
where it was agreed that intelligence was in direct ratio to

the degree of scepticism and nothing was considered real and incontestable except the individual tastes of each person—is no longer that of youth, but a positive, almost a medical philosophy, the philosophy of men who, instead of exteriorising the objects of their aspirations, endeavour to extract from the accumulation of the years already spent a fixed residue of habits and passions which they can regard as characteristic and permanent, and with which they will deliberately arrange, before anything else, that the kind of existence they choose to adopt shall not prove inharmonious. Swann deemed it wise to make allowance in his life for the suffering which he derived from not knowing what Odette had done, just as he made allowance for the impetus which a damp climate always gave to his eczema; to anticipate in his budget the expenditure of a considerable sum on procuring, with regard to the daily occupations of Odette, information the lack of which would make him unhappy, just as he reserved a margin for the gratification of other tastes from which he knew that pleasure was to be expected (at least, before he had fallen in love), such as his taste for collecting or for good cooking.

When he proposed to take leave of Odette and return home, she begged him to stay a little longer and even detained him forcibly, seizing him by the arm as he was opening the door to go. But he paid no heed to this, for among the multiplicity of gestures, remarks, little incidents that go to make up a conversation, it is inevitable that we should pass (without noticing anything that attracts our attention) close by those that hide a truth for which our suspicions are blindly searching, whereas we stop to examine others beneath which nothing lies concealed. She kept on saying: "What a dreadful pity—you never come in the afternoon, and the one time you do come I miss you." He knew very well that she was not sufficiently in love with him to be so keenly distressed merely at having missed his visit, but since she was good-natured, anxious to make him happy, and often grieved when she had offended him, he found it quite natural that she should be sorry on this occasion for having deprived him of the pleasure of spending an hour in her company, which was so very great, if not for her, at any rate for him. All the same, it was a matter of so little importance that her air of unrelieved sorrow began at length to astonish him. She reminded him, even more than usual, of the faces of some of the women created by the painter of the "Primavera." She had at this moment their downcast, heart-broken expression, which seems ready to succumb beneath the burden of a grief too heavy to be borne when they are merely allowing the Infant Jesus to play with a pomegranate or watching Moses pour water into a trough. He had seen the same sorrow once before on her face, but when, he could no longer say. Then, suddenly, he remembered: it was when Odette had lied in apologising to Mme Verdurin on the evening after the dinner from which she had stayed away on a pretext of illness, but really so that she might be alone with Swann. Surely, even had she been the most scrupulous of women, she could hardly have felt remorse for so innocent a lie. But the lies which Odette ordinarily told were less innocent, and served to prevent discoveries which might have involved her in the most terrible difficulties with one or another of her friends. And so when she lied, smitten with fear, feeling herself to be but feebly armed for her defence, unconfident of success, she felt like weeping from sheer exhaustion, as children weep sometimes when they have not slept. Moreover she knew that her lie was usually wounding to the man to whom she was telling it, and that she might find herself at his mercy if she told it badly. Therefore she felt at once humble and guilty in his presence. And when she had to tell an insignificant social lie its hazardous associations, and the memories which it recalled, would leave her weak with a sense of exhaustion and penitent with a consciousness of wrongdoing.

What depressing lie was she now concocting for Swann's benefit, to give her that doleful expression, that plaintive voice, which seemed to falter beneath the effort she was forcing herself to make, and to plead for mercy? He had an idea that it was not merely the truth about what had occurred that afternoon that she was endeavouring to hide from him, but something more immediate, something, possibly, that had not yet happened, that was imminent, and that would throw light upon that earlier event. At that moment, he heard the front-door bell ring. Odette went on talking, but her words dwindled into an inarticulate moan. Her regret at not having seen Swann that afternoon, at not having opened the door to him, had become a veritable cry of despair.

He could hear the front door being closed, and the sound of a carriage, as though someone were going away—probably the person whom Swann must on no account meet—after being told that Odette was not at home. And then, when he reflected that merely by coming at an hour when he was not in the habit of coming he had managed to disturb so many arrangements of which she did not wish him to know, he was overcome with a feeling of despondency that amounted almost to anguish. But since he was in love with Odette, since he was in the habit of turning all his thoughts towards her, the pity with which he might have been inspired for himself he felt for her instead, and he murmured: "Poor darling!" When finally he left her, she took up several letters which were lying on the table, and asked him to post them for her. He took them away with him, and having reached home realised that they were still in his pocket. He walked back to the post office, took the letters out of his pocket, and, before dropping each of them into the box, scanned its address. They were all to tradesmen, except one which was to Forcheville. He kept it in his hand. "If I saw what was in this," he argued, "I should know what she calls him, how she talks to him, whether there really is anything between them. Perhaps indeed by not looking inside I'm behaving shoddily towards Odette, since it's the only way I can rid myself of a suspicion which is perhaps slanderous to her, which must in any case cause her suffering, and which can never possibly be set at rest once the letter is posted."

He left the post office and went home, but he had kept this last letter with him. He lit a candle and held up close to its flame the envelope which he had not dared to open. At first he could distinguish nothing, but the envelope was thin, and by pressing it down on to the stiff card which it enclosed he was able, through the transparent paper, to read the concluding words. They consisted of a stiffly formal ending. If, instead of its being he who was looking at a letter addressed to Forcheville, it had been Forcheville who had read a letter addressed to Swann, he would have found words in it of an altogether more affec-

tionate kind! He took a firm hold of the card which was
sliding to and fro, the envelope being too large for it, and
then, by moving it with his finger and thumb, brought
one line after another beneath the part of the envelope
where the paper was not doubled, through which alone it
was possible to read.

In spite of these manoeuvres he could not make it out
clearly. Not that it mattered, for he had seen enough to
assure himself that the letter was about some trifling incident which had no connexion with amorous relations; it
was something to do with an uncle of Odette's. Swann
had read quite plainly at the beginning of the line: "I was
right," but did not understand what Odette had been
right in doing, until suddenly a word which he had not
been able at first to decipher came to light and made the
whole sentence intelligible: "I was right to open the door;
it was my uncle." To open the door! So Forcheville had
been there when Swann rang the bell, and she had sent
him away, hence the sound that he had heard.

After that he read the whole letter. At the end she
apologised for having treated Forcheville with so little
ceremony, and reminded him that he had left his
cigarette-case at her house, precisely what she had written
to Swann after one of his first visits. But to Swann she
had added: "If only you had forgotten your heart! I
should never have let you have that back." To Forcheville
nothing of that sort: no allusion that might suggest any
intrigue between them. And, really, he was obliged to admit that in all this Forcheville had been worse treated
than himself, since Odette was writing to him to assure
him that the visitor had been her uncle. From which it
followed that he, Swann, was the man to whom she at-

tached importance and for whose sake she had sent the
other away. And yet, if there was nothing between Odette
and Forcheville, why not have opened the door at once,
why have said, "I was right to open the door; it was my
uncle." If she was doing nothing wrong at that moment,
how could Forcheville possibly have accounted for her not
opening the door? For some time Swann stood there, dis-
consolate, bewildered and yet happy, gazing at this envelope which Odette had handed to him without a qualm,
so absolute was her trust in his honour, but through the
transparent screen of which had been disclosed to him,
together with the secret history of an incident which he
had despaired of ever being able to learn, a fragment of
Odette's life, like a luminous section cut out of the unknown. Then his jealousy rejoiced at the discovery, as
though that jealousy had an independent existence,
fiercely egotistical, gluttonous of everything that would
feed its vitality, even at the expense of Swann himself.
Now it had something to feed on, and Swann could begin
to worry every day about the visits Odette received about
five o'clock, could seek to discover where Forcheville had
been at that hour. For Swann's affection for Odette still
preserved the form which had been imposed on it from
the beginning by his ignorance of how she spent her days
and by the mental lethargy which prevented him from
supplementing that ignorance by imagination. He was not
jealous, at first, of the whole of Odette's life, but of those
moments only in which an incident, which he had perhaps misinterpreted, had led him to suppose that Odette
might have played him false. His jealousy, like an octopus
which throws out a first, then a second, and finally a
third tentacle, fastened itself firmly to that particular mo-

ment, five o'clock in the afternoon, then to another, then
to another again. But Swann was incapable of inventing his sufferings. They were only the memory, the per-
petuation of a suffering that had come to him from
without.

From without, however, everything brought him
fresh suffering. He decided to separate Odette from
Forcheville by taking her away for a few days to the
south. But he imagined that she was coveted by every
male person in the hotel, and that she coveted them in return. And so he who in former days, on journeys, used
always to seek out new people and crowded places, might
now be seen morosely shunning human society as if it
had cruelly injured him. And how could he not have
turned misanthrope, when in every man he saw a potential lover for Odette? And thus his jealousy did even more
than the happy, sensual feeling he had originally experienced for Odette had done to alter Swann's character,
completely changing, in the eyes of the world, even the
outward signs by which that character had been intelligible.

A month after the evening on which he had read
Odette's letter to Forcheville, Swann went to a dinner
which the Verdurins were giving in the Bois. As the party
was breaking up he noticed a series of confabulations between Mme Verdurin and several of her guests, and
thought he heard the pianist being reminded to come next
day to a party at Chatou, to which he, Swann, had not
been invited.

The Verdurins had spoken only in whispers, and in
vague terms, but the painter, perhaps without thinking,
exclaimed aloud: "There mustn't be any light, and he

must play the Moonlight Sonata in the dark so that things can become clear."

Mme Verdurin, seeing that Swann was within earshot, assumed an expression in which the two-fold desire to silence the speaker and to preserve an air of innocence in the eyes of the listener is neutralised into an intense vacuity wherein the motionless sign of intelligent complicity is concealed beneath an ingenuous smile, an expression which, common to everyone who has noticed a gaffe, instantaneously reveals it, if not to its perpetrator, at any rate to its victim. Odette seemed suddenly to be in despair, as though she had given up the struggle against the crushing difficulties of life, and Swann anxiously counted the minutes that still separated him from the point at which, after leaving the restaurant, while he drove her home, he would be able to ask her for an explanation, make her promise either that she would not go to Chatou next day or that she would procure an invitation for him also, and to lull to rest in her arms the anguish that tormented him. At last the carriages were ordered. Mme Verdurin said to Swann: "Good-bye, then. We shall see you soon, I hope," trying, by the friendliness of her manner and the constraint of her smile, to prevent him from noticing that she was not saying, as she would always have said hitherto: "Tomorrow, then, at Chatou, and at my house the day after."

M. and Mme Verdurin invited Forcheville into their carriage. Swann's was drawn up behind it, and he waited for theirs to start before helping Odette into his.

"Odette, we'll take you," said Mme Verdurin, "we've kept a little corner for you, beside M. de Forcheville."

"Yes, Madame," said Odette meekly.

"What! I thought I was to take you home," cried Swann, flinging discretion to the wind, for the carriage-door hung open, the seconds were running out, and he could not, in his present state, go home without her.

"But Mme Verdurin has asked me . . ."

"Come, you can quite well go home alone; we've left her with you quite often enough," said Mme Verdurin.

"But I had something important to say to Mme de Crécy."

"Very well, you can write it to her instead."

"Good-bye," said Odette, holding out her hand.

He tried hard to smile, but looked utterly dejected.

"Did you see the airs Swann is pleased to put on with us?" Mme Verdurin asked her husband when they had reached home. "I was afraid he was going to eat me, simply because we offered to take Odette back. It's positively indecent! Why doesn't he say straight out that we keep a bawdy-house? I can't conceive how Odette can stand such manners. He literally seems to be saying, 'You belong to me!' I shall tell Odette exactly what I think about it all, and I hope she'll have the sense to understand me."

A moment later she added, inarticulate with rage: "No, but, don't you agree, the filthy creature . . ." unwittingly using, perhaps in obedience to the same obscure need to justify herself—like Françoise at Combray, when the chicken refused to die—the very words which the last convulsions of an inoffensive animal in its death throes wring from the peasant who is engaged in taking its life.

And when Mme Verdurin's carriage had moved on and Swann's took its place, his coachman, catching sight of his face, asked whether he was unwell, or had heard some bad news.

Swann dismissed him; he wanted to walk, and returned home on foot through the Bois, talking to himself,
aloud, in the same slightly artificial tone he used to adopt
when enumerating the charms of the "little nucleus" and
extolling the magnanimity of the Verdurins. But just as
the conversation, the smiles, the kisses of Odette became
as odious to him as he had once found them pleasing, if
they were addressed to others, so the Verdurins' salon,
which, not an hour before, had still seemed to him amusing, inspired with a genuine feeling for art and even with
a sort of moral nobility, exhibited to him all its absurdities, its foolishness, its ignominy, now that it was another
than himself whom Odette was going to meet there, to
love there without restraint.

He pictured to himself with disgust the party next
evening at Chatou. "Imagine going to Chatou! Like a lot
of drapers after shutting up shop! Upon my word, these
people are really sublime in their bourgeois mediocrity,
they can't be real, they must all have come out of a
Labiche comedy!"

The Cottards would be there; possibly Brichot.
"Could anything be more grotesque than the lives of
these nonentities, hanging on to one another like that.
They'd imagine they were utterly lost, upon my soul they
would, if they didn't all meet again tomorrow at *Chatou!*"
Alas! there would also be the painter, the painter who enjoyed match-making, who would invite Forcheville to
come with Odette to his studio. He could see Odette in a
dress far too smart for a country outing, "because she's so
vulgar, and, poor little thing, such an absolute fool!"

He could hear the jokes that Mme Verdurin would
make after dinner, jokes which, whoever the "bore" might

be at whom they were aimed, had always amused him because he could watch Odette laughing at them, laughing
with him, her laughter almost a part of his. Now he felt
that it was possibly at him that they would make Odette
laugh. "What fetid humour!" he exclaimed, twisting his
mouth into an expression of disgust so violent that he
could feel the muscles of his throat stiffen against his col-
lar. "How in God's name can a creature made in his
image find anything to laugh at in those nauseating witticisms? The least sensitive nose must turn away in horror
from such stale exhalations. It's really impossible to believe that a human being can fail to understand that, in
allowing herself to smile at the expense of a fellow-crea-
ture who has loyally held out his hand to her, she is sinking into a mire from which it will be impossible, with the
best will in the world, ever to rescue her. I inhabit a plane
so infinitely far above the sewers in which these filthy
vermin sprawl and crawl and bawl their cheap obscenities,
that I cannot possibly be spattered by the witticisms of a
Verdurin!" he shouted, tossing up his head and proudly
throwing back his shoulders. "God knows I've honestly
tried to pull Odette out of that quagmire, and to teach
her to breathe a nobler and a purer air. But human patience has its limits, and mine is at an end," he concluded, as though this sacred mission to tear Odette away
from an atmosphere of sarcasms dated from longer than a
few minutes ago, as though he had not undertaken it only
since it had occurred to him that those sarcasms might
perhaps be directed at himself, and might have the effect
of detaching Odette from him.

He could see the pianist sitting down to play the
Moonlight Sonata, and the grimaces of Mme Verdurin in

terrified anticipation of the wrecking of her nerves by Beethoven's music. "Idiot, liar!" he shouted, "and a creature like that imagines that she loves *Art!*" She would say to Odette, after deftly insinuating a few words of praise for Forcheville, as she had so often done for him: "You can make room for M. de Forcheville, there, can't you, Odette?". . . " 'In the dark!' " (he remembered the painter's words) "filthy old procuress!" "Procuress" was the name he applied also to the music which would invite them to sit in silence, to dream together, to gaze into each other's eyes, to feel for each other's hands. He felt that there was much to be said, after all, for a sternly censorious attitude towards the arts, such as Plato adopted, and Bossuet, and the old school of education in France.

In a word, the life they led at the Verdurins', which he had so often described as "the true life," seemed to him now the worst of all, and their "little nucleus" the lowest of the low. "It really is," he said, "beneath the lowest rung of the social ladder, the nethermost circle of Dante. No doubt about it, the august words of the Florentine refer to the Verdurins! When you come to think of it, surely people 'in society' (with whom one may find fault now and then but who are after all a very different matter from that riff-raff) show a profound sagacity in refusing to know them, or even to soil the tips of their fingers with them. What a sound intuition there is in that *'Noli me tangere'* of the Faubourg Saint-Germain."

He had long since emerged from the paths and avenues of the Bois, had almost reached his own house, and still, having not yet shaken off the intoxication of his misery and pain and the inspired insincerity which the counterfeit tones and artificial sonority of his own voice raised

to ever more exhilarating heights, he continued to per-
orate aloud in the silence of the night: "Society people
have their failings, as no one knows better than I; but
there are certain things they simply wouldn't stoop to. So-
and-so" (a fashionable woman whom he had known) "was
far from being perfect, but she did after all have a fundamental decency, a sense of honour in her dealings which
would have made her incapable, whatever happened, of
any sort of treachery and which puts a vast gulf between
her and an old hag like Verdurin. Verdurin! What a
name! Oh, it must be said that they're perfect specimens
of their disgusting kind! Thank God, it was high time
that I stopped condescending to promiscuous intercourse
with such infamy, such dung."

But, just as the virtues which he had still attributed
to the Verdurins an hour or so earlier would not have sufficed, even if the Verdurins had actually possessed them,
if they had not also encouraged and protected his love, to
excite Swann to that state of intoxication in which he
waxed tender over their magnanimity—an intoxication
which, even when disseminated through the medium of
other persons, could have come to him from Odette
alone—so the immorality (had it really existed) which he
now found in the Verdurins would have been powerless,
if they had not invited Odette with Forcheville and without him, to unleash his indignation and make him ful-
minate against their "infamy." And doubtless Swann's
voice was more perspicacious than Swann himself when it
refused to utter those words full of disgust with the Verdurins and their circle, and of joy at having shaken himself free of it, save in an artificial and rhetorical tone and
as though they had been chosen rather to appease his

anger than to express his thoughts. The latter, in fact, while he abandoned himself to his invective, were probably, though he did not realise it, occupied with a wholly different matter, for having reached home, no sooner had he closed the front-door behind him than he suddenly struck his forehead, and reopening it, dashed out again exclaiming, in a voice which, this time, was quite natural: "I think I've found a way of getting invited to the dinner at Chatou tomorrow!" But it must have been a bad way, for Swann was not invited. Dr Cottard, who, having been summoned to attend a serious case in the country, had not seen the Verdurins for some days and had been prevented from appearing at Chatou, said on the evening after this dinner, as he sat down to table at their house: "But aren't we going to see M. Swann this evening? He's quite what you might call a personal friend of . . ."

"I sincerely trust we shan't!" cried Mme Verdurin. "Heaven preserve us from him; he's too deadly for words, a stupid, ill-bred boor."

On hearing these words Cottard exhibited an intense astonishment blended with entire submission, as though in the face of a scientific truth which contradicted everything that he had previously believed but was supported by an irresistible weight of evidence; and bowing his head over his plate with timorous emotion, he simply replied: "Oh—oh—oh—oh—oh!" traversing, in an orderly withdrawal of his forces into the depths of his being, along a descending scale, the whole compass of his voice. After which there was no more talk of Swann at the Verdurins'.

.   .   .

And so that drawing-room which had brought Swann and Odette together became an obstacle in the way of their meeting. She no longer said to him, as in the early days of their love: "We shall meet, anyhow, tomorrow evening; there's a supper-party at the Verdurins'," but "We shan't be able to meet tomorrow evening; there's a supper-party at the Verdurins'." Or else the Verdurins were taking her to the Opéra-Comique, to see *Une Nuit de Cléopâtre*, and Swann could read in her eyes that terror lest he should ask her not to go, which not long since he could not have refrained from greeting with a kiss as it flitted across the face of his mistress, but which now exasperated him. "Yet it's not really anger," he assured himself, "that I feel when I see how she longs to go and scratch around in that dunghill of music. It's disappointment, not of course for myself but for her; I'm disappointed to find that, after living for more than six months in daily contact with me, she hasn't changed enough to be able spontaneously to reject Victor Massé—above all, that she hasn't yet reached the stage of understanding that there are evenings when anyone with the least delicacy of feeling should be willing to forgo a pleasure when asked to do so. She ought to have the sense to say 'I won't go,' if only from policy, since it is by her answer that the quality of her heart will be judged once and for all." And having persuaded himself that it was solely, after all, in order that he might arrive at a favourable estimate of Odette's spiritual worth that he wished her to stay at home with him that evening instead of going to the Opéra-Comique, he adopted the same line of reasoning with her, with the same degree of insincerity as he had used with himself, or even a degree more, for in her case he was yielding also to the desire to capture her through her own self-esteem.

"I swear to you," he told her, shortly before she was to leave for the theatre, "that, in asking you not to go, I should hope, were I a selfish man, for nothing so much as that you should refuse, for I have a thousand other things to do this evening and I shall feel trapped myself, and rather annoyed, if, after all, you tell me you're not going. But my occupations, my pleasures are not everything; I must think of you too. A day may come when, seeing me irrevocably sundered from you, you will be entitled to reproach me for not having warned you at the decisive hour in which I felt that I was about to pass judgment on you, one of those stern judgments which love cannot long resist. You see, your *Nuit de Cléopâtre* (what a title!) has no bearing on the point. What I must know is whether you are indeed one of those creatures in the lowest grade of mentality and even of charm, one of those contemptible creatures who are incapable of forgoing a pleasure. And if you are such, how could anyone love you, for you are not even a person, a clearly defined entity, imperfect but at least perfectible. You are a formless water that will trickle down any slope that offers itself, a fish devoid of memory, incapable of thought, which all its life long in its aquarium will continue to dash itself a hundred times a day against the glass wall, always mistaking it for water. Do you realise that your answer will have the effect—I won't say of making me cease loving you immediately, of course, but of making you less attractive in my eyes when I realise that you are not a person, that you are beneath everything in the world and incapable of raising yourself one inch higher. Obviously, I should have preferred to ask you as a matter of little or no importance to give up your *Nuit de Cléopâtre* (since you compel me to sully my lips with so abject a name) in the hope that you would go to it none the less. But, having decided to make such an issue of it, to draw such drastic consequences from your reply, I considered it more honourable to give you due warning."

Meanwhile, Odette had shown signs of increasing emotion and uncertainty. Although the meaning of this speech was beyond her, she grasped that it was to be included in the category of "harangues" and scenes of reproach or supplication, which her familiarity with the ways of men enabled her, without paying any heed to the words that were uttered, to conclude that they would not make unless they were in love, and that since they were in love, it was unnecessary to obey them, as they would only be more in love later on. And so she would have heard Swann out with the utmost tranquillity had she not noticed that it was growing late, and that if he went on talking much longer she would, as she told him with a fond smile, obstinate if slightly abashed, "end by missing the Overture."

On other occasions he told her that the one thing that would make him cease to love her more than anything else would be her refusal to abandon the habit of lying. "Even from the point of view of coquetry, pure and simple," he said to her, "can't you see how much of your attraction you throw away when you stoop to lying? Think how many faults you might redeem by a frank admission! You really are far less intelligent than I supposed!" In vain, however, did Swann expound to her thus all the reasons that she had for not lying; they might have succeeded in overthrowing a general system of mendacity, but Odette had no such system; she was simply content, whenever she wished Swann to remain in ignorance of anything she had done, not to tell him of it. So that lying was for her an expedient of a specific order, and the only thing that could make her decide whether she should avail herself of it or confess the truth was a reason that was also of a specific or contingent order, namely the chance of Swann's discovering that she had not told him the truth.

Physically, she was going through a bad phase; she was putting on weight, and the expressive, sorrowful charm, the surprised, wistful expression of old seemed to have vanished with her first youth. So that she had become most precious to Swann as it were just at the moment when he found her distinctly less good-looking. He would gaze at her searchingly, trying to recapture the charm which he had once seen in her, and no longer finding it. And yet the knowledge that within this new chrysalis it was still Odette who lurked, still the same fleeting, sly, elusive will, was enough to keep Swann seeking as passionately as ever to capture her. Then he would look at photographs of her taken two years before, and would remember how exquisite she had been. And that would console him a little for all the agony he suffered on her account.

When the Verdurins took her off to Saint-Germain, or to Chatou, or to Meulan, as often as not, if the weather was fine, they would decide to stay the night and return next day. Mme Verdurin would endeavour to set at rest the scruples of the pianist, whose aunt had remained in Paris: "She'll be only too glad to be rid of you for a day.

Why on earth should she be anxious, when she knows you're with us? Anyhow, I'll take full responsibility."

If this attempt failed, M. Verdurin would set off across country to find a telegraph office or a messenger, after first finding out which of the "faithful" had someone they must notify. But Odette would thank him and assure him that she had no message for anyone, for she had told Swann once and for all that she could not possibly send messages to him, in front of all those people, without compromising herself. Sometimes she would be absent for several days on end, when the Verdurins took her to see the tombs at Dreux, or to Compiègne, on the painter's advice, to watch the sunsets in the forest—after which they went on to the Château of Pierrefonds.

"To think that she could visit really historic buildings with me, who have spent ten years in the study of architecture, who am constantly bombarded by people who really count to take them to Beauvais or Saint-Loup-de-Naud, and refuse to take anyone but her; and instead of that she trundles off with the most abject brutes to go into ecstasies over the excrements of Louis-Philippe and Viollet-le-Duc! One hardly needs much knowledge of art, I should say, to do that; surely, even without a particularly refined sense of smell, one doesn't deliberately choose to spend a holiday in the latrines so as to be within range of their fragrant exhalations."

But when she had set off for Dreux or Pierrefonds— alas, without allowing him to turn up there, as though by chance, for that, she said, "would create a deplorable impression"—he would plunge into the most intoxicating romance in the lover's library, the railway time-table, from which he learned the ways of joining her there in

the afternoon, in the evening, even that very morning.
The ways? More than that, the authority, the right to join
her. For after all, the time-table, and the trains themselves, were not meant for dogs. If the public was informed, by means of the printed word, that at eight
o'clock in the morning a train left for Pierrefonds which
arrived there at ten, that could only be because going to
Pierrefonds was a lawful act, for which permission from
Odette would be superfluous; an act, moreover, which
might be performed from a motive altogether different
from the desire to see Odette, since persons who had
never even heard of her performed it daily, and in such
numbers as justified the trouble of stoking the engines.

All things considered, she could not really prevent
him from going to Pierrefonds if he felt inclined to do so.
And as it happened, he did feel so inclined, and had he
not known Odette, would certainly have gone. For a long
time past he had wanted to form a more definite impression of Viollet-le-Duc's work as a restorer. And the
weather being what it was, he felt an overwhelming desire
to go for a walk in the forest of Compiègne.

It really was bad luck that she had forbidden him access to the one spot that tempted him today. Today!
Why, if he went there in defiance of her prohibition, he
would be able to see her that very day! But whereas, if
she had met at Pierrefonds someone who did not matter
to her, she would have hailed him with obvious pleasure:
"What, you here?" and would have invited him to come
and see her at the hotel where she was staying with the
Verdurins, if on the other hand it was himself, Swann,
that she ran into, she would be offended, would complain
that she was being followed, would love him less in con-

sequence, might even turn away in anger when she caught
sight of him. "So, I'm not allowed to travel any more!"
she would say to him on her return, whereas in fact it was
he who was not allowed to travel!

At one moment he had had the idea, in order to be
able to visit Compiègne and Pierrefonds without letting it
be supposed that his object was to meet Odette, of securing an invitation from one of his friends, the Marquis de
Forestelle, who had a country house in that neighbourhood. The latter, whom he apprised of his plan without
disclosing its ulterior purpose, was beside himself with joy
and astonishment at Swann's consenting at last, after fifteen years, to come down and visit his property, and since
he did not (he had told him) wish to stay there, promising at least to spend some days going for walks and excursions with him. Swann imagined himself already down
there with M. de Forestelle. Even before he saw Odette,
even if he did not succeed in seeing her there, what a joy
it would be to set foot on that soil, where not knowing
the exact spot in which, at any moment, she was to be
found, he would feel all around him the thrilling possibility of her sudden apparition: in the courtyard of the
Château, now beautiful in his eyes since it was on her account that he had gone to visit it; in all the streets of the
town, which struck him as romantic; down every ride of
the forest, roseate with the deep and tender glow of sunset—innumerable and alternative sanctuaries, in which,
in the uncertain ubiquity of his hopes, his happy, vaga-
bond and divided heart would simultaneously take refuge.
"We mustn't on any account," he would warn M. de
Forestelle, "run across Odette and the Verdurins. I've just
heard that they're at Pierrefonds, of all places, today. One

has plenty of time to see them in Paris; it would hardly be worth while coming down here if one couldn't go a yard without meeting them." And his host would fail to understand why, once they were there, Swann would change his plans twenty times in an hour, inspect the dining-rooms of all the hotels in Compiègne without being able to make up his mind to settle down in any of them, although they had seen no trace anywhere of the Verdurins, seeming to be in search of what he claimed to be most anxious to avoid, and would in fact avoid the moment he found it, for if he had come upon the little "group" he would have hastened away at once with studied indifference, satisfied that he had seen Odette and she him, especially that she had seen him not bothering his head about her. But no; she would guess at once that it was for her sake that he was there. And when M. de Forestelle came to fetch him, and it was time to start, he excused himself: "No, I'm afraid I can't go to Pierrefonds today. You see, Odette is there." And Swann was happy in spite of everything to feel that if he, alone among mortals, had not the right to go to Pierrefonds that day, it was because he was in fact, for Odette, someone different from all other mortals, her lover, and because that restriction imposed for him alone on the universal right to freedom of movement was but one of the many forms of the slavery, the love that was so dear to him. Decidedly, it was better not to risk a quarrel with her, to be patient, to wait for her return. He spent his days poring over a map of the forest of Compiègne as though it had been that of the "Pays du Tendre,"[13] and surrounded himself with photographs of the Château of Pierrefonds. When the day dawned on which it was possible that she might return, he opened the time-table again, calculated what train she must have taken, and, should she have postponed her departure, what trains were still left for her to take. He did not leave the house for fear of missing a telegram, did not go to bed in case, having come by the last train, she decided to surprise him with a midnight visit. Yes! The front-door bell rang. There seemed some delay in opening the door, he wanted to awaken the porter, he leaned out of the window to shout to Odette if it was she, for in spite of the orders which he had gone downstairs a dozen times to deliver in person, they were quite capable of telling her that he was not at home. It was only a servant coming in. He noticed the incessant rumble of passing carriages, to which he had never paid any attention before. He could hear them, one after another, a long way off, coming nearer, passing his door without stopping, and bearing away into the distance a message which was not for him. He waited all night, to no purpose, for the Verdurins had decided to return early, and Odette had been in Paris since midday. It had not occurred to her to tell him, and not knowing what to do with herself she had spent the evening alone at a theatre, had long since gone home to bed, and was asleep.

As a matter of fact, she had not even given him a thought. And such moments as these, in which she forgot Swann's very existence, were more useful to Odette, did more to bind him to her, than all her coquetry. For in this way Swann was kept in that state of painful agitation which had already been powerful enough to cause his love to blossom, on the night when he had failed to find Odette at the Verdurins' and had hunted for her all evening. And he did not have (as I had at Combray in

my childhood) happy days in which to forget the sufferings that would return with the night. For his days were
spent without Odette; and there were times when he told
himself that to allow so pretty a woman to go out by herself in Paris was just as rash as to leave a case filled with
jewels in the middle of the street. Then he would rail
against all the passers-by, as though they were so many
pickpockets. But their faces—a collective and formless
mass—escaped the grasp of his imagination, and failed to
feed the flame of his jealousy. The effort exhausted
Swann's brain, until, putting his hand over his eyes, he
cried out: "Heaven help me!" as people, after lashing
themselves into an intellectual frenzy in their endeavours
to master the problem of the reality of the external world
or the immortality of the soul, afford relief to their weary
brains by an unreasoning act of faith. But the thought of
the absent one was incessantly, indissolubly blended with
all the simplest actions of Swann's daily life—when he
took his meals, opened his letters, went for a walk or to
bed—by the very sadness he felt at having to perform
those actions without her; like those initials of Philibert
the Fair which, in the church of Brou, because of her
grief and longing for him, Margaret of Austria inter-
twined everywhere with her own. On some days, instead
of staying at home, he would go for luncheon to a restaurant not far off to which he had once been attracted by
the excellence of its cookery, but to which he now went
only for one of those reasons, at once mystical and absurd, which people call "romantic"; because this restaurant (which, by the way, still exists) bore the same name
as the street in which Odette lived: La Pérouse.

Sometimes, when she had been away on a short visit

somewhere, several days would elapse before she thought
of letting him know that she had returned to Paris. And
then she would say quite simply, without taking (as she
would once have taken) the precaution of covering herself,
just in case, with a little fragment borrowed from the
truth, that she had at that very moment arrived by the
morning train. These words were mendacious; at least for
Odette they were mendacious, insubstantial, lacking (what
they would have had if true) a basis of support in her
memory of her actual arrival at the station; she was even
prevented from forming a mental picture of them as she
uttered them, by the contradictory picture of whatever
quite different thing she had been doing at the moment
when she pretended to have been alighting from the train.
In Swann's mind, however, these words, meeting no opposition, settled and hardened until they assumed the
indestructibility of a truth so indubitable that, if some
friend happened to tell him that he had come by the same
train and had not seen Odette, Swann was convinced that
it was the friend who had mistaken the day or the hour,
since his version did not agree with the words uttered by
Odette. These words would have appeared to him false
only if he had suspected beforehand that they were going
to be. For him to be believe that she was lying, an anticipatory suspicion was indispensable. It was also, however,
sufficient. Given that, everything Odette said appeared to
him suspect. If she mentioned a name, it was obviously
that of one of her lovers, and once this supposition had
taken shape, he would spend weeks tormenting himself.
On one occasion he even approached an inquiry agent to
find out the address and the occupation of the unknown
rival who would give him no peace until he could be

proved to have gone abroad, and who (he ultimately
learned) was an uncle of Odette who had been dead for
twenty years.

Although she would not allow him as a rule to meet
her in public, saying that people would talk, it happened
occasionally that, at an evening party to which he and she
had both been invited—at Forcheville's, at the painter's,
or at a charity ball given in one of the Ministries—he
found himself in the same room with her. He could see
her, but dared not stay for fear of annoying her by seeming to be spying upon the pleasures she enjoyed in other
company, pleasures which—as he drove home in utter
loneliness, and went to bed as miserable as I was to be
some years later on the evenings when he came to dine
with us at Combray—seemed to him limitless since he
had not seen the end of them. And once or twice he experienced on such evenings the sort of happiness which
one would be inclined (did it not originate in so violent a
reaction from an anxiety abruptly terminated) to call
peaceful, since it consists in a pacifying of the mind. On
one occasion he had looked in for a moment at a party in
the painter's studio, and was preparing to go home, leaving behind him Odette transformed into a brilliant
stranger, surrounded by men to whom her glances and
her gaiety, which were not for him, seemed to hint at
some voluptuous pleasures to be enjoyed there or elsewhere (possibly at the Bal des Incohérents, to which he
trembled to think that she might be going on afterwards)
which caused Swann more jealousy than the carnal act itself, since he found it more difficult to imagine; he was
already at the door when he heard himself called back in
these words (which, by cutting off from the party that

possible ending which had so appalled him, made it seem innocent in retrospect, made Odette's return home a thing no longer inconceivable and terrible, but tender and familiar, a thing that would stay beside him, like a part of his daily life, in his carriage, and stripped Odette herself of the excess of brilliance and gaiety in her appearance, showed that it was only a disguise which she had assumed for a moment, for its own sake and not with a view to any mysterious pleasures, and of which she had already wearied)—in these words which Odette tossed at him as he was crossing the threshold: "Can't you wait a minute for me? I'm just going; we'll drive back together and you can take me home."

It was true that on one occasion Forcheville had asked to be driven home at the same time, but when, on reaching Odette's door, he had begged to be allowed to come in too, she had replied, pointing to Swann: "Ah! That depends on this gentleman. You must ask him. Very well, you may come in just for a minute, if you insist, but you mustn't stay long, because I warn you, he likes to sit and talk quietly with me, and he's not at all pleased if I have visitors when he's here. Oh, if you only knew the creature as I know him! Isn't that so, my love, no one really knows you well except me?"

And Swann was perhaps even more touched by the spectacle of her addressing to him thus, in front of Forcheville, not only these tender words of predilection, but also certain criticisms, such as: "I feel sure you haven't written yet to your friends about dining with them on Sunday. You needn't go if you don't want to, but you might at least be polite," or, "Now, have you left your essay on Vermeer here so that you can do a little

more of it tomorrow? What a lazy-bones! I'm going to
make you work, I can tell you," which proved that Odette
kept herself in touch with his social engagements and his
literary work, that they had indeed a life in common. And
as she spoke she gave him a smile that told him she was
entirely his.

At such moments as these, while she was making
them some orangeade, suddenly, just as when an ill-ad-
justed reflector begins by casting huge, fantastic shadows
on an object on the wall which then contract and merge
into it, all the terrible and shifting ideas which he had
formed about Odette melted away and vanished into the
charming creature who stood there before his eyes. He
had the sudden suspicion that this hour spent in Odette's
house, in the lamp-light, was perhaps, after all, not an artificial hour, invented for his special use (with the object
of concealing that frightening and delicious thing which
was incessantly in his thoughts without his ever being
able to form a satisfactory impression of it, an hour of
Odette's real life, of her life when he was not there), with
theatrical properties and pasteboard fruits, but was perhaps a genuine hour of Odette's life; that if he himself
had not been there she would have pulled forward the
same armchair for Forcheville, would have poured out for
him, not some unknown brew, but precisely this same orangeade; that the world inhabited by Odette was not that
other fearful and supernatural world in which he spent his
time placing her—and which existed, perhaps, only in his
imagination—but the real world, exhaling no special atmosphere of gloom, comprising that table at which he
might sit down presently and write, this drink which he
was now being permitted to taste, all these objects which

he contemplated with as much curiosity and admiration as gratitude—for if, in absorbing his dreams, they had delivered him from them, they themselves in return had been enriched by them, they showed him the palpable realisation of his fancies, and they impressed themselves upon his mind, took shape and grew solid before his eyes, at the same time as they soothed his troubled heart. Ah, if fate had allowed him to share a single dwelling with Odette, so that in her house he should be in his own, if, when asking the servant what there was for lunch, it had been Odette's menu that he had been given in reply, if, when Odette wished to go for a morning walk in the Avenue du Bois de Boulogne, his duty as a good husband had obliged him, though he had no desire to go out, to accompany her, carrying her overcoat when she was too warm, and in the evening, after dinner, if she wished to stay at home in deshabille, if he had been forced to stay beside her, to do what she asked; then how completely would all the trivial details of Swann's life which seemed to him now so melancholy have taken on, for the very reason that they would at the same time have formed part of Odette's life—like this lamp, this orangeade, this armchair, which had absorbed so much of his dreams, which materialised so much of his longing—a sort of superabundant sweetness and a mysterious density!

And yet he was inclined to suspect that the state for which he so longed was a calm, a peace, which would not have been a propitious atmosphere for his love. When Odette ceased to be for him a creature always absent, regretted, imagined, when the feeling that he had for her was no longer the same mysterious turmoil that was wrought in him by the phrase from the sonata, but affec-

tion and gratitude, when normal relations that would put
an end to his melancholy madness were established between them—then, no doubt, the actions of Odette's
daily life would appear to him as being of little intrinsic
interest—as he had several times already felt that they
might be, on the day, for instance, when he had read
through its envelope her letter to Forcheville. Examining
his complaint with as much scientific detachment as if he
had inoculated himself with it in order to study its effects,
he told himself that, when he was cured of it, what
Odette might or might not do would be a matter of indifference to him. But the truth was that in the depths of his
morbid condition he feared death itself no more than such
a recovery, which would in fact amount to the death of all
that he now was.

After these quiet evenings, Swann's suspicions would
be temporarily lulled; he would bless the name of Odette,
and next day, in the morning would order the finest jewels to be sent to her, because her kindnesses to him
overnight had excited either his gratitude, or the desire to
see them repeated, or a paroxysm of love for her which
had need of some such outlet.

But at other times, his anguish would again take hold
of him; he would imagine that Odette was Forcheville's
mistress, and that when they had both sat watching him
from the depths of the Verdurins' landau in the Bois
on the evening before the party at Chatou to which he
had not been invited, while he implored her in vain, with
that look of despair on his face which even his coachman
had noticed, to come home with him, and then turned
away, solitary and crushed, she must have glanced at
Forcheville, as she drew his attention to him, saying

"Look how furious he is!" with the same expression, sparkling, malicious, sidelong and sly, as on the evening when Forcheville had driven Saniette from the Verdurins'.

At such times Swann detested her. "But I've been a fool, too," he would argue. "I'm paying for other men's pleasures with my money. All the same, she'd better take care, and not push her luck, because I might very well stop giving her anything at all. At any rate, we'd better knock off supplementary favours for the time being. To think that only yesterday, when she said she would like to go to Bayreuth for the season, I was such an ass as to offer to take one of those nice little castles the King of Bavaria has in the neighbourhood for the two of us. However, she didn't seem particularly keen; she hasn't said yes or no yet. Let's hope she'll refuse. Good God! Think of listening to Wagner for a whole fortnight with a woman who takes about as much interest in music as a tone-deaf newt—that would be fun!" And his hatred, like his love, needing to manifest itself in action, he took pleasure in urging his evil imaginings further and further, because, thanks to the perfidies of which he accused Odette, he detested her still more, and would be able, if it turned out—as he tried to convince himself—that she was indeed guilty of them, to take the opportunity of punishing her, and of venting his mounting rage on her. Thus he went so far as to suppose that he was about to receive a letter from her in which she would ask him for money to take the castle near Bayreuth, but with the warning that he was not to come there himself, as she had promised to invite Forcheville and the Verdurins. How he would have loved it if she had had the audacity to do this! How he would have enjoyed refusing, drawing up the vindictive

reply, the terms of which he amused himself by selecting
and declaiming aloud, as though he had actually received
such a letter!

The very next day, he did. She wrote that the Verdurins and their friends had expressed a desire to attend
these performances of Wagner, and that, if he would be
so good as to send her the money, she would at last have
the pleasure, after going so often to their house, of entertaining the Verdurins in hers. Of him she said not a
word; it was to be taken for granted that their presence
would be a bar to his.

Then he had the pleasure of sending round to her
that annihilating answer, every word of which he had
carefully rehearsed overnight without venturing to hope
that it could ever be used. Alas! he felt only too certain
that with the money she had, or could easily procure, she
would be able all the same to take a house at Bayreuth,
since she wished to do so, she who was incapable of dis-
tinguishing between Bach and Clapisson. Let her take it,
then: at least she would have to live in it more frugally.
No chance (as there would have been if he had replied by
sending her several thousand-franc notes) of organising
each evening in some castle those exquisite little suppers
after which she might perhaps indulge the whim (which,
it was possible, had never yet seized her) of falling into
the arms of Forcheville. At any rate it would not be he,
Swann, who paid for this loathsome expedition! Ah! if he
could only manage to prevent it, if she could sprain her
ankle before setting out, if the driver of the carriage
which was to take her to the station would consent (at no
matter what price) to smuggle her to some place where
she could be kept for a time in seclusion—that perfidious

woman, her eyes glittering with a smile of complicity for
Forcheville, that Odette had become for Swann in the last
forty-eight hours!

But she was never that for very long. After a few
days the shining, crafty eyes lost their brightness and
their duplicity, the picture of a hateful Odette saying to
Forcheville "Look how furious he is!" began to fade and
dissolve. Then gradually the face of the other Odette
would reappear and rise before him, softly radiant—that
Odette who also turned with a smile to Forcheville, but
with a smile in which there was nothing but tenderness
for Swann, when she said: "You mustn't stay long, because this gentleman doesn't much like my having visitors
when he's here. Oh! if you only knew the creature as I
know him!"—that same smile with which she used to
thank Swann for some instance of his courtesy which she
prized so highly, for some advice for which she had asked
him in one of those moments of crisis when she would
turn to him alone.

And thinking of this other Odette, he would ask himself what could have induced him to write that outrageous
letter, of which, probably, until then she would never
have supposed him capable, a letter which must have
brought him down from the high, from the supreme place
which by his generosity, by his loyalty, he had won for
himself in her esteem. He would become less dear to her,
since it was for those qualities, which she found neither in
Forcheville nor in any other, that she loved him. It was
for them that Odette so often showed him a reciprocal
warmth which counted for less than nothing in his moments of jealousy, because it was not a sign of reciprocal
desire, was indeed a proof rather of affection than of love,

but the importance of which he began once more to feel in proportion as the spontaneous relaxation of his suspicions, often accelerated by the distraction brought to him by reading about art or by the conversation of a friend, rendered his passion less exacting of reciprocities.

Now that, after this swing of the pendulum, Odette had naturally returned to the place from which Swann's jealousy had momentarily driven her, to the angle from which he found her charming, he pictured her to himself as full of tenderness, with a look of consent in her eyes, and so beautiful that he could not refrain from proffering her his lips as though she had actually been in the room for him to kiss; and he felt as strong a sense of gratitude towards her for that bewitching, kindly glance as if it had been real, as if it had not been merely his imagination that had portrayed it in order to satisfy his desire.

What distress he must have caused her! Certainly he could find valid reasons for his resentment, but they would not have been sufficient to make him feel that resentment if he had not loved her so passionately. Had he not nourished equally serious grievances against other women, to whom he would none the less willingly render a service today, feeling no anger towards them because he no longer loved them? If the day ever came when he found himself in the same state of indifference with regard to Odette, he would then understand that it was his jealousy alone which had led him to find something heinous, unpardonable, in this desire of hers (which was after all so natural, springing from a childlike ingenuousness and also from a certain delicacy in her nature) to be able in her turn, since the opportunity had arisen, to repay the Verdurins for their hospitality, and to play the hostess in a house of her own.

He returned to this other point of view, which was the opposite of the one based on his love and jealousy and to which he resorted at times by a sort of intellectual equity and in order to make allowance for the various probabilities, and tried to judge Odette as though he had not been in love with her, as though she were like any other woman, as though her life (as soon as he was no longer present) had not been different, woven secretly behind his back, hatched against him.

Why should he think that she would enjoy out there with Forcheville or with other men intoxicating pleasures which she had never experienced with him, and which his jealousy alone had fabricated out of nothing? At Bayreuth, as in Paris, if it should happen that Forcheville thought of him at all, it would only be as of someone who counted for a great deal in Odette's life, someone for whom he was obliged to make way when they met at her house. If Forcheville and she gloated at the idea of being there together in spite of him, it was he who would have engineered it by striving in vain to prevent her from going, whereas if he had approved of her plan, which for that matter was quite defensible, she would have had the appearance of being there on his advice, she would have felt that she had been sent there, housed there by him, would have been beholden to him for the pleasure which she derived from entertaining those people who had so often entertained her.

And if—instead of letting her go off on bad terms with him, without having seen him again—he were to

send her this money, if he were to encourage her to undertake this journey and go out of his way to make it
agreeable for her, she would come running to him, happy
and grateful, and he would have the joy of seeing her
which he had not known for nearly a week and which
nothing else could replace. For once Swann could picture
her to himself without revulsion, could see once again the
friendliness in her smile, once the desire to tear her away
from every rival was no longer imposed by his jealousy
upon his love, that love became once again, more than
anything, a taste for the sensations which Odette's person
gave him, for the pleasure he took in admiring as a spectacle, or in examining as a phenomenon, the dawn of one
of her glances, the formation of one of her smiles, the
emission of a particular vocal cadence. And this pleasure,
different from every other, had in the end created in him
a need of her, which she alone by her presence or by her
letters could assuage, almost as disinterested, almost as
artistic, as perverse, as another need which characterised
this new period in Swann's life, when the sereness, the
depression of the preceding years had been followed by a
sort of spiritual overflowing, without his knowing to what
he owed this unlooked-for enrichment of his inner life,
any more than a person in delicate health who from a certain moment grows stronger, puts on flesh, and seems for
a time to be on the road to a complete recovery. This
other need, which developed independently of the visible,
material world, was the need to listen to music and improve his knowledge of it.

And so, through the chemical action of his malady,
after he had created jealousy out of his love, he began
again to manufacture tenderness and pity for Odette. She

had become once more the old Odette, charming and kind. He was full of remorse for having treated her harshly. He wished her to come to him, and, before she came, he wished to have already procured for her some pleasure, so as to watch her gratitude taking shape in her face and moulding her smile.

And consequently Odette, certain of seeing him come to her after a few days, as tender and submissive as before, to plead with her for a reconciliation, became inured, was no longer afraid of displeasing him or even of making him angry, and refused him, whenever it suited her, the favours by which he set most store.

Perhaps she did not realise how sincere he had been with her during their quarrel, when he had told her that he would not send her any money and would do everything he could to hurt her. Perhaps she did not realise, either, how sincere he was, if not with her, at any rate with himself, on other occasions when, for the sake of the future of their relationship, to show Odette that he was capable of doing without her, that a rupture was still possible between them, he decided to wait some time before going to see her again.

Sometimes it would be after several days during which she had caused him no fresh anxiety; and since he knew that he was likely to derive no very great pleasure from his impending visits, but more probably some annoyance which would put an end to his present state of calm, he would write to her saying that he was very busy, and would not be able to see her on any of the days that he had suggested. Meanwhile, a letter from her, crossing his, asked him to postpone one of those very meetings. He wondered why; his suspicions, his anguish, again took

hold of him. He could no longer abide, in the new state
of agitation into which he found himself plunged, by the
arrangements which he had made in his preceding state of
comparative calm; he would hurry round to her, and
would insist upon seeing her on each of the following
days. And even if she had not written first, if she merely
acknowledged his letter, agreeing to his request for a brief
separation, it was enough to make him unable to rest
without seeing her. For, contrary to his calculations,
Odette's acquiescence had entirely changed his attitude.
Like everyone who possesses something precious, in order
to know what would happen if he ceased for a moment to
possess it, he had detached the precious object from his
mind, leaving, as he thought, everything else in the same
state as when it was there. But the absence of one part
from a whole is not only that, it is not simply a partial
lack, it is a derangement of all the other parts, a new state
which it was impossible to foresee in the old.

But at other times—when Odette was on the point of
going away for a holiday—it was after some trifling quarrel for which he had chosen the pretext that he resolved
not to write to her and not to see her until her return,
thus giving the appearance (and expecting the reward) of
a serious rupture, which she would perhaps regard as final, to a separation the greater part of which was the inevitable consequence of her proposed journey, which he
was merely allowing to start a little sooner than it must.
At once he could imagine Odette puzzled, anxious, distressed at having received neither visit nor letter from
him, and this picture of her, by calming his jealousy,
made it easy for him to break himself of the habit of seeing her. At moments, no doubt, in the furthest recesses of

his mind where his determination had thrust it away thanks to the long interval of the three weeks' separation which he had accepted, it was with pleasure that he considered the idea that he would see Odette again on her return; but it was also with so little impatience that he began to wonder whether he would not readily consent to the doubling of the period of so easy an abstinence. It had lasted, so far, but three days, a much shorter time than he had often spent without seeing Odette, and without having, as on this occasion, premeditated it. And yet, suddenly, some minor vexation or physical ailment—by inciting him to regard the present moment as an exceptional one, outside the rules, one in which common wisdom would allow him to take advantage of the soothing effects of a pleasure and, until there was some purpose in a resumption of effort, to give his will a rest—suspended the operation of the latter, which ceased to exert its inhibitive control; or, without that even, the thought of something he had forgotten to ask Odette, such as whether she had decided in what colour she would have her carriage repainted, or, with regard to some investment, whether they were ordinary or preference shares that she wished him to buy (for it was all very well to show her that he could live without seeing her, but if, after that, the carriage had to be painted over again, or if the shares produced no dividend, a lot of good it would have done him)—and suddenly, like a stretched piece of elastic which is let go, or the air in a pneumatic machine which is ripped open, the idea of seeing her again sprang back from the distant depths in which it lay dormant into the field of the present and of immediate possibilities.

It sprang back thus without meeting any further re-

sistance, so irresistible, in fact, that Swann had found it
far less painful to watch the fortnight he was to spend
separated from Odette creeping by day after day than to
wait the ten minutes it took his coachman to bring round
the carriage which was to take him to her, minutes which
he spent in transports of impatience and joy, in which he
recaptured a thousand times over, to lavish on it all the
wealth of his affection, that idea of meeting her again
which, by so abrupt a reversal, at a moment when he
supposed it so remote, was once more present and on the
very surface of his consciousness. The fact was that his
idea no longer found as an obstacle in its course the desire to resist it without further delay, a desire which had
ceased to have any place in Swann's mind since, having
proved to himself—or so at least he believed—that he
was so easily capable of resisting it, he no longer saw any
danger in postponing a plan of separation which he was
now certain of being able to put into operation whenever
he wished. Furthermore, this idea of seeing her again
came back to him adorned with a novelty, a seductive-
ness, armed with a virulence, which long habit had dulled
but which had been retempered during this privation, not
of three days but of a fortnight (for a period of abstinence
may be calculated, by anticipation, as having lasted already until the final date assigned to it), and had converted what had been until then a pleasure in store which
could easily be sacrificed into an unlooked-for happiness
which he was powerless to resist. Finally, the idea returned to him embellished by his ignorance of what
Odette might have thought, might perhaps have done, on
finding that he had given no sign of life, with the result

that what he was going now to find was the entrancing
revelation of an almost unknown Odette.

But she, just as she had supposed that his refusal to
send her money was only a sham, saw nothing but a pretext in the questions he was now coming to ask her, about
the repainting of her carriage or the purchase of shares.
For she could not reconstruct the several phases of these
crises through which he was passing, and the notion she
had formed of them omitted any attempt to understand
their mechanism, but looked only to what she knew beforehand, their necessary, never-failing and always identical termination. An incomplete notion (though possibly
all the more profound in consequence), if one were to
judge it from the point of view of Swann, who would
doubtless have considered himself misunderstood by
Odette, just as a drug-addict or a consumptive, each persuaded that he has been held back, one by some outside
event at the moment when he was about to shake himself
free of his inveterate habit, the other by an accidental
indisposition at the moment when he was about to be
finally cured, feels himself to be misunderstood by the
doctor who does not attach the same importance to these
alleged contingencies, mere disguises, according to him,
assumed, so as to make themselves felt once more, by the
vice of the one and the morbid state of the other, which
in reality have never ceased to weigh heavily and incurably upon the patients while they were nursing their
dreams of reformation or health. And, as a matter of fact,
Swann's love had reached the stage at which the boldest
of physicians or (in the case of certain affections) of surgeons ask themselves whether to deprive a patient of his

vice or to rid him of his malady is still reasonable or indeed possible.

Certainly, of the extent of this love Swann had no direct awareness. When he sought to measure it, it happened sometimes that he found it diminished, shrunk almost to nothing; for instance, the lack of enthusiasm, amounting almost to distaste, which, in the days before he was in love with Odette, he had felt for her expressive features, her faded complexion, returned on certain days. "Really, I'm making distinct headway," he would tell himself next day. "Looking at things quite honestly, I can't say I got much pleasure last night from being in bed with her. It's an odd thing, but I actually thought her ugly." And certainly he was sincere, but his love extended a long way beyond the province of physical desire. Odette's person, indeed, no longer held any great place in it. When his eyes fell upon the photograph of Odette on his table, or when she came to see him, he had difficulty in identifying her face, either in the flesh or on the pasteboard, with the painful and continuous anxiety which dwelt in his mind. He would say to himself, almost with astonishment, "It's she!" as though suddenly we were to be shown in a detached, externalised form one of our own maladies, and we found it bore no resemblance to what we are suffering. "She"—he tried to ask himself what that meant; for it is a point of resemblance between love and death, far more striking than those which are usually pointed out, that they make us probe deeper, in the fear that its reality may elude us, into the mystery of personality. And this malady which Swann's love had become had so proliferated, was so closely interwoven with all his habits, with all his actions, with his thoughts, his health, his sleep, his life, even with what he hoped for after his death, was so utterly inseparable from him, that it would have been impossible to eradicate it without almost entirely destroying him; as surgeons say, his love was no longer operable.

By this love Swann had been so far detached from all other interests that when by chance he reappeared in society, reminding himself that his social relations, like a beautifully wrought setting (although she would not have been able to form any very exact estimate of its worth), might restore something of his own prestige in Odette's eyes (as indeed they might have done had they not been cheapened by his love itself, which for Odette depreciated everything that it touched by seeming to proclaim such things less precious), he would feel there, side by side with his distress at being in places and among people she did not know, the same detached pleasure as he would have derived from a novel or a painting in which were depicted the amusements of a leisured class; just as, at home, he used to enjoy the thought of the smooth efficiency of his household, the elegance of his wardrobe and of his servants' liveries, the soundness of his investments, with the same relish as when he read in Saint-Simon, who was one of his favourite authors, of the mechanics of daily life at Versailles, what Mme de Maintenon ate and drank, or the shrewd avarice and great pomp of Lulli. And to the small extent to which this detachment was not absolute, the reason for this new pleasure which Swann was tasting was that he could take refuge for a moment in those few and distant parts of himself which had remained more or less extraneous to his love and to his pain. In this respect the personality which my great-aunt attributed to him as "young Swann," as distinct from the more individual personality of Charles Swann, was the one in which he was now happiest. Once, wishing to send the Princesse de Parme some fruit for her birthday (and because she could often be of use indirectly to Odette, by letting her have seats for galas and jubilees and the like) and not being quite sure how to order it, he had entrusted the task to a cousin of his mother who, delighted to do an errand for him, had written to him, when sending him the account, to say that she had not ordered all the fruit from the same place, but the grapes from Crapote, whose speciality they were, the strawberries from Jauret, the pears from Chevet, who always had the best, and so on, "every fruit inspected and examined, one by one, by myself." And in the sequel, by the cordiality with which the Princess thanked him, he had been able to judge of the flavour of the strawberries and of the ripeness of the pears. But, most of all, that "every fruit inspected and examined, one by one, by myself" had brought balm to his sufferings by carrying his mind off to a region which he rarely visited, although it was his by right as the heir to a rich, upper-middle-class family in which had been handed down from generation to generation the knowledge of the "right places" and the art of placing an order.

Indeed, he had too long forgotten that he was "young Swann" not to feel, when he assumed the role again for a moment, a keener pleasure than those he might have felt at other times but which had palled; and if the friendliness of the bourgeoisie, for whom he had never been anything else than "young Swann," was less animated than that of the aristocracy (though more flattering, for all that, since with them it is always inseparable from respect), no

letter from a royal personage, whatever princely entertainment it offered, could ever be so agreeable to Swann as a
letter inviting him to be a witness, or merely to be present, at a wedding in the family of some old friends of his
parents, some of whom had kept up with him—like my
grandfather, who, the year before these events, had invited him to my mother's wedding—while others barely
knew him by sight, but considered themselves in duty
bound to show civility to the son, to the worthy successor, of the late M. Swann.

But, by virtue of his intimacy, already time-hon-
oured, with so many of its members, the nobility was in a
certain sense also a part of his house, his domestic estab-
lishment, and his family. He felt, when his mind dwelt
upon his brilliant connexions, the same external support,
the same solid comfort as when he looked at the fine es-
tates, the fine silver, the fine table-linen which had come
to him from his own family. And the thought that, if he
were struck down by a sudden illness and confined to the
house, the people whom his valet would instinctively run
to fetch would be the Duc de Chartres, the Prince de
Reuss, the Duc de Luxembourg and the Baron de Charlus, brought him the same consolation as our old Françoise derived from the knowledge that she would one day
be buried in her own fine sheets, marked with her name,
not darned at all (or so exquisitely darned that it merely
enhanced one's idea of the skill and patience of the seamstress), a shroud from the constant image of which in her
mind's eye she drew a certain satisfactory sense, if not actually of wealth and prosperity, at any rate of self-esteem.
But most of all—since in every one of his actions and
thoughts which had reference to Odette, Swann was con-

stantly obsessed and influenced by the unavowed feeling
that he was, perhaps not less dear, but less welcome to
her than anyone, even the most tedious of the Verdurin
"faithful"—when he betook himself to a world in which
he was the paragon of taste, a man whom no pains were
spared to attract, whom people were genuinely sorry not
to see, he began once again to believe in the existence of a
happier life, almost to feel an appetite for it, as an invalid
may feel who has been bedridden for months, on a strict
diet, when he picks up a newspaper and reads the account
of an official banquet or an advertisement for a cruise
round Sicily.

If he was obliged to make excuses to his society
friends for not visiting them, it was precisely for visiting
her that he sought to excuse himself to Odette. Even so,
he paid for his visits (asking himself at the end of the
month, should he have overtaxed her patience and gone
rather often to see her, whether it would be enough if he
sent her four thousand francs), and for each one found a
pretext, a present that he had to bring her, a piece of information which she required, M. de Charlus whom he
had met actually going to her house and who had insisted
on Swann's accompanying him. And, failing an excuse, he
would ask M. de Charlus to go round to her house and
say to her, as though spontaneously, in the course of conversation, that he had just remembered something he had
to say to Swann, and would she please send a message to
Swann asking him to come to her then and there; but as a
rule Swann waited at home in vain, and M. de Charlus
informed him later in the evening that his ruse had not
proved successful. With the result that, if she was now
frequently away from Paris, even when she was there he

scarcely saw her, and she who, when she was in love with
him, used to say "I'm always free" and "What do I care
what other people think?" now, whenever he wanted to
see her, appealed to the proprieties or pleaded some en-
gagement. When he spoke of going to a charity entertainment, or a private view, or a first-night at which she was
to be present, she would complain that he wished to ad-
vertise their liaison, that he was treating her like a whore.
Things came to such a pitch that, in an effort to avoid
being debarred from meeting her anywhere, Swann, remembering that she knew and was deeply attached to my
great-uncle Adolphe, whose friend he himself had also
been, went to see him in his little flat in the Rue de Belle-
chasse, to ask him to use his influence with Odette. Since
she invariably adopted a poetical tone when she spoke to
Swann about my uncle, saying: "Ah, yes, he's not in the
least like you; it's such an exquisite thing, a great, a beautiful thing, his friendship for me. He's not the sort of
man who would have so little consideration for me as to
let himself be seen with me everywhere in public," this
was embarrassing for Swann, who did not know quite to
what rhetorical pitch he should screw himself up in
speaking of Odette to my uncle. He began by alluding to
her *a priori* excellence, her axiomatic and seraphic super-
humanity, the inspiration of her transcendental, inexpressible virtues. "I should like to speak to you about
her," he went on. "You know what an incomparably superior woman, what an adorable creature, what an angel
Odette is. But you know, also, what life is in Paris. Not
everyone knows Odette in the light in which you and I
have been privileged to know her. And so there are people who think I'm behaving rather foolishly; she won't

even allow me to meet her out of doors, at the theatre. Now you, in whom she has such enormous confidence, couldn't you say a few words for me to her, just to assure her that she exaggerates the harm which my greeting her in public might do her?"

My uncle advised Swann not to see Odette for some days, after which she would love him all the more, and advised Odette to let Swann meet her whenever and as often as he pleased. A few days later Odette told Swann that she had just had a rude awakening, on discovering that my uncle was the same as other men: he had tried to take her by force. She calmed Swann down when he wanted to rush out to challenge my uncle to a duel, but he refused to shake hands with him when they met again. He regretted this rupture all the more because he had hoped, if he had met my uncle Adolphe again a few times and had contrived to talk things over with him in strict confidence, to be able to get him to throw light on certain rumours with regard to the life that Odette had formerly led in Nice. For my uncle Adolphe used to spend the winter there, and Swann thought that it might indeed have been there that he had first known Odette. The few words which someone had let fall in his hearing about a man who, it appeared, had been Odette's lover, had left Swann dumbfounded. But the very things which, before knowing them, he would have regarded as the most terrible to learn and the most impossible to believe, were, once he knew them, absorbed for ever into the general mass of his gloom; he accepted them, he could no longer have understood their not existing. Only, each one of them added a new and indelible touch to the picture he had formed of his mistress. At one point indeed he was

given to understand that this moral laxity of which he
would never have suspected Odette was fairly well
known, and that at Baden or Nice, when she used to go
to spend several months in one or the other place, she
had enjoyed a sort of amorous notoriety. He thought of
getting in touch with one or two pleasure-seekers and in-
terrogating them; but they were aware that he knew
Odette, and besides, he was afraid of putting the thought
of her into their heads, of setting them once more upon
her track. But he, to whom nothing could have seemed
more tedious hitherto than all that pertained to the cos-
mopolitan life of Baden or of Nice, having learned that
Odette had perhaps once led a gay life in those pleasure-
cities, although he could never find out whether it had
been solely to satisfy a need for money which, thanks to
him, she no longer felt, or from some capricious instinct
which might at any moment revive in her, now leaned in
impotent, blind, dizzy anguish over the bottomless abyss
in which those early years of MacMahon's Presidency had
been engulfed, years during which one spent the winter
on the Promenade des Anglais, the summer beneath the
limes of Baden, and he would find in them a painful but
magnificent profundity, such as a poet might have lent
them; indeed he would have devoted to the reconstruction
of the petty details of social life on the Côte d'Azur in
those days, if it could have helped him to understand
something of Odette's smile and the look in her eyes—
candid and simple though they were—as much passion
as the aesthete who ransacks the extant documents of fif-
teenth-century Florence in order to penetrate further into
the soul of the Primavera, the fair Vanna or the Venus of
Botticelli.

Often he would sit, without saying a word, gazing at her dreamily, and she would say: "You do look sad!" It was not very long since he had switched from the idea that she was a really good person, comparable to the nicest he had known, to that of her being a kept woman; conversely, it had happened to him since to revert from the Odette de Crécy who was perhaps too well known to the roisterers, the ladies' men, to this face whose expression was often so gentle and sweet, to this nature so eminently human. He would ask himself: "What does it mean, after all, if everyone at Nice knows who Odette de Crécy is? Reputations of that sort, even when they're true, are always based upon other people's ideas"; he would reflect that this legend—even if it was authentic— was something extraneous to Odette, was not an innate, pernicious and ineradicable part of her personality; that the creature who might have been led astray was a woman with frank eyes, a heart full of pity for the sufferings of others, a docile body which he had clasped in his arms and explored with his hands, a woman whom he might one day come to possess absolutely, if he succeeded in making himself indispensable to her.

She would sit there, often tired, her face momentarily drained of that eager, febrile preoccupation with the unknown things that made Swann suffer; she would push back her hair with both hands, and her forehead, her whole face, would seem to grow larger; then, suddenly, some ordinary human thought, some kindly sentiment such as are to be found in all individuals when, in a moment of rest or reclusion, they are free to express their true selves, would flash from her eyes like a ray of gold. And immediately the whole of her face would light up like a grey landscape swathed in clouds which are suddenly swept aside, leaving it transfigured by the setting sun. The life which occupied Odette at such times, even the future which she seemed to be dreamily contemplating, Swann could have shared with her; no evil disturbance seemed to have left its residue there. Rare though they became, those moments did not occur in vain. By the process of memory, Swann joined the fragments together, abolished the intervals between them, cast, as in molten gold, the image of an Odette compact of kindness and tranquillity, for whom (as we shall see in the second part of this story) he was later to make sacrifices which the other Odette would never have won from him. But how rare those moments were, and how seldom he now saw her! Even in the case of their evening meetings, she would never tell him until the last minute whether she would be able to see him, for, counting on his being always free, she wished first to be certain that no one else would propose coming round. She would plead that she was obliged to wait for an answer that was of the very greatest importance to her, and if, even after she had allowed Swann to come, any of her friends asked her, halfway through the evening, to join them at some theatre or at supper afterwards, she would jump for joy and dress with all speed. As her toilet progressed, every movement she made brought Swann nearer to the moment when he would have to part from her, when she would fly off with irresistible zest; and when at length she was ready, and, peering into her mirror for the last time with eyes tense and bright with anxiety to look well, added a touch of lipstick, fixed a stray lock of hair over her brow, and called for her cloak of sky-blue silk with golden tassels, Swann

looked so wretched that she would be unable to restrain a
gesture of impatience as she flung at him: "So that's how
you thank me for keeping you here till the last minute!
And I thought I was being so nice to you. Well, I shall
know better another time!" Sometimes, at the risk of annoying her, he made up his mind that he would find out
where she had gone, and even dreamed of an alliance with
Forcheville, who might perhaps have been able to enlighten him. In any case, when he knew with whom she
was spending the evening, he was usually able to discover, among all his innumerable acquaintance, someone
who knew—if only indirectly—the man in question, and
could easily obtain this or that piece of information about
him. And while he was writing to one of his friends, asking him to try to clear up some point or other, he would
feel a sense of relief on ceasing to vex himself with questions to which there was no answer and transferring to
someone else the strain of interrogation. It is true that
Swann was no better off for such information as he did
receive. To know a thing does not always enable us to
prevent it, but at least the things we know we do hold, if
not in our hands, at any rate in our minds, where we can
dispose of them as we choose, and this gives us the illusion of a sort of power over them. He was quite happy
whenever M. de Charlus was with Odette. He knew that
between M. de Charlus and her nothing untoward could
ever happen, that when M. de Charlus went out with her,
it was out of friendship for him, and that he would make
no difficulty about telling him everything she had done.
Sometimes she had declared so emphatically to Swann
that it was impossible for her to see him on a particular
evening, she seemed to be looking forward so keenly to

some outing, that Swann felt it really important that M. de Charlus should be free to accompany her. Next day, without daring to put too many questions to M. de Charlus, he would force him, by appearing not quite to understand his first answers, to give him more, after each of which he would feel increasingly relieved, for he very soon learned that Odette had spent her evening in the most innocent of dissipations.

"But what do you mean, my dear Mémé, I don't quite understand . . . You didn't go straight from her house to the Musée Grévin? Surely you went somewhere else first? No? How very funny! You've no idea how much you amuse me, my dear Mémé. But what an odd idea of hers to go on to the Chat Noir afterwards. It was her idea, I suppose? No? Yours? How strange. But after all, it wasn't such a bad idea; she must have known dozens of people there? No? She never spoke to a soul? How extraordinary! Then you sat there like that, just you and she, all by yourselves? I can just picture you. What a nice fellow you are, my dear Mémé. I'm exceedingly fond of you."

Swann was relieved. So often had it happened to him, when chatting with chance acquaintances to whom he was hardly listening, to hear certain detached sentences (as, for instance, "I saw Mme de Crécy yesterday with a man I didn't know"), sentences which dropped into his heart and turned at once into a solid state, grew hard as stalagmites, and seared and tore him as they lay there, irremovable, that the words "She didn't know a soul, she never spoke to a soul" were, by way of contrast, like a soothing balm. How freely they coursed through him, how fluid they were, how vaporous, how easy to breathe! And yet, a

moment later, he was telling himself that Odette must
find him very dull if those were the pleasures she preferred to his company. And their very insignificance,
though it reassured him, pained him as if her enjoyment
of them had been an act of treachery.

Even when he could not discover where she had
gone, it would have sufficed him, to alleviate the anguish
which he then felt, and against which Odette's presence,
the joy of being with her, was the sole specific (a specific
which in the long run served to aggravate the disease, but
at least brought temporary relief to his sufferings), it
would have sufficed him, if only Odette had allowed it, to
remain in her house while she was out, to wait for her
there until the hour of her return, into whose stillness and
peace would have flowed and dissolved those intervening
hours which some sorcery, some evil spell had made him
imagine as somehow different from the rest. But she
would not; he had to return home; he forced himself, on
the way, to form various plans, ceased to think of Odette;
he even succeeded, while he undressed, in turning over
some quite happy ideas in his mind; and it was with a
light heart, buoyed with the anticipation of going to see
some favourite work of art the next day, that he got into
bed and turned out the light; but no sooner, in preparing
himself for sleep, did he relax the self-control of which he
was not even conscious so habitual had it become, than
an icy shudder convulsed him and he began to sob. He
did not even wish to know why, but wiped his eyes and
said, to himself with a smile: "This is delightful; I'm getting neurotic." After which he felt a profound lassitude at
the thought that, next day, he must begin afresh his attempts to find out what Odette had been doing, must use

all his influence to contrive to see her. This compulsion
to an activity without respite, without variety, without results, was so cruel a scourge that one day, noticing a
swelling on his stomach, he felt genuinely happy at the
thought that he had, perhaps, a tumour which would
prove fatal, that he need no longer concern himself with
anything, that illness was going to govern his life, to make
a plaything of him, until the not-distant end. And indeed
if, at this period, it often happened that, without admitting it to himself, he longed for death, it was in order to
escape not so much from the acuity of his sufferings as
from the monotony of his struggle.

And yet he would have liked to live until the time
came when he no longer loved her, when she would have
no reason for lying to him, when at length he might learn
from her whether, on the day when he had gone to see
her in the afternoon, she had or had not been in bed with
Forcheville. Often for several days on end the suspicion
that she was in love with someone else would distract his
mind from the question of Forcheville, making it almost
immaterial to him, like those new developments in a continuous state of ill-health which seem momentarily to
have delivered us from their predecessors. There were
even days when he was not tormented by any suspicion.
He fancied that he was cured. But next morning, when he
awoke, he felt in the same place the same pain, the sensation of which, the day before, he had as it were diluted in
the stream of different daytime impressions. But it had
not stirred from its place. Indeed, it was the sharpness of
this pain that had awakened him.

Since Odette never gave him any information as to
those vastly important matters which took up so much of

her time every day (although he had lived long enough to
know that such matters are never anything else than pleasures), he could not sustain for any length of time the effort of imagining them; his brain would become a void;
then he would draw a finger over his tired eyelids as he
might have wiped his eyeglass, and would cease altogether
to think. There emerged, however, from this terra incog-
nita, certain landmarks which reappeared from time to
time, vaguely connected by Odette with some obligation
towards distant relatives or old friends who, inasmuch as
they were the only people whom she was in the habit of
mentioning as preventing her from seeing him, seemed to
Swann to compose the necessary, unalterable setting of
her life. Because of the tone in which she referred from
time to time to "the day when I go with my friend to the
races," if, having suddenly felt unwell and thought, "Perhaps Odette would be kind enough to come and see me,"
he remembered that it was one of those very days, he
would say to himself: "Oh, no! There's no point in asking
her to come. I should have thought of it before, this is the
day when she goes with her friend to the races. We must
confine ourselves to what's possible; no use wasting time
proposing things that are *ipso facto* unacceptable." And
the duty incumbent upon Odette of going to the races, to
which Swann thus gave way, seemed to him to be not
merely ineluctable in itself, but the mark of necessity with
which it was stamped seemed to make plausible and legit-
imate everything that was even remotely connected with
it. If, having acknowledged a greeting from a passer-by in
the street which had aroused Swann's jealousy, Odette
replied to his questions by associating the stranger with
one of the two or three paramount duties of which she

had often spoken to him—if, for instance, she said:
"That's a gentleman who was in my friend's box at the
races the other day"—this explanation would set Swann's
suspicions at rest; it was, after all, inevitable that this
friend should have other guests than Odette in her box at
the races, though he had never sought to form or succeeded in forming any coherent impression of them. Ah,
how he would have loved to know her, the friend who
went to the races! If only she would invite him there with
Odette. How readily he would have sacrificed all his
grand connexions for no matter what person who was in
the habit of seeing Odette, even if she were a manicurist
or a shop assistant! He would have put himself out for
her, taken more trouble than he would have done for a
queen. Would they not have supplied him, from their
store of knowledge of the life of Odette, with the one ef-
fective anodyne for his pain? With what joy would he
have hastened to spend his days with one or other of
those humble folk with whom Odette kept up friendly relations, either with some ulterior motive or from genuine
simplicity of nature! How willingly would he have taken
up residence for ever in the attic of some sordid but enviable house where Odette went but never took him and
where, if he had lived with the little retired dressmaker,
whose lover he would readily have pretended to be, he
would have been visited by Odette almost daily! In those
almost plebeian districts, what a modest existence, abject
even, but happy, nourished by tranquillity and peace of
mind, he would have consented to lead indefinitely!

It sometimes happened, again, that when, after meeting Swann, she saw some man approaching whom he did
not know, he could distinguish upon Odette's face that

look of dismay which she had worn on the day when he had come to her while Forcheville was there. But this was rare; for on the days when, in spite of all that she had to do, and of her dread of what people might think, she did actually manage to see Swann, what predominated in her attitude now was self-assurance; a striking contrast, perhaps an unconscious revenge for, or a natural reaction from, the timorous emotion which, in the early days of their friendship, she had felt in his presence, and even in his absence, when she began a letter to him with the words: "My dear, my hand trembles so that I can scarcely write" (so, at least, she pretended, and a little of that emotion must have been sincere, or she would not have wanted to feign more). She had been attracted to Swann then. We do not tremble except for ourselves, or for those whom we love. When our happiness is no longer in their hands, how calm, how relaxed, how bold we become in their presence! In speaking to him, in writing to him now, she no longer employed those words by which she had sought to give herself the illusion that he belonged to her, creating opportunities for saying "my" and "mine" when she referred to him—"You are my very own; it is the perfume of our friendship, I shall keep it"—for speaking to him of the future, of death itself, as of a single adventure which they would share. In those early days, whatever he might say to her she would answer admiringly: "You know, you'll never be like other people!"—she would gaze at that long face and slightly bald head, of which people who knew of his successes with women used to think: "He's not conventionally good-looking, if you like, but he has style: that toupee, that eyeglass, that smile!"—and, with more curiosity perhaps to know him

as he really was than desire to become his mistress, she
would sigh: "If only I knew what was in that head of
yours!"

But now, whatever he said, she would answer in a
tone that was sometimes irritable, sometimes indulgent:
"Ah! won't you ever be like other people!" And gazing at
that face which was only a little aged by his recent anxieties (though people now thought of it, by the same mental process which enables one to discover the meaning of
a piece of symphonic music of which one has read the
programme, or the resemblance of a child whose family
one knows: "He's not positively ugly, if you like, but he's
really rather absurd: that eyeglass, that toupee, that
smile!"—adumbrating in their suggestible imaginations
the invisible boundary which separates, at a few months'
interval, the face of a successful lover from that of a cuck-
old), she would say: "Oh, I do wish I could change you,
put some sense into that head of yours."

Always ready to believe in the truth of what he
hoped, if Odette's way of behaving to him left the slightest room for doubt, he would fling himself greedily upon
her words: "You can if you like," he would say to her.

And he tried to explain to her that to comfort him, to
guide him, to make him work, would be a noble task, to
which numbers of other women asked for nothing better
than to be allowed to devote themselves, though it is only
fair to add that in those other women's hands the noble
task would have seemed to Swann a tactless and intolerable usurpation of his freedom. "If she didn't love me just
a little," he told himself, "she wouldn't want to change
me. And to change me, she will have to see me more often." Thus he saw her very reproaches as proofs of her

interest, perhaps of her love; and indeed she now gave
him so few that he was obliged to regard as such the various prohibitions which she imposed on him from time to
time. One day she announced that she did not care for his
coachman, who, she thought, might be setting Swann
against her, and anyhow did not show the promptness
and deference to Swann's orders which she would have
liked to see. She felt that he wanted to hear her say:
"Don't take him again when you come to me," just as he
might have wanted her to kiss him. So, being in a good
mood, she said it: and he was touched. That evening,
talking to M. de Charlus, with whom he had the consolation of being able to speak of her openly (for the most
trivial remarks that he uttered now, even to people who
had never heard of her, always somehow related to
Odette), he said to him: "I believe, all the same, that she
loves me. She's so nice to me, and she certainly takes an
interest in what I do."

And if, when he was setting off for her house, climbing into his carriage with a friend whom he was to drop
somewhere on the way, his friend said: "Hullo! that isn't
Loredan on the box?" with what melancholy joy Swann
would answer him:

"Oh! Good heavens, no! I can tell you, I daren't take
Loredan when I go to the Rue La Pérouse. Odette
doesn't like me to take Loredan, she doesn't think he
treats me properly. What on earth is one to do? Women,
you know, women. My dear fellow, she'd be furious. Oh,
lord, yes; if I took Rémi there I should never hear the last
of it!"

This new manner, indifferent, offhand, irritable,
which Odette now adopted with Swann, undoubtedly

made him suffer; but he did not realise how much he suffered; since it was only gradually, day by day, that Odette
had cooled towards him, it was only by directly contrasting what she was today with what she had been at first
that he could have measured the extent of the change that
had taken place. But this change was his deep, secret
wound, which tormented him day and night, and whenever he felt that his thoughts were straying too near it, he
would quickly turn them into another channel for fear of
suffering too much. He might say to himself in an abstract way: "There was a time when Odette loved me
more," but he never formed any definite picture of that
time. Just as he had in his study a chest of drawers which
he contrived never to look at, which he made a detour to
avoid whenever he went in or out of the room, because in
one of its drawers he had locked away the chrysanthemum which she had given him on one of those first
evenings when he had taken her home in his carriage, and
the letters in which she said: "If only you had forgotten
your heart also. I should never have let you have that
back," and "At whatever hour of the day or night you
may need me, just send me a word, and dispose of me as
you please," so there was a place in his heart where he
would never allow his thoughts to trespass, forcing them,
if need be, into a long divagation so that they should not
have to pass within reach of it; the place in which lingered his memory of happier days.

But his meticulous prudence was defeated one
evening when he had gone out to a party.

It was at the Marquise de Saint-Euverte's, the last,
for that season, of the evenings on which she invited people to listen to the musicians who would serve, later on,

for her charity concerts. Swann, who had intended to go
to each of the previous evenings in turn but never succeeded in making up his mind, received, while he was
dressing for this one, a visit from the Baron de Charlus,
who came with an offer to accompany him to the party, if
this would help him to feel a little less bored and unhappy when he got there. Swann thanked him and said:

"You can't conceive how glad I should be of your
company. But the greatest pleasure you can give me is to
go instead to see Odette. You know what an excellent influence you have over her. I don't suppose she'll be going
anywhere this evening before she goes to see her old
dressmaker, and I'm sure she'd be delighted if you accompanied her there. In any case, you'll find her at home
before then. Try to entertain her, and also to give her a
little sound advice. If you could arrange something for tomorrow that would please her, something we could all
three do together . . . Try to put out a feeler, too, for the
summer; see if there's anything she wants to do, a cruise
that the three of us might take, or something. I don't expect to see her tonight myself; still, if she'd like me to
come, or if you find a loophole, you've only to send me a
word at Mme de Saint-Euverte's up till midnight, and afterwards here. Thank you for all your kindness—you
know how fond I am of you."

The Baron promised to do as Swann wished as soon
as he had deposited him at the door of the Saint-Euverte
house, where Swann arrived soothed by the thought that
M. de Charlus would be spending the evening at the Rue
La Pérouse, but in a state of melancholy indifference to
everything that did not concern Odette, and in particular
to the details of fashionable life, a state which invested

them with the charm that is to be found in anything
which, being no longer an object of our desire, appears to
us in its own guise. On alighting from his carriage, in the
foreground of that fictitious summary of their domestic
existence which hostesses are pleased to offer to their
guests on ceremonial occasions, and in which they show a
great regard for accuracy of costume and setting, Swann
was delighted to see the heirs and successors of Balzac's
"tigers"—now "grooms"—who normally followed their
mistress on her daily drive, now hatted and booted and
posted outside in the roadway in front of the house, or in
front of the stables, like gardeners drawn up for inspec-
tion beside their flower-beds. The tendency he had always had to look for analogies between living people and
the portraits in galleries reasserted itself here, but in a
more positive and more general form; it was society as a
whole, now that he was detached from it, which presented
itself to him as a series of pictures. In the hall, which in
the old days, when he was still a regular attender at such
functions, he would have entered swathed in his overcoat
to emerge from it in his tails, without noticing what had
happened during the few moments he had spent there, his
mind having been either still at the party which he had
just left or already at the party into which he was about
to be ushered, he now noticed for the first time, roused
by the unexpected arrival of so belated a guest, the scattered pack of tall, magnificent, idle footmen who were
drowsing here and there upon benches and chests and
who, pointing their noble greyhound profiles, now rose to
their feet and gathered in a circle round about him.

One of them, of a particularly ferocious aspect, and
not unlike the headsman in certain Renaissance pictures

which represent executions, tortures and the like, advanced upon him with an implacable air to take his things. But the harshness of his steely glare was compensated by the softness of his cotton gloves, so that, as he approached Swann, he seemed to be exhibiting at once an utter contempt for his person and the most tender regard for his hat. He took it with a care to which the precision of his movements imparted something that was almost over-fastidious, and with a delicacy that was rendered almost touching by the evidence of his splendid strength. Then he passed it to one of his satellites, a timid novice who expressed the panic that overpowered him by casting furious glances in every direction, and displayed all the dumb agitation of a wild animal in the first hours of its captivity.

A few feet away, a strapping great fellow in livery stood musing, motionless, statuesque, useless, like that purely decorative warrior whom one sees in the most tumultuous of Mantegna's paintings, lost in thought, leaning upon his shield, while the people around him are rushing about slaughtering one another; detached from the group of his companions who were thronging about Swann, he seemed as determined to remain aloof from that scene, which he followed vaguely with his cruel, glaucous eyes, as if it had been the Massacre of the Innocents or the Martyrdom of St James. He seemed precisely to have sprung from that vanished race—if, indeed, it ever existed, save in the reredos of San Zeno and the frescoes of the Eremitani, where Swann had come in contact with it, and where it still dreams—fruit of the impregnation of a classical statue by one of the Master's Paduan models or an Albrecht Dürer Saxon. And the locks of his

reddish hair, crinkled by nature but glued to his head by
brilliantine, were treated broadly as they are in that Greek
sculpture which the Mantuan painter never ceased to
study, and which, if in its creator's purpose it represents
but man, manages at least to extract from man's simple
outlines such a variety of richness, borrowed, as it were,
from the whole of animate nature, that a head of hair, by
the glossy undulation and beak-like points of its curls, or
in the superimposition of the florid triple diadem of its
tresses, can suggest at once a bunch of seaweed, a brood
of fledgling doves, a bed of hyacinths and a coil of snakes.

Others again, no less colossal, were disposed upon the
steps of a monumental staircase for which their decorative
presence and marmorean immobility might have earned,
like the one in the Palace of the Doges, the name "Staircase of the Giants," and on which Swann now set foot,
saddened by the thought that Odette had never climbed
it. Ah, with what joy by contrast would he have raced up
the dark, evil-smelling, breakneck flights to the little
dressmaker's, in whose attic he would so gladly have paid
the price of a weekly stage-box at the Opera for the right
to spend the evening there when Odette came, and other
days too, for the privilege of talking about her, of living
among people whom she was in the habit of seeing when
he was not there, and who on that account seemed to be
possessed of some part of his mistress's life that was more
real, more inaccessible and more mysterious than anything that he knew. Whereas upon that pestilential but
longed-for staircase to the old dressmaker's, since there
was no other, no service stair in the building, one saw in
the evening outside every door an empty, unwashed milk-
can set out upon the door-mat in readiness for the morn-

ing round, on the splendid but despised staircase which
Swann was now climbing, on either side of him, at different levels, before each anfractuosity made in its walls by
the window of the porter's lodge or the entrance to a set
of rooms, representing the departments of indoor service
which they controlled and doing homage for them to the
guests, a concierge, a major-domo, a steward (worthy men
who spent the rest of the week in semi-independence in
their own domains, dined there by themselves like small
shop-keepers, and might tomorrow lapse to the bourgeois
service of some successful doctor or industrial magnate),
scrupulous in observing to the letter all the instructions
they had been given before being allowed to don the brilliant livery which they wore only at rare intervals and in
which they did not feel altogether at their ease, stood each
in the arcade of his doorway with a pompous splendour
tempered by democratic good-fellowship, like saints in
their niches, while a gigantic usher, dressed Swiss Guard
fashion like the beadle in a church, struck the floor with
his staff as each fresh arrival passed him. Coming to the
top of the staircase, up which he had been followed by a
servant with a pallid countenance and a small pigtail
clubbed at the back of his head, like a Goya sacristan or a
tabellion in an old play, Swann passed in front of a desk
at which lackeys seated like notaries before their massive
register rose solemnly to their feet and inscribed his
name. He next crossed a little hall which—like certain
rooms that are arranged by their owners to serve as the
setting for a single work of art (from which they take
their name), and, in their studied bareness, contain nothing else—displayed at its entrance, like some priceless ef-
figy by Benvenuto Cellini of an armed watchman, a

young footman, his body slightly bent forward, rearing
above his crimson gorget an even more crimson face from
which gushed torrents of fire, timidity and zeal, who, as
he pierced with his impetuous, vigilant, desperate gaze the
Aubusson tapestries screening the door of the room in
which the music was being given, appeared, with a sol-
dierly impassiveness or a supernatural faith—an allegory
of alarums, incarnation of alertness, commemoration of
the call to arms—to be watching, angel or sentinel, from
the tower of a castle or cathedral, for the approach of the
enemy or for the hour of Judgment. Swann had now only
to enter the concert-room, the doors of which were
thrown open to him by an usher loaded with chains, who
bowed low before him as though tendering to him the
keys of a conquered city. But he thought of the house in
which at that very moment he might have been if Odette
had only permitted it, and the remembered glimpse of an
empty milk-can upon a door-mat wrung his heart.

Swann speedily recovered his sense of the general ugliness of the human male when, on the other side of the
tapestry curtain, the spectacle of the servants gave place
to that of the guests. But even this ugliness of faces which
of course were mostly familiar to him seemed something
new now that their features—instead of being to him
symbols of practical utility in the identification of this or
that person who until then had represented merely so
many pleasures to be pursued, boredoms to be avoided,
or courtesies to be acknowledged—rested in the auton-
omy of their lines, measurable by aesthetic co-ordinates
alone. And in these men by whom Swann now found
himself surrounded there was nothing, down to the monocles which many of them wore (and which previously

would at the most have enabled Swann to say that so-
and-so wore a monocle) that, no longer restricted to the
general connotation of a habit, the same in all of them,
did not now strike him with a sense of individuality in
each. Perhaps because he regarded General de Froberville
and the Marquis de Bréauté, who were talking to each
other just inside the door, simply as two figures in a picture, whereas they were the old and useful friends who
had put him up for the Jockey Club and had supported
him in duels, the General's monocle, stuck between his
eyelids like a shell-splinter in his vulgar, scarred and
overbearing face, in the middle of a forehead which it
dominated like the single eye of the Cyclops, appeared to
Swann as a monstrous wound which it might have been
glorious to receive but which it was indecent to expose,
while that which M. de Bréauté sported, as a festive
badge, with his pearl-grey gloves, his crush hat and white
tie, substituting it for the familiar pair of glasses (as
Swann himself did) when he went to society functions,
bore, glued to its other side, like a specimen prepared on
a slide for the microscope, an infinitesimal gaze that
swarmed with affability and never ceased to twinkle at the
loftiness of the ceilings, the delightfulness of the entertainment, the interestingness of the programmes and the
excellence of the refreshments.

"Hallo, you here! Why, it's ages since we've seen
you," the General greeted Swann and, noticing his drawn
features and concluding that it was perhaps a serious illness that had kept him away, added: "You're looking
well, old man!" while M. de Bréauté exclaimed: "My dear
fellow, what on earth are you doing here?" to a society
novelist who had just fitted into the angle of eyebrow and

cheek a monocle that was his sole instrument of psychological investigation and remorseless analysis, and who
now replied with an air of mystery and self-importance,
rolling the "r": "I am observing!"

The Marquis de Forestelle's monocle was minute and
rimless, and, by enforcing an incessant and painful contraction of the eye in which it was embedded like a superfluous cartilage the presence of which is inexplicable and
its substance unimaginable, gave to his face a melancholy
refinement, and led women to suppose him capable of
suffering greatly from the pangs of love. But that of M.
de Saint-Candé, encircled, like Saturn, with an enormous
ring, was the centre of gravity of a face which adjusted itself constantly in relation to it, a face whose quivering red
nose and swollen sarcastic lips endeavoured by their grimaces to keep up with the running fire of wit that
sparkled in the polished disc, and saw itself preferred to
the most handsome looks in the world by snobbish and
depraved young women whom it set dreaming of artificial
charms and a refinement of sensual bliss. Meanwhile, behind him, M. de Palancy, who with his huge carp's head
and goggling eyes moved slowly through the festive gathering, periodically unclenching his mandibles as though in
search of his orientation, had the air of carrying about
upon his person only an accidental and perhaps purely
symbolical fragment of the glass wall of his aquarium, a
part intended to suggest the whole, which recalled to
Swann, a fervent admirer of Giotto's Vices and Virtues at
Padua, that figure representing Injustice by whose side a
leafy bough evokes the idea of the forests that enshroud
his secret lair.

Swann had gone forward into the room at Mme de

Saint-Euverte's insistence, and in order to listen to an air from *Orfeo* which was being rendered on the flute, had taken up a position in a corner from which, unfortunately, his horizon was bounded by two ladies of mature years seated side by side, the Marquise de Cambremer and the Vicomtesse de Franquetot, who, because they were cousins, spent their time at parties wandering through the room each clutching her bag and followed by her daughter, hunting for one another like people at a railway station, and could never be at rest until they had reserved two adjacent chairs by marking them with their fans or handkerchiefs—Mme de Cambremer, since she knew scarcely anyone, being all the more glad of a companion, while Mme de Franquetot, who, on the contrary, was extremely well-connected, thought it elegant and original to show all her fine friends that she preferred to their company that of an obscure lady with whom she had childhood memories in common. Filled with melancholy irony, Swann watched them as they listened to the pianoforte intermezzo (Liszt's "Saint Francis preaching to the birds") which had succeeded the flute and followed the virtuoso in his dizzy flight, Mme de Franquetot anxiously, her eyes starting from her head as though the keys over which his fingers skipped with such agility were a series of trapezes from any one of which he might come crashing a hundred feet to the ground, stealing now and then a glance of astonishment and unbelief at her companion, as who should say: "It isn't possible, I'd never have believed that a human being could do that!", Mme de Cambremer, as a woman who had received a sound musical education, beating time with her head, transformed for the nonce into the pendulum of a metronome, the sweep and rapid-

ity of whose oscillations from one shoulder to the other
(performed with that look of wild abandonment in her eye
which a sufferer shows when he has lost control of himself and is no longer able to master his pain, saying
merely "I can't help it") so increased that at every moment her diamond earrings caught in the trimming of her
bodice, and she was obliged to straighten the bunch of
black grapes which she had in her hair, though without
any interruption of her constantly accelerated motion. On
the other side (and a little way in front) of Mme de Franquetot was the Marquise de Gallardon, absorbed in her
favourite subject of meditation, namely her kinship with
the Guermantes family, from which she derived both
publicly and in private a good deal of glory not unmin-
gled with shame, the most brilliant ornaments of that
house remaining somewhat aloof from her, perhaps because she was boring, or because she was disagreeable, or
because she came of an inferior branch of the family, or
very possibly for no reason at all. When she found herself
seated next to someone whom she did not know, as she
was at this moment next to Mme de Franquetot, she suffered acutely from the feeling that her own consciousness
of her Guermantes connexion could not be made exter-
nally manifest in visible characters like those which, in
the mosaics in Byzantine churches, placed one beneath
another, inscribe in a vertical column by the side of some
holy personage the words which he is supposed to be uttering. At this moment she was pondering the fact that
she had never received an invitation, or even a call, from
her young cousin the Princesse des Laumes during the six
years that had elapsed since the latter's marriage. The
thought filled her with anger, but also with pride; for, by

dint of telling everyone who expressed surprise at never seeing her at Mme des Laumes's that it was because of the risk of meeting the Princesse Mathilde there—a degradation which her own ultra-Legitimist family would never have forgiven her—she had come to believe that this actually was the reason for her not visiting her young cousin. She remembered, it is true, that she had several times inquired of Mme des Laumes how they might contrive to meet, but she remembered it only confusedly and, besides, more than neutralised this slightly humiliating reminiscence by murmuring, "After all, it isn't for me to take the first step; I'm twenty years older than she is." And fortified by these unspoken words she flung her shoulders proudly back until they seemed to part company with her bust, while her head, which lay almost horizontally upon them, was reminiscent of the "detachable" head of a pheasant which is brought to the table regally adorned with its feathers. Not that she in the least resembled a pheasant, having been endowed by nature with a squat, dumpy and masculine figure; but successive mortifications had given her a backward tilt, such as one may observe in trees which have taken root on the edge of a precipice and are forced to grow backwards to preserve their balance. Since she was obliged, in order to console herself for not being quite the equal of the rest of the Guermantes clan, to repeat to herself incessantly that it was owing to the uncompromising rigidity of her principles and pride that she saw so little of them, the constant iteration had ended up by remoulding her body and giving her a sort of presence which was accepted by bourgeois ladies as a sign of breeding, and even kindled at times a momentary spark in the jaded eyes of old club-

SWANN IN LOVE   469

men. Had anyone subjected Mme de Gallardon's conversation to that form of analysis which by noting the relative frequency of its several terms enables one to discover
the key to a coded text, they would at once have remarked that no expression, not even the commonest,
occurred in it nearly so often as "at my cousins the
Guermantes'," "at my aunt Guermantes's," "Elzéar de
Guermantes's health," "my cousin Guermantes's box."
If anyone spoke to her of a distinguished personage, she
would reply that, although she was not personally acquainted with him, she had seen him hundreds of times
at her aunt Guermantes's, but she would utter this reply
in so icy a tone, in such a hollow voice, that it was clear
that if she did not know the celebrity personally it was by
virtue of all the stubborn and ineradicable principles
against which her shoulders leaned, as against one of
those ladders on which gymnastic instructors make us
stretch in order to develop the expansion of our chests.

As it happened, the Princesse des Laumes, whom no
one would have expected to appear at Mme de Saint-Euverte's, had just arrived there. To show that she did not
wish to flaunt her superior rank in a salon to which she
had come only out of condescension, she had sidled in
with her arms pressed close to her sides, even when there
was no crowd to be squeezed through and no one attempting to get past her, staying purposely at the back,
with the air of being in her proper place, like a king who
stands in the queue at the doors of a theatre where the
management have not been warned of his coming; and,
restricting her gaze—so as not to seem to be advertising
her presence and claiming the consideration that was her
due—to the study of a pattern in the carpet or her own

skirt, she stood there on the spot which had struck her as
the most modest (and from which, as she very well knew,
a rapturous exclamation from Mme de Saint-Euverte
would extricate her as soon as her presence there was noticed), next to Mme de Cambremer, whom she did not
know. She observed the dumb-show by which her neighbour was expressing her passion for music, but she refrained from imitating it. This was not to say that, having
for once consented to spend a few minutes in Mme de
Saint-Euverte's house, the Princesse des Laumes would
not have wished (so that the courtesy she was doing her
hostess might, so to speak, count double) to show herself
as friendly and obliging as possible. But she had a natural
horror of what she called "exaggerating," and always
made a point of letting people see that she "had no desire" to indulge in displays of emotion that were not in
keeping with the tone of the circle in which she moved,
although on the other hand such displays could not help
but make an impression upon her, by virtue of that spirit
of imitation, akin to timidity, which is developed in the
most self-confident persons by contact with an unfamiliar
environment, even though it be inferior to their own. She
began to ask herself whether these gesticulations might
not, perhaps, be a necessary concomitant of the piece of
music that was being played—a piece which did not quite
come within the scope of the music she was used to hearing—whether to abstain from them might not be evidence of incomprehension as regards the music and of
discourtesy towards the lady of the house; with the result
that, in order to express by a compromise both of her
contradictory inclinations in turn, at one moment she
would confine herself to straightening her shoulder-straps

or feeling in her golden hair for the little balls of coral or
of pink enamel, frosted with tiny diamonds, which formed
its simple but charming ornament, scrutinising her impassioned neighbour with cold curiosity the while, and at the
next would beat time for a few bars with her fan, but, so
as not to forfeit her independence, against the rhythm.
The pianist having finished the Liszt intermezzo and begun a prelude by Chopin, Mme de Cambremer turned to
Mme de Franquetot with a fond smile of knowing satisfaction and allusion to the past. She had learned in her
girlhood to fondle and cherish those long sinuous phrases
of Chopin, so free, so flexible, so tactile, which begin by
reaching out and exploring far outside and away from the
direction in which they started, far beyond the point
which one might have expected their notes to reach, and
which divert themselves in those byways of fantasy only
to return more deliberately—with a more premeditated
reprise, with more precision, as on a crystal bowl that re-
verberates to the point of making you cry out—to strike
at your heart.

Brought up in a provincial household with few connexions, hardly ever invited to a ball, she had revelled, in
the solitude of her old manor-house, in setting the pace,
now slow, now breathlessly whirling, for all those imaginary waltzing couples, in picking them off like flowers,
leaving the ball-room for a moment to listen to the wind
sighing among the pine-trees on the shore of the lake, and
seeing all of a sudden advancing towards her, more different from anything one has ever dreamed of than earthly
lovers are, a slender young man with a slightly sing-song
voice, strange and out of tune, in white gloves. But nowa-

days the old-fashioned beauty of this music seemed to
have become a trifle stale. Having forfeited, some years
back, the esteem of the connoisseurs, it had lost its distinction and its charm, and even those whose taste was
frankly bad had ceased to find in it more than a moderate
pleasure to which they hardly liked to confess. Mme de
Cambremer cast a furtive glance behind her. She knew
that her young daughter-in-law (full of respect for her
new family, except as regards the things of the mind,
upon which, having got as far as Harmony and the Greek
alphabet, she was specially enlightened) despised Chopin,
and felt quite ill when she heard him played. But finding
herself free from the scrutiny of this Wagnerian, who was
sitting at some distance in a group of her own contempo-
raries, Mme de Cambremer let herself drift upon a stream
of exquisite sensations. The Princesse des Laumes felt
them too. Though without any natural gift for music, she
had had lessons some fifteen years earlier from a piano-
teacher of the Faubourg Saint-Germain, a woman of genius who towards the end of her life had been reduced to
penury and had returned, at seventy, to instruct the
daughters and granddaughters of her old pupils. This
lady was now dead. But her method, her beautiful tone,
came to life now and then beneath the fingers of her
pupils, even of those who had become in other respects
quite mediocre, had given up music, and hardly ever
opened a piano. Thus Mme des Laumes could wave her
head to and fro with complete conviction, with a just ap-
preciation of the manner in which the pianist was rendering this prelude, since she knew it by heart. The closing
notes of the phrase that he had begun sounded already on

her lips. And she murmured "How *ch*arming it is!" with
a double *ch* at the beginning of the word which was a
mark of refinement and by which she felt her lips so ro-
mantically crinkled, like the petals of a beautiful, budding
flower, that she instinctively brought her eyes into harmony with them, illuminating them for a moment with a
vague and sentimental gaze. Meanwhile Mme de Gallardon was saying to herself how annoying it was that she
had so few opportunities of meeting the Princesse des
Laumes, for she meant to teach her a lesson by not acknowledging her greeting. She did not know that her
cousin was in the room. A movement of Mme Franquetot's head disclosed the Princess. At once Mme de Gallardon dashed towards her, disturbing everybody; although
determined to preserve a distant and glacial manner which
should remind everyone present that she had no desire to
be on friendly terms with a person in whose house one
might find oneself cheek by jowl with the Princesse
Mathilde, and to whom it was not for her to make advances since she was not "of her generation," she felt
bound to modify this air of dignity and reserve by some
non-committal remark which would justify her overture
and force the Princess to engage in conversation; and so,
when she reached her cousin, Mme de Gallardon, with a
stern countenance and one hand thrust out as though she
were trying to "force" a card, said to her: "How is your
husband?" in the same anxious tone that she would have
used if the Prince had been seriously ill. The Princess,
breaking into a laugh which was characteristic of her and
was intended at once to draw attention to the fact that she
was making fun of someone and also to enhance her

beauty by concentrating her features around her animated
lips and sparkling eyes, answered: "Why, he's never been
better in his life!" And she went on laughing.

Whereupon Mme de Gallardon drew herself up and,
putting on an even chillier expression, though still apparently concerned about the Prince's health, said to her
cousin:

"Oriane," (at once Mme des Laumes looked with
amused astonishment towards an invisible third person,
whom she seemed to call to witness that she had never
authorised Mme de Gallardon to use her Christian name)
"I should be so pleased if you would look in for a moment tomorrow evening, to hear a clarinet quintet by
Mozart. I should like to have your opinion of it."

She seemed not so much to be issuing an invitation as
to be asking a favour, and to want the Princess's opinion
of the Mozart quintet just as though it had been a dish
invented by a new cook, whose talent it was most important that an epicure should come to judge.

"But I know that quintet quite well. I can tell you
now—that I adore it."

"You know my husband isn't at all well—his liver
. . . He would so much like to see you," Mme de Gallardon went on, making it now a charitable obligation for
the Princess to appear at her party.

The Princess never liked to tell people that she would
not go to their houses. Every day she would write to express her regret at having been kept away—by the sudden arrival of her husband's mother, by an invitation
from her brother-in-law, by the Opera, by some excursion
to the country—from some party to which she would
never have dreamed of going. In this way she gave many

people the satisfaction of feeling that she was on intimate terms with them, that she would gladly have come to their houses, and that she had been prevented from doing so only by some princely obstacle which they were flattered to find competing with their own humble entertainment. And then, as she belonged to that witty Guermantes set in which there survived something of the mental briskness, stripped of all commonplace phrases and conventional sentiments, which goes back to Mérimée and has found its final expression in the plays of Meilhac and Halévy, she adapted it even for the purposes of her social relations, transposed it into the form of politeness which she favoured and which endeavoured to be positive and precise, to approximate itself to the plain truth. She would never develop at any length to a hostess the expression of her anxiety to be present at her party; she thought it more amiable to put to her a few little facts on which it would depend whether or not it was possible for her to come.

"Listen, and I'll explain," she said to Mme de Gallardon. "Tomorrow evening I must go to a friend of mine who has been pestering me to fix a day for ages. If she takes us to the theatre afterwards, with the best will in the world there'll be no possibility of my coming to you; but if we just stay in the house, since I know there won't be anyone else there, I shall be able to slip away."

"Tell me, have you seen your friend M. Swann?"

"No! my beloved Charles! I never knew he was here. I must catch his eye."

"It's odd that he should come to old Saint-Euverte's," Mme de Gallardon went on. "Oh, I know he's very clever," meaning by that "very cunning," "but that makes no difference—the idea of a Jew in the house of a sister and sister-in-law of two Archbishops!"

"I'm ashamed to confess that I'm not in the least shocked," said the Princesse des Laumes.

"I know he's a convert and all that, and even his parents and grandparents before him. But they do say that the converted ones remain more attached to their religion than the practising ones, that it's all just a pretence; is that true, d'you think?"

"I can throw no light at all on the matter."

The pianist, who was to play two pieces by Chopin, after finishing the Prelude had at once attacked a Polonaise. But once Mme de Gallardon had informed her cousin that Swann was in the room, Chopin himself might have risen from the grave and played all his works in turn without Mme des Laumes paying him the slightest attention. She belonged to that half of the human race in whom the curiosity the other half feels about the people it does not know is replaced by an interest in the people it does. As with many women of the Faubourg Saint-Germain, the presence in any room in which she might find herself of another member of her set, even though she had nothing in particular to say to him, monopolised her attention to the exclusion of everything else. From that moment, in the hope that Swann would catch sight of her, the Princess spent her whole time (like a tame white mouse when a lump of sugar is put down before its nose and then taken away) turning her face, which was filled with countless signs of complicity, none of them with the least relevance to the sentiment underlying Chopin's music, in the direction where Swann was standing and, if he moved, diverting accordingly the course of her magnetic smile.

"Oriane, don't be angry with me," resumed Mme de Gallardon, who could never restrain herself from sacrificing her highest social ambitions, and the hope that she might one day dazzle the world, to the immediate, obscure and private satisfaction of saying something disagreeable, "people do say about your M. Swann that he's the sort of man one can't have in one's house; is that true?"

"Why, you of all people ought to know that it's true," replied the Princesse des Laumes, "since you must have asked him a hundred times, and he's never been to your house once."

And leaving her cousin mortified, she burst out laughing again, scandalising everyone who was trying to listen to the music, but attracting the attention of Mme de Saint-Euverte, who had stayed, out of politeness, near the piano, and now caught sight of the Princess for the first time. Mme de Saint-Euverte was all the more delighted to see Mme des Laumes as she imagined her to be still at Guermantes, looking after her sick father-in-law.

"My dear Princess, you here?"

"Yes, I tucked myself away in a corner, and I've been hearing such lovely things."

"What, you've been here for quite a time?"

"Oh, yes, a very long time which seemed very short, long only because I couldn't see you."

Mme de Saint-Euverte offered her own chair to the Princess, who declined it, saying:

"Oh, please, no! Why should you? I don't mind in

the least where I sit." And deliberately picking out, the
better to display the simplicity of a really great lady, a
low seat without a back: "There now, that pouf, that's all
I need. It will make me keep my back straight. Oh! good
heavens, I'm making a noise again; they'll be telling you
to have me chucked out."

Meanwhile, the pianist having redoubled his speed,
the musical excitement was at its height, a servant was
handing refreshments round on a salver, and was making
the spoons rattle, and, as happened every week, Mme de
Saint-Euverte was making unavailing signs to him to go
away. A recent bride, who had been told that a young
woman ought never to appear bored, was smiling vigorously, trying to catch her hostess's eye so as to flash her a
look of gratitude for having "thought of her" in connexion with so delightful an entertainment. However, although she remained calmer than Mme de Franquetot, it
was not without some uneasiness that she followed the
flying fingers, the object of her concern being not the pianist but the piano, on which a lighted candle, jumping at
each fortissimo, threatened, if not to set its shade on fire,
at least to spill wax upon the rosewood. At last she could
contain herself no longer, and, running up the two steps
of the platform on which the piano stood, flung herself on
the candle to adjust its sconce. But scarcely had her hand
come within reach of it when, on a final chord, the piece
came to an end and the pianist rose to his feet. Nevertheless the bold initiative shown by this young woman and
the brief promiscuity between her and the instrumentalist
which resulted from it, produced a generally favourable
impression.

"Did you see what that girl did just now, Princess?"

asked General de Froberville, who had come up to Mme
des Laumes as her hostess left her for a moment. "Odd,
wasn't it? Is she one of the performers?"

"No, she's a little Mme de Cambremer," replied the
Princess without thinking, and then added hurriedly: "I'm
only repeating what I've heard—I haven't the faintest notion who she is; someone behind me said that they were
neighbours of Mme de Saint-Euverte in the country, but I
don't believe anyone knows them, really. They must be
'country cousins'! By the way, I don't know whether
you're particularly familiar with the brilliant society which
we see before us, because I've no idea who all these astonishing people can be. What do you suppose they do
with themselves when they're not at Mme de Saint-Euverte's parties? She must have ordered them along with
the musicians and the chairs and the food. 'Universal
providers,' you know. You must admit they're rather
splendid, General. But can she really have the heart to
hire the same 'supers' every week? It isn't possible!"

"Oh, but Cambremer is quite a good name—old,
too," protested the General.

"I see no objection to its being old," the Princess answered dryly, "but whatever else it is it's not *euphonious*,"
she went on, isolating the word euphonious as though between inverted commas, a little affectation to which the
Guermantes set were addicted.

"You think not, eh! She's a regular little peach,
though," said the General, whose eyes never strayed from
Mme de Cambremer. "Don't you agree with me,
Princess?"

"She thrusts herself forward too much. I think, in so
young a woman, that's not very nice—for I don't suppose

she's my generation," replied Mme des Laumes (this expression being common, it appeared, to Gallardon and Guermantes). And then, seeing that M. de Froberville was still gazing at Mme de Cambremer, she added, half out of malice towards the latter, half out of amiability towards the General: "Not very nice . . . for her husband! I'm sorry I don't know her, since you've set your heart on her—I might have introduced you to her," said the Princess, who, if she had known the young woman, would probably have done nothing of the sort. "And now I must say good night, because one of my friends is having a birthday party, and I must go and wish her many happy returns," she explained in a tone of modest sincerity, reducing the fashionable gathering to which she was going to the simple proportions of a ceremony which would be boring in the extreme but which it was obligatory and touching to attend. "Besides, I must pick up Basin who while I've been here has gone to see those friends of his—you know them too I believe—who are called after a bridge—oh, yes, the Iénas."

"It was a victory before it was a bridge, Princess," said the General. "I mean to say, to an old soldier like me," he went on, wiping his monocle and replacing it, as though he were laying a fresh dressing on the raw wound beneath, while the Princess instinctively looked away, "that Empire nobility, well of course it's not the same thing, but, after all, taking it for what it is, it's very fine of its kind—they were people who really did fight like heroes."

"But I have the deepest respect for heroes," the Princess assented with a faint trace of irony. "If I don't go with Basin to see this Princess d'Iéna, it isn't at all because of that, it's simply because I don't know them. Basin knows them, and is deeply attached to them. Oh, no, it's not what you think, it's not a flirtation. I've no reason to object. Besides, what good has it ever done when I have objected," she added in a melancholy voice, for the whole world knew that, ever since the day when the Prince des Laumes had married his ravishing cousin, he had been consistently unfaithful to her. "Anyhow, it isn't that at all. They're people he has known for a long time, he takes advantage of them, and that suits me down to the ground. In any case, what he's told me about their house is quite enough. Can you imagine it, all their furniture is 'Empire'!"

"But, my dear Princess, that's only natural; it belonged to their grandparents."

"I don't say it didn't, but that doesn't make it any less ugly. I quite understand that people can't always have nice things, but at least they needn't have things that are merely grotesque. I'm sorry, but I can think of nothing more pretentious and bourgeois than that hideous style—cabinets with swans' heads, like baths!"

"But I believe, all the same, that they've got some fine things; why, they must have that famous mosaic table on which the Treaty of . . ."

"Oh, I don't deny they may have things that are interesting enough from the historic point of view. But things like that can't ever be beautiful . . . because they're simply horrible! I've got things like that myself, that came to Basin from the Montesquious. Only, they're up in the attics at Guermantes, where nobody ever sees them. But in any case that's not the point, I would rush round to see them with Basin, I'd even go to see them

among all their sphinxes and brasses if I knew them,
but—I don't know them! D'you know, I was always
taught when I was a little girl that it wasn't polite to call
on people one didn't know." She assumed a tone of childish gravity. "And so I'm just doing what I was taught to
do. Can't you see those good people, with a totally
strange woman bursting into their house? Why, I might
get a most hostile reception."

And she coquettishly enhanced the charm of the
smile which that supposition had brought to her lips, by
giving to her blue eyes, which were fixed on the General,
a gentle, dreamy expression.

"My dear Princess, you know that they'd be simply
wild with joy."

"No, why?" she inquired with the utmost vivacity, either to give the impression of being unaware that it would
be because she was one of the first ladies in France, or in
order to have the pleasure of hearing the General tell her
so. "Why? How can you tell? Perhaps they might find it
extremely disagreeable. I don't know, but if they're anything like me, I find it quite boring enough to see the
people I do know, and I'm sure if I had to see people I
didn't know as well, even if they had 'fought like heroes,'
I should go stark mad. Besides, except when it's an old
friend like you, whom one knows quite apart from that,
I'm not sure that heroism takes one very far in society.
It's often quite boring enough to have to give a dinner-
party, but if one had to offer one's arm to Spartacus to go
into dinner . . . Really, no, it would never be Vercinge-
torix I should send for to make a fourteenth. I feel sure I
should keep him for grand receptions. And as I never
give any . . ."

"Ah! Princess, it's easy to see you're not a Guermantes for nothing. You have your share of it, all right,
the wit of the Guermantes!"

"But people always talk about the wit of *the* Guermantes in the plural. I never could make out why. Do
you really know any *others* who have it?" she rallied him,
with a rippling flow of laughter, her features concentrated,
yoked to the service of her animation, her eyes sparkling,
blazing with a radiant sunshine of gaiety which could be
kindled only by such observations—even if the Princess
had to make them herself—as were in praise of her wit or
of her beauty. "Look, there's Swann talking to your Cambremer; over there, beside old mother Saint-Euverte,
don't you see him? Ask him to introduce you. But hurry
up, he seems to be just going!"

"Did you notice how dreadfully ill he's looking?"
asked the General.

"My precious Charles? Ah, he's coming at last. I was
beginning to think he didn't want to see me!"

Swann was extremely fond of the Princesse des
Laumes, and the sight of her reminded him of Guermantes, the estate next to Combray, and all that country
which he so dearly loved and had ceased to visit in order
not to be separated from Odette. Slipping into the manner, half-artistic, half-amorous, with which he could always manage to amuse the Princess—a manner which
came to him quite naturally whenever he dipped for a
moment into the old social atmosphere—and wishing also
to express in words, for his own satisfaction, the longing
that he felt for the country:

"Ah!" he began in a declamatory tone, so as to be au-
dible at once to Mme de Saint-Euverte, to whom he was

speaking, and to Mme des Laumes, for whom he was speaking, "Behold our charming Princess! Look, she has come up on purpose from Guermantes to hear Saint Francis preach to the birds, and has only just had time, like a dear little titmouse, to go and pick a few little hips and haws and put them in her hair; there are even some drops of dew upon them still, a little of the hoar-frost which must be making the Duchess shiver. It's very pretty indeed, my dear Princess."

"What! The Princess came up on purpose from Guermantes? But that's too wonderful! I never knew; I'm quite overcome," Mme de Saint-Euverte protested with quaint simplicity, being but little accustomed to Swann's form of wit. And then, examining the Princess's head-dress, "Why, you're quite right; it is copied from . . . what shall I say, not chestnuts, no—oh, it's a delightful idea, but how can the Princess have known what was going to be on my programme? The musicians didn't tell me, even."

Swann, who was accustomed, when he was with a woman whom he had kept up the habit of addressing in terms of gallantry, to pay her delicate compliments which most society people were incapable of understanding, did not condescend to explain to Mme de Saint-Euverte that he had been speaking metaphorically. As for the Princess, she was in fits of laughter, both because Swann's wit was highly appreciated by her set, and because she could never hear a compliment addressed to herself without finding it exquisitely subtle and irresistibly amusing.

"Well, I'm delighted, Charles, if my little hips and haws meet with your approval. But tell me, why did you pay your respects to that Cambremer person, are you also her neighbour in the country?"

Mme de Saint-Euverte, seeing that the Princess seemed quite happy talking to Swann, had drifted away.

"But you are yourself, Princess!"

"I! Why, they must have 'countries' everywhere, those people! Don't I wish I had!"

"No, not the Cambremers; her own people. She was a Legrandin, and used to come to Combray. I don't know whether you're aware that you are Comtesse de Combray, and that the Chapter owes you a due."

"I don't know what the Chapter owes me, but I do know that I'm touched for a hundred francs every year by the Curé, which is a due that I could do very well without. But surely these Cambremers have rather a startling name. It ends just in time, but it ends badly!" she said with a laugh.[14]

"It begins no better." Swann took the point.

"Yes; that double abbreviation!"

"Someone very angry and very proper who didn't dare to finish the first word."

"But since he couldn't stop himself beginning the second, he'd have done better to finish the first and be done with it. I must say our jokes are in really charming taste, my dear Charles . . . but how tiresome it is that I never see you now," she went on in a winning tone, "I do so love talking to you. Just imagine, I couldn't even have made that idiot Froberville see that there was anything funny about the name Cambremer. Do you agree that life is a dreadful business. It's only when I see you that I stop feeling bored."

Which was probably not true. But Swann and the Princess had a similar way of looking at the little things of life, the effect—if not the cause—of which was a close analogy between their modes of expression and even of pronunciation. This similarity was not immediately striking because no two things could have been more unlike than their voices. But if one took the trouble to imagine Swann's utterances divested of the sonority that enwrapped them, of the moustache from under which they emerged, one realised that they were the same phrases, the same inflexions, that they had the style of the Guermantes set. On important matters, Swann and the Princess had not an idea in common. But since Swann had become so melancholy, and was always in that tremulous condition which precedes the onset of tears, he felt the same need to speak about his grief as a murderer to speak about his crime. And when he heard the Princess say that life was a dreadful business, it gave him a feeling of solace as if she had spoken to him of Odette.

"Yes, life is a dreadful business! We must meet more often, my dear friend. What is so nice about you is that you're not cheerful. We might spend an evening together."

"By all means. Why not come down to Guermantes? My mother-in-law would be wild with joy. It's supposed to be very ugly down there, but I must say I find the neighbourhood not at all unattractive; I have a horror of 'picturesque spots'."

"Yes, I know, it's delightful!" replied Swann. "It's almost too beautiful, too alive for me just at present; it's a country to be happy in. It's perhaps because I've lived there, but things there speak to me so. As soon as a breath of wind gets up, and the cornfields begin to stir, I feel that someone is going to appear suddenly, that I'm going to hear some news; and those little houses by the water's edge . . . I should be quite wretched!"

"Oh! my dear Charles, look out, there's that appalling Rampillon woman; she's seen me; please hide me. Remind me what it was that happened to her; I get so confused; she's just married off her daughter, or her lover, I don't know which; perhaps the two of them . . . to each other! Oh, no, I remember now, she's been dropped by her prince . . . Pretend to be talking to me, so that the poor old Berenice shan't come and invite me to dinner. Anyhow, I'm going. Listen, my dearest Charles, now that I've seen you for once, won't you let me carry you off and take you to the Princesse de Parme's? She'd be so pleased to see you, and Basin too, for that matter—he's meeting me there. If one didn't get news of you, sometimes, from Mémé . . . Imagine, I never see you at all now!"

Swann declined. Having told M. de Charlus that on leaving Mme de Saint-Euverte's he would go straight home, he did not care to run the risk, by going on now to the Princesse de Parme's, of missing a message which he had all the time been hoping to see brought in to him by one of the footmen during the party, and which he might perhaps find with his own porter when he got home.

"Poor Swann," said Mme des Laumes that night to her husband, "he's as charming as ever, but he does look so dreadfully unhappy. You'll see for yourself, as he has promised to dine with us one of these days. I do feel it's absurd that a man of his intelligence should let himself suffer for a woman of that sort, and one who isn't even

interesting, for they tell me she's an absolute idiot!" she
added with the wisdom invariably shown by people who,
not being in love themselves, feel that a clever man
should only be unhappy about a person who is worth his
while; which is rather like being astonished that anyone
should condescend to die of cholera at the bidding of so
insignificant a creature as the comma bacillus.

Swann wanted to go home, but just as he was making
his escape, General de Froberville caught him and asked
for an introduction to Mme de Cambremer, and he was
obliged to go back into the room with him to look for
her.

"I say, Swann, I'd rather be married to that little
woman than slaughtered by savages, what do you say?"

The words "slaughtered by savages" pierced Swann's
aching heart; and at once he felt the need to continue the
conversation. "Ah!" he began, "some fine lives have been
lost in that way . . . There was, you remember, that
navigator whose remains Dumont d'Urville brought back,
La Pérouse . . ." (and he was at once happy again, as
though he had named Odette). "He was a fine character,
and interests me very much, does La Pérouse," he added
with a melancholy air.

"Oh, yes, of course, La Pérouse," said the General.
"It's quite a well-known name. There's a street called
that."

"Do you know anyone in the Rue La Pérouse?" asked
Swann excitedly.

"Only Mme de Chanlivault, the sister of that good
fellow Chaussepierre. She gave a most amusing theatre-
party the other evening. That'll be a really elegant salon
one of these days, you'll see!"

"Oh, so she lives in the Rue La Pérouse. It's attractive, a delightful street, so gloomy."

"Not at all. You can't have been in it for a long time; it isn't gloomy now; they're beginning to build all round there."

When Swann did finally introduce M. de Froberville to the young Mme de Cambremer, since it was the first time she had heard the General's name she offered him the smile of joy and surprise with which she would have greeted him if no one had ever uttered any other; for, not knowing any of the friends of her new family, whenever someone was presented to her she assumed that he must be one of them, and thinking that she was showing evidence of tact by appearing to have heard such a lot about him since her marriage, she would hold out her hand with a hesitant air that was meant as a proof at once of the inculcated reserve which she had to overcome and of the spontaneous friendliness which successfully overcame it. And so her parents-in-law, whom she still regarded as the most eminent people in France, declared that she was an angel; all the more so because they preferred to appear, in marrying their son to her, to have yielded to the attraction rather of her natural charm than of her considerable fortune.

"It's easy to see that you're a musician heart and soul, Madame," said the General, alluding to the incident of the candle.

Meanwhile the concert had begun again, and Swann saw that he could not now go before the end of the new number. He suffered greatly from being shut up among all these people whose stupidity and absurdities struck him all the more painfully since, being ignorant of his

love and incapable, had they known of it, of taking any
interest or of doing more than smile at it as at some
childish nonsense or deplore it as an act of folly, they
made it appear to him in the aspect of a subjective state
which existed for himself alone, whose reality there was
nothing external to confirm; he suffered above all, to the
point where even the sound of the instruments made him
want to cry out, from having to prolong his exile in this
place to which Odette would never come, in which no
one, nothing was aware of her existence, from which she
was entirely absent.

But suddenly it was as though she had entered, and
this apparition was so agonisingly painful that his hand
clutched at his heart. The violin had risen to a series of
high notes on which it rested as though awaiting something, holding on to them in a prolonged expectancy, in
the exaltation of already seeing the object of its expectation approaching, and with a desperate effort to last out
until its arrival, to welcome it before itself expiring, to
keep the way open for a moment longer, with all its remaining strength, so that the stranger might pass, as one
holds a door open that would otherwise automatically
close. And before Swann had had time to understand
what was happening and to say to himself: "It's the little
phrase from Vinteuil's sonata—I mustn't listen!", all his
memories of the days when Odette had been in love with
him, which he had succeeded until that moment in keeping invisible in the depths of his being, deceived by this
sudden reflection of a season of love whose sun, they supposed, had dawned again, had awakened from their slumber, had taken wing and risen to sing maddeningly in his

ears, without pity for his present desolation, the forgotten
strains of happiness.

In place of the abstract expressions "the time when I
was happy," "the time when I was loved," which he had
often used before then without suffering too much since
his intelligence had not embodied in them anything of the
past save fictitious extracts which preserved none of the
reality, he now recovered everything that had fixed unal-
terably the specific, volatile essence of that lost happiness;
he could see it all: the snowy, curled petals of the
chrysanthemum which she had tossed after him into his
carriage, which he had kept pressed to his lips—the address "Maison Dorée" embossed on the note-paper on
which he had read "My hand trembles so as I write to
you"—the contraction of her eyebrows when she said
pleadingly: "You won't leave it too long before getting in
touch with me?"; he could smell the heated iron of the
barber whom he used to have singe his hair while
Loredan went to fetch the little seamstress; could feel the
showers which fell so often that spring, the ice-cold
homeward drive in his victoria, by moonlight; all the network of mental habits, of seasonal impressions, of sensory
reactions, which had extended over a series of weeks its
uniform meshes in which his body found itself inextrica-
bly caught. At that time he had been satisfying a sensual
curiosity in discovering the pleasures of those who live for
love alone. He had supposed that he could stop there,
that he would not be obliged to learn their sorrows also;
yet how small a thing the actual charm of Odette was
now in comparison with the fearsome terror which extended it like a cloudy halo all around her, the immense

anguish of not knowing at every hour of the day and
night what she had been doing, of not possessing her
wholly, always and everywhere! Alas, he recalled the accents in which she had exclaimed: "But I can see you at
any time; I'm always free!"—she who was never free
now; he remembered the interest, the curiosity she had
shown in his life, her passionate desire that he should do
her the favour—which it was he who had dreaded at that
time as a possibly tedious waste of his time and disturbance of his arrangements—of granting her access to his
study; how she had been obliged to beg him to let her
take him to the Verdurins'; and, when he allowed her to
come to him once a month, how she had had to repeat to
him time and again, before he let himself be swayed,
what a joy it would be to see each other daily, a custom
for which she longed when to him it seemed only a tiresome distraction, which she had then grown tired of and
finally broken while for him it had become so irresistible
and painful a need. Little had he suspected how truly he
spoke, when at their third meeting, as she repeated: "But
why don't you let me come to you oftener?" he had told
her, laughing, and in a vein of gallantry, that it was for
fear of forming a hopeless passion. Now, alas, it still happened at times that she wrote to him from a restaurant or
hotel, on paper which bore a printed address, but printed
in letters of fire that seared his heart. "It's written from
the Hôtel Vouillemont. What on earth can she have gone
there for? With whom? What happened there?" He remembered the gas-jets being extinguished along the
Boulevard des Italiens when he had met her against all
expectations among the errant shades on that night which
had seemed to him almost supernatural and which

indeed—a night from a period when he had not even to ask himself whether he would be annoying her by looking for her and finding her, so certain was he that she knew no greater happiness than to see him and to let him take her home—belonged to a mysterious world to which one never may return again once its doors are closed. And Swann could distinguish, standing motionless before that scene of remembered happiness, a wretched figure who filled him with such pity, because he did not at first recognise who it was, that he had to lower his eyes lest anyone should observe that they were filled with tears. It was himself.

When he had realised this, his pity ceased; he was jealous, now, of that other self whom she had loved, he was jealous of those men of whom he had so often said, without suffering too much: "Perhaps she loves them," now that he had exchanged the vague idea of loving, in which there is no love, for the petals of the chrysanthemum and the letterhead of the Maison Dorée, which were full of it. And then, his anguish becoming too intense, he drew his hand across his forehead, let the monocle drop from his eye, and wiped its glass. And doubtless, if he had caught sight of himself at that moment, he would have added, to the collection of those which he had already identified, this monocle which he removed like an importunate, worrying thought and from whose misty surface, with his handkerchief, he sought to obliterate his cares.

There are in the music of the violin—if one does not see the instrument itself, and so cannot relate what one hears to its form, which modifies the tone—accents so closely akin to those of certain contralto voices that one has the illusion that a singer has taken her place amid the orchestra. One raises one's eyes, and sees only the wooden case, delicate as a Chinese box, but, at moments, one is still tricked by the siren's deceiving call; at times, too, one thinks one is listening to a captive genie, struggling in the darkness of the sapient, quivering and enchanted box, like a devil immersed in a stoup of holy water; sometimes, again, it is in the air, at large, like a pure and supernatural being that unfolds its invisible message as it goes by.

As though the musicians were not nearly so much playing the little phrase as performing the rites on which it insisted before it would consent to appear, and proceeding to utter the incantations necessary to procure, and to prolong for a few moments, the miracle of its apparition, Swann, who was no more able to see it than if it had belonged to a world of ultra-violet light, and who experienced something like the refreshing sense of a metamorphosis in the momentary blindness with which he was struck as he approached it, Swann felt its presence like that of a protective goddess, a confidante of his love, who, in order to be able to come to him through the crowd and to draw him aside to speak to him, had disguised herself in this sweeping cloak of sound. And as she passed, light, soothing, murmurous as the perfume of a flower, telling him what she had to say, every word of which he closely scanned, regretful to see them fly away so fast, he made involuntarily with his lips the motion of kissing, as it went by him, the harmonious, fleeting form. He felt that he was no longer in exile and alone since she, who addressed herself to him, was whispering to him of Odette. For he had no longer, as of old, the impression that

Odette and he were unknown to the little phrase. Had it not often been the witness of their joys? True that, as often, it had warned him of their frailty. And indeed, whereas in that earlier time he had divined an element of suffering in its smile, in its limpid, disenchanted tones, tonight he found there rather the grace of a resignation that was almost gay. Of those sorrows which the little phrase foreshadowed to him then, which, without being affected by them himself, he had seen it carry past him, smiling, on its sinuous and rapid course, of those sorrows which had now become his own, without his having any hope of being ever delivered from them, it seemed to say to him, as once it had said of his happiness: "What does it all matter? It means nothing." And Swann's thoughts were borne for the first time on a wave of pity and tenderness towards Vinteuil, towards that unknown, exalted brother who must also have suffered so greatly. What could his life have been? From the depths of what well of sorrow could he have drawn that god-like strength, that unlimited power of creation?

When it was the little phrase that spoke to him of the vanity of his sufferings, Swann found a solace in that very wisdom which, but a little while back, had seemed to him intolerable when he fancied he could read it on the faces of indifferent strangers who regarded his love as an insignificant aberration. For the little phrase, unlike them, whatever opinion it might hold on the transience of these states of the soul, saw in them something not, as all these people did, less serious than the events of everyday life, but, on the contrary, so far superior to it as to be alone worth while expressing. It was the charms of an intimate sadness that it sought to imitate, to re-create, and their

very essence, for all that it consists in being incommuni-
cable and in appearing trivial to everyone except him who
experiences them, had been captured and made visible by
the little phrase. So much so that it caused their value to
be acknowledged, their divine sweetness savoured, by all
those same onlookers, if they were at all musical—who
then would fail to recognise them in real life, in every individual love that came into being beneath their eyes.
Doubtless the form in which it had codified those charms
could not be resolved into rational discourse. But ever
since, more than a year before, discovering to him many
of the riches of his own soul, the love of music had, for a
time at least, been born in him, Swann had regarded musical motifs as actual ideas, of another world, of another
order, ideas veiled in shadow, unknown, impenetrable to
the human mind, but none the less perfectly distinct from
one another, unequal among themselves in value and significance. When, after that first evening at the Verdurins',
he had had the little phrase played over to him again, and
had sought to disentangle from his confused impressions
how it was that, like a perfume or a caress, it swept over
and enveloped him, he had observed that it was to the
closeness of the intervals between the five notes which
composed it and to the constant repetition of two of them
that was due that impression of a frigid and withdrawn
sweetness; but in reality he knew that he was basing this
conclusion not upon the phrase itself, but merely upon
certain equivalents, substituted (for his mind's convenience) for the mysterious entity of which he had become
aware, before ever he knew the Verdurins, at that earlier
party when for the first time he had heard the sonata
played. He knew that the very memory of the piano falsi-

fied still further the perspective in which he saw the elements of music, that the field open to the musician is not
a miserable stave of seven notes, but an immeasurable
keyboard (still almost entirely unknown) on which, here
and there only, separated by the thick darkness of its unexplored tracts, some few among the millions of keys of
tenderness, of passion, of courage, of serenity, which
compose it, each one differing from all the rest as one
universe differs from another, have been discovered by a
few great artists who do us the service, when they awaken
in us the emotion corresponding to the theme they have
discovered, of showing us what richness, what variety lies
hidden, unknown to us, in that vast, unfathomed and for-
bidding night of our soul which we take to be an impenetrable void. Vinteuil had been one of those musicians. In
his little phrase, although it might present a clouded surface to the eye of reason, one sensed a content so solid, so
consistent, so explicit, to which it gave so new, so original
a force, that those who had once heard it preserved the
memory of it on an equal footing with the ideas of the intellect. Swann referred back to it as to a conception of
love and happiness whose distinctive character he recognised at once as he would that of the *Princesse de Clèves*,
or of *René*, should either of those titles occur to him.
Even when he was not thinking of the little phrase, it existed latent in his mind on the same footing as certain
other notions without material equivalent, such as our notions of light, of sound, of perspective, of physical pleasure, the rich possessions wherewith our inner temple is
diversified and adorned. Perhaps we shall lose them, perhaps they will be obliterated, if we return to nothingness.
But so long as we are alive, we can no more bring our-

selves to a state in which we shall not have known them than we can with regard to any material object, than we can, for example, doubt the luminosity of a lamp that has just been lit, in view of the changed aspect of everything in the room, from which even the memory of the darkness has vanished. In that way Vinteuil's phrase, like some theme, say, in *Tristan*, which represents to us also a certain emotional accretion, had espoused our mortal state, had endued a vesture of humanity that was peculiarly affecting. Its destiny was linked to the future, to the reality of the human soul, of which it was one of the most special and distinctive ornaments. Perhaps it is not-being that is the true state, and all our dream of life is inexistent; but, if so, we feel that these phrases of music, these conceptions which exist in relation to our dream, must be nothing either. We shall perish, but we have as hostages these divine captives who will follow and share our fate. And death in their company is somehow less bitter, less inglorious, perhaps even less probable.

So Swann was not mistaken in believing that the phrase of the sonata really did exist. Human as it was from this point of view, it yet belonged to an order of supernatural beings whom we have never seen, but whom, in spite of that, we recognise and acclaim with rapture when some explorer of the unseen contrives to coax one forth, to bring it down, from that divine world to which he has access, to shine for a brief moment in the firmament of ours. This was what Vinteuil had done with the little phrase. Swann felt that the composer had been content (with the musical instruments at his disposal) to unveil it, to make it visible, following and respecting its outlines with a hand so loving, so prudent, so delicate and so sure that the sound altered at every moment, softening and blurring to indicate a shadow, springing back into life when it must follow the curve of some bolder projection. And one proof that Swann was not mistaken when he believed in the real existence of this phrase, was that anyone with the least discernment would at once have detected the imposture had Vinteuil, endowed with less power to see and to render its forms, sought to dissemble, by adding a counterfeit touch here and there, the flaws in his vision or the deficiencies of his hand.

The phrase had disappeared. Swann knew that it would come again at the end of the last movement, after a long passage which Mme Verdurin's pianist always skipped. There were in this passage some admirable ideas which Swann had not distinguished on first hearing the sonata and which he now perceived, as if, in the cloak-room of his memory, they had divested themselves of the uniform disguise of their novelty. Swann listened to all the scattered themes which would enter into the composition of the phrase, as its premisses enter into the inevitable conclusion of a syllogism; he was assisting at the mystery of its birth. "An audacity," he exclaimed to himself, "as inspired, perhaps, as that of a Lavoisier or an Ampère—the audacity of a Vinteuil experimenting, discovering the secret laws that govern an unknown force, driving, across a region unexplored, towards the one possible goal, the invisible team in which he has placed his trust and which he may never discern!" How beautiful the dialogue which Swann now heard between piano and violin, at the beginning of the last passage! The suppression of human speech, so far from letting fancy reign there uncontrolled (as one might have thought), had elim-

inated it altogether; never was spoken language so in-
exorably determined, never had it known questions so
pertinent, such irrefutable replies. At first the piano complained alone, like a bird deserted by its mate; the violin
heard and answered it, as from a neighbouring tree. It
was as at the beginning of the world, as if there were as
yet only the two of them on the earth, or rather in this
world closed to all the rest, so fashioned by the logic of
its creator that in it there should never be any but themselves: the world of this sonata. Was it a bird, was it the
soul, as yet not fully formed, of the little phrase, was it a
fairy—that being invisibly lamenting, whose plaint the
piano heard and tenderly repeated? Its cries were so sudden that the violinist must snatch up his bow and race to
catch them as they came. Marvellous bird! The violinist
seemed to wish to charm, to tame, to capture it. Already
it had passed into his soul, already the little phrase which
it evoked shook like a medium's the body of the violinist,
"possessed" indeed. Swann knew that the phrase was going to speak to him once again. And his personality was
now so divided that the strain of waiting for the imminent
moment when he would find himself face to face with it
again shook him with one of those sobs which a beautiful
line of poetry or a sad piece of news will wring from us,
not when we are alone, but when we impart them to
friends in whom we see ourselves reflected like a third
person whose probable emotion affects them too. It reappeared, but this time to remain poised in the air, and to
sport there for a moment only, as though immobile, and
shortly to expire. And so Swann lost nothing of the precious time for which it lingered. It was still there, like an
iridescent bubble that floats for a while unbroken. As a

rainbow whose brightness is fading seems to subside, then
soars again and, before it is extinguished, shines forth
with greater splendour than it has ever shown; so to the
two colours which the little phrase had hitherto allowed to
appear it added others now, chords shot with every hue in
the prism, and made them sing. Swann dared not move,
and would have liked to compel all the other people in
the room to remain still also, as if the slightest movement
might imperil the magic presence, supernatural, delicious,
frail, that was so soon to vanish. But no one, as it happened, dreamed of speaking. The ineffable utterance of
one solitary man, absent, perhaps dead (Swann did not
know whether Vinteuil was still alive), breathed out above
the rites of those two hierophants, sufficed to arrest the
attention of three hundred minds, and made of that platform on which a soul was thus called into being one of
the noblest altars on which a supernatural ceremony could
be performed. So that when the phrase had unravelled itself at last, and only its fragmentary echoes floated among
the subsequent themes which had already taken its place,
if Swann at first was irritated to see the Comtesse de
Monteriender, famed for her naïveties, lean over towards
him to confide her impressions to him before even the
sonata had come to an end, he could not refrain from
smiling, and perhaps also found an underlying sense,
which she herself was incapable of perceiving, in the
words that she used. Dazzled by the virtuosity of the performers, the Comtesse exclaimed to Swann: "It's astonishing! I've never seen anything to beat it . . ." But a
scrupulous regard for accuracy making her correct her
first assertion, she added the reservation: "anything to
beat it . . . since the table-turning!"

From that evening onwards, Swann understood that
the feeling which Odette had once had for him would
never revive, that his hopes of happiness would not be realised now. And on the days on which she happened to
be once more kind and affectionate towards him, had
shown him some thoughtful attention, he recorded these
deceptive signs of a change of feeling on her part with the
fond and sceptical solicitude, the desperate joy of people
who, nursing a friend in the last days of an incurable illness, relate as facts of infinitely precious insignificance:
"Yesterday he went through his accounts himself, and actually corrected a mistake we had made in adding them
up; he ate an egg today and seemed quite to enjoy it, and
if he digests it properly we shall try him with a cutlet tomorrow"—although they themselves know that these
things are meaningless on the eve of an inevitable death.
No doubt Swann was assured that if he had now been living at a distance from Odette he would gradually have
lost interest in her, so that he would have been glad to
learn that she was leaving Paris for ever; he would have
had the heart to remain there; but he hadn't the heart to
go.

He had often thought of going. Now that he was once
again at work upon his essay on Vermeer, he needed to
return, for a few days at least, to The Hague, to Dresden,
to Brunswick. He was convinced that a picture of "Diana
and her Companions" which had been acquired by the
Mauritshuis at the Goldschmidt sale as a Nicholas Maes
was in reality a Vermeer. And he would have liked to be
able to examine the picture on the spot, in order to but-
tress his conviction. But to leave Paris while Odette was
there, and even when she was not there—for in strange

places where our sensations have not been numbed by
habit, we revive, we resharpen an old pain—was for him
so cruel a project that he felt capable of entertaining it
incessantly in his mind only because he knew he was determined never to put it into effect. But it sometimes happened that, while he was asleep, the intention to travel
would reawaken in him (without his remembering that it
was out of the question) and would actually take place.
One night he dreamed that he was going away for a year;
leaning from the window of the train towards a young
man on the platform who wept as he bade him farewell,
he was trying to persuade this young man to come away
also. The train began to move, he awoke in alarm, and remembered that he was not going away, that he would see
Odette that evening, and the next day and almost every
day. And then, being still deeply affected by his dream,
he thanked heaven for those special circumstances which
made him independent, thanks to which he could remain
close to Odette, and could even succeed in getting her to
allow him to see her sometimes; and, recapitulating all his
advantages: his social position—his wealth, from which
she stood too often in need of assistance not to shrink
from the prospect of a definite rupture (having even, so
people said, an ulterior plan of getting him to marry
her)—his friendship with M. de Charlus, which, it was
true, had never won him any very great favour from
Odette, but which gave him the consolatory feeling that
she was always hearing complimentary things said about
him by this friend in common for whom she had so great
an esteem—and even his intelligence, which was exclusively occupied in devising each day a fresh scheme which
would make his presence, if not agreeable, at any rate

necessary to Odette—remembering all this, he thought of what might have become of him if these advantages had been lacking; it struck him that if, like so many other men, he had been poor, humble, deprived, forced to accept any work that might be offered to him, or tied down by parents or by a wife, he might have been obliged to part from Odette, that that dream, the terror of which was still so recent, might well have been true; and he said to himself: "People don't know when they're happy. One is never as unhappy as one thinks." But he reflected that this existence had already lasted for several years, that all he could now hope for was that it would last for ever, that he would sacrifice his work, his pleasures, his friends, in fact the whole of his life to the daily expectation of a meeting which, if it occurred, could bring him no happiness; and he asked himself whether he was not mistaken, whether the circumstances that had favoured his liaison and had prevented its final rupture had not done a disservice to his career, whether the outcome to be desired might not have been that as to which he rejoiced that it had happened only in a dream—his own departure; and he said to himself that people did not know when they were unhappy, that one is never as happy as one thinks.

Sometimes he hoped that she would die, painlessly, in some accident, since she was out of doors, in the streets, crossing busy thoroughfares, from morning to night. And as she always returned safe and sound, he marvelled at the strength and the suppleness of the human body, which was able continually to hold at bay, to outwit all the perils that beset it (which to Swann seemed innumerable since his own secret desire had strewn them in her path), and so allowed mankind to abandon itself, day after day, and almost with impunity, to its career of mendacity, to the pursuit of pleasure. And Swann felt a very cordial sympathy with the sultan Mahomet II whose portrait by Bellini he admired, who, on finding that he had fallen madly in love with one of his wives, stabbed her to death in order, as his Venetian biographer artlessly relates, to recover his peace of mind. Then he would be ashamed of thinking thus only of himself, and his own sufferings would seem to deserve no pity now that he himself held Odette's very life so cheap.

Unable to cut himself off from her irrevocably, if at least he had seen her continuously and without separations his anguish would ultimately have been assuaged, and his love, perhaps, have died. And since she did not wish to leave Paris for ever, he hoped that she would never leave it. As he knew that her one prolonged absence, every year, was in August and September, at least he had abundant opportunity, several months in advance, to dissolve the bitter thought of it in all the Time to come which he stored up inside himself in anticipation, and which, composed of days identical with those of the present, flowed through his mind, transparent and cold, nourishing his sadness but without causing him any intolerable pain. But that inner future, that colourless, free-flowing stream, was suddenly convulsed by a single remark from Odette which, penetrating Swann's defences, immobilised it like a block of ice, congealed its fluidity, froze it altogether; and Swann felt himself suddenly filled with an enormous and infrangible mass which pressed on the inner walls of his being until it almost burst asunder; for Odette had said to him casually, observing him with a malicious smile: "Forcheville's going on a fine trip at

Whitsun. He's going to Egypt!" and Swann had at once understood this to mean: "I'm going to Egypt at Whitsun with Forcheville." And in fact, if, a few days later, Swann said to her: "About that trip you told me you were going to take with Forcheville," she would answer carelessly: "Yes, my dear boy, we're starting on the 19th; we'll send you a view of the Pyramids." Then he was determined to know whether she was Forcheville's mistress, to ask her point-blank, to insist upon her telling him. He knew that, superstitious as she was, there were some perjuries which she would not commit, and besides, the fear, which had hitherto restrained his curiosity, of making Odette angry if he questioned her, of making her hate him, had ceased to exist now that he had lost all hope of ever being loved by her.

One day he received an anonymous letter telling him that Odette had been the mistress of countless men (several of whom it named, among them Forcheville, M. de Bréauté and the painter) and women, and that she frequented houses of ill-fame. He was tormented by the discovery that there was to be numbered among his friends a creature capable of sending him such a letter (for certain details betrayed in the writer a familiarity with his private life). He wondered who it could be. But he had never had any suspicion with regard to the unknown actions of other people, those which had no visible connexion with what they said. And when he pondered whether it was beneath the ostensible character of M. de Charlus, or of M. des Laumes, or of M. d'Orsan that he must seek the uncharted region in which this ignoble action had had its birth, since none of these men had ever, in conversation with Swann, given any indication of approving of anony-

mous letters, and since everything they had ever said to
him implied that they strongly disapproved, he saw no
reason for associating this infamy with the character of
any one of them rather than the others. M. de Charlus
was somewhat inclined to eccentricity, but he was fundamentally good and kind; M. des Laumes was a trifle hard,
but sound and straightforward. As for M. d'Orsan,
Swann had never met anyone who, even in the most depressing circumstances, would approach him with more
heartfelt words, in a more tactful and judicious manner.
So much so that he was unable to understand the rather
indelicate role commonly attributed to M. d'Orsan in his
relations with a certain wealthy woman, and whenever he
thought of him he was obliged to set that evil reputation
on one side, as being irreconcilable with so many unmistakable proofs of his fastidiousness. For a moment Swann
felt that his mind was becoming clouded, and he thought
of something else so as to recover a little light, until he
had the strength to return to these reflections. But then,
having been unable to suspect anyone, he was forced to
suspect everyone. After all, though M. de Charlus was
fond of him, was extremely good-hearted, he was also a
neurotic; tomorrow, perhaps, he would burst into tears on
hearing that Swann was ill, and today, from jealousy, or
anger, or carried away by a sudden whim, he might have
wished to do him harm. Really, that kind of man was the
worst of all. The Prince des Laumes was certainly far less
devoted to Swann than was M. de Charlus. But for that
very reason he did not suffer from the same susceptibili-
ties with regard to him; and besides, his was a nature
which, though no doubt cold, was as incapable of base as
of magnanimous actions. Swann regretted not having

formed attachments only to such people. Then he reflected that what prevents men from doing harm to their
neighbours is fellow-feeling, that he could only, in the last
resort, answer for men whose natures were analogous to
his own, as was, so far as the heart went, that of M. de
Charlus. The mere thought of causing Swann so much
distress would have revolted him. But with an insensitive
man, of another order of humanity, as was the Prince des
Laumes, how was one to foresee the actions to which he
might be led by the promptings of a different nature? To
have a kind heart was everything, and M. de Charlus had
one. M. d'Orsan was not lacking in heart either, and his
relations with Swann—cordial if not intimate, arising
from the pleasure which, holding the same views about
everything, they found in talking together—were more
restful than the overwrought affection of M. de Charlus,
capable of being led into acts of passion, good or evil. If
there was anyone by whom Swann had always felt himself
understood and discriminatingly liked, it was M. d'Orsan.
Yes, but what of the disreputable life he led? Swann regretted that he had never taken any notice of those rumours, had often admitted jestingly that he had never felt
so keen a sense of sympathy and respect as in the company of a scoundrel. "It's not for nothing," he now assured himself, "that whenever people pass judgment on
their fellows, it's always on their actions. It's only what
we do that counts, and not at all what we say or what we
think. Charlus and des Laumes may have this or that
fault, but they are men of honour. Orsan may not have
these faults, but he's not a man of honour. He may have
acted dishonourably once again." Then Swann suspected
Rémi, who, it was true, could only have inspired the let-

ter, but he now felt himself for a moment to be on the right track. To begin with, Loredan had reasons for bearing a grudge against Odette. And then, how could one not suppose that servants, living in a situation inferior to our own, adding to our wealth and our weaknesses imaginary riches and vices for which they envy and despise us, must inevitably be led to act in a manner abhorrent to people of our own class? He also suspected my grandfather. Every time Swann had asked a favour of him, had he not invariably refused? Besides, with his ideas of middle-class respectability, he might have thought that he was acting for Swann's good. He went on to suspect Bergotte, the painter, the Verdurins, pausing for a moment to admire once again the wisdom of society people in refusing to mix with those artistic circles in which such things were possible, perhaps even openly avowed as good jokes; but then he recalled the traits of honesty that were to be observed in those Bohemians and contrasted them with the life of expedients, often bordering on fraudulence, to which the want of money, the craving for luxury, the corrupting influence of their pleasures often drove members of the aristocracy.

In a word, this anonymous letter proved that he knew a human being capable of the most infamous conduct, but he could see no more reason why that infamy should lurk in the unfathomed depths of the character of the man with the warm heart rather than the cold, the artist rather than the bourgeois, the noble rather than the flunkey. What criterion ought one to adopt to judge one's fellows? After all, there was not a single person he knew who might not, in certain circumstances, prove capable of a shameful action. Must he then cease to see them all? His

mind grew clouded; he drew his hands two or three times
across his brow, wiped his glasses with his handkerchief,
and remembering that, after all, men as good as himself
frequented the society of M. de Charlus, the Prince des
Laumes and the rest, he persuaded himself that this
meant, if not that they were incapable of infamy, at least
it was a necessity in human life, to which everyone must
submit, to frequent the society of people who were perhaps not incapable of such actions. And he continued to
shake hands with all the friends whom he had suspected,
with the purely formal reservation that each one of them
had possibly sought to drive him to despair.

As for the actual contents of the letter, they did not
disturb him since not one of the charges formulated
against Odette had the slightest verisimilitude. Like many
other men, Swann had a naturally lazy mind and lacked
imagination. He knew perfectly well as a general truth
that human life is full of contrasts, but in the case of each
individual human being he imagined all that part of his or
her life with which he was not familiar as being identical
with the part with which he was. He imagined what was
kept secret from him in the light of what was revealed. At
such times as he spent with Odette, if their conversation
turned upon an indelicate act committed or an indelicate
sentiment expressed by some third person, she would
condemn them by virtue of the same moral principles
which Swann had always heard expressed by his own parents and to which he himself had remained faithful; and
then she would arrange her flowers, would sip her tea,
would inquire about Swann's work. So Swann extended
those attitudes to fill the rest of her life, and reconstructed
those actions when he wished to form a picture of the

moments in which he and she were apart. If anyone had
portrayed her to him as she was, or rather as she had
been for so long, with himself, but had substituted some
other man, he would have been distressed, for such a portrait would have struck him as lifelike. But to suppose
that she went to procuresses, that she indulged in orgies
with other women, that she led the crapulous existence of
the most abject, the most contemptible of mortals—what
an insane aberration, for the realisation of which, thank
heaven, the remembered chrysanthemums, the daily cups
of tea, the virtuous indignation left neither time nor place!
However, from time to time he gave Odette to understand that people maliciously kept him informed of everything that she did; and making opportune use of some
detail—insignificant but true—which he had accidentally
learned, as though it were the sole fragment which he had
involuntarily let slip of a complete reconstruction of her
daily life which he carried secretly in his mind, he led her
to suppose that he was perfectly informed upon matters
which in reality he neither knew nor even suspected, for if
he often adjured Odette never to swerve from the truth,
that was only, whether he realised it or not, in order that
Odette should tell him everything that she did. No doubt,
as he used to assure Odette, he loved sincerity, but only
as he might love a pimp who could keep him in touch
with the daily life of his mistress. Thus his love of sincerity, not being disinterested, had not improved his character. The truth which he cherished was the truth which
Odette would tell him; but he himself, in order to extract
that truth from her, was not afraid to have recourse to
falsehood, that very falsehood which he never ceased to
depict to Odette as leading every human creature down

to utter degradation. In a word, he lied as much as did Odette because, more unhappy than she, he was no less egotistical. And she, when she heard him repeating thus to her the things that she had done, would stare at him with a look of distrust and, at all hazards, of indignation, so as not to appear to be humiliated and to be blushing for her actions.

One day, during the longest period of calm through which he had yet been able to exist without being over-taken by an access of jealousy, he had accepted an invita-tion to spend the evening at the theatre with the Princesse des Laumes. Having opened his newspaper to find out what was being played, the sight of the title—*Les Filles de Marbre*, by Théodore Barrière—struck him so cruel a blow that he recoiled instinctively and turned his head away. Lit up as though by a row of footlights, in the new surroundings in which it now appeared, the word "mar-ble," which he had lost the power to distinguish, so ac-customed was he to see it passing in print beneath his eyes, had suddenly become visible again, and had at once brought back to his mind the story which Odette had told him long ago of a visit which she had paid to the Salon at the Palais de l'Industrie with Mme Verdurin, who had said to her, "Take care, now! I know how to melt you, all right. You're not made of marble." Odette had assured him that it was only a joke, and he had attached no im-portance to it at the time. But he had had more confi-dence in her then than he had now. And the anonymous letter referred explicitly to relations of that sort. Without daring to lift his eyes towards the newspaper, he opened it, turned the page so as not to see again the words *Filles de Marbre*, and began to read mechanically the news from the provinces. There had been a storm in the Channel, and damage was reported from Dieppe, Cabourg, Beuzeval . . . Suddenly he recoiled again in horror.

The name Beuzeval had reminded him of another place in the same area, Beuzeville, which carried also, bound to it by a hyphen, a second name, to wit Bréauté, which he had often seen on maps, but without ever previously remarking that it was the same as that of his friend M. de Bréauté, whom the anonymous letter accused of having been Odette's lover. After all, in the case of M. de Bréauté, there was nothing improbable in the charge; but so far as Mme Verdurin was concerned, it was a sheer impossibility. From the fact that Odette occasionally told a lie there was no reason to conclude that she never told the truth, and in those remarks she had exchanged with Mme Verdurin and which she herself had repeated to Swann, he had recognised the meaningless and dangerous jokes which, from inexperience of life and ignorance of vice, are often made by women whose very innocence is revealed thereby and who—as for instance Odette—are least likely to cherish impassioned feelings for another of their sex. Whereas the indignation with which she had rejected the suspicions which for a moment she had unintentionally aroused in his mind by her story fitted in with everything that he knew of the tastes and the temperament of his mistress. But now, by one of those inspirations of jealousy analogous to the inspiration which reveals to a poet or a philosopher, who has nothing, so far, to go on but an odd pair of rhymes or a detached observation, the idea or the natural law which will give him the power he needs, Swann recalled for the first time an observation which Odette had made to him at least two

years before: "Oh, Mme Verdurin, she won't hear of anyone just now but me. I'm a 'love,' if you please, and she
kisses me, and wants me to go with her everywhere, and
call her *tu*." So far from seeing at the time in this observation any connexion with the absurd remarks intended to
simulate vice which Odette had reported to him, he had
welcomed them as a proof of Mme Verdurin's warm-
hearted and generous friendship. But now this memory of
her affection for Odette had coalesced suddenly with the
memory of her unseemly conversation. He could no
longer separate them in his mind, and he saw them
assimilated in reality, the affection imparting a certain se-
riousness and importance to the pleasantries which, in return, robbed the affection of its innocence. He went to see
Odette. He sat down at a distance from her. He did not
dare to embrace her, not knowing whether it would be affection or anger that a kiss would provoke, either in her
or in himself. He sat there silent, watching their love expire. Suddenly he made up his mind.

"Odette, my darling," he began, "I know I'm being
simply odious, but I must ask you a few questions. You
remember the idea I once had about you and Mme Verdurin? Tell me, was it true, with her or with anyone
else?"

She shook her head, pursing her lips, a sign which
people commonly employ to signify that they are not going, because it would bore them to go, when someone has
asked, "Are you coming to watch the procession go by?",
or "Will you be at the review?". But this shake of the
head thus normally applied to an event that has yet to
come, imparts for that reason an element of uncertainty to
the denial of an event that is past. Furthermore, it sug-

gests reasons of personal propriety only, rather than of
disapprobation or moral impossibility. When he saw
Odette thus signal to him that the insinuation was false,
Swann realised that it was quite possibly true.

"I've told you, no. You know quite well," she added,
seeming angry and uncomfortable.

"Yes, I know, but are you quite sure? Don't say to
me, 'You know quite well'; say, 'I have never done anything of that sort with any woman.' "

She repeated his words like a lesson learned by rote,
in a sarcastic tone, and as though she hoped thereby to be
rid of him: "I have never done anything of that sort with
any woman."

"Can you swear to me on the medal of Our Lady of
Laghet?"

Swann knew that Odette would never perjure herself
on that.

"Oh, you do make me so miserable," she cried, with
a jerk of her body as though to shake herself free of the
constraint of his question. "Haven't you had enough?
What's the matter with you today? You seem determined
to make me hate you. I wanted to be friends with you
again, for us to have a nice time together, like the old
days; and this is all the thanks I get!"

However, he would not let her go but sat there like a
surgeon waiting for a spasm to subside that has interrupted his operation but will not make him abandon it.

"You're quite wrong to suppose that I'd bear you the
least ill-will in the world, Odette," he said to her with a
persuasive and deceitful gentleness. "I never speak to you
except of what I already know, and I always know a great
deal more than I say. But you alone can mitigate by your

confession what makes me hate you so long as it has been reported to me only by other people. My anger with you has nothing to do with your actions—I can and do forgive you everything because I love you—but with your untruthfulness, the ridiculous untruthfulness which makes you persist in denying things which I know to be true. How can you expect me to go on loving you when I see you maintain, when I hear you swear to me a thing which I know to be false? Odette, don't prolong this moment which is agony for us both. If you want to, you can end it in a second, you'll be free of it for ever. Tell me, on your medal, yes or no, whether you have ever done these things."

"How on earth do I know?" she exclaimed angrily. "Perhaps I have, ever so long ago, when I didn't know what I was doing, perhaps two or three times."

Swann had prepared himself for every possibility. Reality must therefore be something that bears no relation to possibilities, any more than the stab of a knife in one's body bears to the gradual movement of the clouds overhead, since those words, "two or three times," carved as it were a cross upon the living tissues of his heart. Strange indeed that those words, "two or three times," nothing more than words, words uttered in the air, at a distance, could so lacerate a man's heart, as if they had actually pierced it, could make a man ill, like a poison he has drunk. Instinctively Swann thought of the remark he had heard at Mme de Saint-Euverte's: "I've never seen anything to beat it since the table-turning." The agony that he now suffered in no way resembled what he had supposed. Not only because, even in his moments of most complete distrust, he had rarely imagined such an extrem-

ity of evil, but because, even when he did try to imagine
this thing, it remained vague, uncertain, was not clothed
in the particular horror which had sprung from the words
"perhaps two or three times," was not armed with that
specific cruelty, as different from anything that he had
known as a disease by which one is struck down for the
first time. And yet this Odette from whom all this evil
sprang was no less dear to him, was, on the contrary,
more precious, as if, in proportion as his sufferings increased, the price of the sedative, of the antidote which
this woman alone possessed, increased at the same time.
He wanted to devote more care to her, as one tends a disease which one has suddenly discovered to be more serious. He wanted the horrible things which, she had told
him, she had done "two or three times," not to happen
again. To ensure that, he must watch over Odette. People
often say that, by pointing out to a man the faults of his
mistress, you succeed only in strengthening his attachment to her, because he does not believe you; yet how
much more if he does! But, Swann asked himself, how
could he manage to protect her? He might perhaps be
able to preserve her from the contamination of a particular woman, but there were hundreds of others; and he realised what madness had come over him when, on the
evening when he had failed to find Odette at the Verdurins', he had begun to desire the possession—as if that
were ever possible—of another person. Happily for
Swann, beneath the mass of new sufferings which had entered his soul like an invading horde, there lay a natural
foundation, older, more placid, and silently industrious,
like the cells of an injured organ which at once set to
work to repair the damaged tissues, or the muscles of a

paralysed limb which tend to recover their former movements. These older, more autochthonous inhabitants of
his soul absorbed all Swann's strength, for a while, in that
obscure task of reparation which gives one an illusory
sense of repose during convalescence, or after an operation. This time it was not so much—as it ordinarily
was—in Swann's brain that this slackening of tension due
to exhaustion took effect, it was rather in his heart. But
all the things in life that have once existed tend to recur,
and like a dying animal stirred once more by the throes of
a convulsion which seemed to have ended, upon Swann's
heart, spared for a moment only, the same agony returned
of its own accord to trace the same cross. He remembered
those moonlit evenings, when, leaning back in the victoria
that was taking him to the Rue La Pérouse, he would
wallow voluptuously in the emotions of a man in love,
oblivious of the poisoned fruit that such emotions must
inevitably bear. But all those thoughts lasted for no more
than a second, the time that it took him to press his hand
to his heart, to draw breath again and to contrive to
smile, in order to hide his torment. Already he had begun
to put further questions. For his jealousy, which had
taken more pains than any enemy would have done to
strike him this savage blow, to make him forcibly acquainted with the most cruel suffering he had ever
known, his jealousy was not satisfied that he had yet suffered enough, and sought to expose him to an even
deeper wound. Thus, like an evil deity, his jealousy inspired Swann, driving him on towards his ruin. It was not
his fault, but Odette's alone, if at first his torment was
not exacerbated.

"My darling," he began again, "it's all over now. Was it with anyone I know?"

"No, I swear it wasn't. Besides, I think I exaggerated, I never really went as far as that."

He smiled, and went on: "Just as you like. It doesn't really matter, but it's a pity that you can't give me the name. If I were able to form an idea of the person it would prevent my ever thinking of her again. I say it for your sake, because then I shouldn't bother you any more about it. It's so calming to be able to form a clear picture of things in one's mind. What is really terrible is what one can't imagine. But you've been so sweet to me; I don't want to tire you. I do thank you with all my heart for all the good that you've done me. I've quite finished now. Only one word more: how long ago?"

"Oh, Charles, can't you see you're killing me? It's all so long ago. I've never given it a thought. Anyone would think you were positively trying to put those ideas into my head again. A lot of good that would do you!" she concluded, with unconscious stupidity but intentional malice.

"Oh, I only wanted to know whether it had been since I've known you. It's only natural. Did it happen here? You can't give me any particular evening, so that I can remind myself what I was doing at the time? You must realise that it's not possible that you don't remember with whom, Odette, my love."

"But I don't know; really, I don't. I think it was in the Bois, one evening when you came to meet us on the Island. You'd been dining with the Princesse des Laumes," she added, happy to be able to furnish him with a precise detail which testified to her veracity. "There was a woman at the next table whom I hadn't seen for ages. She said to me, 'Come round behind the rock, there, and look at the moonlight on the water!' At first I just yawned, and said, 'No, I'm too tired, and I'm quite happy where I am.' She assured me there'd never been any moonlight to touch it. 'I've heard that tale before,' I said to her. I knew quite well what she was after."

Odette narrated this episode almost with a smile, either because it appeared to her to be quite natural, or because she thought she was thereby minimising its importance, or else so as not to appear humiliated. But, catching sight of Swann's face, she changed her tone:

"You're a fiend! You enjoy torturing me, making me tell you lies, just so that you'll leave me in peace."

This second blow was even more terrible for Swann than the first. Never had he supposed it to have been so recent an event, hidden from his eyes that had been too innocent to discern it, not in a past which he had never known, but in the course of evenings which he so well remembered, which he had lived through with Odette, of which he had supposed himself to have such an intimate, such an exhaustive knowledge, and which now assumed, retrospectively, an aspect of ugliness and deceit. In the midst of them, suddenly, a gaping chasm had opened: that moment on the island in the Bois de Boulogne. Without being intelligent, Odette had the charm of naturalness. She had recounted, she had acted the little scene with such simplicity that Swann, as he gasped for breath, could vividly see it: Odette yawning, the "rock, there," . . . He could hear her answer—alas, how gaily—"I've heard that tale before!" He felt that she would tell him

nothing more that evening, that no further revelation was
to be expected for the present. He was silent for a time,
then said to her:

"My poor darling, you must forgive me; I know I've
distressed you, but it's all over now; I won't think of it
any more."

But she saw that his eyes remained fixed upon the
things that he did not know, and on that past era of their
love, monotonous and soothing in his memory because it
was vague, and now rent, as with a gaping wound, by
that moment on the Island in the Bois, by moonlight, after his dinner with the Princesse des Laumes. But he was
so imbued with the habit of finding life interesting—of
marvelling at the strange discoveries that there are to be
made in it—that even while he was suffering so acutely
that he did not believe he could bear such agony much
longer, he was saying to himself: "Life is really astonishing, and holds some fine surprises; it appears that vice is
far more common than one has been led to believe. Here
is a woman I trusted, who seems so simple, so straightforward, who, in any case, even allowing that her morals are
not strict, seemed quite normal and healthy in her tastes
and inclinations. On the basis of a most improbable accu-
sation, I question her, and the little that she admits reveals far more than I could ever have suspected." But he
could not confine himself to these detached observations.
He sought to form an exact estimate of the significance of
what she had just told him, in order to decide whether
she had done these things often and was likely to do them
again. He repeated her words to himself: "I knew quite
well what she was after." "Two or three times." "I've
heard that tale before." But they did not reappear in his

memory unarmed; each of them still held its knife, with
which it stabbed him anew. For a long time, like a sick
man who cannot restrain himself from attempting every
minute to make the movement that he knows will hurt
him, he kept on murmuring to himself: "I'm quite happy
where I am," "I've heard that tale before," but the pain
was so intense that he was obliged to stop. He was
amazed to find that acts which he had always hitherto
judged so lightly, had dismissed, indeed, with a laugh,
should have become as serious to him as a disease which
may prove fatal. He knew any number of women whom
he could ask to keep an eye on Odette, but how was he to
expect them to adjust themselves to his new point of
view, and not to look at the matter from the one which
for so long had been his own, which had always guided
him in sexual matters; not to say to him with a laugh:
"You jealous monster, wanting to rob other people of
their pleasure!" By what trap-door suddenly lowered had
he (who had never had hitherto from his love for Odette
any but the most refined pleasures) been precipitated into
this new circle of hell from which he could not see how
he was ever to escape. Poor Odette! He did not hold it
against her. She was only half to blame. Had he not been
told that it was her own mother who had sold her, when
she was still hardly more than a child, at Nice, to a
wealthy Englishman? But what an agonising truth was
now contained for him in those lines of Alfred de Vigny's
Journal d'un Poète which he had previously read without
emotion: "When one feels oneself smitten by love for a
woman, one should say to oneself, 'Who are the people
around her? What kind of life has she led?' All one's future happiness lies in the answer." Swann was astonished

that such simple sentences, spelt over in his mind, as "I've heard that tale before" or "I knew quite well what she was after," could cause him so much pain. But he realised that what he thought of as simple sentences were in fact the components of the framework which still enclosed, and could inflict on him again, the anguish he had felt while Odette was telling her story. For it was indeed the same anguish that he now was feeling anew. For all that he now knew—for all that, as time went on, he might even have partly forgotten and forgiven—whenever he repeated her words his old anguish refashioned him as he had been before Odette had spoken: ignorant, trustful; his merciless jealousy placed him once again, so that he might be pierced by Odette's admission, in the position of a man who does not yet know; and after several months this old story would still shatter him like a sudden revelation. He marvelled at the terrible re-creative power of his memory. It was only by the weakening of that generative force, whose fecundity diminishes with age, that he could hope for a relaxation of his torments. But, as soon as the power of any one of Odette's remarks to make Swann suffer seemed to be nearly exhausted, lo and behold another, one of those to which he had hitherto paid little attention, almost a new observation, came to reinforce the others and to strike at him with undiminished force. The memory of the evening on which he had dined with the Princesse des Laumes was painful to him, but it was no more than the centre, the core of his pain, which radiated vaguely round about it, overflowing into all the preceding and following days. And on whatever point in it his memory sought to linger, it was the whole of that season, during which the Verdurins had so often gone to dine on

the Island in the Bois, that racked him. So violently that
by slow degrees the curiosity which his jealousy aroused
in him was neutralised by his fear of the fresh tortures he
would be inflicting upon himself were he to satisfy it. He
recognised that the entire period of Odette's life which
had elapsed before she first met him, a period of which
he had never sought to form a picture in his mind, was
not the featureless abstraction which he could vaguely see,
but had consisted of so many definite, dated years, each
crowded with concrete incidents. But were he to learn
more of them, he feared lest that past of hers, colourless,
fluid and supportable, might assume a tangible and monstrous form, an individual and diabolical countenance.
And he continued to refrain from seeking to visualise it,
no longer from laziness of mind, but from fear of suffering. He hoped that, some day, he might be able to hear
the Island in the Bois or the Princesse des Laumes mentioned without feeling any twinge of the old heartache;
and meanwhile he thought it imprudent to provoke
Odette into furnishing him with new facts, the names of
more places and different circumstances which, when his
malady was still scarcely healed, would revive it again in
another form.

But, often enough, the things that he did know, that
he dreaded, now, to learn, were revealed to him by
Odette herself, spontaneously and unwittingly; for the gap
which her vices made between her actual life and the
comparatively innocent life which Swann had believed,
and often still believed his mistress to lead, was far wider
than she knew. A vicious person, always affecting the
same air of virtue before people whom he is anxious to
keep from having any suspicion of his vices, has no gauge

at hand from which to ascertain how far those vices, whose continuous growth is imperceptible to himself, have gradually segregated him from the normal ways of life. In the course of their cohabitation, in Odette's mind, side by side with the memory of those of her actions which she concealed from Swann, others were gradually coloured, infected by them, without her being able to detect anything strange in them, without their causing any jarring note in the particular surroundings which they occupied in her inner world; but if she related them to Swann, he was shattered by the revelation of the way of life to which they pointed. One day he was trying—without hurting Odette—to discover from her whether she had ever had any dealings with procuresses. He was, as a matter of fact, convinced that she had not; the anonymous letter had put the idea into his mind, but in a mechanical way; it had met with no credence there, but for all that had remained, and Swann, wishing to be rid of the purely material but none the less burdensome presence of the suspicion, hoped that Odette would now extirpate it for ever.

"Oh, no! . . . Not that they don't pester me," she added with a smile of self-satisfied vanity, quite unaware that it could not appear justifiable to Swann. "There was one of them waited more than two hours for me yesterday—offered me any money I asked. It seems there's an ambassador who said to her, 'I'll kill myself if you don't bring her to me.' They told her I'd gone out, but she waited and waited, and in the end I had to go and speak to her myself before she'd go away. I wish you could have seen the way I went for her; my maid could hear me from the next room and told me I was shouting

at the top of my voice: 'But haven't I told you I don't
want to! It's just the way I feel. I should hope I'm still
free to do as I please! If I needed the money, I could understand . . .' The porter has orders not to let her in
again; he's to tell her I'm out of town. Oh, I wish I could
have had you hidden somewhere in the room while I was
talking to her. I know you'd have been pleased, my darling. There's some good in your little Odette, you see, after all, though people do say such dreadful things about
her."

Besides, her very admissions—when she made any—
of faults which she supposed him to have discovered,
served Swann as a starting-point for new doubts rather
than putting an end to the old. For her admissions never
exactly coincided with his doubts. In vain might Odette
expurgate her confession of all its essentials, there would
remain in the accessories something which Swann had
never yet imagined, which crushed him anew, and would
enable him to alter the terms of the problem of his jealousy. And these admissions he could never forget. His
soul carried them along, cast them aside, then cradled
them again in its bosom, like corpses in a river. And they
poisoned it.

She spoke to him once of a visit that Forcheville had
paid her on the day of the Paris-Murcie Fête. "What! you
knew him as long ago as that? Oh, yes, of course you
did," he corrected himself, so as not to show that he had
been ignorant of the fact. And suddenly he began to
tremble at the thought that, on the day of the Paris-Murcie Fête, when he had received from her the letter which
he had so carefully preserved, she had perhaps been having lunch with Forcheville at the Maison Dorée. She

swore that she had not. "Still, the Maison Dorée reminds me of something or other which I knew at the time wasn't true," he pursued, hoping to frighten her. "Yes, that I hadn't been there at all that evening when I told you I had just come from there, and you'd been looking for me at Prévost's," she replied (judging by his manner that he knew) with a firmness that was based not so much on cynicism as on timidity, a fear of offending Swann which her own self-respect made her anxious to conceal, and a desire to show him that she could be perfectly frank if she chose. And so she struck with all the precision and force of a headsman wielding his axe, and yet could not be charged with cruelty since she was quite unconscious of hurting him; she even laughed, though perhaps, it is true, chiefly in order not to appear chastened or embarrassed. "It's quite true, I hadn't been to the Maison Dorée. I was coming away from Forcheville's. I really had been to Prévost's—I didn't make that up—and he met me there and asked me to come in and look at his prints. But someone else came to see him. I told you I'd come from the Maison Dorée because I was afraid you might be angry with me. It was rather nice of me, really, don't you see? Even if I did wrong, at least I'm telling you all about it now, aren't I? What would I have to gain by not telling you that I lunched with him on the day of the Paris-Murcie Fête, if it was true? Especially as at the time we didn't know one another quite so well as we do now, did we, darling?"

He smiled back at her with the sudden, craven weakness of the shattered creature which these crushing words had made of him. So, even in the months of which he had never dared to think again because they had been too happy, in those months when she had loved him, she was already lying to him! Besides that moment (that first evening on which they had "done a cattleya") when she had told him that she was coming from the Maison Dorée, how many others must there have been, each of them also concealing a falsehood of which Swann had had no suspicion. He recalled how she had said to him once: "I need only tell Mme Verdurin that my dress wasn't ready, or that my cab came late. There's always some excuse." From himself too, probably, many a time when she had glibly uttered such words as explain a delay or justify an alteration of the hour fixed for a meeting, they must have hidden, without his having the least inkling of it at the time, an appointment she had with some other man, some man to whom she had said: "I need only tell Swann that my dress wasn't ready, or that my cab came late. There's always some excuse." And beneath all his most tender memories, beneath the simplest words that Odette had spoken to him in those early days, words which he had believed as though they were gospel, beneath the daily actions which she had recounted to him, beneath the most ordinary places, her dressmaker's flat, the Avenue du Bois, the race-course, he could feel (dissembled by virtue of that temporal superfluity which, even in days that have been most circumstantially accounted for, still leaves a margin of room that may serve as a hiding place for certain unconfessed actions), he could feel the insinuation of a possible undercurrent of falsehood which rendered ignoble all that had remained most precious to him (his happiest evenings, the Rue La Pérouse itself, which Odette must constantly have been leaving at other hours than those of which she told him) everywhere disseminat-

ing something of the shadowy horror that had gripped
him when he had heard her admission with regard to
the Maison Dorée, and, like the obscene creatures in the
"Desolation of Nineveh," shattering stone by stone the
whole edifice of his past . . . If, now, he turned away
whenever his memory repeated the cruel name of the
Maison Dorée, it was because that name recalled to him
no longer, as, but recently, at Mme de Saint-Euverte's
party, a happiness which he had long since lost, but a
misfortune of which he had just become aware. Then it
happened with the Maison Dorée as it had happened with
the Island in the Bois, that gradually its name ceased to
trouble him. For what we suppose to be our love or our
jealousy is never a single, continuous and indivisible passion. It is composed of an infinity of successive loves, of
different jealousies, each of which is ephemeral, although
by their uninterrupted multiplicity they give us the impression of continuity, the illusion of unity. The life of
Swann's love, the fidelity of his jealousy, were formed of
the death, the infidelity, of innumerable desires, innumerable doubts, all of which had Odette for their object. If he
had remained for any length of time without seeing her,
those that died would not have been replaced by others.
But the presence of Odette continued to sow in Swann's
heart alternate seeds of love and suspicion.

On certain evenings she would suddenly resume towards him an amenity of which she would warn him
sternly that he must take immediate advantage, under
penalty of not seeing it repeated for years to come; he
must instantly accompany her home, to "do a cattleya,"
and the desire which she claimed to have for him was so
sudden, so inexplicable, so imperious, the caresses which

she lavished on him were so demonstrative and so un-
wonted, that this brutal and improbable fondness made
Swann just as unhappy as any lie or unkindness. One
evening when he had thus, in obedience to her command,
gone home with her, and she was interspersing her kisses
with passionate words, in strange contrast to her habitual
coldness, he suddenly thought he heard a sound; he rose,
searched everywhere and found nobody, but hadn't the
heart to return to his place by her side; whereupon, in the
height of fury, she broke a vase and said to him: "One
can never do anything right with you!" And he was left
uncertain whether she had not actually had some man
concealed in the room, whose jealousy she had wished to
exacerbate or his senses to inflame.

Sometimes he repaired to brothels in the hope of
learning something about Odette, although he dared not
mention her name. "I have a little thing you're sure to
like," the bawd would greet him, and he would stay for
an hour or so chatting gloomily to some poor girl who sat
there astonished that he went no further. One of them,
who was quite young and very pretty, said to him once:
"Of course, what I'd like would be to find a real friend—
then he might be quite certain I'd never go with any
other men again."

"Really, do you think it possible for a woman to be
touched by a man's loving her, and never to be unfaithful
to him?" asked Swann anxiously.

"Why, of course! It all depends on people's characters!"

Swann could not help saying to these girls the sort of
things that would have delighted the Princesse des
Laumes. To the one who was in search of a friend he said

with a smile: "But how nice, you've put on blue eyes to go with your sash."

"And you too, you've got blue cuffs on."

"What a charming conversation we're having for a place of this sort! I'm not boring you, am I; or keeping you?"

"No, I'm not in a hurry. If you'd have bored me I'd have said so. But I like hearing you talk."

"I'm very flattered . . . Aren't we having a nice chat?" he asked the bawd who had just looked in.

"Why, yes, that's just what I was saying to myself, how good they're being! But there it is! People come to my house now just to talk. The Prince was telling me only the other day that it's far nicer here than at home with his wife. It seems that, nowadays, all the society ladies are so flighty; a real scandal, I call it. But I'll leave you in peace now," she ended discreetly, and left Swann with the girl who had the blue eyes. But presently he rose and said good-bye to her. She had ceased to interest him. She did not know Odette.

The painter having been ill, Dr Cottard recommended a sea-voyage. Several of the "faithful" spoke of accompanying him. The Verdurins could not face the prospect of being left alone in Paris, so first of all hired and finally purchased a yacht; thus Odette went on frequent cruises. Whenever she had been away for any length of time, Swann would feel that he was beginning to detach himself from her, but as though this moral distance were proportionate to the physical distance between them, whenever he heard that Odette had returned to Paris, he could not rest without seeing her. Once, when they had gone away ostensibly for a month only, either

they succumbed to a series of temptations, or else
M. Verdurin had cunningly arranged everything beforehand to please his wife, and disclosed his plans to the
"faithful" only as time went on; at all events, from Al-
giers they flitted to Tunis; then to Italy, Greece, Constantinople, Asia Minor. They had been absent for nearly
a year, and Swann felt perfectly at ease and almost happy.
Although Mme Verdurin had endeavoured to persuade
the pianist and Dr Cottard that their respective aunt and
patients had no need of them, and that in any event it
was most rash to allow Mme Cottard to return to Paris
which, so M. Verdurin affirmed, was in the throes of revolution, she was obliged to grant them their liberty at
Constantinople. And the painter came home with them.
One day, shortly after the return of these four travellers,
Swann, seeing an omnibus for the Luxembourg approaching and having some business there, had jumped on it
and found himself sitting opposite Mme Cottard, who
was paying a round of visits to people whose "day" it
was, in full fig, with a plume in her hat, a silk dress, a
muff, an umbrella-sunshade, a card-case, and a pair of
white gloves fresh from the cleaners. Clothed in these re-
galia, she would, in fine weather, go on foot from one
house to another in the same neighbourhood, but when
she had to proceed to another district, would make use of
a transfer-ticket on the omnibus. For the first minute or
two, until the natural amiability of the woman broke
through the starched surface of the doctor's-wife, not being certain, moreover, whether she ought to talk to Swann
about the Verdurins, she proceeded to hold forth, in her
slow, awkward and soft-spoken voice, which every now
and then was completely drowned by the rattling of the

omnibus, on topics selected from those which she had picked up and would repeat in each of the score of houses up the stairs of which she clambered in the course of an afternoon.

"I needn't ask you, M. Swann, whether a man so much in the swim as yourself has been to the Mirlitons to see the portrait by Machard which the whole of Paris is rushing to see. Well and what do you think of it? Whose camp are you in, those who approve or those who don't? It's the same in every house in Paris now, no one talks about anything else but Machard's portrait. You aren't smart, you aren't really cultured, you aren't up-to-date unless you give an opinion on Machard's portrait."

Swann having replied that he had not seen this portrait, Mme Cottard was afraid that she might have hurt his feelings by obliging him to confess the omission.

"Oh, that's quite all right! At least you admit it frankly. You don't consider yourself disgraced because you haven't seen Machard's portrait. I find that most commendable. Well now, I have seen it. Opinion is divided, you know, there are some people who find it a bit over-finical, like whipped cream, they say; but I think it's just ideal. Of course, she's not a bit like the blue and yellow ladies of our friend Biche. But I must tell you quite frankly (you'll think me dreadfully old-fashioned, but I always say just what I think), that I don't understand his work. I can quite see the good points in his portrait of my husband, oh, dear me, yes, and it's certainly less odd than most of what he does, but even then he had to give the poor man a blue moustache! But Machard! Just listen to this now, the husband of the friend I'm on my way to see at this very moment (which has given me the very great pleasure of your company), has promised her that if he is elected to the Academy (he's one of the Doctor's colleagues) he'll get Machard to paint her portrait. *There's* something to look forward to! I have another friend who insists that she'd rather have Leloir. I'm only a wretched Philistine, and for all I know Leloir may be technically superior to Machard. But I do think that the most important thing about a portrait, especially when it's going to cost ten thousand francs, is that it should be like, and an agreeable likeness."

Having delivered these words, to which she had been inspired by the loftiness of her plume, the monogram on her card-case, the little number inked inside each of her gloves by the cleaner, and the embarrassment of speaking to Swann about the Verdurins, Mme Cottard, seeing that they had still a long way to go before they would reach the corner of the Rue Bonaparte where the conductor was to set her down, listened to the promptings of her heart, which counselled other words than these.

"Your ears must have been burning," she ventured, "while we were on the yacht with Mme Verdurin. We talked about you all the time."

Swann was genuinely astonished, for he supposed that his name was never uttered in the Verdurins' presence.

"You see," Mme Cottard went on, "Mme de Crécy was there; need I say more? Wherever Odette is, it's never long before she begins talking about you. And you can imagine that it's never unfavourably. What, you don't believe me!" she went on, noticing that Swann looked sceptical.

And, carried away by the sincerity of her conviction, without putting any sly meaning into the word, which she

used purely in the sense in which one employs it to speak
of the affection that unites a pair of friends: "Why, she
adores you! No, indeed, I'm sure it would never do to say
anything against you when she was about; one would
soon be put in one's place! Whatever we might be doing,
if we were looking at a picture, for instance, she would
say, 'If only we had him here, he's the man who could
tell us whether it's genuine or not. There's no one like
him for that.' And all day long she would be saying,
'What can he be doing just now? I do hope he's doing a
little work! It's too dreadful that a fellow with such gifts
as he has should be so lazy.' (Forgive me, won't you.) 'I
can see him this very moment; he's thinking of us, he's
wondering where we are.' Indeed, she made a remark
which I found absolutely charming. M. Verdurin asked
her, 'How in the world can you see what he's doing,
when he's a thousand miles away?' And Odette answered,
'Nothing is impossible to the eye of a friend.' No, I assure you, I'm not saying it just to flatter you; you have a
true friend in her, such as one doesn't often find. I can
tell you, besides, that if you don't know it you're the only
one who doesn't. Mme Verdurin told me as much herself
on our last day with them (one talks freely, don't you
know, before a parting), 'I don't say that Odette isn't
fond of us, but anything that we may say to her counts
for very little beside what Swann might say.' Oh, mercy,
there's the conductor stopping for me. Here I've been
chatting away to you, and would have gone right past the
Rue Bonaparte and never noticed . . . Will you be so
very kind as to tell me if my plume is straight?"

And Mme Cottard withdrew from her muff, to offer it to Swann, a white-gloved hand from which there

floated, together with a transfer-ticket, a vision of high
life that pervaded the omnibus, blended with the fragrance of newly cleaned kid. And Swann felt himself
overflowing with affection towards her, as well as towards
Mme Verdurin (and almost towards Odette, for the feeling that he now entertained for her, being no longer
tinged with pain, could scarcely be described, now, as
love) as from the platform of the omnibus he followed her
with fond eyes as she gallantly threaded her way along
the Rue Bonaparte, her plume erect, her skirt held up in
one hand, while in the other she clasped her umbrella and
her card-case with its monogram exposed to view, her
muff dancing up and down in front of her as she went.

To counterbalance the morbid feelings that Swann
cherished for Odette, Mme Cottard, a wiser physician, in
this case, than ever her husband would have been, had
grafted on to them others more normal, feelings of gratitude, of friendship, which in Swann's mind would make
Odette seem more human (more like other women, since
other women could inspire the same feelings in him),
would hasten her final transformation back into the
Odette, loved with an undisturbed affection, who had
taken him home one evening after a revel at the painter's
to drink a glass of orangeade with Forcheville, the Odette
with whom Swann had glimpsed the possibility of living
in happiness.

In the past, having often thought with terror that a
day must come when he would cease to be in love with
Odette, he had determined to keep a sharp look-out, and
as soon as he felt that love was beginning to leave him, to
cling to it and hold it back. But now, to the diminution of
his love there corresponded a simultaneous diminution in

his desire to remain in love. For a man cannot change, that is to say become another person, while continuing to obey the dictates of the self which he has ceased to be. Occasionally the name glimpsed in a newspaper, of one of the men whom he supposed to have been Odette's lovers, reawakened his jealousy. But it was very mild, and, inasmuch as it proved to him that he had not completely emerged from that period in which he had so greatly suffered—but in which he had also known so voluptuous a way of feeling—and that the hazards of the road ahead might still enable him to catch an occasional furtive, distant glimpse of its beauties, this jealousy gave him, if anything, an agreeable thrill, as, to the sad Parisian who is leaving Venice behind him to return to France, a last mosquito proves that Italy and summer are still not too remote. But, as a rule, with this particular period of his life from which he was emerging, when he made an effort, if not to remain in it, at least to obtain a clear view of it while he still could, he discovered that already it was too late; he would have liked to glimpse, as though it were a landscape that was about to disappear, that love from which he had departed; but it is so difficult to enter into a state of duality and to present to oneself the lifelike spectacle of a feeling one has ceased to possess, that very soon, the clouds gathering in his brain, he could see nothing at all, abandoned the attempt, took the glasses from his nose and wiped them; and he told himself that he would do better to rest for a little, that there would be time enough later on, and settled back into his corner with the incuriosity, the torpor of the drowsy traveller who pulls his hat down over his eyes to get some sleep in the railway-carriage that is drawing him, he feels, faster

and faster out of the country in which he has lived for so
long and which he had vowed not to allow to slip away
from him without looking out to bid it a last farewell. Indeed, like the same traveller if he does not awake until he
has crossed the frontier and is back in France, when
Swann chanced to alight, close at hand, on proof that
Forcheville had been Odette's lover, he realised that it
caused him no pain, that love was now far behind, and he
regretted that he had had no warning of the moment
when he had emerged from it for ever. And just as, before kissing Odette for the first time, he had sought to
imprint upon his memory the face that for so long had
been familiar before it was altered by the additional memory of their kiss, so he could have wished—in thought at
least—to have been able to bid farewell, while she still
existed, to the Odette who had aroused his love and jealousy, to the Odette who had caused him to suffer, and
whom now he would never see again.

He was mistaken. He was destined to see her once
again, a few weeks later. It was while he was asleep, in
the twilight of a dream. He was walking with Mme Verdurin, Dr Cottard, a young man in a fez whom he failed
to identify, the painter, Odette, Napoleon III and my
grandfather, along a path which followed the line of the
coast, and overhung the sea, now at a great height, now
by a few feet only, so that they were continually going up
and down. Those of the party who had reached the
downward slope were no longer visible to those who were
still climbing; what little daylight yet remained was failing, and it seemed as though they were about to be
shrouded in darkness. From time to time the waves
dashed against the edge, and Swann could feel on his

cheek a shower of freezing spray. Odette told him to wipe
it off, but he could not, and felt confused and helpless in
her company, as well as because he was in his nightshirt.
He hoped that, in the darkness, this might pass unnoticed; Mme Verdurin, however, fixed her astonished gaze
upon him for an endless moment, during which he saw
her face change shape, her nose grow longer, while beneath it there sprouted a heavy moustache. He turned
round to look at Odette; her cheeks were pale, with little
red spots, her features drawn and ringed with shadows;
but she looked back at him with eyes welling with affection, ready to detach themselves like tears and to fall
upon his face, and he felt that he loved her so much that
he would have liked to carry her off with him at once.
Suddenly Odette turned her wrist, glanced at a tiny
watch, and said: "I must go." She took leave of everyone
in the same formal manner, without taking Swann aside,
without telling him where they were to meet that evening,
or next day. He dared not ask; he would have liked to follow her, but he was obliged, without turning back in her
direction, to answer with a smile some question from
Mme Verdurin; but his heart was frantically beating, he
felt that he now hated Odette, he would gladly have
gouged out those eyes which a moment ago he had loved
so much, have crushed those flaccid cheeks. He continued
to climb with Mme Verdurin, that is to say to draw further away with each step from Odette, who was going
downhill in the other direction. A second passed and it
was many hours since she had left them. The painter remarked to Swann that Napoleon III had slipped away immediately after Odette. "They had obviously arranged it
between them," he added. "They must have met at the

foot of the cliff, but they didn't want to say good-bye together because of appearances. She is his mistress." The strange young man burst into tears. Swann tried to console him. "After all, she's quite right," he said to the young man, drying his eyes for him and taking off the fez to make him feel more at ease. "I've advised her to do it dozens of times. Why be so distressed? He was obviously the man to understand her." So Swann reasoned with himself, for the young man whom he had failed at first to identify was himself too; like certain novelists, he had distributed his own personality between two characters, the one who was dreaming the dream, and another whom he saw in front of him sporting a fez.

As for Napoleon III, it was to Forcheville that some vague association of ideas, then a certain modification of the baron's usual physiognomy, and lastly the broad ribbon of the Legion of Honour across his breast, had made Swann give that name; in reality, and in everything that the person who appeared in his dream represented and recalled to him, it was indeed Forcheville. For, from an incomplete and changing set of images, Swann in his sleep drew false deductions, enjoying at the same time, momentarily, such a creative power that he was able to reproduce himself by a simple act of division, like certain lower organisms; with the warmth that he felt in his own palm he modelled the hollow of a strange hand which he thought he was clasping, and out of feelings and impressions of which he was not yet conscious he brought about sudden vicissitudes which, by a chain of logical sequences, would produce, at specific points in his dream, the person required to receive his love or to startle him awake. In an instant night grew black about him; a tocsin sounded, people ran past him, escaping from their blazing houses; he could hear the thunder of the surging waves, and also of his own heart, which with equal violence was anxiously beating in his breast. Suddenly the speed of these palpitations redoubled, he felt an inexplicable pain and nausea. A peasant, dreadfully burned, flung at him as he passed: "Come and ask Charlus where Odette spent the night with her friend. He used to go about with her in the past, and she tells him everything. It was they who started the fire." It was his valet, come to awaken him, and saying:

"Sir, it's eight o'clock, and the barber is here. I've told him to call again in an hour."

But these words, as they plunged through the waves of sleep in which Swann was submerged, did not reach his consciousness without undergoing that refraction which turns a ray of light in the depths of water into another sun; just as, a moment earlier, the sound of the door-bell, swelling in the depths of his abyss of sleep into the clangour of a tocsin, had engendered the episode of the fire. Meanwhile, the scenery of his dream-stage scattered into dust, he opened his eyes, and heard for the last time the boom of a wave in the sea, now distant. He touched his cheek. It was dry. And yet he remembered the sting of the cold spray, and the taste of salt on his lips. He rose and dressed himself. He had made the barber come early because he had written the day before to my grandfather to say that he was going to Combray that afternoon, having learned that Mme de Cambremer— Mlle Legrandin that had been—was spending a few days there. The association in his memory of her young and charming face with a countryside he had not visited for so long offered him a combined attraction which had made

him decide at last to leave Paris for a while. As the different circumstances that bring us into contact with certain
people do not coincide with the period in which we are in
love with them, but, overlapping it, may occur before love
has begun, and may be repeated after it has ended, the
earliest appearances in our lives of a person who is destined to take our fancy later on assume retrospectively in
our eyes a certain value as an indication, a warning, a
presage. It was in this fashion that Swann had often re-
verted in his mind to the image of Odette encountered in
the theatre on that first evening when he had no thought
of ever seeing her again—and that he now recalled the
party at Mme de Saint-Euverte's at which he had introduced General de Froberville to Mme de Cambremer. So
manifold are our interests in life that it is not uncommon,
on the self-same occasion, for the foundations of a happiness which does not yet exist to be laid down simultaneously with the aggravation of a grief from which we are
still suffering. And doubtless this could have occurred to
Swann elsewhere than at Mme de Saint-Euverte's. Who
indeed can say whether, in the event of his having gone
elsewhere that evening, other happinesses, other griefs
might not have come to him, which later would have appeared to him to have been inevitable? But what did seem
to him to have been inevitable was what had indeed taken
place, and he was not far short of seeing something providential in the fact that he had decided to go to Mme de
Saint-Euverte's that evening, because his mind, anxious to
admire the richness of invention that life shows, and incapable of facing a difficult problem for any length of time,
such as deciding what was most to be wished for, came to
the conclusion that the sufferings through which he had

passed that evening, and the pleasures, as yet unsuspected, which were already germinating there—the exact
balance between which was too difficult to establish—
were linked by a sort of concatenation of necessity.

But while, an hour after his awakening, he was giving
instructions to the barber to see that his stiffly brushed
hair should not become disarranged on the journey, he
thought of his dream again, and saw once again, as he
had felt them close beside him, Odette's pallid complexion, her too thin cheeks, her drawn features, her tired
eyes, all the things which—in the course of those successive bursts of affection which had made of his enduring
love for Odette a long oblivion of the first impression that
he had formed of her—he had ceased to notice since the
early days of their intimacy, days to which doubtless,
while he slept, his memory had returned to seek their exact sensation. And with the old, intermittent caddishness
which reappeared in him when he was no longer unhappy
and his moral standards dropped accordingly, he exclaimed to himself: "To think that I've wasted years of
my life, that I've longed to die, that I've experienced my
greatest love, for a woman who didn't appeal to me, who
wasn't even my type!"

Part Three

PLACE-NAMES · THE NAME

Among the rooms which used most commonly to take shape in my mind during my nights of sleeplessness, there was none that differed more utterly from the rooms at Combray, thickly powdered with the motes of an atmosphere granular, pollinated, edible and devout, than my room in the Grand Hôtel de la Plage, at Balbec, the ripolin-painted walls of which enclosed, like the polished sides of a bathing-pool in which the water glows blue, a finer air, pure, azure-tinted, saline. The Bavarian upholsterer who had been entrusted with the furnishing of this hotel had varied his scheme of decoration in different rooms, and in that which I found myself occupying had set against the walls, on three sides of it, a series of low book-cases with glass fronts, in which, according to where they stood, by a law of nature which he had not perhaps foreseen, was reflected this or that section of the ever-changing view of the sea, so that the walls were lined with a frieze of sea-scapes, interrupted only by the polished mahogany of the actual shelves. So much so that the whole room had the appearance of one of those model bedrooms which are to be seen in exhibitions of modern housing, decorated with works of art calculated by their designer to gladden the eyes of whoever may ultimately sleep therein, the subjects being in keeping with the locality and surroundings of the houses for which the rooms are planned.

And yet nothing could have differed more utterly, ei-

ther, from the real Balbec than that other Balbec of which
I had often dreamed, on stormy days, when the wind was
so strong that Françoise, as she took me to the Champs-
Elysées, would advise me not to walk too close to the
walls or I might have my head knocked off by a falling
slate, and would recount to me, with many a groan, the
terrible disasters and shipwrecks that were reported in the
newspaper. I longed for nothing more than to behold a
stormy sea, less as a mighty spectacle than as a momentary revelation of the true life of nature; or rather there
were for me no mighty spectacles save those which I
knew to be not artificially composed for my entertainment, but necessary and unalterable—the beauty of landscapes or of great works of art. I was curious and eager to
know only what I believed to be more real than myself,
what had for me the supreme merit of showing me a fragment of the mind of a great genius, or of the force or the
grace of nature as it appeared when left entirely to itself,
without human interference. Just as the beautiful sound of
her voice, reproduced by itself on the gramophone, would
never console one for the loss of one's mother, so a mechanical imitation of a storm would have left me as cold as did
the illuminated fountains at the Exhibition. I required
also, if the storm was to be absolutely genuine, that the
shore from which I watched it should be a natural shore,
not an embankment recently constructed by a municipal-
ity. Besides, nature, by virtue of all the feelings that
it aroused in me, seemed to me the thing most diametrically opposed to the mechanical inventions of mankind.
The less it bore their imprint, the more room it offered
for the expansion of my heart. And, as it happened, I
had preserved the name of Balbec, which Legrandin had

cited to us, as that of a seaside place in the very midst of "that funereal coast, famed for the number of its wrecks, swathed, for six months of the year, in a shroud of fog and flying foam from the waves."

"You still feel there beneath your feet," he had told me, "far more than at Finistére itself (and even though hotels are now being superimposed upon it, without power, however, to modify that oldest ossature of the earth) you feel there that you are actually at the land's end of France, of Europe, of the Old World. And it is the ultimate encampment of the fishermen, the heirs of all the fishermen who have lived since the world's beginning, facing the everlasting kingdom of the sea-fogs and shadows of the night."

One day when, at Combray, I had spoken of this seaside resort of Balbec in the presence of M. Swann, hoping to learn from him whether it was the best point to select for seeing the most violent storms, he had replied: "Yes indeed I know Balbec! The church there, built in the twelfth and thirteenth centuries, and still half Romanesque, is perhaps the most curious example to be found of our Norman Gothic, and so singular that one is tempted to describe it as Persian in its inspiration."

And that region which, until then, had seemed to me to be nothing else than a part of immemorial nature, that had remained contemporaneous with the great phenomena of geology—and as remote from human history as the Ocean itself or the Great Bear, with its wild race of fishermen for whom no more than for their whales had there been any Middle Ages—it had been a great joy to me to see it suddenly take its place in the order of the centuries, with a stored consciousness of the Romanesque epoch, and to know that the Gothic trefoil had come to diversify those wild rocks too at the appointed time, like those frail but hardy plants which in the Polar regions, when spring returns, scatter their stars about the eternal snows. And if Gothic art brought to those places and people an identification which otherwise they lacked, they too conferred one upon it in return. I tried to picture how those fishermen had lived, the timid and undreamt-of experiment in social relations which they had attempted there, clustered upon a promontory of the shores of Hell, at the foot of the cliffs of death; and Gothic art seemed to me a more living thing now that, detached from the towns in which until then I had always imagined it, I could see how, in a particular instance, upon a reef of savage rocks, it had taken root and grown until it flowered in a tapering spire. I was taken to see reproductions of the most famous of the statues at Balbec—the shaggy, snub-nosed Apostles, the Virgin from the porch—and I could scarcely breathe for joy at the thought that I might myself, one day, see them stand out in relief against the eternal briny fog. Thereafter, on delightful, stormy February nights, the wind—breathing into my heart, which it shook no less violently than the chimney of my bedroom, the project of a visit to Balbec—blended in me the desire for Gothic architecture as well as for a storm upon the sea.

I should have liked to take, the very next day, the fine, generous 1.22 train, whose hour of departure I could never read without a palpitating heart on the railway company's bills or in advertisements for circular tours: it seemed to me to cut, at a precise point in every afternoon, a delectable groove, a mysterious mark, from which the diverted hours still led, of course, towards evening,

towards tomorrow morning, but an evening and morning
which one would behold, not in Paris, but in one of those
towns through which the train passed and among which it
allowed one to choose; for it stopped at Bayeux, at
Coutances, at Vitré, at Questambert, at Pontorson, at Balbec, at Lannion, at Lamballe, at Benodet, at Pont-Aven,
at Quimperlé, and progressed magnificently overloaded
with proffered names among which I did not know the
one to choose, so impossible was it to sacrifice any. But
even without waiting till next day, I could, by dressing
with all speed, leave Paris that very evening, should my
parents permit, and arrive at Balbec as dawn spread west-
ward over the raging sea, from whose driven foam I
would seek shelter in that church in the Persian style. But
at the approach of the Easter holidays, when my parents
had promised to let me spend them for once in the North
of Italy, suddenly, in place of those dreams of tempests
by which I had been entirely possessed, not wishing to
see anything but waves dashing in from all sides, mounting ever higher, upon the wildest of coasts, beside
churches as rugged and precipitous as cliffs, in whose
towers the sea-birds would be wailing, suddenly, effacing
them, taking away all their charm, excluding them because they were its opposite and could only have weak-
ened its effect, was substituted in me the converse dream
of the most colourful of springs, not the spring of Combray, which still pricked sharply with all the needle-points
of the winter's frost, but that which already covered the
meadows of Fiesole with lilies and anemones, and gave
Florence a dazzling golden background like those in Fra
Angelico's pictures. From that moment onwards, only
sunlight, perfumes, colours, seemed to me of any worth;

for this alternation of images had effected a change of front in my desire, and—as abrupt as those that occur sometimes in music—a complete change of key in my sensibility. Then it came about that a simple atmospheric variation was sufficient to provoke in me that modulation, without there being any need for me to await the return of a season. For often in one we find a day that has strayed from another, that makes us live in that other, evokes at once and makes us long for its particular pleasures, and interrupts the dreams that we were in process of weaving, by inserting out of its turn, too early or too late, this leaf torn from another chapter in the interpolated calendar of Happiness. But soon, in the same way as those natural phenomena from which our comfort or our health can derive but an accidental and all too modest benefit until the day when science takes control of them and, producing them at will, places in our hands the power to order their appearance, free from the tutelage and independent of the mandate of chance, so the production of these dreams of the Atlantic and of Italy ceased to depend exclusively upon the changes of the seasons and of the weather. I need only, to make them reappear, pronounce the names Balbec, Venice, Florence, within whose syllables had gradually accumulated the longing inspired in me by the places for which they stood. Even in spring, to come upon the name Balbec in a book sufficed to awaken in me the desire for storms at sea and for Norman Gothic; even on a stormy day the name Florence or Venice would awaken the desire for sunshine, for lilies, for the Palace of the Doges and for Santa Maria del Fiore.

But if these names thus permanently absorbed the image I had formed of these towns, it was only by transforming that image, by subordinating its reappearance in me to their own special laws; and in consequence of this they made it more beautiful, but at the same time more different from anything that the towns of Normandy or Tuscany could in reality be, and, by increasing the arbitrary delights of my imagination, aggravated the disenchantment that was in store for me when I set out upon my travels. They magnified the idea that I had formed of certain places on the surface of the globe, making them more special and in consequence more real. I did not then represent to myself cities, landscapes, historical monuments, as more or less attractive pictures, cut out here and there of a substance that was common to them all, but looked on each of them as on an unknown thing, different in essence from all the rest, a thing for which my soul thirsted and which it would profit from knowing. How much more individual still was the character they assumed from being designated by names, names that were for themselves alone, proper names such as people have! Words present to us a little picture of things, clear and familiar, like the pictures hung on the walls of schoolrooms to give children an illustration of what is meant by a carpenter's bench, a bird, an anthill, things chosen as typical of everything else of the same sort. But names present to us—of persons, and of towns which they accustom us to regard as individual, as unique, like persons—a confused picture, which draws from them, from the brightness or darkness of their tone, the colour in which it is uniformly painted, like one of those posters, entirely blue or entirely red, in which, on account of the limitations imposed by the process used in their reproduction or by a whim on the designer's part, not only the sky

and the sea are blue or red, but the ships and the church
and the people in the streets. The name of Parma, one of
the towns that I most longed to visit after reading the
Chartreuse, seeming to me compact, smooth, violet-tinted
and soft, if anyone were to speak of such or such a house
in Parma in which I should be lodged, he would give me
the pleasure of thinking that I was to inhabit a dwelling
that was compact, smooth, violet-tinted and soft, that
bore no relation to the houses in any other town in Italy,
since I could imagine it only by the aid of that heavy first
syllable of the name of Parma, in which no breath of air
stirs, and of all that I had made it assume of Stendhalian
sweetness and the reflected hue of violets. And when I
thought of Florence it was of a town miraculously scented
and flower-like, since it was called the City of the Lilies,
and its cathedral, Our Lady of the Flower. As for Balbec,
it was one of those names in which, as on an old piece of
Norman pottery that still keeps the colour of the earth
from which it was fashioned, one sees depicted still the
representation of some long-abolished custom, of some
feudal right, of the former status of some locality, of an
obsolete way of pronouncing the language which had
shaped and wedded its incongruous syllables and which I
never doubted that I should find spoken there even by
the inn-keeper who would serve me coffee on my arrival,
taking me down to watch the turbulent sea in front of the
church, and to whom I would ascribe the disputatious,
solemn and mediaeval aspect of some character in an old
romance.

If my health had grown stronger and my parents allowed me, if not actually to go down to stay at Balbec, at
least to take, just once, in order to become acquainted

with the architecture and landscapes of Normandy or of
Brittany, that 1.22 train into which I had so often clambered in imagination, I should have wished to stop, for
preference, at the most beautiful of its towns; but in vain
did I compare and contrast them—how to choose, any
more than between individual persons who are not interchangeable, between Bayeux, so lofty in its noble coronet
of russet lacework, whose pinnacle was illumined by the
old gold of its second syllable; Vitré, whose acute accent
barred its ancient glass with wooden lozenges; gentle
Lamballe, whose whiteness ranged from egg-shell yellow
to pearl grey; Coutances, a Norman cathedral which its final consonants, rich and yellowing, crowned with a tower
of butter; Lannion with the rumbling noise, in the silence
of its village street, of a coach with a fly buzzing after it;
Questambert, Pontorson, ridiculous and naïve, white
feathers and yellow beaks strewn along the road to those
well-watered and poetic spots; Benodet, a name scarcely
moored that the river seemed to be striving to drag down
into the tangle of its algae; Pont-Aven, pink-white flash
of the wing of a lightly posed coif, tremulously reflected
in the greenish waters of a canal; Quimperlé, more firmly
anchored, ever since the Middle Ages, among its babbling
rivulets threading their pearls in a grey iridescence like
the pattern made, through the cobwebs on a church window, by rays of sunlight changed into blunted points of
tarnished silver?

These images were false for another reason also—
namely, that they were necessarily much simplified.
Doubtless whatever it was that my imagination aspired to,
that my senses took in only incompletely and without any
immediate pleasure, I had committed to the safe custody

of names; doubtless, because I had accumulated there a
store of dreams, those names now magnetised my desires;
but names themselves are not very comprehensive; the
most that I could do was to include in each of them two
or three of the principal "curiosities" of the town, which
would lie there side by side, without intermediary; in the
name of Balbec, as in the magnifying glasses set in those
penholders which one buys at seaside places, I could distinguish waves surging round a church built in the Persian style. Perhaps, indeed, the enforced simplicity of
these images was one of the reasons for the hold that they
had over me. When my father had decided, one year, that
we should go for the Easter holidays to Florence and
Venice, not finding room to introduce into the name of
Florence the elements that ordinarily constitute a town, I
was obliged to evolve a supernatural city from the impregnation by certain vernal scents of what I supposed to
be, in its essentials, the genius of Giotto. At most—and
because one cannot make a name extend much further in
time than in space—like some of Giotto's paintings
themselves which show us at two separate moments the
same person engaged in different actions, here lying in his
bed, there getting ready to mount his horse, the name of
Florence was divided into two compartments. In one, beneath an architectural canopy, I gazed at a fresco over
which was partly drawn a curtain of morning sunlight,
dusty, oblique and gradually spreading; in the other (for,
since I thought of names not as an inaccessible ideal but
as a real and enveloping atmosphere into which I was
about to plunge, the life not yet lived, the life, intact and
pure, which I enclosed in them gave to the most material
pleasures, to the simplest scenes, the same attraction that

they have in the works of the Primitives), I moved swiftly—the quicker to arrive at the lunch-table that was spread for me with fruit and a flask of Chianti—across a Ponte Vecchio heaped with jonquils, narcissi and anemones. That (even though I was still in Paris) was what I saw, and not what was actually round about me. Even from the simplest, the most realistic point of view, the countries which we long for occupy, at any given moment, a far larger place in our actual life than the country in which we happen to be. Doubtless, if, at that time, I had paid more attention to what was in my mind when I pronounced the words "going to Florence, to Parma, to Pisa, to Venice," I should have realised that what I saw was in no sense a town, but something as different from anything that I knew, something as delicious, as might be, for a human race whose whole existence had passed in a series of late winter afternoons, that inconceivable marvel, a morning in spring. These images, unreal, fixed, always alike, filling all my nights and days, differentiated this period in my life from those which had gone before it (and might easily have been confused with it by an observer who saw things only from without, that is to say who saw nothing), as in an opera a melodic theme introduces a novel atmosphere which one could never have suspected if one had done no more than read the libretto, still less if one had remained outside the theatre counting only the minutes as they passed. And besides, even from the point of view of mere quantity, in our lives the days are not all equal. To get through each day, natures that are at all highly strung, as was mine, are equipped, like motor-cars, with different gears. There are mountainous, arduous days, up which one takes an infinite time to climb, and downward-sloping days which one can descend at full tilt, singing as one goes. During this month—in which I turned over and over in my mind, like a tune of which one never tires, these visions of Florence, Venice, Pisa, of which the desire that they excited in me retained something as profoundly personal as if it had been love, love for a person—I never ceased to believe that they corresponded to a reality independent of myself, and they made me conscious of as glorious a hope as could have been cherished by a Christian in the primitive age of faith on the eve of his entry into Paradise. Thus, without my paying any heed to the contradiction that there was in my wishing to look at and to touch with the organs of my senses what had been elaborated by the spell of my dreams and not perceived by my senses at all—though all the more tempting to them, in consequence, more different from anything that they knew—it was that which recalled to me the reality of these visions that most inflamed my desire, by seeming to offer the promise that it would be gratified. And for all that the motive force of my exaltation was a longing for aesthetic enjoyments, the guide-books ministered even more to it than books on aesthetics, and, more again than the guide-books, the railway time-tables. What moved me was the thought that this Florence which I could see, so near and yet inaccessible, in my imagination, if the journey which separated it from me, in myself, was not a viable one, could yet be reached circuitously were I to take the plain, terrestrial route. True, when I repeated to myself, giving thus a special value to what I was going to see, that Venice was the "School of Giorgione, the home of Titian, the most complete museum of the domestic architecture of the Middle

Ages," I felt happy. But I was happier still when, out on an errand and walking briskly on account of the weather, which, after several days of a precocious spring, had relapsed into winter (like the weather we invariably found awaiting us at Combray in Holy Week)—seeing on the boulevards that the chestnut-trees, though plunged in a glacial atmosphere that soaked through them like water, were none the less beginning, punctual guests, arrayed already for the party and admitting no discouragement, to shape and chisel and curve in its frozen lumps the irrepressible verdure whose steady growth the abortive power of the cold might hinder but could not succeed in restraining—I reflected that already the Ponte Vecchio was heaped high with an abundance of hyacinths and anemones, and that the spring sunshine was already tingeing the waters of the Grand Canal with so deep an azure and such noble emeralds that when they washed against the foot of a Titian painting they could vie with it in the richness of their colouring. I could no longer contain myself for joy when my father, in the intervals of tapping the barometer and complaining of the cold, began to look out which were the best trains, and when I understood that by making one's way after luncheon into the coal-grimed laboratory, the wizard's cell that undertook to contrive a complete transmutation of its surroundings, one could wake up next morning in the city of marble and gold, "its walls embellished with jasper and its streets paved with emeralds." So that it and the City of the Lilies were not just artificial scenes which I could set up at will in front of my imagination, but existed a certain distance from Paris which must inevitably be traversed if I wished to see them, at a particular place on the earth's surface and

at no other—in a word, were entirely real. They became
even more real to me when my father, by saying, "Well,
you can stay in Venice from the 20th to the 29th, and
reach Florence on Easter morning," made them both
emerge, no longer only from the abstraction of Space, but
from that imaginary Time in which we place not one
journey at a time but others simultaneously, without too
much agitation since they are only possibilities—that
Time which reconstructs itself so effectively that one can
spend it again in one town after one has already spent it
in another—and assigned to them some of those actual,
calendar days which are the certificates of authenticity of
the objects on which they are spent, for these unique days
are consumed by being used, they do not return, one cannot live them again here when one has lived them there. I
felt that it was towards the week that would begin with
the Monday on which the laundress was to bring back the
white waistcoat I had stained with ink that they were hastening to absorb themselves, on emerging from that ideal
Time in which they did not yet exist—those two queens
of cities of which I was soon to be able, by the most
thrilling kind of geometry, to inscribe the domes and towers on a page of my own life. But I was still only on the
way to the supreme pinnacle of happiness; I reached it finally (for not until then did the revelation burst upon me
that on the clattering streets, reddened by the light reflected from Giorgione's frescoes, it was not, as I had
continued to imagine despite so many admonitions, men
"majestic and terrible as the sea, bearing armour that
gleamed with bronze beneath the folds of their blood-red
cloaks" who would be walking in Venice next week, on
Easter eve, but that I myself might be the minute person-

age whom, in an enlarged photograph of St Mark's that had been lent to me, the illustrator had portrayed, in a bowler hat, in front of the portico) when I heard my father say: "It must be pretty cold, still, on the Grand Canal; you'd do well, just in case, to pack your winter greatcoat and your thick suit." At these words I was raised to a sort of ecstasy; I felt myself—something I had until then deemed impossible—to be penetrating indeed between those "rocks of amethyst, like a reef in the Indian Ocean"; by a supreme muscular effort, far in excess of my real strength, divesting myself, as of a shell that served no purpose, of the air in my own room which surrounded me, I replaced it by an equal quantity of Venetian air, that marine atmosphere, indescribable and peculiar as the atmosphere of dreams, which my imagination had secreted in the name of Venice; I felt myself undergoing a miraculous disincarnation, which was at once accompanied by that vague desire to vomit which one feels when one has developed a very sore throat; and I had to be put to bed with a fever so persistent that the doctor declared not only that a visit now to Florence and Venice was absolutely out of the question, but that, even when I had completely recovered, I must for at least a year give up all idea of travelling and be kept from anything that was liable to excite me.

And alas, he also imposed a formal ban on my being allowed to go to the theatre to hear Berma. The sublime artist whose genius Bergotte had proclaimed might, by introducing me to something else that was perhaps as important and beautiful, have consoled me for not having been to Florence and Venice, for not going to Balbec. My parents had to be content with sending me every day to the Champs-Elysées, in the custody of a person who would see that I did not tire myself; this person being none other than Françoise, who had entered our service after the death of my aunt Léonie. Going to the Champs-Elysées I found unendurable. If only Bergotte had described the place in one of his books, I should no doubt have longed to get to know it, like so many things else of which a simulacrum had first found its way into my imagination. This breathed life into them, gave them a personality, and I sought then to rediscover them in reality; but in this public garden there was nothing that attached itself to my dreams.

One day, as I was bored with our usual place beside the roundabout, Françoise had taken me for an excursion—across the frontier guarded at regular intervals by the little bastions of the barley-sugar women—into those neighbouring but foreign regions where the faces of the passers-by were strange, where the goat-carriage went past; then she had gone back to collect her things from her chair that stood with its back to a shrubbery of laurels. While I waited for her I was pacing the broad lawn of meagre, close-cropped, sun-baked grass, dominated, at its far end, by a statue rising from a fountain, in front of which a little girl with reddish hair was playing battledore and shuttlecock, when from the path another little girl, who was putting on her coat and covering up her racquet, called out sharply: "Good-bye, Gilberte, I'm going home now; don't forget we're coming to you this evening, after dinner." The name Gilberte passed close by me, evoking all the more forcefully the girl whom it labelled in that it did not merely refer to her, as one speaks of someone in

his absence, but was directly addressed to her; it passed
thus close by me, in action so to speak, with a force that
increased with the curve of its trajectory and the proximity of its target—carrying in its wake, I could feel, the
knowledge, the impressions concerning her to whom it
was addressed that belonged not to me but to the friend
who called it out, everything that, as she uttered the
words, she recalled, or at least possessed in her memory,
of their daily intimacy, of the visits that they paid to each
other, of that unknown existence which was all the more
inaccessible, all the more painful to me from being, conversely, so familiar, so tractable to this happy girl who let
it brush past me without my being able to penetrate it,
who flung it on the air with a light-hearted cry—wafting
through the air the exquisite emanation which it had dis-
tilled, by touching them with the utmost precision, from
certain invisible points in Mlle Swann's life, from the
evening to come, just as it would be, after dinner, at her
home—forming, on its celestial passage through the
midst of the children and their nursemaids, a little cloud,
delicately coloured, resembling one of those clouds that,
billowing over a Poussin landscape, reflect minutely, like
a cloud in the opera teeming with chariots and horses,
some apparition of the life of the gods—casting, finally,
on that ragged grass, at the spot where it was at one and
the same time a scrap of withered lawn and a moment in
the afternoon of the fair battledore player (who continued
to launch and retrieve her shuttlecock until a governess
with a blue feather in her hat had called her away) a marvellous little band of light, the colour of heliotrope, impalpable as a reflection and superimposed like a carpet on
which I could not help but drag my lingering, nostalgic

and desecrating feet, while Françoise shouted: "Come on,
do up your coat and let's clear off!" and I remarked for
the first time how common her speech was, and that she
had, alas, no blue feather in her hat.

But would *she* come back to the Champs-Elysées?
Next day she was not there; but I saw her on the following days, and spent all my time revolving round the spot
where she played with her friends, to such effect that
once, when they found that there were not enough of
them to make up a prisoner's base, she sent one of them
to ask me if I cared to complete their side, and from that
day I played with her whenever she came. But this did
not happen every day; there were days when she was prevented from coming by her lessons, by her catechism, by
a tea-party, by the whole of that life, separated from my
own, which twice only, condensed into the name Gilberte,
I had felt pass so painfully close to me, in the hawthorn
lane near Combray and on the grass of the Champs-
Elysées. On such days she would tell us in advance that
we would not be seeing her; if it was because of her
lessons, she would say: "It's too tiresome, I shan't be able
to come tomorrow; you'll all be enjoying yourselves here
without me," with an air of regret which to some extent
consoled me; if, on the other hand, she had been invited
to a party, and I, not knowing this, asked her whether she
was coming to play with us, she would reply: "I should
jolly well hope not! I hope Mamma will let me go to my
friend's." But on these days I did at least know that I
would not see her, whereas on others, without any warning, her mother would take her shopping, and next day
she would say: "Oh, yes! I went out with Mamma," as
though it had been the most natural thing in the world,

and not the greatest possible misfortune for someone else. There were also the days of bad weather on which her governess, afraid on her own account of the rain, would not bring Gilberte to the Champs-Elysées.

And so, if the sky was overcast, from early morning I would not cease to examine it, observing all the omens. If I saw the lady opposite putting on her hat beside her window, I would say to myself: "That lady is going out; so it must be weather in which one can go out. Why shouldn't Gilberte do the same as that lady?" But the weather would cloud over. My mother would say that it might clear again, that one burst of sunshine would be enough, but that more probably it would rain; and if it rained, what was the use of going to the Champs-Elysées? And so, from lunch-time onwards, my anxious eyes never left the unsettled, clouded sky. It remained dark. The balcony in front of the window was grey. Suddenly, on its sullen stone, I would not exactly see a less leaden colour, but I would feel as it were a striving towards a less leaden colour, the pulsation of a hesitant ray that struggled to discharge its light. A moment later, the balcony was as pale and luminous as a pool at dawn, and a thousand shadows from the iron-work of its balustrade had alighted on it. A breath of wind would disperse them, and the stone darkened again, but, as though they had been tamed, they would return; imperceptibly the stone whitened once more, and as in one of those uninterrupted crescendos which, in music, at the end of an overture, carry a single note to the supreme fortissimo by making it pass rapidly through all the intermediate stages, I would see it reach that fixed, unalterable gold of fine days, on which the clear-cut shadow of the wrought iron of the

balustrade was outlined in black like some capricious vegetation, with a delicacy in the delineation of its smallest
details that seemed to indicate a deliberate application, an
artist's satisfaction, and with so much relief, so velvety a
bloom in the restfulness of its dark, felicitous masses that
in truth those broad and leafy reflections on that lake of
sunshine seemed aware that they were pledges of tranquillity and happiness.

Brief, fading ivy, climbing, fugitive flora!—the most
colourless, the most depressing, to many minds, of all
that creep on walls or decorate windows; to me the dearest of them all ever since the day when it appeared upon
our balcony, like the very shadow of the presence of
Gilberte, who was perhaps already in the Champs-
Elysées, and as soon as I arrived there would greet me
with: "Let's begin at once; you're on my side"; frail,
swept away by a breath, but at the same time in harmony, not with the season, but with the hour; promise of
that immediate happiness which the day will deny or fulfil, and thereby of the one paramount immediate happiness, the happiness of love; softer, warmer upon the stone
even than moss; robust, a ray of sunlight sufficing for it
to spring into life and blossom into joy, even in the heart
of winter.

And even on those days when all other vegetation
had disappeared, when the fine green hide which covered
the trunks of the old trees was hidden beneath the snow,
and, though the latter had ceased to fall, the sky was still
too overcast for me to hope that Gilberte would venture
out, then suddenly—inspiring my mother to say: "Look,
it's quite fine now; I think you might perhaps try going
to the Champs-Elysées after all"—on the mantle of snow

that swathed the balcony, the sun would appear and weave a tracery of golden threads and black shadows. On one such day we found no one, or only a solitary little girl on the point of departure, who assured me that Gilberte was not coming. The chairs, deserted by the imposing but shivering assembly of governesses, stood empty. Alone, beside the lawn, sat a lady of a certain age who came in all weathers, dressed always in an identical style, splendid and sombre, to make whose acquaintance I would at that time have sacrificed, had it lain in my power, all the greatest advantages and privileges of my future life. For Gilberte went up to greet her every day; she used to ask Gilberte for news of her "adorable mother"; and it struck me that, if I had known her, I should have been for Gilberte someone wholly different, someone who knew people in her parents' world. While her grandchildren played together at a little distance, she would sit and read the *Journal des Débats*, which she called "My old *Débats*," and with aristocratic affectation would say, speaking of the policeman or the woman who let the chairs, "My old friend the policeman," or "The chair-keeper and I, who are old friends."

Françoise found it too cold to stand about, so we walked to the Pont de la Concorde to see the Seine frozen over, which everyone, even children, approached fearlessly, as though it were an enormous whale, stranded, defenceless, and about to be cut up. We returned to the Champs-Elysées; I was growing sick with misery between the motionless roundabout and the white lawn, caught in the black network of the paths from which the snow had been cleared, while the statue that surmounted it held in its hand a long pendent icicle which seemed to explain its gesture. The old lady herself, having folded up her *Débats*, asked a passing nursemaid the time, thanking her with "How very good of you!" then begged the road-sweeper to tell her grandchildren to come, as she felt cold, adding: "A thousand thanks. I am sorry to give you so much trouble!" Suddenly the sky was rent in two; between the Punch-and-Judy and the horses, against the opening horizon, I had just seen, like a miraculous sign, Mademoiselle's blue feather. And now Gilberte was running at full speed towards me, sparkling and rosy beneath a cap trimmed with fur, animated by the cold, her lateness and the desire for a game; shortly before she reached me, she slid along the ice and, either to keep her balance, or because it appeared to her graceful, or else pretending that she was on skates, it was with outstretched arms that she smilingly advanced, as though to embrace me. "Bravo! bravo! that's splendid; 'topping,' I should say, like you—'sporting,' I suppose I ought to say, only I'm a hundred-and-one, a woman of the old school," exclaimed the old lady, uttering, on behalf of the voiceless Champs-Elysées, their thanks to Gilberte for having come without letting herself be frightened away by the weather. "You are like me, faithful at all costs to our old Champs-Elysées. We're two brave souls! You wouldn't believe me, I dare say, if I told you that I love them, even like this. This snow (I know you'll laugh at me), it makes me think of ermine!" And the old lady began to laugh herself.

The first of these days—to which the snow, a symbol of the powers that could deprive me of the sight of Gilberte, imparted the sadness of a day of separation, almost the aspect of a day of departure, because it changed the outward form and almost forbade the use of the cus-

tomary scene of our only encounters, now altered, covered, as it were, in dust-sheets—that day, none the less,
marked a stage in the progress of my love, for it was like
a first sorrow that we shared together. There were only
our two selves of our little company, and to be thus alone
with her was not merely like a beginning of intimacy, but
also on her part—as though she had come there solely to
please me in such weather—it seemed to me as touching
as if, on one of those days when she had been invited to a
party, she had given it up in order to come to join me in
the Champs-Elysées; I acquired more confidence in the
vitality, in the future of a friendship which could remain
so enduring amid the torpor, the solitude, the decay of
our surroundings; and while she stuffed snowballs down
my neck, I smiled lovingly at what seemed to me at once
a predilection that she showed for me in thus tolerating
me as her travelling companion in this new and wintry
land, and a sort of loyalty which she cherished for me
through evil times. Presently, one after another, like shyly
hopping sparrows, her friends arrived, black against the
snow. We got ready to play and, since this day which had
begun so sadly was destined to end in joy, as I went up,
before the game started, to the friend with the sharp voice
whom I had heard the first day calling Gilberte by name,
she said to me: "No, no, I'm sure you'd much rather be
in Gilberte's camp; besides, look, she's signalling to you."
She was in fact summoning me to cross the snowy lawn
to her camp, to "take the field," which the sun, by casting
over it a rosy gleam, the metallic lustre of old and worn
brocades, had turned into a Field of the Cloth of Gold.

This day which I had so dreaded was, as it happened,
one of the few on which I was not unduly wretched.

For, although I now no longer thought of anything save not to let a single day pass without seeing Gilberte (so much so that once, when my grandmother had not come home by dinner-time, I could not resist the instinctive reflection that if she had been run over in the street and killed, I should not for some time be allowed to play in the Champs-Elysées; when one is in love one has no love left for anyone) yet those moments which I spent in her company, for which I had waited so impatiently all night and morning, for which I had quivered with excitement, to which I would have sacrificed everything else in the world, were by no means happy moments; and well did I know it, for they were the only moments in my life on which I concentrated a scrupulous, unflagging attention, and yet could not discover in them one atom of pleasure.

All the time I was away from Gilberte, I felt the need to see her, because, constantly trying to picture her in my mind, I ended up by being unable to do so, and by no longer knowing precisely what my love represented. Besides, she had never yet told me that she loved me. Far from it: she had often boasted that she knew other boys whom she preferred to myself, that I was a good companion, with whom she was always willing to play, although I was too absent-minded, not attentive enough to the game; indeed, she had often shown signs of apparent coldness towards me which might have shaken my faith that I was for her a person different from the rest, had that faith been founded upon a love that Gilberte felt for me and not, as was the case, upon the love I felt for her, which strengthened its resistance to the assaults of doubt by making it depend entirely on the manner in which I was

obliged by an internal compulsion to think of Gilberte.
But I myself had not yet ventured to declare my feelings
towards her. True, on every page of my exercise-books I
wrote out, in endless repetition, her name and address,
but at the sight of those vague lines which I traced without her thinking of me any the more on that account,
which made her take up so much apparent space around
me without her being any the more involved in my life, I
felt discouraged, because they spoke to me, not of
Gilberte, who would never so much as see them, but of
my own desire, which they seemed to show me in its true
colours, as something purely personal, unreal, tedious and
ineffectual. The important thing was that we should see
each other, Gilberte and I, and should have an opportunity of making a mutual avowal of our love which, until
then, would not officially (so to speak) have begun.
Doubtless the various reasons which made me so impatient to see her would have appeared less urgent to a
grown man. As life goes on, we acquire such adroitness in
the cultivation of our pleasures, that we content ourselves
with the pleasure we derive from thinking of a woman, as
I thought of Gilberte, without troubling ourselves to ascertain whether the image corresponds to the reality, and
also with the pleasure of loving her without needing to be
sure that she loves us too; or again that we renounce the
pleasure of confessing our inclination for her, so as to preserve and enhance her inclination for us, like those
Japanese gardeners who, to obtain one perfect blossom,
will sacrifice several others. But at the period when I was
in love with Gilberte, I still believed that Love did really
exist outside ourselves; that, allowing us at the most to
surmount the obstacles in our way, it offered its blessings

in an order to which we were not free to make the least
alteration; it seemed to me that if I had, on my own initiative, substituted for the sweetness of avowal a pretence
of indifference, I should not only have been depriving
myself of one of the joys for which I most longed, but
fabricating, quite arbitrarily, a love that was artificial and
valueless, that bore no relation to the true one, whose
mysterious and foreordained ways I should thus have
ceased to follow.

But when I arrived in the Champs-Elysées—and, as
at first sight it appeared, was in a position to confront my
love, so as to make it undergo the necessary modifica-
tions, with its living cause, independent to myself—as
soon as I was in the presence of that Gilberte Swann on
the sight of whom I had counted to revive the images that
my tired memory could no longer recapture, of that
Gilberte Swann with whom I had played the day before,
and whom I had just been prompted to greet and recognise by a blind instinct like that which, when we are
walking, sets one foot before the other without giving us
time to think what we are doing, then at once it became
as though she and the little girl who was the object of my
dreams had been two different people. If, for instance, I
had retained in my memory overnight two fiery eyes
above full and rosy cheeks, Gilberte's face would now offer me with overpowering insistence something that I distinctly had not remembered, a certain sharp tapering of
the nose which, instantaneously associating itself with certain other features, assumed the importance of those characteristics which in natural history define a species, and
transformed her into a little girl of the kind that have
pointed snouts. While I was getting ready to take advan-

tage of this longed-for moment to effect, on the basis of
the image of Gilberte which I had prepared beforehand
but which had now gone from my head, the adjustment
that would enable me, during the long hours I must
spend alone, to be certain that it was indeed her that I
had in mind, that it was indeed my love for her that I
was gradually putting together as one composes a book,
she passed me a ball; and, like the idealist philosopher
whose body takes account of the external world in the reality of which his intellect declines to believe, the same
self which had made me greet her before I had identified
her now urged me to seize the ball that she handed to me
(as though she were a companion with whom I had come
to play, and not a sister-soul with whom I had come to be
united), made me, out of decorum, address a thousand
and one polite and trivial remarks to her until the time
came when she had to go, and so prevented me either
from keeping a silence during which I might at last have
laid hands once more on the urgent truant image, or from
uttering the words which might have brought about the
decisive progress in the course of our love the hope of
which I was always obliged to postpone until the following afternoon.

It did, however, make some progress. One day, we
had gone with Gilberte to the stall of our own special
vendor, who was always particularly nice to us, since it
was to her that M. Swann used to send for his ginger-
bread, of which, for reasons of health (he suffered from
ethnic eczema and from the constipation of the prophets),
he consumed a great deal, and Gilberte pointed out to me
with a laugh two little boys who were like the little artist
and the little naturalist in the children's story-books. For

one of them would not have a red stick of barley sugar because he preferred the purple, while the other, with tears in his eyes, refused a plum which his nurse was buying for him because, as he finally explained in passionate tones: "I want the other plum; it's got a worm in it!" I purchased two ha'penny marbles. With admiring eyes I gazed at the agate marbles, luminous and imprisoned in a bowl apart, which seemed precious to me because they were as fair and smiling as little girls, and because they cost sixpence each. Gilberte, who was given a great deal more pocket money than I ever had, asked me which I thought the prettiest. They had the transparency and mellowness of life itself. I would not have had her sacrifice a single one of them. I should have liked her to be able to buy them, to liberate them all. Still, I pointed out one that had the same colour as her eyes. Gilberte took it, turned it round until it shone with a ray of gold, fondled it, paid its ransom, but at once handed me her captive, saying: "Here, it's for you. Keep it as a souvenir."

Another time, being still obsessed by the desire to hear Berma in classic drama, I had asked her whether she had a copy of a booklet in which Bergotte spoke of Racine, and which was now out of print. She had asked me to let her know the exact title of it, and that evening I had sent her an express letter, writing on its envelope the name, Gilberte Swann, which I had so often traced in my exercise-book. The next day she brought me the booklet, for which she had instituted a search, in a parcel tied with mauve ribbon and sealed with white wax. "You see, it's what you asked me for," she said, taking from her muff the express letter that I had sent her. But in the address on the pneumatic message[15]—which, only yesterday, was nothing, was merely a *petit bleu* that I had written, and which, after a messenger had delivered it to Gilberte's porter and a servant had taken it up to her room, had become that priceless thing, one of the *petits bleus* that she had received in the course of the day—I had difficulty in recognising the futile, straggling lines of my own handwriting beneath the circles stamped on it at the post-office, the inscriptions added in pencil by a postman, signs of effectual realisation, seals of the external world, violet bands symbolical of life itself, which for the first time came to espouse, to maintain, to lift, to gladden my dream.

And there was another day when she said to me: "You know, you may call me 'Gilberte.' In any case, I'm going to call you by your first name. It's too silly not to." Yet she continued for a while to address me by the more formal *"vous,"* and when I drew her attention to this, she smiled and, composing, constructing a phrase like those that are put into the grammar-books of foreign languages with no other object than to teach us to make use of a new word, ended it with my Christian name. Recalling, some time later, what I had felt at the time, I distinguished the impression of having been held for a moment in her mouth, myself, naked, without any of the social attributes which belonged equally to her other playmates and, when she used my surname, to my parents, accessories of which her lips—by the effort she made, a little after her father's manner, to articulate the words to which she wished to give a special emphasis—had the air of stripping, of divesting me, like the skin from a fruit of which one can swallow only the pulp, while her glance, adapting itself to the same new degree of intimacy as her speech, fell on me also more directly and testified to the consciousness, the pleasure, even the gratitude that it felt by accompanying itself with a smile.

But at the actual moment I was unable to appreciate the value of these new pleasures. They were given, not by the little girl whom I loved to the "me" who loved her, but by the other, the one with whom I used to play, to that other "me" who possessed neither the memory of the true Gilberte, nor the inalienably committed heart which alone could have known the value of a happiness which it alone had desired. Even after I had returned home I did not savour these pleasures, since every day the necessity which made me hope that on the morrow I should arrive at a clear, calm, happy contemplation of Gilberte, that she would at last confess her love for me, explaining why she had been obliged hitherto to conceal it from me, that same necessity forced me to regard the past as of no account, to look ahead of me only, to consider the small favours she had granted me not in themselves and as if they were self-sufficient, but as fresh rungs of the ladder on which I might set my feet, which would enable me to advance one step further towards the final attainment of that happiness which I had not yet encountered.

If at times she showed me these marks of affection, she pained me also by seeming not to be pleased to see me, and this happened often on the very days on which I had most counted for the realisation of my hopes. I was sure that Gilberte was coming to the Champs-Elysées, and I felt an elation which seemed merely the anticipation of a great happiness when—going into the drawing-room in the morning to kiss Mamma, who was already dressed to go out, the coils of her black hair elaborately built up, and her beautiful plump white hands fragrant still with soap—I had been apprised, on seeing a column of dust standing up by itself in the air above the piano, and on hearing a barrel-organ playing beneath the window *En revenant de la revue*, that the winter had received, until nightfall, an unexpected, radiant visit from a day of spring. While we sat at lunch, the lady opposite, by opening her window, had sent packing in the twinkling of an eye from beside my chair—sweeping at one bound across the whole width of our dining-room—a sunbeam which had settled down there for its midday rest and returned to continue it a moment later. At school, during the one o'clock lesson, the sun made me sick with impatience and boredom as it trailed a golden glow across my desk, like an invitation to festivities at which I could not myself arrive before three o'clock, until the moment when Françoise came to fetch me at the school-gate and we made our way towards the Champs-Elysées through streets bejewelled with sunlight, dense with people, over which the balconies, detached by the sun and made vaporous, seemed to float in front of the houses like clouds of gold. Alas! in the Champs-Elysées I found no Gilberte; she had not yet arrived. Motionless on the lawn nurtured by the invisible sun which, here and there, kindled to a flame the point of a blade of grass, while the pigeons that had alighted upon it had the appearance of ancient sculptures which the gardener's pick had heaved to the surface of a hallowed soil, I stood with my eyes fixed on the horizon, expecting at every moment to see Gilberte's form, following that of her governess, appearing from behind the statue that seemed to be holding out the glistening

child it carried to receive the sun's benediction. The old
lady who read the *Débats* was sitting on her chair, in her
invariable place, and had just accosted a park attendant
with a friendly wave of her hand as she exclaimed "What
a lovely day!" And when the chair-keeper came up to collect her fee, with an infinity of simperings she folded the
ticket away inside her glove, as though it had been a posy
of flowers for which she had sought, in gratitude to the
donor, the most becoming place upon her person. When
she had found it, she performed a circular movement with
her neck, straightened her boa, and fastened upon the collector, as she showed her the edge of a yellow paper that
stuck out over her bare wrist, the bewitching smile with
which a woman says to a young man, pointing to her bosom: "You see I'm wearing your roses!"

I dragged Françoise, in the hope of meeting Gilberte
halfway, as far as the Arc de Triomphe; we did not meet
her, and I was returning towards the lawn convinced,
now, that she was not coming, when, in front of the
roundabout, the little girl with the sharp voice flung herself upon me: "Quick, quick, Gilberte's been here a quarter of an hour. She's going soon. We've been waiting for
you to make up a prisoner's base."

While I had been going up the Avenue des Champs-
Elysées, Gilberte had arrived by the Rue Boissy-d'Anglas,
Mademoiselle having taken advantage of the fine weather
to do some shopping for her; and M. Swann was coming
to fetch his daughter. And so it was my fault; I ought
not to have strayed from the lawn; for one never knew for
certain from what direction Gilberte would appear, and
whether she would be early or late, and this perpetual
tension succeeded in making more thrilling not only the

entire Champs-Elysées and the whole span of the afternoon, like a vast expanse of space and time on every point
and at every moment of which it was possible that
Gilberte's form might appear, but also that form itself,
since behind that form I felt that there lay concealed the
reason why it had flashed into my presence at four o'clock
instead of at half-past two, crowned with a formal hat instead of a playtime beret, in front of the Ambassadeurs
and not between the two puppet-shows, I divined one of
those occupations in which I might not follow Gilberte
and which forced her to go out or stay at home, I was in
contact with the mystery of her unknown life. It was this
mystery, too, that troubled me when, running at the
sharp-voiced girl's bidding to begin our game without
further delay, I saw Gilberte, so brusque and informal
with us, making a curtsey to the old lady of the *Débats*
(who acknowledged it with "What a lovely sun! You'd
think it was a fire") and speaking to her with a shy smile,
with an air of constraint which called to my mind the
other little girl that Gilberte must be when at home with
her parents, or with friends of her parents or paying calls,
in the whole of that other existence of hers which eluded
me. But of that existence no one gave me so strong an
impression as did M. Swann, who came a little later to
fetch his daughter. For he and Mme Swann—inasmuch
as their daughter lived with them, and her lessons, her
games, her friendships depended upon them—contained
for me, like Gilberte, perhaps even more than Gilberte, as
befitted gods with an all-powerful control over her, in
whom it must have had its source, an undefined, an inaccessible quality of melancholy charm. Everything that
concerned them was the object of so constant a preoccu-

pation on my part that the days on which, as on this day,
M. Swann (whom I had seen so often in the past without
his having aroused my curiosity, when he was still on
good terms with my parents) came to fetch Gilberte from
the Champs-Elysées, once the violent throbbing of my
heart provoked by the appearance of his grey hat and
hooded cape had subsided, the sight of him still impressed me as might that of an historic personage about
whom one has just been reading a series of books and the
minutest details of whose life and person intrigue us. His
relations with the Comte de Paris, which, when I heard
them discussed at Combray, had left me indifferent, became now in my eyes something to be marvelled at, as if
no one else had ever known the House of Orleans; they
made him stand out vividly against the vulgar background of pedestrians of different classes who encum-
bered that particular path in the Champs-Elysées, in the
midst of whom I admired his condescending to figure
without claiming any special deference, which as it happened none of them dreamed of paying him, so profound
was the incognito in which he was wrapped.

He responded politely to the salutations of Gilberte's
playmates, even to mine, for all that he had fallen out
with my family, but without appearing to know me. (This
reminded me that he had seen me quite often in the
country; a memory which I had retained, but kept out of
sight, because, since I had seen Gilberte again, Swann had
become to me pre-eminently her father, and no longer the
Combray Swann; since the ideas to which I now connected his name were different from the ideas in the system of which it was formerly comprised, ideas which I no
longer utilised when I had occasion to think of him, he

had become a new, another person; nevertheless, I attached him by an artificial, secondary and transversal thread to our former guest; and since nothing had henceforth any value for me except so far as my love might profit by it, it was with a spasm of shame and of regret at not being able to erase them that I recalled the years in which, in the eyes of this same Swann who was at this moment before me in the Champs-Elysées and to whom, fortunately, Gilberte had perhaps not mentioned my name, I had so often, in the evenings, made myself ridiculous by sending to ask Mamma to come upstairs to my room to say good night to me, while she was drinking coffee with him and my father and my grandparents at the table in the garden.) He told Gilberte that she had his permission to play one game, that he could wait for a quarter of an hour; and, sitting down just like anyone else on an iron chair, paid for his ticket with that hand which Philippe VII had so often held in his, while we began our game upon the lawn, scattering the pigeons whose beautiful, iridescent bodies (shaped like hearts and, as it were, the lilacs of the feathered kingdom) took refuge as in so many sanctuaries, one on the great stone basin, to which its beak, as it disappeared below the rim, imparted the gesture and assigned the purpose of offering in abundance the fruit or grain at which it appeared to be pecking, another on the head of the statue, which it seemed to crown with one of those enamelled objects whose polychrome varies the monotony of the stone in certain classical works, and with an attribute which, when the goddess bears it, earns her a particular epithet and makes of her, as a different Christian name makes of a mortal, a new divinity.

On one of these sunny days which had failed to fulfil my hopes, I could not conceal my disappointment from Gilberte.

"I had so many things to ask you," I said to her; "I thought that today was going to mean so much in our friendship. And no sooner have you come than you go away! Try to come early tomorrow, so that I can talk to you."

Her face lit up and she jumped for joy as she answered: "Tomorrow, you may depend upon it, my dear boy, I shan't be coming. I've got a big tea-party. The day after tomorrow I'm going to a friend's house to watch the arrival of King Theodosius from the window—won't that be splendid?—and the day after that I'm going to *Michel Strogoff*, and then it will soon be Christmas and the New Year holidays! Perhaps they'll take me to the Riviera—wouldn't that be nice? though I should miss the Christmas-tree here. Anyhow, if I do stay in Paris, I shan't be coming here, because I shall be out paying calls with Mamma. Good-bye—there's Papa calling me."

I returned home with Françoise through the streets that were still gay with sunshine, as on the evening of a holiday when the merriment is over. I could scarcely drag my legs along.

"I'm not surprised," said Françoise, "it's not the right weather for the time of year; it's much too warm. Oh dear, oh dear, to think of all the poor sick people there must be everywhere. It's like as if everything's topsy-turvy up there too."

I repeated to myself, stifling my sobs, the words in which Gilberte had given utterance to her joy at the prospect of not coming back for a long time to the

Champs-Elysées. But already the charm with which, by
the mere act of thinking, my mind was filled as soon as it
thought of her, and the special, unique position, however
painful, in which I was inevitably placed in relation to
Gilberte by the inner constraint of a mental habit, had
begun to lend a romantic aura even to that mark of her
indifference, and in the midst of my tears my lips shaped
themselves into a smile which was simply the timid ad-
umbration of a kiss. And when the time came for the
postman to arrive I said to myself, that evening as on every other: "I'm going to get a letter from Gilberte; she's
going to tell me at last that she has never ceased to love
me, and explain to me the mysterious reason why she has
been forced to conceal it from me until now, to pretend to
be able to be happy without seeing me, the reason why
she has assumed the form of the other Gilberte who is
simply a playmate."

Every evening I would beguile myself by imagining
this letter, believing that I was actually reading it, reciting
each of its sentences in turn. Suddenly I would stop in
alarm. I had realised that if I was to receive a letter from
Gilberte, it could not, in any case, be this letter, since it
was I myself who had just composed it. And from then
on I would strive to divert my thoughts from the words
which I should have liked her to write to me, for fear
that, by voicing them, I should be excluding just those
words—the dearest, the most desired—from the field of
possibilities. Even if, by some improbable coincidence, it
had been precisely the letter of my invention that Gilberte
addressed to me of her own accord, recognising my own
work in it I should not have had the impression that I
was receiving something that had not originated from me,

something real, something new, a happiness external to
my mind, independent of my will, a true gift of love.

Meanwhile, I re-read a page which, although it had
not been written to me by Gilberte, at least came to me
from her, that page of Bergotte's on the beauty of the old
myths whence Racine drew his inspiration, which (with
the agate marble) I always kept close at hand. I was
touched by my friend's kindness in having procured the
book for me; and as everyone needs to find reasons for his
passion, to the extent of being glad to recognise in the
loved one qualities which (he has learned from literature
or conversation) are worthy of love, to the extent of as-
similating them by imitation and making them additional
reasons for his love, even though these qualities are diametrically opposed to those his love would have sought
after as long as it was spontaneous—as Swann, before my
day, had sought to establish the aesthetic basis of
Odette's beauty—I, who had at first loved Gilberte, from
Combray onwards, on account of all the unknown element in her life in which I longed to be immersed, rein-
carnated, discarding my own as a thing of no account, I
thought now, as of an inestimable privilege, that of this
too familiar, despised life of mine Gilberte might one day
become the humble servant, the kindly and comforting
collaborator, who in the evenings, helping me in my
work, would collate for me the texts of rare pamphlets.
As for Bergotte, that infinitely wise, almost divine old
man, because of whom I had first loved Gilberte, before I
had even seen her, now it was above all for Gilberte's
sake that I loved him. With as much pleasure as the
pages that he had written about Racine I studied the
wrapper, folded under the great white seals of wax tied

with festoons of mauve ribbon, in which she had brought
them to me. I kissed the agate marble, which was the better part of my love's heart, the part that was not frivolous
but faithful, and which, for all that it was adorned with
the mysterious charm of Gilberte's life, dwelt close beside
me, inhabited my room, shared my bed. But the beauty
of that stone, and the beauty also of those pages of
Bergotte which I was glad to associate with the idea of my
love for Gilberte, as if, in the moments when it seemed
no more than a void, they gave it a kind of consistency,
were, I perceived, anterior to that love and in no way resembled it; their elements had been determined by the
writer's talent or the laws of mineralogy before ever
Gilberte had known me; nothing in book or stone would
have been different if Gilberte had not loved me, and
nothing, consequently, authorised me to read in them a
message of happiness. And while my love, incessantly
waiting for the morrow to bring the avowal of Gilberte's
for me, destroyed, unravelled every evening the ill-done
work of the day, in some shadowed part of my being an
unknown seamstress refused to abandon the discarded
threads, but collected and rearranged them, without any
thought of pleasing me or of toiling for my happiness, in
the different order which she gave to all her handiwork.
Showing no special interest in my love, not beginning by
deciding that I was loved, she gathered together those of
Gilberte's actions that had seemed to me inexplicable and
her faults which I had excused. Then, one and all, they
took on a meaning. It seemed to tell me, this new arrangement, that when I saw Gilberte, instead of coming
to the Champs-Elysées, going to a party, or going shopping with her governess, or preparing for an absence that

would extend over the New Year holidays, I was wrong in thinking: "It's because she's frivolous or docile." For she would have ceased to be either if she had loved me, and if she had been forced to obey, it would have been with the same despair in her heart that I felt on the days when I did not see her. It showed me further, this new arrangement, that I ought after all to know what it was to love, since I loved Gilberte; it drew my attention to the constant anxiety that I had to shine in her eyes, by reason of which I tried to persuade my mother to buy Françoise a waterproof coat and a hat with a blue feather, or, better still, to stop sending me to the Champs-Elysées in the company of a servant with whom I blushed to be seen (to which my mother replied that I was unjust to Françoise, that she was an excellent woman and devoted to us all), and also that exclusive need to see Gilberte, the result of which was that, months in advance, I could think of nothing else but how to find out when she would be leaving Paris and where she was going, feeling that the most attractive country in the world would be a place of exile if she was not to be there, and asking only to be allowed to stay for ever in Paris so long as I might see her in the Champs-Elysées; and it had little difficulty in making me see that neither my anxiety nor my need could be justified by anything in Gilberte's conduct. She, on the contrary, appreciated her governess, without troubling herself over what I might choose to think about her. It seemed quite natural to her not to come to the Champs-Elysées if she had to go shopping with Mademoiselle, delightful if she had to go out with her mother. And even supposing that she had allowed me to spend my holidays in the same place as herself, when it came to choosing that place she would consider her parents' wishes, and the various amusements of which she had been told, and not at all that it should be the place to which my family were proposing to send me. When she assured me (as she sometimes did) that she liked me less than some other of her friends, less than she had liked me the day before, because by my clumsiness I had made her side lose a game, I would ask her forgiveness, would beg her to tell me what I must do in order that she should begin to like me again as much as, or more than anyone else; I wanted her to tell me that that was already the case, I besought her as though she were capable of modifying her affection for me as she or I chose, in order to please me, simply by the words she would utter, as my good or bad conduct should deserve. Did I not then know that what I felt for her depended neither upon her actions nor upon my will?

It showed me finally, the new arrangement devised by the invisible seamstress, that, if we find ourselves hoping that the actions of a person who has hitherto caused us pain may prove not to have been sincere, they shed in their wake a light which our hopes are powerless to extinguish and to which we must address ourselves, rather than to our hopes, if we are to know what will be that person's actions on the morrow.

My love listened to these new counsels; they persuaded it that the morrow would not be different from all the days that had gone before; that Gilberte's feeling for me, too long established now to be capable of alteration, was indifference; that in my friendship with Gilberte, it was I alone who loved. "It's true," my love answered, "there is nothing more to be made of that friendship. It will not alter now." And so, as from the very next day (or

from the next public holiday, if there was one in the off-
ing, or an anniversary, or the New Year, perhaps—one of
those days which are not like other days, on which time
starts afresh, casting aside the heritage of the past, de-
clining its legacy of sorrows) I would ask Gilberte to ter-
minate our old friendship and to join me in laying the
foundations of a new one.

I always had within reach a plan of Paris which, because I could see on it the street in which M. and Mme
Swann lived, seemed to me to contain a secret treasure.
And for pure pleasure, as well as from a sort of chivalrous
loyalty, on no matter what pretext I would utter the name
of that street until my father, not being, like my mother
and grandmother, apprised of my love, would ask me:
"But why are you always talking about that street?
There's nothing wonderful about it. It's a very agreeable
street to live in because it's only a few minutes walk from
the Bois, but there are a dozen other streets to which the
same applies."
I went out of my way to find occasions for my parents to pronounce Swann's name. In my own mind, of
course, I never ceased to murmur it; but I needed also to
hear its exquisite sound, to have others play to me that
music the voiceless rendering of which did not suffice me.
Moreover, the name Swann, with which I had for so long
been familiar, had now become for me (as happens with
certain aphasiacs in the case of the most ordinary words)
a new name. It was for ever present in my mind, which
could not, however, grow accustomed to it. I analysed it,
I spelt it; its orthography came to me as a surprise. And
together with its familiarity it had simultaneously lost its

innocence. The pleasure that I derived from the sound of it I felt to be so sinful that it seemed to me as though the others read my thoughts and changed the conversation if I tried to guide it in that direction. I fell back on subjects which still concerned Gilberte, I repeated over and over again the same words, and although I knew that they were only words—words uttered in her absence, which she could not hear, words without virtue in themselves, repeating what were facts but powerless to modify them—it seemed to me none the less that by dint of thus manipulating, stirring up everything that had reference to Gilberte, I might perhaps elicit from it something that would bring me happiness. I told my parents again that Gilberte was fond of her governess, as if that proposition, voiced for the hundredth time, would at last have the effect of making Gilberte suddenly burst into the room, come to live with us for ever. I had already sung the praises of the old lady who read the *Débats* (I had hinted to my parents that she was an ambassadress, if not actually a Highness) and I continued to descant on her beauty, her splendour, her nobility, until the day I mentioned that, from what I had heard Gilberte call her, she appeared to be a Mme Blatin.

"Oh, now I know who you mean," exclaimed my mother, while I felt myself blushing with shame. "On guard! on guard!—as your poor grandfather would have said. So she's the one you find so beautiful! Why, she's perfectly horrible, and always has been. She's the widow of a bailiff. Don't you remember, when you were little, all the trouble I used to go to in order to avoid her at your gym lessons, where she was always trying to get hold of me—I didn't know the woman, of course—to tell me that you were 'too beautiful for a boy.' She has always had a mania for getting to know people, and she really must be a sort of maniac, as I've always thought, if she does in fact know Mme Swann. For even if she does come from a very common background, I've never heard anything against her. But she must always be forcing herself upon strangers. She really is a horrible woman, frightfully vulgar, and affected as well."

As for Swann, in order to try to resemble him, I spent all my time at table pulling my nose and rubbing my eyes. My father would exclaim: "The child's an idiot, he'll make himself quite hideous." More than anything else I should have liked to be as bald as Swann. He seemed to me a being so extraordinary that I found it miraculous that people of my acquaintance knew him too and in the course of the day might run into him. And once my mother, while she was telling us, as she did every evening at dinner, where she had been and what she had done that afternoon, merely by the words: "By the way, guess whom I saw in the Trois Quartiers—at the umbrella counter—Swann!" brought forth in the midst of her narrative (an arid desert to me) a mystic blossom. What a melancholy pleasure to learn that Swann, that very afternoon, his supernatural form silhouetted against the crowd, had gone to buy an umbrella. Among the events of the day, great and small, but all equally insignificant, that one alone aroused in me those peculiar vibrations by which my love for Gilberte was perpetually stirred. My father complained that I took no interest in anything because I did not listen while he was speaking of the political consequences that might follow the visit of King Theodosius, at the moment in France as the nation's guest and (it was claimed) ally. But how I longed, on the other hand, to know whether Swann had been wearing his hooded cape!

"Did you speak to him?" I asked.

"Why, of course I did," answered my mother, who always seemed afraid lest, were she to admit that we were not on the best of terms with Swann, people would seek to reconcile us more than she cared for, in view of Mme Swann, whom she did not wish to know. "It was he who came up and spoke to me. I hadn't seen him."

"Then you haven't quarrelled?"

"Quarrelled? What on earth makes you think we've quarrelled?" she briskly parried, as though I had cast doubt on the fiction of her friendly relations with Swann, and tried to bring about a reconciliation.

"He might be cross with you for never asking him here."

"One isn't obliged to ask everyone to one's house, you know. Has he ever asked me to his? I don't know his wife."

"But he often used to come at Combray."

"Yes, I know he used to come at Combray, and now, in Paris, he has other things to do, and so have I. But I can promise you, we didn't look in the least like people who had quarrelled. We were kept waiting there for some time, while they brought him his parcel. He asked after you; he told me you played with his daughter," my mother went on, dazzling me with the stupendous revelation that I existed in Swann's mind; even more, that I existed in so complete, so material a form that when I stood before him, trembling with love, in the Champs-Elysées, he had known my name, and who my mother was, and

had been able to bring together around my capacity as his
daughter's playmate certain facts with regard to my
grandparents and their connexions, the place where we
lived, and certain details of our past life which were perhaps unknown even to me. But my mother did not seem
to have discovered a particular charm in that counter at
the Trois Quartiers where she had represented to Swann,
at the moment when he caught sight of her, a definite
person with whom he had sufficient memories in common
to impel him to go up to her and greet her.

Nor did either she or my father seem to find, in
speaking of Swann's family, or the title of honorary stockbroker, a pleasure that surpassed all others. My imagination had isolated and hallowed in social Paris a certain
family, just as it had set apart in structural Paris a certain
house, whose entrance it had sculpted and its windows
bejewelled. But these ornaments I alone had eyes to see.
Just as my father and mother regarded the house in which
Swann lived as identical with the other houses built at the
same period in the neighbourhood of the Bois, so Swann's
family seemed to them to be in the same category as
many other families of stockbrokers. They judged it more
or less favourably according to the degree to which it
shared in merits that were common to the rest of the universe and saw nothing unique in it. On the contrary, what
they appreciated in it they found in equal if not superior
degree elsewhere. And so, after admitting that the house
was in a good position, they would go on to speak of
some other house that was in a better, but had nothing to
do with Gilberte, or of financiers who were a cut above
her grandfather; and if they had appeared for a moment
to be of my opinion, that was through a misunderstand-

ing which was very soon dispelled. For in order to distinguish in everything that surrounded Gilberte an indefinable quality analogous in the world of the emotions to what in the world of colours is called infra-red, my parents would have needed that supplementary sense with which love had temporarily endowed me.

On the days when Gilberte had warned me that she would not be coming to the Champs-Elysées, I tried to arrange my walks so that I should be brought into some kind of contact with her. Sometimes I would take Françoise on a pilgrimage to the house in which the Swanns lived, making her repeat to me unendingly all that she had learned from the governess with regard to Mme Swann. "It seems she's got great faith in medals. She wouldn't think of starting on a journey if she'd heard an owl hoot, or a sort of tick-tock in the wall, or if she'd seen a cat at midnight, or if the furniture had creaked. Oh yes! she's a most religious lady, she is!" I was so madly in love with Gilberte that if, on our way, I caught sight of their old butler taking the dog out, my emotion would bring me to a standstill and I would gaze at his white whiskers with eyes filled with passion. Françoise would say: "What's wrong with you now?"

Then we would continue on our way until we reached their gateway, where a porter, different from every other porter in the world and saturated, down to the very braid on his livery, with the same melancholy charm that I sensed in the name of Gilberte, looked as though he knew that I was one of those whose natural unworthiness would for ever prohibit from penetrating into the mysteries of the life which it was his duty to guard and upon which the ground-floor windows appeared conscious of being

protectingly closed, with far less resemblance, between the
nobly sweeping arches of their muslin curtains, to any
other windows in the world than to Gilberte's glancing
eyes. On other days we would go along the boulevards,
and I would take up a position at the corner of the Rue
Duphot, along which I had heard that Swann was often to
be seen passing on his way to his dentist; and my imagination so far differentiated Gilberte's father from the rest
of humanity, his presence in the midst of the real world
introduced into it such an element of wonder, that even
before we reached the Madeleine I would be trembling
with emotion at the thought that I was approaching a
street from which that supernatural apparition might at
any moment burst upon me unawares.

But most often of all—on days when I was not to see
Gilberte—as I had heard that Mme Swann went for a
walk or a drive almost every day in the Allée des Acacias,
round the big lake, and in the Allée de la Reine Marguerite, I would lead Françoise to the Bois de Boulogne.
It was to me like one of those zoological gardens in which
one sees assembled together a variety of flora and contrasted landscapes, where from a hill one passes to a
grotto, a meadow, rocks, a stream, a pit, another hill, a
marsh, but knows that they are there only to enable the
hippopotamus, zebra, crocodile, albino rabbit, bear and
heron to disport themselves in a natural or a picturesque
setting; it, the Bois, equally complex, uniting a multitude
of little worlds, distinct and separate—alternating a plan-
tation of redwood trees and American oaks, like an exper-
imental forest in Virginia, with a fir-wood by the edge of
the lake, or a grove from which would suddenly emerge,
in her raiment of soft fur, with the large, appealing eyes

of a dumb animal, a hastening walker—was the Garden
of Woman; and like the myrtle-alley in the *Aeneid*,
planted for their delight with trees of one kind only, the
Allée des Acacias was thronged with the famous beauties
of the day. As, from a long way off, the sight of the jutting crag from which it dives into the pool thrills with joy
the children who know that they are going to see the seal,
so, long before I reached the acacias, their fragrance
which, radiating all around, made one aware of the approach and the singularity of a vegetable personality at
once powerful and soft, then, as I drew near, the glimpsed
summit of their lightly tossing foliage, in its easy grace,
its coquettish outline, its delicate fabric, on which hundreds of flowers had swooped, like winged and throbbing
colonies of precious insects, and finally their name itself,
feminine, indolent, dulcet, made my heart beat, but with
a social longing, like those waltzes which remind us only
of the names of the fair dancers, called aloud as they enter the ballroom. I had been told that I should see in the
alley certain women of fashion, who, in spite of their not
all having husbands, were habitually mentioned in con-
junction with Mme Swann, but most often by their professional names—their new names, when they had any,
being but a sort of incognito, a veil which those who
wished to speak of them were careful to draw aside in order to make themselves understood. Thinking that
Beauty—in the order of feminine elegance—was gov-
erned by occult laws into the knowledge of which they
had been initiated, and that they had the power to realise
it, I accepted in advance like a revelation the appearance
of their clothes, of their carriages and horses, of countless
details in which I placed my faith as in an inner soul

which gave the cohesion of a work of art to that ephemeral and shifting pageant. But it was Mme Swann whom I wished to see, and I waited for her to go past, as thrilled as though she were Gilberte, whose parents, impregnated, like everything that surrounded her, with her own special charm, excited in me as keen a passion as she did herself, indeed a still more painful agitation (since their point of contact with her was that intimate, that internal part of her life from which I was excluded), and furthermore (for I very soon learned, as we shall see in due course, that they did not like my playing with her) that feeling of veneration which we always have for those who hold, and exercise without restraint, the power to do us harm.

I assigned the first place in the order of aesthetic merit and of social grandeur to simplicity, when I saw Mme Swann on foot, in a polonaise of plain cloth, a little toque on her head trimmed with a pheasant's wing, a bunch of violets in her bosom, hastening along the Allée des Acacias as if it had been merely the shortest way back to her house, and acknowledging with a wink the greetings of the gentlemen in carriages who, recognising her figure at a distance, raised their hats to her and said to one another that there was never anyone so well turned out as she. But instead of simplicity it was to ostentation that I must assign the first place if, after I had compelled Françoise, who was worn out and complained that her feet were "killing" her, to stroll up and down with me for another hour, I saw at length emerging from the Porte Dauphine—figuring for me a royal dignity, the passage of a sovereign, an impression such as no real queen has ever since been able to give me, because my notion of their

power has been less vague, more founded upon experience—borne along by the flight of a pair of fiery horses,
slender and shapely as one sees them in the drawings of
Constantin Guys, carrying on its box an enormous coachman furred like a cossack, and by his side a diminutive
groom like "the late Beaudenord's tiger," I saw—or
rather I felt its outlines engraved upon my heart by a
clean and poignant wound—a matchless victoria, built
rather high, and hinting, through the extreme modernity
of its appointments, at the forms of an earlier day, in the
depths of which Mme Swann negligently reclined, her
hair, now blonde with one grey lock, encircled with a narrow band of flowers, usually violets, from which floated
down long veils, a lilac parasol in her hand, on her lips an
ambiguous smile in which I read only the benign condescension of Majesty, though it was pre-eminently the
provocative smile of the courtesan, which she graciously
bestowed upon the men who greeted her. This smile was
in reality saying, to one: "Oh yes, I remember very well;
it was wonderful!" to another: "How I should have loved
to! It was bad luck!" to a third: "Yes, if you like! I must
just follow in the procession for a moment, then as soon
as I can I'll break away." When strangers passed a lazy
smile still played about her lips, as though in expectation
or remembrance of some friend, which made people say:
"What a lovely woman!" And for certain men only she
had a sour, strained, shy, cold smile which meant: "Yes,
you old goat, I know that you've got a tongue like a
viper, that you can't keep quiet for a moment. But do you
suppose that I care what you say?" Coquelin passed,
holding forth among a group of listening friends, and
with a sweeping wave of his hand bade a theatrical good

day to the people in the carriages. But I thought only of
Mme Swann, and pretended not to have seen her yet, for
I knew that when she reached the pigeon-shooting ground
she would tell her coachmen to "break away" and to stop
the carriage, so that she might come back on foot. And on
days when I felt that I had the courage to pass close by
her I would drag Françoise off in that direction; until the
moment came when I saw Mme Swann, trailing behind
her the long train of her lilac skirt, dressed, as the popu-
lace imagine queens to be dressed, in rich finery such as
no other woman wore, occasionally looking down at the
handle of her parasol, and paying scant attention to the
passers-by, as though her sole object was to take exercise,
without thinking that she was being observed and that every head was turned towards her. Sometimes, however,
when she had looked back to call her dog, she would cast,
almost imperceptibly, a sweeping glance round about her.

Even those who did not know her were warned by
something singular, something exorbitant about her—or
perhaps by a telepathic suggestion such as would move an
ignorant audience to a frenzy of applause at moments
when Berma was being sublime—that she must be someone well known. They would ask one another, "Who is
she?", or sometimes would interrogate a passing stranger,
or would make a mental note of how she was dressed as
an indication for some better-informed friend who would
at once enlighten them. Another pair of strollers, half-
stopping in their walk, would say to each other:

"You know who that is? Mme Swann! That conveys
nothing to you? Odette de Crécy, then?"

"Odette de Crécy! Why, I thought as much. Those
sad eyes . . . But I say, you know, she can't be as young

as she was once, eh? I remember I slept with her on the day MacMahon resigned."

"I shouldn't remind her of it, if I were you. She's now Mme Swann, the wife of a gentleman in the Jockey Club, a friend of the Prince of Wales. But she still looks superb."

"Oh, but you should have known her then. How pretty she was! She lived in a very odd little house with a lot of Chinese stuff. I remember we were bothered all the time by the newsboys shouting outside; in the end she made me get up and go."

Without hearing these reflections, I could feel all about her the indistinct murmur of fame. My heart throbbed with impatience when I thought that a few seconds must still elapse before all these people, among whom I was dismayed not to find a certain mulatto banker by whom I felt I was despised, would see the unknown youth, to whom they had not as yet paid the slightest attention, salute (without knowing her, it was true, but I felt that I was authorised to do so because my parents knew her husband and I was her daughter's playmate) this woman whose reputation for beauty, misconduct and elegance was universal. But I was now close to Mme Swann, and I doffed my hat to her with so lavish, so prolonged a gesture that she could not repress a smile. People laughed. As for her, she had never seen me with Gilberte, she did not know my name, but I was for her— like one of the keepers in the Bois, or the boatman, or the ducks on the lake to which she threw scraps of bread— one of the minor personages, familiar, nameless, as devoid of individual character as a stage-hand in a theatre, of her daily walks in the Bois.

On certain days when I had missed her in the Allée des Acacias I would sometimes meet her in the Allée de la Reine Marguerite, where women went who wanted to be alone, or to appear to want to be alone; she would not be alone for long, being soon overtaken by some friend, often in a grey "topper," whom I did not know, and who would talk to her for some time, while their two carriages crawled behind.

That complexity of the Bois de Boulogne which makes it an artificial place and, in the zoological or mythological sense of the word, a Garden, came to me again this year as I crossed it on my way to Trianon, on one of those mornings early in November when, in Paris, if we stay indoors, being so near and yet excluded from the transformation scene of autumn, which is drawing so rapidly to a close without our witnessing it, we feel a veritable fever of yearning for the fallen leaves that can go so far as to keep us awake at night. Into my closed room they had been drifting already for a month, summoned there by my desire to see them, slipping between my thoughts and the object, whatever it might be, upon which I was trying to concentrate them, whirling in front of me like those brown spots that sometimes, whatever we may be looking at, will seem to be dancing or swimming before our eyes. And on that morning, no longer hearing the splash of the rain as on the preceding days, seeing the smile of fine weather at the corners of my drawn curtains, as at the corners of closed lips betraying the secret of their happiness, I had felt that I might be able to look at those yellow leaves with the light shining through them, in their supreme beauty; and being no more able to restrain myself from going to see the trees than, in my childhood days, when the wind howled in the chimney, I had been able to resist the longing to visit the sea, I had risen and left the house to go to Trianon via the Bois de Boulogne. It was the hour and the season in which the Bois seems, perhaps, most multiform, not only because it is the most subdivided, but because it is subdivided in a different way. Even in the unwooded parts, where the horizon is large, here and there against the background of a dark and distant mass of trees, now leafless or still keeping their summer foliage unchanged, a double row of orange-red chestnuts seemed, as in a picture just begun, to be the only thing painted so far by an artist who had not yet laid any colour on the rest, and to be offering their cloister, in full daylight, for the casual exercise of the human figures that would be added to the picture later on.

Further off, at a place where the trees were still all green, one alone, small, stunted, lopped, but stubborn in its resistance, was tossing in the breeze an ugly mane of red. Elsewhere, again, might be seen the first awakening of this Maytime of the leaves, and those of an ampelopsis, a smiling miracle like a red hawthorn flowering in winter, had that very morning all "come out," so to speak, in blossom. And the Bois had the temporary, unfinished, artificial look of a nursery garden or a park in which, either for some botanic purpose or in preparation for a festival, there have been embedded among the trees of commoner growth which have not yet been transplanted elsewhere, a few rare specimens, with fantastic foliage, which seem to be clearing all round themselves an empty space, making room, giving air, diffusing light. Thus it was the time of

year at which the Bois de Boulogne displays more separate characteristics, assembles more distinct elements in a
composite whole than any other. It was also the time of
day. In places where the trees still kept their leaves, they
seemed to have undergone an alteration of their substance
from the point at which they were touched by the sun's
light, still, at this hour in the morning, almost horizontal,
as it would be again, a few hours later, at the moment
when in the gathering dusk it flames up like a lamp, pro-
jects afar over the leaves a warm and artificial glow, and
sets ablaze the few topmost boughs of a tree that itself remains unchanged, a sombre incombustible candelabrum
beneath its flaming crest. At one point it thickened the
leaves of the chestnut-trees as it were like bricks, and, like
a piece of yellow Persian masonry patterned in blue, ce-
mented them crudely against the sky; at another, it detached them from the sky, towards which they stretched
out their curling, golden fingers. Half-way up the trunk
of a tree draped with Virginia creeper, it had grafted and
brought to blossom, too dazzling to be clearly distinguished, an enormous bouquet as of red flowers, perhaps
a new variety of carnation. The different parts of the
Bois, so easily confounded in summer in the density and
monotony of their universal green, were now clearly divided. Open spaces made visible the approach to almost
every one of them, or else a splendid mass of foliage
stood out before it like an oriflamme. One could make
out, as on a coloured map, Armenonville, the Pré Catelan,
Madrid, the Race Course and the shore of the lake. Here
and there would appear some meaningless erection, a
sham grotto, a mill for which the trees made room by
standing aside from it, or which was borne upon the soft

green platform of a grassy lawn. One sensed that the Bois was not only a wood, that it existed for a purpose alien to the life of its trees; the exhilaration that I felt was due not only to admiration of the autumn tints but to an obscure desire—wellspring of a joy which the heart feels at first without being conscious of its cause, without understanding that it results from no external impulse. Thus I gazed at the trees with an unsatisfied longing that went beyond them and, without my knowledge, directed itself towards that masterpiece of the fair walkers which the trees enshrine for a few hours each day. I walked towards the Allée des Acacias. I passed through groves in which the morning light, breaking them into new sections, lopped and trimmed the trees, united different trunks in marriage, made nosegays of their branches. It would skilfully draw towards it a pair of trees; making deft use of the sharp chisel of light and shade, it would cut away from each of them half of its trunks and branches, and, weaving together the two halves that remained, would make of them either a single pillar of shade, defined by the surrounding sunlight, or a single luminous phantom whose artificial, quivering contour was encompassed in a network of inky shadows. When a ray of sunshine gilded the highest branches, they seemed, soaked and still dripping with a sparkling moisture, to have emerged alone from the liquid, emerald-green atmosphere in which the whole grove was plunged as though beneath the sea. For the trees continued to live by their own vitality, which, when they had no longer any leaves, gleamed more brightly still on the nap of green velvet that carpeted their trunks, or in the white enamel of the globes of mistletoe that were scattered among the topmost boughs of the poplars, rounded like the sun and moon in Michelangelo's "Creation." But, forced for so many years now, by a sort of grafting process, to share in the life of feminine humanity, they called to my mind the figure of the dryad, the fair worldling, swiftly walking, brightly coloured, whom they shelter with their branches as she passes beneath them, obliging her to acknowledge, as they themselves acknowledge, the power of the season; they recalled to me the happy days of my unquestioning youth, when I would hasten eagerly to the spots where masterpieces of female elegance would be incarnate for a few moments beneath the unconscious, accommodating boughs. But the beauty for which the firs and acacias of the Bois de Boulogne made me long, more disquieting in that respect than the chestnuts and lilacs of Trianon which I was about to see, was not fixed somewhere outside myself in the relics of an historical period, in works of art, in a little temple of love at whose door was piled an oblation of autumn leaves ribbed with gold. I reached the shore of the lake; I walked on as far as the pigeon-shooting ground. The idea of perfection which I had within me I had bestowed, in that other time, upon the height of a victoria, upon the raking thinness of those horses, frenzied and light as wasps on the wing, with bloodshot eyes like the cruel steeds of Diomed, which now, smitten by a desire to see again what I had once loved, as ardent as the desire that had driven me many years before along the same paths, I wished to see anew before my eyes at the moment when Mme Swann's enormous coachman, supervised by a groom no bigger than his fist and as infantile as St George in the picture, endeavoured to curb the ardour of the quivering steel-tipped pinions with which they thundered over the ground. Alas! there was nothing now but motor-cars driven each by a moustached mechanic, with a tall footman towering by his side. I wished to hold before my bodily eyes, to see whether they were indeed as charming as they appeared to the eyes of memory, little women's hats, so low-crowned as to seem no more than garlands. All the hats now were immense, covered with all manner of fruits and flowers and birds. In place of the beautiful dresses in which Mme Swann walked like a queen, Graeco-Saxon tunics, pleated à la Tanagra, or sometimes in the Directoire style, accentuated Liberty chiffons sprinkled with flowers like wallpaper. On the heads of the gentlemen who might have been strolling with Mme Swann in the Allée de la Reine Marguerite, I no longer found the grey "toppers" of old, nor indeed any other kind of hat. They went out bare-headed. And seeing all these new components of the spectacle, I had no longer a belief to infuse into them to give them consistency, unity and life; they passed before me in a desultory, haphazard, meaningless fashion, containing in themselves no beauty which my eyes might have tried, as in the old days, to re-create. They were just women, in whose elegance I had no faith, and whose clothes seemed to me unimportant. But when a belief vanishes, there survives it—more and more vigorously so as to cloak the absence of the power, now lost to us, of imparting reality to new things—a fetishistic attachment to the old things which it did once animate, as if it was in them and not in ourselves that the divine spark resided, and as if our present incredulity had a contingent cause—the death of the gods.

How horrible! I exclaimed to myself. Can anyone find

these motor-cars as elegant as the old carriage-and-pair? I dare say I am too old now—but I was not intended for a world in which women shackle themselves in garments that are not even made of cloth. To what purpose shall I walk among these trees if there is nothing left now of the assembly that used to gather beneath this delicate tracery of reddening leaves, if vulgarity and folly have supplanted the exquisite thing that their branches once framed. How horrible! My consolation is to think of the women whom I knew in the past, now that there is no elegance left. But how could the people who watch these dreadful creatures hobble by beneath hats on which have been heaped the spoils of aviary or kitchen-garden, how could they even imagine the charm that there was in the sight of Mme Swann in a simple mauve bonnet or a little hat with a single iris sticking up out of it? Could I even have made them understand the emotion that I used to feel on winter mornings, when I met Mme Swann on foot, in an otter-skin coat, with a woollen cap from which stuck out two blade-like partridge-feathers, but enveloped also in the artificial warmth of her own house, which was suggested by nothing more than the bunch of violets crushed into her bosom, whose flowering, vivid and blue against the grey sky, the freezing air, the naked boughs, had the same charming effect of using the season and the weather merely as a setting, and of living actually in a human atmosphere, in the atmosphere of this woman, as had, in the vases and jardinières of her drawing-room, beside the blazing fire, in front of the silk-covered settee, the flowers that looked out through closed windows at the falling snow? But it would not have sufficed me that the costumes alone should still have been the same as those in

distant years. Because of the solidarity that binds together
the different parts of a general impression that our memory keeps in a balanced whole of which we are not permitted to subtract or to decline any fraction, I should
have liked to be able to pass the rest of the day with one
of those women, over a cup of tea, in an apartment with
dark-painted walls (as Mme Swann's were still in the year
after that in which the first part of this story ends) against
which would glow the orange flame, the red combustion,
the pink and white flickering of her chrysanthemums in
the twilight of a November evening, in moments similar
to those in which (as we shall see) I had not managed to
discover the pleasures for which I longed. But now, even
though they had led to nothing, those moments struck me
as having been charming enough in themselves. I wanted
to find them again as I remembered them. Alas! there was
nothing now but flats decorated in the Louis XVI style,
all white, with a sprinkling of blue hydrangeas. Moreover,
people did not return to Paris, now, until much later.
Mme Swann would have written to me from a country
house to say that she would not be in town before February, long after the chrysanthemum season, had I asked
her to reconstruct for me the elements of that memory
which I felt to belong to a particular distant year, a particular vintage towards which it was forbidden me to as-
cend again the fatal slope, the elements of that longing
which had itself become as inaccessible as the pleasure
that it had once vainly pursued. And I should have required also that they should be the same women, those
whose costume interested me because, at the time when I
still had faith, my imagination had individualised them
and had provided each of them with a legend. Alas! in the

acacia-avenue—the myrtle-alley—I did see some of them again, grown old, no more now than grim spectres of what they had once been, wandering, desperately searching for heaven knew what, through the Virgilian groves. They had long since fled, and still I stood vainly questioning the deserted paths. The sun had gone. Nature was resuming its reign over the Bois, from which had vanished all trace of the idea that it was the Elysian Garden of Woman; above the gimcrack windmill the real sky was grey; the wind wrinkled the surface of the Grand Lac in little wavelets, like a real lake; large birds flew swiftly over the Bois, as over a real wood, and with shrill cries perched, one after another, on the great oaks which, beneath their Druidical crown, and with Dodonian majesty, seemed to proclaim the inhuman emptiness of this deconsecrated forest, and helped me to understand how paradoxical it is to seek in reality for the pictures that are stored in one's memory, which must inevitably lose the charm that comes to them from memory itself and from their not being apprehended by the senses. The reality that I had known no longer existed. It sufficed that Mme Swann did not appear, in the same attire and at the same moment, for the whole avenue to be altered. The places we have known do not belong only to the world of space on which we map them for our own convenience. They were only a thin slice, held between the contiguous impressions that composed our life at that time; the memory of a particular image is but regret for a particular moment; and houses, roads, avenues are as fugitive, alas, as the years.

NOTES · SYNOPSIS

1 (p. 17) Bressant: a well-known actor (1815–1886) who introduced a new hair-style which involved wearing the hair short in front and fairly long behind.

2 (p. 35) *O ciel, que de vertus vous nous faites haïr.* From Corneille's *Mort de Pompée.*

3 (p. 36) *à contre-coeur*: reluctantly.

4 (p. 38) *Le Miracle de Théophile*: verse play by the thirteenth-century troubadour, Rutebeuf. *Les quatres fils Aymon* or *Renaud de Montauban*: twelfth-century *chanson de geste.*

5 (p. 108) *bleu*: express letter transmitted by pneumatic tube (in Paris).

6 (p. 191) The first edition of *Du côté de chez Swann* had "*pour Chartres*" instead of "*pour Reims.*" Proust moved Combray (which as we know was modelled on Illiers, near Chartres) to the fighting zone between Laon and Rheims when he decided to incorporate the 1914–1918 war into his book.

7 (p. 204) Indirect quotation from Racine's *Phèdre*, Act I, Scene 3:
Que ces vains ornements, que ces voiles me pèsent!
Quelle importune main en formant tous ces noeuds
A pris soin sur mon front d'assembler mes cheveux?

8 (p. 269) In English in the original. Odette's speech is peppered with English expressions.

9 (p. 276) "Home" is in English in the original, as is "smart" on p. 276.

10 (p. 348) *La Reine Topaze*: a light opera by Victor Massé presented at the Théâtre Lyrique in 1856.

11 (p. 349) *Serge Panine*: play by Georges Ohnet (1848–1918), adapted from a novel of the same name, which had a great success in 1881 in spite of its mediocre literary qualities.
Olivier Métra: composer of such popular works as

La Valse des Roses and a famous lancers quadrille, and conductor at the Opéra-Comique.

12 (p. 374) *Serpent à sonnettes* means rattlesnake.

13 (p. 418) *Pays du Tendre* (or, more correctly, *Pays de Tendre*): the country of the sentiments, the tender emotions, mapped (the *carte de Tendre*) by Mlle de Scudéry in her novel, *Clélie* (1654–1670).

14 (p. 485) The rather forced joke on the name Cambremer conceives of it as being made up of abbreviations of *Cambronne* and *merde* (shit). *Le mot de Cambronne* (said to have been flung defiantly at the enemy by a general at Waterloo) is the traditional euphemism for *merde*.

15 (p. 573) *Pneumatique* or *petit bleu*: see note to p. 108 above.

COMBRAY

SWANN IN LOVE

bad impression on her (307). The little seamstress; Swann agrees to meet Odette only after dinner (307). Vinteuil's little phrase, "the national anthem of their love" (308). Tea with Odette; her chrysanthemums (311). Faces of today and portraits of the past: Odette and Botticelli's Zipporah (314). Odette, a Florentine painting (316). Love letter from Odette written from the Maison Dorée (319). Swann's arrival at the Verdurins' one evening after Odette's departure (320); anguished search in the night (323). The cattleyas (328); she becomes his mistress (331). Odette's vulgarity (341); her idea of "chic" (344). Swann begins to adopt her tastes (348) and considers the Verdurins "magnanimous people" (352). Why, nevertheless, he is not a true member of the "faithful," unlike Forcheville (355). A dinner at the Verdurins': Brichot (356), Cottard (357), the painter (361), Saniette (370). The little phrase (374). Swann's jealousy: one night, dismissed by Odette at midnight, he returns to her house and knocks at the wrong window (387). Forcheville's cowardly attack on Saniette, and Odette's smile of complicity (393). Odette's door remains closed to Swann one afternoon; her lying explanation (394). Signs of distress that accompany Odette's lying (398). Swann deciphers a letter from her to Forcheville through the envelope (400). The Verdurins organise an excursion to Chatou without Swann (403). His indignation with them (406). Swann's exclusion (410). Should he go to Dreux or Pierrefonds to find Odette? (415). Waiting through the night (419). Peaceful evenings at Odette's with Forcheville (424). Recrudescence of anguish (426). The Bayreuth project (427). Love and death and the mystery of personality (438). Charles Swann and "young Swann" (440). Swann, Odette, Charlus and Uncle Adolphe (442). Longing for death (451).

An evening at the Marquise de Saint-Euverte's. Detached from social life by his love and his jealousy, Swann can observe it as it is in itself (458): the footmen (459); the monocles (463); the Marquise de Cambremer and the Vicomtesse de Franquetot listening to Liszt's "St Francis" (466); Mme de Gallardon, a despised cousin of the Guermantes (467). Arrival of the Princesse des Laumes (469); her conversation with Swann (483). Swann introduces the young Mme de Cambremer (Mlle Legrandin) to

PLACE-NAMES·THE NAME

reader of the *Débats* (Mme Blatin) (565; cf. 587). Marks of friendship: the agate marble, the Bergotte booklet, "You may call me Gilberte" (573); why they fail to bring me the expected happiness (574). A spring day in winter: joy and disappointment (575). The Swann of Combray has become a different person: Gilberte's father (578). Gilberte tells me with cruel delight that she will not be returning to the Champs-Elysées before the New Year (580). "In my friendship with Gilberte, it was I alone who loved" (585). The name Swann (586; cf. 202). Swann meets my mother in the Trois Quartiers (588). Pilgrimage with Françoise to the Swanns' house near the Bois (591).

The Bois, Garden of Woman. Mme Swann in the Bois (594). A walk through the Bois one late autumn morning in 1913 (598). Memory and reality (606).

A NOTE ON THE TYPE

The principal text of this Modern Library edition
was composed in a digitized version of
Horley Old Style, a typeface issued by
the English type foundry Monotype in 1925.
It has such distinctive features
as lightly cupped serifs and an oblique horizontal bar
on the lowercase "e."